Angels on the Head of a Pin

# Yuri Druzhnikov
# Angels on the Head of a Pin
## A novel

Translated from the Russian by
**Thomas Moore**

**PETER OWEN**
London and Chester Springs

UNESCO Publishing
Paris

PETER OWEN PUBLISHERS
73 Kenway Road, London SW5 0RE

Peter Owen books are distributed in the USA by
Dufour Editions Inc., Chester Springs, PA 19425-0007

Translated from the Russian *Angely na konchike igly*
© Yuri Druzhnikov 1979
First published in Great Britain 2002
English translation © UNESCO/Peter Owen 2002

UNESCO COLLECTION OF REPRESENTATIVE WORKS

ISBN 0 7206 1170 9
UNESCO ISBN 92 3 103837 0

A catalogue record for this book is available from the British Library

Printed and bound in India
by Thomson Press Ltd

# Contents

The number of angels that can fit on the head of
a pin is equal to the square root of two.
– Scholasticist textbook. Year and page forgotten

Readers are requested not to look for people they
know under the fictitious names in this book, as
no good can come of it.

# 1

# At the Main Entrance

He came to a halt between the two guards and presented his dark-red identification card. While one of them studied his photograph and checked it against its original, the other one attentively looked over Igor Makartsev from head to foot. The second nodded to the first, and the first returned the document.

'If you please.'

Mechanically putting the ID into his pocket, Makartsev moved towards the exit. Before, he always used to say goodbye, but now he only nodded with dignity. As he walked, he wound his scarf around his neck and buttoned up his overcoat. Pulling the inner door towards him, he could feel the light pressure of warm air from underneath the wooden grating. Giving the outer door a shove, he went out on to the footpath.

The cold, wet air tickled his nostrils, filled his lungs. His eyes took in the Polytechnic Museum, the pot-bellied monument to the grenadiers who fell at Plevna, and Old Square, deserted – if you didn't count several special-detachment traffic inspectors – and cut off by a solid row of parked cars. To the right, overtaking one another, more cars tore along downhill to the Chinese Way. Not for the first time the fleeting thought struck Makartsev that the thoroughfare's name was a patent misnomer. The street should have been renamed long before. What nonsense: the road leading straight up to the most important building in the country being called the Chinese Way!

Makartsev's appearance on the deserted footpath didn't remain unnoticed by the traffic wardens, nor by the various people in civilian

clothes standing around unobtrusively. Moreover, every passer-by was
stared at by the chauffeurs who were waiting for their masters and from
time to time warming up their engines. It was beginning to get dark, and
a light snow was falling, but the street lights hadn't yet come on and the
drivers were straining their eyes not to miss their charges.

Aleksey Dvoyeninov, brisk and sharp-nosed, now and again ran his
eyes from door to door. Even though Makartsev more often than not went
in and out through the main entrance, his pass let him through any of
the building's entryways. Catching sight of his boss, Aleksey instantly
started up the engine and turned on the heater, but he didn't open the
door for Makartsev straight away because he wanted to keep the passenger
cabin from getting cold. It hadn't been likely that his boss was going to
show up soon. He would always say he wouldn't be long, and then he
would sit around in there for two hours, sometimes up to four.

Makartsev cut across the footpath and had already stepped out on to
the square when suddenly, feeling a stab in his heart, he stopped, throwing his head back. It had been acting up from time to time, and after
standing still for a moment he decided against breathing too deeply. It was
as if an electric current had hit him in the shoulder, the pain momentarily
running down into his stomach.

Makartsev tried to moan, but all that came out was a wheeze. He
clutched a hand to his chest, trying to undo a button. Spots rippled in front
of his eyes, the Polytechnic building tilted over to one side and the cars
started up, heading all in a bunch straight for Makartsev. He realized he
was losing consciousness. Both his legs lost their strength and his knees
buckled. Saving his head from hitting the pavement, he got his hands
behind him and sat up. Consciousness stayed with him.

The first thing he noticed when he was on the ground was the sharp
odour of urine. The wind, mixed with snow, was blowing from a corner
of the Polytechnic Museum, carrying with it the fug from a public lavatory. There was nobody near him to give him a hand up or call for help.
And pain, pain enough to make you gasp. His only chance of salvation
was a rapid return to the door that he'd just come through.

The pain became unbearable; his arms ached. His body contorted, refusing to obey him, and Makartsev fell back. Gritting his teeth, he slowly rolled over on to one side and got to his knees. Now he had to get up on to the footpath. But the snow was melting, and his hands slipped. For an instant he felt the idiocy of his position: a man of his rank crawling into the Central Committee building on all fours. They would see him, they would spread it around, and his authority would be weakened. They might even report him to Himself. But the pain was making him forget about everything else. The important thing was to get to a doctor. They would save him! The door was heavy, it wasn't something he could just shove open. He was going to have to reach the door-handle. He moved towards the door on all fours, very slowly.

Having noticed Makartsev crossing the footpath Aleksey had turned on the engine and the heater and had bent over to open the heating vent a bit wider: Makartsev loved to warm his legs in the flow. The vent was jammed. When Aleksey, with a jerk, finally shifted it and once more looked out his boss was nowhere to be seen. Had he mistaken somebody else for him? Then he saw someone crawling on all fours in the twilight, towards the door over which, in gold letters, was written the legend 'Communist Party Central Committee'. Another few moments passed before Aleksey caught on.

With his last strength Makartsev clawed at the edge of the door, whimpering, and collapsed on to the wet, bristly mat they used to wipe their feet on. The guards stepped over and lifted him up. One of them pressed a button. Makartsev failed to notice anything else: he was unconscious.

'One of ours,' said a guard, glancing at his blackening face. The second adroitly unbuttoned Makartsev's overcoat and pulled his identification card out of his pocket. He did it as briskly and skilfully as if he'd been the one who'd put it there. He dutifully checked the photograph on it against the original lying in front of him and nodded to the doctors. 'You can take him in.'

They picked him up by the arms and legs and put him on a stretcher.

He groaned. Within a minute and forty seconds they had him off the stretcher and on to the operating table in the emergency surgery, equipped with the latest American-made apparatus.

Makartsev lay there in his dark suit, clean but threadbare, ten years out of fashion. His black half-boots were neatly shined, but the heels were slightly worn. This uniform, stitched up in the Central Committee's own tailor shop, was especially for those days when he went to the Big House. It wasn't the thing to stand out, either from a too bright tie or too carefully ironed trousers, and his wife, knowing that, always ironed the trousers of his Central Committee suit with a dry cloth instead of a wet one. They covered the patient with a sheet, and two emergency doctors from the Fourth Chief Directorate of the Ministry of Health – keeping their round-the-clock duty watch here – bent over him.

Slipping into the space before the inner door, Aleksey only managed to catch a glimpse of his boss, like a dead person, being put on a stretcher and carried off.

'I need to know. I'm a chauffeur, his driver . . .'

'Driver? Then get back to your car!'

'Yes, but what's going on with him?'

'They'll inform you when they can.'

He turned off his engine, and, wrapping his arms around the wheel, rested against it. *Drive back to the office and tell them the chief is sick? Or first rush over to his house and inform his wife? But then I'll have to drive her here and then maybe somewhere else. He'll lie around in there for a while and then come out. His car won't be here, and there'll be a panic all over Moscow. It'd be better for me to just sit here, snooze a bit . . .*

Aleksey had already had enough sleep (he'd shown up early at work and slept his fill behind the wheel, in expectation of his boss's arrival), and now he'd turned on the engine six times or so to warm up. The cars parked next to him left, and others pulled in to their places. He smoked his last cigarette, although he usually always hung on to the last one, since the time the year before last he'd driven Makartsev back from a reception at the *dacha* of somebody in government. Makartsev, a bit tipsy, searched for a cigarette in his pockets and then asked Aleksey for one, but Aleksey didn't have any fags left either.

'What kind of a chauffeur are you if you can't hang on to a cigarette for me?' Makartsev gave Aleksey a fatherly tug on the ear.

The Volga had come to a sudden halt in front of a traffic cop – there were more of them on Uspenskoye Chaussee than there were mushrooms in the woods. Aleksey, indicating his boss with a toss of the head, asked for a cigarette. The portly lieutenant, getting on in years (on routes maintained for government use their ranks were usually higher than was indicated on their shoulderboards), looked askance at the car's licence plate, with its double-zero first two digits. They had no right to stop a car with those zeroes on it, and Aleksey had a card appended to his licence that allowed him to break the traffic laws, so long as he kept within the bounds of safety. Saluting, the traffic cop silently pulled out a pack of cigarettes, and Aleksey, winking, took two of them. From that day on Aleksey had always held on to his last one. But Makartsev never once asked him for a cigarette; on the contrary, he himself would give his driver a present of a pack of American ones or sometimes even two. But now Aleksey had smoked his hold-out, so he decided to drive to the office and come back again if he had to.

Because the chauffeur was alone they didn't bother switching the lights to green for him right away. Aleksey rolled along towards Dzerzhinsky Square unhurriedly, although he was used to chasing around Moscow at over sixty miles an hour. At a trolleybus stop he was flagged down by a thickset man with a suitcase who looked like someone on a business trip.

'I'll pay you to take me to Kursk Station. I'm late.'

Aleksey drove him to Kursk Station in silence. When he got close, he turned the car around on the Garden Ring and said: 'Settle up with me in advance, or someone at the station will nick me for doing a job on the side.'

The passenger nodded and held out a three-rouble note – lunch for Aleksey. Aleksey never wasted his wage-packet but saved his money for the extension to his parents' house. Not so that he could go to live in the country but so that his wife and child would have somewhere to go in summer. He didn't want to live any worse than other people. The side trip took ten minutes, no longer. Spinning his keys around a finger, Aleksey took the lift to the fourth floor, where the editor-in-chief's office was. Walking into reception, he'd already opened his mouth to say the phrase that he had ready when Anna attacked him in a whisper.

'Where did you disappear to?! You should have taken Makartsev's wife to him right away. They were looking for you all over the building and in the garage. They sent Yagubov's car, and he himself has to get to the city council right away.'

'I'll take him,' said Aleksey. 'What's the matter with him, with Makartsev?'

'Did you just come from the moon? A myocardial infarct, a bad one. The posterior wall, and something else, too . . . He's in the Kremlin hospital, in a room, I've forgotten what it's called. And where have you been? Have you been moonlighting again?'

She disappeared into the office of the deputy editor-in-chief, Yagubov.

'In-farct,' Aleksey mouthed carefully, not investing the word with any understanding.

The reception area was empty. He looked at the secretary's desk. On the desk calendar today was Wednesday, 26 February 1969 – a black border had been drawn around it. Anna had already marked the day of the editor-in-chief's sudden illness for future reference. Returning, she informed him that he had to chauffeur Yagubov in ten minutes. Aleksey started telling Anna how he'd been waiting in front of the Central Committee building. Anna was supposed to be in the know about absolutely everything, and she listened attentively, memorizing the new details.

'So why did you keep quiet when I was telling you off?'

'. . . and he crawled like a dog up to the door,' Aleksey finished his tale, not answering her.

'And he was wise to do so,' Anna said approvingly. 'If Makartsev had stayed lying in the square a city ambulance would have had to pick him up. And it takes so long just to get one. It would have come thirty minutes later and then taken another half an hour to find space in a city hospital – he'd probably have been left somewhere in a corridor. And then if they'd transferred him to the Kremlin – he would have been jolted around. They say that if he hadn't crawled as far as that door he would never have come round again!'

'But why would he have a heart attack? He was just as happy as ever.'

She didn't answer, but he didn't repeat the question. Closing his eyes, Aleksey thought lazily of how immeasurably happier he was – an ordinary chauffeur – than Makartsev. That fellow had nothing but fuss, duties and cares – more than you could count. How much better it was to just take people somewhere and bring them back and live for yourself. No, he wouldn't want to be in the editor's place!

Despite that, Aleksey did have his own aspirations. And they were no less important than other people's.

# 2

# The Rise and Fall of
# Aleksey Dvoyeninov

Nikanor Dvoyeninov had come back to his village from the Second World War among the first of the few villagers to return at all. The whole town had poured out on to the street when, his medals clinking, he marched up the hill to his house on the outskirts, rubbing his wounded thigh. He had left the place as a boy, but he'd gone quite bald, even though the war hadn't harmed him too much. He'd had to hang about in the military hospital for a while with a slight wound, but his life had not been in danger. His baldness had either come about from his constant fright or the hairs had simply been worn off by the winter cap he hadn't taken off once in three years.

All day until late people came from the neighbouring village of Padikovo, where Nikanor had half a street full of relatives, to touch him, the survivor. Nikanor took off his jodhpurs, keeping on only his sweat-soaked blue underpants. And suddenly Klavdiya from next door threw herself to her knees, sobbed and, embracing Nikanor's legs, started covering his scarred thigh with kisses. They barely managed to pull her off and make her drink icy spring water.

But, in any case, Nikanor – crazed with his own joy, everyone's attention and the illicitly distilled *samogon* vodka – was lost to Klavdiya that very evening. When they sat down to his feast she contrived to sit right next to him and never took a step away from him. Every so often, as if by accident, she would touch his thigh. She looked at him with moist, devoted eyes, and he could scarcely say a word without her bursting into laughter. Klavdiya had long ago reached womanhood and would go off into the woods with any passing stranger whenever the opportunity arose. But, owing to the total lack of men in Anosino during recent times, she was starved of sex and so was particularly hot for him.

Nikanor's old folks, having waited out their son's absence, died of pure joy three months apart from each other, leaving the young people their rotting, straw-thatched hut. Nikanor and Klavdiya themselves took apart the log cabin and reassembled it to get rid of the rot. Then, nine months later to the day, Klavdiya gave birth to a son. God alone knew how they managed to rear him, he was so pale and rickets-raddled. Nobody got paid any wages on the collective farm, in either money or potatoes, and you had to work for your electricity. If you didn't show up in the fields with your scythe they would cut your cable at the power-pole and you would be left in the dark.

Klavdiya dragged herself the mile and a half to the convent spring for some holy water to bathe her son in. The Anosino convent itself had been turned into the collective farm's garage: in it were two ton-and-a-half trucks, overgrown by tall weeds, that hadn't gone off to war by virtue of their extreme age. The convent icons had long since been stolen. Klavdiya's mother, Agafya, who had been the senior beggar at the convent before its spoliation, had hidden away part of the smashed iconostasis in her own home.

'There hasn't been any God for a long time,' Nikanor explained to the women. 'You should read the newspapers!'

Klavdiya believed only in her own desires and never paid any heed to her man. She needed God to save her son, and so she frequented her mother's hut to pray alongside her on their knees. A faded portrait of Stalin in a frame of paper funeral flowers had been stuck with horseshoe nails just above the gate-icon of Our Lady on the convent gates, not far from the Dvoyeninov home. But the old folks in Anosino assured everyone that this was just to put people off the scent and continued to say their prayers at the gates. Klavdiya, too, would make the sign of the cross whenever Nikanor wasn't looking, so that the Lord wouldn't forget about her son.

And Aleksey had grown up – even though feeble – almost healthy and happy, in defiance of hunger and poverty. It was as if in Anosino they lived the way life was supposed to be, like in the films that they showed at the community club (the former convent refectory). Aleksey's parents and his grandma Agafya hadn't spared themselves in his service: he was the only one they had left. Nikanor, true, still wanted to make more babies: their allotment was giving them enough potatoes to feed more mouths. In Germany, he told the two women, all parents without exception had three kids. But Klavdiya had fallen ill with some sort of female complaint, and the doctor told Nikanor that she could never have any more children – how she had managed to give birth at all was a phenomenon, a mystery of medical science. Nikanor didn't have a clue about whatever it was that the doctor had noticed was wrong with Klavdiya, but she really never did get pregnant again; evidently she'd put everything into that first occasion.

When her son finally reached the age of conscription and the local military enlistment board had shaven his head, Klavdiya had grieved and wept to the jolly martial music of the brass band, as if out of some sort of precognition. In 1964 there was a shortfall in the call-up owing to the low wartime birth rate, and the health of all the conscripts was poor because of the post-war famine. But inasmuch as the speedy development of jet aircraft and atomic submarines for defence against American imperialism demanded personnel, as Nikanor explained it, the medical board temporarily lowered its strict standards. So Aleksey had been classified as an extra-healthy specimen, highly qualified, and wound up at an aviation academy for supersonic MiG pilots.

Aleksey Dvoyeninov was embarking on military service in an epoch when people were no longer considered to be mere cogs. Moreover, they had become the most advanced and most conscious people in the world – the Soviet nation. Their highs and lows, deeds and misdemeanours, victories and defeats, their straight lines, their parabolas, their ellipses – that is, the entire geometry of their lives – depended on the Motherland, which determined Aleksey's path along with the orbits of all the other Alekseys. Gagarin had been launched into orbit, inducted into the Party while still in orbit and had come back to earth to be greeted with glory. But they could just as well not have inducted him and not greeted him, or let anyone else know about it, or not have made him a hero at all – the Motherland decided everything: the Motherland to whom, according to the song, every Tom, Dick and Aleksey was in eternal debt.

He never thought about this and accepted his fate. Even though discipline at the academy was as tight as a taut bowstring he was even happy at the thought that others were responsible for all his decisions. Your life didn't belong to you but to the Soviet homeland. Aleksey was proud of that. He liked flying, but he saw only the whitewashed fuel bunkers at the military airfields and the bomb magazines behind their barbed-wire fences – everything else was hidden by clouds. That was how he imagined the Soviet landscape: airstrips, bomb dumps and Anosino village and their house on the knoll above the purest river in the world, the Istra.

Either the designers had failed to take something into account or the workers had been skiving at the aircraft plant, though, because a glitch hit him soon enough. One day his engine revolutions fell sharply during a flight. Aleksey – in accordance with instructions – quickly informed the control tower.

'Give us your coordinates,' the tower demanded.

He made a turn over the Swedish island of Åland and flew towards the coast of Poland, so he could then turn towards Kaliningrad. An order came from his flight leader: 'Find out what's wrong, you motherfucker!'

'I can't find anything,' Aleksey reported. 'Negative on that.'

'We'll ask base.'

There was a long pause. Both parties were operating in strict accordance with instructions, but somehow this didn't help. His engine fell silent, and a hush ensued.

'The commander is cancelling the mission,' Aleksey heard over his helmet radio. 'Jettison your canopy and reserve tanks.'

Aleksey understood from the two foreign airliners flashing past that he was in a civilian aviation zone. He continued losing altitude.

He felt cold, not because of his approaching end but from the deathly silence. It would be better to die in a roar and screech of rending metal where you couldn't hear your own last guttural shriek. It was sad that he'd never had any leave to go home to Anosino to his mother and father, that nobody in the village had ever seen him in his officer's uniform. Life, if you looked into it, wasn't all that precious. But it was too bad about the leave time. Well, and there *was* another duty he'd left unfulfilled.

Duty – that was something Aleksey was aware of. If they'd taught it to him it meant he had to do it. He was obliged to try to save the aeroplane entrusted to him by Party and government. But how was he going to do that, when the plane had already stopped obeying?

The order came. 'Eject!'

He'd done training ejections twice. Both times successfully, if you didn't count the vomiting and vertigo from the light concussion that he'd had to carefully conceal from his superiors. This time he felt the strong upward jolt – he was being flung out together with his seat. The short-term loss of consciousness owing to the ebbing of blood from his head could be ignored. Aleksey was hanging in a damp mass that was pasted to the visor of his helmet. Going by the altimeter that he had glanced at just before ejecting, there was no distance at all left to the ground – or, more precisely, to the water. The plane disappeared, dissolving into the clouds, as if it had never been.

'I'm alive!' howled Aleksey, happily raving. 'Alive!'

The clouds barely let the lieutenant pass through them: he saw nothing more than a solid grey mass. Aleksey felt first a jolt, and then he was twisting around in his shroud lines. Now the rain was coming down heavily, slantwise, together with Aleksey. The grey mass below was churning in all directions, sucking him into it. A wave caught him and dragged him down, but then itself pushed him up out of the deep. The lieutenant pressed the valve on his tank of compressed air, and the orange raft opened out, quickly blowing up full, and stood vertically out of the water. He pushed it down and lay sprawled flat on it, spreading his legs for balance.

'Alive!' Aleksey repeated once more, checking himself over.

The raft rose up on the crests of the waves and fell back down into the troughs. He could only guess that he was about two-thirds of the way between the island of Åland and the Polish coastline, and he felt sub-consciously that he was being carried either to the south or to the south-west. *Either way is fine: Poland is ours, and the GDR is ours, too. Just have to wait.*

Aleksey dragged his helmet off his head; it was getting heavy, but it was cold without it. At first he held the helmet against the raft with one hand, and then he got tired and the helmet was washed away by the water. *Surely our lads are already out looking for me.* Aleksey broke the seal on his signal flare and got ready to launch it, but there was no one in the vicinity and it would have been useless to set it off. He listened carefully to the sounds around him and didn't hear anything except the splashing of the waves. He was getting rolled around a lot, and he felt a bit seasick. He swallowed his emergency rations and drank some rainwater, turning his face to the sky and scraping the moisture from his cheeks and forehead with one hand. As he dozed off, Aleksey heard the chugging of an engine. He'd never once doubted that they would find him. His first shot didn't go off – the flare gun misfired. He thought it might have got too damp. But the second time he heard a hissing, and a red flame fanned out above the water.

They'd noticed him. In the twilight Aleksey could make out the gunwale of a fishing boat.

'*Pan tonie?*' a voice asked, magnified by a speaking trumpet. 'Who are you, *pan?*'

'I'm Russian!' Aleksey howled. 'I've had an accident! Help!' *Our lads – they lend a helping hand to the whole world, and everyone on earth greets our lads with pride, sure as God made little green apples!*

'*Ryoosky?*' the man on the seiner asked again. '*Sovyetsky?*'

'Soviet, Soviet!' Aleksey nodded and got up on his knees on the raft so they could see him, the Soviet, better.

'Sovyetskies having to go back. Go to the Bolsheviks. Let them to help. *Proshu, pane!*' The man on the seiner lowered his megaphone and went into his wheelhouse.

'Hey,' yelled Aleksey, not understanding a thing. 'Wait a minute! I've been hanging on here for more than nine hours already.'

The sound of the engine grew louder and drowned out his words. The seiner disappeared.

'What a fascist!' Aleksey muttered. 'And we liberated them, after all!'

He shivered, a light tremor. He clenched his teeth and tried moving his arms and legs to keep himself warm, but didn't have the strength to do it. Night fell. Aleksey passed out and came back around from the pain in his spine. He groaned and opened his eyes. The film was winding backwards. Aleksey once again hung above the grey mass of water with its white foam, the wind rocking him from side to side. The endless grey mass of water was receding from him. His leg got tangled in his parachute shroud lines, and he tried to free it. But here his delirium ended. He was being hoisted, all hunched up, into the hatch of a helicopter.

He came to in a military hospital. He'd been bobbing about on the waves for thirty-six hours. They had informed the commander of the Baltic military district about him, who in turn had reported to the commander-in-chief of the combined forces of the Warsaw Pact countries, Marshal Grechko, in Moscow. Moscow had sent a coded message to the coastal military bases in East Germany. A helicopter had been sent for him from there.

Aleksey was taken to the Ministry of Defence hospital for officers with psychological disorders at Pavshino, outside Moscow, with a diagnosis of hallucinatory-delirious psychosis. Aleksey had insomnia, he felt hungry even after eating, and he had constant headaches and fears. Fear of falling, fear of looking down from a window, fear of being alone in the ward. He would scream at night – and his healthier neighbours in the ward would shake him by the shoulder. He was being treated with peace and quiet and chemicals to reduce his fears.

Nobody had informed his parents of anything. They were sure their son was doing his duty. Aleksey had seldom written home even before this. But now he was in hospital right near his home: you can get to Pavshino on a bike from the village of Anosino. He came to terms with his life being arranged differently and was even happy about it. So Klavdiya cried a bit and sighed a bit, but the trouble was already behind them, thank God.

He didn't have any superiors to tell him what to do any more, so Aleksey was forced to figure things out for himself. The first thing he did as a civilian was to get married. Hurriedly, just like his father, out of the blue. He married Lyuba, the girlfriend of a friend of his from school, who was working now as a metalworker in a car factory. His friend was fed up with Lyuba. She herself felt like there was nothing doing there and invited the demobilized Aleksey to a dance in the Culture Park. Lyuba lived with her father and mother in Moscow, in a hundred-and-seventy-square-foot room in a communal apartment in an old building in Plyushchikha. She explained straight away that if they got him registered as one more resident in their room they would be put on a waiting-list for a new apartment. Aleksey always got rooted to the spot whenever he touched Lyuba, and he agreed. Klavdiya alone was categorically opposed.

'She's got him wound around her finger – he's just a boy!' she complained to her neighbours. 'Wound around her finger!'

'But he's getting a residence permit for Moscow,' her neighbours objected.

'Residence permit? Any woman would like to marry him – he's an officer! He could have shopped around and picked one of the best. And how are they going to live now? God knows when they're going to get a new apartment! Right now they're sleeping bed-to-bed with her parents. They can't even move on the bed. For shame!'

His friend not only left Lyuba to him but his job as well. The shop boss asked Aleksey for his particulars. 'Right, so you mean you're some kind of hero?'

Aleksey shrugged his shoulders. 'Hero-schmeero. A hero's someone who's done something. And what am I? It just happened that way.'

'No! Anybody else, probably, would have been captured by the enemy or drowned, but you . . . you couldn't save your plane, but you did save your inflatable dinghy. And it wasn't even your dinghy. It was the government's!'

It wasn't clear if his new boss was joking or serious, but Aleksey was

pleased. He had completely recovered. After working for a while as a metalworker he took a driving course. They put his picture up on the Honour
Board. Soon after that the three best drivers were summoned to district
Party headquarters and offered a transfer to a special garage. The pay there
was higher and the work less

Aleksey was assigned to the *Trudovaya Pravda* editor, Makartsev, who
was content with him. Aleksey liked the work, but the people around him
were all striving for higher pay and newer apartments, they were buying
good furniture, while he and Lyuba (she was studying in her final year
at a financial college) had nothing. And now that his son had been born
everything was harder still. Everyone else used connections to get
ahead, but Aleksey didn't know how. This he understood: you're better
off giving the impression that you're stupid. Then the demands on you
are fewer and life is easier. But, reading the papers while he waited for
the editor, he took to recalling his heroic deed more and more often and
wondered how he could use it to his advantage.

One day on the Minsk Chaussee Aleksey was stopped by the driver
of a heavy refrigerator truck. Aleksey had just taken Makartsev to his *dacha*;
he was in no hurry and lent the other driver his spark-plug wrench. They
had a chat during a smoke break. The refrigerator truck had just come
from Hungary.

'You bring something back with you every time. No comparison with
what you get for Soviet money! Of course, it'd be best of all to go to a capitalist country, but even the socialist ones aren't bad.'

'So how do you get a job like that?'

'Join the Party. Without that you're just pissing in the wind. Well, and
get somebody to help you . . .'

Aleksey was itching to transfer to work at Sovtransavto. But getting
a job there turned out to be more complicated than the fellow had been
saying. Party membership was all well and good, but they were looking
only for experienced drivers – first-class, married ones. For that reason
Aleksey took a first-class drivers' course. He became an active member
of the Young Communist League in his garage and soon got elected sec-

retary. That was a step towards Party candidacy, and Aleksey got accepted as someone with a heroic past and a conscientious present. He was relying on his record, but he remembered that he was going to need a helping hand. One day he was impertinent enough to ask Makartsev, who was in a good mood, for a favour.

'You don't like driving me around?'

'Come on! Driving you is great, but I have to grow, too, you know. Right?'

'I was just joking. How are you coming along with the Party?'

'Fine! My candidacy probation period is almost over.'

'Well, see: you and I are both candidates. You for the Party, me for the Party Central Committee. OK! I'll give Foreign Trade a call. You get ready.'

Aleksey had got himself ready. But the realization of his dream was now to be postponed.

# — 3 —
# A Classic Infarct

Makartsev opened his eyes, then screwed them up at the whiteness around him. The sun shone through the window, something that he had become unused to over the winter. It was impossible for him to work out how long he'd remained in a state of oblivion. He was lying flat on his back, and he wanted to raise his hand to look at the time, but his arm was strapped to the bed and he could feel that his watch wasn't on it. An intravenous drip stood alongside his bed, and a tube ending in a fine needle came down from it to a vein in his arm. His breathing was all right: oxygen was barely audibly seeping into his nose, coming from another tube.

He turned his gaze from the IV to the ceiling, dappled with sunlight, reflecting off the phials standing on the glass-covered table and off the screen of the television in the corner. His eyes tired of the work, and he closed them.

'Does it hurt?' he heard a rather hoarse female voice say.

So he wasn't alone. He once more raised his eyelids with an effort and saw a thick-lipped girl in a white smock and cap.

'What's the date?' he asked.

'The twenty-seventh. Do you need anything?'

'A phone.'

'Go on!' The nurse flapped her chubby arms and adjusted his oxygen hose. 'No telephone for you! They had to wheel you into the emergency ward again last night. The department head said that you were to lie back and think of something pleasant.'

'It hurts.' His tongue felt thick, so he had to speak in short bursts.

'Where does it hurt?'

'My shoulder. Stomach. Back.'

'That's what it seems like to you. It's your heart.'

'My heart doesn't hurt.'

'And good thing, too! You have a classic infarct. I'll give you a shot for the pain right now.'

She was repeating the doctors' words. Lifting up the edge of his blanket the nurse bared his buttocks.

'Ow!' exclaimed Makartsev, like a little boy, when he felt the pain of the needle. 'I'm thirsty!'

She brought him a cup with a long spout: the water trickled between his lips, spilling down his cheek on to his pillow, but some got to his mouth.

'Your wife came to visit,' the nurse recalled. 'She said that everything was fine at home and at work, too. She's coming back again tomorrow. You just relax. If you need something, just press that button.'

Makartsev lay in semi-oblivion, listening to his heart. *Why am I here?* swam into his consciousness. *Am I going to have to lie here for long, like a useless idiot? Where's my wife – surely she could have forced her way in? I don't even know what they put in our last issue.*

The nurse had hit the nail on the head. Like a lot of Party members in his position who had lain in this ward before him, he knew neither how to be ill nor how to relax. He never went on vacation. At first his wife used to go with their son, but as soon as he'd grown up and refused to go with her any more she'd been going off to the Central Committee health resorts on her own. Makartsev was always at work.

On an external level this meant taking part in the preparation of decisions for the highest levels of authority, learning what those decisions actually were, working towards their execution, following up on their execution and reporting back on whatever work had been accomplished. There was constant tension, especially during the first and last steps. What happened in between, that is, the publishing of the newspaper, was the productive outcome of the first step and was done for the sake of the last.

To people at a lower level, understanding – or even more so, evaluating – the reasoned strictness and precision of the Party apparatus was quite impossible: to do that you would have to be at a particular height above sea level yourself.

The internal level that the outer one rested on consisted of his personal connections, meetings, banquets, trips. At every step there was some discussion of things that weren't written down, but frequently (for important reasons) asserting the contrary to what did get recorded. This level of affairs was just as serious as the first one. No less. But no more either. Those who considered that personal ties were the more important thing usually burned out before their time. Makartsev's scales held identical weights in each pan.

On both levels of activity you had your own patterns of behaviour, your own responsibility for every task entrusted to you and your directives, both official and personal. Otherwise, it was too easy to deviate. A Party activist of Makartsev's rank always had to think about what was going to happen if he deviated, and how to skirt around such danger zones. Someone who deviated in his ideological labours would never get on in the world. Despite all the humanism of the Soviet system that would never happen. Truth to tell, Makartsev had the firm conviction that he would never find himself in that position.

All by themselves his thoughts ran down the rut formed by his decades of activity among the leadership. The record that had been put on the turntable in his youth played on, and the needle was still sharp, still kept meticulously to the groove; the melody was the kind that became a habit, learned by rote. But every time it came to one particular point, now, there was a breakdown, and this endlessly repeating combination of *farct-in-farct* followed. His heart attack had come out of nowhere, unplanned for, like some kind of force that could never have manifested itself – in principle, from a normal point of view. That is, the point of view of the philosophy of materialism.

The most terrible thing for Makartsev, worse than death itself, had always been the possibility of making a wrong guess about what the party line was going to be in any concrete circumstance. And now it had come to pass that he was alive, that he had made no mistake in any way, but he was none the less getting shoved to one side. The heart attack hadn't coordinated its appearance with anyone, neither with him nor with the Central Committee. The whole of yesterday evening and this morning Makartsev had *not* been taking the pulse of Party life. Everyone else was there, and he wasn't. Things were coming to fruition, getting decided, being implemented – all without him. If things would stop there, too, just for a while – but no, they were going ahead! The heart attack was his alone. He – a necessary link in that living chain – had fallen, and the link was restored, without him! When would their arms ever open up to receive him again?

He'd heard a lot about heart attacks in other people, but he had been certain that he himself had some kind of immunity against them. And even now he still didn't want to admit that he'd been mistaken. No, they would never be able to make do without him. He'd done so much, could still do so much more. Their arms might have linked up again without him, but they would soon be feeling the lack of that one particular human force. Even though he was only a candidate member of the Central Committee, he'd been made a candidate because the Central Committee needed his brains.

He had to get back on his feet as quickly as possible. Where were the professors? The specialist physicians? What were they all off doing? Why hadn't they learned how to treat heart attacks swiftly, at least in important cases? Couldn't they understand that he had to get better quickly, to begin to take charge of things from here? Let them at least hook up a telephone for him!

'Please,' he mumbled, half alive, to his wife through his wan and disobedient lips, as soon as they let her in to see him for a moment. 'Make sure it doesn't get about too much that I've had a heart attack. Tell them that there was a suspicion, but it hasn't been confirmed.'

'Of course. What do you take me for, a fool?'

She didn't tell him that the hospital had immediately informed the

Central Committee, as well as the *Trudovaya Pravda* office, the Journalists'
Union – everybody. She quietly left the room.

How could he have had a heart attack, let alone a *classic* one? Was that
good or bad? Probably good. If it was the classic kind, surely you could
hope that they had learned how to treat it! And why had it happened –
did they know? His heart had always been healthy. If it hadn't been, even
to the slightest degree, Makartsev would never have received a directive
to prepare the documents necessary to obtain a diplomatic passport. Even
before now he had been using a special gate, his baggage not subject to
inspection. Now he could expect to be met by his personal car right beside
the gangway. But was his health going to permit him to travel? While the
doctors were taking their time Makartsev decided to analyse his own affairs
and establish the reason for his heart attack, so he would know who the
enemy was and how to beat him.

# — 4 —
## Makartsev's Own
## Flights and Falls

Makartsev considered himself a lucky man and felt he could rightfully count on more. At every stage in his life's history, though, when he'd spread his wings and flown to a perch closer to the top of the tree one of his wings had hit something. Because of that, his flights seemed to him not as magnificent as he had intended. And there had been the danger of breaking a wing every time.

His father, Ivan Makartsev, the German teacher at the St Petersburg Gymnasium (on Vasilyevsky Island), had named his son Hans, thereby expressing his respect for German culture. It would have been better if he'd just taught him German. If the young Makartsev had been born a couple of years later, when St Petersburg was renamed Petrograd, they wouldn't have named him Hans, and that would have made the future flapping of his wings easier. Hans's parents died in the Civil War, and the ten-year-old boy was taken in by kinsfolk. His formerly middle-class uncles and aunts passed him from family to family in those disordered years, feeding him with whatever they could.

A boy scout troop became his second home. He would joyfully put on his blue uniform, sewn out of rough canvas, and his light-blue neckerchief, in which he would tie a new knot after every good deed. And then the Yookies came along – young people from the Communist Youth League, the *Komsomol* – and scout troops were banned. He proudly joined them instead. Igor Makartsev was well liked in the Young Communist cells for his open disposition and his energy, and they always elected him leader.

He was finishing his university studies and working actively in the Young Communists when Kirov was assassinated. Makartsev, already in the Party, was offered the chair of the editor of the Leningrad *Komsomol* newspaper, *Smena*. The editorship had recently been liberated from an enemy of the people. Makartsev liked to write, too – he was best at ringing articles on international themes. His articles were reprinted several times in *Pravda*, and he was offered a transfer to Moscow.

The subjects for his articles were now being given to him by the People's Commissariat for International Affairs, which was where he took what he'd written. Some bits got taken out, and some bits were suggested to him in addition. Unexpectedly, the publishing department recommended that he sign one of his articles not just with the initial H by itself, but with his full name: Hans Makartsev. The Bureau of Information disseminated his article abroad. This was soon after 16 August 1939, the day Von Ribbentrop arrived in Moscow.

He had been brought up through his childhood and youth on antifascism. And now? Outwardly everything seemed to stay the same, but inwardly things were different. He felt that he would be on top of things if only he could understand what was going on in Comrade Stalin's current policy. His entire path after that – opportunities for a maximal output to the Party – now depended on how faithfully he could put into practice what was evidently a brilliant idea from the most important person in the Party, the country and the whole world, judging by its boldness. It couldn't have been just an accident that Stalin had declared fascism to be a historically progressive system, serving as an intermediate step between capitalism and socialism, after all. So, now one had to work hand in hand with the fascists. Out of the blue, Makartsev had been included in the list of people accompanying Molotov to Berlin. As the translator Berezhkov said at the time: 'You've got a nice name for this trip.'

The start of the war had been a blow for Makartsev, although he could have foreseen it. *We helped Hitler, and he turned out to be an ingrate!* Makartsev had believed too absolutely in what he was writing in his articles. He quickly made the adjustment and never again erred through such sincerity. However, he had developed a great flair for the necessary spirit in which to write, and just as before it didn't let him down. At the beginning of the war he'd heard about arrests and deportation of people with German first and last names, although he didn't believe it could happen to him. Just in case, he filed a request to change his German name, Hans, to the Russian Igor. After that was done he asked his local recruitment office to send him to the front. They didn't: he was already *nomenklatura*, on the staff of the Central Committee. He never knew that he stayed at large thanks to Molotov, who had read his articles.

'Makartsev, who went with us to see that rascal Hitler,' said Molotov, 'understood the right way to make propaganda under novel conditions. He's got a nose for it. Put him on the list.'

Thus Makartsev's name was among those receiving the first medals to be awarded during the war. At the end of the war, when they were gearing up ideological work, restarting newspapers in the regions that had earlier been occupied by the Germans, he was made an instructor in the newspaper division of the Central Committee apparatus.

His thirty-first year had come and gone when he suddenly began thinking, seriously to the point of sickliness, about the fact that he was alone. The homes of the people around him were comfortable, with children in them, and he had never tasted that particular joy. In a little while it would be too late. The country had lost over twenty million lives in the war, and everyone was hastening to reproduce (and Makartsev was a son of his country). Because of that, and because the time was ripe, he decided to get married.

He met Zina on a bench by the pond at the Central Committee health centre at Barvikha. She'd already been married once before. Given her beauty and intelligence, this was unsurprising. He was tactful and never asked about her first husband. The place where they met was entirely proper; they had gone twice to the Bolshoi Theatre and once to the Moscow Arts Academy Theatre. He was eager to get married: he fell in love with Zina.

Makartsev would come home late at night, as was the norm in those years. He would stand for a long time by his son's cot, joyfully listening to the baby's even breathing. He worked so hard, though, that he didn't even have any time to play with his growing son.

In the middle of February 1953 he was asked to complete a new questionnaire in the personnel department for management cadres. After attentively reading it, the examiner asked: 'What's your wife's maiden name?'

'Zhevnyakova.'

'And her name from her first marriage?'

Makartsev didn't know – after divorcing her first husband Zina had retaken her maiden name. But he couldn't say that he didn't know, so he was at a loss.

'Does this really matter?'

'I'm just doing my job,' the examiner answered. 'Her first husband's name was Fleytman.'

'But she's a Russian, not a Jew!' He leaped to her defence, feeling the fright covering his face with a flush of guilt.

Makartsev's duties had brought him face to face with this problem when selecting personnel – in accordance with the spirit of the times – for the regional newspapers. He'd never felt there was any need for it, though. On the contrary, an unpleasant feeling of guilt, even, overcame him every time the issue came up. He had explained this phenomenon to himself as a provincial prejudice, as something having to do with the ill-bred personnel who had flooded into the Party after the Purge. Stalin, of course, didn't know about it.

'She's a pure-blooded Zhevnyakova!' he repeated.

'That's not the point. Are you acquainted with her former husband?'

'No! I've never seen him and never asked about him. What's going on?'

'Surely you're aware that proceedings are now under way against the doctors who've been plotting to give improper treatment to our leaders. And former Professor Fleytman worked in the same clinic with those enemies of the people.'

'But my wife doesn't have anything to do with that. I know that as an absolute certainty.'

'For now there's only one thing that's absolutely certain: we have received a personal directive with regard to this Doctors' Plot.'

Makartsev sat in shock. One thought ran feverishly around his mind in an artless groove, hedged with thorns on every side. He could already imagine his wife being taken away from him, maybe even their proposing that he divorce her. He thought of calling his patron, but Molotov had already demonstrated great principle in denouncing his wife, Zhemchuzhina, as an enemy of the people.

'Who can I talk to about this?'

'Who would you talk to,' the instructor answered with a question, 'when we have already got a directive on it?'

'Whose directive?'

'Don't you understand?' The instructor raised his eyes skywards and then looked at Makartsev with compassion.

And that was why he had taken a clumsy step – out of despair, surely. He requested a holiday at a health resort, since he hadn't taken any time off in five years and wasn't feeling too well. That made them smile: arresting someone at a health resort was considered more convenient than doing it where they worked.

After booking a place in the Caucasus he had left with his wife and son. At Kursk Makartsev had grabbed their suitcase and shoved the perplexed Zina off the train, explaining to the woman conductor that he had to get back to Moscow. An hour later they were travelling in a third-class carriage in sweltering heat, among people with sacks, and Zina was looking wide-eyed at her husband. He understood, though: they would find him sooner or later, anywhere. He just didn't want it to happen right then. At a village market full of ragged people an old forester who had come to town to buy a piglet hove into sight. Makartsev identified himself by a different name and complained that his sick son had been told by the doctors that he needed some forest air. He could pay well.

The forester's hut smelt of soured milk and chicken droppings:

chickens were kept indoors in winter. Through the nights Makartsev waited. But no one took any interest in them. They lived without any extravagance, eating bread and pork fat, sleeping on wooden shelves. With nothing to do Makartsev was in torment. The forester didn't take any newspapers, and the radio blared away, talking about grandiose accomplishments in the Socialist countries and about strikes in other ones, testifying to the imminent collapse of the capitalist system. Listening to it, Makartsev thought the propaganda being put out was very monotonous, without much flexibility. With a tremor in his soul, he suppressed any thoughts about the looming end to his holiday. When his host woke him up early one morning and told him in a whisper that the radio was saying that Stalin was dying, Makartsev grew even more afraid.

'This is the end!' he told his wife.

'How innocent you are! I never gave a damn about Stalin. You're the one who's precious to me!'

'Quiet!' He shut her mouth with his hand, but she pushed him away and got down from the shelf.

'Don't you understand. This is our only salvation!'

Makartsev asked the old man to take him to town. He telephoned his boss from there.

The man was surprised. 'Where have *you* been? They've been looking for you.'

'My son fell ill on the way.'

'Come back as soon as you can. You're needed. It was just a mistake.'

On the way back to the forester's hut he snatched the reins from the old man and himself urged on the horse with words and whip.

'The Doctors' Plot has been dropped,' he yelled to Zina across the threshold.

'What did I tell you?'

The Makartsevs went home. Outwardly everything was calm, but everyone's nerves were on edge. Makartsev was one of the most active in the preparations for the Twentieth Party Congress. He worked with animation, energy and once again a clear conscience. When they transferred many people out of the Central Committee to other jobs – people whose pasts were stained by their connection with the Cult of Personality – he wasn't touched.

He never took a liking to the people to whom he was now subordinate. The world had been turned upside down, and they had risen from the bottom. They had stood around the speechless Stalin when he was lying on the floor, weeping after his stroke. Now the throne was left empty. Wary of one another, they began talking of collective leadership. Nobody wanted to lose, and Makartsev depended on them utterly. At any moment your past could be used as evidence against you, or it could work to your advantage. Fortunately, he was a workhorse on the Central Committee, on that large team to which the Politburo entrusted its work, leaving themselves only the one thing – power. With the expert secretaries' group he wrote entire chapters of Khrushchev's speeches. Khrushchev himself laughed long when he heard by accident of how Makartsev had hidden out at the forester's hut. After one of his trips abroad, during which Makartsev was in charge of feeding the proper information to the press, Khrushchev offered Makartsev a newspaper. Not long before this the previous editor had raised a question – in that narrow circle of people – about Khrushchev's name being mentioned too often in print and on very minor grounds and had been packed off into retirement.

After being made editor-in-chief Makartsev thought more and more often that the Stalinist repressions hadn't been as terrible for Party members who were devoted to the cause as was sometimes bruited about. He worked for Khrushchev and then for Brezhnev and did it selflessly. In his youth Makartsev had been famous for knowing how to spot someone's striking characteristic, and nicknames that he'd devised frequently stuck to their owners. He was the one who'd named Brezhnev 'Thick Eyebrows', and this characterization then took on a life of its own, giving birth to the famous joke about Stalin's moustache reappearing on a higher plane.

Makartsev himself suspected that his strength lay in the access that he had in some strange way, even during Stalin's time, to the eternal

Politburo member, Suslov. Makartsev understood that this elder of the apparatus, whom he had given the nickname Comrade Skinny, was a unique personality. His was a pure, old-fashioned style. He considered himself one of Lenin's Guards, although he'd never had anything to do with that body. Now he held in his hands every thread of internal and external ideology, and his very inconspicuousness gave him special satisfaction.

Makartsev could only guess how he had managed to attract attention to himself. But one day he'd been invited to Comrade Skinny's *dacha*. The man had Igor meet him in his private park. Suslov was in a long gabardine Chinese cloak, holding an umbrella, even though it was a sunny June day. They drank tea *al fresco* under the lime trees. Makartsev tried to give the impression that he was no fool, that he was modest and that he could guess what he might be needed for. His host told him how he had stopped smoking and offered him the post of assistant.

'I need an employee who knows how to write and understands what he's writing for.'

This was even more unexpected: everyone thought Comrade Skinny was the only one who wrote his own speeches. Since that time Makartsev would periodically drop in for tea (his host never drank anything stronger). Over the years the teas became more and more rare, but they kept going.

Their relationship was neither that of friends nor something obligatory, like that between a boss and his subordinate. It was more like a mutually convenient symbiosis. At tea Makartsev would sniff out certain things in the air, things that were coming up at the top, and Skinny, preferring to keep to the shadows, learned what was roiling around below. For him, Makartsev was a Party man occupying a level to which he never lowered himself. Makartsev kept this connection a secret even from Zina. It seemed to him that the tea parties under the limes demeaned him in some way, but how, exactly, he didn't want to explain to himself.

Makartsev was in his fifties, and he had something to lose. Material well-being he didn't especially value, but he still cared about his position.

He could feel stability only in upward movement, but in recent times that had slowed down. After all, as soon as you come to a stop you're going to start rolling back downhill. His health wasn't what it had been. Every day, even though he tried not to think about it, something hurt: now his back (an incrustation of salts, the doctors said), now his liver. He loved to eat, and he overate. He loved to drink. As for women, whenever conversation in masculine company turned to them, he would say with a smile that in old age he understood the simple truth: they were built the same, one and all. As the old forester from Tambov had put it, however hard you look you'll never find one that goes sideways.

Makartsev understood that the position he was occupying wasn't any kind of barrier, but a certain apathy – and other, external reasons that were unclear to him – stopped him from being more active. He comforted himself with the fact that he didn't push himself forward like some people did, stepping on the toes of his rivals. Despite everything, he believed in the ultimate triumph of Communism. Not in the means (they had long since been compromised) but in the ends, in the happiness that had to come sooner or later. Not for him – for others.

In the days of the events in Czechoslovakia in the previous year, 1968, Makartsev had been thinking: *We won't go to the brink, we won't send in the troops. Even under Stalin we couldn't do that with Yugoslavia. If I were in charge I wouldn't allow it.* He liked Dubcek, only it was so deep within him that he didn't admit it even to himself. Makartsev didn't share the complacency of the present-day leaders, for whom Party functions were higher than human ones. Indulgence frightened them. He would surely behave differently, in a more cultured fashion. We can't know what notions would have occurred to Makartsev, though, had he climbed the remaining steps to the top. He was afraid of rejection even inside himself and much more so outside of him. It wasn't so much inertia as common sense that was stronger than he was, that dictated his actions and his behaviour. Whatever anyone else's abilities, Makartsev certainly couldn't help foreseeing the currents beneath the surface. He understood that ideological muscles were tensing up after the Czech events. He calmed himself with the idea that it was unavoidable, that he wouldn't lose his head. In the middle of December 1968, though, Makartsev had something to be nervous about.

For nearly two weeks his mother-in-law had been visiting from Rostov-on-Don. She went to all the museums; she delighted in the length of the queues everywhere.

'My son-in-law is such a responsible person, he hasn't got time to talk,' she grumbled jokily. 'I'm on the go all the time, too, though . . .'

'Don't stand in queues. Make a shopping list, and I'll send my chauffeur.'

'Don't think of it! It wouldn't do to go adding to your troubles.'

His mother-in-law was five years older than he was and constantly stressed it. Once when he came home from chairing a conference at Journalists' House on ideological work, he was tired and wanted to go straight to bed. But in addition to his mother-in-law there was an unfamiliar man with a short sailor's beard sitting in the room, a man who looked like some kind of modern-day scientist. So Ma-in-law had got herself a boyfriend!

The visitor rose from his chair, stretched out a hand and, looking him attentively in the eye, pronounced in a sharp voice: 'Aleksandr.'

'Igor,' Makartsev answered straight away, although he hadn't made someone's acquaintance in such an informal way for a long time.

'My sister was in the same class as he was,' his mother-in-law explained. 'They came to be friends, played together. I last saw him just before the war. He was graduating from college. I managed to find him. But I wouldn't have recognized him on the street. Igor, are you hungry?' She went out into the kitchen.

'What did you study at university?' Makartsev asked his guest. He wasn't asking out of curiosity but for conversation's sake. 'Physics?'

'Physics and mathematics,' said the guest.

Makartsev didn't even congratulate himself for his perspicacity. Whatever else he might not be able to do, he was quick to size people up. His mother-in-law set a plate down in front of him: a cold chicken leg and two tomatoes – just the way he liked it.

'And are you going to have something?'

'Most gracious,' the guest growled. He wasn't very talkative.

'He doesn't want anything,' his mother-in-law explained. 'He says he's full. And I have to watch my waist at night. As the French say, a moment on your tongue, the rest of your life on your hips.'

'Are you an editor?' The guest shifted his eyes to the fresh, red, December tomatoes. It wasn't clear whether he wanted to ask for something in connection with the query (there are quite a few things to ask the editor-in-chief of a newspaper for – this didn't surprise Makartsev, who took it as a duty and helped however he could) or was asking out of politeness.

'Yes, I'm a journalist,' Makartsev corrected him slightly and recited:

> *'At thirty you'll be buying glasses,*
> *Thirty-five, it's cataracts,*
> *At forty it's "Goodbye, sweet lasses,"*
> *Forty-five – you're dead or whacked.'*

'Who wrote that?'

'It's folk wisdom. That's what young newspapermen sing in their cups. But older men who've turned *that* corner keep quiet.'

'How old are you?'

'I'm fifty-six.'

'So not all prophecies come true,' said the guest, again eyeing the scarlet tomatoes.

'Well, I do have back trouble, and my liver is acting up,' smiled Makartsev.

'In physics there's a concept called a *threshold*. Water, water, then suddenly, across the threshold, there's ice, a qualitative difference. People have thresholds that are more relative, I think.'

'And how is your health?' his mother-in-law asked their guest.

'Ten years ago I thought I'd reached my threshold. The doctors spooked me: doomed, they said. But, as you can see, I managed to pull myself out of it. Well, it's time for me to go. I've been working evenings as well.'

'In a secret institute?' asked Makartsev, once again certain that he wasn't mistaken, since the majority of research institutions were clandestine.

'Almost!' his guest nodded, getting up. 'Take care!'

They shook hands with one another, and his mother-in-law went to see her sister's classmate to the door. Their hushed voices, and their laughter, could be heard in the corridor. Makartsev put his plate to one side, poured himself a glass of mineral water, drank it down and waited for the burp, pulled a cigarette out of the pack with his lips and took a luxuriant drag on it. His mother-in-law came back.

'Did you like my visitor?'

'On the whole . . .' Makartsev muttered politely, already thinking of his own affairs.

'But what a modest man! The whole world is talking and writing about him, after all!'

'The whole world?' Makartsev pulled the cigarette out of his mouth. 'Just who is he, then?'

'You surprise me sometimes! Solzhenitsyn.'

'Sol— ?!' Makartsev had a coughing fit.

'What's surprising about that?'

'Nothing, nothing at all . . .' He got up and went to hide in the bedroom.

Suslov had given Makartsev a copy of *Cancer Ward* when the question of its publication in *Novy Mir* was being debated. Makartsev had returned the galley proofs three days later.

'Well, what do you think?' Suslov asked.

'I don't know. If we cut out some of the allusions, maybe it'll be cleared?'

'You and I would understand it properly. But the masses? And, besides, if we allow it – tomorrow they'll want something spicier! Solzhenitsyn isn't on our side.'

Most of all he felt resentment at his mother-in-law. After pacing around his bedroom he came back out again. She was washing dishes in the kitchen.

'Keep in mind that *that* man' – he consciously didn't want to pronounce his name – 'is going to be expelled from the Writers' Union soon for anti-Sovietism!'

'That'll be a big mistake. In their time everybody knocked Yesenin, Pasternak and Bulgakov – and now?'

'Don't you know that he has connections abroad and that the KGB has him under surveillance?'

'That's just stupid! He's an honest man, more honest than any of us. They wanted to give him the Lenin Prize not long ago.'

'Yes, he hugged Khrushchev.'

'And he's not talented, then, without Khrushchev around?'

'I don't want to argue about his talent. But do you realize what kind of a spot you're putting me in, bringing him here?'

'Oh, that's what you're on about!'

'Let's grant you don't give a damn about me,' he said, not giving her a chance to make any excuses, 'but what about your daughter and grandson? Their situation depends on me as well, you know!'

'As far as I can tell, it's not 1937 any more.'

'A lot you know! Maybe I even like your damned Solzhenitsyn. He could conceivably be the next Leo Tolstoy. Be that as it may, leave it to our descendants to figure it out. You're a literature teacher, and I, in a manner of speaking, am a responsible Party worker, damn it! My sympathies and antipathies are defined neither by you nor your classmate!'

'Not mine, my sister's!'

'All right, your sister's!'

'I get you. We don't have to engage in a political catechism. You won't hear another word about him. I mean, you won't hear it from me.' And his mother-in-law made a dignified exit.

'Sorry for being sharp,' he called after her.

But he was furious with her the next day, too. Of course she was going to tell Zina and her grandson about it. It would be the last straw if his son began despising him for cowardice!

Did *they* know that Solzhenitsyn had been to his home? It would be wise to take out a little insurance. He'd been thinking all night how best to do it, and the answer came that morning when Makartsev was driving to the Central Committee. Walking down the corridor he told himself he had a right to suppress his cultural sentiments on ideological grounds and, keeping in mind their tea parties under the lime trees, he stuck his head into the office of Suslov's assistant.

Khomutilov, the media assistant, was dry and long, a lot like his master, and he spoke softly and unhurriedly. They had known each other since the end of the thirties. Makartsev asked if he could find out whether Himself could see him for a moment on an important matter.

He was received that same night. Makartsev claimed that a huge number of letters condemning Solzhenitsyn had been coming in to his office. The newspapers had kept their silence so far, but maybe now it was time to print a few of the comments? Makartsev understood that *they* might not like the idea of his giving them advice on ideological policy, but he was insuring himself against any accusation of sympathy for Solzhenitsyn just in case. During the meeting, though, Suslov didn't give away his own opinion but simply wanted to look at the correspondence.

Back in his office Makartsev called for the acting head of the Communist Education department, Rappoport, and suggested that he get together some of the commentary right away. An hour and a half later the pieces lay on Makartsev's desk, under the heading 'Shame on Solzhenitsyn!' Their texts said everything necessary about the writer. Makartsev crossed out the heading and wrote: 'We Object to Solzhenitsyn!' He knew that a campaign would catch fire only gradually, and you had to keep some kerosene in reserve.

The following day Khomutilov telephoned Makartsev and gave him permission to put the material in the next issue. The newspaper came out, and he expected that his mother-in-law wouldn't be able to restrain herself but would come up with something offensive. That evening, though, his wife told him she'd put her mother on the train. Her mother had wanted to stay for the New Year, but today she had suddenly changed her mind.

'She could at least have telephoned to say goodbye,' he said, glad at heart that she hadn't.

'She asked me to give you a kiss.' So his mother-in-law hadn't said anything to Zina.

'She could move in with us permanently.'

'You know how independent she is!'

All the other newspapers, TASS and the foreign Communist press took up the campaign against Solzhenitsyn. The correctness of Makartsev's line came in for praise at the Central Committee ideological conference. There was a particular joy in outcomes like that: you always acted the way the Party wanted you to, even though you personally might disagree with something or even think the opposite. *Yes, the opposite – because you're not a machine, you're a living member of the Party. But, of course, you disagree in your heart, without expressing it. You have to act as the Party considers necessary. And therein lies the root of the difference between Leninist adherence to principles and an abstract adherence to principles, an apolitical conscientiousness.*

In his youth Makartsev had sometimes suffered from the feeling that he had demeaned his sense of self-respect by having to carry out, from necessity, some absurd order. But he had figured a way out of it: his self-respect never suffered in cases where he himself, prior to some decree, could grasp what was Party-wise and what was not at that given moment. The dull-witted Party leader was the poor one who waited for directions. And although in the final analysis the result was the same – since foreseeing meant acting in accordance with a decree that hadn't yet been received – the difference of principle was unquestionable.

# Icebergs

It seemed to Makartsev that he was lying in semi-oblivion, but his brain was working overtime. The electrocardiograph machine alongside his bed hummed away quietly, registering every beat of the editor's heart, and the hum didn't bother him: it even helped him think. Breathing was easier in the oxygen tent.

It was now Thursday, 27 February 1969. The trouble had started on Wednesday.

Makartsev began his recollection of the preceding days with Monday, since on Sunday his wife had insisted that they finally go for a one-day health-centre visit and go walking in the pine forest at Barvikha. They wandered around the park, took in the holiday luncheon in honour of Soviet Army Day and then relaxed in a two-room apartment with a television. Makartsev was given a massage, and he had a yoga exercise recommended for his spreading paunch, and they assigned an individual trainer to him in the swimming-pool. Out of long habit, though, Makartsev was scornful of all the blessings of being served that were on offer for someone like him. And, scorning them, he was singling himself out from everyone else and making enemies – but he couldn't have done otherwise.

After a whole day of it he was worn out, a nervous wreck, faint from inactivity. For the last third of that Sunday he'd sat down at the telephone, anyway, and made decisions on a whole range of issues, talking to whoever was necessary. Zina looked at him, telephone in his hand, with reproach.

'What's wrong with you?' he asked.

'Are you going to take a phone to the grave with you?'

Their chauffeur drove the Makartsevs home; they were rather exhausted but none the less rested. They went to bed that night before twelve. So he decided to start his recollections from Monday, because everything the week before had been calm and quiet, and on Sunday he had become a bundle of nerves only from the inactivity. But he was certain that his heart attack hadn't arisen out of that.

So, on Monday, 24 February 1969, at 9.45 in the morning Makartsev had phoned his secretary, Anna. The working day at *Trudovaya Pravda* began at eleven; the majority of the employees would have made their appearance by noon, and it was only the typing pool that started at ten. Anna would show up at reception at 9.30 so that she could air her editor's smoky office and select the papers that urgently needed his signature and the ones that were for his eyes only.

The newspaper's routine was never really any concern of Makartsev's. He could read the already composed pages in the evening. Or not read anything at all. Putting things in, taking things out, checking them over, adding to them or shortening something – that could all be done by people at the newspaper without any input from him. He would only look over the articles that were obviously important before they were set in type. But Makartsev lived by the traditions of the thirties; he loved the newspaper's kitchen-like atmosphere, he liked going into things with a fine-toothed comb.

He would go around the various departments asking how people were getting along; he could strike up conversations even with rank-and-file employees, the majority of whom he knew by face and last name. The deputies were his shadows: he did their work, and in their offices they made up minor jobs for themselves. Makartsev loved it when they were concisely relaying the essence of an article to him and he would catch them in mid-word and hurry them on: 'What comes next? What's the conclusion?' Of course, what worried him most was the strategy of the whole thing, that is, the topics that stretched from issue to issue over the long term, as well as the planned *absence* of other topics, another strategy of this newspaper that had been entrusted to him. The sense of this strategy and its larger goals were not to be grasped at editorial board meetings. Therefore he had telephoned on Monday morning for them not to wait for him: he was going to be at the ideological conference. He had already driven to the Central Committee, even though there were still two hours to go before it started.

In the corridors of the Central Committee he always encountered his old comrades. Many of them were of sufficiently academic bent to have defended their dissertations, but they, too, sat at their desks from morning till night, bending to the unbreakable discipline, ready to leap at a bell, developing nervous disorders. He wouldn't be subordinate to them now. No. He, Makartsev, had done the right thing, leaving their ranks for his newspaper: there was more independence there, and the work was lively and evident to the people at large.

The time remaining before the conference was more important than the conference itself. In private conversations, cigarette breaks and corridor encounters he would clear up a range of matters that were neither spoken of from the stage nor written down in sealed documents. These were the hints that everything else depended on, including the decisions taken at the conference and the strategy for all the newspapers. Like an iceberg, this was almost entirely underwater. But there is something that is the opposite of an iceberg, something that cannot exist in the ocean: the top part moves in one direction, while the underwater, invisible part is moving to one side or even in the opposite direction. A newspaper was that sort of bifurcated iceberg. In particular, Makartsev had found that, while *Trudovaya Pravda* might be singled out for praise in a speech at the conference, tomorrow he could be hauled on to the carpet for inadequacies, and there was no contradiction in this. You had to be ready for everything, find out what the criticism was about and make sure your defence was commensurate with the obligatory admission of guilt, thus underlining the wisdom of the leadership.

The newspaper was praised at the conference. It was gratifying to hear them call it not *Trudovaya Pravda* but 'Makartsev's newspaper', even though the masthead always carried the cold words 'Board of Editors'. He considered the newspaper to be his, just the way they say 'Tupolev aeroplanes'. Makartsev loved his newspaper, got upset over any errors and never considered that he was the one who put it together. He himself, whenever he spoke about the newspaper or gave some account of it, would say not '*Trudovaya Pravda*' but 'the team'.

He had returned to the office in a good frame of mind. Anna had laid out the still-damp page proofs on his desk, after carefully folding up the bottom edges. He would start reading from the top down and might stain his cuffs with the black ink. He drew his glasses out of his pocket and, after looking at the proofs, stood up, holding them by the margins so as not to stain his hands. This issue was being edited by the editorial board's chief secretary, Polishchuk, so Makartsev went to see him with the proofs. He discussed a number of transpositions on the front page, found out what was to be in the blank spot on page three, asked about the score of a football match for which they'd left a blank line and ordered Polishchuk to think up a less-hackneyed headline for the article entitled 'America: Poverty and Tears'.

Right away they retitled the article 'America – a Sea of Lawlessness'. Makartsev made a face, but waved his hand and went off to do the rounds of the departments. The duty personnel were working away and the rest were getting ready to go home, even though their working day hadn't ended yet. Makartsev considered journalism to be a creative business. Whoever didn't want to work, or didn't know how, was not going to, even under the strictest of regimes. He demanded a conscious output, that is, copy and not just the wearing out of one's pants at the office. Moreover, work discipline was the concern of the managing editor, Kashin, and not the editor-in-chief.

After another half hour Makartsev suddenly put on his coat and headed for the lift.

'Why are you so early today?' asked Aleksey in surprise as they drove through the small park on to the street.

'Don't you think I'm entitled to any personal life at all?'

Taking his foot off the accelerator abruptly, Aleksey tore his eyes from the road. 'Then where am I taking you?'

'Home, Aleksey, home,' grinned his master. 'My personal life, brother, is at home.'

The editor wasn't disposed to talk nonsense, so Aleksey kept quiet. Makartsev was thinking that today he would finally talk to his son. His wife had long ago asked him to, but he and Boris never managed to get together. On those infrequent days when the father came home a bit earlier than usual, the son would roll home past midnight.

This time, too, he wasn't at home, and Makartsev chewed his dinner alone. Following her mother's example, Zina had stopped eating at night to preserve her figure. She sat and watched her husband eat. In his heart of hearts Makartsev was actually glad that Boris wasn't there again and there wouldn't be any conversation. They had had a falling out, although Makartsev tried not to show it. It had become impossible to explain anything to his son. As a father, he couldn't come up with convincing words, or would start treating him like a child or would get irritated, and his son would slip away every time. Boris had grown his hair down to his shoulders and a thin moustache down to his chin; he went around in trousers made by God-alone-knew-who, and his manners had become a mixture of musketeer and hoodlum. He would show up at home reeking of alcohol. In his room he would crank up his Grundig stereo full blast irrespective of the time of day.

Makartsev had already calmed down, since there wasn't going to be any chat, and rechannelled his train of thought. He was going to make two or three essential calls and go to bed. Just lie there and look at the ceiling. Then Boris showed up. Without saying hello, he threw open the door into the living-room, glanced fleetingly at his father, threw his blue bag with its long strap and the legend 'Sabena' under the coat rack in the corridor and went to his room.

'We haven't seen each other for a while,' his father muttered after him.

His son didn't answer. Without slackening his pace, he disappeared.

Nobody else in the world displayed that kind of boorishness to Makartsev, not even his superiors. But he held back, he didn't shout: he got up and opened the door to his son's room. He was deafened by an avalanche of noise: Boris had already put on a reel-to-reel tape.

'We haven't talked to each other for a long time, son,' said Makartsev, trying to outshout the Beatles, a record he himself had brought Boris from London, to his detriment.

'And what are we supposed to talk about?'

'Well, who knows . . . How are you getting along, I'd like to know?'

'I'm not getting any regularly, Pop.'

'What a wit!'

'What are you pestering me for? Haven't you got anything else to do? Go the hell back where you came from. Boss *them* around!'

'You've misunderstood me. I'm not going to boss you around. But we are relatives, after all.'

'You have your door, I have mine. Close mine on your way out.'

'No . . . hey, hold on a minute! He who pays the piper calls the tune. If family relations seem atavistic to you, just you remember who supports you financially.'

'Huh, you do keep harping on about that dumb shit . . .'

'Turn off that damned noise! So if I'm wrong, show me.'

'I already told you: you're never going to get it anyway. You're a conformist.'

'Me? You're just an immature kid who doesn't know anything about the complexities of life! Grow up enough to appreciate the blessings your mother and I put warm in your mouth. Other people's children don't even dream about what you've got.'

'To hell with your blessings!'

'Hell?'

'See, I told you so: you don't get it!'

Walking over to the window, Boris examined the dark sky. Makartsev looked around. His wife was leaning an elbow against the doorway at the other end of the corridor and listening attentively to the conversation, making a wry face at the Beatles' hysterical shouting.

'Let's establish diplomatic relations anyway,' the father appealed. 'If you've got nothing to say, then at least hear me out. But please turn that row down!'

His son looked at him, shrugged his shoulders and went over to the tape recorder. With a sharp movement he twisted the knob. Makartsev shuddered: the sound that had already been loud turned into an unbearable roar, full of hisses and whistling that his eardrums couldn't endure.

'Looks like you're not in the mood.' He had to back into the corridor. 'Fine. We'll talk another time.'

His words were drowned out by the din. Zina had disappeared, so that her husband wouldn't be ashamed that she'd witnessed his defeat. He went to his bedroom, placed an anti-angina tablet under his tongue and lay down, without undressing, on the just-folded-back, snow-white sheets.

He calmed himself with the idea that what he had experienced was only to be expected. *Teenagers! I must have been one, too. But this generation is a lot more complicated. We're to blame, of course, somehow. It's been too easy for them to overthrow authority. Injustice has given rise to further injustice. True, the authorities themselves are guilty of a great deal, but we just have a bout of self-criticism and we're fine! A man is an iceberg, the greater part of him invisible. Under Communism people are going to be utterly open to one another, and then they won't be able to have any inadequacies. Ultimately, the core of my son is healthy, I'm certain of that. But we do have to have a discussion some other time.*

So, he persuaded himself. He spat out the tablet into an ashtray. Now, in hospital, it was absurd to think that the fight with his son had been the reason for his heart attack. Scenes like that happened all the time. *And they'll keep on happening until, as Zina says, Boris settles down with his own family, and we'll be needed once again – to give, to fetch, to nurse.* That night Makartsev never noticed that he had fallen asleep. He woke around one in the morning, undressed and went back to bed. Zina could hear him undressing, but she pretended to be asleep.

# The Grey Folder

On Tuesday morning came a feeling of a change in the weather, and the Makartsev iceberg rocked. There was a general dressing-down in the Propaganda department. He was reprimanded for letting slide the newspaper's standards of what was newsworthy, for raising secondary issues that were obscuring the main thrust of the ideological struggle while there was still some danger of a relapse in Czechoslovakia. A whole range of industries weren't fulfilling their five-year plan – and that was the fault of the press as well. As a matter of urgency the newspaper's plans had to be reviewed and resubmitted to the Central Committee. It was clear that the Politburo needed to find scapegoats. The departments of the Central Committee were the driving force, and hiving off the guilt for some short-coming in their propaganda work on to the shoulders of the newspapers was perfectly natural.

Makartsev got back to the office while a planning session was under way. The first deputy editor, Yagubov, was leading the discussion. He was the new man on the editorial staff, appointed a mere four months earlier. Makartsev was helping him to get into the swim of things as quickly as possible, although he felt some resistance. He was looking after his deputy benevolently and guardedly, and he felt a lack of contact. The general tone of the meeting, through the half-open door to Yagubov's office, was even and businesslike. Makartsev took off his overcoat in his office and on his way to Yagubov's walked past Anna, who was about to run to him with a folder. On the wall there, pinned up with thumbtacks, hung dummies of all four pages, prettily drawn in coloured marker-pen.

Makartsev had brought the pens back from Japan for his sub-editors. Catching sight of his editor-in-chief at the doorway, Yagubov stopped in mid-sentence and declared joyfully: 'And here comes our chief, comrades. So, are you going to take it from here? Actually, we're just winding things up.'

Makartsev waved that he should continue.

'Then should I run over the salient points for you?'

'No, carry on, carry on. I'll have a look later.'

He looked around for a free chair. Yagubov's office was less than two-thirds the size of his own, and he couldn't see anywhere to sit. The managing editor, Kashin, got up, sat Makartsev down and went to get himself another chair from reception.

When the topics under discussion had been dealt with, Yagubov looked inquiringly at his editor in case he wanted to add something. Makartsev asked the editorial board members and department editors to stay behind.

'Everyone else is free to go,' Yagubov concluded.

'I want you to concentrate your attention on your departmental plans one more time,' the editor-in-chief said when the others had left.

'But we've already handed them in!' pointed out the sharp-tongued Kachkareva indignantly. She was a thickset, masculine creature in a dress, the editor of the arts and literature department, eternally at odds with everyone over trifles.

'You're right, you did. The plans aren't bad, on the whole. But the leadership of the newspaper' – Makartsev glanced at Yagubov, and the latter, not knowing yet what was going on, nodded – 'thinks that certain policies should be given more depth. More attention to fulfilling the five-year plan . . .'

'Don't we come up with enough articles?' said the industrial department editor, Alekseyev, in surprise.

'A lot, but not enough,' Makartsev replied, more firmly this time.

'Right!' As untidy and conscientious as a schoolteacher, Alekseyev was grieved by the fact that, instead of producing living and breathing article, he would now have to spend another three hours sweating over the refashioning of a plan that nobody really needed. His editor-in-chief also understood that the plans weren't going to get any better, but he had to pass on the directive that he'd received.

'And now it's up to you to carry the ball,' Makartsev paused and moved his eyes over the individuals present. 'Anna is going to pass back the old plans to all the departments. Please bring them back, updated, before the planning session tomorrow.'

'Is that everything?' Yagubov asked.

Makartsev nodded and was the first to stand. Everyone streamed through the door. The editor's deputy understood that, although it hadn't been said out loud, the reproof about their plan had been handed down from Upstairs. He was thinking that Makartsev was going to hang back and add something else to him one-on-one, but he refrained from asking questions. His boss didn't lay down any more cards, though, and just went back to his own office.

'Send in Kakabadze,' Makartsev ordered his secretary. 'Have him bring his camera.'

He pulled two questionnaire forms out of his desk drawer, an old one and a new one, and started filling in the new one, copying down from the old so that there wouldn't be any discrepancies.

'May I?' Kakabadze, a young photo-journalist, opened the office door. 'Who are we going to shoot?'

'Me. A picture for my passport. You'll have to excuse me for exploiting you.'

'Come on! I collect photos of everyone in charge. No, seriously. A whole collection, and I haven't got one of you yet.'

Kakabadze placed his camera bag on the floor, took out a camera with a big portrait lens and moved stealthily around, as light and flexible as a panther.

'Go over to the window but not all the way . . . a little further. Turn to this side – there'll be softer shadows. Tighten your tie, the knot's worked loose. Look at me, a teeny bit higher . . .'

'Yes, sir!'

'Damn, it's good to boss your superiors around!' Kakabadze snapped away several times, placed his camera back in the bag and took out another one. 'And now, for insurance, let's change the pose. Turn this way. Right!'

'Thanks. Are you in a hurry?' The director put an arm around the photographer's shoulders and led him over to his side-table, where only members of the editorial board were welcome. Here were special goodies – American cigarettes, chewing-gum.

'Thanks. I don't smoke,' Kakabadze said, embarrassed.

'Go ahead, take something! You can treat your girlfriends.'

Kakabadze selected a pack of Camels. Makartsev took a pack of Marlboros for himself. Kakabadze shook out his black curls and disappeared, dragging his camera bag behind him.

The second half of the editor-in-chief's day slipped by in trivial and utterly uncreative work. He signed the list of royalty payments for the first half of February, documents for employees' wages, retouchers' and artists' accounts, without even looking at the figures; then he read the readers' letters that had been pulled out for him, ones that could be used as topics for future articles.

He respected the ordinary reader and demanded the same respect from his staff: *We all live and work for our readers!* He personally signed the most significant outgoing letters. In addition to that, he had meetings scheduled with employees of various ranks – he made no exception – and then he did his rounds of the offices and returned.

'Have some tea,' Anna said, quickly snatching a sweet-wrapper off her desk.

'Uh-huh!' he said, happily. 'Nice and strong!'

'Aren't you worried about drinking it strong? What about your heart?'

'I have a heart of iron,' he said and patted Anna on the shoulder.

When Anna had gone out he unbuttoned his jacket and, slackening his belt, pulled up his trousers, tucking in his white shirt, already wrinkled after the long day. *Paunchy, paunchy* – he caught sight of himself in the mirror. As he ran his fingers through his hair, his legs heading for his armchair, his eyes, still not seeing anything, were already roving over the proof pages on his desk. He sat and clapped his palm on his desk where his glasses were supposed to be. They were right there. 'Order broadens thought' was his favourite aphorism. Unfortunately he couldn't follow that piece of wisdom because he was too busy.

His glasses were lying on top of something. Makartsev wanted to move that something to one side so he could get down to his reading. It was a file folder, a plump grey folder with black calico sides, tightly tied with green ribbon-ties. Some kind of annual report? These absent-minded people could never get things done on time! He shifted the folder to one side (*Damn, that's heavy!*), put on his glasses and addressed himself to the front-page proof. He ran his eyes over the main headline: 'Communism – The Radiant Future for All Mankind!' He looked over the headlines of all the articles, even the smallest. Everything was fine. Makartsev pressed the intercom buttons on his telephone for his deputy director, his managing editor, his deputy, the duty editor and the print-production manager. The howl of the linotypes broke into his office from the typesetting shop, separated from the compositors' tables by a glass partition.

The editor spoke to the four of them at once over the PA system: 'How's it going? Report!' From the general muttering he understood that the layout was going according to schedule, no deviations.

'But there will be some,' Polishchuk warned. 'TASS just informed us. We typeset the Secretary General's speech yesterday, but today there'll be some corrections.'

'Big ones?'

'A lot of them, something like a hundred and fifty so far. And they're still coming in. They are redoing the corrections that they made us do earlier back to the way they had it before. We'll have to delay the front page and page two for an hour.'

'Right.' Makartsev suppressed a sigh. 'Hey, about the front page. That banner headline: whose idea was that?'

'Mine,' admitted Polishchuk.

'Fine! But get rid of the word "all"! Why wave a red flag in front of a bull? It's not time! The remainder of my comments are on the proof pages. That's all!'

The phone rang. Anna put his wife through to him.

'Why aren't you coming home for dinner?'

'Things are pretty hectic here . . .'

'Will you be back late?'

'Probably not. What are you up to?'

'Watching television, as usual.'

'Is Boris home?'

'Not yet. You finish your talk with him, will you?'

'Of course. Just don't nag me about it.'

'I'm not nagging, but time's passing. You know, he came home drunk at midday and passed out.'

'All right. I'll deal with it later. I'm busy now.'

*Zina spoiled our son, and now she wants me to straighten him out.* He lit a cigarette, grabbed the page proofs with one hand and called Anna. She took them out to the sub-editors. His desk was suddenly free – *Order broadens thought*. But his gaze once again alighted on the thick grey folder.

The phone beeped. Makartsev picked up the receiver.

'What is this crap?' he muttered irritably, pulling the folder towards him.

'What crap? This is Volobuyev. Good evening, chief. Sorry to bother you . . .'

'Go ahead,' he told his censor.

'I have a complaint about the sports department. I've told them a hundred times: they can't mention the Khimik sports societies in any of their articles. They're defence industry factories. And today there's yet another Khimik on page four. I don't want to get a reprimand!'

'I'll deal with it. Is that all?'

'Not quite. There are new limitations on the publication of certain materials.'

'Fine. When I'm free, you can fill me in.' He buzzed the sports desk duty editor on the intercom and tore a strip off him.

Just at that moment his hands untied the ribbon-tapes on the grey folder. He finally opened it and discovered a typed manuscript. '*Russia in 1839*,' he read, looked closer and saw the legend '*Samizdat*'. The text went on.

'Gibberish!' said Makartsev, out loud.

Out of the habit shared by everyone who reads a lot because they have to, he first glanced at the ending. The manuscript was over five hundred pages long. Makartsev popped an anti-angina tablet under his tongue. Anna's unexpected appearance made him shrink rather than start. She waited for him to look at her, while he took her unexpected appearance as an infringement upon the secrecy of his affairs.

'I'm busy!' It seemed to him that she was trying to discover what was lying on his desk.

'Excuse me. One of our typists has taken ill. She's pregnant, and all our cars are out. Can we send her home in yours?'

*Depends on who made her pregnant*, he would have joked in a different, better mood, but now he just nodded, saying: 'Just tell Aleksey to get back as quick as he can.' He hesitated over whether to ask her something, then asked: 'Was anyone in my office while I was out?' He looked at her closely.

'No one was,' she replied, alarmed. 'I brought in the page proofs myself. Has something happened? Is something missing? Would you like me to look for something? I can get it in a flash.'

Ordinarily quite restrained, he burst out: 'How many times have I asked you to keep my desk clear, Anna? How many times?'

'But you tell me not to take things away. You say you won't be able to find anything you need later on. Auntie Masha, who cleans up in the morning, doesn't touch your desk. I only take away the tea leaves and empty the ashtrays. Has something gone missing?'

'Nothing. But something could go missing in a mess like this. Visitors come in, they leave things here instead of taking them to the relevant department. If I'm preoccupied with personal issues . . .'

'I understand, excuse me.'

He'd blown off steam and now he calmed down.

'You know,' she recalled, embarrassed, 'I actually ran off to the canteen when you weren't here – they were throwing out some smoked sausage. Just for five minutes, no longer. But Aleksey sat there in my place while I was gone. I'll find out, right now.' She ran out without closing the door.

'Aleksey!' Her words carried back to him. 'When I was out, did anyone go into his office?'

'No, nobody.'

'Would you go in and tell him yourself? And then take the typist home. But come back as soon as you can, will you?'

Aleksey had never gone into his boss's office. He coughed and knocked on the door.

'Did you call for me?'

'Yes, I already heard you, I heard you!'

Anna returned to the office to put an end to the conflict. In her agitation she was blushing, her breath rapid. She stood beside him, short, nicely built, a little plump – but even that suited her.

# 7

# The Joys and Sorrows of
# Anna Lokotkova

Everyone at the office, even students from the journalism faculty who were there to gain practical experience, considered the secretary Anna Lokotkova a second-rate creature. Makartsev was the exception and now his new deputy, Yagubov, as well, neither of whom permitted anyone to take liberties with her. She was a woman of indeterminate age (you definitely wouldn't be able to say forty-three), carefully maintained, dressed inexpensively but with some taste, cosmetics in the same vein, thick-set rather than plump, a sort of tasty cupcake – you'd fancy a bite, and people who didn't know her would think this cupcake was easy enough to get. But not a bit of it! Anna knew how to stand on her feminine dignity, probably even too sharply, way over the top, so that she had more than once in life done herself out of her fair share. But she could never have done otherwise.

She appeared to everyone to be upbeat, and nobody knew that she had an unremitting complex, absurd and insurmountable, about her womanly misfortunes.

Of course, her work was efficient and dependable; otherwise she wouldn't have been in her position. Makartsev valued her, and she valued her position very highly, sincerely (and justly) certain that she could do more even than the editor himself, in certain areas. She permitted herself to be curious only to the extent that he needed it, she put up with his irritability, and she never forgot anything he told her to do. Makartsev was being misled, however: although Anna never revealed it by so much as a single twitch, she was greatly curious about his private life.

She was always undone by her ingenuousness. She considered it to be just feminine pride, but she hadn't managed to rid herself of it even by her present forty-third year. At every new job, sooner or later she would get into some relationship that was nervy and tormenting for her and which she was sure would be the real one, the one to last to the end of her days. She never fell in love herself – she would give in to others' being in love with her, or at least that was what she persuaded herself. There was always one single man that she loved, the father of her future child, who would appear to her in various guises. For the sake of the child she dreamed about at night – that tiny bundle of joy – she would give in to their importunities, dreaming the while of just one thing – getting pregnant as soon as possible. After that, His Majesty the Male wouldn't be of any more use to her, so she could just break up with him calmly and not even tell him she was in the family way. Out of her candour, though, she would start talking too soon to her new friend about liking children and how she could never have an abortion – that would be a sin, after all, since it was already a living little creature.

'And do you like children yourself?' she'd asked each one of the ten men who had passed through her and stepped over her.

And each of them had said of course but that, in general, it would be better not to rush into things, why think about such things right now, let's just love each other. And so she would, and they would, too, but a cooling-off would quickly set in and the relationship turn sour. Turn very sour indeed when Anna would start pondering out loud about what sexual positions would be best for getting pregnant. To calm herself down she would tell herself that this friend of hers was just too inexperienced, but things would work out properly with the next one, if it was serious. Not with any old somebody, no (there was no question of that!) but with a suitable father, who would be worthy in features, body and mind. The rest, found unworthy, were turned away from her door.

And that's what she did every time: after each love affair fell through she would go and get a job somewhere else. It had to be somewhere else! At the old job everyone would already know, and any other love affair would be doomed to a short life and would doubtless end up again without any issue. She would once again go on to her new job – which was always secretarial: and she was a fine secretary, well built and pert-bosomed (a brassiere only distorted their shape). She sewed her own clothes and wasn't too lazy to unpick the stitches and redo them as much as ten times to get a perfect fit. The shoes that she bought had to be imported, even if they were second hand, and she would pay up to three-quarters of her wages for them. She kept her figure slim on the remaining money.

And it always happened that a new love would come along, after a brief selection period. Although the war had decimated Anna's male contemporaries, it had apparently not thinned the ranks of her admirers. Both older and younger men fawned over her – she was ageless, after all! In a word, a cupcake – it wasn't hard to be ten years off the mark. Lying in bed, relaxed, she liked to make them guess her age and confuse them with the truth. But why bother concealing it – after all, she didn't want to get married. She just wanted a baby, a little bundle of joy!

For some reason, though, a baby never happened. Anna had sat in the queues at the district clinic and borne the unimaginable pain when they insufflated her Fallopian tubes. For four years in a row she'd travelled to Kislovodsk for the mud-baths, on her union-organized holidays: the first two times for free, the last two half price. They just kept on telling her about some blockage of her tubes. There was one elderly gentleman, a private doctor of high academic status, and she got to see him only after pulling some major strings: after taking twenty-five roubles off her he reassured her that it might work out, that the important thing was not to lose hope and try even harder to get pregnant.

She tried with all her might, but her hopes for success grew smaller and smaller. When Anna moved to *Trudovaya Pravda*, she told herself straight off: 'Makartsev is the best man here!'

Right away she tried to make herself indispensable to him. He wouldn't be able to take a step without her. If she were even once to fall ill with a cold, she was sure the paper wouldn't come out that day. Anna was on fire at work, not sparing herself. He would have just lifted a finger to push the button for her and she would already be opening the door and looking in, ready for anything. She would unerringly divine whenever he was hungry or thirsty, or had a headache, and straight away bring him tea and a sandwich, or mineral water, buying it all out of her modest assets. He never inquired about it – he didn't have time to think about trifles.

Anna wasn't the least bit put off by his wife. On the contrary, she was happy that he wasn't neglected in her absence, that he was fed and had a change of shirt every day. Of course, *she* would have ironed his collar better and wouldn't have forgotten about the lapels of his jacket and would have sewn new cuff-tapes on his trousers (the old ones were getting frayed and threads were visible, hanging from his left trouser-leg).

She spoke to his wife in a half-whisper before connecting her to her husband: 'Makartsev had a pain in his side after lunch, so I gave him a pill, just in case. Don't give him anything rich this evening.'

She was passing the baton to Makartsev's wife, so she could take it back in her tenacious little hands the next morning. She was certain that both in spirit and physically she was considerably younger, and her character softer, and she was more caring. Whenever Makartsev worked late Anna would stay behind, and at the slightest hint would run into his office, tightly closing both doors behind her. She dressed for work as if for a night out, with a deep décolletage and, when it became fashionable, in a maximally mini skirt. If he asked for anything she would come around behind his desk and as if by accident bend low and blow the ashes from his cigarette off the table. Trembling so hard that her vocal chords would go into spasm, she would feel how his eyes turned and looked at her neck and lower. She waited for his hand to touch her waist, and then she was going to say, shivering: 'Oh, no! I'm afraid . . . here . . .'

But instead she heard: 'Run down to the typesetters and have them pull one more galley proof!'

So she would run down to the typesetters, at a loss from the misunderstanding and exhausted by the absence of any prospects whatsoever. She wanted to acquire something like Makartsev's understanding of international and domestic affairs. With his approval she attended the municipal House of Political Enlightenment in the evening and would earnestly sit through the lectures while others slipped off to do their shopping after checking in. But after she'd finished – *da-daaaah!* – two years at the University of Marxism-Leninism he didn't even pat her on the back.

This was the first time anything like this had happened in her life, and it was serious, and she was deeply unhappy. Anna even secretly took pride in her unhappiness. After all, for her he was the kind of man nobody could compare to, never mind replace. She couldn't even look at anybody else any more. But she was getting older, wasn't she? Were her four trips to the health spa going to be in vain? She couldn't even find out if the insufflation and mud-baths had helped!

Seven years had passed this way, without any progress. Then the year before last a short-statured visitor had strode decisively into reception with a folder under his arm, intending to walk straight into the editor-in-chief's office. Anna leaped up and just as decisively barred the door.

'The editor is busy. What business are you here on, young man?'

'On a matter of indecency! Step aside!'

'Step aside? I'm the one in charge here. Until you tell me what's going on I won't be able to tell him, and until I can do that he's not going to see you. What organization are you from?'

'I'm a writer,' he yelled. 'Do you understand what that is? Inform your editor: I want to tell him what I think of him!'

'You tell me, and I'll pass it on to him.'

He laughed in her face, sprinkling her with saliva. Then he suddenly stopped. Anna could tell that he was attracted to her.

'All right,' he gave in. 'It's only out of respect for the fact that you –'

'That's got nothing to do with this.' Her eyes dropped.

'How do you know? What if I got married?'

'What's that got to do with me?'

'Got married to you, I mean!'

'Listen,' she told him. 'There are lots of young girls over there. They're all keen to make friends with young men like you.'

'I don't like young ones,' he said. 'They only take and can't give anything back in exchange.'

'And what do you want to get back?'

'Your soul.'

'What are you, the devil?'

'That's what your editor is – the devil!'

'Cut that out!'

'He's just that, the devil! They asked me for an article – at first they praised me for it, and then they made me rework it three times. Everything I wanted to say was cut out, what I didn't want to say they put in, and now they're stringing me along: tomorrow, tomorrow . . .'

'The editor doesn't know anything about it. If he did, he'd have done something.'

'What are you defending him for?' He looked at Anna in a way that made her blush. 'As if he's going to do something for you! Hey, he's no match for you!'

'So . . . who *is* a match for me, then?'

'Me!'

Her guiding thread snapped that day. It suddenly came to Anna that she was being silly about Makartsev. Basically there was nothing going on, after all! He really was no match for her. He wasn't the kind to have an affair. That was clear as a bell – how come she hadn't understood it before? Once she had realized this she thought about it all day and the whole of the following night. What was she going to do now? Leave, like she always did? But nothing had happened. And besides, where was she going to go, with her incomplete higher education, after such a prestigious organization? Probably to a lower-level position. And that wouldn't do – the newspaper had just given her a room in Tyoply Stan, and she and her mother had moved there from the school cupboard they'd been living in. It was a long way out, to be sure, but if Makartsev hadn't phoned the Moscow city council she wouldn't even have got that. He would regret that he hadn't got any pleasure from her in those seven years. He would be sorry, but it would be too late.

So she had stayed on.

The next day the persistent young man (he turned out, unluckily, to be a whole sixteen years younger than Anna) phoned up and suggested a date. Since Anna's love for Makartsev had ended the day before, she agreed. They went to a Caucasian-style barbecue. They didn't have any *shashlyk* there, so they ate *lyulya-kabobs* instead and drank a bottle of Gamza wine. Then Semyon suggested they go to his modest penthouse and have some tea.

She went up with him to the fourth floor of an old building on Kirov Street, to a communal apartment with a long corridor crammed with wardrobes. He'd scarcely closed the door when he pulled Anna towards him, without turning out the light, and with feverish hands began checking out her quantities of this and that.

'Everything's where it belongs,' she said proudly, fending off his determined hands. 'But you mustn't do that! Otherwise I'll leave. It's not good to do that sort of thing right away. It's not serious. You might think I'm frivolous.'

'I'd never think that, for the world!' he said, freeing his hands from hers and resuming his impertinence. 'But then I knew yesterday that this was serious.'

'Do you like children, Semyon?' she whispered, already trembling and losing her cold calculation, together with any hope of an honest answer.

After all, throughout her seven years of abstinence she had been dreaming at night of orgies at which she would be surrounded by five men, all of them manifesting their intentions, and her allowing them to do things that embarrassed her when she recalled them the next day.

'Why don't you say something? I'm asking, do you like children?'

'I do. But dogs more.'

'Hey, wait, don't tear my blouse. I'll take it off.'

Anna moved in with him, and it soon became clear that the treatment hadn't helped. Semyon bought himself a German shepherd puppy and grew very fond of it. The puppy messed everywhere he could and ate Anna's expensive stockings. She started coming home earlier and spending the whole evening tidying up their room, because Semyon didn't have the time. He would play with the dog and in the breaks tap away at his typewriter on a film script that nobody was going to take. He wore western-style pyjamas, lace-trimmed and with gold buttons, that he'd bought in a second-hand shop. He smoked a pipe and made coffee ten times a day, of which he bought a fresh supply every day from the neighbourhood shop, which was called Tea. And he was 'married' to Anna, as he explained to her, because she conformed to the Balzac standard.

Anna was happy to so conform. She still maintained the same efficient relationship with Makartsev, but now she was doing a lot of it without the same spirit. She convinced herself that all her life she had simply wanted to get married, like everyone else, and a child – that was just some unconscious desire. She had someone to fuss over now, she had a man, and her man had a dog. One thing alone offended her: how come Semyon didn't propose that they register their marriage? Of course, she would say it wasn't necessary – what difference did it make, if they were in love? But why didn't he, all the same? On the other hand, though, there was some comfort even in that. If they registered Anna would have to start paying a six per cent tax for childlessness, which would be really stupid, given the size of her wages.

# 8

# A Little Night Reading

Makartsev was fairly tired, although he'd grown accustomed to being around people from morning till night, making a string of decisions in quick succession and visiting a variety of places. Now he stood in his office at a loss, not knowing what to do next. After hesitating a moment, he took a key out of his pocket and opened the safe in which he kept his secret documents. On the inner side of the safe door was glued a piece of paper printed in red ink with a reminder that all the documents in the safe were secret and it was forbidden to hand them over to anyone else.

He had placed the heavy grey folder on the upper shelf, towards the back. On that shelf lay TASS documents A and AB, intended for the editors of central newspapers. The white TASS hand-outs, for members of the editorial board, he only glanced at, while he actually read the other documents. He wasn't offended by the fact that he wasn't supposed to read red TASS documents. That's what discipline was all about. It just passed through his mind that there was a large backlog of papers he had already read and should have handed back by now. He locked the safe and rang home.

'Shall I cook you some meat?' his wife asked.

'Yes. Er, no, to hell with it! Just make me some coffee.'

'You won't sleep.'

'Just make it! And go to bed, Zina. I'm going to have to work at home for a while.'

'It'll get cold – are you going to drink it cold?'

'Yes, cold.'

Throwing down the receiver he unlocked his safe again. Since he had the folder he should at least know what it contained. Maybe after he read the thing it would be clearer why it had shown up here. Makartsev never carried a briefcase, so he wrapped the folder up in an old issue of *Izvestia*.

Putting on his coat, he called for Aleksey.

'Are you done?' asked Anna.

'Yes. If anything comes up, have them ring me at home.'

'What about your hat? You've forgotten your hat. It's snowing, sleet . . .'

Anna disappeared into his office and brought out his fawn-skin hat. She was carrying the latest galley proofs from the print shop, assuming the editor would like to take another look, even if he was on his way out.

'Give them to Yagubov,' he ordered, contrary to his usual practice.

In the car he put the bundle mechanically on the rear seat, but then picked it up again straight away. He'd heard a lot about how people passed *samizdat* works to one another and how dangerous it was. Until now he'd always laughed at them. Aleksey looked askance at his boss and kept silent.

Zina wasn't waiting for him, so she must have gone to bed. Lately she'd often gone to bed early: she would say she was tired, although what did *she* do to get tired from? Boris had also come home – Makartsev could hear music, but for a change it was wonderfully soft. Boris didn't emerge from his room, and Makartsev didn't look in on him. The child had calmed down, and thank God for that.

Pushing aside the unwashed dishes in the kitchen, Makartsev took the cold pot off the stove and poured himself some coffee. A few grounds dripped out of the spout. His son had got to the coffee first. Makartsev cursed, though without much feeling, grabbed his bundle and went off to his study. He pulled a bottle of Kubanskaya export-quality vodka out of his cabinet and poured himself a shot. He noticed a bottle of heart medicine sitting there, something that wasn't available at the chemist's. That meant that his wife had made a special trip to the polyclinic. He squirted twenty drops of the medicine into the vodka, made a wry face, drank it down, turned on his wall lamp and lay down on the couch.

He didn't feel like starting to read it. In the line of duty Makartsev had run his eyes over thousands of lines of print over the years. With articles for his newspaper and material for the Central Committee he knew in advance what he was going to be reading, and only things that 'deviated' grabbed his attention.

He'd lost his taste for reading, and he loved his newspaper as an object irrespective of its contents. He was sure that even the obligatory material in it was more attractive, more effective, than in the other newspapers. Makartsev was somewhat contemptuous of the famous Soviet writers who gave him presentation copies of their books with generous inscriptions. He would take home to his wife the rare foreign novels that they kept aside for him at the book distributors'. Strictly speaking, he didn't read at all any more, he just carried out his Party duty. He could evaluate reading material by weight or by column inch. Like a shackled slave, he was obliged to drag his stones around. He always tried to overcome his resistance: he would skim through something to lighten the load, then he would quickly glance at the end, just to make sure of its correctness, and sign off on it.

How much more did he dislike reading books like this! They were unsettling. He caught himself thinking he'd lost the art of arguing on issues of principle, even with himself. For decades he had been full of certainty: everything was going as it should and it couldn't be otherwise – he would get irritated whenever he read someone saying things were wrong. He simply switched off the moment he read that everything was wrong. In the final analysis, wasn't that his right – to hold on to the convictions he'd held for so long? He poured himself another shot of vodka for encouragement and knocked it back, not eating anything with it, just grimacing. Stretching out on his stomach, he turned the wall lamp away from him so that the light didn't hurt his eyes and began to read the contents of the grey folder.

# 9

# A Visit by
# the Marquis de Custine

We recommend that whoever strives to understand the present should turn to the past. Reading the Marquis de Custine's book, *Russia in 1839*, Emperor Nicholas threw it to the floor and shouted: 'It's my fault! Why did I have to talk to that scoundrel?' Incidentally, he had spoken to Custine in an effort to present himself and Russia in a good light.

The commentaries of the French traveller, who visited St Petersburg, Moscow, Yaroslavl, Nizhny Novgorod and Vladimir, have been published many times, in all European languages. They were banned immediately in Russia, and this work by the Marquis de Custine, which Herzen called without any doubt the most remarkable and intelligent book written about Russia by a foreigner, was inaccessible. Some of Custine's thoughts were prophetic, others showed that nothing in our fatherland has ever got any better since the time of Ioann Barklay (seventeenth century), who wrote: 'This is a nation [the Muscovites] born for slavery and fiercely opposed to any manifestation of freedom; they are otherwise meek when oppressed and do not balk at the yoke.'

Our work on the translation of the book *La Russie en 1839, par Le Marquis de Custine*, is going slowly, considering the conditions, but we are hurrying to propagate this first draft version by *samizdat*.

Here Makartsev yawned. He was reading superficially, leaping from paragraph to paragraph and from habit dividing whatever phrases he picked up into 'permitted' and 'forbidden'. He had an amazing nose for what was 'forbidden'. Towards the end of the foreword Makartsev made a face: what could this old fart have to say about a long-gone Russia that he'd ridden through in his carriage?

'Quite a bit!' said a resounding voice. 'Unfortunately, things have got even worse.'

'Who's there?' asked Makartsev, his throat taut with fear.

He turned his head: before him stood a shortish man of middle age, strangely dressed for the present day. He was wearing an unbuttoned blue frock coat with breeches to his knees, a light-blue-striped vest, black stockings and shoes with high heels, buckles and spurs. A luxuriously lacy snow-white shirt with diamond cufflinks was set off by a large light-blue bow at his neck. At his side hung a rapier. Makartsev breathed in the stupefying smell of strong perfume.

'Sorry for intruding on you without an invitation,' said the Marquis de Custine. 'But I am curious about you, for you are a clever man, indeed one who wields some authority. This is why I have decided to share the reading of my book with you.'

'But – you're a foreigner!' Makartsev said indignantly. 'I have to report first thing tomorrow that you were in my apartment, otherwise . . .'

'Oh, don't worry, Monsieur Makartsev,' de Custine replied soothingly. 'Nobody knows I'm here. Learning from bitter experience, I entered your country this time through a hole in the atmospheric ozone layer. And there aren't any border-guard bloodhounds there or any custom-agent thieves. If you permit me, I'll take a seat, and you continue reading. Never fear, just read . . . I'm interested in your reaction, that's all.'

De Custine sat down in the armchair, making a gesture with his hands to calm Makartsev down, closed his eyelids and dozed off, as it seemed. Makartsev obediently began to read the manuscript.

My carriage and all my baggage were aboard the *Nikolay I*, a Russian ship, 'the best in the world'. The Russian grandee Prince K. addressed me by name and expounded his views on the character of the people and institutions in his native land.

'The merciless despotism that holds sway over us arose in a time when serfdom had already been abolished throughout the rest of Europe. From the time of the Mongol invasion, the Slavs, formerly the freest people in the world, were turned into slaves, first of their conquerors and then of their princes. Serfdom has so degraded the human word that it has turned into a snare. The government in Russia lives by a lie, for both tyrant and slave fear the truth. Our autocrats became acquainted at some point with the power of tyranny out of their own experience. They learned well the power of despotism from their own slavery, then vented the malice generated by their own humiliation, taking revenge upon the innocent. Think about every step you take when you're among this Asiatic people.

'Religious intolerance is a key factor in Russian politics. Things that could happen in Europe only in the Middle Ages are occurring in Russia in our day. Russia has fallen four centuries behind the West in everything.'

We foreigners were detained for over an hour on deck without any shade, in the full blaze of the sun. Then we had to appear before the tribunal that was sitting in the wardroom.

'What, precisely, is your business in Russia?'

'We wish to become acquainted with the country.'

'But that isn't a reason for travelling!'

'I, however, have no other.'

'Who do you think you will be meeting in St Petersburg?'

'Everyone who will permit me to make their acquaintance.'

'How long a time do you intend being in Russia?'

'I don't know.'

'Approximately, then?'

'Several months.'

'Are you perhaps on some sort of diplomatic mission?'

'No.'

'Perhaps a secret one?'

'No.'

'Some sort of scientific purpose?'

'No.'

'Have you been sent by your government to study our social and political system?'

'No.'

'Do you have any sort of commercial mission?'

'No.'

'So, you are travelling exclusively out of curiosity?'

'Yes.'

'But why Russia, specifically?'

'I don't know . . .'

'Have you any letters recommending you to anyone?'

I had been warned beforehand of the undesirability of a too-sincere answer to this question. The bloodhounds of the Russian police have exceptional noses, and, in accordance with the personality of every passenger, they examine their passports with greater or lesser severity. A certain Italian commercial traveller who preceded me was mercilessly searched. He was forced to open his wallet, and they ransacked all of his clothing, inside and out, not leaving even his underwear unexamined. They began rooting around in my things and particularly among my books. The latter were nearly all taken from me. Russia is a country of completely useless formalities.

Here Makartsev tore his eyes from the manuscript and sighed.

'Well, what do you think?' the Marquis de Custine asked him at once.

He was sitting elegantly in the armchair, one leg crossed over the other, observing Makartsev.

'Of course, there's a lot you, the French, don't understand,' Makartsev immediately began explaining to him. 'Why should we, the Russians, organize ourselves according to *your* traditions? We live under completely different conditions! Besides, it's not surprising that we could overdo things, that we wouldn't know how to treat foreigners with respect. Of course you do treat us well in your country.'

Something like approval flashed in de Custine's black eyes. He nodded and asked: 'And your own?'

'What?' Makartsev didn't understand.

'I mean: isn't respect a requisite in dealing with your own people?'

Makartsev was at a loss for an answer. He muttered something like 'Well, you know . . .' and went back to reading. He didn't notice how his indifference to reading was being replaced by curiosity, and how his mind had leaped from the nineteenth century back to the twentieth without any trouble. The Marquis was helping him, of course. Makartsev was imperceptibly becoming accustomed to his presence and was reading voluntarily now or at least without anybody forcing him. He could have set it aside – it was obvious what it was about! – but he read on. His heart wasn't troubling him, nor his head, and he didn't feel like sleeping. He read with interest, and the scepticism that had long lain dormant in him only increased his interest.

'Wait a second.' Makartsev, hesitating, suddenly interrupted himself and looked at de Custine. 'Are you trying to pull the wool over my eyes?'

'Pull the . . . what?' asked the Marquis.

'I'm saying this whole thing is a hoax! Who's going to believe that you wrote this thing a hundred years ago?'

'A hundred and thirty,' corrected de Custine.

'A hundred and thirty, then, damn you! This is all just blatant anti-Sovietism, anyway!'

'Excuse me, Monsieur Makartsev! I wrote this a hundred years before Stalin's Great Terror! That is a historical fact.'

Makartsev was at a loss what to answer and silently buried his head in the manuscript.

The things that he was used to reading, saying and hearing were completely absent here, without any compromises. And those harmful things that had been condemned once and for all as impeding the forward progress of the nation, things he knew perfectly well how to avoid and eliminate, knew how not to hear – they stood out glaringly. Makartsev started reading with more and more indignation and therefore more actively. He would go back to something, then rush ahead impatiently. The steps in the reasoning didn't interest him. He was sure he could pick out the essentials more quickly than the author was managing to expound it. Meanwhile the Marquis de Custine himself sat quietly in the armchair, observing his reader.

Every foreigner who crosses the Russian border is assessed in advance as a criminal. Here, you may nowise move around, even breathe, except with the Tsar's permission or on his command. Everything is gloomy, suppressed, and a deathly silence stifles all life. It is as if the shadow of death hangs over this entire section of the earthly globe.

Poverty, however thoroughly it is hidden away, gives birth to a melancholy tedium in any case. It is impossible to be merry on command. Dramas are played out in real life – while in the theatres vaudeville reigns supreme, frightening no one. Empty amusements are the only thing permitted. The words 'peace' and 'happiness' are as indeterminate here as the word 'paradise'. An unrestrained laziness, an alarming idleness – those are the inevitable result of an autocracy.

The day some minister or other falls from favour, his friends must become mute and blind. He is considered dead and buried the moment he appears to have been disgraced.

The Russians have names for everything, but they have nothing in reality. Russia is a country of façades. Read the labels: they have civilization, society, literature, theatre, art, science, while in reality they do not even have any doctors: if you fall ill, you can consider yourself a dead man!

The Russian court reminds one of a theatre in which the actors busy themselves exclusively with dress rehearsals. No one knows his role well, and opening night never comes, because the theatre director is dissatisfied with the acting of his players. The players and the director spend their entire lives in fruitless preparation, correcting and improving their endless public comedy. In Russia, everyone fulfils their destiny to the last of their strength.

'Who's this theatre director?' asked Makartsev aloud, involuntarily.

'Surely you understood what was meant?' said de Custine, answering the question with a question, and laughed.

'It's easy for you fault-finders to give advice. You want Communism handed to you on a plate! But where are we going to get it from, ready-made?'

'We have no need of your Comnism,' said de Custine sadly, not catching the word. 'And I don't know at all what it is you need. I'm simply a writer, and I'm expressing my own opinion, the truth as I understand it, that's all.'

Makartsev was growing angry and getting more and more carried away as a result. He couldn't help admitting that this was a clever book, because there was no cheap abuse in it at all. He, Makartsev, a representative of the ruling party and therefore responsible to some extent for the greatest events of the century, wasn't being reproached personally.

'As a matter of fact, if you want to know,' said Makartsev, 'I've always tried to improve things, to make things more cultured, to be fairer, more humane, that is, to be a real Communist.'

'I see that, monsieur,' nodded de Custine. 'That is why I have come to you.'

'If I had more power, the system wouldn't be what it is. But what can I do on my own?'

'I'm not here to judge you,' sighed de Custine. 'Just read on . . .'

There are no great people in Russia because there are no independent characters, with the exception of a few favoured personages, too small in number to have any influence on their surroundings. The most insignificant person, if he knows how to please his sovereign, could become the first in the nation tomorrow. Every deed that transcends blind and slavish obedience becomes onerous and suspicious to the monarch. These exceptional incidents remind him of someone's claims on him, claims remind him of people's rights, while, under a despot, any subject who even dreams of his rights is already a mutineer.

The majestic boulevard extends – gradually becoming more deserted, uglier and more sorrowful – to the very borders of the city, and little by little it is swallowed up in the waves of Asiatic barbarism that flood St Petersburg from all sides, and recede in all directions along the several post-highways whose construction has only just begun in this primordial country. The city is surrounded by a horrible muddle of hovels and shanties, shapeless crowds of cabins of unknown purpose, nameless wastes full of every possible kind of rubbish – sickening garbage, piled up over a hundred years by the disorderly and filthy-natured populace. The Russians have borrowed science and art from outside. They are not devoid of natural wit, but the wit that they have is imitative.

Contempt for whatever is unknown seems to me to be the dominant feature of the Russian national character. Their quick and disdainful gaze slides indifferently over everything that has over the centuries been created by human genius. They consider themselves above everybody else in the world, because they despise everything. Their praises sound like insults. Instead of trying to understand, the Russians prefer to mock. The irony of the upstart can become the destiny of the entire nation. The influence of the Tatars outlived the thrown-off yoke. Surely you did not drive them off just so you could imitate them? You will not get far if you keep on abusing what you do not understand.

Makartsev stopped. He took off his glasses and pressed two fingers against his eyelids, so as to give his eyes a rest. De Custine, who'd seemed to be dozing in the armchair, looked silently at him.

'What's the difference,' Makartsev said out loud, not addressing him, 'if this was written now or in 1839? This is all taken down very perspicaciously!'

'You find that, do you?' the marquis noted in satisfaction.

'Yes, damn it! To be frank with you, we do have all of these abominations! It's high time we changed it all. What are we afraid of? Why don't we want to hear anything else?'

'Indeed, why not?' asked de Custine and roared with laughter.

'I don't see anything funny,' responded Makartsev drily and went back to his reading.

How does this crowd that is called a nation represent itself? Do not deceive yourself for nothing: they are the slaves of slaves. A person in Russia knows neither the elevated joys of a cultured life, nor the full and coarse freedom of the savage, nor yet the independence and irresponsibility of the barbarian. The burdensome feeling that has never left me since I came to Russia is strengthened by the fact that everything speaks to me of the natural talents of this downtrodden nation. The thought of what might have been achieved if they had been free is driving me mad. The people drown their anguish in silent drunkenness, the higher classes in noisy revelry. This nation lacks one vital spiritual quality – the ability to love.

The traveller, with the greatest of efforts, distinguishes at every step between two nations, fighting one against the other: Russia the way it is in reality, and a different one – Russia the way it wants to be seen in Europe. The travellers who enjoy the greatest reputations are those who are more easily deceived than others. Always and everywhere, I have felt the concealed, hypocritical cruelty, worse than in the time of the Tatar yoke: modern Russia is much closer to that period than they want us to believe. Everything here comes down to one single feeling – fear.

If you run your eyes over the headlines alone, everything will seem wonderful. But be careful to look beyond the chapter headings. Open the book and you will find out for certain that there is nothing in it: all the chapters are merely designations, and they have yet to be written. How many forests are really swamps, where you would not find a bundle of brushwood? How many regiments in remote localities, where you will not find a single soldier! How many towns and roads exist only as plans! The entire nation, in essence, is nothing other than a poster pasted up across a Europe that is deceived by a diplomatic fiction.

Political superstition lies at the heart of this society. The autocrat, totally irresponsible from a political point of view, is responsible for everything. Up until now I have always thought that truth is as necessary to mankind as air, as sunlight. My trip around Russia has disabused me of this. Lying, here, means to protect things; telling the truth means to rock the foundations.

'Watch out, don't say too much!' is the inevitable refrain in the mouths of Russians or acclimatized foreigners.

The Russian people are a nation of mutes. A Russian receives in his lifetime no fewer blows than the number of times he bows down for them. The one and the other are both uniformly used here as methods for the social education of the people. They tremble to the point that they hide their fear under a mask of tranquillity, something that is dear to the oppressor and suitable for the oppressed. Tyrants love it when everyone around is smiling. Thanks to the terror hanging over everyone's heads, a slavish submissiveness becomes the unbreakable rule of behaviour. Victims and executioners alike are certain of the necessity for blind obedience.

It appears simply to be in the order of things to beat a person, without trial or investigation, in broad daylight in front of hundreds of passers-by. In civilized countries a citizen is protected by the whole community from arbitrary actions on the part of the representatives of authority; here officials are arbitrarily protected from the justified protests of those they offend against. There can be no advocacy in a country where justice is absent. Whence is the middle class to come, the class that forms the basic force of society and without which a nation is transformed into a herd that can be kept under control by a well-trained sheepdog?

The ways of the Russians, contrary to all the claims of this half-barbarian tribe, are still very cruel and will continue to be cruel for a long time to come. Beneath the veneer of European elegance, the majority of these parvenus of civilization have preserved a bearskin pelt – they have put it on with the fur inside. But just scratch one of them, and you will see how the fur comes sticking back out, all bristly. Russians do not so much want to be truly civilized as to appear as if they are. Basically they remain barbarians. Unfortunately, these barbarians are familiar with firearms. This is a nation formed into regiments and battalions, under a military regime which governs society as a whole, even the estates that have nothing to do with soldiering.

From this organization of society springs such a fever of envy, such a frenzy of ambition, that the Russian people are now capable of nothing except the conquest of the world. My thoughts constantly return to that, because no other goal could explain the limitless sacrifices made by the state and individual members of society. Evidently, the nation has sacrificed its freedom in the name of victory. A serious question arises: is the dream of world domination fated to remain just a dream, capable of stirring the imagination of a half-savage people for years to come, or can it come true some fine day? I will say just one thing: since I have been in Russia the future of Europe has appeared to me in a gloomy light.

The destiny of Russia, they assure me, is to conquer the East and then fall to pieces. A nation that is powerless to teach those nations that it is going to conquer will not remain the strongest for long. A state that has not tasted freedom since its inception, a state in which all serious political crises have been provoked by foreign influences – such a state has no future.

This lovely country is organized in such a way that, without direct assistance from the representatives of authority, it is impossible for a foreigner to travel around in it without inconvenience and even danger. You come to the conclusion that it would be better not to see a great deal, rather than having to ask endlessly for permission – that is the first benefit of the system. You will always be under close observation, the only contacts you will be able to maintain will be official ones with every possible high official – and you will be conceded only a single freedom: the freedom to express your admiration for the lawful authorities. Here everyone engages in spying out of love for the art, often not expecting any reward for it.

I make my notes and carefully hide them. An ambush might await me in the forest: I will be attacked, my briefcase that I never part with for a moment will be snatched from me, and I will be killed like a dog. If you hear nothing about me, you will know that I have been sent to Siberia.

The quays of St Petersburg are among the most beautiful structures in Europe. Thousands of people died constructing them. No matter! To make up for it, we will have a European capital, the glory of a great city. Weeping over the inhumane cruelty with which the edifice was built, I admire its beauty, none the less.

'At last!' Makartsev exclaimed.

The Marquis de Custine was curious: 'What, exactly?'

'At last you've found something to praise! I was born in Petersburg, after all, and I love that city.'

'I'm glad to have brought you some joy,' sneered the marquis, 'but I doubt that it's going to be for long. I should add – unfortunately.'

Political beliefs here are hardier and stronger than the religious. There will come a day when the seal of silence will be torn from the lips of the people, and the amazed world will think this is a second Tower of Babel. Out of religious differences, someday a social revolution will arise in Russia, and this revolution will be the worse for the fact that it is done in the name of religion. The ferocity that is being manifested by both sides tells us what the final outcome will be. This is probably not going to happen very soon: with nations ruled by methods like these, passions seethe before they can burst out. Danger is approaching with every hour, but the crisis is delayed and the evil seems endless.

This is an unfortunate country, where every foreigner looks like a saviour to the crowds of the oppressed because he represents truth, openness and freedom to a people deprived of all of these bounties. This terrible society abounds in contrasts: many talk among themselves as freely as if they lived in France. Secret freedom consoles them for the blatant slavery that is the shame and misfortune of their homeland.

The Kremlin makes a journey to Moscow worth while! It is the very boundary between Europe and Asia. Under the successors of Genghis Khan, Asia threw itself upon Europe for the last time; retreating, it stamped its foot – and there the Kremlin sprang up. To live in the Kremlin means not to live but to defend oneself. Ivan the Terrible was the ideal tyrant, and the Kremlin the ideal palace for a tyrant. Putting it simply, it is a dwelling-place for ghosts. The cult of the dead serves as a pretext for popular amusement. The glory arising from slavery – this is the allegory expressed by this satanic architectural memorial. Two towns live alongside one another in Moscow: a city of executioners and a city of their victims. For want of anything better, Moscow has been transformed into a commercial and industrial city. It takes pride in the growth of its factories.

Society here, it could be said, began with abuse. Having once resorted to deceit in order to rule the people, it is difficult to get off that slippery path. A new campaign is a new lie. And the machinery of the state continues with its work. Complete uniformity overwhelms everything here, freezing the pedantry that is inseparable from their idea of order, as a result of which you find yourself hating everything that, in essence, deserves your affection. Russia, that child-nation, is nothing other than an immense school. Everything in it takes place as in a military academy, with the single difference that the pupils do not graduate until death itself.

With such a feeble body, this giant, scarcely emerged from the depths of Asia, makes an effort today to throw all of its weight on to the scales of European politics and dominate the congresses of Western countries, ignoring all the successes of European diplomacy over the past thirty years. Our diplomacy has become sincere, but here sincerity is valued only in others.

The Russians are the greatest actors in the world. They forget about you as soon as they have said goodbye. They are all frivolous, they live only in the present and forget today what they thought yesterday. They live and die without taking any notice of the serious sides of human existence. Nowhere is the influence of the unity of a form of rule and the unity of education proclaimed with such force as in Russia. Every single soul here wears a uniform. The climate destroys the physically weak, and the government does the same for the morally weak. Only bred-in-the-bone beasts survive, individuals strong in both good and bad parts of their nature.

Russians have such a sad and crestfallen appearance that they probably relate with equal indifference to their own and to others' downfall. The life of a human being has no value of any sort here. Existence is surrounded by such constraints that everyone, I imagine, treasures secret dreams of leaving, leaving for wherever their noses lead them, but that dream is fated never to come to pass in this life. Noblemen are not granted passports, peasants have no money, and everyone stays where they are, sitting in their corners with the patience and fortitude of despair.

The issue here is not political liberty, but personal independence, the possibility of travel and even the spontaneous expression of natural human feelings. Peace or the lash! That is the dilemma for everybody. What a country! Grey village hovels seem to be growing into the ground, and every thirty to fifty miles a city lies dead, as if abandoned by its inhabitants, also pressed into the ground, also grey and downcast, the buildings looking like temporary barracks thrown up for manoeuvres. That is Russia for you, for the hundredth time, the way it is. Winter and death, it seems, hang continuously over this country. The northern sun and climate give a sepulchral hue to everything.

Everything is sacrificed to the future. In this sepulchral citadel the dead seem freer than the living. It is hard to breathe under the mute vault of the sky. The stamp of despondency and an uncertainty about tomorrow lie over everything. Tolerance is guaranteed neither by public opinion nor by governmental laws. Everything depends on the mercy granted by a single person who could tomorrow snatch away what he gave today. If there are not enough criminals, they make some more. The victims of arbitrariness have no graves. The children of convicts are convicts themselves. All of Russia is one big prison, and what is more terrible, it is so huge and so difficult for anyone to reach its borders and cross them.

'State criminals . . .' If these unfortunates could appear out of the ground now, they would rise up like avenging ghosts and root the despot himself to the spot, and the edifice of despotism would be shaken to its foundations. Everything can be defended by beautiful phrases and convincing arguments. But whatever they might say, a regime that has to be supported by these means is deeply depraved. If the Russian people could muster the strength to make a real revolution, beating would be as regular as military executions. Villages would be transmuted into barracks, and organized murder – pouring out of the hovels fully armed – would make an orderly advance; in a word, the Russians would perpetrate a massacre from Smolensk to Irkutsk.

'Hey, my dear boy,' sneered Makartsev, 'you're being somewhat naive here!'

'I am curious to know – in what way?' asked the marquis.

'You don't understand the strength and resilience of our ideology. Even though the Twentieth Party Congress was a major shock, the Party still retained its strength, not the people rehabilitated from the camps. It's easy to offer advice about all this from the sidelines, to crack cheap jokes. You should try ruling our immense country yourself!'

'Not on your life!' de Custine exclaimed in fright. 'I just suggested what would happen, and now I can tell you: I'm dispirited by what I see. Read on, monsieur!'

The contemporary political situation in Russia can be defined in a few words: this is a country in which the government says whatever it wants, because it alone has the right to speak. In order to live in Russia, it is not enough just to conceal your thoughts – you have to know how to pretend. The first is useful, the second necessary.

Historical truth is afforded no more respect in Russia than is the sanctity of an oath. The authenticity of stones is as impossible to establish here as the credibility of the spoken or written word. The Russians know no rivals in the art of faking history. Like parvenus without a past, they replace with ephemeral decorations that which, by its very nature, inspires thought about a lengthy existence. The mania for public show, parades and manoeuvres is an epidemic in Russia.

When the sun of openness finally rises over Russia, it will illumine so many injustices, so much monstrous cruelty, that the entire world will shudder.

I will never forget the feeling that seized me as I crossed the Neman. I can say and write whatever I like! You must live in that desert without peace, in that prison without rest that is called Russia, in order to feel all the freedom that is provided to the peoples in the other countries of Europe, regardless of the form of rule. If your children ever think of grumbling about France, please follow my advice and tell them: 'Go to Russia!' Such a journey would be good for any European. Anyone with an intimate acquaintance of Russia would be glad to live in any other country. It is always useful to know that there exists a state in the world in which happiness is unthinkable, for by his very nature a human being cannot be happy without freedom.

'Well, what do you think now?' asked the Marquis de Custine, squinting slyly. 'Doesn't it seem to you . . . ?'

'Do you drink vodka?' Makartsev interrupted.

His guest took fright. 'No! I would prefer some burgundy. But unfortunately it's time for me, as you say hereabouts, to clear off. I know what you think of my book, my friend. If you didn't like it, you wouldn't have been reading it until dawn.'

Makartsev had meanwhile got up off the couch with a grunt and went to the refrigerator, pulled out the bottle and filled himself a third of the teacup that was sitting on the table. He made a face at the smell and drank the whole thing down in one. When he had put the cup down and made to answer de Custine, the armchair was empty. The marquis had disappeared as imperceptibly as he had come – through that hole in the ozone layer, evidently.

# 10

# Towards Morning

'So . . .' Makartsev muttered.

He seemed to recall who he was and how he was supposed to read things. A candidate member of the Central Committee of the Communist Party of the Soviet Union, he became pensive, in official mode. *The weakness of the author in his Partyless, classless position. Should we reject what we ourselves accepted in 1917? Unwise. Unprincipled.* He experienced no more wavering. No affection for the written thoughts was left in him. He was somehow keeping himself aloof from the author for whom he'd felt affection a moment ago. The editor-in-chief in him had awoken again. Once again he was thinking Party-wise, as he should.

Tying up the folder's ribbons, he became filled with indignation. *How could anybody mix up all that was holy to us, all of us, with such muck? It's not about criticism. This manuscript is entirely alien to us, ideologically. It keeps us from moving forward. By law, something like this requires . . . by the way, what is required?*

He took a small booklet off the shelf and looked up Article No. 70: 'Agitation or propaganda conducted for the purposes of undermining or weakening Soviet power . . . the distribution for the same purposes of slanderous inventions that defame the Soviet state and public order, as well as the distribution or preparation or possession with those same purposes of literature with those contents is punishable by . . . up to seven years, and with a further five years in exile . . .'

Suddenly he turned his attention to the word 'possession'. *Is it 'possession' in my case as well? After all, I'm only holding on to the manuscript in the course of my job! No, it shouldn't have any bearing on me!* Roused by his discovery, Makartsev glanced at his watch: it was nearly 4 a.m.

Picking up the manuscript, he went out into the kitchen. He spread a newspaper out on the table, so as not have to take out a plate. He noticed that he'd spread out *Trudovaya Pravda*, so he replaced it with *Sotsialisticheskaya Industriya*, and then sliced himself a chunk of black bread. He opened the refrigerator and saw a jar of pickled tomatoes. He tilted it over and, after spilling some of the juice on the floor, fished out a tomato. Puckering from the sourness, he swallowed it whole and, staggering, made his way to the bedroom. He put the folder on top of the pile on the table at the side of the bed, and underneath the folder he tucked his glasses so that when he looked for them in the morning he wouldn't forget the folder. Zina, sensing that he was beside her, put her hand on his shoulder near his neck. He rubbed his stubbly chin against her hand and touched her breast. She removed his hand and turned her back to him.

'Go to sleep, Makartsev! There isn't anything you want now.'

He sighed and didn't insist, then lay there for a while gazing at the ceiling, trying to dispel his thoughts. Sleep didn't come. Makartsev blindly opened the drawer of the bedside table and took out the imported sedatives that always worked for him. The tablet was somewhat bitter, and he pushed it around with his tongue until it melted. He soon fell asleep and slept for a whole four hours. In the morning he threw on his bathrobe without doing it up and walked around the apartment. The radio was reviewing the central newspapers. They mentioned an article in *Trudovaya Pravda*.

Boris had already gone. Zina was busy in the kitchen.

'Something has happened to you.'

Makartsev had long since broken himself of the habit of telling her his troubles. He only told her about the good things, thinking that this would enhance his authority in her eyes. He knew that this was stupid, but it was what he was now used to.

'Overwork,' he said. 'As always, overwork . . .'

He stood underneath the shower, the water as hot as he could stand it, to clear his head. His wife had prompted him with what he'd been unable to tell himself: something had really happened, after all. *What employees I've got! It's a good thing they didn't leave it somewhere else. I'm going to tear it up into little pieces right away and drop it down the rubbish chute, just as if it had never been.*

But as he stood naked under the shower and the water poured off him, running down his somewhat sunken chest and rounded stomach, another side of the affair occurred to him. *Why was it accidentally forgotten in my office? I'm the bungler, not them, hanging on to my naivety until I'm old and grey. Of course, they planted it on me with quite definite intentions! I know what kind of rubbish they talk about in the departments when nobody else is around. Everybody's walking on a knife edge. The photo lab printed up a bunch of copies of Solzhenitsyn's portrait – I blew my top, demanded the negative and burned it right in front of them! Even in our planning sessions they heckle me. Whenever I'm being nice, they call me a liberal, but as soon as I'm not – right away I'm a Stalinist. It's high time they enlightened me as to what they think I am. But they don't take time into consideration. That's just rudeness on their part! There's no reason for them to be rude to me. When it comes down to it I'm not just their editor but an old comrade to many of them. For their sake I close my eyes to certain things that I shouldn't be closing them to. But what should I do in this case?*

*Wait, though! Would somebody risk doing this in order to expose me to it? After all, the manuscript could turn up in somebody else's hands. But to get me compromised – there could be people who want to do that.*

His thoughts whirled around this version of events. *Somebody was entrusted with the job of putting it there. He was sent by people who are especially engaged in this. Is it possible that everything is coming full circle – and once again they're spying on devoted Party workers? Or is it just a little check-up – of my vigilance, my drive, my principles – just that and nothing else? But now they'll think I've hidden it, or passed it on to someone else to read, in other words that I'm guilty of distributing it. I haven't informed them about it, after all! (On the contrary, they'll think that I've hidden it, or passed it on*

*to someone else to read, that is, that I'm guilty of distributing it. I myself haven't
informed them about it, after all!)*

If it was the KGB running some kind of check-up on him, though,
they were obliged to coordinate it with other people. Or, rather, why would
they *not* coordinate it? Someone must have given a direct order. If that
were so, he, Makartsev, would come out on top. *They've started a game
they'll be sorry for. Uppity young bastards!* He would teach them a lesson
on a higher level than they'd expect. He would even tell Comrade Skinny
himself about it! Let him dole out a proper punishment to these people
who were trying too hard. He was the man who put together a Party newspaper that was read in a hundred and two countries across the world. He
was the wrong person to pick a fight with! While Makartsev was getting
dressed he made the decision that as soon as he got into the office he would
immediately phone one of the deputy chairmen of the KGB on the secure
line.

Makartsev cheered up, his dismay a thing of the past. He was already
whistling as he put on his tie.

# 11

# Who To Talk To?

That morning Anna had barely managed to close the ventilator pane and leave the room after airing it before Makartsev was stashing the grey folder away in his safe. He needed to consider the tone for his conversation and ring the place that he had decided to call on the secure line. He pressed the buzzer.

'Where's my car?'

'Aleksey still hasn't come back from the KGB.'

Every morning his secretary would take a fresh copy of *Trudovaya Pravda* from a bundle, stick it into an envelope, and, when Aleksey had brought Makartsev to work, get him to take it to the KGB. Of course, the aforementioned institution, like any other, could have subscribed to *Trudovaya Pravda*, and the postman would have delivered it every morning. But that's the way things were. Should he send the grey folder straight there with Aleksey? But then he remembered that he'd decided to ring them about it.

He put his hand on the receiver of the secure phone, but his attention was distracted by a pile of snapshots on his blotter. Kakabadze had brought them to Anna that morning, and she'd left them in a prominent spot. Makartsev raked the photographs into the middle of his desk with his palm and distractedly looked at his own image, multiplied twenty times for his selection. Opening the middle drawer of his desk, he swept the photographs into it so that they wouldn't be in his way. He wasn't up to dealing with them.

So the train of conversation would go like this: *Although I'm very busy,*

*I cannot leave this issue unattended, even though it is probably of little consequence. A manuscript of a particular content was planted in my office. If you want, have someone take care of it. After all, that's what your lads get paid for. If not, I'll just throw it out. I have more important Party and government affairs to attend to.*

In a side drawer lay the red telephone directory. Makartsev looked up a four-digit number in it and lifted the receiver of the secure line. But then he replaced it in its cradle. They would come around straight away after his call; for sure, because it was a candidate-member of the Central Committee who was ringing. They would talk tediously to him, pretend to be detectives, tear him away from his work for half a day. Then they would start searching for the source. Financial auditors would appear at the office, the Party Control Commission for Letters-to-the-editor, locksmiths and floor-swabbers. They would check up on all the people that he had personally recruited on to his staff. Even ask for their agents to be hired as temporary correspondents. Telephones would be tapped unselectively. And people here in the office said such awful things! If they didn't find anything on the desks of his employees (but they would, after all!), they would try to prove that they hadn't been working in vain, and they would report to the Central Committee, bandy his name about. *No way – call them? Not likely!* Shop his own newspaper? Whatever was going on there, he wasn't going to do that. Whatever else happened, he wouldn't be accused of a lack of decency.

*So, I'm not going to make the call.* What if the manuscript had been placed as bait, and they wanted to see how he was going to react? What if they knew more about his employees than he did? Tomorrow, Bespakbayev from the district KGB office would drop in on him during office hours and say, 'By the way, did you find a grey folder? According to our information, a certain reader with anti-Soviet sympathies was trying to get to see you.' Or he'd simply telephone and start asking questions.

*This is all so stupid!* He struck his fist against the door of the safe containing the grey folder. The blow was muffled. The safe didn't rock, didn't rattle, didn't react in any way. And they really might telephone, after all. What would he tell them? His tone, of course, would have to be calm, confident –that was the most important thing.

The phone buzzed. *This is it.*

'Sorry to bother you in the morning.' It was the voice of his wife. She was asking for the car. If he didn't need it right then Aleksey could take her to see a sick friend.

'Yes, of course,' he sighed in relief. 'I'll send him.' He called in his secretary. 'Anna, would you send Aleksey to my place? Don't put anyone else through, except from the Central Committee, don't let anybody in, except the people I ask for myself. I'm getting ready for the plenum.'

'And questions about the next issue?'

'I'll deal with them tonight.'

He looked her in the eye. *Is she the one who was told to plant the thing? Too obvious. Maybe Aleksey? That's a possibility, but he's just small fry. One of the 'fresh heads', sitting in my office at the intercom that evening. But it was planted before I left – so it was meant for me! And maybe they've already noticed that I took it home with me. Damn, what stupid thoughts are running around my brain!*

Makartsev was left alone and, rubbing his cheeks, he thought tensely of whom he should talk to about this. *Yagubov's untested in taking joint responsibility for something dangerous. He might try to use the information for his own ends, if not now, then later on; therefore he's out. Polishchuk? He wouldn't tell anyone, of course. But what kind of advice would he give, with his Young Communist fervour? A simple approach has to be taken here. Simple but precise, like a snooker ball dropping into the pocket. Otherwise, distrust. And what could be more terrible than distrust?*

But he wasn't necessarily obliged to ask someone in the office. He had friends.

Relatively recently Makartsev had been tracked down by his former schoolmates, and, nostalgic for his youth, he'd gone off to Leningrad for a reunion party organized in the banquet hall of the Moskovskaya Hotel. More than a third of the class was there, the rest having disappeared into prison or in the war. They drank heavily, and, one after another, in front of their ageing female classmates, boasted about who had achieved what. They had become public figures, some of them defending their doctoral theses, some were colonels, some directors, many had their own cars. One had even made it as far as organizing the next life: he was in charge of funerals for Leningrad VIPs. But, of course, nobody had climbed as high as Makartsev. That was why he spoke the most modestly of all. Of their classmates, only Volodya Bezrukov hadn't achieved anything, and he kept silent, sitting in a ragged pea-jacket. And he had sat behind the same desk as him for six years! Bezrukov shone with erudition – at one point he had studied with Makartsev at the university; he'd been imprisoned twice for revisionism, had been sentenced to be shot and, after several spells in labour camps, had worked as a lathe operator in a factory and was now living as ascetically as Schopenhauer. Makartsev asked Bezrukov several times to come to Moscow, promising to help him. But the latter turned him down flat. Living the Schopenhauer way wasn't for everyone. His drunken classmates agreed to meet regularly and promptly forgot about it. What kind of advice would he get from them?

But Makartsev did have a huge number of Party comrades. He had connections, more or less, with all of them; he had scratched their backs, and they his. But the norms of Party ethics were always observed in their relations: the person to make the call was the one lower in rank. Whoever was higher would answer 'I'll think about it', and whoever was lower would say, 'Yes, sir!' To cross the line into personal affairs was improper until one was firmly ensconced in one's place. Asking for advice meant that you were in trouble.

Out of the blue he regretted that he had no mistress, an intelligent woman, genuine, quiet, faithful, one who would sympathize with him. His worries always seemed like nonsense to Zina: she was a rational person. He had no secret love. Whenever desire would raise its head and rouse him to action, either he wouldn't have the time or he would be afraid of it getting out. And now it was a bit late. His thoughts came back to where he had started, but they hadn't come full circle in vain. Now he came to a conclusion: it would be best to feel out what was known about the folder in the office, carefully. He glanced at the steel door, as if wanting to make sure that the folder was in a safe place. Anna's buzzer went, she jumped up and went in to the editor.

'Is Kashin in? Send him here!'

# — 12 —
# The Parabola of
# Valentin Kashin

Russians always shake hands to say hello, and Kashin always did it with his left hand, but everyone in the office was used to it and nobody took offence. He would smile politely at the people he met, he eagerly fulfilled any request, cracking jokes the while, and easily managed to get everything done on time.

At first they thought there was something wrong with his right hand (he limped on his right leg, too). It turned out, though, that he always had a bunch of keys clutched in his right hand. These keys were all needed from moment to moment – the key to the teletype room, to the storeroom, to the safe. Which key would be needed next he never knew, but it would always be needed in a hurry, so there wasn't time to stuff them in his pocket. Fortunately Kashin was left-handed and signed all his documents with this hand. He said his signature was harder to forge that way. In order to shake hands with his right he had to transfer the keys to the other hand, which he did only for Makartsev and Yagubov – and that was out of respect for the leadership, not to be a lickspittle.

According to the staff rolls, Makartsev had five assistants: the first, third and fourth were assistants to the editorial board secretary, Polishchuk, and their job was to oversee the production of the newspaper in shifts. The fifth was the managing editor, in effect the plant manager, and finally there was Kashin, the second assistant, who was head of the personnel department. By tradition, though, the second assistant simultaneously carried out the functions of the fifth and was called the managing editor, although first and foremost he was the personnel chief.

Kashin knew every corner of the office, even the women's toilet, which he found it necessary to inspect regularly as part of his duties — whether to check that the mirror was hung properly or when completing a work order for running (literally) repairs to the toilet.

If the managing editor wasn't sitting with some documents in his little cubby-hole (desk, safe, bookcase and just enough space for one visitor) or running around the office, favouring his right leg and rattling his keys, or driving with Aleksey in the editor's Volga to buy a trophy cup for the victors of the *Trudovaya Pravda* Round-Kremlin bicycle race, he would be sitting in the secretarial pool, telling the tender-hearted typists about his unhappy family life. His favourite refrain was: 'Try trusting a woman after that!'

The typists would agree, although they added that there were instances when men, too, shouldn't be trusted. But in this particular context, of course, women were guilty across the board. Imagine throwing over a guy like that: not only didn't he drink, he was thrifty, too. He was always unlucky with women, though; he didn't complain about anything else in his life and even related to it with a good bit of humour, although he refrained from sharing that humour with anyone else.

In his school years Kashin had liked playing hockey out of doors more than anything else. When he finished the ninth grade his father took him to his factory. It was a military plant, and after he'd been vetted Kashin became an apprentice radio-assembler. He took apart American radios, unsoldering their components and sorting them into groups by type, so they could be used for the production of Soviet goods. He joined the Young Communists, and then, when he was a grade eight radio-assembler, the Party itself. They offered to make him a foreman, but he had refused: the pay would be less, the headaches would last until night-time, and, even worse, he would be responsible for any stolen parts.

Unexpectedly he was summoned to the plant KGB office. Two unfamiliar people, of medium height, were sitting there. They talked to him about his life plans and, looking at one another, offered him training in a KGB school, with work afterwards outside the country.

'We need mature people who know what's what. And you know all about radio equipment. Your references are good. Your wife won't object, will she?'

'The Party calls, the Young Communist answers "Yes, sir!" as he's trained to!'

'Well, talk it over, anyway.'

At the time he was married to his first wife, Zoya, a copyist in the design office, but they were nursing grievances against each other. She would sulk for three days in a row without any evident reason. Kashin was delighted that he'd have to part from her. When he talked it over with his father, the latter said: 'They'll pay you well and let you jump the queue for an apartment – that's the most important thing. They won't make you the same offer again, and you'll just fade into the factory, like me.'

The school trained personnel for technical work in legal Soviet institutions outside the country. He was well fed and coached in Spanish and English conversation; he easily picked up the cipher techniques. Just before the end of the course he suddenly came a cropper, absurdly: during training to shoot at sounds in complete darkness a bullet ricocheted off a steel plate and hit him in the knee, shattering his kneecap. He underwent two operations in the hospital; but even though he was left with a limp they hadn't taken him off the active duty roster.

Kashin was liable to dismissal, though, anyway, with a written undertaking not to divulge any of the knowledge he had gained, on pain of criminal liability. He was rescued by Fidel Castro, who had just then decided that his provisional revolutionary government should be styled a permanent one. There was an immediate demand for KGB communications personnel at the Soviet embassy in Cuba, in line with an increase in the number of military specialists and the planned construction of bases for intercontinental ballistic missiles aimed at the United States. KGB Junior Lieutenant Kashin was sent, as an exception, to a desk job in Havana.

He wasn't happy for very long. The secret service agents weren't often allowed out into the city to check out the pretty Cubanas, and even when they were they had to stay in groups and under armed KGB guard. They were given very little money. On top of that, there was hardly any work to do. The cipher clerks sat in a damp, stuffy room without any windows. To keep their communications in constant readiness the cipher clerks had to train by encoding excerpts from Sholokhov and other such wonderful Soviet writers. And Lt Col. Vinogradov, the deputy chief of the Central Cipher Group, compared their decoded messages in Moscow against the original text and didn't let a single error get past him.

Once, after getting in trouble for some minor inaccuracy (which was Sholokhov's fault, for trying to express himself in too highfalutin a way), Kashin wrote in a fit of temper, 'Vinogradov is a daehtihs' in tiny letters on the margin of the cipher logbook. He'd forgotten about it before the day was out, but Lt Col. Vinogradov soon after flew in to Cuba on an inspection. The word 'daehtihs' he could figure out without the help of a cipher clerk, reading it from the end.

Junior Lieutenant Kashin was sent back to Moscow on the return flight of the same IL-62 that had brought the lieutenant colonel. Vinogradov called for his removal from the intelligence service and his expulsion from the Party. Kashin's opposite number in Moscow, a cipher clerk named Uterin, suffered as well, because it came out in their face-to-face inter-rogation that Kashin had transmitted that description of the lieutenant colonel unencoded, so it could have been intercepted by the intelligence agencies of the imperialist autocracies. Kashin and Uterin were stripped of their officers' rank and their right to work outside the country. However, taking into consideration their sincere repentance, their punishment was confined to strong reprimands in their Party files and a transfer to the tenth section of the *Semyorka* – the Seventh Operational Directorate, the inter-nal monitoring service.

Kashin never did a single day's work in that section, though. When his new boss caught sight of him limping to his desk he said, without hid-ing his irritation: 'Just what I needed, a lame flatfoot.'

There was no lower position in the KGB than flatfoot, so he was assigned to civilian staff work at the offices of *Trudovaya Pravda*. He was sorry he had been kicked out of the KGB: a year's work there counted as two for pension purposes, and the work wasn't dusty. The only comfort was that he'd already got his one-room apartment, and a modest addition to his salary continued coming in regularly. Conditions would change, and he would get back to working for them again.

Zoya had left Kashin while he was still at the KGB school and married an engineer; so on his return to Moscow from Cuba Kashin married his neighbour. Lydia turned out to be a lot older than him, and at first she was satisfied with everything, but then she started complaining that she couldn't see how he was ever going to earn much (he spent all their money on stamps and on his aquariums) and that their life together wasn't filled with any of the joys he'd hinted at when they were courting. Had he worn himself out in Cuba, where, they say, Fidel Castro permits free love? Even if the wages of love had to be handed over to the state, at least in Cuba you got some pleasure out of it. These opinions went against Kashin's convictions. For whatever reason, Lydia started betraying him shamelessly, and he decided to split up, since their views on happiness were so different, to say nothing of their sex life.

Kashin had brought back a small collection of beautiful postage stamps from Cuba and, a bachelor again, he turned to collecting them with redoubled energy. At the Philatelists' Society he was held in respect as a newspaperman and was elected to the board. He'd also brought back from Cuba an aquarium with striped tropical fish. He fed his fish, trained them, built little grottoes for them on the bottom. When he read in a magazine that looking at fish was good for raising work performance, he had set up an aquarium at the office. He spoke with pleasure of the character, habits and breeding of fish, showing how they learned to swim towards the fish food. As he sprinkled the dried food out of a little packet Kashin would even put his keys down on the desk for a bit in order to free up his other hand.

Evil tongues at the newspaper said that the fish were more important than people to the managing editor. Fish were fauna, a part of nature, that you should love and look out for, while people were just personnel. But this was an exaggeration. Kashin didn't treat the staff at the office any worse than his fish.

# — 13 —
## Everyone Has Their
## Own Functions

'Did you call, chief?' Ready to smile, Kashin's round, kindly face stuck through the half-open door.

'Have a seat.'

The editor shook his hand amicably. While Kashin was sitting himself down, Makartsev looked him over, as if meeting him for the first time, thinking how best to conduct the conversation. Kashin was wearing his habitual dark trousers and the American checked jacket that he'd brought back with him from Cuba and was already getting a bit worn. He always wore one and the same – but clean – Finnish white nylon shirt with red cufflinks. He washed it out himself every night and hung it up to dry in his bathroom. He also wore a tie with a permanent knot fastened with a hook under his collar in the back. The knot was pulled a little to one side and Kashin straightened it, waiting attentively to hear what his editor was going to ask him. His face, simple and open, was disposed towards complete sincerity. A person like that simply couldn't be devious, even if he wanted to be.

'How are things in the secretarial pool?' asked Makartsev, since he hadn't come up with a better opener.

'Do you mean the order about the typing samples?' Kashin smoothed back his hair and coughed, ready to report. 'Well, there was certainly an uproar! I sweated my guts out until all the documents had been checked. I've finished them all. I wouldn't have waited, I'd have taken them away, but they have to have your signature . . . here.'

Kashin opened out a loose-leaf binder and placed a sheaf of papers down in front of his editor.

'Why so many?'

'They had to be done on every typewriter, separately. For the test, I suppose. To keep things straight.'

'Leave it here. I'll sign it later. Listen . . .' He looked at Kashin searchingly. 'You haven't forgotten about our understanding, have you?'

Long before, sure that Kashin was in the office to gather information, Makartsev had asked him to keep an unobtrusive eye on the behaviour of the employees: how they behaved in their everyday relations, who was hitting the bottle. 'We're a national newspaper, in the public eye, after all. So we must keep everything straight internally here. A Party sort of a job, but just between the two of us.' This sort of method was something that would be categorically objected to in principle by Makartsev, but this was diplomacy. The managing editor had to engage in it anyway, whatever the editor's wishes might be. Besides, Makartsev could keep his finger on the pulse of things, so that if anything happened he could step in and avert any disasters. He couldn't just demand straight out that Kashin tell him, the editor, what he was reporting on to the KGB. But this way, asking the personnel chief to keep tabs on the personal affairs of their employees to help promote workplace discipline, that was in the line of duty for a good manager. And Kashin would want to work in harmony with his editor-in-chief.

'You mean, as far as our set-up goes?' he ventured. 'Well, it's like this. There have been several separate instances of people hitting the bottle during working hours. I called them in and warned them about it. I didn't take things any further, not without your input. True, they don't make any trouble when they drink, and they can always find some excuse: a birthday here, something else there. Especially, of course, the youngsters in the print shops, the typesetters and the compositors. But these lads have their own boss, and I warn him about every case. But here in the office there's also . . . and now we're talking about amorality, so to speak. They do chase around, of course! And there's all the talk that goes on!'

'Talk?'

'There always is. Right now, it's a bit less. Or else they've already said it all. Truth to tell, I've been informed that there's some kind of stuff going around, connected with Solzhenitsyn. *Cancer Ward*, maybe, and minor stories is what they're saying. And some shorthand notes from trials. A lot of that sort of material gets confiscated in searches. But I haven't seen any here. They tell jokes but mostly ones about women. They wouldn't appeal to you.'

'No? Why not?'

'Well, I'd tell them to you, but I haven't got the gift for telling jokes. But here's a new political one about Lenin. An old friend came up to Rappoport in the Communist Education Department, a long-haired fellow named Sagaydak, and he told the joke to the whole department. "On what date are the Americans planning to launch their Apollo rocket to the moon?"'

'What date then?'

'On the hundredth anniversary of Lenin's conception.'

'Surely that's nine months before he was born?'

'Exactly! I checked it out on the calendar myself!'

'Yes . . .' Makartsev sighed. 'Anyway, you and I don't work enough at raising the level of political ideology among our employees, do we?'

There was no answer forthcoming, but this was the right way anyway: making the managing editor not simply a trusted administration official but a participant in the workforce's slackness, feeling responsibility not just for listening to jokes but for their being told as well. It was as if Makartsev was equating Kashin's responsibility in this with his own.

'So nobody in the office is reading any typewritten manuscripts?' he said, point-blank.

'Nobody. I'd be the one to know! That's a matter for . . . I mean, that sort of thing is the KGB's business.'

'I'm glad you understand that. I've been promised bonuses for Press Day, and I've got to decide ahead of time who to give them to. The candidates all have to be one-hundred-per-centers. Draw me up a list.'

'Yes, sir!'

'As far as a bonus for you goes, don't worry.'

'Steady on, chief!'

'I'm going to include you on the administration list. By the way' –
Makartsev again skilfully changed the subject – 'how's my new assistant
getting along? Has he found any common ground with the employees?
If there's anything wrong, you'll have to help him out, make the right suggestions to him. We have our own customs here at the paper – familiarize
him with them so he doesn't foul anything up.'

It was important to get something across to Yagubov through Kashin,
as though Makartsev himself had nothing to do with it.

'Yagubov's on our side,' Kashin reassured Makartsev. 'He's got a strong
grip on things. Getting himself acquainted. He spent half a day reading
the personal files. He says you've got to know who you're dealing with.'

*Everybody these days says someone is 'on our side', and everyone gives it
their own twist.* 'That's right,' Makartsev noted aloud, 'we have to know
everyone's function and capabilities. Well, that's about it!'

Kashin got up from his chair, nodded and silently went out, trying
not to drag his foot. Makartsev waited until the door closed, then decided
to compare the typewritten pages collected by Kashin against the
Marquis de Custine's text. He got the grey folder out of the safe and
opened the manuscript at one of the first pages. He didn't know how to
do it, so he devised a method all by himself: find some defect on each typewriter – a broken or sprung letter – and check that letter against the same
one in the manuscript. The tables that Kashin had neatly drawn up suggested which letters to compare.

The editor set aside all the pages with the particular letters he wanted,
but he failed to glean any correspondences. That meant that the manuscript hadn't been reproduced on any office typewriter. It made things
easier. Hiding the folder back in the safe, Makartsev signed Kashin's tables
where it said 'Signature of manager of enterprise (institution)' and called
Anna in to take the sheets to Kashin. Makartsev knew that he had reassured himself in vain. If Kashin didn't know about the manuscript (he
would hardly have concealed it), that meant that it probably hadn't been

the Moscow directorate of the KGB that had planted it but the central directorate, which would be much worse. It was likely that there were still several other people at the office reporting back to the KGB independently and doing jobs for them, but Makartsev didn't know who, exactly, however hard he tried to figure it out.

The huge grandfather clock in the corner of the office, with its glittering pendulum, struck noon. A little longer and it would be a whole twenty-four hours since that damned folder had been left lying in his office, and he still hadn't figured out what to do. The KGB would be thinking he'd passed it on to someone to read or got scared or was at a loss. If anybody asked, he had to have at least some sort of respectable answer to hand. Who could he trust on this ticklish issue? He had to move quickly before it was too late. He decided there was only one person to get sensible, practical advice from, not just anybody but a man from his own office – Rappoport.

Should he go to Rappoport's department himself? *Call him out into the corridor and talk to him? But contact like that will attract unwelcome attention. It would be better here – an everyday chat about production.* Just then Makartsev wondered for the umpteenth time if his office was bugged. *They would hardly start bugging their own dedicated Party people just like that, though. That sort of thing won't be happening again, not just yet.* Hesitating over whether to call in Rappoport through Anna or over the intercom, the editor lifted the receiver of his regular telephone.

'Rappoport,' he said, with an awkwardness that he couldn't hide (*stupid, of course!*). 'You couldn't come up to my office, could you?'

# The Free Fall of
# Yakov Rappoport

You might not believe this, but Rappoport knew by heart absolutely every answer to the questions on the good few hundred personal history forms – or maybe even more – that he had ever filled in. He maintained that every Soviet man and woman had to remember the answers to those questions, even after their demise, since no one knew if Russians (to say nothing of Jews) were accepted into Hell without the right forms – but they definitely wouldn't get into Heaven.

Rappoport also had to remember his responses on the questionnaires because he wasn't capable of answering *yes* or *no* to a single question, not even the simplest. In every *no* there was a teeny *yes*, and in every *yes* a certain percentage of *no*. He considered that the truest answers were what he'd written on the latest form and could only guess at whether the rest was better known – or not known at all – to some organization or other than it was to himself. It was only his present *nom de plume* that he could indicate with confidence, although in this case as well, of course, it was one per cent here and one per cent there.

His mother, Sarra Rappoport, had been born in the Ukraine, in the very Pale of Jewish Settlement. She told her son the story of how she – an active member of the Russian Social Democratic Workers' Party – had had to go to Berlin in her youth. Until then she'd been living illegally in St Petersburg following her exile, and there the police had begun tailing her. In Berlin she met a real German Communist. It was possible that he was Jewish, too, but perhaps not. Sarra Rappoport recalled to her boy how the rabbi in a Berlin synagogue had circumcised him on 13 January

1917 at the insistence of her parents (Sarra's father owned a watchmaker's shop), and recorded him in the book as being born on this date under the name of Yankel.

'And ever since the rabbi started the ball rolling,' complained Rappoport, 'I keep getting circumcised by anyone who feels like it.'

When he got his internal passport in 1933 in Moscow he registered as Yakov. Sarra called her former husband Mark, his comrades called him Meyer. His real name was never used. At the synagogue Yankel had been registered in his father's name, but while the boy was still young his father's name was never mentioned at home; he had stayed behind in Germany, and Sarra, on her return to Russia after the Revolution, was afraid that her son would blurt it out. She assumed that since his father wasn't writing it meant that he'd gone underground. And for that reason she gave her son her own name.

One day a foreigner came to see them. Sarra was working as a typist at the Council of People's Commissars. He could just about speak Russian, and he passed on greetings and a parcel. He tried to talk Rappoport's mother into joining his father, who, as it turned out, had long before emigrated to the United States and had his own small business there.

'He's probably forgotten that he's a Communist!' Sarra yelled at her guest in irritation. 'But you can tell him that I'm not about to change *my* convictions!'

'You don't have to,' the American tried to persuade her. 'You'll be a Communist in America. Here in Russia there's a lot of Communists, and we have only a few. And then . . . he's the father of your child, after all. He loves you!'

'If he loves me, let him come here and build Communism!'

Yakov never heard anything more about his father. In order to avoid misunderstandings he never inquired about him, and in personal history forms would write that he had no relatives outside the country. When he got his internal passport at the age of sixteen, since he didn't have a birth certificate he named another city, Berdichev, instead of Berlin, as his birthplace, because they both started with *Ber*. And that was a very far-sighted act, as he later became convinced. What sort of documents was he able to present to the police? Only Sarra's old passport, on which she had left the country and come back before the Revolution. And whenever you present any kind of document right away the confusion begins. In her passport it read: 'Religion: Judaean.'

'So what exactly is your mother?' asked the police officer.

'A Jew.'

'And where does it say that, I ask you?'

'Judaean – that's Jewish.'

'You're not lying, are you?' The officer looked at him mistrustfully.

'Young Communist's honour!'

'But surely "Judaean" isn't any worse than "Jew", is it?'

'Not really, no, not worse.'

'Let's write down "Judaean", then, just to be precise.'

But the woman who filled in Yakov's passport details wrote down 'Indaean' in her beautiful hand instead of 'Judaean'. And when he expressed surprise she reassured him. 'Does it really make any difference to you, my boy? All nations are equal here.'

So you can understand how Rappoport was neither Yakov, nor Markovich, nor Rappoport. He'd been born not-sure-exactly-when and certainly not in Berdichev. He wasn't a member of any one of the existing ethnic groups, and the only thing left for him to do was become the progenitor and representative of a new nation – the Indaeans.

When, following the murder of Comrade Kirov in 1935, Comrade Stalin was studying the list of upper-echelon people in charge and not-so-in-charge that had been presented to him, and was ticking off certain of their names, he put a blue pencil mark next to Sarra Rappoport's. He fell into thought and even sucked his pipe. He knew Sarra very well. They'd seen a lot of each other before the Revolution. He'd taken her for a Georgian and pursued her just a bit. At the time she'd been practically a little girl, slender as a grapevine, with a black plait, and when she came back to Russia in 1919 she had filled out after giving birth, even getting a tiny bit curvaceous. Stalin ran into her at the Central Committee, put a comradely hand on her shoulder and offered her a job as a typist at his secretariat.

'It's not that easy to find good staff,' he said in his thick Georgian accent.

After giving Sarra her job Stalin started inviting her to the *dacha* in Barvikha and strolling with her in the woods. Once, on the path, when Stalin had as if by accident put his hand below Sarra's waist, Lenin appeared in front of them. He stopped and with his characteristic bluntness and craftiness shook a finger at them: 'I think you're having a little petty-bourgeois relationship, eh?'

Knowing that it wouldn't work out any other way Stalin proposed to her, promising that if she agreed he would divorce his wife. But for some reason Sarra turned him down. Stalin never asked her on a picnic again.

'Just think about it!' Rappoport reflected later. 'Stalin could have adopted me! And I would have called him "Comrade Daddy".'

The very first thing that Stalin recalled, after marking his blue pencil dot, was that Sarra Rapport had had very lovely skin in her youth. And then – the insult she'd dealt him. He thought a bit longer, then placed a tick on the list next to the name Rappoport and wrote slantwise: 'Isn't she connected with the attempt on Lenin's life?'

Yakov's mother was arrested. She wrote an indignant letter to Stalin from Lubyanka prison: 'Koba! I demand that you set me free at once! This is just vile – to settle a personal grudge against a woman!' For the words 'vile' and 'demand' Sarra Rappoport was shot.

At this point Yakov Rappoport was a student. He dreamed of becoming a monumental sculptor. His degree work was entitled *Lenin and Stalin at Gorki*. Stalin is paying a visit, they're sitting on a bench, and Lenin is inspiredly talking about the future while Stalin inspiredly works out Lenin's tenets. Rappoport was stretching the historical record a tiny bit: at the time he was fixing for eternity, Lenin was already unable to talk. But everything was correct from the point of view of socialist realism, though.

At the institute Yakov managed to keep the fact of his mother's arrest hidden, and everything else went fine. The only pity was that he, the son of revolutionaries, was never able to write anything about it, at first because he was the son of a foreign father, then because he was the son of a purged mother and after that so as not to be accused of hiding the truth before. Rappoport was no slower than anyone else to grasp the fact that a complete personal history form was essentially a denunciation of oneself, and he was in no hurry to fill in the details. But he stopped hurrying only after he'd already burned his fingers.

He'd been sent straight from the Institute to sculpt a 330-foot statue of Lenin for the roof of the Palace of Soviets. The palace was being built on the banks of the Moscow river, on the site of the demolished Cathedral of Christ Saviour. The sculptors whose backgrounds were more worker-peasant than his began to tease Rappoport about his being an Indaean, and for the first and last time in his life he was disturbed by ethnic feelings. So he went to the police to file a request to change his ethnic designation, so that 'Jew' would be written in his passport or, failing that, he was willing to accept any other ethnic designation so long as it actually existed.

'How do you mean – any other? And what are you really?'

'A Jew, a yid . . .'

'Really – a Jew?'

'Just take a look at me.'

They promised to sort the matter out for him and handed him a new form to fill in. They came for him that night. He found out during one of his interrogations that he was engaged in espionage on behalf of the Indaean Republic. They didn't even beat him. They gave him a break from food and water for two days and then fed him salt herring. Two days later, yearning for water, he remembered that he really was the agent-in-residence of the state security service of the bourgeois Republic of Indaea. Rappoport was only afraid that they would try to make him point out Indaea on the map. But that hadn't been called for.

'You're not the agent-in-residence,' the interrogator corrected, 'but somebody recruited by agents-in-residence. Got that?'

That was better, anyway. The other sculptors from the studio, as it tran-
spired later, had deliberately sculpted a statue that was too heavy. The
palace was being built in a swampy area, and Lenin wound up crashing
down on to the House of Government across the way. So Yakov
Rappoport had got off relatively easily. Convicted without a trial by a
special court, he got the ten years' servitude due to him for betrayal of the
Motherland, aggravated by his utterances offensive to the friendship of
the peoples of the Soviet Union (he'd called himself a yid); from
Lubyanka prison he'd been sent to the Krasnopresnenskaya transit camp
and from there to the transit camp at Vtoraya Rechka, near Vladivostok.

Early on at the camp Rappoport had got a fright that lasted for a long
time. On his very first day, as he was standing in line for his rations, something heavy piled into him. Rappoport buckled under the weight, and
behind him they laughed. A man frozen stiff as a board, who was being
held up from behind by two crooks – actually they'd failed to keep hold
of him – had fallen on top of him. Rappoport got to his feet and held up
the stiff to the distribution window, out of which the unsuspecting sim-
pletons handed the dead man his rations, skilfully snatched by the crooks.

For two days the dead man got his rations, while the crooks hid him
away at night. The dead prisoner's face began to seem familiar to
Rappoport. He was in no doubt that it was a Jew. His supposition was
confirmed on the third day, when the guards discovered the body and figured out its name by its number. It was the prisoner Osip Mandelstam.
It was rumoured that the crooks had killed him as a favour to the authorities. Rappoport didn't match up the poet Mandelstam with this
Mandelstam right away. He was only sorry that they hadn't met sooner.

Rappoport himself told the story of how he had been in prison with
Mandelstam, but it was possible that it hadn't happened, or it hadn't happened quite like he said, or it had been another Mandelstam, just with
the same name as the great Russian poet. This was because Rappoport,
a talented actor, was always acting a little bit in his real life, even over-
acting.

Of course, he'd wanted to stay alive and had sought out the best ways of doing that, keeping an eye out for any real opportunity. He put together a wall-newspaper called *For Shock Labour* and wrote pieces for it about how labour shocked the prisoners, as he put it. In addition, he modelled a bust of the camp boss out of clay, but the clay dried out and the boss started cracking all over.

One day the convicts were washing themselves in the bathhouse. Rappoport was left alone, covered in soap. Just then they let the women into the bathhouse. What saved him was that he lost his head. Already clean but still going through the motions of washing himself, he was sitting all covered in soap when someone shouted from the door that the war had begun. If it hadn't been for the soap Rappoport could have acquired a harem of his own. And he could have heroically perished in it if he'd been discovered by the sex-starved women

Penal battalions for the front were being recruited from among the camp thieves. As a political prisoner Rappoport shouldn't have been afforded that kind of trust, but there weren't enough young thieves to fill the quota. However, the personal representative of Rokossovsky's staff knew that the soldiers of the penal battalion were to be garlanded with bottles full of flammable liquid and thrown under German tank tracks, so he was more interested in how fast they could run than in what their views were. So the politicals were lined up in ranks and given the command: 'At the double – quick march!' Rappoport reached the finishing line third out of his rank; they took the fastest three from each one, and he wound up at the front.

Private Yakov Rappoport received three and a half ounces of alcohol internally and a quart of kerosene in two bottles in his hands, lay down in the path of a tank and waited. But the tank that was bearing down on him stopped two yards away: its fuel supply had run out a bit before Rappoport's did. Rappoport stood up and tried to get back to his own side but was shot down by the Russian machine-gunners walking in a rank behind them for the purpose of encouraging the penal battalion's labours.

And again Rappoport had a lucky break: he'd received only two light wounds, and he wasn't even sent from the field hospital to the rear. The surgeon turned out to be Jewish, too, and ordered him to put out a hospital newspaper called *Back into Action!* The newspaper was seen by the adjutant to the head of the Front Political Directorate, who was there getting injections for an accidentally acquired social disease. This officer had been instructed to come up with an article for *Pravda*. Lying in bed, with a guaranteed three meals a day, Rappoport wrote the article in a single day and a week later was reading it in *Pravda* over the signature of Marshal Rokossovsky himself.

They were supposed to send Rappoport back to his front-line unit, but the adjutant to the head of the Political Directorate had a brainstorm: his superiors might possibly need to have yet more articles written. Discovering that Private Rappoport understood German, he took him along with him to front headquarters. Rappoport's old guilt was written off. He was reassigned and placed at the disposal of the Propaganda Department.

The broadcaster's seat was next to the driver's in the cabin of the sound truck. The vehicle, fitted with loudspeakers, would creep up as close as possible to the boundary between the armies, camouflage themselves at the edge of a wood and call on the Germans to give themselves up, since the war for them was lost anyway. The voice of the former convict, the hireling of the counter-intelligence service of the bourgeois Republic of Indaea, was fully audible to the Russian side, and with a following wind even carried as far as the enemy. But his knowledge of a foreign language hadn't been indicated with utter precision on the questionnaire: Yakov Rappoport, would-be instructor to the enemy forces on their demoralization, spoke German with a thick accent. And the Germans in the trenches took his calls to desert to be comedy broadcasts, and that only raised the morale of the German army.

Rappoport also once found himself somehow accidentally in enemy-occupied territory, although he never wrote that down in his personal forms. The truck got stuck one night on the rain-sodden clay road. Through his little viewing hatch, like a funnel, Rappoport could see that he was surrounded by a platoon of German soldiers. Fortunately they were all well stewed. Rappoport turned his loudspeaker to full power:

'*Kameraden! Achtung!*' he pronounced in solemn tones, trying to speak without an accent. '*Wir sind von der PK. Sonderauftrag des Oberkommandos. Eingähender darf ich nicht sagen. Wir müssen noch heute im Rücken der Iwans sein . . . Doch diese verdammten Landstrassen! Los! Greift alle zu! Feste! Der deutsche Soldat muss mit dem russischen Strassendreck fertig werden. Hei-Ruck.*

The engine revved up, the soldiers began to shout encouragement to one another. The wheels sank into the brown slush, but it wasn't far to a cobbled stretch of road. Feeling firm ground under the wheels, Rappoport took the mike in his hand once again.

'*Danke, Kameraden!*' he yelled. '*Sieg heil!*'

'*Heil!*' the soldiers shouted, throwing their hands out in front of them.

They drove back home as if nothing had happened. No one had noticed their absence, and they themselves didn't whisper a word about it. No one would have believed them anyway, and Rappoport would have got another ten years in the camps. Truth to tell, this story seemed pretty far-fetched to many at the office, but that was the way Rappoport told it, and who else would you believe if not him? A whole year before the Great Victory he was reinstated in the Party as a reward.

Throughout the war he had been corresponding with a classmate of his, a girl named Asya Rabinovich. There had been nothing going on between them, but she had brought him parcels after his arrest. Asya had been evacuated to Altay, and she was now living in Biysk, after getting a job as a drawing instructor at a school there. After the end of the war with Germany, the units that Rappoport had been fighting in were sent over to the Japanese front. By the time they arrived that war was drawing to a close, too, and they were soon demobilized. From the Far East he set off, naturally, for Biysk, but on the way, in Barnaul, he met another classmate, Vasya Kuptsov, who had become the chief director of the theatre there. He helped Rappoport get a job on the local newspaper. Asya moved to Barnaul, and they got married.

Rappoport the front-line veteran went around in an officers' tunic without shoulderboards and rose rapidly in the newspaper to become head of the arts and literature section, around the time the fight against Rootless Cosmopolitans began. Rappoport willingly wrote articles about these lick-spittles of the West.

'If you don't want to be called an anti-Semite, call a yid a Cosmopolitan,' was how he explained the Party's policy to Asya at home.

Rappoport started a column entitled 'But They Eat Russian Fatback', taking the line from a fable that was well known at the time, and he enriched the column with living examples from the lives of Cosmopolitans in Altay Territory. There wasn't any fatback – dried pork crackling – to be had in Altay, but the column heading sounded good. Despite every-thing, Rappoport still remained naive and never suspected that articles, poems and even overheard utterances were as much denunciations as per-sonal history questionnaires ever were. And they affected more than just himself.

The wonderful poet Aleksandr Zharov came from Moscow to take up the fight against the Rootless Cosmopolitans in Altay, accompanied by a KGB art expert in civilian clothes. According to the plan, the Cosmopolitans were supposed to be all the cultural and artistic figures in Altay Territory who belonged to that well-known ethnic group. Party Territorial Committee First Secretary Belyayev looked over the prepared list along with both visitors. When they got to Rappoport's name, the Secretary scratched his cheek for a moment and crossed it out.

'That can't be right!' objected Zharov. 'Surely this one's a Cosmo-politan, too!'

'We know better than you who the Cosmopolitans around here are!' Belyayev cut him short. Rappoport wrote all the Secretary's speeches and addresses.

'But what about the total number?' asked Zharov.

'We have a real Cosmopolitan here, even though he's a Russian. That's the drama theatre director, Kuptsov. We'll put him into this empty slot.'

Belyayev's daughter had graduated from the Theatrical Academy the year before, but Kuptsov had stubbornly resisted letting her play any of the main roles.

Soon the Cosmopolitans were sent off to build railways in Siberia. But now all his acquaintances started thinking that, since Rappoport had been left alone, there had to be a reason for it, and they began to steer clear of him.

'Have no fear,' he tried to reassure them. 'They'll put me in jail soon enough!'

'Keep your trap shut!' Asya exclaimed. 'It would be better to let them think the worst.'

His own troubles were kept off for less than a year. In one of his articles he mentioned that the word *tovarishch* – 'comrade' in Russian – is of Turkic origin. Where he had read that he didn't even remember for sure, probably in an etymological dictionary. But the most important thing was – why had he read it? And what had possessed him to go messing around in philological research? He was called in for questioning. On the desk of the handsome young investigator lay the article and the file of a case already opened on his remarks against the word *tovarishch*. The article, by the way, said that the Russian language was the greatest, mightiest, fairest and freest in the world, but now that was of no interest to the investigator. This time he wasn't allowed any parcels, and Asya was very rudely thrown out.

Since Secretary Belyayev was also arrested at this time they simultaneously recalled that Yakov Rappoport had earlier tried to escape his just deserts, for he was indeed a Rootless Cosmopolitan. During the search of his home they found a box full of German medals that Rappoport had brought back from the front. They confiscated it, and a complete list of Iron Crosses of every class was included in the case against him, medals awarded to the accused, former Junior Lieutenant Rappoport, for espionage, but in this case on behalf of Nazi Germany. The recidivist confessed to everything again, of course, and the investigator asked: 'Do you know any jokes? Come on, tell me some.'

He was afraid to tell jokes, more than anything.

'You bugger!' said the investigator. 'If anyone knows any good jokes I give him ten years, and everyone else gets twenty-five. And you a Cosmopolitan, too!'

Rappoport wound up in Karaganda, where the German prisoners-of-war were serving out their sentences. It goes without saying that he was commissioned to carry on propaganda among them in German, to get them to stay in Kazakhstan for ever and build a Communist society there. In addition to that, he once again published a wall-newspaper, this time called *For an Early Release!* Political prisoners were never granted release ahead of schedule, but from the point of view of the education of the New Man it was necessary to write about it. He served only four years in all before getting released this time, although he had to stay in exile.

The first thing Rappoport did was go to the library, where he learned that the Turkic word *tovarishch* came from the words *tovar* and *is* – roots meaning *beast* and *friend* respectively. That radically changed the matter. It meant that comrades were friends who acted beastly. 'A true friend is the one', Rappoport would say, 'who first of all learns everything about you and only then informs on you.'

Asya came to live with him, and together they waited out his rehabilitation.

'What kind of ethnic group is that, Indaean?' the police once again asked him, looking over his camp documents.

'A Red Indian Jew,' he explained gloomily. And that's what they put down after his rehabilitation.

The Rappoports started life anew. They managed to get registered in Moscow and in time received a one-room apartment. Asya, now fat and considerably older, went to work as a teacher in a nursery school. Rappoport, having thought up a *nom de plume* for himself, began writing articles for newspapers and magazines. He refrained from recollecting old times. Only when he sat down to write would he first slice some chunks off a loaf of white bread, put some sausage and cheese on each slice and arrange them like chessmen around him on his desk. He would write a few lines and then say, 'Check!', at which he would move one of the sausage sandwiches into his mouth. In the camps he'd had to rake potato peelings out of the garbage heap with a shovel and then cook them on the shovel over an open fire. Years later the feeling of hunger never left him, even after a sumptuous dinner.

They readily printed his articles, and everywhere they let him fill in their personal history forms, but they wouldn't make him a full-time staffer, even on wretched little factory newspapers. Makartsev, only recently appointed editor-in-chief of *Trudovaya Pravda* and even more energetic and bold than at present, offered him the post of literary contributor. The pay was miserly but regular, and Rappoport instantly agreed. At this time he was striving in vain to be reinstated in the Party.

The matter was complicated by the fact that he'd been imprisoned twice, and the relevant Party committee was hanging fire on his application. Once again Makartsev came to his aid, but with his new Party card all his Party seniority disappeared. That was the unkindest cut of all: Rappoport had been dreaming of getting to the time when he would become an Old Bolshevik and receive a personal pension.

He was well known in the newspaper world, and nobody was surprised that he soon took over the duties of editor of the Communist Education desk. Departments like this were being established in all newspapers now that Communism had entered a period of all-out attack on all fronts. It was necessary work, thought Rappoport. After all, the Party – and this was straight from Khrushchev's mouth – was giving notice that even today's present generation of Indaeans would one day be living under pure Communism. The department's task was to get the old people ready for their new labours. Without any such preparation they were bound to be in a tight spot.

Rappoport regarded Makartsev highly, remembering the good the editor had done him, and slaved away for him. The only thing he couldn't stand was being sent off on assignment.

'I'm not going to write about anything I see there,' he explained. 'And I can make up everything here just as well.'

Best of all, Rappoport adored making up readers' letters. Oh, he was the King of Letters to the Editor! After every event, when a command would come down from on high to express some nationwide sentiment in their newspaper, he would sit down by the telephone and track down suitable candidates from among plant directors, house painters, artistes, academicians and taxi drivers. In a brisk patter he would read them over the phone the opinions they were supposed to express and say: 'Everything civilized! Nothing bogus, you understand, eh?'

And he would invoice a fee for himself – five roubles per opinion.

'Letters to the editor – I tell you! That's the *vox populi*,' he explained to a student intern from the journalism faculty. 'What, tell me, do our marvellous Soviet authors write? Correct! Letter-novels, letter-stories. Poetry – of course! Sure, I could write them better, but I phone them to give the youngsters a piece of the action. And the best thing is this: you speak in the name of the people, but you bear the responsibility for nothing at all! I have to tell you, though, that writing for other people requires real artistry. Any fool can write for himself. But here you have to play a role. Ah, letters to the editor – that, children, is great literature. Just look!'

And he would show them samples of his artistry. 'We unanimously approve (condemn, protest, hold up to shame, demand).' 'On the subject of the launching of our sputnik, the launching of an atomic icebreaker, a speech by whoever and wherever, court trials of writers here or of Communists somewhere else, aggression by the American imperialists, etc.'

Sometimes he would mysteriously disappear from the office. Only Makartsev knew that he was at the district committee or at the Central Committee itself. If they needed something to be written by someone of low rank they would say, 'You'll have to help him write it.' If they were middle-ranking, it would be: 'Go see him, he'll help you write something.' In other words, 'He'll tell you how he would write it himself, if he knew how.'

One morning he was summoned peremptorily to the Kremlin Palace of Congresses and commissioned to write folk ditties for the Yaroslavl Lads singing group, to which Khrushchev had taken a liking.

That evening the lads from Yaroslavl were to put on a show. To Rappoport's chagrin they threw out his best verse:

> *A rocket to the moon will be how*
> *Rocketeers do well, they hope:*
> *Our achievements will be seen, now,*
> *Only through a telescope.*

He expressed the thoughts of the workers' vanguard and Party men, milkmaids and pig girls, factory directors and shop managers, Party and trade-union members, war leaders and heroes, laureates and deputies, writers and composers, as well as veterans saluting young people and Young Pioneers entrusted with the salutation of veterans. He wrote speeches for the Party Secretaries of African and Asian countries. He could have written a speech for the president of the Republic of Indaea, if such a one ever turned up. The orator himself would get the fee and take it as his due. Rappoport might sometimes receive a handshake.

Reading not-himself in the newspapers, he would speedread down the familiar columns, smirk if something had been 'corrected' and chuck the newspaper into the wastepaper bin.

'Did you see that?' he would growl. 'What the hell were they thinking of? They redid it. They think they know the Party line better than me!'

He made doll's houses out of children's blocks: 'The pig girl gives me two, the milkmaid gives me three – five paragraphs of Christmas present, all – for – thee,' he would purr, working away with his scissors at the threshold of the latest assembly, meeting, conference, council, rally, session, forum, seminar, symposium, colloquium, congress or even convention. Reports, speeches, talks, addresses, collective letters, resolutions, salutations of all kinds, mandates for posterity and so on, etc. etc. – he hoisted them all on high. If anyone had suggested that there weren't any Party conferences, activist assemblies or plenums that didn't go *entirely* according to scenarios written by Rappoport, that comrade would have been an anti-Semite. Well, except for when the chairperson would ask at the end, impromptu: 'All in favour? Passed unanimously.' But then he would once again glance at his approved thought-guide: 'Allow me, comrades, warmly to thank in your name the Central Committee of our dear Party, and personally . . .'

'I'll tell you what, little ones,' Rappoport would say to the office youngsters. 'If there is anybody in the world that Rappoport hasn't written something for, you'll know that they aren't on the same path we are! And if they are, they won't be for much longer!' Like all very great people, he sometimes spoke of himself in the third person.

Usually, when his participation was urgently called for, they would meet him halfway, creating the proper conditions for him to work in. And if they let him avail himself of their private delicatessen, he would have a speech for them in next to no time and exactly what was needed. He always knew better than they did exactly what they needed. However, if they tried to phone him and ask him to bring the finished report round, he would answer that of course he would try to write it but that here at the office there were absolutely no conditions for such responsible work. 'This is a newspaper, you understand! Noise, din, hullabaloo . . .' And he would drag things out until the very last moment, when they would write him out a pass. Once inside their premises he would first visit the delicatessen and buy Asya a can of crabmeat, a piece of whitefish, smoked sausage – and, in winter, fresh tomatoes and bananas. When he had filled his briefcase with these scarcities he would take out the box that held his CAVIAR. CAVIAR, or his Compendium of Applicable Variations on the Ideological Arguments of Rappoport, was a collection of words, phrases, quotations and entire paragraphs cut out of newspapers and arranged by subject in a cardboard box that had once held Krasnaya Moskva perfume.

When he was given the task of preparing an article or speech Rappoport would 'spawn', that is, get thoughts on the required subject out of his CAVIAR box. He would update the old Party Congress number with the current one, and with great reluctance he would, if he had to, beef it up with facts by means of an up-to-the-minute phone call. Rappoport didn't have any copyright on his material, and anybody could use his methods and materials without citing their sources.

Once they sent round a car for him. An ideological conference dedicated to dealing with young people had already begun in the Colonnade Hall, and a number of the speeches were in urgent need of replacement. He searched out the delicatessen first thing, anyway. The hall was full of people sitting and waiting. But the delicatessen turned out to be closed. Rappoport went into the panellists' lounge, put his briefcase down immediately beside him (in case anybody walked off with it), took out the box with all his CAVIAR and, after establishing what the subject of the conference was to be, began dictating the chairman's opening address to a typist. As soon as Rappoport had finished the chairman began his speech. Everything went smoothly from then on: whoever's text he finished, that orator would raise his hand and clamber up to the lectern.

Yuri Gagarin was the guest of honour at the conference, and he arrived at the end. He'd already had to speak at two other meetings that day and had been held up. Rappoport was no less tired than Gagarin, but while the audience was greeting the jolly cosmonaut – bedecked with the medals of every country in the world, from his speech organs down to his reproductive ones – with a standing ovation, Rappoport managed to dictate the first page of his speech: 'On behalf of my comrades, the pilot-cosmonauts, and for myself personally . . . As if it were today I remember my first space flight . . . "The eaglets are learning to fly . . ."' This page was delivered to Gagarin by a duty attendant in a red armband, and, while the cosmonaut was reading it from the lectern, Rappoport was dictating page two – only he didn't manage it this time. Gagarin got to the end of the first page too soon and looked over at the Presidium. The audience started clapping.

Tyazhelnikov, the first secretary of the Young Communists' League, went out to the lobby personally to find out what was going on. He came to a stop next to Rappoport, who was droning something or other to the typist and out of curiosity fell to observing the process.

'Is there a hold-up?' asked Tyazhelnikov.

'Don't bother me,' Rappoport brushed him off. 'Get back on the stage!'

'Fine, fine!' the man said, embarrassed, and went back in.

The audience kept on clapping until the duty attendant brought Gagarin page two. 'Right now, when our Party and the entire Soviet nation . . .' The crowd held its breath. Rappoport was by this time feverishly dictating page three. 'You have today, doubtless, heard many an interesting and useful fact, but you're tired. Therefore allow me to be brief. I wish you all . . .'

When the session was over, muttering curses under his breath, he gathered up into his briefcase his copies of the dictated speeches (they would come in handy for his CAVIAR). There was a reason for his ire. On orders from above the delicatessen and the kiosk full of scarcities had been closed because nobody had wanted to go into the hall and everyone was crowding around the counters. The participants had been given coupons for the goodies after the meeting. Rappoport wasn't a participant at the conference, so he wasn't entitled to any coupons.

Gagarin walked past him, stopped and turned. 'Was that you who wrote my speech?'

'Yeah, that was me.'

'The best thing about it was that it was short. One, two – and applause, already.'

'It would have to be short, when there's fuck all to be had at the delicatessen!' Rappoport was thinking about his own needs.

'Really? Come with me!'

Gagarin led Rappoport to the banquet table and sat him down next to him. Then he poured him a drink. Around them sat the entire cohort of panellists. Toasts were being proposed in hierarchical order. Rappoport clinked glasses and stood up when everyone else rose but didn't drink anything himself. His stomach had got in a terrible state in the camps. If Asya hadn't been making him oatmeal water every morning and thin pudding every night Rappoport – with his creeping stomach ulcer, cholecystitis, constant constipation and haemorrhoids such as God forbid you should even dream about – would never have got out of hospital.

'To be cured in Russia you have to have an iron constitution,' he used to say. Lots of people nowadays quote that maxim without knowing that its author was none other than Rappoport himself. Fortunately, everyone else at the long table so lavishly spread with tasty wonders was knocking back the booze, and nobody paid any attention to the Great Teetotaller of the age. Trying as hard as he could to avoid the spicy dishes, he managed to fill up to his heart's content on the scarcities that they wouldn't supply him with at the delicatessen counter. But the cosmonaut, a man who had passed through a special selection process and pre-flight training, had sharper eyes than Rappoport supposed.

'What, aren't you drinking?' asked Gagarin, putting his arm around Rappoport's shoulder. 'You're going to knock one back right now. A directive from on high, all right?'

He stood up, hiccupped and said, hushing the speakers with one hand: 'Comrades! Allow me to propose a toast to the most modest fellow sitting at our table. We don't know him, but he knows us: he wrote all our speeches today. This is . . . what's your name?'

'Tavrov,' growled Rappoport.

'To Comrade Tavrov! Hurrah!'

'You can do that without a script?' said Rappoport in surprise.

'What did you think? Maybe I'm just pulling your leg. Hey, drink up, just like we agreed. Bottoms up!'

That evening, thanks to Gagarin, Rappoport felt light and breezy. *How right people are who drink!* Even though he had lived until his hair was pure white that happiness had passed him by.

Only Rappoport had no personal driver waiting for him. Supporting him by one arm, Gagarin led him out on to the street. Taxi drivers recognized him at once. The cars darted forward, their doors opening while the vehicles were still moving.

Gagarin said to the first driver: 'Listen, friend! Take this cosmonaut home. He's a little under the weather. Here, take this!' And Gagarin held out a wrinkled five-rouble note to the driver. He was in post-flight condition himself, too.

'Hey, Tavrov, Tavrov!' he said dreamily, kissing Rappoport three times,

'I'd really like to send you to where I come from, Klushino village in Gzhatsk district – actually, it's called Gagarinsk now.'

'What for?'

'You'd make a good collective farm chairman. You don't know how to drink, but you know how to put the screws on people.'

'It's a good thing you're not Khrushchev or I'd be on my way!'

'Well, so long, Tavrov!' Gagarin hugged and kissed him again. 'Do I get some respect or what? Here's a souvenir for you, mate!'

He ripped something off his chest and placed it in Rappoport's hand, closing the fingers himself. In the half-light Rappoport raised his palm to his eyes.

'But this is the Order of Lenin!' He took fright, because he'd already done a stretch on account of medals. 'You're off your trolley!'

'Keep it, keep it! I've got hundreds of boxfuls of that rubbish. Don't believe me? Come to Star City, I'll write you out a pass, show you around. Wherever I go the crowds swarm all over me, happy as larks. By order of the Supreme Soviet they made me a bunch of fake medals. If one gets ripped off the wife polishes up another one and screws it on.'

'And the foreign ones?'

'Even the foreign ones are just churned out – brass and glass. What did you think they were? Diamonds? Well, be seeing you!'

At that moment Rappoport wouldn't have been sorry to give Gagarin his real medal back. But he was no longer in possession of either of the government awards he mentioned on his personal history forms: both his medals had been confiscated following his second arrest, along with his Nazi crosses.

Asya heard a strange rustling. Her husband was sitting on the stairs with an Order of Lenin on his chest, scraping his fingernails against the wall. Although she was sick herself, Asya got him into bed. A very intelligent, very ugly, fat and kind woman, Asya was the only person in the world devoted to Rappoport. For a year and a half she'd been eaten away by breast cancer. They did the operation too late (Asya had been afraid to tell them she had a tumour), and far from helping her it only hastened her end.

Without noticing it, Rappoport let himself go to pieces after her death. He washed his shirts more and more seldom, while his trousers never got ironed at all. The women in the typing pool sewed on his buttons, and he never changed his socks until they got holes in them, and then he would buy new ones, putting them on under his desk at work.

But one day when he was in a shop he asked about a fur hat. His old hat had shrunk and didn't fit his large head any more, and it was too cold to go around in a cap. They didn't have any fur hats in the shop, of course, but they'd got a delivery of imported English hats of large, irregular sizes; Rappoport got in line and bought one because everyone else was. He never guessed what effect it would have. His new hat was widely discussed at *Trudovaya Pravda*. People dropped in on him, felt it, asked to try it on for a stroll. The grey hat with its black band was intended for funerals in England, but in Moscow everyone was delighted with it.

Because of his new hat the deficiencies in the rest of Rappoport's dress began attracting attention. He was advised to buy a new suit ('There are some cheap Polish ones now'). People offered to go shopping with him and to lend him money. He pulled some strings and ended up buying himself a Yugoslav overcoat – grey, too. The women in the typing pool threw in two roubles each to buy him a present of a green-checked scarf from Korea for his birthday. Two roubles apiece wasn't enough, though, so they had to extract some money from the birthday boy himself.

'Now, Rappoport, you can go wherever you like. Go abroad, get married.'

'They aren't going to let me out of the country, girls. And I won't let myself get married. Anyway, I've bought all this stuff for the last time in my life, so that I'll have something to be buried in. I just hope I can manage to pay back everything I owe! Why did I splurge on this hat? Now I have to think about clothes, too. When am I going to get any work done?'

But severe frosts soon took the shape out of the hat, his overcoat grew shabby from riding the metro, his suit got shiny, his shoes ran down at the heels and, after tearing off its tight collar, Rappoport started wearing his East German shirt as an undershirt, putting on his dirt-proof dark-grey sweater over it. And everything settled back into its rut again.

Three years had passed since Rappoport buried his wife, and he still couldn't get back to normal. Imagine that: he continued to love her and wrote about her on his personal history forms as if she were alive. The fact that nobody ever once pointed this out to him was proof that people in Russia *were* capable of trust. But then again there were untruths in his questionnaire answers regarding his son as well.

Kostya was actually the son of a classmate of Asya and Yakov, the stage artist Vanya Dedov, and his wife Rita, an actress who looked like a madonna, who had both been arrested before Rappoport. Instead of the NKVD sending the boy straight to their children's reception centre he'd been left alone in his apartment. The Rappoports decided to make themselves his guardians but not to adopt him, for fear of ruining his life, God forbid!

Now Kostya had already turned twenty-one. He lived apart from his father, although he often visited him. Rappoport paid the rent on Kostya's room or, more accurately, the kitchen of a one-bedroom apartment: the registered tenants had left for the north for three years after locking up their things in their bedroom, and they rented out the separate kitchen with its couch and gas hob for thirty-five roubles a month. Once again unpleasantness lay in wait for Rappoport. After graduating from the Institute with a degree in dam-building Kostya Dedov had suddenly changed the direction of his young life.

The company he kept seldom showed up at the Rappoports' home. They weren't by any stretch of the imagination hooligans, as you might imagine. All of them were from good families. They were studying Hebrew, working on their lessons in each other's homes. Not long before, Kostya had come by his father's and asked from the front door: 'Dad, could you let me have four hundred roubles? Once we raise some money, we'll pay you back. The lads have found a Jewish encyclopaedia.'

'Son, where am I going to get money like that? You know we spent everything on presents for the doctors when your mum was sick. So – would tomorrow be too late? I'll have to borrow it. But what good is an encyclopaedia to you anyway? I'll let you know when Purim comes round.'

'You're so strange, Dad. Are you still so naive as to think that anti-Semitism is going to be abolished as of April the first? Even if that did happen, it would just be an April Fools' joke.'

'I don't think that at all, my boy. But what business is it of yours? Your father and mother, fortunately, were Russians.'

'I think I've already explained it, Father: they aren't my parents. They're just portraits and nothing more!'

'So be it! But you're in the Young Communists, you're going to be an engineer. In any case, that's cleaner than ideology. You'll be joining the Party – if, of course, you haven't been photographed around the synagogue yet. Or don't you know that possessing a Hebrew textbook will get you a stretch, like any other anti-Soviet act? Maybe you want to wind up in the international Zionist network?'

'You see, Dad, this is hard to explain. Mum said that the Russian wives of Jewish husbands consider themselves to be Jews.'

'Are you getting married, Son?'

'That's not it! I'm ashamed of being Russian. It would have been better if you'd adopted me!'

'Not at all! Believe me, in this country it's better being just a Russian.'

'But what if I don't want to be in this country? My friends all have hopes of leaving. By registering me as a Russian you and Mum wrecked any hopes I might have had!'

'Excuse me, Son. Is this all my fault? I'm only asking you to do one thing: be careful. If you forget about the danger for even one minute you'll be heading down the road I took. Look at this!'

With a jerk, Rappoport pulled up his shirt and, turning his back to Kostya, showed him the jagged scars.

'This is what my prison boss did to me with the iron buckle on his belt, beating me up just a little bit for including the Jews among all the rest of the amicable peoples of our country in my wall-newspaper.'

'I've seen these scars of yours a hundred times already.' Kostya clapped his father on the back and pulled down his shirt. 'But after all, now, you yourself . . .'

'Yes, I talk rot, and I spit on them, Son, because I've nothing to lose. I'm in my sixth decade, and I'm a senile old man. I'm not a person even with a small *p*. If you look into it, I'm not even a Jew.'

'You're a Jew!'

'Fine, I'm a Jew. Where I end up – on this side of the camp barbed wire or the other – makes no difference to me. They can shoot in both directions from the watchtowers. But you . . .'

'They don't put you away just like that any more!'

'He knows all about it! Maybe they don't put away that many people. But what does that mean? It means that the daily lives of those of us out here have become that little bit more prison-like, that's all. So just listen: sit tight and . . .'

'Sit tight and don't make a peep? Thanks.'

'Am I trying to talk you out of it, Kostya? I'm begging you. Sitting behind bars, believe me, is an altogether different proposition from sitting on the outside!'

'All right. Don't worry, you dear Jew of mine, you!'

Rappoport maintained that if he was paid the average staff royalty at *Trudovaya Pravda* for all the questionnaires, life histories and character references he'd composed about himself, the money would buy him a *dacha*. For all his dislike of personal history forms he would joyfully answer certain questions, though. He would write without the slightest hesitation that he hadn't suffered any judicial persecution before 1917 and had never served in the forces of any White government, because he had only been born just about then.

'I'm the same age as the October Revolution,' Rappoport would introduce himself when he met someone. 'I'm the herald of the beginning of the New Era. And you? Were you before or after?'

And he had never belonged to any other party, inasmuch as there couldn't be any. He was very sorry that in recent times the question 'Have you ever hesitated to carry out the policies of the Party?' had disappeared from the personal histories. For to this question Rappoport the Communist could answer firmly and with pride, at any time of the day or night, in any period of history: 'Never!' If he ever had hesitated, it was, as they say, only in line with policy.

Other questions on the endless forms weighed heavily on him, though, forcing him into cohabitation with untruth. It wasn't the untruth that was the burden. It was just that he was heaped with praise for all the other lies that he wrote. For lying on a questionnaire they could put the squeeze on him. On one occasion he had made a mistake: in response to the question 'Party membership', he'd written: 'Never subjected to it.' That night he hadn't slept, and in the morning he'd run unshaven into the managing editor's office and succeeded in correcting it, but he spent the rest of the day with his hand clutched to his heart.

'Be a good lad, Rappoport!' people would say as they asked him for something.

'I'm first of all a Communist', he would say, 'and only then a good lad!'

Or: 'Tell the truth, Rappoport!'

'Which one?' Rappoport would instantly react. 'I've got two of them, the Party one and my own.'

'Tell us yours!'

'I will, but bear in mind that mine belongs to the Party, too.'

He tried to avoid deeds altogether, dragging things out until there was no need for a decision any more. But he knew better than anyone how to tell other people what to do. But here he would add: 'Don't tell a soul that I was the one who told you that!'

That was the kind of person Rappoport was, well known to the readers of *Trudovaya Pravda* under his *nom de plume* of 'Tavrov'.

## — 15 —

## Playing by the Rules

Kicking the door behind him and staring fastidiously straight ahead, Rappoport shambled corpulently into the office, not uttering a word the while. He was generally impolite and sullen, and in his relations with his superiors had for some time now especially emphasized this. This was how he combated his own cowardice.

'Pardon me for tearing you away from work, Rappoport,' Makartsev said, rising half out of his seat and shaking the limp hand stretched towards him. 'Cigarette?' he offered, then went over and pushed the inner door closed. It hadn't closed from Rappoport's kick.

'Who do I have to write for?'

Makartsev lit his cigarette and smiled. Pulling a piece of chocolate out of his pocket Rappoport unwrapped it and threw the paper on the floor, stuck the piece into his mouth whole and started slowly sucking it.

'Don't be embarrassed,' said Rappoport, chewing. 'Or do you think I just write speeches off the top of my head? I've got calluses there. Yet another swine is going to be making a speech? So what? The lectern's made of oak, it'll survive. It's heard worse things than this! If I had to write a speech for a decent man, I'd probably refuse.'

'Why?' Makartsev asked artlessly.

'Well, a decent man can say what he thinks without my help. But there aren't any of those left.'

Hearing that from anybody else Makartsev would probably have reacted. But Rappoport had indifferently established an obvious fact. It would be sillier to get angry than to keep quiet. So the editor, taking what had been said as an unavoidable deficiency in his employee, just waved towards a chair.

'I've got something to talk to you about.'

'Good or bad?'

Rappoport always got nervous if the wait dragged on and would hurry to get to the point. His breathing was still heavy: he was panting after climbing the stairs. It would have taken too long to wait for a lift on the middle floors. He sat in the armchair and stared vacantly at the wall past Makartsev with his catastrophically weak, protruding eyes, enlarged by the thick lenses of his glasses, aware that nothing good was coming anyway and that there was no point hiding from the bad.

Makartsev looked at Rappoport as if he hadn't seen him for a long time. His face was a mess. Wrinkles furrowed his skin even in places they didn't have to be. Bags under his eyes, a long nose hanging down over his mouth, badly shaven cheeks and around his gigantic bald dome the remnants of his grey hair, uncut even once since the death of his wife. Rappoport couldn't abide barbers. Asya herself had sometimes sat him down in the kitchen on a stool and trimmed his hair. Rappoport slouched so badly that he looked like a hunchback. His jacket, of indeterminate colour and covered with dandruff on the shoulders and back, hung down unbuttoned, partly concealing his wide, wide trousers. Whenever his body moved his jacket would fly open, hiding his arms. There was something about him of a sick and bedraggled eagle with broken wings, one that was allowed to wander free around the zoo because it couldn't fly any more.

Makartsev wanted to begin right off with the folder, but first he spoke about something else so that Rappoport wouldn't realize how vitally important the issue was to him.

'What's going on with Katukov? Have things settled down?'

Rappoport shrugged. Not long before Soviet Army Day a cadence-counting officer had marched into his room, saluted, and asked: 'You – are you the head of the Communist Education Department?'

'How can I be of service?'

'Here are the memoirs of Armoured Forces Marshal Katukov. Print them up for Soviet Army Day.'

The adjutant placed the manuscript down on his desk and, after saluting again, marched off. Rappoport had heaps of wartime memoirs lying in his office. All the marshals, generals and even lesser ranks wanted to figure in history. All the memoirs were similar, one to the other. Without reading it Rappoport threw Marshal Katukov's memoirs on top of the heap. But when he found himself later without an appropriate article for the next Soviet Army Day Rappoport took Katukov's from the top of the heap and, after cutting it down to a fifth of its original size, he sent it off to the compositors.

Editorial board secretary Polishchuk was shocked. 'Katukov? What's the matter with you, Rappoport? The censor's never going to pass that. He's been mentally ill ever since his automobile accident. Did you know what kind of job they thought up for him? Military Inspector – an adviser to a group of inspector-generals at the Ministry of Defence. A jolly band of marshals all out of their minds.'

So Rappoport had been forced to get someone else's memoirs ready. But on the morning of 23 February Rappoport's door opened and the officer appeared in front of him. He saluted, clicked his heels and bawled out: 'Armoured Forces Marshal Katukov is here to see you.' The officer snapped to attention as the marshal came through the door.

'Is this Rappoportov?' the marshal inquired of his adjutant.

'Affirmative, sir!' the officer reported.

'Comrade Rappoportov!' Katukov heaved his massive chest, festooned with medals, on to Rappoport's desk. 'Why hasn't my article been published?'

All the marshal had to do was pull out his pistol and shoot, and there wouldn't be anyone to feed the cats impatiently awaiting Rappoport's return.

He started casting around for a way out. 'Well, you see . . . your material was already ready for printing – here are the galley proofs – but . . .'

'But what?' the marshal's hand crept towards his holster, or at least it seemed that way to the head of the Communist Education Department.

'Well, the newspaper directors decided that . . . your memoirs are so interesting that . . . they've kept them back for Victory Day, 9 May. That's even more honorific!'

'Right. But bear this in mind: if the article doesn't show up on the ninth of May I'm sending in my tanks!' The marshal made an about-face and, counting cadence, left, escorted by his adjutant.

'What do you think, Rappoport – is he going to complain?' Makartsev asked now, since Rappoport had yet to reply.

'He won't until the ninth of May. I made him a promise, after all.'

'And you were right to. Then we'll see what happens.'

Makartsev once again fell silent, thinking that Rappoport would interpret his silence as a bureaucratic habit. *The subordinate feels humiliated, expecting you to give him a bashing or hand him some disgusting chore – something really revolting.* The editor decided to pat him on the back and say something pleasant.

'Have you noticed how procrastination has been on the increase in the office? We say, "I'll do it," and then immediately forget all about it. Directives get thwarted, chores are left undone, deadlines get missed – and that's a fact! It's like a disease! The only businesslike person here, a man with a sense of responsibility who knows how to work effectively – is Rappoport.'

Rappoport slowly transferred his gaze from the wall to his editor. 'What – are you getting ready to fire me?'

'Where did you get that from?'

'Then you must be in some kind of personal trouble. Otherwise what would you have called me on the phone for and then apologized for tearing me away from work?'

'You're telepathic, Rappoport!'

'I'm just *a part of you* . . .' he said, half in English.

'Which is?'

'A Party Jew.'

'It's too bad I speak only Russian.'

'Bullshit! Do you think we publish a Russian-language newspaper?'

'Well, then, what language do we use?'

'Party language. Tell me what you want, don't drag things out.'

Once more Makartsev hesitated. *Why does he despise me so much? I've only ever done him good, after all! He certainly has changed a lot. He was a first-class journalist, he knew how to liven up any boring topic that the leadership thought important. He used to be interesting to talk to.* Makartsev still remembered Rappoport's tales of the camps that he'd unfortunately had to spend time in. *But his humour has gradually become more peevish, and his journalistic talent has deteriorated into blatant hackwork.* Rappoport was corrupting all the youngsters at the office. He didn't believe in anything himself and made fun of anyone who didn't have the same outlook. Rappoport's off-the-cuff comments had frightened the editor more than once. *Of course, this is just on the surface, echoes of what he's lived through, but at heart Rappoport is a true Communist. Nevertheless you have to think about what you're saying!* He would tell his terrifying jokes to the first person he met. And what was most offensive – he sneered at his own articles. He had even quoted Makartsev passages out of old speeches made by today's leadership that now sounded like something you would rather not recall.

Makartsev was struck by an idea: should he get rid of Rappoport, to stay out of harm's way? But the editor hadn't been acting against his conscience when he praised him for his efficiency. Makartsev knew that Rappoport always unflinchingly supported him, unlike other journalists who didn't care whether they kept their jobs or not. Most importantly, it was precisely thanks to his cynicism that he was so dependable. What was left in him was his decency, which was why Makartsev had decided to seek advice from Rappoport in particular.

'Rappoport, I need to ask you for some advice. But just between the two of us, on your word of honour . . .'

Rappoport didn't raise an eyebrow. He continued staring past Makartsev at some indistinct spot on the wall. Makartsev glanced in that direction but didn't see anything.

'Why so quiet? Won't you give me your word?'

Rappoport's shoulders barely rose in a shrug and then fell back. 'What for? If I give you my word, can't I sell you out just the same? If you've made up your mind – speak. If you've thought twice about it, I'll go.'

'No, just give me your word as a Communist anyway.'

'All right.' Rappoport smacked his lips. 'You've got it.'

It was too late to get out of it, so Makartsev told him in detail about the grey folder and his suspicions.

Once again there was an awkward pause. 'Is that all?'

'What, don't you think this is something serious?'

Rappoport breathed heavily for a bit. 'How would I know if this is serious or not?' he finally squeezed out. 'Ask *them*! Or are you afraid to?'

'Them, them! But what if it'd been planted on *you*?'

'On me? Depends! Let me have a look.'

After hesitating a moment Makartsev opened his safe and took out the folder. Rappoport opened it out on his lap, glanced cursorily at the title, put his thumb on the first page and read the names Djilas, Orwell, Solzhenitsyn. Makartsev looked at him and waited patiently. Rappoport's face didn't give anything away. He flipped through another fifty pages and then once more got stuck into the text. He snorted, harrumphed.

'What's that?'

'M-m-m-m.' After mooing for a moment Rappoport suddenly read aloud: '*Who shall tell me what can a society come to that has no human dignity at its base?*'

'See?' Makartsev exclaimed. 'What did I tell you?'

Rappoport slammed the folder shut, neatly tied up the ribbons and handed it back without saying a word.

'Did you have it for a while, too?' asked Makartsev.

'No!' Rappoport cut across him. 'For the word "have", which can be construed to mean "possession", you get a seven-year stretch.'

'I know!'

'And for the word "too" they'll give us hard labour – now it's a group thing. And another five years on the horns.'

'What do you mean – "on the horns"?'

'*You* will no longer have the right to elect Deputy Makartsev to the Supreme Soviet. You won't have *any* civil rights. I don't give a damn! I'll go back to the Zone after losing my 200-rouble pay-cheque, which doesn't buy me anything anyway! But you . . .'

'All right, let's say I really do have more to lose. What would you do in my place?'

'In your place?' Rappoport chuckled. "But you wouldn't do what I would, anyway!'

'I will. Just tell me!'

'Do you have a friend? You know, the editor of some little newspaper or other?'

'I do, more than one.'

'Then here's what you do: drive over to his place, have a chat about something or other and on your way out accidentally forget the folder on his desk.'

'You're joking!' Makartsev said furiously. 'But I'm serious. It seems to me you didn't learn anything from your stretch in prison.'

'We'll see how much you get out of it if you're inside as long as I've been!'

'Me?' Makartsev's eyes grew mean.

'Fine!' Rappoport backed off. 'It's easy. Give the folder to me.'

'To you?'

'Sure! If anything happens I'll admit that I took it from your office to read it without your permission. But you never laid eyes on it!'

Makartsev looked searchingly at Rappoport, trying to understand the degree of seriousness of the proposition this time. 'Aren't you scared?'

'Maybe they won't send me back a third time.'

'Nonsense!' pronounced the editor, realizing that however convenient it would be for him he couldn't agree to this. 'Out of the question!'

'You're probably right,' Rappoport agreed. 'Anyway, that would be dissemination of anti-Soviet literature through your office, which comes under the same Article Seventy. But you're a better man than I thought, Makartsev.'

'Really?' he smiled, flattered.

'Seriously! After all, I seldom praise anyone. It's just that you're always afraid people might suddenly think you really are a better man than you are. You're like the dog in the well-known riddle.'

'Which riddle?'

'How do you make a dog eat mustard? If you just give it to him he'll never eat it. But if you smear it on his arse he'll lick it all up. Lick away!'

'If that's so,' Makartsev bristled, 'they're doing the right thing, putting away the mustard-smearers.'

'Now you're changing your tune! We're talking about dogs here. People – they like licking up mustard. Are you going to decide for them what they should and shouldn't eat? If anyone wants mustard – put him in the slammer? They're too embarrassed to do that just now. But just you wait! A new personality cult is coming, and then . . .'

'Hang on! *Why* is one coming?'

'Our cults always start with blood. The cult of Lenin began after the civil war. Stalin's came after the liquidation of the *kulaks*, and his second cycle was after the war. The Corn Man had his after the tanks rolled over Hungary. Today's . . .'

'You think – after Czechoslovakia?'

'You bet!'

'Then you'd consider that the cult has already started,' frowned Makartsev. 'They've been recommending that we enlarge the size of his photographs and print them more often.'

'Wouldn't you just know it! I keep thinking: what do you, Makartsev, lack that keeps you from becoming a real tyrannosaurus? You don't like blood? Nonsense, you'd learn to like it if you had to. They're all hayseeds, come here to be masters of the world, but you – an intellectual, a Petersburger? No – better people than you have turned nasty! You're not an anti-Semite? Non-anti-Semites fall into two categories. The first never notice whether you're Jewish or not, the second wait for the pogroms so they can help the Jews. You don't belong to either of those categories, since you're a high-ranking Party member. If the Party commands – you'll be an anti-Semite!'

'Me? I've never fired a single Jew!'

'Don't get hot under the collar. How many have you hired then? Do you consider yourself ninety per cent honest? But that means that you're a whole hundred-per-cent liar!'

'So what *do* I lack, according to you?'

'When I figure it out I'll tell you right away. You'll make it. Tyrannosaurs take a million years to die out.'

'Well, let's not go on about that,' Makartsev interrupted, smiling acidly. 'I think it's easier to see things from the vantage of the Central Committee than from down here anyway. You look at a lot of things differently from up there. And it's not all that simple. We'd better think about specific issues of life.'

'Specific issues? That's just a game!'

'But a big one. And as long as the rules of the game are what they are we'll play it by those rules. If the rules change, then we'll play it differently.'

'And who do you think is supposed to change the rules?'

'Don't you see, as far as I'm concerned – speaking between ourselves – I'm ready to carry out any sort of democratization and to take it as far as it can go. But first they have to call me up and tell me that I can. And that's enough about that. Better tell me what to do now.' He'd always felt it: Rappoport despised him. He took comfort only in the fact that Rappoport despised everybody, including himself. 'What if I just pretend I never noticed the folder?'

'They won't believe you.'

'You know yourself what it's like, being on the hook. You *must* know how to act in circumstances like these!'

'For God's sake! You're not going to leave me be, are you! Well, all right, I'll tell you so you'll let me go. I've got a lot of work to do. Don't get too smart, keep it simple. So . . .' And in a few words Rappoport let his editor in on what he had to do.

'That's a really good solution!' Makartsev was delighted. 'I should have figured that out myself. Rappoport, you're too much!'

The editor brightened up, his tension fell away. Rappoport grabbed the arms of the chair to help his feeble body up. Makartsev stopped him with a gesture.

'Hang on just a minute more. There's never enough time to ask you about your personal life. I live like a horse in a circus ring. How are things with you? How come you're still alone? You could get married. It's not even too late to have another child. I could help you get a better place to live.'

'As some sort of compensation for my advice? No, I'll go on living in my old warren along with my Spidola radio – nothing stops me listening to that except the jamming. As for children, it's too late for that.'

'Why do you want to act as if you're an old man, Rappoport? I'm older than you – and I feel young!'

'And I feel old. Jews usually grow old early. You're a Russian – you're lucky!'

'Hmm. Well, never mind – wives, children. But do you have any dreams?'

'What?' Rappoport threw the question back, and stared at Makartsev as if he really had turned into a circus horse.

'I'm asking you about your dreams.' Makartsev threw himself back in his chair and took off his glasses, deftly throwing them on to the desk and blinking his eyes like a child. 'I've been dreaming recently. And about just one thing . . .'

'About what, I wonder?'

'I dream about living on a lake somewhere or other, far away. A place that no roads go to. And there's a boat lying on the grass. And fog. And on the porch a big jug of milk. Somebody brings it around every morning. Who, you never know. Maybe a shy young woman. She brings it around and leaves right away, no stopping her. And I don't even try. Most important is the lake, and no roads.'

'And the fog?' Rappoport inquired.

'Yeah, fog, for sure. What do you think – could a dream like that come true?'

'No. Not for you.'

'Not for me,' Makartsev agreed. 'But you know how pleasant it is to have a dream! Don't you dream about anything at all?'

'Only about one thing. About not writing bullshit or having to read it.'

'Well, that's totally unrealistic!'

'Totally.'

Rappoport stood up sharply, as if he'd suddenly got younger, and walked out without looking at his editor, leaving the inner door open. Makartsev stretched, straightening out his kinks, and pressed the buzzer. Anna hurried in.

'Bring me a big thick envelope. The biggest you can find in the letters department.'

She ran out. He rubbed his hands together, drew the folder over to him, untied it, looked at it, leafed through it. His gaze suddenly came to a halt at a paragraph that had seemed to him earlier, last night, to be offensive to the honour of his country. Now he read it again. And the truth of it, to be fair, was the truth, after all. But it was an unneeded truth – that was the problem!

Anna appeared again and put a snow-white envelope down on his desk, one with a legend in bold across the top: '*Trudovaya Pravda*. Organ of the Central Committee of the CPSU.'

'Is the planning session going to be in here?' She laid on his desk the plan for the next issue of the newspaper, which he'd already approved. He looked at his watch – ten minutes left before the meeting. 'Do you want me to send that off right away?'

'No, that's not necessary. You can go now.'

The envelope bulged; it was hard to seal it, but the folder fitted inside. Makartsev took his pen and wrote on the envelope in medium-sized letters: 'Inform the Committee for State Security, ask them what steps to take.' He weighed the labelled envelope in his hands, lightly hefting it. *A heavy*

*burden but an easy way out! If I'd had to I could have shown some initia-*
*tive myself. I was just distracted by things – more important Party and*
*government affairs . . . If somebody from here planted the folder, we'll just*
*let it lie there.* He, Makartsev, wasn't going to turn anybody in. Pulling
open the middle drawer of his desk, he took out an old newspaper that
was there and, putting the heavy envelope in the drawer, replaced the paper
on top of it – as if, in his hurry, he had accidentally forgotten to inform
anyone about the grey folder.

Makartsev leaned back against his armchair, breathed in as much air
as he could and, eyes closed, began slowly releasing it. He'd read somewhere that this was the best way to calm yourself down.

'I should like to compliment you. A correct decision!'

Makartsev started, opened his eyes: the Marquis de Custine was coming towards him. As before, he was elegant, and redolent of expensive
cologne.

'Is it you again?' the editor asked, in surprise and fright.

De Custine's sword clanked off the parquet flooring, and the marquis
lifted it up with a finger, but then, sitting down in the chair, he placed it
between his knees and leaned on the hilt.

It occurred to Makartsev that his secretary would come in now, catch
sight of his strange visitor, and word about him would spread through the
office. De Custine, it seemed, read his thoughts.

'I am desolate, monsieur, that you might get in trouble. You must pardon me.'

'No – you must pardon me!' Makartsev raised his voice, feeling considerably surer of himself here in his editor's office than last night at home.
'On what grounds are you persecuting me, Marquis? What do you want?'

'Perhaps it has occurred to you,' asked de Custine, 'that it was I who
planted the folder?'

'You?'

'For myself, monsieur, I would not stoop to such intrigues. I felt
you personally at the time, because you began reading me, taking me for
a contemporary author. This does me some honour, but, alas, I died a

hundred and twelve years ago. I can only be proud that my thoughts live on.'

'And you decided to share your faith with me? To convince me that you're right?' Makartsev's fists clenched involuntarily, as if he were getting ready for a fight.

'Not at all!' de Custine said soothingly. 'I have nothing to say to you aloud that would add to what I wrote in 1839. The details of my journey I have completely forgotten in the hundred and so years that have passed since then. I am in no condition to argue with so competent a fellow as yourself.' With his fingers, the marquis tweaked his sword out of its scabbard by the hilt and then snapped it back in again.

'Then why did you pick on me, as they say?'

De Custine grinned. 'It occurred to me that you might need my moral support. Since the time you read my book, a forbidden act here among you people, you and I have been forged into a single chain, so to speak, even if you do not share my ideas. When I last saw you I wanted to say that I would be deeply grateful if you would pass this folder on to someone in the leadership of the country, since you're so well *in* with them.'

'You're out of your mind! Pass it on yourself, if you can.'

'There you go! I didn't expect any other sort of answer.' De Custine smiled. 'Forget about any such awkward notion. I see now that you have dealt with the mysterious folder in the very best way. If the police search the premises it's vitally important that you bluff your way out of it. After all, you never know what to expect from them. I wouldn't like to be the cause of any trouble for you. From the bottom of my heart, I wish you prosperity!'

His sword rattling on the parquetry, the Marquis de Custine got up from his chair, bowed to Makartsev, took several steps in the direction of the door and disappeared without opening it.

Makartsev sat for a while unmoving, at a loss, staring at the point where his uninvited French guest had faded from sight.

# 16

# The Planning Session

Towards twelve thirty the spacious office of the editor-in-chief began to fill up with bureau editors, various editorial board members and secretariat newspaper employees. They came in by ones and twos. If they hadn't seen each other yet today they said their hellos, conversing in low tones, and settled into their favourite seats. Without looking up, Makartsev nodded to them all. He was skimming over the plan for the next day's issue, marking stumbling points in the margins with the necessary corrections. His mood had brightened, as if his perplexity had never been. Finishing his inspection, he put the plan aside and looked around at his employees happily, waiting until everyone was present.

Deputy editor Yagubov appeared. He said a courteous hello to everyone and, setting the reworked combined plan of the Central Committee paper down in front of Makartsev, sat down next to his chief. The art editor, Ikunenko, ran in, long, thin and pimply-faced, with a pile of photographs that he threw on to the floor beside his chair. Kashin, the managing editor, hefting his ringful of keys in his hand, looked around, smiling affably. Last in, a little late, breathing heavily, came the acting Communist Education editor, Rappoport, with his jacket flapping open, his hands clasped behind his back. He found himself space in a corner and stood with a gloomy look, as if awaiting his usual scolding. Anna walked in quietly behind him with her notepad and pen, after assuring herself that everyone who should be there was already seated and nobody needed any more reminders over the phone. She firmly closed the outer and inner doors and took her seat beside the editor at the low telephone table. The bureau chiefs waited while Makartsev, thumbing his lighter, lit up a cigarette. That was the signal to begin conversation. Only the chief got to smoke at planning sessions.

'Everybody here?'

The conversations died down. Yezikov, the tall and thin-as-a-rail deputy to the editorial board secretary, stood up. He coughed, raised his red marker pen like a pointer and aimed it at the first of four pages of the dummy, prettily drawn and tacked on to a special panel on the wall.

'Issue for Thursday, 27 February,' Yezikov coughed. 'Page one – a banner headline the whole width of the page. Above the *Trudovaya Pravda* logo we'll print 'The Ideas of Lenin the Great Will Be Victorious Throughout the Ages!' in archaic typeface. Next . . .'

Makartsev was nodding along, but only listening with half an ear. Everything they were talking about was habitual, inexorable. The things that happened in your life could change spontaneously. The things that the newspaper wrote about changed only by order. And that gave certainty to the correctness of his actions. Individual matters could be short-changed; there could be negligence, even outright mistakes, but there was always something to lean on. Therefore Makartsev wasn't afraid of adding something beyond what was agreed, in particular why it was necessary to (or why they shouldn't) publish one thing or another. Moreover, real events could, in the opinion of the editor, help the newspaper safely negotiate some sharp corners. In his own way Makartsev loved to tell the truth. But he divided truth up into the broad truth, the narrow truth and the absolute truth.

On his return from a three-week trip to the USA he had told them he was ill and hadn't shown up at work for a week. He was weighing the truth and sorting it out under its various headings. Once he'd weighed everything up he returned to work as optimistic and authoritative as ever, and he was as restrained and businesslike as ever at the Central Committee.

He had held discussions about his trip to the USA and his meetings there for the benefit of the mass of rank-and-file employees. Each episode

Makartsev preceded with these words of warning: 'America is a sick society. Seriously ill, comrades. It's being eaten up by contradictions. Judge for yourself.' And he would cite gloomy examples of crime and poverty. 'Although they have goods in their stores, by no means everyone has the necessary purchasing capacity.' Makartsev's articles (he hadn't written any for a long time, but if he were to write any) would also be full of the broad truth but without the first half of that last quotation.

The narrow truth had considerably larger gradations. The editorial board members and bureau chiefs got to hear a more substantive account from him. ('Automobiles, roads – they really do have the best in the world – we're a long way off from that.' 'Drugs are the real ulcer of capitalism.' 'Unfortunately there aren't many Communists there, especially youngsters.') A small group of trustworthy people from the office got to hear an addition to that last phrase, in the course of a private conversation: 'They say that, among Communists there, 51 per cent are FBI agents. But, in general, they aren't afraid of saying anything, absolutely anything. They curse their president out loud, on the subway. Newspapers make policy, not the other way round, with politicians putting out newspapers.'

The narrow truth for Makartsev was multifaceted: there was one kind for foreign Communists, another for his fellow journalists, for his Party colleagues, for the instructors at the Central Committee, and the Secretariat there, for Comrade Skinny, who preferred to stay in the shadows, for Makartsev's wife . . . Makartsev never mixed up the people he expressed his narrow truth to with those he shouldn't or how much he spoke aloud with how much he kept to himself. It had become a part of his profession – not to say too much, to understand when to say something entirely other than what you knew, when to say things almost not quite so, not entirely so or almost nearly so, but never the whole thing, in any case. As a reward to subordinates you could say a bit more, and as a punishment you could do them out of their share. The narrow truth was currency.

Makartsev considered absolute truth to be bits of information for himself alone, entrustable to no one else. They concerned certain moments in his personal life, in particular his wife's misunderstanding of several things he'd done and the uncontrollability of their son. But this was second-degree absolute truth. The more important bits were when he speculated about the verities that were sometimes thrown up into his consciousness, demanding to be re-examined. This was the set of values that in his life up to now Makartsev had supposed to be unshakeable.

At times he felt like thinking in some other sorts of categories. But he forbade himself to do so. He persuaded himself that he was not a philosopher but a practitioner, a Party worker, and that it was too late to re-examine his convictions. He'd shouldered the burden, he couldn't get out from under it now. And so much had been gained that it would be stupid to throw it away. To hell with it – that sort of absolute truth would probably turn into something else tomorrow. And maybe it was nowhere on earth to be found in any case. But even if it did exist, it always aligned itself so closely with manifestations of bourgeois ideology that even he, Makartsev, was incapable of telling them apart. Let it go whichever way it had before.

'So that's it for the front page, then?' he said, cutting off Yezikov, who loved to talk. 'So, as far as industry goes, there's nothing except the conveyor belt that runs to music? But where's the working class, Alekseyev? Where's the socialist competition for the masses?'

Alekseyev, the industry and transport editor, sighed guiltily and was ready to answer but then closed his dropsical eyes and waited until his boss was through.

'Why aren't we running any of the campaigns that get the people going?' continued the editor. 'Never mind new ones – how many times have we agreed that campaigns have to be carried through from issue to issue so that they're not forgotten?'

'It's our fault.'

'It's no easier for me to escape your culpability. We're talking about the prestige of the newspaper here! You hardly get going, and right away it's a fiasco. We only glimpse your exemplary workers for a second. What does the reader think? That they aren't exemplary any more!'

'Makartsev is trying to teach us that the newspaper's heart has to beat arrhythmically,' said Yezikov, and everyone smiled, except for their editor-in-chief.

'You're talking about the quantity of interesting material, the "hooks". Campaigns are completely different. Where, for instance, is Galina Arefyeva? Is she still alive?'

'She got married,' Alekseyev said gloomily, blushing as if it were his own fault. 'Changed her name to her husband's.'

'There you go!' Makartsev barely managed to get out. 'How could something that stupid happen?'

'Well, what could we do?'

Alekseyev had celebrated the assembly-line worker Galina Arefyeva in a series of articles. She and her girlfriends had undertaken to produce faultless appliances above the output norm. Alekseyev, who had come up with the campaign, had only a dim idea of how this could be done in practice, but the campaign found favour at the top. Galina Arefyeva, who was contributing a distinguished amount to the material base of the five-year plan, stared out from a multitude of photographs. After the *Trudovaya Pravda* articles appeared she had been made a delegate to the Young Communist League congress, and articles about her began to pop up in the pages of other newspapers. They wrote about the thousands of young female patriots extending the light-bulb factory campaign. Alekseyev had ridden in from the rank and file to become the editor of his department on the back, so to speak, of Arefyeva. Suddenly – there wasn't any Arefyeva, just some Kirillova person!

'Maybe she could change her name back again?' suggested Yagubov. 'Would it make any difference to her?'

'We tried to talk her into it,' Alekseyev said, with a dismissive wave of his hand, 'but she stuck to her guns! "I love my husband!" she said.'

'What's the matter with her – doesn't she have any ambition?'

'Tell you what,' said Makartsev, finding a way out. 'It's no good just to give up on the campaign, but nobody will understand if we call her

Kirillova now. So call her Arefyeva only in the past tense, but for all present-tense purposes call her Galina.'

'How's that?' Alekseyev, the old hand, exclaimed in surprise.

'Just that! Write: "the campaign that Arefyeva started", "Arefyeva's team" and things like that. The main thing for us is not to go deep but to keep going. It's not her so much that we need now but her campaign, which has already spread over the whole country, right?'

'Right, but, anyway . . .' Alekseyev hemmed and hawed.

'Our campaigns camp the economy's pains,' Rappoport muttered, but so quietly that nobody heard him.

No jokes were allowed at planning sessions. The vocabulary was exclusively Party-minded. It was better to keep any ironies to yourself and preserve a stony face, bearing in mind that there were sure to be informers present at the session.

'That's settled.' Makartsev cut him short. 'We won't flog that horse any more. Come on, Yezikov, what have you got on page two?'

The deputy secretary, turning his stork-like neck, named the topics, pausing briefly after each one in case Makartsev wanted to amplify or object to anything. Makartsev finally interrupted Yezikov when he mentioned an article called 'The Pointer Swings Back and Forth'.

'Who sent that material? What's it about?'

'The business bureau. Sales clerks are short-weighting their customers,' Yezikov answered both questions at once. 'The author is a volunteer consumers' inspector.'

'Which shop is giving short weight – does it say?'

'I don't remember for sure.'

'Does it name the store manager? Find out. If it's not there, put it in. Otherwise the readers aren't going to know who's responsible for the short-weighting, and they might think the Soviet regime is at fault. By the way, whenever we criticize something we have to keep *that* point in mind – whose concrete fault it is. We don't need any scattershot here. And here's something else, Yezikov: don't put those two critical pieces alongside each other – the one about the poor job the housing administration is doing and the one about the short weight. That could create an oppressive impression. Is that all for page two? On to page three then.'

'Foreign,' said Yezikov. That's what all foreign news and information – provided by the wire agencies of the world and culled for the Soviet readership – was called for short at the newspaper. In addition, large newspapers like *Trudovaya Pravda* maintained their own correspondents in the major countries. 'In the middle of the page there's a satirical article by our special correspondent Ovcharenkov that we got over the phone: "They Threaten Us With Their Big Stick". The militarization of West Germany is continuing: they've issued a stamp showing Hitler's personal plane.'

'That's not very much,' Makartsev said. 'He seldom writes anything, and when he does it's usually superficial. Go on.'

The narrow truth about special correspondent Ovcharenkov that Makartsev had just articulated was only for those who were present at the planning session. Most of *Trudovaya Pravda*'s special correspondents outside the country had never once set foot in the editorial offices and never wrote anything. Sometimes, however, articles under their names were dropped off in envelopes by a courier. The correspondents' bureau chief knew the phone numbers and contact details of only a few of the paper's special correspondents abroad. Ovcharenkov in Bonn was one of that select band and really did send in material. It wasn't done at the office to criticize the work of the foreign correspondents, though. Makartsev alone could afford to do it. The gradations of his truth were these:

For the newspaper's readership, the Bonn special correspondent unmasked West German imperialism (the broad truth). For editorial board members and bureau chiefs (as Makartsev had noted) he wrote shallowly, he should be deeper. For Ovcharenkov's KGB bosses: 'Doesn't it raise suspicions in the West that *Trudovaya Pravda* special correspondents write so little and so badly?' Give them some indication that they shouldn't forget the paper. 'For instance, we sorely need an article unmasking the machinations of Western politicos' (a certain kind of truth). For the Central Committee: 'It's a bit expensive for the newspaper to maintain special correspondents outside the country – it eats up all the hard currency we're allowed. Would it be permissible to increase our funding just a bit?' For friends and colleagues: 'Your wife is going to West Germany? I'll call our special correspondent, Ovcharenkov, tell him to meet her, show her around, so she doesn't have to go around in a crowd with the rest of her tour group.' For his wife: 'That Ovcharenkov is a loafer. He copies things out of German newspapers that I can get translated here at the international bureau. I pay him one salary, a second one goes automatically into his savings account from the KGB, and the parasite doesn't do a damned thing!'

As far as he himself was concerned, Makartsev had a general notion of what the function of their special correspondents was: providing financial support for Communist and terrorist organizations abroad, secret propaganda and disinformation for the press and diplomatic corps about events inside Russia, recruitment of foreigners, communications with Russian agent-in-residence 'moles' in foreign Communist and other parties and in the offices of newspapers and publishers, communication with specialists in political assassination, and special missions from KGB Centre. Makartsev understood that all of this absolute truth was necessary to the grand policies of the state and didn't go into it any further. Let whoever answered for it have the headaches.

Meanwhile, Yezikov had reported about sport, literature and various other things and fallen silent.

'Any suggestions?' Makartsev asked. 'Questions?'

He reminded them of the directive to use no more than one photograph per page, in order to use the newspaper's space for propaganda the more effectively. Yezikov nodded: he'd already taken that into account. Makartsev made a few more general remarks, principally about how important it was to report on the preparations for Lenin's centenary more and, more seriously, without repeating themselves but finding new angles.

'Let's think about it, comrades! What if we introduce this as a rubric: "Only So-and-So Many Days Left Until the Centenary!" It's modest, it's significant, and it'll gradually build anticipation. Well – that's it for me!'

Rappoport was the first to leave, silently, clasping his hands behind his back, *zek*-style. The rest strung along after him, talking among themselves. The last one to rise was Anna.

'Anna,' Makartsev asked, 'what business do I have left? I need to get off to the Central Committee, unless there's something else.'

She brought in a folder with papers that were awaiting his signature: two assignments, a character reference for his district committee for Skobtsov, the sports bureau chief, so he could get to the world ice hockey championships in Sweden. Skobtsov was politically literate, ideologically restrained, morally steady and didn't drink more than anybody else. Moreover, he had already been outside the country. Makartsev signed them. Yagubov brought in the proofs of some articles that he wanted to get some advice on.

'Later,' his editor stopped him. 'I'm off to the Central Committee.'

Aleksey ran off to warm up the engine, and then he drove off with his boss. Makartsev had lunch in the Central Committee dining-room, where he managed to have a few words with some useful people, and then set off for the press section with his newspaper plan. His heart wasn't causing him any pain. He hadn't recalled the grey folder even once either during the planning session or afterwards. Now, in his hospital bed, a suspicion crept into his mind that it was the damned grey folder's fault. What else could it be if it wasn't that?

'Why did you do it?' Makartsev moved his lips, although there wasn't anyone in the ward. 'If I'm bad for you, who would be better?'

Just then he remembered that he needed to have positive emotions. But he didn't have any. His train of thought was unexpectedly broken by the doctors' coming into the ward. They surrounded his bed in a tight circle. Makartsev answered the questions of the consultation group, his tongue scarcely moving, but his thoughts stayed with the folder. He'd never been so suspicious before. He'd done the right thing, sticking that damned manuscript into the envelope. Just a trifle, all in all, but it was his only salvation, especially now, when he was lying here and it was lying there.

But either he couldn't forget about the Marquis de Custine, or de

Custine couldn't forget about him – thoughts about what he'd read ate into his memory and periodically swam up into his consciousness, imposing themselves on Makartsev's own experience and the facts of life surrounding him. And this dispirited him. He assured himself that nothing could be changed, but after reading the book *Russia in 1839* he felt that he could now no longer think the way he had before. The crack in the ice was spreading, the thawed stretch was widening. The internal conflict made him angry: he wasn't ready to jump into the open water, and his fear wouldn't go away.

Makartsev looked around the room, because he had the feeling that someone had made an appearance. He was trying to figure out who it was when he suddenly realized that security wouldn't let anybody into the Kremlin hospital who didn't belong there.

In fact, the Marquis de Custine failed to appear. But Makartsev was waiting for him.

# 17

# The Passion of
# St Rappoport

Entry to the *Trudovaya Pravda* offices was open to everyone, without need of any pass. A security guard would ask for your identification if you tried to get near the printing presses. But in the office lobby there was just an elderly lady on duty, whose name nobody knew, dozing behind an old desk next to the lift. Casual visitors – authors, people with complaints – would wake her up to ask how to get to which department or to drop off envelopes addressed to various employees. At her own discretion, she would divide visitors into the serious and the non-serious. The former she sent on to the editorial departments, the latter to the advice bureau in the public reception room.

When the planning session in Makartsev's office ended at a quarter to two, Rappoport had felt an urgent need for something to eat. He kept an electric hotplate under his desk on which he could boil a kettle. He threw a pinch of tea into a glass and poured in some hot water and then poured the tea into another glass, so that the tea leaves were left behind in the first one. He bit off a piece of cheese, carefully chewed it up with his dentures (Rappoport's teeth, the ones that hadn't been knocked out in the camps, had all been wasted by scurvy) and was sucking away on a lump of sugar and sipping tea when someone knocked at his door.

'Come in!' he barked.

The door slowly opened and the narrow, shaven head of a visitor thrust through it.

'Where'd you get such awful manners – knocking on my door?'

Rappoport grumbled. 'What, do you think this is my bedroom? This is an institution, and it's working hours. What do you want?'

The visitor stood guiltily in the doorway, holding a thin briefcase under one arm. 'You'll be the editor of the Communist Education Department if I'm not mistaken?'

Rappoport continued methodically chewing his cheese and sugar, and, once they were well chewed, bellowed: 'Sit down in the chair!'

'You see . . .' the entrant said, obediently sitting and placing his brief-case on his lap.

'I haven't seen anything yet.'

'I wanted to offer you an article on a vitally important – I would even say topical – subject.'

'And just who are you?'

'I'm Shaten. Yevgeny Shaten. Not Sha-*nine* but Sha-*ten*! That way it's easier for you to remember.'

'All right. Well, what is it?'

'Perhaps you've heard about my invention of an electronic musical instrument that produces sound induced by proximity. I have a patent on it . . . here . . .'

Rappoport didn't look at the stamped sheet of paper that was placed in front of him.

'So what?'

'Just imagine,' his visitor dreamily pronounced, 'people can ballet dance around my instrument and the sound will follow their movements. My instrument is called a Danshaten.'

'Danshaten? That's original!'

'You said it! A completely new art form. True, nobody quite needs one yet . . .'

'And you think we need some ballet here at *Trudovaya Pravda*?'

'No! I've written a piece about something else. I called in to the indus-trial bureau, but they sent me to you. I'll tell you about it.'

Drinking down his tea, Rappoport wadded up the paper with the cheese rind and tossed it into his waste bin. His stomach had stopped whining with hunger, and his mood had improved.

'I'll read it myself, no need to tell it to me,' Rappoport said, licking his lips. 'And anyway I don't hear so well with my bad ear.'

'No, allow me to, anyway – I'll lay the whole thing out for you in brief. I'm a lonely man, with no children. My son died at the front, and where he's buried I have no idea. I buried my wife two years ago, and this year my mother died. She was ninety-four, would you believe. I decided that it would be too hard on me to be left entirely alone, so I made a little niche above the head of my bed. I put a natural-light lamp in it, so it would look nice, and I put the two urns in it, with the ashes of my mother and my wife. Now they're with me for ever!'

'And you consider that it's better that way?' Rappoport said, looking closely into his visitor's eyes.

'Of course! If someone close to you should die – God forbid! – put their urn in your room, and you'll see! Whenever I'm depressed I walk up to my Danshaten, make a few passes with my hands, and music comes out. And Mama and my wife hear the music together with me. It's possible that my son, the one who was killed at the front, flies to us, as well. I mean, his spirit does.'

'You should get your . . . to that school next door, go see those young technicians. You could teach them how to build your instrument!'

'I went there! And what happened? Do you think those children understand my music? No! They laughed at me! But Mama and my wife understand it! Recently I've perfected my system: the light in the niche comes on only when the music plays. And the louder it gets, the brighter the light gets on the jars with the ashes of my wife and my mama. Maybe you'd like to take a look? I live in a communal apartment with six neighbours, but it's not very far away.'

'Can't right now! So, your article is about how the ashes of your wife and your mother respond to the music?' He was already about to fob his visitor off on to the arts and literature department.

'Not quite! That would be too intimate. You see, I want to raise the issue in your newspaper of the inexpediency of the existence of cemeteries in general. They take up a lot of land, and funerals cost working people a lot of money. It'd be better not to bury them!'

'In general?' Rappoport queried. 'How do you mean?'

'The ashes should be kept by relatives. Then, except for crematoriums, the state wouldn't have to worry about anything. Not about cemeteries or graves or columbaries. I've already talked my neighbour into it. He and his wife have set aside a shelf on their sideboard and have already bought jars.'

'Who for?'

'Themselves, of course. I know you always launch useful campaigns in your newspaper. The whole country gets caught up in them. What if you and I start a new campaign: "For the Non-Occupancy of Cemetery Plots"?'

'So *Trudovaya Pravda* is to come out with a full-page headline that says, "Keep Your Corpses at Home"? What – do you want *my* ashes?'

'N-n-no! Why corpses? Just their ashes. Look: on the scale of our country, I figure, there would be a savings of two and a half billion roubles. But the most important thing is that, from the point of view of our Communist morals – just what you need to bring to the thing that you're always writing about – faithfulness to the precepts of our hero forefathers.'

'Yeah, those who are *heroes!*'

'Forgive me, here I will allow myself to disagree with you. Anyone can become a hero these days!'

'Give me your article!' Rappoport said, grinding his teeth.

He ran his eyes fleetingly over the lines, feeling how attentively their author was following the expression on his face. If he offered to improve the article, the fellow would come bothering him again. If he praised it and took it, and then later held it back, the fellow would annoy him until he turned into ashes himself. No, he was going to have to cut him off straight away.

So, setting the article down to one side, he said: 'Here's what, Shaten! Other people, less principled than I am, would probably jerk you around, but I'll tell you frankly. Everything we print in this newspaper is crap. What you've written is crap, too. But this isn't the kind of crap that we print!'

'Excuse me!'

'I won't do it! I have no personal objection to your initiating a campaign. But screw around somewhere else! We write only about the heroic present and the shining future. Not about corpses of any sort!'

The insulted author picked his article up off the desk, shoved it into his briefcase and walked out without saying goodbye. But visitors weren't even giving Rappoport a chance to breathe. There were already three moonfaced young men sitting around his desk, following his every movement without taking their eyes off him. Two of them were dressed in black suits and ties, the third in a grey suit with red pinstripes, also wearing a tie. Rappoport shrank.

'What can I do for you, young men?'

'Your newspaper', the one in grey started, without any prologue, 'has got to cover a particular story. When can you do it?'

'And you yourselves are from where?'

'We're from the central committee of the Young Communist League.'

'Well, then, colleagues – you have your own newspaper. And it needs young authors!'

'We've already put it into our newspaper,' said the young man in grey. 'If we have to, we'll bring pressure to bear.'

'Pressure isn't necessary, I'm not an insect. But what's the deal, exactly?'

'You know, of course, that mountain-climbing is a manly sport.'

'Of course! I've seen it on television.'

'Climbing is done without any lofty goals, though. Or, rather, with the goal of simply conquering the summit.'

'That's right!' agreed Rappoport. 'And you . . . ?

'We're organizing a climb in honour of Lenin's hundredth anniversary. A group of Young Communists led by Sports Master Stepanov here is going to carry a bust of Lenin to the summit of Mount Communism and set it up there. For eternity. I'm the group's political leader. We want your newspaper to report to readers regularly on our preparations for this unparalleled feat.'

'And is the bust heavy?'

'Tell him, Stepanov!' ordered the political leader.

'Fifty-five pounds, five ounces.'

'And are you, the political leader, going to carry the bust as well?'

'No. According to the plan I'm going to be coordinating the assault from the base.'

'Right! So who's carrying it?'

'Stepanov.'

'And the others?'

'We're the organizers responsible for the climb,' the political leader explained. 'We take care of the propaganda measures. After all, the climb is of the highest order of difficulty! Well, and the political significance . . .'

'Clear as a bell!' snorted Rappoport. 'I salute your undertaking, young fellows! Only, boys, let's agree to do it this way. I'm already completely on your side. But what if you don't manage to get the bust to the top? Why get yourselves into a mess? I'm sure everything's going to be all right. Take the thing to the top – and we'll tell everyone about it right away. I'm giving you my word as a Soviet newspaperman!'

Not waiting for the three to find anything to say in objection, he stood up and began warmly shaking their hands.

'I wish you luck! The Young Communist League has thought up something great! But just think about the fact that it's fifty-five pounds, five ounces, right?'

Clapping the mountain climbers on the shoulder, he pushed them out the door.

'Rappoport, did you hear?' asked Alekseyev, the industry bureau chief, running past. 'Makartsev's had a heart attack!'

'You're joking!'

'He collapsed coming out of the Central Committee. But then he crawled back inside on all fours. A will of iron! There you are: you go on with your daily life and you never know where you'll catch it.'

The news about their chief ran through the office with the speed of electricity. The employees of the various bureaus poured into the corridors to find out the details. Everyone had information, suppositions, fears about the future. As it happened, it was only information that was in short supply. Whoever had heard something or other was able to come up with their own details, after repeated retellings.

'A man has to pay for responsibility with his health,' pronounced Alekseyev philosophically. 'The country doesn't just hand out money for free.'

'What does responsibility have to do with it? They've probably punished him for *King Chanticleer*, and he's collapsed because of it. Remember that phone call? We gave it a bad review, but Comrade Skinny actually liked the film. How could Makartsev have guessed that?'

'What did he like about it?'

'The heroine has big jugs, the way he likes them.'

'The way he used to like them,' Special Correspondent Ivlev pointed out coldly.

'Knock it off.' Rappoport reined him in and glanced around. 'It wasn't the jugs he liked but the fact that the director was a Spanish Communist.'

'In my opinion,' said Deputy Secretary Yezikov, 'it's Makartsev's own fault. He tried to be nice to everybody.'

Rappoport was listening. In general he hated talking in front of such a large number of ears. He looked around at the people standing there. Who could have planted the folder? Who had driven a good man to a heart attack?

'It's his own fault, you say?' Rappoport stepped closer to Yezikov. 'So what are you accusing him of? Being soft?'

Yezikov retreated. 'I'm not accusing him of anything! Him a softie? That's a laugh!'

'That may be a laugh to you,' said Inna, the typist, butting in on the conversation. 'You've never had and never will have a soft spot. But Makartsev is a terrific guy! It's not his fault things sometimes didn't work out.'

'What didn't work out?' asked Yezikov.

'Anything! Do you remember what happened with the canteen?'

'And how!' said Kakabadze. 'I personally took part in that assignment, for the Young Communist League.'

One day Makartsev had asked at a planning session where Alekseyev was. 'He went home,' they answered him. 'Something he ate in the office canteen disagreed with him.' That lunchtime Makartsev went down to the canteen himself. He stood in line with his tray, sat down at a table, sniffed the soup, set it to one side, then picked at the meat rissole with his fork. He almost threw up, but he was obliged to contain himself for the sake of the Party. He called Kashin over.

'What the hell is this! Why is it so revolting?'

'They're stealing, apparently,' surmised Kashin.

'Why should we take it lying down? We're journalists! How can we demand anything of others if we can't fix our own problems?'

'You're the editor-in-chief. You try.'

'I won't just try! I'll go ahead and do it!'

The editor called the head of the city police on the hot line. That very same day a proper-looking young man, modestly dressed, appeared at the *Trudovaya Pravda* office exit. He politely asked every woman coming down the stairs with a heavy bag: 'Excuse me, do you work in the canteen?' If she nodded, he would ask her to step into the next room. There were two policemen and representatives of the People's Inspection there, standing around a weighing scale. They plucked the stolen food out of the bags, weighed it and wrote out a charge sheet. The next day the entire canteen staff, from dishwashers to manager, had been replaced, and everything was so clean and tasty that the newspaper employees went to lunch two and three times in a row. By the following day the soup had got less tasty and two days later the main entrée as well. Within a week everything had gone back to the way it had been before. Makartsev drove over to the Central Committee dining-room and never returned to the issue.

'Our business sure is a roostery sort of thing,' said Ivlev. 'We crow away to beat the band, but whether dawn comes or not we don't care!'

'It wasn't Makartsev's fault,' said Anna, offended.

'Of course not!' Rappoport calmed her down. 'Why blame somebody for having good impulses? Other people don't have any impulses at all.'

'What's the argument about, comrades?' Kashin appeared in the corridor.

'We're just musing,' said Yezikov, 'on how to work without a head.'

'The leadership is worried about that, too,' Kashin said, looking around at everyone. 'I telephoned the hospital. We can't count on Makartsev for another two months or so, maybe even three whole months. As far as a temporary replacement for him goes, the Central Committee has already given the nod to Yagubov.'

# 18

# The Ups and Downs of
# Stepan Yagubov

Stepan Yagubov, although short of stature, looked like an athlete and appeared considerably younger than his forty-eight years. He looked after himself, shaving meticulously and with pleasure morning and evening (in the morning for himself, at night for his wife), and took exercise twice a week, even after a night shift, swimming in the Ministry of Defence pool. He never got sick, never caught a cold. Holidaying in the autumn at the Central Committee seaside health spa in Riga, he wouldn't swim in the pool – he swam in the icy Baltic – and never a twinge of rheumatism, never a head cold. Whenever anyone complained of a headache, he would sympathetically – even sincerely – ask: 'What's that like, then?' His head, its neatly trimmed black mane without a single white hair, had never ached even once in his life. Whenever it was necessary he drank exactly as much as everyone else, so that nobody would think he was just pretending to drink, but he never drank too much.

Makartsev chuckled at that: 'Are you off to join the ranks of the righteous, Yagubov?'

Yagubov smiled politely, trying the while not to look askance at the editor's large paunch. His own father, Trofim Yagubov, had never known what his father's first name was. In the well-to-do Cossack town of Nagutskaya he'd had no kinsfolk and was considered a stranger, even though he couldn't complain about his land or his house. He was a dry, laconic man, and he got around on a crutch: his leg had been broken under the wheel of a cart, and the bones had never knitted properly. The Yagubovs were fairly well off. They'd had three children to begin with, but they'd ended up burying two of them in an epidemic. Trofim Yagubov hadn't wanted to be liquidated with the rich peasants, the *kulaks*. So he'd signed up on a collective farm, joined the Party and helped in the process of collectivization. Those of their neighbours who were left alive after the collectivization were afraid of Trofim Yagubov and would start bowing from afar. His family, too, had starved in the famine. Yagubov himself, when he'd grown enough, helped his father with everything. He took pride in telling about the times his father, already an old man, would say: 'The Party commanded – Trofim answered, "Yes, sir!"'

But the decisive factor in Yagubov's ascent to the professional heights he currently occupied turned out to be neither his splendid upbringing nor even the qualities instilled in him but how tall he was. Or wasn't.

Yagubov had suffered since childhood from the fact that he'd been endowed with a height of just four feet and nine inches. Although he would always respond to gibes with the standard 'Little man, big dick', it was still painful to endure the taunts of his comrades, and he wore shoes with thick soles that he had tacked on himself, but it didn't help much.

After finishing high school, Yagubov, sharp in mind and quick on the uptake, had managed to procure the necessary document and left the collective farm. In Moscow he had entered the Aviation Institute. But he got kicked out after his first year: he'd failed to get a 'satisfactory' grade in any single subject except Party history, something that his father would read aloud in the evening at home. His paternal uncle, who had managed to become somebody, helped Yagubov get a job as a policeman on point duty. If it hadn't been for his uncle's pressure and connections, they would never have taken someone as short as him for anything. Yagubov then moved on to a job with the NKVD.

Standing his post as a policeman, Yagubov had stopped feeling himself inadequate. On the contrary, he came to acquire a sense of his superiority over the people he could order around. They were just citizens – he represented the Soviet regime. If he felt like it he could stop them, check their papers, even haul them off to the station if he felt like it. Everyone except his superiors was obliged to respect him, but even his superiors did, too, because he respected them. Contrary to all possibility, he had all the qualities needed to grow, and he was ready to grow.

Yagubov never suspected that his height (all those four feet, nine inches) was registered in a special card catalogue. As an A-student in Communist political studies, Yagubov was sent to an academy in the Moscow suburbs, after an additional test. The cadets there were taught to shoot pistols at moving human silhouettes and to speak English and German. Moreover, Yagubov completed around sixty parachute jumps, teasing those of his comrades who turned pale as soon as the plane had barely started to climb. Soon Yagubov found out that the courses were being run by a different department of the NKVD – the GUGB, the Chief Directorate of State Security. However, the fact that they were all being taught in one bunch, and not singly at secret hideaways, foretold that Yagubov was not being trained to be an intelligence agent, as he'd dreamed of.

The cadets felt nothing of the war. Life flowed by at a measured pace, interrupted only for field exercises. These exercises consisted of the cadets being sent to guard special sites or taking measures for the liquidation or resettlement of inimically inclined ethnic minorities. Thus Yagubov and his comrades evicted from their Volga homesteads the Germans he had hated since childhood. Shoving the crowd of women with their howling children and old folk, the cadets filled the covered trucks with them, freeing up their homes for genuine Soviet people.

A framed portrait of Stalin stood constantly on the table next to Yagubov's bed in their hostel. On one occasion the whole academy was roused and taken to an airfield. On the field stood two aeroplanes whose engines, they said, were working around the clock. A rumour went around that Stalin himself was going to be evacuated by air to the east. The cadets were kept in a *cordon sanitaire* around the planes for about three hours, then assembled and taken away. They said Stalin had flown off from a different airfield. But later it became known that the Leader had stayed behind in Moscow. Yagubov was hoping that the academy would be lined up in a Seventh of November or May Day parade. He would see Comrade Stalin right away. The Greatest Leader of All Times and Peoples would be taller than anyone else standing on the balcony of Lenin's tomb. And his surmise, in fact, was true.

For Stalin, who was five feet, two inches tall, they always set up a stool upholstered in multi-layered carpeting, with two short banisters on either side, so that he wouldn't fall over right there on the balcony. Stalin suffered from a height complex much bigger than Yagubov's, just because he was Stalin. Any newspaper photographs that showed people around him taller than the Leader of the World Proletariat were doctored in TASS, the Soviet press agency, in accordance with an unwritten rule that Comrade Stalin had to be shown that little bit taller than anyone else. The seams where the films were sliced and repositioned were carefully retouched. Stalin couldn't bear it if any of his servants were taller than him. Therefore, since the time of the Latvian commander of his personal bodyguard, Salpeter, who was imprisoned in 1938, Stalin had maintained a system of selecting bodyguards – and secretaries, cooks, waiters, bath attendants, gardeners, drivers and all the rest of his retinue – who were no more than five feet, one inch in height. Comrade Stalin himself decided the fate of companions-in-arms who were taller than he was.

Meanwhile, among Yagubov's teachers there appeared an ever-smiling and impeccably dressed man with a pencil moustache immediately above his lip and a bow tie.

'Let's say you can call me Kudrevatykh.'

The cadets smiled: Kudrevatykh was bald, unlike his name, which meant 'curly'. They heard that this was the former Soviet agent-in-residence in Berlin. He had been working as a waiter in a restaurant that was frequented by personages of the Reich, but his cover had been blown and he had managed to get back home. Kudrevatykh taught them etiquette, how to set a table with both three-crystal-glass settings and seven-crystal ones for the more formal occasions. He also showed them how best to listen to what the guests were saying, standing half turned away and showing a deliberately indifferent expression on your face. The cadets could only guess at where and for what they were being prepared.

Unexpectedly, an order was read out that they were to be given the rank of junior lieutenants and issued new uniforms: black vests with black trousers, snow-white dickeys and bow ties. When the pupils had changed into their new uniforms and were once again lined up, they were acquainted with their task: to wait on foreigners at a government reception. They were supposed to smile and pretend that they didn't understand a thing. In case of any difficulty they were to call on the *maître d'hôtel*, who would interpret for them and go away again. Their task entailed listening to what the foreigners were saying among themselves, going out to the kitchen and quickly and precisely relating it all without omitting any details to the *maître d'*, a lieutenant colonel, the head of the waiters' group. The guests were to be referred to by number.

Their bus, with curtained windows that they were forbidden to open, drove into Moscow. But they could see a little something anyway, whenever the bus braked and the curtains rocked back and forth: the glass on the buildings all paper-taped crosswise, sandbags blocking shop windows, anti-aircraft batteries. The bus drove up to some gates, and the curtains rocked. Yagubov instantly reckoned that they were being taken into the Kremlin. The cadet's heart beat joyfully: *This is how high you've flown, Yagubov! If only the village girls could see you now.* Yagubov glanced sideways at his neighbours. They were sitting with stern faces, looking straight ahead, just as the drill manual required them to. Yagubov looked straight ahead, too.

The reception got under way. Yagubov meticulously carried out his work, standing behind No. 14, a fat Englishman, the new press attaché, who looked more like a juggler that Yagubov had seen at the circus as a boy. The Englishman nattered away to the American next to him, all sorts of nonsense about women, but wasn't in any hurry to reveal any state secrets. Suddenly a wave of excitement swept through the hall, and everyone stood. Yagubov hadn't been warned how to behave in a circumstance like this, and he asked his neighbour, the one waiting on No. 15, the American, in a whisper: 'Petya, why are they standing up?'

'Blockhead! Can't you see – Stalin!' The great man, accompanied by his comrades-in-arms, walked along, his right hand between the buttons of his jacket, his thumb sticking out. With his left hand every now and then he stroked the medals on the breast of his new tunic, its gold shoulderboards gleaming brightly. Yagubov had seen Stalin only in portraits, and he was surprised to see him now, in real life, wearing trousers instead of riding breeches and boots.

Stalin had in truth worn boots his entire life, from early on, and didn't recognize any other footwear. For that reason a considerable percentage of the planned output of footwear from the country's factories was boots. The Leader's feet had been accustomed to such enslavement and endured it for years. And then they suddenly gave up. The second and third toes on his left foot, congenitally joined, hurt in particular. Doctors had long discussed the causes of the pain, and they carefully recommended that, in order to avoid thrombophlebitis, he wear lighter footwear so that his extremities could breathe.

Special shoes were cobbled together for Stalin, made of leather from Swanetia, in his native Georgia. They were cobbled on Stalin's boot lasts, as always with high heels, only with tops like shoes, without laces, but with stretchy rubber on the sides. Stalin asked them to take newsreel footage of him so he could see what he looked like in his trousers and new shoes. The film pleased him, and its destruction was ordered. On 17 January 1943 an order was issued for the introduction of a new army uniform – tunics and trousers.

Today Stalin was attending a reception wearing shoes for the first time. To him it seemed as if, without boots, he lacked confidence in the absolute rightness of every step that he took. He realized he was the only one feeling that way; his comrades-in-arms had no suspicion of the trauma in his soul. They were thinking that the Leader was simply the first to set a new example. Nobody else could change the places of cause and effect as skilfully as he could.

From that day forth, in millions of photographs and portraits distributed throughout the world by TASS, Stalin would be wearing his service jacket and trousers. It goes without saying that thenceforth policemen, railworkers, prosecutors, aviators and miners all wore shoes and trousers instead of boots and riding breeches. The country made itself over in the image of the Leader. All that was to come later, but today Stalin was praying to God that nobody in the world would guess the reason for his changing from boots to shoes. The enemies of the Party were just waiting for him to get sick somehow. He wasn't going to let himself weaken. He was thinking of the People, who needed to be saved. He had to get manufactured goods from the West, military equipment, to talk them into opening a second front, to scare them with the fact that he could capture all of Europe if victory was his alone.

Stalin passed so close to Yagubov that he could have touched him. Yagubov noticed that his torso was short and narrow and his arms were too long. His teeth were uneven and bad. Stalin was afraid of pain in his teeth and never had them looked after. By the time war came he had grown a large stomach – he ate a lot but didn't get around much. His hair had got thin, and his cheeks flaccid – his face had an indoor-Kremlin colouring from his night-time perch in his various offices and boardrooms. Yagubov exulted. Stalin turned out to be not that much taller than he was! The Great Leader was sitting across from Yagubov's press attaché, No. 14. A waiter he hadn't seen before stood behind Stalin's chair. Stalin pointed a finger at his wine glass, and it was instantly filled with dry wine.

'Cold water, please,' his No.14 Englishman said, in English, of course. Yagubov stood rooted, under Stalin's spell.

'Water! Pour him some water!' whispered the *maître d'*, appearing from God knows where.

Only then did Yagubov catch on. He grabbed a bottle of mineral water, wrapped it in a white napkin and poured half a glass for the Englishman, who nodded and drank it down.

'Have you noticed, my dear friend,' whispered Englishman No. 14 to American No. 15, 'how Russians are struck dumb whenever they see Stalin? He hypnotizes them with his dyed moustache. Look at that fool of a waiter!'

*You scum, you goddamned imperialist*, thought Yagubov, offended. *He thinks I don't understand English. I'll get you, you vermin!*

Stalin stooped slightly to one side (his left arm and shoulder had been slow to respond ever since a childhood accident); he coughed and stood up with his glass in hand. Yagubov sprang to attention. But the *maître d'* touched his elbow and commanded Yagubov to follow him into the kitchen. 'Well, what?' he asked, along the way.

Yagubov decided to add a little colour, to get revenge on the English imperialist. 'Number Fourteen spoke in a manner critical of Comrade Stalin . . .'

'That information is unnecessary,' the *maître d'* answered drily, glancing to one side. 'He didn't reveal any facts or figures?'

'Not yet,' answered Yagubov, sensing that he'd screwed things up and, to set things right, asked: 'Any new instructions?'

'Put his main course on your tray!'

He came back into the hall just as everyone was applauding. Stalin was calmly listening to the foreigners, puffing on his Dunhill pipe. Suddenly he turned his tenacious little eyes on the English press attaché and asked: 'And you, sir: what are you drinking?'

'Mineral water,' Englishman No. 14 answered him in Russian. 'But now, perhaps, I'll try some brandy . . .'

'Brandy?' Stalin thought it over. 'Armenian or Georgian?' And once again he gazed fixedly at the Englishman, probing his thoughts. The man didn't know what to answer and smiled guiltily.

'Although I'm a Georgian,' said Stalin, 'Armenian brandy is better. As you can see, ethnic rivalries don't exist among Communists. For example, all of us, the Soviet people, love Soviet champagne from the Crimea.'

It crossed the press attaché's mind that he might have been placing too much trust in his English newspapers. Stalin was in reality much more democratic, and his face much less strongly disfigured by smallpox scars, than they wrote in the West. He would have to tell the journalists that.

Stalin meanwhile continued: 'We consider the best of all to be champagne from Crimean vaults, bottled at the end of the last century by Greek winemakers for the Russian aristocracy. Now it is drunk by the working class and the labouring peasants. You drink it, too. Don't be shy!'

Stalin indicated the bottle with his eyes and snapped his fingers. Yagubov and two other waiters leaped to carry out the order. Yagubov was the quickest off the mark. He got to the bottle first and was already about to pour some into Stalin's glass. But Stalin pointed at the Englishman's glass. By the time Yagubov had poured and turned back to him, Stalin's waiter was already holding another bottle just like it in his hands. He poured a swallow into a little shot glass, drank it and then poured Stalin some.

The champagne tickled the Englishman's nostrils; it seemed uncloying and light. He didn't even put his glass back down on the table but held it out for Yagubov to pour him some more without looking around. Yagubov was standing sideways, as he had been taught, the better to hear the dinner conversation. Thinking quickly, he grabbed the glass, but either he wasn't holding it firmly enough or the Englishman let go of it too soon. The goblet fell to the carpet.

Yagubov looked around the diners out of the corner of his eye to see if anybody had noticed his blunder and kicked the glass under the table with the toe of his shoe. He quickly snatched a clean glass from the tray and poured champagne into it. The Englishman sipped a bit and, addressing Stalin, praised the Crimean wine and the good taste of the ordinary Soviet people, who knew what to drink.

'I told you so!' observed Stalin with satisfaction and stroked his moustache with his thumb.

When Beria was briefing Stalin the following day on what the diplomats had been talking about among themselves, Stalin drew something in a notebook. Beria craned his neck and saw that Stalin was drawing a football.

Suddenly he interrupted Beria in Georgian: 'By the way, what's the name of that footballer?'

'From which team?'

'Don't turn away, look me in the eye. You're getting absent-minded lately.' Stalin picked up his pipe from the desk, poked down the dottle with his finger, fired up his lighter and puffed away. 'What's the name of that soccer player who passed the glass underneath the table?'

It turned out that nobody had noticed a thing. But Stalin loved startling people with his powers of observation. Beria told him the man's name a little later over the phone.

'I have to point out that this Yagubov is useless as a waiter,' Stalin said. 'Far too nervous. Maybe he's too handy for this sort of work, eh?'

'We'll get rid of him.'

'You surprise me! I know without your telling me that you're going to get rid of him. I've been worried for a long time about how easy it is for you to get rid of people. People – those are our *personnel*.'

Beria could hear Stalin smacking his lips on the other end, relighting his pipe.

'Here's what,' Stalin advised. 'Give the footballer a job that fits his profile.'

Beria, screwing up his face, recalled the bloodthirsty dwarf Yezhov, who had been found by Stalin himself in the provinces and promoted to the top. In general, Stalin seemed to like going by the proverb, 'Taken from the slough-mud, made into a blue-blood.' That meant it wasn't by chance that he was interested in Yagubov. So he would have to be careful with this boy. General Chernov, the head of Beria's chancellery, received a directive, and Yagubov was made one of the directors of the NKVD stadium, Dinamo. The next day he'd already got down to business: standing in front of Yagubov, who was sitting in his chair, his predecessor told Yagubov what his duties were. The former director was sent off to the front. There wasn't much work for the new director to do. The gyms and dressing-rooms beneath the stadium stands were all occupied. A school had been set up in them to train saboteurs to be dropped in the enemy's rear. The school was under the command of other people.

Stalin never remembered this particular joke, although in general he loved to check out the results of his jokes from time to time. The Leader was distracted by the construction of an underground tunnel, down which he could drive from his house in Kuntsevo into the Kremlin. The tunnel was completed by the regular metro builders. Stalin inspected his new route, but it seemed to him that he could suffocate inside the tunnel if a cave-in ever happened, whether accidentally or on purpose. He thought about it a little longer and then issued a directive for the tunnel to be used as a metro line. The newspapers wrote stories about the Great Leader's latest concern for the well-being of the people.

So Yagubov never did find out who it was who had ever-so-slightly manipulated his fate. All the other people who had been involved in getting him his job were later executed but not because of Yagubov, of course. In his position as stadium director Yagubov didn't just get a taste for being kowtowed to. He became a member of the *nomenklatura*, the high and mighty. He soon became acquainted with Nina, the daughter of a Central Committee department head. Nina had come to the Dinamo stadium to play tennis. She wasn't that much taller than Yagubov. Yagubov devised a special regime for her, assigning her his best personal trainer. He came himself to observe how Nina's training was going, and in the process of observation got interested in her. Sometime later he succeeded in getting into Nina's pants, which made marrying her all the easier.

His father-in-law, after squaring the matter with Beria and the Central Committee propaganda department, managed to get Yagubov a transfer: from being one of the directors of the stadium, he was now sent over to bolster the newspaper *Sovietsky Sport*. By this time Yagubov had already graduated from the Higher Party School. That was how he had become a journalist. Now he had the opportunity to explain to the broad masses that sport was a Party matter, a political matter, a mighty means of instilling Soviet patriotism. Sport could also ideologically strengthen the multimillion-strong army of sports fans. Yagubov's father-in-law was pensioned off. He tried to press some advice on to Yagubov about how to behave with superiors and subordinates, but Yagubov cut him off, clapping him on the shoulder with a smile.

'Your old-fashioned methods won't do, Pops. What we need is people who know how to work, not blather. Look how many mistakes you've made – so you just hush, now!'

Yagubov himself, though, was hanging by a thread. Among some others being sent further away from Moscow at Beria's behest, just in case, Yagubov wound up working in Hungary. This decision of Beria's killed two birds with one stone. He was sending away people who'd been in favour under Stalin, to show that he himself had been against Stalin. But he was also tucking away these experienced personnel in such a way that, as soon as the situation changed in his favour, he could bring them back quick as a flash.

The thirty-three-year-young stud Yagubov arrived at the Soviet embassy in Hungary and swam into Ambassador Kegelbanov's ken as the embassy's second secretary. His wife stayed behind in Moscow with her parents. Yagubov hastened to cheer Kegelbanov up: 'Hey, you and I are *zemlyaki* – we're from the same neck of the woods!'

Kegelbanov had already familiarized himself with his new employee's personal file. He couldn't help but appreciate the businesslike character and expeditiousness of his second secretary. Yagubov's job was to keep an eye on the embassy employees and on Soviet citizens there on business: engineers, athletes, artistes, Party and Young Communist League officials. He had had some modest experience in this sphere: he knew how to eavesdrop half turned away. Ambassador Kegelbanov was extremely punctilious with Yagubov and not because they'd been born in the same village. He knew that his countryman was watching him, too, and as a *zemlyak* would know more than anyone else. Understanding this, Yagubov hastened to prove to the ambassador by his deeds that, quite the contrary, he could appreciate the care he lavished on Yagubov and would never rat on him.

By the time Beria was executed, Yagubov was already feeling himself to be a Kegelbanov man. And he wasn't mistaken: on the list of state security agents secretly awarded medals for skilful leadership in the suppression of the counter-revolution in Budapest in 1956 Kegelbanov topped the list and Yagubov was at the bottom of it. Soon afterwards, Ambassador Kegelbanov – his hands covered with blood, according to Western newspapers – had to be withdrawn from Hungary. Yagubov occupied himself with more modest affairs and night-time ones at that. He was in charge of clearing the corpses from the streets. Western newspapers didn't write anything about him. He stayed behind to serve at the embassy, although he did dream of going back to Moscow, too.

Yagubov's father-in-law was in retirement, strolling about at his *dacha*. It wasn't very far from Khrushchev's, though, and they became friends. He told Khrushchev that his daughter was pining for her husband. The purge of the Party apparatus that was so necessary to Khrushchev was proceeding with difficulty. He needed some people of his own. Khrushchev phoned Kegelbanov to find out who this Yagubov was – the name seemed somehow familiar. Kegelbanov was by this time heading a department at the Central Committee and reminded Khrushchev about the list of people honoured for their role in Hungary.

'I remember,' said Khrushchev. 'But what sort of fellow is he?'

'He's proved himself by his deeds. He's one of ours!' concluded Kegelbanov, who needed his own people, too.

Three days later Yagubov had been called back 'for transfer to another position' and had landed in Moscow. There the old Bureau of Information was being reorganized into the *Novosti* press agency. Khrushchev included his son-in-law Adzhubey on the administrative staff and Yagubov, too. At *Novosti* Yagubov got to show off his experience as an organizer. The *Novosti* press began distributing propagandizing literature for free. Under the direction of various Soviet embassies, *Novosti* offices were set up throughout the world, staffed by KGB delegates and selected local Communists.

Yagubov's having been abroad – even if it was just Hungary – and his high-level work couldn't help but change his outward appearance and range of interests. A certain bumpkin-like quality in him disappeared entirely. His understanding of life deepened. He dressed modestly and well, was a pleasant conversationalist, had a sense of humour and knew just when to stop. He never made any errors over whom to call personally and whom to talk to through their secretary and what tone of voice to talk to them in. He became a character whose opinion of himself and whose real achievements, although not completely equivalent, were none the less close. He could understand that his further growth depended on the results of his propaganda efforts only indirectly – but directly on his mutual relations with his superiors. Yagubov even had his own subordinates, dedicated to him. His children were growing up healthy and obedient and were doing well at school. His wife didn't work very much after graduating from the Institute of Physical Culture, but she did play tennis with their children with pleasure. He loved his children, played with them at night and in the summer sent them off to the old folks in the Kuban with his wife so that they would get the habit of labour from childhood. In a word, Yagubov had good grounds to consider that everything in his life was coming together unsurpassably well.

The only thing that grieved him was his hastiness, probably arising from his small stature. He spoke and walked too quickly. Haste diminished his dignity. He was having to stop himself, make pauses and only then speak and move slower, without any fuss, in accordance with his present position. And it occurred to him more and more frequently that it was time to make a new leap. Had they forgotten about him?

When Czechoslovakia came up, it would have been the best thing to send Kegelbanov there right away as ambassador, him having such huge experience in the similar situation in Hungary. But that would have provoked an undesirable reaction. The Politburo had appointed Kegelbanov chairman of the KGB, and the prophylactic measures being taken in Prague were organized under his command from Moscow. Kegelbanov had need of additional personnel. The list of people awarded medals in Hungary was lying in front of him on his desk. Kegelbanov was assessing not only his comrades' work experience in Hungary but also their work afterwards – after all, twelve years had gone by.

Kegelbanov's assistant, Shamayev, rang Yagubov – with whom he'd been on personal terms in Hungary – and warned him that he might be needed.

'Always ready!' Yagubov answered with the Pioneer greeting, simply and even happily, rising slightly out of his seat.

'You're not going on holiday?'

'That'll depend on what my orders are.'

'Then you'll have to put off your holiday for a bit.'

'Yes, sir,' he answered, not guessing what was in store for him.

Events played themselves out, and they managed to get along at the Lubyanka without him. Incidentally, Yagubov had never liked saying 'the Lubyanka'. He usually just said 'the apparatus', in a businesslike and modest fashion. On the morning of 21 August Yagubov heard over the radio the TASS bulletin about extending urgent fraternal assistance to the Czechoslovak people.

Shamayev rang him again and told him to drive down to Nogina Square and park near the Chinatown wall. Yagubov had scarcely driven up when a man stepped up to him and asked him to get into another car, one with curtains. Five minutes later the car was diving into the main building of 'the apparatus', through the gates around from the square. They went silently up to the third floor in the lift and walked down a long, deserted corridor with light-green walls. Guards stood in every corner. Yagubov didn't ask a thing. He saw the plaque reading 'Chairman' as they went through the door.

In an immense anteroom, behind an enormous desk with multi-coloured telephones on it, sat an elderly clerk in a major's uniform. Yagubov's escort disappeared. On the control panel a red light came on. The clerk silently got up and opened the door. Behind the desk far down the spacious office, its redwood-panelled walls hung with oriental carpets since Beria's day, Yagubov saw the familiar face with its gold-rimmed spectacles. The office's owner straightened his cuffs. Kegelbanov had gone grey, his hair was thinner, his glasses didn't conceal the bags under his eyes. He got up and said hello reservedly, inquiring into Yagubov's health. Yagubov, as already mentioned, was always healthy. The thought flashed through Yagubov's mind that he was going to be sent to Czechoslovakia for the kind of prophylactic work that he had coped with so successfully in Hungary. But then it occurred to him at once: since they had brought him straight to 'the apparatus' they weren't about to send him abroad.

'I recommended you, Comrade Yagubov,' said Kegelbanov, looking him straight in the eye, 'for the preparation of an appeal for assistance from a group of members of the Central Committee of the Communist Party of Czechoslovakia, the government and the national assembly of the Czechoslovakian Socialist Republic. As you know, that assistance was already given last night.'

'I'm aware of that,' nodded Yagubov, even though he wasn't completely in the know. 'When do I get down to it?'

'Right now.' Kegelbanov pushed a button, and when the elderly major appeared at the door, standing at attention, he added: 'Give him the material.'

'One small thing,' Yagubov said, guiltily, waiting until the major had gone. 'I don't speak Czech.'

'I know.' Yagubov felt the irony in Kegelbanov's voice. 'I think we'll be able to find a translator. Sit down and get to work.'

The chairman unlocked his secret side-door and left. Yagubov shifted his weight from foot to foot, not daring to sit behind the chairman's desk, with its six telephones. He hunched down next to it, at the long green-baize-covered conference table. A portrait of Dzerzhinsky stared fixedly at Yagubov. The sunlight was blinding, reflecting on the ceiling in long rectangles from the windows, making him squint.

Even in his excitement, Yagubov didn't lose his ability to reason. He didn't think about why such a responsible mission had fallen to his lot specifically. He didn't doubt his own irreplaceability. He knew how to work effectively. Back in Budapest, Yagubov hadn't let his soldiers sleep, urging on the trucks, and by dawn all the corpses had been loaded up, taken away and buried in pits. They'd even managed to wash down the streets. Yagubov himself hadn't got any sleep, either, driving in his jeep from Buda to Pest and back again, even though they were still shooting from the windows. No, the issue wasn't just his effectiveness: the important thing now was that he was a journalist, too. But surely Kegelbanov had a lot of personnel who were capable of carrying out tasks like this? It was also important that he, Yagubov, be outside the loop. Kegelbanov's man but, at the same time, not his man. Reliable but not *from* the apparatus itself. The decision to bring in *him* in particular was not only logical but the only correct one. He never suffered any doubts, not Yagubov! But even that was a bonus: once he'd convinced himself of it, he always carried out the work even more steadfastly.

The major brought in bound copies of *Pravda* for the month of July and half of August of the present year, 1968. Yagubov moved a pad of blank paper closer to him. His task was complicated by the fact that he had never written a thing in his life, if you didn't count dictation in school. He hadn't even tried. Everything that he needed was written for him, at his command. He was capable of a lot more than mere writing: he knew what was supposed to be written and why. He could create a multitude of articles simultaneously, fill in the text of entire newspapers, publish dozens of books. To write for himself was as awkward as having to sweep up his own office. Lackeys were on hand to do the writing.

Yagubov sighed and started leafing through *Pravda*. Czechoslovakia had disappeared from the pages of the newspaper in July. They were afraid of the decisions reached by the Extraordinary Session of the Communist Party of Czechoslovakia and were trying to talk them out of it. They had asked Dubcek nicely to come to Moscow, but then they'd had to go to see him in Cerna-on-Tissa themselves. What kind of a Communist was this Dubcek, to be harbouring doubts? What were they hinting at, these Czechs, talking about socialism with a human face? It had got to the point where they'd opened their borders up, and people were free to come and go as they wanted! Communists, and behaving like children! And here was what Yagubov needed right now: a letter from the Czechoslovakian workers at the Avto-Praga factory – a facsimile with ninety-nine signatures. There'd be no such facsimile at the bottom of his

letter. *There, that's the important thing: 'The holy duty of every Communist'*
*– a theoretical article. The fundament of the Czechs' massive appeal to*
*us.*

Yagubov remembered everything he was looking at but continued to
page through *Pravda* up to the last issue, to the TASS announcement. The
Party and governmental leaders of the Czechoslovakian Socialist
Republic, it said, appealed to the Soviet Union and other allied states
. . . *They've already appealed, and here the text of the appeal hasn't been pre-*
*pared yet – there's a cock-up for you! Now the important thing is to get started.*
Suddenly the salutation of it flooded into his mind by itself: 'Brothers and
Sisters!'

He liked that sort of beginning. That was the way Stalin had
addressed the people at the start of the war. Afterwards, when Yagubov
opened *Pravda*, he saw that they had rewritten his salutation: 'Men and
Women!' But he stuck to his opinion, anyway, that it was better written
in Stalin's and his version.

But while he was doing it he sensed the he shouldn't concentrate too
hard on the politics of it: he had to play on the national pride of the Czechs.
They had to be talked into it politely, without force, so that they would
be deciding, as it were, independently. The more so, since the troops had
already been sent in and there was nothing to worry about in that regard.
'We appeal to you, dear citizens,' Yagubov continued to write. He
approached ready-made formulae with a certain creativity. 'The ire and
indignation of the entire Soviet people', 'crazed mercenaries', 'instigators',
'revanchists', 'a wild outburst of reaction' – he threw them all out, choos-
ing softer words, merely preserving a firm Party standpoint. After the first
agonizing attempts the writing got easier, his pen gliding over the paper.
His writing done, Yagubov called in the major and said that he needed
a typist. 'One who can spell!' he added.

The major nodded and went off and after a moment came back in with
a typewriter in his hands. He clattered away like a real machine-gun, and
soon the text was lying on the table. On top was written: 'Not for distribution out of this office.' The very same escort took Yagubov out through

the gates. When Yagubov transferred into the waiting Volga, his chauffeur had merely shrugged a shoulder.

'You tired, eh?' asked Yagubov. 'Never mind! The human being is a hardy creature.'

Yagubov was in a festive mood. He'd taken part, to put it into newspaper language, in the salvation of a socialist country from ignominy – leaving the Communist camp. Later even the Czechs themselves would realize that. Yagubov was entering their history, he was going to become a national hero of theirs. Some day the whole of progressive mankind was going to know this, but for now not even his wife knew.

Yagubov was needed again the next day. He was appointed editor of the newspaper *Praci*, published by patriotic Czechs, that was being printed in Dresden and handed out free in Czechoslovakia, now liberated by Soviet troops. This Czech-patriot newspaper was actually being put together in Moscow, at the *Novosti* press where Yagubov worked. The Dresden edition was carried in on military helicopters. The journalist Karl Nepomnyashchy was killed on one of them, crushed under a load of newspapers. He was buried in Moscow, the cause of his death concealed. Yagubov worked day and night, personally checking and coordinating every line. He grew pale and thin. The Czechs didn't want to read his newspaper.

When the situation in Czechoslovakia had normalized, the necessity for a Czech patriots' strategic body declined. Having fulfilled his historic mission, Yagubov felt certain that he deserved a reward. But the secrecy of the whole operation had been so great that there was no way to reward him directly. He came to the conclusion that he could expect some sort of promotion. He wasn't in suspense for long. In October he was allowed to go away on holiday. He set out for the airport with his wife and a new assignment: after his holiday he would get down to work as first deputy to the editor of *Trudovaya Pravda*.

In his résumés and personal histories, Yagubov never indicated that he'd been a point-duty policeman. He wrote that he had 'occupied a post in the NKVD system'. All real KGB men had a concealed contempt for policemen in their hearts. Yagubov understood that he was lucky but considered that this luck was something natural, a consequence of his peculiar qualities. Therefore he considered every job that he got to be temporary, a step from which he could rise to the next. He was striving towards more responsible work, he wanted to be higher than other people, and, if he were to be given the chance to rule everyone, he would do it more wisely and correctly than those who were now ruling. Neither did Yagubov deny his ambition. He could well accept honours, see his portrait everywhere; just for fun he thought about how the village of Nagutskaya was going to become the city of Yagubov. The future occupied his thoughts a lot less than the present did, though.

One concrete way to get ahead was to become an assistant to some Politburo member or Central Committee secretary or, best of all, to the one in charge of international affairs where he, Yagubov, was already an expert. But you didn't get appointed to a post like that; you got elected. And there was only one voter in those elections. Assistants got their jobs in order to give their bosses additional grey matter. That was what Yagubov had. This rapid growth was impeded by only one serious deficiency – his perfect health. People of too healthy an appearance were not liked by Politburo members, so, in order to rise to the top, Yagubov still had getting sick and getting old in store for him.

But even his present-day appointment to *Trudovaya Pravda* was a serious promotion. Only people who had worked for the Central Committee – so their work would be personally known – were appointed editors-in-chief or their assistants. An exception had been made for Yagubov in consideration of his services. He even saw some danger in it: Makartsev had earlier worked in the Central Committee apparatus and consequently had connections there. Yagubov could be turned into a whipping boy. At one time he'd been a good parachutist, though, and he had always pulled his ripcord at the right moment.

But the best-laid plans ... Soon after his transfer to *Trudovaya Pravda*, Yagubov was assigned, via a phone call from the Central Committee, to welcome a Journalists' Union guest – the new (after the events in Czechoslovakia) deputy editor-in-chief of the Czech newspaper *Rude Pravo*. They were nearly the same age, but the Czech was a foot taller. Their itinerary took them to Central Asia. It was a trio, though, that took in the sights of Samarkand – their interpreter, Marina, a tall dyed blonde, well built and dressed in imported clothes, came along. There they were, dining in the restaurant of the Intourist Hotel, Samarkand. The Czech screwed up his face against the flies and said that he liked it there a lot. They each drank two shot-glasses of vodka. Marina unhurriedly drained the rest of the bottle by herself. When they parted in the corridor, Yagubov noticed the interpreter going into the Czech's room and then leaving after an animated conversation with him.

The deputy editor of *Rude Pravo*, who had come to the Soviet Union in accordance with his convictions, and also being afraid of an insufficient display of them, had apparently turned down Marina's further services and bade her a good night. Marina hadn't expected an insult like that and, going to Yagubov's room to ask for a cigarette, suggested: 'Do you want to have a look?'

He failed to understand. 'At what?'

She undressed and stood there, giving him time to catch on. 'Well, what do you think?'

Yagubov tried to chuck her out into the corridor, but she spun away with a laugh, and he couldn't make her put her clothes back on. Besides, she wasn't bad-looking at all, and he wasn't made of stone. The tall woman (he'd always been afraid of them) conducted herself superlatively well. Yagubov enjoyed that sort of activity, but he usually tried to restrain himself. An hour and a half later, after coming back to his senses, he tried to talk Marina into leaving.

'I like you,' she protested, and fell asleep on his arm.

Next morning he looked out into the corridor, and, after letting her out, sighed. Back in Moscow, Marina telephoned Yagubov at work. He was such a lofty person that he wouldn't even remember some people he knew. But she had the key to a new private one-room apartment, and she invited Yagubov to come and see it. He spoke drily to her in return and

politely turned down the invitation to see the apartment, referring to his
workload. On the desk in front of Marina at that moment lay her report
on the *Rude Pravo* deputy editor-in-chief's trip to Central Asia. Putting
down the phone, Marina thought for a little bit, and then, after giving the
Czech Communist a short, positive character reference, she added at the
end: 'Com. S. Yagubov was politically proper but morally unsteady on the
trip.'

If he'd known that, Yagubov would surely have gone to inspect the
new apartment. Politically he was indeed proper – impeccable, even. When
some Swedish journalists visited the *Trudovaya Pravda* office, Yagubov
met them, owing to Makartsev's illness. Anna ran down to the private buf-
fet for some coffee and cakes. Certain issues were disturbing the Swedish
journalists a great deal.

'Can you tell us, Mr Yagubov, why Soviet newspapers torment individual writers from time to time?'

He answered straight away: 'We can't forbid newspapers to express
their opinion. We have a free press here, too, gentlemen!'

'So what would one do if one's own convictions diverged from whatever is the current position of your Party?'

'You see,' explained Yagubov, 'my thoughts belong to the Party. I'm at
its disposal, so there can never be any divergence between it and me.'

'But mightn't there be, with individual people in the Party?' one of
the journalists tried to pin him down, swallowing some coffee to give
Yagubov time to think.

Yagubov was surprised that his Swedish colleague couldn't understand
elementary things like this but went on to explain it calmly.

'If such a Party member were to be higher in rank than me,' he said,
'there couldn't be any divergence. After all, a directive from them is a directive from the Party, for me.'

'You have said that you were a simple peasant, Mr Yagubov. How have
you managed to make a career?'

'In our country you can't make a career. You can only grow,' Yagubov
patiently explained. 'In our country all those who are dedicated to the Party

and to our ideals grow quickly.' And Yagubov smiled his charming smile – a simple, open, Russian fellow from Stavropolye.

'Your parents – who are they?' asked another Swede.

'I've already told you, they're peasants,' chuckled Yagubov. 'In our language, collective farmers – *kolkhozniki*. I love them a great deal. Every spring I fly down there for a day or two, bring a lot of food with me, dig in the garden, fix the roof – that's hard for the old folks ... I always manage to get down there unless I'm on duty over the May Day holiday. Business before anything else, gentlemen!'

# 19

# Heading Off on a Mission

Yagubov had started off at his editorship duties quietly enough but without any familiarity. He'd decided to introduce a polite but businesslike Western style of interrelation with his subordinates. If he forgot and got too familiar then, remembering, he would return to the designated etiquette. He divided journalists into two categories: the irresponsible, who wrote things, and the responsible, who signed off on things. Yagubov was one of those who had to sign off. Now, in the absence of his editor-in-chief, the burden of responsibility lay on him in full measure.

'Whatever else goes on in the universe,' declared Yagubov at his first planning session in Makartsev's absence, 'our subscribers have to read that everything in this country is fine.'

The new man in the office, he understood that the drive belts all led to Makartsev. Ahead of him lay the task of determining who it was that he could rely on to make their individual belts temporarily lead to him and which of them he could later leave attached to him for good. In front of him lay a list of staff members with an indication of their positions, their work experience and their wages. His eyes slid from name to name. He tried to remember what he had heard about this or that employee and what was the opinion of them that he'd formed so far. After a cursory browse, the deputy editor marked two names: Kashin and Rappoport. Both of them for contradictory reasons.

Makartsev evidently didn't like the managing editor, Kashin, very much but never expressed it aloud. On the contrary, he would remark on his efficiency and steady character. But Yagubov reckoned, based on the ironic tone that crept into Makartsev's voice, that he despised his managing editor. Evidently he felt himself to be sufficiently firmly in place that he didn't need Kashin for support. Makartsev considered him the managing editor and just forgot about the fact that it was the the KGB that had given Kashin his mission of keeping track of the editorial staff and not Makartsev. People usually tried to work better when they felt relied on, and Yagubov decided to show Kashin that he relied on him.

As far as the other employee went, Rappoport's motivating factors were more complicated. To Yagubov, personally, the untidily dressed, poorly shaven and always grumbling Communist Education Department acting editor was unattractive. And the antipathy was evidently mutual. Rappoport's way of constantly objecting, of stretching out the execution of any directives that he didn't like, was doubtlessly explained by his lack of the chief quality of a journalist – an internal Party-mindedness. If Yagubov had been the editor-in-chief he would have long before brought in someone more ideologically restrained, to say nothing of possessing a more attractive biography.

However, Makartsev had frequently praised Rappoport to Yagubov: his wit, his professionalism, his dependability in carrying out the subtlest of tasks. Nor could it be excluded that Rappoport had connections of his own. Through Rappoport, Yagubov would be able to learn about the weak sides of their temporarily absent editor-in-chief. Rappoport had authority. This was especially so in connection with the part of the workforce that made itself out to be intellectual and reasoned more than it should. The circumstance of Yagubov's establishing contact with a Jew would have a salutary effect on that part of the staff and put paid to any rumours that might arise. He asked for Kashin to be sent in to him first.

Holding back for a moment, Anna asked: 'Aren't you going to move to Makartsev's office?'

Yagubov had been waiting for the suggestion but raised his eyebrows in surprise. 'Why would I do that?'

Anna was embarrassed. 'Well, it's easier for me to get to that office. It's closer.'

'That's all right, Anna. It's not the two of *us* who decide these things. And Makartsev will be back soon. For now you'll just have to make the trip. Get me Kashin!'

She nodded understandingly and ran off. Yagubov, on the other hand, really did think that it was more convenient to manage the newspaper from the editor-in-chief's office. It was spacious, and that was where the secure line was. Yagubov had to go there whenever he needed to call anyone. But Makartsev himself would have to suggest the move into his office.

'May I?'

Kashin entered with small steps, trying to drag his leg unobtrusively, which made his lameness even more obvious. Under his arm he had a thin red folder with the gold-embossed legend 'To Be Reported'.

'Please!' Yagubov pointed to the chair and adroitly rolled his cigarette from one corner of his mouth to the other with his tongue.

Kashin smiled and swept his gaze solicitously around the deputy editor's office. 'You see how it goes. I'd got up and was coming to see you, and there Anna was, calling me here. Telepathy! I gave an order for the curtains in your office to be changed. It's too dark in here.'

Yagubov nodded, smoking, not in any hurry to ask anything. Kashin felt that, in view of Yagubov's history, he was going to be able to establish closer ties with him than with Makartsev. Now Kashin looked temporizingly at the deputy editor, hesitating over whether or not to bring it up himself or to wait for a corresponding offer.

'What's on your mind?' Yagubov asked, crushing out his cigarette in the ashtray. He didn't want to take the initiative from the managing editor.

'According to the new directive,' Kashin began, having received permission to speak, 'I'm obliged to make you aware of the fact that there's a manuscript going around the office, a *samizdat*.'

'Have you found it?'

'I've never held it in my hands, myself. They say it's in a grey folder. People are discussing the contents – but what they are I still haven't clearly determined. In a word, it's anti-Soviet.'

Yagubov was silent, thinking. Then he said: 'The reason why I asked if you'd found the manuscript was this. I've already been informed, so I do know about it.' Nobody had informed him about anything, but Yagubov was letting him know right away that he, Yagubov, was in charge. 'What about Makartsev?' he added, after a pause. 'Have you informed him about it?'

Any further trust between them depended on the answer to this. Kashin understood. 'I never got to inform him. But Makartsev always considered this kind of work to be secondary. He would know better, of course. But maybe that was an underestimation?' That was how cautiously and half-inquiringly Kashin ended up, leaving it to the new boss to decide the issue.

'Makartsev is a pure Party worker. He considers that ideological work alone is enough. But you and I', he allowed himself to move to a confidingly familiar level and underlined the 'you and I' with a pause, 'are in the know on a different side of the issue. So that part of the responsibility will be ours. Makartsev will simply be grateful to us if we help him to manage the part of the newspaper that he hasn't got time for.'

'Right,' nodded Kashin.

'But,' Yagubov paused again, underlining the importance of the following thought, 'of course, we don't need to fuss or panic. The body of the newspaper is healthy, I hope. And, if necessary, we can look closely at individual comrades. Here's what you can do. Have a look at who's doing this. I mean reading . . . well, and, as they say, leftish conversations. Otherwise, what sort of managers are we if we don't know our people?'

'As far as that goes, I've got you – I'll be heading that way . . .' Kashin hesitated, not knowing if he should say anything further. But he decided that trust had been established and needed to be developed. 'Makartsev left me two jobs. One concerns the bonuses for Publishing Day. Should I give you the list?'

'Leave it here. I'll have a look.'

'And the other is a delicate subject. Makartsev requested information on people's morality. Well, to put it simply, who's living with who. So, here,

I made a list. Not everyone, of course. Just the ones being talked about.'

'Makartsev asked for this?' Yagubov repeated, not showing his surprise. 'Evidently he had something in mind.'

'The ones who drink have asterisks after their names.'

'You didn't make any copies for yourself, I hope?'

'No. Why would I?'

'Good man!'

'No problem!'

'Well, I'm happy that we have a complete mutual understanding. You can count on my support.'

'Thank you!'

'And here's another thing: order me a hard cushion for my chair – that's what I'm used to.'

Yagubov followed Kashin with his eyes to see whether he closed the door behind him, fastidiously picked up the list of names, so accurately noted down by Kashin in pairs, and, without reading it, scrunched it up indignantly and chucked it into the wastepaper bin. He hadn't expected that sort of thing from Makartsev. No, he, Yagubov, wasn't going to stoop to that sort of thing! If someone fell in love and a personal relationship came out of it, let it happen! If it didn't interfere with the work, and there wasn't any scandal, there was no reason to get involved. Kashin wouldn't raise the issue again. Makartsev with his heart attack wasn't going to be up to moralizing. *What does he need it for, I wonder? What's he going to get out of it? Is he jealous of somebody and just wants to settle accounts? Or maybe he's got some other idea in mind? One way or another, the issue is over and done with!*

Thus making up his mind, Yagubov energetically bent over and pulled the crumpled sheet out of the basket. He smoothed it out against the glass and started looking it over, just to check his intuition and powers of observation, to see who at the office, after all, was sleeping with whom. He covered the right-hand column with his hand, reading the men's names on the left and trying to guess what women's names could be underneath his palm. But out of the nearly twenty names he guessed right about only

two of them and another two whose relationships were evident to everyone, even without the list. The list wasn't worth much. *What does 'live
with' mean? A permanent or a temporary union? Do they have a family, or
not? Do they have affairs with anyone else at the same time? Where do they
meet? How often do these women change their men or the men the
women? Kashin should have acquainted himself with sociology before taking up this job! Kashin's a fool, an obliging fool. I should bear that in mind
and not overestimate him. Evidently, it wasn't just because of his injuries and
particular mistakes that he got transferred from the KGB to a civilian job.*
After memorizing the names Yagubov carefully tore the sheet into small
pieces and threw them back into the basket. He called for Anna. She
wasn't on the list.

'Get me Rappoport, please.'

She nodded and ran off, almost noticeably swaying her hips. Yagubov
lit another cigarette. He was being obliged to assert his authority at the
office in short order. People like Rappoport, known as 'unofficial leaders' in sociology, represented the greatest danger for him. The authority
of an unofficial leader, especially when he was such an ironical cynic,
would work against Yagubov's authority. He had to try to get Rappoport
moving down the desired channel. *It's a pity he wasn't on Kashin's list.*

'Hello.' Yagubov greeted Rappoport first, as he came in the door.
'Please, have a seat.'

Crossing the parquet with big, heavy steps Rappoport weightily tum-
bled into the armchair in the far corner of the office.

'What's up?' he muttered discontentedly, not saying hello back, half
looking at Yagubov and half at Lenin's portrait hanging above Yagubov.

Yagubov took it in his stride, as if it was supposed to be that way. 'The
newspaper's left without a head.'

'What does that have to do with me?'

'You and I are members of the newspaper's Party bureau,' Yagubov
reminded him. 'The main thing for us is not to let the level of the newspaper drop during the editor's absence. Don't you agree?'

Rappoport had completely given up looking at Yagubov and was now attentively peering at the window, even though there was nothing visible but greyish sky, since the lower panes were covered over for winter with paper strips. Feeling no contact with his visitor, Yagubov got even more tense but continued speaking without raising his voice.

'Makartsev considers you to be one of the most experienced journalists on the paper, while I'm just the new boy. Can I lean on you, count on you for support?'

'On me?' Rappoport raised his eyebrows. 'I can barely stand, myself!'

'Well, on whom, then, in your opinion?'

'Find something a bit younger.'

'No objection,' chuckled Yagubov, understanding that he wouldn't be able to catch Rappoport on his hook right away. 'We can draw in someone younger, too. But you – you're the brains here!'

Rappoport's lips twisted, preparing to issue something sarcastic. But his internal censor came on at that instant and prevented him from saying what had come into his mind.

'I may be laying it on thick,' said Yagubov, 'but I feel that we've just been playing games recently. We get blasted for that, Upstairs, and – let's be self-critical here – that is what we deserve; they are not being unfair. Let's think about it, have a discussion.'

'About what?'

'About initiating a big campaign. One that'll get *Trudovaya Pravda* talked about high and low. After all, I know it was you who suggested to Makartsev starting up the Movement for Communist Labour.'

Rappoport shrugged his shoulders. Once again he wanted to answer but held himself back. He just wheezed like an old clock that wanted to strike the hour but whose cogs wouldn't mesh and chimes wouldn't strike.

'When do you want to start your campaign?' asked Rappoport, suddenly. 'After Makartsev's return or before?'

The word 'your' stuck in Yagubov's craw. But the question had been asked in a businesslike fashion. 'Immediately!' he answered. 'If we've got an idea, why let it float around until some other newspaper picks up on it?'

Having answered, Yagubov realized that Rappoport's question had contained a dirty trick. Realizing what the trick was, he hurriedly added: 'Of course, all of our undertakings will go through Makartsev and be on his behalf. That's obvious.'

'That's what I was thinking.'

Yagubov got angry with himself for failing to best Rappoport, who was making God knows what out of himself. He couldn't resort to provocation, though.

'I don't respect Makartsev any less than you do,' he smiled affably, 'although I do know that you're on excellent terms with him.'

'I'm not on any terms with Makartsev!' Rappoport refused to acknowledge it, just in case. 'I wanted to clear up, as technical executive, whether or not your commission differs in any way from the editor's position, so that I won't be slogging away for nothing.'

'In what sense?'

'Recently Makartsev – even though he was talking about hot topics – was thinking that the newspaper shouldn't be making too much noise. Do you get me? In other words, we should be trying *not* to stand out. We made the paper no worse, but no better, than the others. You're proposing that we get talked about. But what if they talk in the wrong place, the wrong way?'

'Right!' Yagubov's ears pricked up, and he threw himself back in his chair in relief. 'The campaign that we're going to conduct will be, as I imagine it, not just worked out carefully but also carefully agreed to with the Big House. I'll take that on myself. So there shouldn't be any reason for you to worry.'

'I'm not worried for myself,' Rappoport noisily let the air out through his nose. 'For you.'

Yagubov couldn't understand whether Rappoport was saying this seriously or was mocking him. But he decided it would be better to take it seriously.

'So, we're in agreement?' He rose from behind the desk. 'Whenever they're needed, I'll allocate as many people for you as you want from other departments. The important thing is the idea!'

'Why exploit people?' Rappoport rose as well. 'I'll manage it myself, somehow.'

Yagubov spread his arms and said that any variant would suit him, and then firmly shook Rappoport's limp, gnarled hand. At the door Rappoport collided with Anna, running in at Yagubov's call.

'Your union dues haven't been paid for three months,' she whispered. Rappoport didn't answer; he'd vanished.

'Anna,' Yagubov asked immediately. 'What do you think: could I have a talk with Makartsev? Will the doctors let me?'

'I don't think so! Makartsev's wife told me that the doctors aren't letting anybody say a word to him – complete rest! Do you really need to? If so, maybe I should call his wife and ask.'

'It's not worth it. I'll go to the hospital myself. If anyone asks for me here at the office, tell them that I'm with Makartsev. Have them pull me some proofs of the pages that have already been typeset. I'll take them with me. And I'll be driving to the Big House from there, so I'll be away for a while.'

Yagubov spent less than ten minutes in the Kremlin hospital. He wrote out a note saying that he'd come to visit, that everything was fine at the paper and that the staff were waiting for their editor to get well as soon as possible.

He drove off with the sense of a duty fulfilled and the unpleasant acceptance that hospitals should have to exist at all. He was certain that they weren't for him. He was sorry for Makartsev. *Becoming a reserve player is a risky business. After an injury it isn't that easy to get back on to the front bench. Without a doubt, Makartsev was an honourable Party worker, but he was too sensitive. He acted like an intellectual, that is, he was simply behind the times. He worried about things immoderately, which was why he got sick.* Yagubov caught himself thinking about his editor in the past tense and decided that that was wrong. Makartsev would get better.

He drove to the Big House to coordinate plans. The sharp pine cones that had been falling on Makartsev's head would now fall on his. But he was certain that he would bear it more lightly and get more out of it. If only his staff didn't let him down. But not all of them were as undisciplined as Rappoport. And Yagubov, doubtless, had managed to draw him into the necessary furrow.

Coming out of Yagubov's office, Rappoport, drawn into the necessary furrow, tramped slowly down the corridor, the flaps of his unbuttoned jacket touching oncomers. The brains of the journalist Rappoport had already sifted through the peelings of his conversation, highlighted what was important and got to work, although externally Rappoport seemed as sleepy as always; he was thinking of accidental things that had no relation to the newspaper or to himself. Recently, ever since reading the entry in the *Great Soviet Encyclopaedia*, he had been thinking about the Fiji Islands. The country was a paradise. It was always warm there, and backs never cried out from the damp. There they had everything in the shops. And, most important, they retired at an early age. It would be even better, thought Rappoport, if there wasn't any written language on Fiji. That was how he took his holiday, on the hoof, wending his way back to his department. His stomach whined, demanding sustenance. Somebody called out to him just as he got to his door. He looked around. Nadya Sirotkina from the letters department was hurrying towards him.

'Can I come in?'

'Why the hell not? Come on in!' He waved a hand invitingly and slouched through the door first.

# 20

# Ascentless, Descentless
# Nadya Sirotkina

Whenever a new typist appeared at the newspaper, employees of the male gender would soon come up with a terrific need for the immediate dictation of an urgent article. Whoever was first to get the *Urgent/Today's Issue* pass from the secretarial office would then become possessor of whatever initial information there was about the new girl. Regardless of whether or not he was mistaken, or the typist just turned out not to be his type, his opinion would long define the relations of the male half of the newspaper to the new typist.

Nadya hadn't been lucky. Even though she was eighteen and a half when she arrived at the typing pool, she reeked of a thirteen-year-old naivety so strong that you couldn't even laugh at her. On her first day, when Nadya Sirotkina showed up at the typists' pool in the morning, the fat woman who ran it, Nonna Abeleva (everybody at the newspaper called her Colonel Abel, which really suited her), had sat her down at a desk and herself taken the cover off her Kontinental typewriter.

'I barely got here!' Nadya told her neighbours, who were restoring their makeup after their own journeys. 'It's terribly stuffy on the metro, so crowded, and they jam their elbows into your stomach! But, most of all, I was ashamed to be riding on it!'

'What do you mean, ashamed?'

'Everyone was looking at me and thinking: "The poor thing, she hasn't got money for a taxi!"'

There were all sorts of women among the newspaper's typists, except happy ones and well-to-do ones. Her carefree phrase had flown around the office even before the most curious of the men got his *Urgent/Today's Issue* pass. Nobody wanted to have anything to do with the daughter of a general.

Nadya was short and thin, maybe too thin. As a result of this, her breasts, which pointed to either side, seemed bigger than they really were, giving her a certain sexiness. She had a pleasant face, her brow and nose were straight, her cheeks and lips fresh, almost childlike. And her slender hands with their long fingers and her long legs could simply be considered beautiful. You could sense a lightness and simplicity about her. As for Nadya's way of thinking, it was something like a dandelion that nobody had blown on yet.

Nadya's mother had been a strong-willed person, and she had followed a programme for raising her daughter that she herself had never doubted. School: she had to get perfect grades; music: she had to play for four hours every day and give concerts on Sundays. For culture, visits to the Conservatory; for health, summers in the country and good food. If she was reading something, she had to say what it was. If she made friends with another girl, she had to tell who she was. Her mother had let the nearly grown Nadya out to see Moscow with her father on only one single occasion, while she stayed behind for another week at the health resort. She had written out daily schedules for her daughter, intending to check up on her at the end of the week. But the landing gear failed on the plane bringing her home. Nadya's father goaded the best medical help around into action, but her mother died without regaining consciousness. Nadya was a year away from finishing secondary school. Her father had always worked hard, and now he stopped sparing himself at all.

In accordance with her mother's dreams – that Nadya *had* to make come true – her prospects were entry either into the Conservatory or the Gnesin Academy. At the time she still looked on her classmates through her mother's eyes: they were wasting their time, not striving towards any goals. These qualities gradually began to assume a charm for Nadya, though: strolling the streets mindlessly was a hundred times more interesting than practising musical passages. But she was jangling away at the piano for four hours a day. Nadya continued to be governed by her mother's will even after her death, so she did apply to the Conservatory, but she failed her creativity examination. She tried her luck with the Gnesin Academy, but that didn't work either. Her father, using his connections, could have helped her get into some other college, but he refused to, now.

Nadya would get up late and slouch around the apartment all day. She was sick of striving. She was in a fortunate milieu, and she was living in the world's most advanced country, and she could enter any college she wanted to the following year. But she was existing in a vacuum right now. She was a Cinderella, an ugly duckling, and looking at herself in the mirror was the most revolting thing she could do. She kept the wardrobe door in her room open, so that its mirror was turned towards the wall.

One morning, when Nadya was wandering around the apartment in search of the source of a strange smell, she glanced into her father's room. On his bedside table stood a perfume flagon with a sharp odour. On the sofa next to it lay a glossy magazine. Nadya immediately discerned a naked woman on the cover in a pose that left no doubt about her intentions and two men ready to help her to realize them. Nadya threw the magazine across the room. Her head was spinning, and if she hadn't sat down right away on her father's bed she would have fallen unconscious to the carpet. After sitting awhile, Nadya again picked up the magazine and, in order to check out a suspicion that had crept into her mind, started looking for more such magazines in her father's room. There was a whole pile of them inside his bedside table. *That's how Father is amusing himself – shame on him! Mama would never have forgiven him for this!* Carrying the pile of magazines into her room she climbed back under her covers. Her heart was pounding, her head wouldn't stop spinning, she was trembling and couldn't get warm. Suddenly she imagined herself in the place of that woman, seized by those hairy arms. She wanted to scream, but she burst into tears. Nadya was shaking, the magazine trembled, but she kept leafing through the pages. She was almost eighteen, and no one had even kissed her on the mouth, to say nothing of the kind of kissing on display here in these magazines. Nadya would die from a single kiss like that; she wouldn't be able to go on living. But what if she remained alive? That would be even worse. Because she wouldn't be able to go on living like before.

Nadya leafed through the pages in a sort of trance. She fell asleep, slept for a while, then got up and looked over her features carefully in the mirror, as if she were meeting herself for the first time. She took the magazines back to her father's room. Her head was throbbing with pain. Nadya chewed an aspirin tablet, then made herself a cup of coffee. She gradually calmed down, but now thoughts about her not being a woman yet, while life kept going on anyhow, kept running through her mind. How could she have remained a child until she was fully grown? She was getting older, after all. Nadya went out and wandered around the streets, not knowing why, looking over the men and women. She rang her school girlfriends, but they were busy. A day later, though, Nadya managed to see one of them, Katya, to share her alarm. They went to the Kosmos café on Gorky Street, and each ordered ice cream and a glass of champagne.

'What are you, from the moon?'

It turned out that Katya had tried everything, more than once. They talked about jobs. Katya's mother worked as a proofreader at the *Trudovaya Pravda* office.

'Go there. Mama said they need typists. There's lots of men there, all kinds.' Katya burst out laughing.

That evening Nadya told her father that she was going to get a job.

'What do you want to do that for?'

'I want to be a journalist, Papa! I've thought things through. This is my calling.'

Her father looked at her attentively. 'But you don't know how to do anything!'

'I'll learn. My fingers are nimble enough – and I've heard that they need typists at the newspaper. They won't take me in off the street, but if you . . .'

'All right, I'll try.'

Kashin, the managing editor, got a phone call asking him to take on a typist who had no experience but who was educated and from a good background. As a result of the typists' discussions about relationships with men, Nadya grew up quickly, but she remained strictly a theorist without experience. Any ease she had in sexual relations was only in words. In reality, she wanted to get hooked up with some man, to think about him, talk to him. Some did make advances, although they were afraid of her naivety. But she thought that if they weren't serious that meant that something was lacking in her. They gradually stopped calling her the general's daughter, although sometimes her father's chauffeur would still give her a lift to work.

On the recommendation of the newspaper she entered night school at Moscow University's journalism faculty. She could have enrolled in the day course, but she didn't feel like leaving the office. She'd been promoted to the position of tally clerk in Letters, and she'd started earning ten roubles more per month. Her wages were enough for the nylons that she snagged every day. When they had ladders she would throw nylons away that others would have stitched up.

Nadya's views were taking shape. Politics – that was what everyone wrote about and talked about, all around her. It didn't concern her. She lived by butterfly logic: live for the day! What kind of joy had there been today? Who did you like? Who liked you? Out of worries such as these Nadya grew prettier; she started demanding nice things from her father more often. She held on to her desires and waited. But you can't go on like that endlessly.

Nadya was afraid even to say his name to herself. What made it worse was that there was nothing special about him. He related to her amicably enough but without any special marks of attention. He was the one who had advised her to take the journalism course, but then he never even asked if she had gone ahead and done it. Nadya knew that he was married and that he had a six-year-old son. He could walk on foot with her through half of Moscow, chatting away, but later on not even notice her in the corridor for two weeks.

Now she never opened the magazines kept in her father's bedside table any more. 'It could only be that way with *him*, with Ivlev!' Nadya told herself. For a long time now she'd been ready either for an ascent or a fall. But no one had invited her for the one or the other.

# 21

# The Secret of the Magic Trick

Nadya went in behind Rappoport and stopped at the door in indecision.

'There's a letter . . . Everyone's laughing, nobody wants to take it. I thought maybe you could sign for it? It's right for an article.'

'What sort of letter, little one?'

'A girl in her last year of secondary school writes that she's dreaming of becoming a journalist.'

Rappoport, stretching out one hand to Nadya as if asking a boon, pulled his glasses out of his jacket pocket with the other and glanced at the return address recorded by Nadya on the receipt card. 'Oh, Nadya, Nadya, you merchant's daughter! I wish I had problems like yours, mademoiselle!' Rappoport was just grumbling in passing, tenderly, his thoughts not concentrated on the letter. Nevertheless, he unfolded the exercise-book page and started reading it aloud.

'"*Dear Sir or Madam: Please advise me how to become a real journalist. What attracts me to this profession? I want to see life, I want to love people, I want to write for them. Not a day without a line that someone needs! Lots of people will say that this is the romanticism of youth. But I love the smell of a just-received newspaper, I love the rustle of its all-knowing pages. And it seems to me that I will be able to extract the truth from life and present to people what I have managed to absorb from reading your newspaper. Valya Kozlova.*"'

'Naive, eh?' asked Nadya.

Rappoport set aside the sheet of paper and, removing his glasses, scrutinized Sorotkina attentively – her skinny knees, her too-sharp shoulders, her disproportionately large bosom and her pretty head, framed by her unbound hair.

'Not in the slightest! A very intelligent letter. Surely you and I want to see life and love people? And want to write for them? She should be informed that if she becomes a journalist she will really very soon extract all the truth from life and give other people the gift of whatever she's managed to absorb. As for the smell of the newspaper, that's just poetic licence. There's a smell all right and what a one! As a budding journalist you're quite capable of answering it yourself.'

'I've wanted to ask you for a long time,' Nadya took the letter he was holding out. 'Don't you believe in what you're writing about? How can you write it if you don't?'

'How charming you are!'

'How can you do that, understanding everything?'

'That's just it – understanding everything, I understand that I have to do what everyone does! You're surprised that I write. Well, I'm surprised that people stand in queues for their newspapers and read what I write! Give me your word that you won't tell your highly placed papa what I'm going to tell you now.'

'I don't tell him anything!' Nadya pouted, offended.

'Good girl! Here's what: as a friend of mine said – I used to be a Communist, but now I'm a "Come-money-ist".'

'What's that?'

'Something. Like your reader, I love to hear the rustle. Only not of pages but of banknotes!'

'You're slandering yourself! Or do you take me for an idiot?'

'Well, what is a newspaper? Have they told you at the journalism department?'

'Sort of . . .'

'Sort of like this: the original form of the word "gazette" in the eighteenth century, in Italy, I think, signified "small coins". And so people who make newspapers are small-coiners. And who writes letters to newspapers?'

'Well, people with complaints . . .' Nadya started enumerating. 'And those who aren't very bright ask for advice about how to live. And semi-literate pensioners with nothing to do passionately support and approve of things . . .'

'Nadya, you're almost a sociologist!' Rappoport said approvingly. 'I underestimated you. And what do you do with letters criticizing . . . er . . . our beloved Soviet system?'

'I don't register them, and I give them to the department editor?'

'And what does he do?'

'I think he takes them to the deputy editor-in-chief.'

'You think? You're such a charmer, Nadya! But do you remember the letter about how our Leader should retire? Where's the author of that letter? He's in jail, Nadya. Who put him in jail? Have you thought about that? And the lecturer from the Yaroslavl Institute who wrote to our newspaper suggesting that food from the provincial committee refreshment room be sent to nursery schools? We forwarded the letter to the provincial committee, and the committee expelled the poor lecturer from the Party for slandering them. His students went to the committee to explain that their instructor was a good man, but they locked them into a room and called for a KGB squad. They aren't students any more, Nadya. And you say "I think".'

'What am I supposed to do, then?'

'You? I don't know. You need a man, Nadya.'

'What do you mean?' she blushed instantly.

'Here's what. A normal, cynical man, something like myself. Only twenty years or so younger. He'll explain it all to you. Readers' letters won't help you grow up. True, naivety is a compensation. Whoever wins you will get a cornucopia of delight.'

'I'm an old maid.'

'That deficiency, Nadya, can be overcome in the shortest time possible, believe me! One *subbotnik* – and everything's sorted. Kiss-kiss!'

Escorting Nadya to the door with his eyes, he thought that he wouldn't mind a piece of this spotless and good-looking girl. The obstacle wasn't that she was young enough to be his son's girlfriend. It was in his internal indifference. *Old age isn't years of age. Old age is when you ask, 'What do I need this for?'* Rappoport stretched out luxuriously, clasping his hands behind his head. His gaze fell on his desk calendar. *Is there any sort of date there that I could peg something on? Yagubov is raring to plunge ahead while Makartsev's still confined to his bed. How to avoid helping* Parteigenosse *Yagubov?*

Out of an utter absence of fresh ideas Rappoport began leafing through the calendar. He came to a halt at the date of the Paris Commune. *Maybe we could call on the Soviet people to join in a little rebellion as a gesture of solidarity with the French proletariat?* The idea wasn't bad, but his back still hadn't recovered from the bunks in the camps. *Maybe everyone should blast off into space on 12 April in honour of the first flight of my friend Gagarin? But if there isn't anything here to guzzle down, there isn't even anything to breathe, up there! And what's this?* 'On the night of 13–14 April 1919 twenty Communists at the Moscow Sorting Depot repaired steam locomotives for free.' That was the first *subbotnik*, a wageless field-day where everybody pitched in. *Wait a minute! Exactly fifty years ago. So, what if . . . Nadya, my precious, you've given me an idea!* Across the top of the front page of that morning's *Trudovaya Pravda* was an enormous picture of the Soviet leaders embracing the new Czech ones who had made the trip to Moscow unlike their predecessor.

'Dear hearts!' Rappoport said tenderly to them all. 'I'll invite you, too, to come and work on my *subbotnik*.'

Pulling a ten-rouble note out of his wallet, he transferred it to his pocket. That was the advance that Rappoport immediately paid himself for the idea. The articles calling people to the *subbotnik* would go on the front page, jumping the queue. He'd have to come to some arrangement with Yagubov to be paid the maximum rate, taking into account his efficiency. *Subbotniks* were unpaid, therefore it would be better to earn more before it started.

Rappoport was an experienced campaign-deployment specialist; he knew that the preparation for one consisted of three acts. Act One was thinking up a new campaign and getting the Party organs to agree to it. Act Two demanded first of all the clandestine definition of the candidacy of those who would pick up on the slogan as if it were their own and then those who, with great fervour, would latch on to the patriotic summons of the first lot. Then came Act Three: the newspaper openly wrote about it, and the Party organs would publicly approve the popular campaign.

The journalist Rappoport had no real desire to be the inventor of the latest dirty trick to be played on the Soviet people. He decided to assign himself the role of eyewitness. Therefore he dug around in his notebooks and found a phone number for Balyakin, the Party committee secretary for the Moscow Sorting Depot.

'Listen. We've heard about your idea for holding a *subbotnik* in honour of the fiftieth anniversary of Lenin's first unpaid Saturday overtime. So I just want to tell you: the paper's with you all the way. Just keep me posted.'

Party Committee Secretary Balyakin didn't have any such notion. But he had already been in his position for two years and dreamed of getting on the district committee. He interpreted the *Trudovaya Pravda* idea as a guide to action and began picking out people for it. An hour later he called Rappoport back. They agreed that the depot's Party committee would prepare a plan of action and get it approved at the city committee. And Rappoport would send along a reporter.

'So which Saturday is it going to be on?' asked Balyakin.

Rappoport leafed through his desk calendar.

'Let's do it on the one closest to the anniversary – 19 April. Get a log ready.'

'What log?'

'Well, Lenin personally carried a log at his *subbotnik*. It could be that some of the most important comrades might come by.'

Rappoport rapped on the hook with his finger and straight away dialled another number.

'Zakamorny? Did I wake you? Good thing I've scared you up, old man. Did you say you needed some money? Come on over, pal.'

# — 22 —
## The Ellipse of
## Maksim Zakamorny

Zakamorny was a man with quirks. This had been observable in him since his childhood.

His father, Pyotr Zakamorny, drafted into the army from the Vinnitsa region, rose to the rank of commissar in the border-guard troops of the OGPU thanks to his wits and energy, and was sent on a special mission to the Far East. From the very furthest point of the country, separated from Alaska by the narrow Bering Strait, had come denunciations about the local inhabitants – Eskimos who earned their living hunting and catching fish – who, despite the propaganda that had been disseminated in their Little Red Schooltents, were brazenly crossing the strait to see their relatives in Alaska and coming back again. It fell to Commissar Pyotr Zakamorny to end this violation of the Soviet border, which was supposed to be locked up tight.

One day the motor launch of the border guards (organized locally by the commissar) was chasing after a boatload of Eskimos. The latter got angry about these busybodies intruding into their personal lives, passed down to them by the traditions of their ancestors, and started shooting. Commissar Zakamorny was seriously wounded. But he turned out to be the only one left alive on the border-guard launch. The Eskimos had never learned how to shoot to miss. The Commissar, unconscious from loss of blood, was picked up by them and taken to Alaska. There they took care of him, and when he had recovered they brought him back. The polar night had set in. Vessels, rare enough when it was warm, had by now completely stopped coming. The daughter of the Little Red Skin-tent's owner looked after Pyotr. She attached herself to him and never let him out of her sight. Soon a baby was born – Maksim. The Eskimos offered to let Pyotr stay, but duty called the commissar back to the OGPU. Returning to Moscow with his wife and son in just over a month, he went with his entire family to report his survival to his superiors. The boy was about two years old.

At Lubyanka Square the son plucked at his father's hand. Pyotr unbuttoned his son's trousers and positioned him near the wall, so as not to intrude on passers-by, and a thin stream ran down the pavement. Instantly a man in a dark overcoat and cap appeared. 'What are you doing?' he demanded. 'Don't you know what building this is?'

'I know,' said Zakamorny. 'But the boy couldn't hold it any longer.'

'You knew, but you did it anyway? Let's go.'

They detained the three of them. Pyotr Zakamorny was no shrinking violet, though. He demanded that they contact his superiors. The heads of the border guards were surprised that Commissar Zakamorny was still alive. They freed him straight away, but the sky darkened when the commissar, not concealing anything, told the unvarnished truth. As it happened, the Eskimo voyages abroad were continuing, and not long before they had shot down a coastguard plane. It turned out that Commissar Zakamorny had not only left his mission unfulfilled but had run off abroad with the criminals.

OGPU Commissar Pyotr Zakamorny – it came out at the same time that he was the son of a *kulak*, a member of the proscribed rich peasant class – was sentenced to be shot, while his wife was given imprisonment for a ten-year stretch, to which was added a further ten years. She died somewhere in Vorkuta. Maksim Zakamorny turned out to be the best off of the three hundred children at the KGB orphanage in the Arkhangel province town to which they sent him: at least he had his own first and last name. In addition, his parents had left him in good physical and spiritual health, which helped him overcome not only hunger and rickets but the mental poverty of the people who were raising him, as well. An orphanage creature, Zakamorny always wrote in his documents that he was a former homeless waif who had been set on the straight and narrow by the Soviets. Thanks to that, he was able to enrol at Timiryazev Agricultural Academy after the war.

There, a year before the end of his studies at the academy, he accidentally found himself at a *soirée* organized, as it turned out, by some comrades from the MGB, who had been given the task of uncovering some kind of student anti-Soviet organization. During the subsequent investigation he learned that he had been plotting an attempt on the lives of Comrade Lysenko and other leading representatives of the agrobiological sciences when he was sitting at the table and drinking while the others danced. The evidence was irrefutable: everyone else had been with their girlfriends, while he had not. His life history came to light, too. Six of them got ten years each; Zakamorny, as leader of the organization and a plutocrat stooge to boot, got twenty years. In the Vorkuta camps Zakamorny had searched the faces of oncoming women, looking for his mother.

He left his health behind in the construction of mineshafts for underground nuclear tests (there was secrecy about that in the release certificate as well, since the prisoners had only been digging coal, supposedly, at the institution indicated in his record). But they hadn't managed to irradiate him; the tests began later on. Released from the camps, Zakamorny lucked into a job as the manager of a dance hall for freelance civilian workers at the settlement for Mineshaft No. 40 of the Vorkutugol complex. He'd picked up a Bible from an exiled priest, and he read it during the evening to the strains of foxtrots and tangos, sitting in his tiny cubicle, tearing himself away only to change the records.

The dance-hall manager had even more free time daily before 7 p.m. With nothing to do, he started reading the English-language textbooks of his landlady's son and soon started talking English to himself. Zakamorny would pace around his room, shifting flashcards made of little bits of paper from pocket to pocket, and later on taught himself French and German, too. The further he got, the faster he went, language after language. He would draw hieroglyphs all over his hands.

Zakamorny discovered from the newspapers that his father had been posthumously rehabilitated. He was made a Hero of the Civil War, a liberator of the Ukraine from the Whites. As it says in Luke, '*And the Last shall be the First.*' Twenty-nine years after his birth Zakamorny was now the son of a hero. He decided to return to Moscow, to enrol back in (with difficulty) and graduate from (without difficulty) the academy that he had been snatched out of.

The former dance-hall manager brought along a little weakness with him from Vorkuta. There he had learned to drink glassfuls of badly filtered Moskovskaya vodka, the product of the local Vorkuta spirituous-liquors plant. He would drink it along with the other plutocrat stooges. Those of them who were left alive shook it off little by little, crawling out from under the Lysenko rubbish compactor.

The old experimental genetics laboratory was reborn in Moscow in the guise of an essentially new organization. Zakamorny was taken on there, but he had neither a residence permit nor a flat to live in. They told him that it would be easier for him to defend his dissertation and get a residence permit if he joined the Party. And, true, he did defend it easily enough and organized a grand banquet at the Praga restaurant, something that the geneticists recalled with a special tenderness in later days when banquets like that were forbidden. Zakamorny himself didn't remember it: out of happiness and hunger he had got drunk at the beginning of the ceremonies, passed out in the men's lavatory and been carried home by his friends.

The subject of his dissertation concerned him personally as well. According to Zakamorny (supported by statistics and the theory of prob-ability), the mass exterminations of the foremost representatives of culture, art and science as well as that part of the population who were the more industrious and goal-oriented in the country – peasants, workers, administrators, and military – had resulted in the entire genotype of people who were the most expedient for the development and flourish-ing of the state being exterminated as well. The worst were left, and they began reproducing their kind, filling up the vacuum. The train had been derailed and was heading for the precipice. Society was degenerating at an accelerated socialistic pace.

None of this found its way into his dissertation, of course. The work was of a purely academic character, drily relating the multiplication and degeneration of *drosophilus* flies, which, as it said in the foreword, was a species that lent itself to the execution of any task entrusted to science at the recent Party congress.

Meanwhile, Zakamorny had grown a beard and was scraping by, every six months extending his temporary Moscow residence permit by means of a bribe. He rented a room in a communal apartment on Malaya Gruzinskaya, not far from the Tishinsky market, a triangular room with a window looking out on a narrow courtyard. Because he didn't have a permanent residence permit his landlady took a ten-rouble bill off him in addition, splitting it with the local policeman.

'*In that selfsame city*,' as it says in Luke, '*there dwelt a widow*.' Our polyglot geneticist's lab assistant introduced him to her. Zakamorny's new acquaintance hadn't been married for very long, you could almost say she hadn't been at all – her husband had drowned when drunk shortly after they got married. But she worked as a *manekenshchitsa* at the Central Models' House on Kuznetsky Most and was preparing to become a fashion-design artist. Long-legged and somewhat mannered, which really rather suited her, she looked best of all from a distance and from a little below, as if she had been born especially for the catwalks of Models' House. She called Zakamorny a great scientist.

In the tiny room that he took her back to after the Yakor restaurant, which was located not very far from his building, she sat on the edge of his bed with her knees clenched tightly together. The biological sciences doctoral candidate had barely tried passing a hand through her airspace when she moved away.

'You're going to spoil the whole thing! It'd be better if you told me about yourself.'

There was a husband candidate in him, she felt. And the poet in him woke up. Zakamorny got down on his knees and, in a whisper, so that his landlady wouldn't hear, intoned:

> *'Eyes front, my heart all stormy,*
> *Your tender mouth I spy before me,*
> *Eyes down, my shame so vast,*
> *I see your soul-beguiling arse.'*

'Wonderful,' she laughed resonantly. 'But "arse" – surely you can't put that in a poem?'

'Yours I can!'

He stretched out on the floor, admiring her from below, foreshortened, which really suited her. They went down to the registry office, and then the happy couple set off to spend their honeymoon in Pitsunda on their own. On the third day, lying on the sand at the seashore, his wife took out a sheet of paper and a pen and started writing a letter to a girlfriend.

'Don't distract me!' she said, turning away from him. 'When you look at me like that, my thoughts go all over the place.'

'Fine. I won't,' he said, smiling, and went in for a swim.

That evening some people they had met on the beach invited them out to a restaurant. Zakamorny said that he'd forgotten to shine his shoes and went back to their place. He opened up her bag and took out the letter. *'We've had good luck with the weather,'* he read. *'As far as Zakamorny goes, you're right, after all: he's a nothing.'* At dinner Zakamorny was cheerful; he recited them some new poems, and at the end he poured everyone a drink himself and solemnly declared: 'Ladies and gentlemen, I ask you to raise your glasses. Let's drink to my wife's and my divorce!'

He took the letter out of his pocket, held it in his hands. He read the fright in her eyes, so he didn't read the letter aloud but tore it into pieces and dropped them into the ashtray.

*'Yea, some amongst our womenfolk have astounded us,'* he quoted from Luke sadly, then quietly walked out and flew back to Moscow.

Having lost faith in women, Zakamorny became, in his own expression, a 'mass-licker'. He wrote an amusing and popular book about genetics, won a prize for it and stayed drunk for a whole month on the prize money.

When Zakamorny, disillusioned with all women, met an actress from the Central Children's Theatre who played boys' parts – a boyish-looking matchstick who burst into flame at his touch – he tried to escape from her, but she telephoned him. 'Everything that's mine is yours,' she said. He had nearly acquired an inferiority complex, but with the boy-actress's help he realized that he wasn't a loser, after all, but a man. They saw each other during the day, in between her rehearsals and her shows. He grew younger in her company, began to have faith in himself and decided that he wouldn't ever get married again, so that he wouldn't have to worry about getting a divorce. He worked out a formula by which fat women were what he needed in winter and thin ones in summer. In winter he would cultivate a beard for warmth, and in summer he would shave. He would drink eighty-proof booze in winter, while in summer he could have fortified wines, too, because Hippocrates himself had said that in summer you add wine to water, while in winter you add water to wine. All his remaining aims were abolished, since they fettered his freedom of desire.

There had been changes, meanwhile, at the laboratory where Senior Scientific Worker Zakamorny was paid the salary necessary for the realization of certain of his desires. The boss had made his peace with the Lysenkoites, entered the ranks of academicians and been appointed director of an institute. A former Party organizer, who was aiming to be a corresponding member of the Academy of Sciences, became director of the laboratory. He took up Zakamorny's old topic and included it in his plan, formulated thus: 'The genetic basis of *Homo sovieticus*, the builder of Communism, as the summit of the range of human genotypes.'

'Genotypes is your topic?' the new lab head asked Zakamorny.

'Topic seems to be mine. But the conclusions . . .'

'The conclusions need not worry you! You lay down the basics, and we'll find somebody else to reach the conclusions. We've included your topic under Position Six, so that bourgeois scientists won't be able to use your discoveries to improve their own genotypes. Fill out the form, and we'll get you access to your stuff.'

After a four-month check Zakamorny was allowed access to his own material, which now bore the legend 'Top Secret'.

But he never started work on it. That day there was a rally at the lab, dedicated to the workers' unanimous approval of fraternal aid for the Czechs. Zakamorny, sitting in the back row, was still preoccupied by the fate of his genotypes and didn't notice how all the rest of his scientific co-workers had begun their unanimous vote of approval.

'Any abstentions?' asked the former Party organizer and present lab head, just to be able to declare instantly, 'Adopted unanimously!'

Zakamorny mechanically raised his hand, which looked as though he was the only one to abstain, and that meant that he didn't approve the resolution. Truth to tell, he got a fright himself. But the Party organizer decided that, as someone of greater ideological conviction, he would be better at finishing the work on the *Homo sovieticus* genotype and Zakamorny would only get in the way. Zakamorny's abstention became known to the various authorities, after which he was expelled from the Party, fired from his job and deprived of his rank as doctoral candidate in biological sciences.

He was left with his own sense of propriety. He came to the conclusion that this unpleasantness had befallen him just in time. It even started to seem to him that he had abstained on purpose during the voting and had proven that the genotype of M. Zakamorny was a top-notch one. And the others were all just 'money-changers in the Temple'. Freedom from the obligation of putting in his hours at the lab opened up two paths before him: he could become a thoroughgoing drunk or else take up theology. He decided to go down both roads. Zakamorny – alternately carried away and cooling off – was by turns a Christian, a Buddhist, a yogi, a Zionist, a Nietzschean and a Seventh-Day Adventist; he com-bined the philosophies of Schopenhauer, Leontiev and Berdyaev. Whoever's book was the latest he succeeded in obtaining on the sly was the man he worshipped.

'In essence, I'm a Marxist-anti-Communist and an atheist-believer,' he would explain to his friends over a bottle. 'Most of all, I'm grateful to the Party for kicking me out. Life isn't that complicated, after all: drunk in the morning, free all day.'

Zakamorny liked to waste time on things that were absolutely unnecessary. He had been turning sour from constraints. His tastes fluctuated. Just yesterday he had been demanding a new revolution for Russia, while today he was enthused with the idea of erecting a monument to the unmasked Comrade Stalin.

'Just think! After all, nobody has ever promoted the discrediting of an ideal the way he has!'

Afraid of forgetting it, he hurried to impart this fleeting notion to others as quickly as possible. With the man sitting next to him on the metro he discussed the issue of whether or not to write a letter proposing the introduction of new badges of rank. On the shoulderboards of state security officers, replace the little stars with little keyholes: one keyhole for a major, three for a colonel.

'You realize they're going to put you away,' his friends warned.

And at that he bawled: 'You're a bunch of scaredy-cats! It's because of you they get to do that sort of thing!' As a result, his friends became a lot fewer, then few, and finally he had none at all.

At the cafeteria, the out-patient clinic and the shop that he patronized, where they would call him names, Zakamorny would pull a sticker out of his pocket that said 'Boors at work here' and slap it on the wall. He got away with it. But then one day he went out of his house with his beard, his moustache and his hair completely shaven off the left half of his face and head, the right side with its normal growth. This was, from his point of view, a way of proclaiming the new two-faced mode, peculiarly Russian. He was taken down to the police station, where they shaved off the rest of his hair, put him in the slammer for fifteen days for minor hooliganism and threatened to exile him from Moscow for parasitism. His landlady refused to give him back his room. He spent his nights after that at his lady friends', compiling a list a month in advance and giving them due warning when he would be sleeping at their place.

His money ran out, and he went to the *Trudovaya Pravda* office to see if he could write something or translate something from 'foreign' into 'Soviet'. Rappoport would print the stuff over one of the multitude of Zakamorny's pen names or without any signature at all. Zakamorny had left genetics behind, left politics behind and had no faith in any trendy theory of activity. The night before, he had written in green marker pen on the belly of his new lover, just a little below her navel: 'Can't get better than this.' She understood it in her own way and was happy.

# School for Canaries

'Anybody else around?'

Zakamorny stuck his flat head through the partly open door. It looked as though somebody had squeezed it and his head had been flattened. Coming further in, he leaned against the doorway. Rappoport took off his glasses and wiped his eyes wearily. It suddenly occurred to him that Makartsev's grey folder might well have been planted on him by Zakamorny. Everything fitted: the naivety of it, the impudence and the knowledge of French. *Maybe I should ask him straight? But Zakamorny's eccentric, he won't give me a straight answer. If he wanted to, he'd say something about it himself.* And, besides, what business was it of Rappoport's?

'Come in, my good friend,' Rappoport said cordially. 'There's a chance of some work for you.'

'The dustman wants to form a co-op with the jeweller!'

'Hang on!' Rappoport glanced at his watch. 'Indifferent health – that's the only thing I have left.' He pulled a little packet of cheese out of his briefcase and tossed a pinch of tea each into two cups. He poured the boiling water into them and cut the cheese in half.

'You got anything to drink? My head's still splitting from yesterday's hangover.'

'A healthy head, if you can stand it long enough. Wait a bit longer, old friend, until you earn something – and then get drunk.'

'Get drunk? I'm giving up drink entirely! Tell me, where is the money?'

'You can help us organize a *subbotnik.*'

'A *subbotnik* is unpaid. And I'm serious.'

'It's unpaid for other people. But for you and me it's serious. There was a fire chief doing time in the camp with me. One day he'd got a call from a newspaper, and they said that the city Party committee had noted the good work of the fire department and decreed that it be covered in the press. So a reporter would be coming by to photograph the firemen at work. The fireman told them: "You're welcome, to be sure. Come on by. But we don't have any fires for you." "Why not?" they asked. "Because we do good work." "All right," the newspaper people responded, "we'll wait. If something catches fire, call us at once." They called him back two days later. "You're lucky. There's a fire. We're on our way." "Fine," said the people at the newspaper, "but don't put it out until we get there. Remember: this is by direction of the city committee!" The firemen laughed. The reporter showed up, but the fire was already extinguished.'

'So what did they put away the fire chief for?'

'For frustrating a decree of the city Party committee. What else? So get out there while there's still a fire burning, and work it up.'

'How much do you want me to *fartlander* up?'

'What?' Rappoport didn't understand.

'Write up.'

'Did you think that up yourself? I'll put it to good effect! Two hundred lines, nothing less. I've already organized a rally for you.'

'I never understood before', mused Zakamorny, 'how these semi-literate people manage to regurgitate from the lectern whole ready-made chunks of whatever it is they're expected to.'

'And now you get it?' asked Rappoport with a smirk.

'Yep. Do you know how they teach young canaries to sing? They put one into a cage with experienced ones who know how to sing. And the youngster begins to copy the older ones. Our journalists are typical canaries. They hear something and then they repeat it, over and over, never going into the significance of it. Did you ever give any thought, Rappoport, to where executive types come from?'

'Another biological association, I guess?'

'They used to get rid of rats aboard ship this way. First the sailors would catch four rats in traps, then move the traps together in pairs and open up the doors. The rats would throw themselves on each other, and the two that were the strongest and most vicious would bite the weaker ones to death. Then they'd catch two more rats and stick them in the cages. And then another two. The remaining two most bloodthirsty and aggressive rats were set free, starving. They would disappear down the rat-holes and kill any rat who wasn't ready to fight.'

'I'm sick of your biology!' muttered Rappoport. He started thinking about the grey folder again. *Well, you keep samizdat in a safe place. Why come out with it? It'll just start plaguing everybody.* 'Have you heard that there's a manuscript doing the rounds here?'

'I haven't. If you come across it, give it to me. I'm off to your *subbotnik* now.'

'Hang on! It won't ring any bells without a photo. I'll call Kakabadze.'

# The Theory and Practice of
# Sasha Kakabadze

The previous year Kakabadze had spent his annual holiday in the town of Gagry in the Caucasus. When the resort season was over, he and his mother had rented a small room by the sea. By day he and his mother would go to the market, and Kakabadze would cautiously avoid the barrel of wine where a lively Azerbaijani dealt his wares. The man's donkey was tied up alongside. On the day of their arrival Kakabadze had gone up to the barrel to sample a glass of real country wine. The queue was moving unhurriedly. A portrait of Stalin had been stuck to the barrel. Everyone who got to try the wine first had to toast the Leader, hopping the rim of their glass off the forehead of the portrait and only then drinking it down. But Kakabadze lifted his glass straight to his lips.

'Why you no go and toast Stalin?' the salesman shouted. 'You no like Georgian, right?'

'I *am* a Georgian,' said Kakabadze. 'And you're not.'

'I Azerbaijan man, right? That Caucasus, too. Russia spoil you. Who live in Caucasus must to love Stalin!'

Shrugging his shoulders, Kakabadze toasted the portrait with the rest of his wine and drank to the repose of his soul. But he didn't want to do it again, because of his father, Shalva Kakabadze. His father had been an art historian. In the thirties he'd been the first to propose the removal from the Museum of Pictorial Arts in Tbilisi of the canvases of those artists whose works didn't reflect the image of Lenin's most faithful pupil.

By a happy coincidence, the museum was located in the same building that had earlier been the Tiflis Seminary. As it became known from the autobiography of the Great Leader of All Peoples, written by the man himself, while the other seminarists were praying the Leader was off organizing Marxist study groups. The museum had filled up with canvases portraying Comrade Stalin at various ages. True, this didn't save Shalva Kakabadze from arrest. Kakabadze was about a year old when his father was imprisoned.

Aida, his frail wife, who had worked in the museum as well, was helped by relatives to get a job selling things at the bazaar. Aida began earning lots of money, but it wasn't enough for her. She did things energetically: she gave short weight, sold black market goods, learned how to short-change people. Kakabadze's mother saved up a whole fortune and – who knew what could happen? – travelled off to the camp her husband was in and bought his freedom. According to the documents, the prisoner Shalva Kakabadze had been killed during an escape attempt. But Shalva Kakabadze himself, with the passport of one Pavel Korkia – who had in fact served out his sentence for swindling but had been murdered by thieves – was released from custody. Back in Tbilisi this passport was exchanged for another with a different birthplace, once again for large sums of money. His mother then registered her marriage for the second time.

They left Georgia for the Urals, so as not to run into any acquaintances. After the war they moved to Moscow, where his father taught the history of Soviet pictorial art at a theatre school. When Kakabadze was full grown his father left them and married one of his students. Kakabadze junior wasn't about to get married, though, even if Aida very much wanted him to.

'Look how many girls there are in Moscow,' she would say. 'Even your father couldn't restrain himself. And you? If I could persuade him to leave me, it's long past time that you did! Your father, when he was young, had a whole harem, and I never objected because I knew he loved me most of all! What kind of a Kakabadze are you if you can't seduce girls?'

'Calm down, Ma,' Kakabadze tried to make her see reason. 'I could, but I don't have the time.'

His time did, strangely, fly. This completely impractical and quiet

Georgian would suddenly announce things to the whole office – such as his being able to lift a barbell weighing two and a quarter hundredweight. 'You don't believe me, I'll make you a bet!'

Three people eagerly took the bet and then four. These were the conditions: if Kakabadze couldn't lift a barbell with the designated weight he would pay them ten roubles apiece. They all got into a taxi and drove off to the Palace of Weight Lifting. They went to the manager and showed him their newspaper credentials. He laughed when he learned what the request was for and led them into the gym. Muscular sportsmen hung the required weights on the barbell and stepped aside. Puny Kakabadze was left one on one on the dais with the barbell. He bravely laid his slender hands on it, with a jerk heaved away at it and, making a supreme effort, tried to get it up to his chest. After two or three tries he silently stepped off the dais, red and blotchy.

'I'll give you your money on payday, lads.'

So he paid up the ten roubles to everyone, honest as could be. He didn't say anything to his mother, so as not to upset her, and earned some money on the side to get her money to her as usual. He himself starved until his next payday. But three days after getting their pay packets he discovered that he could read thoughts at a distance. They waved him away, sorry for him. But he wouldn't give ground: 'Honest to God, I'll give you every second thought you have. Don't you want to bet? If I lose, I'll pay up, five roubles apiece to everybody.'

Kakabadze had become a photographer by accident. After his ten years of secondary school he was conscripted into the army, and he took his camera with him. His favourite trick was taking people's pictures without any film in his camera. But then his division commander ordered him to photograph his family, and any trickery would have landed him in a punishment cell. So he had to put some film in the camera. To the surprise of Kakabadze, the pictures turned out quite well. From that time on there was no retreating from his officers. The division newspaper started printing his photos. When a reporter from *Trudovaya Pravda* showed up, they wouldn't allow him to photograph anything inside the base without a special permit. But Kakabadze's ready-made photographs at the paper's office were already cleared by the military censors.

So *Trudovaya Pravda* started printing Private Kakabadze's photographs after that, whenever there was a military holiday. After demobilization he was taken on as a freelance by the art department. He worked without wages but received a royalty for any pictures of his that were published.

He easily learned how to take pictures of whatever was called for. Exemplary workers, who, smiling, either gazed at their machines or stood with their backs to them (there couldn't be any third variant), builders, collective farmers – he brought them all in on miles of film, printed them up in batches, never grudged the rejections and was ready once again to go wherever he had to. But as soon as Kakabadze had mastered his profession it started to bore him. He would rather have published the candid photographs that were taking up more and more of his time. Street scenes, paupers, the beggars at small-town bazaars, the stupid faces on the drunken workers who, cackling, had surrounded them during the photographing of an exemplary worker nominated by the local Party committee. But Kakabadze only ever saw candid shots like that in foreign magazines. For amusement he'd started collecting photos of Party and government personages he had had to photograph at various sessions and ceremonies and during meetings with the heads of foreign states. Kakabadze picked out the most expressive shots, the ones that should have been destroyed immediately.

'What do you need them for?' people would ask him. 'Surely you get sick of looking at them!'

'Really sick!' he would answer merrily. 'But this is for our descendants. A certain person advised me to collect them.'

'Who?'

'That's not important. "What if our descendants", he said to me, "feel like having their own Nuremberg trials here in Moscow?" If they do – here they are!'

# I'm a Fish

Catching sight of Nadya Sirotkina at the end of the hall Kakabadze dropped his heavy case full of camera equipment, stopped and spread his skinny arms from wall to wall. He stood there and waited. Nadya, pale from the lengthy absence of the sun, could have slipped past anywhere, it seemed. Just not past Kakabadze. Her steps grew smaller and smaller, and she finally came to a halt.

'Let me by, please,' she requested unemotionally. 'I'm in a hurry.'

'Nadya!' Kakabadze spoke with a reproach in his voice.

'What?' She looked wearily at him.

'Nadya! Today is eight months and four days since I've liked you.'

'And I like you. Let me past!'

'"Let me past!" Where to? Always just "Let me past!" Please! Nobody's detaining you! How old are you anyway?'

'Twenty-three.'

'And what about me?'

'Twenty-eight, I'd say.'

'There, you see! An ideal alignment of forces.'

'So what?'

'What do you mean, "So what"? Let's go.'

'Go where?'

'Go get married, what else?'

'And then what?'

'Then? You're making me blush, Nadya. Then everyone does the one and the same thing.'

'There, you see! And I don't want any of that one and the same thing.'

'Oh, all right. I agree. It'll be otherwise, with us. One and the same way for everyone except us. Only I beg one thing of you: that we have children, just like everybody else. I want two. How about you?'

'I want two as well.'

'That's four in all. Agreed, Nadya! Let's go!'

'Where?'

'There you go with your "Where?" again. To the registry office.'

'I don't want to.'

'All right – let's do it without any registry office. We'll just write on the wall – "Nadya plus Sasha equals love." What do you say?' Kakabadze stretched out his hand to her. She pushed it away.

'I can't take any more. So, let's write it on the wall. Just don't pester me any more! You're looking at me way too seriously.'

'And that's what – bad, right?' He pouted like a child whose feelings are hurt. He leaned back against one wall, folding his arm over his chest. He bowed his head, and his long, curly hair fell forward over his face.

'Go ahead,' he said, not looking at Nadya. 'I know that you're squeamish about me. Because I'm a Georgian, right?'

She laughed. 'You're like a little boy. The fact that you're a Georgian is your biggest virtue.'

Kakabadze looked at her with disbelief. 'By the way, you know that Yagubov is an anti-Semite: he doesn't like Georgians. I told that to Rappoport, and he answered, "Anti-Semite – that's something to be proud of!" So if you have any doubts, just say it straight out!'

'What are you saying! I myself have always dreamed of being a Georgian woman! But for there to be something between us I have to *relate* to you.'

'What do you mean, relate?'

'Just relate, that's all. Right now, I'm not relating to you. I'm like a fish, understand? A frozen fish. A filet. What am I to you? You've dreamed me up, and I'm just a salt fish. See how my bones stick out.' She drew her fingers along her collarbone.

'Filet, salt fish, a whole damned fish shop!' Kakabadze kicked at his heavy case. 'I love you, Nadya. And you're going to love me.'

'No way!'

'Then you'll see! We'll go to Tbilisi, have a modest wedding, only for my very closest friends – seven hundred guests, no more.'

'Again?'

'All right, all right! I've waited eight months and four days – I'll wait a little longer.'

Kakabadze gritted his teeth and picked up the heavy case full of apparatus, three-quarters of which was never needed and was brought along just for effect. Flinging open the door he burst into Rappoport's office.

'You are', Rappoport said to him in greeting, 'the most businesslike man in this brothel of an office.'

'You're always praising me. What for?'

Rappoport didn't waste any time explaining what he meant. Instead, he briefly explained what and where to shoot. It would be best just to photograph the work at those sectors where preparation was being carried out for the Lenin *subbotnik*. The photos would do for later on, as if they had been taken at the *subbotnik* itself. It was desirable to have a look behind the placards that would summon people to wherever they were needed.

'By the way, there's a manuscript going around the office. Have you seen it yet?'

'What a question! Just like that, right between the eyes, the old-fashioned way! If I didn't know you, Rappoport, I'd think you were a grass – or maybe even a KGB informer!'

He affably waved a hand and disappeared. Nadya had meanwhile run to the other end of the corridor. There she almost imperceptibly looked around to see if Kakabadze was watching her and then stopped in front of a door with a sign saying 'Special Correspondents'. She caught her breath, straightened her blouse and froze in indecision: go into Ivlev's office or not?

# 26

# The Demeanours and Misdemeanours of
# Special Correspondent Ivlev

'Ma, what do you think you should do if a friend of yours is saying something bad?'

'He'd have to be set right, Son.'

'But he just laughs. And says it again!'

'Says what again?'

'Well, you know, terrible things – about Stalin and whatnot.'

'That's awful! It's Khokhryakov, isn't it? Of course, by law you should tell on him, otherwise you're guilty as well. But telling on him is perilous, too. What times these are! They'll make you testify – and with exams coming up . . .'

'So what should I do?'

'Maybe you can re-educate him in your Young Communist group? Talk about it at the meeting. You heard it from somebody and then repeated it.'

'Repeated this?

> *'Stalin and Gottwald kicked over their traces,*
> *Exceptional times setting in with those blips.*
> *Now that we're rid of those steely old faces,*
> *When are the rest going to cash in their chips?'*

His mother blanched. 'Hush your mouth! And swear to me on your Young Communist's honour that you will never – do you understand me? – ever in your life say that again! I'm not even going to tell it to your father.'

Ivlev, teachers' pet and hope, was about to graduate from his ten-year secondary school. He was a straight-A student, a Young Communist organizer, captain of the basketball team, the foremost student expert on international affairs, entrusted by the principal with reading the newspaper over the school public-address system during the lunch break. His family was respectable, his parents both Communists. In a word, a shoo-in for his class gold medal. Only one thing was causing him any hesitation: deciding whether to choose history or philosophy as his main subject at university.

Ivlev brought pressure to bear on Khokhryakov. 'Hey, that jingle of yours. Did you tell it to anybody else?'

'What if I did?'

'You'd better shut up is what. And bear in mind that the death of Stalin is a tragedy for the whole of mankind, while you just –

'So we're forbidden to talk at all? Fuck off!'

'Do you want us to put it to the committee?'

'Put it wherever you want. That's just something you have to do to earn your medal.'

Ivlev didn't bring it up in the committee but not out of principle. His mother was right: it could hurt him, too. Besides, other events were occupying the attention of Committee Secretary Ivlev. At the May Day parade the final-year school students, off to buy some ice cream, crowded around a policeman and someone yelled: 'Long live the Soviet Militia!'

They solicitously tossed the policeman in the air. He flew up, hanging on to his holster and came down again just as gently.

'Hey, what's the matter with you kids? I'm on my beat!'

The incident was seen by Krestovsky, the school principal. He ran over, returned the pupils to their column and after the holidays called Ivlev out of his class and ordered him to bring before the committee the issue of the expulsion of the participants from the Young Communist League, which would mean losing their chance of going to university and conscription straight into the army. Some of the very best pupils were among those expelled. Of course Khokhryakov was involved, too. Krestovsky named him the malicious instigator of the incident, and Ivlev was given a directive to expel him from the Young Communist League.

'Hey, Ma, the gold medal's in my pocket!'

'I've made up my mind: go into philosophy, Son. Marxism-Leninism is the soundest choice. You become a theoretician, and I'll have peace of mind.'

Ivlev was used to submitting to his mother's authority. It was hard not to submit to her. His father always obeyed her as well, thereby affording his son an example. She was a beautiful woman, now slightly plump. She carefully kept secret the fact that at one time she had been a rabid Christian. Her family was of noble blood, and she had gone on foot in rags to Zagorsk for some holy water from Nadkladeznaya church. She was seventeen at the time, just over three years had passed since the Revolution and she had decided to enter a convent and take the veil. But she didn't stay there long. It had been looted with the assistance of the neighbouring army unit. The nuns had been raped, the mother superior sent to the wall.

A little later on Tatyana became a Young Communist, just as rabidly a believer in Lenin. She actively propagandized for free love, the kind written about in the Manifesto of the Communist Party and the kind that there would be under pure Communism. Sergey Ivlev had married her when she was already nearly thirty. She was really good-looking, and she left him at one time but came back. Ivlev senior was an engineer with a job in the Design Bureau, working on atomic energy, and he never talked about what he was doing. He lived a measured life: home, work, reading *Pravda*. Ivlev didn't have anything to talk to his father about.

Ivlev was supposed to go on to graduate school. He had already cleared the theme of his dissertation: 'The Struggle of the Communist Party to Strengthen the Leninist Norms of Party Life'. True, the norms of Ivlev's own life hadn't changed. Ivlev, like his mother, believed that food products from abroad that appeared in Russian shops held danger: they could be poisoned. And, meanwhile, several distant relations of Sergey's had returned from places of incarceration. Tatyana asserted that the Party knew whom it was imprisoning, and evidently they'd been sinners of some sort. His father agreed with her, but her son suddenly began to dispute her.

Not long before this Ivlev had run into Khokhryakov. They dived into a beer hall and got a mug each. Khokhryakov had succeeded in concealing his expulsion from the Young Communist League and had entered a teachers' college. He had studied in the English department, listened to foreign radio stations and related what he heard to his fellow students, for which he'd been expelled. After suffering hardship for half a year he'd landed a cushy job at a library.

'I'll soon be handing out your works, you Party philosopher! But it looks like you aren't all that pure, after all.'

Now Ivlev saw him in a different light. They took to hanging out together. It was interesting to be around Khokhryakov. At one of their meetings Ivlev said: 'You'll have to forgive my idiocy at school. I understand now. Forgive me.'

'I can't forgive you,' Khokhryakov replied immediately, as if his answer had been prepared in advance. 'And what good would it do you, forgiveness? But if you understand it now, good for you. I used to think that people like you could never grow any wiser.'

Khokhryakov picked amusing pieces out of foreign magazines, translated them and took them around to the newspapers, earning a little on the side to fill out his meagre library wage. He took Ivlev to meet Rappoport. The philosopher Ivlev got taken on as a writer at *Trudovaya Pravda*. All around him everything was reeling, in a ferment. Ivlev was unable to comprehend what was going on. The thread on his bolt was gradually wearing out, ring by ring, until the nut dropped off. Special-correspondent assignments helped the process, too. On the eve of Soviet Army Day he was sent off to cover the Northern Fleet exercises.

'Ivlev, what's with you?' Inna the typist was first to ask, when he was dictating his material to her after returning from the assignment. 'Your temples have gone grey.'

'I was on exercises, military exercises.'

'Just exercises, after all – you weren't in a war!'

The destroyer that was taking Special Correspondent Ivlev out to the exercises received notification that the hypothetical enemy was located within firing range.

'Rocket projectiles – fire!'

The launch, however, didn't happen. The projectiles were jammed in the launcher. There was nothing to do except knock them out with a sledgehammer.

'Who's going to volunteer?' asked the captain. Those wanting to were nowhere to be found. He picked up a chisel and a sledgehammer. Instantly the entire crew hit the deck. Ivlev threw himself down with the rest of them.

'What are you afraid of, you cretins?' the captain said, turning his head. 'If this thing goes, nobody here will be left anyway.' He started knocking the stuck missiles out of their tubes carefully, with light blows of the sledgehammer.

Everything turned out all right. The destroyer, taking no further part in the exercises, returned to base. There it came to light that they had obtained missiles of the wrong calibre.

'Who loaded them up? Court-martial them!'

'How could this have happened?' said Ivlev, in surprise, in a conversation with the captain. 'What if it was a real war?'

'You are *so* naive! And when you go to the grocer's, are there sometimes rotten cabbages there?'

'Sometimes.'

'How come they get to have fuck-ups at a vegetable store but we can't on a military base? People are the same everywhere!'

In Ivlev's article, 'On Guard at Our Borders', everything was written as it was supposed to be: the destroyer, putting the hypothetical enemy to rout, returned victorious to its native shore. Mighty Soviet missiles were ready at any minute to strike at any enemy. Ivlev went down to the military censor's office on Kropotkin Street and got his 'Publication Permitted' stamp. The piece came in for praise at a special meeting. But it was a long time before Special Correspondent Ivlev could forget lying on the steel deck of the destroyer, covering his head with his hands.

Rappoport laughed at Ivlev's doubts. He gave him some Solzhenitsyn to read. Rappoport brought to a head the condition that had been set going by Khokhryakov. Ivlev shook off his mesmerization by the past that his mother had so carefully instilled in him, shook off the philosophy faculty. He keenly assured his friends that Solzhenitsyn was real literature, that everything else was just a waste of time. Hearing that Solzhenitsyn's fiftieth birthday had come Ivlev sent a telegram to Ryazan: 'Happy birthday to the hope and pride of Russian literature. Ivlev.'

About three weeks later Ivlev received a summons to appear before the KGB. The building was old-fashioned, with plaster moulding on the walls and ceiling. A pleasant young man of Young Communist age sat, smiling cordially, in the office to which they brought Ivlev. After asking him for certain particulars, he asked curiously: 'Do you know Solzhenitsyn?'

'Yes, I do.'

'Have you been acquainted for long?'

'We aren't.'

'Have you ever met?'

'No, I've never met him.'

'Then name some of your mutual friends.'

'He and I don't have any mutual friends.'

'That's not true! People who aren't acquainted don't send each other birthday greetings by telegram.'

'He's a famous Soviet writer, and therefore –'

'What have you read?'

'I've read –' Ivlev quickly cut out everything that he'd read in manuscript form, '*One Day in the Life of Ivan Denisovich* and *Matryona's Home* . . .'

'*Cancer Ward*?'

'No.'

'But you do know that Solzhenitsyn is carrying on activities that play into the hands of enemies of our Party. So it turns out that you're a supporter of his?'

'Probably I didn't express myself very clearly,' said Ivlev, trying surreptitiously to squeeze his hands into fists to keep them from shaking. 'Solzhenitsyn gets published in *Novy Mir*. I presumed that if he was being published, then I could read him, and I could like it or not myself.'

'You don't want to understand,' the investigator continued. 'It's not whether you like his stuff or not. It's the fact that you, a journalist, a worker on the ideological front, support a writer who gets praised by the bourgeois press. Did you never wonder who gets praised by our enemies and why? We have data supporting the fact of your acquaintance with him.'

'I told you, we're not personally acquainted, I've never seen him.'

'And that portrait photo – did he give it to you?'

'What portrait?'

'The one that's hanging in your apartment.'

That portrait had been blown up by Kakabadze from a candid shot and given as presents to Ivlev and Rappoport.

'Why are you silent? Speak up!'

'The portrait I bought. I bought it from a hawker next to the bookseller's.'

'Who did you buy it from? Describe him.'

'A little guy with a beard, some kind of student.'

'We'll take your word for it. And certainly you can tell us more than that.'

They let him go, after warning him that they were going to call him back. He was very frightened. He told no one about his conversation, decided not to worry even his wife about it. But the next day he was summoned to the editor's office. His heart pounding, he went in to see Makartsev.

'Sit!' Makartsev left off what he was doing at once. 'Well, what have you gone and done. Spit it out!'

Ivlev shrugged and told him.

'You fool!' Makartsev rose out of his chair. 'You idiot! Did Solzhenitsyn need your damned birthday greetings? You've very nearly done for us all! I don't want to, but it looks like I'm going to have to fire you. Get out!'

I'm going to talk to somebody about this. Get out, go on, get out of my sight!'

'Couldn't you have guessed that this would happen?' Rappoport said to Ivlev. 'Naturally they want to get rid of Solzhenitsyn. Only not right away. First they'll torment him, take bites out of him, smear him with some dirt, until he's isolated. Then they'll lynch him publicly, after declaring that he, all by himself, is against the whole nation. You're in deep shit!'

'But just –'

'Quiet. Don't get your back up. You sent the telegram supposing that it was some sort of audacious move. But did Solzhenitsyn even get it? Suppose he did. Even without you he already knows he's somebody. The entire world – risking nothing – supports him. What would your birthday telegram mean to him? It would just make him think that they were going to keep an eye on him even more, now that he's so popular. But in fact Solzhenitsyn never got your telegram. They put it on a spike at the KGB. Right?'

'Let's say they did. And what happens then?'

'Just imagine that I'm the KGB colonel charged with keeping on top of this. I divide all the telegrams up into piles. Twenty of them from writers. Sure! Are there like-minded people in the Writers' Union? – we'll keep an eye on them, not let them get published, not let them speak out in public. We'll just put some more grasses in Authors' House. Two hundred telegrams from intellectuals. We'll hound them out of their jobs, expel them from the Party, so they'll never get back up again. Two hundred from students. These youngsters we'll expel publicly, so that the mass of students will take note.'

'Right!'

'Hang on, I haven't finished. I'm a colonel in the KGB. I'm thinking – how does Solzhenitsyn come by all this popularity? What it means is that the birthday greeters are all reading *samizdat*. I'll dig deeper. If it doesn't help – put them away. It turns out, Ivlev, that by your telegram you've helped them compile a list of suspects, so it'll be easier to keep an eye on them. The telegram was a provocation – and you're a provocateur.'

'How can you say that?'

'Never mind the fact, Ivlev, that you've put your friends on the spot: they'll be watched, too, from now on. If you want to be a hero, do it some other way.'

'Like what?'

'Go abroad or write some *samizdat* on the quiet. Just don't get your friends tangled up in your affairs! Everyone's like that: they keep their silence, and then they ask why everything around them is so awful. Sometimes it seems to me that there is no Solzhenitsyn. He's a mirage, a fantasy. How *can* a single man stand up against the machine?'

Ivlev kept silent and looked at Rappoport.

'All right, Ivlev, I'm not going to argue with you,' said the latter and turned towards the window, giving the impression that he didn't want to discuss the matter further.

'The way your mind works, things will never improve in this country!'

Rappoport turned and stared fixedly at Ivlev.

'Improve? And what kind of improvement are you trying to make with your telegram? I advise you to repent and condemn Solzhenitsyn with all your might. If you do manage to save yourself – remember: this is a signal. Don't get involved again! If you can't keep quiet, speak out, but only to a very few. And actually to perform heroic deeds – that, brother, is some kind of anachronism. In my opinion you've learned your Marx and Lenin too well and taken their revolutionary notions too literally.'

Makartsev went to see the district Party committee secretary about the affair of Party member Ivlev. Makartsev had done him a favour when the man was still just Party secretary at his automobile plant. Now grown fat, the man listened to Makartsev's request guardedly.

'He's still young,' Makartsev assured him. 'A good Communist, a conscientious worker. Some devil made him do it. He's got talent. We need talented people.'

The district secretary had been listening silently, but now he smiled.

'Talented? The Party doesn't need people who are simply talented. The Party needs talents who understand what we want from them.'

'He does understand, believe me. Ivlev does a lot for the paper. At the end of the day, who decides things now – us or the KGB?'

'We decide this, all of us together,' the secretary clarified. 'This isn't just childishness, it's Czechoslovak-style recidivism. They went and liberalized – and look what it came to.'

'By the way,' said Makartsev, 'Ivlev has been planning some useful pieces about your factory.'

'That's the ticket – send him to the factory, see how things work!'

'If we don't ruin him he'll be a loyal worker. He'll come in handy. Let's punish him according to Party policy – but not too hard, just as a deterrent to others. What are we – don't we know our own personnel better than the KGB does? If anything happens I'll bring it up with the Central Committee.'

The district Party secretary didn't answer. There was a long pause. 'All right,' he said finally, shifting his gaze to one side. 'Out of respect for you personally, Makartsev. But you'll have to ring the KGB yourself.'

When Makartsev got back to the office he summoned Ivlev in again. The latter entered, sullen and ready for the worst.

'Consider yourself incredibly lucky,' said Makartsev. Everybody stood up for you. We'll have a Party meeting in a few days. Do you know what to say?'

'I understand.'

'Sure you understand, now! But as far as work goes, here you're going to have to prove yourself. Get busy writing a clever article on the irreconcilability of the two ideologies. Its author is supposed to be the district Party secretary. Write it from the heart. Were they wasting their time teaching you philosophy?'

Ivlev, happy now, went down to see Rappoport.

'Congratulations!' Rappoport came to life. 'The meeting – that's just *pro forma*. Truth to tell, I didn't think they were going to let you off the hook so easily. In my time, I –'

'Times are changing!'

'Probably.'

This all took place on the eve of 1969. But in early January, before the Party meeting, the investigator again telephoned Ivlev and asked him to come once more to Dzerzhinsky Street. A pass had already been ordered for him.

'So, you've thought about it, and you understand that Solzhenitsyn is just an enticement for the weak?' he inquired. 'Well, that's certainly correct. Judge for yourself – what do you want to mess up your record for? We never even doubted that the telegram was just a chance happening. But since you *have* made a mistake, you're going to have to prove, as a Communist, that you realize it. You're a journalist, you know how to write. It isn't hard for you.'

'So what am I supposed to do?'

'It's not complicated, and you yourself will soon find out that Solzhenitsyn is a nobody, someone completely sold out for German dollars –'

'Marks,' Ivlev corrected him.

'Exactly,' the investigator smiled. 'You do write short stories, after all.'

'Bad ones. I've given up on them.'

'That's not too bad. Take some of your stories and go see Solzhenitsyn in Ryazan.'

'Me?'

'What are you afraid of? We'll pay for the trip. You'll say that you've come looking for advice as a first-time author. You can even slag off something or other, if necessary.'

'And then what?'

'Nothing! Get acquainted with the hope of Russian literature, as you put it in your telegram. Then come back here and give me a call.'

Ivlev was silent, his head bowed. He cautiously looked out at the investigator from under his eyebrows. He had expected anything but this. He nodded, so as not to antagonize the investigator, while he thought with a shudder how it would be impossible to refuse now.

'So, is it agreed?'

'Excuse me, I didn't understand exactly. What am I supposed to get acquainted with Solzhenitsyn for?'

'You're a Communist? Just consider this a Party mission. And we'll include you on the staff of the Young Writers' Conference.'

'You see, I'm not really up to it. I might tell him something I shouldn't.'

'That's no problem.'

'I might blow the gaff.'

'You can't say that *we* asked you to go there!'

'The thing is that I *might* do something. You know, I'm really not up to this. No way!'

'All right! So, all your repentance was just for appearance's sake. Well, the Party meeting still hasn't taken place . . .'

A bead of sweat ran down Ivlev's forehead to the bridge of his nose and then down on to his cheek. 'You didn't quite understand me,' he said. 'I *would* agree to do it, but I'm afraid I'd just mess the whole thing up.'

'Well, then, here's what. Sign this slip that says for the unauthorized disclosure of our conversation you're subject to punishment under article 184 of the Criminal Code. Then you can go!'

The Party meeting, as the all-powerful Makartsev had promised, severely reprimanded Ivlev, with an entry in his record and a warning that for any further violations he would be expelled from the Party. As far as the mission that he'd turned down went, they weren't yet bothering him about it. They'd probably found a more likely candidate.

# 27

# What Are You Scared Of?

Nadya stood in front of the door with the *Special Correspondents* sign. She didn't grasp the handle right away. She looked once again at the letters she held in her hand, sorted through them, straightened her hair, and, finally making up her mind, opened the door. Ivlev, sitting behind his desk, was figuring something, turning over the pages on his desk calendar. He didn't even look up at Sirotkina.

'Are you busy?' she asked softly. 'If so I'll come back later.'

'Letters?' he didn't turn his head. 'Leave them here.'

Nadya didn't want just to leave them there, because after that she wouldn't have any excuse to come by. And then she'd have to go back to counting the days. Nadya shifted from foot to foot. *He's in a really bad mood, now,* she told herself, *get out of here. You'll ruin everything, don't force yourself on him. I'm not forcing myself on him. It's just that he's so lonely and helpless, like never before. Walk up to him. Put your hand on his head. Or at least say something to him. Come on, think of something!*

'Do you have a lot to do? Maybe I could help.'

She frightened herself with what she was saying. *Now he'll laugh, and then I'd better never catch his eye again.*

'Help me how?'

He stopped leafing through his calendar and, putting a finger on the page, looked attentively at her, raising his eyebrows as if seeing her for the first time. She was too slender. But there was something about her, and now, when he noticed this something – Nadya understood straight away – it interested him.

Nadya quietly waited while he looked her over and wasn't disconcerted. She'd just had her hair done, which was why she had been late for work. She had carefully done her eyelashes in the ladies' room, with real French mascara. Her suede skirt looked good on her, that's what all the girls were saying. Her long, slender neck extended from her blouse with its high collar, round cut-out décolletage and appliqué holes around the edge of the cut-out – everything was visible to an inquisitive observer more than a man would expect from a first look. He hemmed, and she understood that he liked her. At long last!

'Don't look at me like that!' she said, pouting, so that she could be certain of her victory by his answer. She was flirting with all her might.

'Can't I?'

'You can't!' she pronounced; now she could allow herself to put on airs and change the subject. 'What are you figuring out?'

'Age.'

'What of it?'

'It's just that I have five more years to go before I grow any wiser.'

'How old *are* you?'

'Thirty-three.'

'The same age as Jesus Christ. That's all? You're only nine years older than me. And I was thinking . . .'

'What?'

'You look older.'

'For ten years in school and five at the institute they bash your head in, to break you of the habit of thinking. And to forget all of that it takes another fifteen years. I have five years left.'

'Why should you get any wiser? Things will just get harder.'

'Any easier is boring.'

'I envy you! When I get out of the journalism faculty I won't have to relearn anything: I haven't got anything to forget.' She gazed at him and suddenly, not realizing what she was saying until it was too late, she said: 'I'll go, if you don't need me.'

'Why go?'

Nadya blushed and turned her back on him, hoping to be saved somehow. Her voice became thick, wouldn't obey her. 'Do you want me to bring you some books? Foreign ones. My father has a good library. I can feed you and do your cleaning . . .'

'I have a wife to do that for me.'

*Not that you'd notice,* she thought but didn't say it. Nadya didn't want to insult his wife.

'She hasn't got the time; she's got a child. How old is your son?'

'Six.'

'That's a pity: have to wait a long time, otherwise I'd marry him. Kick me out of here, I'm an idiot!'

'Come on, stop that!'

She carried on standing with her back towards him. He got up out of his chair to calm her down, put his hands on her shoulders, and, feeling the hot skin underneath her thin blouse, moved his hands up to her neck. Ivlev felt a tremor under his fingers – she swallowed and turned sharply, sticking her nose into his shoulder.

'The door! The door, you crazy wench!' he said to her, kissing her neck, her ear, her cheek.

'Lock it!' She pushed his hands apart and stood with her eyes closed, unmoving, just smiling a vacant and somewhat impudent smile.

Turning the key in the lock, he shook his head in an attempt to come to his senses. What did he need this for? Why was he wilfully running up against gossip? She would cling to him like a leech; he'd be walking around with a tail. It was terrible around her, with the sort of artlessness she had. *No! I'll just do this without any boorishness, so as not to offend her.*

'Nadya,' he said, firmly.

She took three uncertain steps forward, like someone coming down off a merry-go-round, and put her hands over his ears.

'You're yelling like we're in the woods. I'm right here.' Her breath was warm against his throat.

'What am I to you? There's Kakabadze – single, good-looking, twenty-eight, his children would be a lovely sight! And I'm five minutes to bald!'

'Cut it out,' Nadya said sternly. 'I can flirt with you, to catch your eye, but you flirt with me? – never. What are you scared of? I don't love you in the least. I get intimate quickly, but then I get bored. I don't need your love. Just you. And not for long. You need me, too, I can feel it – you need me!

'And you're shaking for that reason? What are we going to do?'

Nadya shrugged. But now all his previous conceptions had got tangled up, fused together, then fallen away like something that didn't deserve any attention. Ivlev pulled her to him by the elbows in an abrupt movement, as if she would have lost her balance and fallen if he had been a second later. And she fell against him, obeying his hands, soft, pliant, boneless. She bent to him, with her last strength trying not to lose contact with his lips, as if without them she would suffocate. He moved her away, looking for her breasts, but she didn't understand and pressed herself against him, getting in his way, afraid that he was trying to pluck her away from him.

'You're kissing me as if I was naked,' she whispered, when their lips finally came apart.

'Don't you want to be naked?'

'I do,' she laughed. 'The girls have been talking about it so much. And here . . .'

'Here what?'

'I'm waiting for what you're going to do.'

'What everybody does.'

'What does everybody do?'

'Listen! I'm not cut out to be a teacher!'

'You are, too! You're cut out for any role you want!'

'You're cracked!'

'Uh-huh. And you? Aren't you going to get undressed?'

She had no more than a third of her clothes still on when someone knocked at the door.

'Ivlev! Are you there?' Rappoport's voice carried through the door. 'Come on, let me in.'

Nadya pressed her hands to her flaming cheeks. Ivlev went to fasten his belt; it jingled. Rappoport knocked one more time, coughed and said gloomily: 'When you're free, come and see me.'

Nadya squatted down on her haunches behind the desk, so that Ivlev wouldn't see her half dressed and hurriedly pulled on her tights. It would be hard to imagine a position less suitable for doing this manoeuvre.

'I'm not looking. Don't worry.'

Ivlev turned away and stood waiting. The telephone rang, banishing his nerves, forcing him to think and act quicker. He picked up the phone.

'Ivlev, why didn't you open the door? I need you!'

'I'm coming right now.'

He unlocked the door and peeked out. Nadya squeezed past him, imperceptibly tracing her fingers along his cheek, on which there was a day's growth of stubble. Only the barely perceptible odour of very good soap was left behind, and it suddenly became a necessity to Ivlev.

# 28

# An Imperishable Thing

'What was going on in your office, Ivlev?'

'I was doing some work.'

'That's what I thought.'

'Did something happen?'

'Nothing significant. Everything all right at home?'

'Of course! Why do you ask?'

'No reason. Maybe we could go for a stroll? I have a splitting headache.'

Three minutes later, dressed for the outdoors, they went out on the boulevard across from the newspaper office. Here it was possible to converse more freely. The spring sunshine was blinding, and the two of them squinted like cats who had just crawled out of a shed.

'Ivlev, do you like Yagubov?' Rappoport asked as they walked out on to the dry pavement.

'You want a straight answer?' asked Ivlev, steering the other by one arm around a puddle. 'We'll see what we'll see. What about it?'

'For a long time I've been keeping two ledgers, writing down people's names in them. In one – good people; in the other – scum. Which one should I put Yagubov in?'

'Which one did you put me in?'

'The good one. But that doesn't mean it's for ever.'

'And which book did you put yourself in?'

'My name is the first one in both books. I should think that's not too immodest of me, eh?'

'Not at all, professor! You know what I think about you! Although I could allow that you might have some sins that you're punishing yourself for.'

'Everybody's a sinner, Ivlev.' Rappoport wasn't about to enlarge on that theme. 'I make my entries not for the quantity or absence of their sins but for their life-position. Their personality – human or some kind of slime.'

'In any case, you're a somebody!'

'For sure, Ivlev. If only there was a bit more reasonableness spread around in nature I'd be the editor of the paper and Makartsev and Yagubov would be running errands for *me*.'

'That's a career! And you're just a human being. And, after that, a journalist. Millions read your every word.'

Was he was joking or talking seriously? Rappoport looked askance at him over his glasses and made a face.

'I don't know what kind of profession that is, journalist, Ivlev,' he muttered. 'Me personally, by profession – I'm a liar. And any other kind of "journalist" – as you allow yourself to put it – isn't to be met with anywhere in this country, and surely they're not about to let me into some other one. But I'm not ashamed of being a liar; I'm proud of it.'

'Proud?'

'Why not? Let's say I wanted to write what I see and what I think. I can't! I can't do what I love, but I love what I do. I work creatively, giving myself to it completely; I create something imperishable. My lies are pure, without the slightest taint of the truth. *Herr Doktor* Goebbels maintained that a lie has to be a big one before people would believe it. That's not quite right. It's not the quantity, Ivlev, but the possibility of comparison. If the reader has no way to compare things, that means that he won't have any doubts. As they put it in Indian philosophy, a man who doesn't understand that he sees the colour blue can't even see it. Newspaper philosophy has to be accessible to fools. On orders from above, I invent a past, suck pseudo-heroes and the pseudotask of modernity – things like this *subbotnik* – out of my fingers, and then I myself depict the nationwide rejoicing. On this sham fundament I promise a firm future. Or isn't that so?'

'By the way, how's it going with the *subbotnik*?'

'It's approved on high. They've decided to make my *subbotnik* Moscow-wide. Professors will be chopping ice off the pavements. Writers will clean cages at the zoo. Artists will cart off rubbish heaps from court-yards. The entire proletariat of this city will be coming out to work for nothing!'

'Not all of them, Rappoport.'

'The majority! Because, steeped in propaganda, Ivlev, the people are becoming even worse than their government. Toilers write letters demanding that Solzhenitsyn be locked up, even though they've never read a word of his. We have accustomed people to the idea that they're warmed by the sun of the Soviet constitution, in the warm beams of whose articles a rich harvest is ripening. And they consider the real sun to be a poorer thing.'

'There *are* failures, too.'

'There are. See how they got worked up and had to explain how Stalin was a little bit wrong. And do you think everybody believed it? On the contrary! They accuse Khrushchev of slander. And why? Because the truth interferes with their blind faith, the way it was before. They understood that lying has to be total, all the time, and not just now and then. No safety valves!'

'But you understand that you're lying, don't you?'

'I'm a different case. I'm a professional liar. I transform the old lie into a new one, and that way I bury the truth even deeper.'

'So truth exists! Of course, the means besmirch themselves, but the goal, it seems to me, is a good one. It's just the getting there.'

'Forget it. It's only you and I, professionals, who need the truth and the goal, in order to understand why we lie. The naive journalist – as you allowed yourself to put it – striving to get rid of the conflict between his conscience and his Party membership, will lie sincerely for the sake of over-coming the discrepancies along the road to the radiant summit. And then what? If he does, he only besmirches both the summit and himself.'

'You're laying it on a bit thick!' Ivlev objected. 'Even those Party workers who just ten years ago were yelling that they had to inform the KGB organs about every joke they heard are now hiding from their wives in the bathroom listening to the BBC. They're trying to understand.'

'Not to understand – they've just got more cynical. Get this, my lad: the cult and the dictatorship are advantageous both to those at the top and those below. Personal responsibility gets shucked off. Do what you're ordered to, and don't worry about it.'

'But society can't function without morals. It degenerates. Where's the progress?'

'Right, old boy.'

'So, the complete devotion that we're standing up for turns a man into a sheep!'

'Who's arguing with you? Of course, propaganda is one of the most amoral things known to humankind. The very existence of it testifies to just one thing: our leaders grasp that people are not going to trample along after them voluntarily. Yes, it's vile to foist your views on other people. And me? After all, it's not my own views that I'm foisting on other people. And somehow that's easier. I lie and don't worry about observing the proprieties. I write parodies, but they get taken seriously.'

'You're talented, Rappoport. Are you sorry for yourself?'

'I'm not sorry for that sort of talent. Rightish thoughts I write with my left hand, leftish thoughts with my right. But I myself am absolutely in the middle.'

They had walked down to the end of the boulevard, to the tram terminus, and now turned back. Mischief glittered in Ivlev's eyes.

'And could you write an article that didn't have a single thought of yours in it?'

'You imbecile! All of my articles are exactly that. That's the Tavrov-Rappoport Basic Law: "Not a line with a thought in it!" I create a sea of lies, I bathe the leaders in it. They suck up the lies, masticate them thoroughly and belch them back up again. I understand them, I sympathize with them. The more they get knocked outside the country, the stronger their desire is to be praised, here on the inside. And there you go: when they read that their lies are the truth, they themselves start to think they're not lying. And, after they calm down, they lie even more, completely parting ways with reality. It's a vicious circle: they think upstairs that the lie is necessary down below; downstairs, they think the ones on top want to be lied to. And they need me: they themselves can only lie semi-literately. That's why I'm reckoned among the best Party scribblers.'

'As Khrushchev put it, Party journeymen.'

'Journeymen . . . That word belittles me, Ivlev. You shouldn't use us like prostitutes, pushing us up against the entryway wall. Good liars belong to the Party elite – as longs as they're not Jews, of course. Our epoch, though, has created what is in principle a new type of Jew.'

'The Jewish anti-Semite?'

'Uh-huh! The kind who are ready to trample on their own tribe. That's not me, mind you. I'm just a liar.'

'And your own personal convictions?'

'My own? In the first place, the ones I had were beaten out of me with a steel buckle. But, to be honest, I'm not sorry I lost those convictions.'

'Any other ones?'

'Hmm. If people in our profession, old man, have any convictions at all, they're *always* only other ones.'

'Dostoevsky said that there are people who can preach with foam coming out of their mouths, trying to bring people to their faith. And who themselves don't believe. "Then why do you try to persuade others?" "I want to persuade myself."'

'My boy, I'd like to end my days in the kind of penal servitude Dostoevsky vacationed in when he was forging his views. I was left with one single conviction: you've got to think in unison with your superiors. Let people like you, Ivlev, go ahead and struggle. As far as I'm concerned, I've used up all my principles in difficult circumstances. One thing alone consoles me: we ignore the truth, try to liquidate it. But the lie drags you down like quicksand.'

'And it drags *you* down, too! You're sinking. Maybe it would be better to drown in the truth?'

'What? Write the truth, for yourself? For myself, I already know it well. And if I wrote it for other people – they'd put me away again.'

'And what if a crack appears?'

'A crack, so you could bark and then go hide in it? A crack . . . And where *is* truth anyway? And whose is it? Yours? Mine? Theirs? Feuchtwanger got across to the world that the Nazis were transforming Germany into a madhouse. But then he comes here, to a country where the dictatorship is even more refined than the fascists' and starts blowing bubbles. You know yourself, Ivlev, what I think of Solzhenitsyn. Is it due just to his talent alone that he and nobody else became the spokesman for our concentration-camp epoch? No, it was just a coincidence. I know an old writer who has a story similar to *One Day in the Life of Ivan Denisovich,* only it was written earlier. And from the point of view of truth-lovers like you, it's much stronger and gloomier. The story never made it as far as Tvardovsky and higher up. And even if it *had* made it that far, they wouldn't have printed it, because the hero of the story is a Jew and he gets brutally murdered, and when they're carting his corpse out of the camp the guard sticks him in the heart with his bayonet, just to make sure. There isn't any optimism to be had in it. Solzhenitsyn managed to wriggle through the crack, and thank God for that. But a lot of others were left behind, and the door slammed shut.'

'Who is this fellow?'

'That's not a tactful question, my boy.'

'Excuse me,' said Ivlev, embarrassed. 'I was thinking that it's possible I know the author.'

'If you know him, figure it out. Let's sit down for a bit – there's an empty bench – I'm tired of marching around.'

Rappoport took a folded copy of *Trudovaya Pravda* out of his pocket, spread it out and sat down on it, breathing heavily.

'Fine.' Ivlev sat down next to him. 'Let's say you haven't got any convictions, but integrity – is there such a thing as simple human integrity?'

'Hah! Integrity. Who needs it? Can your body be jaundiced and healthy at the same time? No, I want to drown in the quicksand of lies along with everyone that I've wasted my life on. Talking this rubbish about shining ideals over and over, day after day, I'm dragging them into the slough with all my might. Integrity would just slow me down.'

'So what about conscience?'

'Conscience?' Rappoport fell silent, and his eyes grew wicked. His face twisted with pain, and he took a sweet out of his pocket, unwrapped it and started sucking on it. The juices in his stomach strained. Rappoport belched and felt better. 'You, Ivlev, have never seen my conscience, and neither have I. If I ever had one, it's been directed down the proper channel long since. My mother served her time in Tsarist exile so that I could be free. And me? I was ordered to tell more or they'd put away my wife, too. I graduated from the University of Conscience there. But from my son I hear now that I'm guilty for the fact that our freedom is worse than jail, and I blame my mother for that. The chain has been locked around us. What do I need to torture myself with conscience for? I spend the remnants of my strength on proving that our Soviet paralysis is the most progressive of all.'

'Well, you're Mr Mystificator!'

'Me? Well, that's the times for you. If our descendants decide a name for our era it won't be the Atomic Age or the Space Age but the Age of the Great Sham. And as its son I don't get my daily bread for nothing. I'm needed. Makartsev supports me because he's comfortable with me. He's a nobody himself, although he makes out that he's a decent guy. And Yagubov's just a worm without me! He should pray to me, not Lenin. I wouldn't ever have hired Lenin, with his confusion of ideas, as a writer on *Trudovaya Pravda*. He would have been put away a long time ago for left or right deviationism. The present regime can exist only thanks to vermiform people like me. Any questions?'

Ivlev turned his attention to a young woman pushing a pram; he looked at her well-shod long legs and said: 'It's nonsense, of course, but I'll ask anyway. What if the impossible happened?'

'Curious! Over how long a time – fifty years or five hundred? This land, friend, perhaps like no other, deserves a more worthy regime from God, by virtue of its sufferings and its patience. Not to mention a press. But . . .'

'And you?'

Rappoport covered his eyes with his hand and gave it a thought.

'Me? I'm a part of this system and, of this country, a cog. Where else could I get to while I'm still alive? I think one thing, I say another, I write still a third. What a rich intellectual life! No, our press has a unique atmosphere, and it's only in it here that I can breathe deeply.'

'So what would you do if it did happen?'

An old pensioner, rapping his cane, walked up to the bench, coughed and sat down carefully on the edge. Rappoport didn't answer but stood up, folded his newspaper and stuck it away in his pocket. They resumed their walk up the boulevard and only then did Rappoport rasp: 'What would I do, personally? Are you serious? You know they'll open the borders up. I'll emigrate, probably, then – if I live long enough, of course.'

'You? Run away from freedom? But where to?'

'What? In the West they think that the ideology here attracts indigent people. In reality, it attracts only ambitious, aggressive people, ours and others'. These lads understand how easy it is to trick backward people. Not only that, there are lots of naive people in the world who are sick of prosperity.'

'Surely our own zoo here has taught them something?'

'You can only sense a cage from inside it. And they're just itching for the chain out there. They've got a sweet presentiment of how great a stimulus you can get from a whipping. There are lots of ambitious people with a thirst for power everywhere on earth. The first thing they do is cut themselves off from the rest of the world with barbed-wire fences and start publishing – guess what? – *Pravda*, the "Truth".'

'*Trudovaya Pravda*, "the Hard-Won Truth"?'

'I'm not saying no! In any case, what's needed right away is professional liars.'

'But you don't even know any other languages.'

'And I don't need to. I'll only be needed when everybody's already been made to crow in Russian. My function is to fool the masses, to develop their herd instincts, to set one bunch of people against another. In my time, I've had a lot of that work. Without lies, Ivlev, people forget for some reason that there's truth on this earth. Although I've got no conscience of my own, I'm the person who acts as the conscience of progressive mankind. That's the way things are, old boy. You'll just have to excuse me for my frankness. And, in general, listen to me a bit less; after all, I can't *not* tell lies. I hope this is all going to stay between the two of us? The more so since we have good cause to keep quiet about it.'

'Cause? It's always been this way!'

Rappoport rubbed his once more aching stomach. 'Investigator Chaly, I'll never forget the man, was the nicest person. He spoke tenderly to you: he understood. He'd talk about his children – he loved them deeply. And in order to see me better at our confidential discussions he'd turn the table lamp straight into my eyes, right up close. And keep it there up to six hours at a time. That was like ten of the suns that you're looking at right now. If I closed my eyes he'd break off from writing notes and stick his pen in my throat. There they are, blue spots, see? I'm not sorry about the fact that I was left with fifty per cent of the sight in one of my eyes and twenty-five per cent in the other. And not for the fact that no one wants to grind the right lenses for me whenever I have to order glasses. I'm sorry about the fact that my eyes hurt in advance – somebody just walks up to the switch to turn on the light, and it's like an electric shock to me. Nothing I can do about it! I try to turn on lights myself and distract my attention by various means.'

'What are you telling me this for?'

'Because I have this same sort of presentiment just before getting arrested. My hands stretch out behind me and my fingers clasp together: now they're going to lead me off . . . Have you heard about some manuscript that's doing the rounds at work?'

'Not yet. I'm hoping it won't escape me.'

'Be a little more careful, Ivlev, I don't like that.'

'What's the matter with you? It's not 1952.'

'And it's not 1957 either! I think they're starting to stir again. By the way, how about you going off on an assignment?'

'Do you want me to lie low? But I haven't got anything to be scared of!'

'There's nobody who isn't scared. Why are you always looking around at women like you've never seen one before? Yes, and I meant to tell you: it's better to do your copulating at home.'

Ivlev scratched his nose, and then muttered: 'At whose home?'

'At mine. If you need to, don't be shy. Just take the key.'

# 29

# The Sabbath

The grey folder was being read in the evenings by everyone who was the 'fresh head' proofreader (according to the schedule under the glass on Anna's desk) instead of their looking for errors in the galley proofs. And everyone, after discovering the thing for themselves, came to the conclusion that it would be better not to mention it: it was almost certain that the manuscript in the envelope in the desk of the editor-in-chief had been put there especially to catch someone on that primitive hook. If it was Makartsev himself who turned out to be the leftist, he wouldn't keep the *samizdat* in his office. Some other ideas crossed people's minds as well. What if Makartsev had thought up some new way of educating his employees and was calculating to increase his prestige thereby? Or maybe there was something going on among the higher-ups and there was hope for some indulgence? It was only Rappoport who had no illusions. He was vacillating between his editor's trust in him and the necessity of warning his friends.

But errors were cropping up thick and fast in the pages of *Trudovaya Pravda*, and Yagubov couldn't understand what was going on. The Party secretary of an automobile plant and its manager had their initials mixed up. A People's Artist of the USSR got offended when he was called a lower-ranking Distinguished Artist instead. The scores from two ice hockey matches in different cities got mixed up, and a sports-desk worker had to man the telephone until eleven o'clock that night. Several readers threatened to cancel their subscriptions to *Trudovaya Pravda* because of the hockey scores. There wasn't any danger in that: the paper's print run was established from on high and depended on the amount of paper bought in Finland. The reduction in subscribership increased retail street sales, that was all. The errors didn't earn them any pats on the back, though. Yagubov asked for Lenin's portrait on the subscribers' page to be cropped so that Lenin would look into the distance instead of downwards. The make-up man cropped the image but cut off a chunk of the back of Lenin's head, and Yagubov had to explain himself to the Central Committee. The make-up man was fired; the duty editors received reprimands.

Kashin hung up Yagubov's reprimand orders in a prominent place, although a day hadn't passed before there were new errors. The duty 'fresh head' proofreader, after getting engrossed in the manuscript in Makartsev's office, had checked the galleys carelessly. It was a good thing that God spared them from any huge ideological blunders. There wouldn't have been any irate phone calls from readers – a call from on high would have had everyone in big trouble.

Rappoport was puffing over his pieces on the *subbotnik*. Each day saw articles and information going into the issue. Yagubov was demanding a broadness of scope and – what irritated Rappoport the most – a creative approach. That was why when Anna walked up to him Rappoport asked: 'See Yagubov again? Don't you think I'm fed up with him?'

'Your intercom is always busy. Maybe it's out of order?'

'It's working fine!' muttered Rappoport, getting up.

In reality he had pulled one of the wires of the intercom out of its socket, on the assumption that Yagubov or someone else was listening to what went on in the departments. Rappoport plodded off to the deputy editor right behind Anna, unceremoniously scrutinizing her legs and things located higher up. On the stairs he couldn't resist it and gently patted her on her attractively protruding bottom.

'What are you doing?' she asked sternly.

'Oh, Anna . . . Recollections of youth.'

Anna giggled but for the sake of propriety said reprovingly: 'I might expect someone else to do that, but it's entirely out of character for you.'

'Out of character, out of character,' he agreed straight away. 'Out of my line of sight is what it should be.'

Yagubov was pacing around his office, full of excitement. Catching sight of Rappoport in the doorway he smiled joyfully.

'Come in, come in,' he said, rubbing his hands. 'Have I got news for you!'

*He's not going to give me hell,* Rappoport thought fleetingly. *But what's he so happy about?* 'Did they telephone down from Upstairs about the *sub-botnik*?'

'You already know? And do you know who called?'

Rappoport could of course have figured it out (it wasn't a big deal), but Yagubov didn't give him time to think.

'Comrade Khomutilov just called on the secure line. He asked me to pass on that they'd reported our campaign to his boss, and he had informed – you yourself understand *who* –' Yagubov paused dramatically. 'And from there came an order to congratulate all of us here at the newspaper. A great honour! We're on the right path – the Politburo is going to decide to make our *subbotnik* nationwide in the next few days.'

'I'm happy for you,' Rappoport noisily let the air out through his nose.

Yagubov didn't pay any attention to his last words. 'All of this is a great honour, but it obliges us to a lot of things, too. The press run is nine million – the whole country is reading us!'

'Can you be more specific?' Rappoport interrupted.

'More specific? Let's work away in a manner to justify their faith in us.'

'My *subbotnik* is already under way.'

'Exactly!' Yagubov picked it up. 'You put that very well. A Politburo member – they haven't yet said who – is personally going to put an article on the *subbotnik* in our paper, and *you're* the one who'll write the article.'

'Well, that's certainly more specific,' said Rappoport approvingly.

Yagubov, waiting for Rappoport to comprehend his responsibility, walked over to his desk and picked up some galleys. 'Oh, yes, while I still remember! About the jubilee anniversary of the Paris Commune: clean up this piece, please. We don't need any barricades, and a bit less about the rebellion and crowds of people out in the streets. That sort of stuff is of merely historical interest, after all. And add something about the new, strong regime that was necessary. Got that?'

Rappoport nodded again, silently took the article out of Yagubov's hands and went straight to the reference library. Ivlev was there, sitting at a table.

'They went for it?' exclaimed Ivlev and dropped his voice to a whisper. 'They just have nothing to do. Their education doesn't let them make sense out of politics or economics, but an unpaid Saturday field-day for everybody else and they're able to get stuck into it. But our descendants . . . Generations to come will loathe you, Rappoport, for this dirty trick.'

'Inasmuch as you're younger and you will have a chance to meet them, you can tell our descendants that in the Politburo members' articles I used purely Nazi phraseology: "the struggle for our ideals", "the great victory" and whatnot. It's only a little thing, but it's pleasant.'

'There's where they are!' The shout rang out through the reading room.

Zakamorny's beard stood out vividly in the doorway.

'Quiet,' Rappoport reasoned with him, 'what's the orgy about?'

'The orgy's still ahead of us.'

'You know already?'

'"*The day that was past was Friday, and the day beginning was the Sabbath day*." The gospel according to Luke. You owe me a drink now.'

'But you've given up drinking.'

'I gave up *not* drinking. Let's go!'

Zakamorny, Rappoport and Ivlev left the library in single file and set off for the Communist Education department. Once inside Rappoport turned the key so that passers-by wouldn't disturb them, and a bottle of vodka appeared on his desk, pulled by Zakamorny out of the pocket of his tattered overcoat.

'What energy!' Rappoport said with delight. 'Well, sirs, let's divide up the honours: I'll pour, you two drink.'

The tea dregs from one of his cups got chucked under his desk. He took the other cup off the windowsill and filled them both up.

'Pour yourself one, too,' said Ivlev.

Rappoport looked at his watch.

'As my friend Misha Svetlov said, I don't drink between five minutes to four and four o'clock.'

Zakamorny raised his cup and scratched the end of his nose with it. 'Well, let's drink to that which in whose name we, despite everything –'

'– and to us always going to birthday parties and to our enemies having to go on crutches,' Rappoport joined in.

This was a ritual of theirs, a prayer and tribute all at once. Ivlev didn't get to the bottom of his drink. He choked on it; there was a little left in his glass. He tore off a piece of clean paper from a sheet on Rappoport's desk, chewed it and spat it into a corner. Zakamorny, tossing his drink down in one gulp, breathed in forcefully and deeply, yoga-style, making do with oxygen as his *hors d'oeuvre*.

'Well, what? Did the wind-up frog jump?' asked Zakamorny.

'Surely it could have been no other way,' Rappoport replied, as if in surprise. 'There are three stages to newspaper publishing, according to Rappoport's Law: stage one is universal chaos and muddle. Stage two: the beating of the innocents. Stage three: the rewarding of non-participants.'

'We're non-participants?!' said Ivlev in exasperation. 'Wasn't it you who sucked us into this *subbotnik* escapade?'

'I never suck anyone into anything, Ivlev. I go with the flow, avoiding the white water. In the present instance, I merely called something by its own name.' Rappoport pointed a finger at the telephone and finished what he was saying in a whisper. 'I openly said that labour in this country was slavery, and they yell "hurrah!" for some reason.'

'I can't believe it!' muttered Ivlev. 'To make the two-hundred-and-fifty-million-strong Soviet populace drudge away for free, worse still on a Saturday when by all Jewish laws it's a sin to work! And our Rappoport, the simple Soviet, has done it!'

'It says in the Bible,' Zakamorny noted, 'that man is not for Saturday but Saturday for man. Rappoport has corrected the Bible: man *is* for Saturday!'

'Just wait, there's more to come!' Rappoport said gloomily. 'On Saturdays there'll be *subbotniks* and on Sundays – *voskresniks*! We'll join up holidays to vacations, vacations to retirement. We'll spend our retirement in treatment.'

'How can the people stand you?' asked Zakamorny.

'The people? The people love me.' He tenderly stroked the telephone.

'If you were to make nails out of these people, there'd be lots more nails for sale!' declaimed Ivlev.

'You're repeating yourself, Ivlev,' observed Zakamorny. 'I'll pour some more, if you'll allow me . . .'

He raised the bottle to his eyes, estimated the volume and in two sharp tilts of the neck exactly divided up the remaining contents between Ivlev and himself.

'This *subbotnik* is the robbery of the century!' Zakamorny theatrically pronounced. 'Let's drink then, Ivlev, to the author of this audacious project that will soon extract billions from the pocket of the people. It's too bad it's not for himself. He himself remains a pauper. He doesn't even have enough to pay his Party dues with. To Tavroport, our leader and teacher!'

He drank his down and slouched off around the room. Ivlev sipped a bit and lit a cigarette.

'You're not going to finish it?' Zakamorny asked Ivlev. 'Then I'll –' And he drained what was left in Ivlev's cup.

'Being an alcoholic doesn't suit you, Zakamorny,' Rappoport observed. 'You're going downhill.'

'Nonsense! I'm doing exactly what you're doing, only by a different means. We alcoholics speed up our death pangs, and that means that we're promoting progress.'

'Hang on a minute!' Rappoport implored. 'The phone is ringing with painful persistence.'

He bent down over the desk, made a sign with his hand for them to keep quiet and picked up the phone.

'Is this Rappoport?' asked a chesty female voice.

'What if it is?' he answered somewhat irritatedly.

'This is Makartseva.'

'Who?'

'Zina, Makartsev's wife.'

'Oh, forgive me. I didn't catch your name right away. We're having a little meeting here. How's . . . feeling?' He nearly said his name.

'He's better. They've allowed him to talk to people. He asked for you to come by, although he doesn't want anybody at the office to know. For some reason he needs you. They transferred him today from Granovsky to Rublyov Chaussee.'

'Right! I'll go tomorrow.'

'Thanks. Your pass is waiting for you. Do you need a car?'

'No, I'll make my own way.'

Rappoport stood for a while in thought.

'Makartsev's wife?' asked Ivlev.

'What did you get that from?'

'It wasn't hard to twig. What does she want?'

'The boss wants to congratulate me.'

'Is that all?'

'Isn't that enough? To your horses, Chekists! Speaking in Russian, that's *shabash*!'

'*Shabash* a Russian word?' said Zakamorny in surprise. 'Nothing of the sort! It's originally an ancient Hebrew word that means "Saturday".'

'But it's a Russian word in the dictionary. And that keeps it from the people.'

'It's with your help, Rappoport, that it's been Russified.'

'Let's split up, children, before Kashin snitches on our little drunken session.'

Zakamorny grabbed the empty bottle off the desk and stuck it into the inside pocket of his overcoat.

# — 30 —
# Cold Glass

This particular night the 'fresh head' edition checker was Nadya Sirotkina. It was torture for her to do overnight duty on the next day's issue. Nadya was gregarious, and the office emptied out at night. So she had to store up information, hanging on to her news until the next day. And that bored her to tears. After Yagubov passed the pages for press, everyone went home, and Nadya was left alone in the office.

Anything else that needed changing on the passed pages was taken care of in the compositors' shop, then the galleys were taken away to make up the matrix. The next morning, when they were already out of date, the galleys of the now unnecessary pages (if there hadn't been any emergency) would be taken back and pied. But now the matrices went to the stereotype shop. The ink-smeared stereotypists would cast the semicircular panels, and insubstantial words on insubstantial paper would acquire a metallic ring. The transporter hooks carried the stereotypes to the rotary press plant. There they were mounted on the press and register-adjusted; paper was fed in between the cylinders, and the printers would have a go at starting up the plant. The ink would print unevenly on the paper. They would stop the presses, take off the stereotypes, stuff in wads of newsprint under the spot where the ink was uneven, put them back in place again and start the presses up once more. Then the bustle would start again with the registration of the second colour, red, for printing slogans or borders around especially important pieces of news. And the precious night hours, a time for rosy dreams and partying, would simply drain away.

Nadya was sitting in empty expectation. There wasn't even anyone to telephone and unbosom herself to. Everyone was long asleep. She was sitting in the commodious armchair behind the editor-in-chief's desk. Makartsev, that democrat, considered that his employees' sense of responsibility would be increased by that sort of trust in the 'fresh head'. The doors to Makartsev's second, personal, study and his rest room with its separate exit were both locked, of course. To the left sat the dead intercom switchboard: whichever department you buzzed there was nobody to answer, even though a penetrating ringing resounded throughout the office. The clock pendulum swung slowly first to one side and then the other. Nadya was growing older there in the office, and nobody could care less.

She started pulling open the desk drawers. In them lay Central Committee, city committee and Moscow city council telephone books with the legend 'For Official Use Only', as if there could be anyone in the world who would read them for pleasure. There were bundles of leaflets and advertising brochures from tourist agencies of the many countries that the editor travelled to, and Nadya leafed through them without any special interest. Then came copies of bookkeeping accounts for the newspaper's expenditures, mixed up with New Year's cards to the editor and Soviet Army Day greetings that hadn't been thrown out yet by Anna. Nadya put all of these things into a single pile.

Suddenly her gaze fell on a thick envelope, and she took it out of the desk. She decided to find out what the editor wanted to consult the KGB about. She pulled out the Marquis de Custine and started reading him, forgetting about everything else. She tore herself away at about one in the morning. There was only a little time left before the rotary presses started up. Nadya's thoughts returned to Ivlev. She blushed when she recalled what she'd got up to during the day and told herself firmly that it wouldn't happen again. 'Swear it won't!' she told herself.

'Cross my heart!' she answered herself.

At this point both the doors comprising the antechamber of Makartsev's office flew open, and Ivlev appeared. Nadya's eyes opened wide, and she once more felt herself blushing. Nadya would have been less surprised if Jesus Christ himself had appeared. But today Ivlev meant more to her than Christ. Christ was someone incorporeal to her, and, even though nothing had happened, she belonged to Ivlev now.

While Nadya was coming to her senses Ivlev kept his hand on the door handle. Only women are quick-witted enough to turn an unexpected situation into an ordinary one, as if everything is clear to them beforehand.

'Who are you looking for?' asked Nadya unflappably, and her eyes glinted archly in the light from the desk lamp. 'I didn't send for you. What are you here for?'

He had come himself, and finally she had an opportunity to pretend that she didn't need him at all, that she was absolutely indifferent to him. Just think! Several hours earlier she'd had to be both woman and man, to overcome herself and win him, ashamed of herself . . . And now he was standing there, regarding her closely – nervous even, it seemed.

'Are you busy?'

She didn't answer; just blinked her eyes, checking to make sure that it wasn't a dream.

'Are you tired? Want to get some sleep?'

He was stupid apparently. She hadn't closed her eyes for that reason! 'Miaow!' she said, stretching languidly. 'So what's your reason for coming to see me?'

'It's personal,' he explained. 'May I?'

Ivlev moved closer, bent down and placed his hands on hers where they lay on the cold glass of Makartsev's desk. She felt the weight of his hands and instantly became as submissive as she had been earlier that day, in his room. All her good intentions evaporated; her heart beat faster. She waited. Letting go of one of her hands, he pressed the switch on the desk lamp with a finger. It got darker. From the window a diffuse light fell, softening the contours of Nadya's face in the yellow half-light. He pulled her to him by her fingers. Nadya rose from her chair and smoothly floated across the desk, just like someone being led in an unknown dance.

'Yes?' he asked. That 'yes' carried to her from afar, as if flying for a long time through the editor's office, echoing off the walls and ceiling before reaching her ears.

'Yes, what?' she asked him back soundlessly, just her lips moving.

'You haven't changed your mind?'

Smiling with the corners of her mouth, she slowly shook her head in condemnation of his doubts and, tilting back her head, offered him her half-open mouth. Ivlev kissed the corners of her mouth, still afraid of a no. Taking fright at the notion that he might mistake her shyness for a lack of desire, and recalling what he had done with her that day, she passed her hands up and down his back and then, moving them around to his chest and shifting his tie to one side, undid his shirt buttons one by one, thrusting her hands inside. She abruptly got up and started taking her clothes off. Tidily taking off each article of clothing, she held it out to Ivlev, kissing him after handing over every piece.

'Now I love you,' he said.

She nodded, as if it went without saying that now he loved her. *Now you can't help loving me.* But she didn't stir, she just stood a step away from Ivlev, hot and bothered and draped with her things. He looked around for a place to put her clothes and placed them down on the long, narrow table around which the bureau editors gathered at their planning sessions. Then he grabbed Nadya by the elbows, lifted her up and sat her down on Makartsev's desk.

'You'll catch cold, standing around barefoot,' he explained.

'You think the glass on this desk is warmer than the floor?' she asked shivering.

He tried to prop her up off the glass of the desk with his hands, without success. Then he shifted the thick grey folder lying on the desk, to place it underneath her. Nadya was warmer straight away. Ivlev roughly groped her, and Nadya, who belonged to him now, was silent and submissively expectant. He began to do the deed. Nadya suddenly raised her eyes in fright: 'Oh, no! He's looking at us! I'm scared.'

A portrait photo of a half-smiling Lenin, blown up at Makartsev's special request by the photographer, Kakabadze, hung above the editor's desk.

'Look at me and not at him,' Ivlev suggested. He snatched Nadya's knickers off the pile of underclothing, climbed up on the desk and hung them over the upper half of the Leader's face.

'Is that all right?'

'Yes, that's better.'

He began to kiss her knees, her belly, her neck. She flinched from the pain, trying not to moan, and he stopped.

'Haven't you ever . . . ?' He was surprised at this.

'Never,' she explained. 'Do you despise me? Just don't leave me; the glass has warmed up and I'm warm.'

He was touching Nadya lightly again when the phone rang. Nadya stretched over to reach it.

'Yes. I'll be right there.' She hung up.

'It'll be too bad if we don't do this again,' she said.

'But doesn't it hurt?'

'It hurts. But it'll be too bad anyway.'

'We'll do this again.' He grinned. 'Why wouldn't we?'

'Just not today.'

'Not today?' He was offended. 'Why not today? When?'

'Whenever you want. Let me up! I'm frozen. And I have to pass the issue for press.'

'Don't forget your knickers!'

In the shimmering light from the street Lenin winked at them, and the smile froze on his lips. Nadya dressed in a flash. She turned on the desk lamp and pulled the middle drawer out, to hide away the envelope with the grey folder.

'What's that?'

Nadya wondered if she should say something to Ivlev about the folder but decided not to distract his attention from her.

'I was rooting around in the desk out of boredom,' she said carelessly. 'Maybe you should get dressed, too. Or have you decided to change jobs and become Apollo?'

Standing in the middle of the office he studied her. 'I still love you!' he said.

She ran over to him, got down on her knees and kissed him.

'You know, when it's little it's even cuter! It looks like the handle on a toilet chain.'

'And me!' he said. 'Kiss me, too!'

'You have nothing to do with this!' she whispered archly.

In the lift she glanced at herself in the mirror and recoiled: her blouse was unbuttoned, her hair dishevelled, there were red spots on her cheeks, and her lips were swollen from kisses. In those several seconds it took the lift to deliver her down to the print shop she managed to button herself up, tug her skirt around so that the zip was properly positioned at the back, smooth down her hair and do a quick finger-massage of her face to even out the red spots with the surrounding paleness – at least a little bit.

In the printing plant all the presses were running, and the rumble spread into every nook and cranny – the stairway railings, the doors and the windowsills all vibrated, and her feet could feel the minute vibration of the concrete floor. Nadya was instantly deafened. The rumble of the revolving rollers bore down relentlessly, depriving her of reason. With a speed that defied the eyes' ability to follow it, a river of paper was flowing, pouring out on to the rollers from under the floor. Suddenly and instantly it was filled with text and photographs, chopped into lengths, folded and sent crawling up through the crack in the ceiling as the latest issue of *Trudovaya Pravda*. Eight German rotary presses, removed from Germany in 1945 as war reparations, were already in their twenty-fourth year of fulfilling their function in another propaganda machine and doing it with the thoroughness characteristic of their creators. Thirty thousand copies per hour in total, a print run of a million in four hours and twenty minutes. According to the schedule, everything had to be finished at four forty in the morning, and at five thirty the last of the mail trucks had to leave the publisher's courtyard. A report on how the schedule had gone, signed by the head of the printing plant, was on the desk of the editor's secretary every day at ten o'clock in the morning. If everything went to schedule that night Anna would simply fasten the slip into the report folder. If the schedule wasn't adhered to, Anna would underline the name of the guilty party in red pencil and leave it on the editor's desk.

On this occasion everything went according to schedule. Cautiously avoiding the rubbish bins and fire extinguishers, Nadya made her way to the desk of the shop foreman. The corpulent foreman, dressed in an oil-smeared coverall, nodded indifferently to her, wiped his hands on a petrol-soaked rag and deftly pulled out a copy of the issue from under the legs of the conveyor belt. Nadya unfolded the pages with the tips of her fingers, and after laying the issue out on the desk carefully pressed her little finger against the edge of the text to see if the ink had dried. The letters imprinted themselves on her skin. Nadya began checking over the headlines, trying to penetrate their meaning, spot (in the wake of dozens of other people who did this all day and more sedulously) any errors, non-sensicalities or blunders. She checked as she should to see if any of the type plates were upside down, if the names underneath the photos corresponded to the faces shown in them, simultaneously wondering whether Ivlev was going to wait for her as she rooted around down here or leave.

The foreman stood alongside Nadya, regarding her with a smirk. Not waiting for her to finish, he pulled a paper carton of milk out of a drawer in his desk, bit off a corner and started drinking, throwing back his head sharply enough to cause drops of milk to fall on the paper. He then flung the empty carton into a corner. Without asking, Nadya took a pen out of his breast pocket, wrote something in tiny letters, signed it and, after glancing at the foreman, wrote down the time as 00.30, as the schedule demanded, although it was already 00.45. She stuck the pen back into his pocket and ran to the lift. When the gates clattered shut she sighed with relief – at the quiet, at the possibility of calming down. Thank God, the slog was over!

Ivlev wasn't there. Nadya locked up the office, hid the key in Anna's desk and went downstairs. The special correspondents' office was locked as well. Nadya heaved a sigh and told herself that she had been expecting this, donned her fur coat, powdered her face and put on lipstick. That was something she hardly ever did, even though she always carried around French powder and lipstick. The last office car and driver was waiting to take her home. Once she was in the passenger's seat alongside the driver she caught sight of Ivlev. He was sitting on a wet bench in the public garden under an old, gnarled maple, lit by a dim street lamp swaying in the wind. His collar was raised, and he was in an old-womanish pose with his hands tucked into opposite sleeves. *Frozen stiff, the poor thing, waiting.* The chauffeur lifted his head off the steering wheel, reached a hand to the key and wiped his eyes with the other.

'I'm not going,' Nadya said suddenly. 'My place isn't far from here. I'll walk.'

He nodded, pulled out a trip ticket and held it out for her to sign. 'Put the time as a little later,' he requested.

Nadya signed quickly, and he closed the door and drove off. She quietly stole up on Ivlev from behind, turned down his collar and blew into his ear. Not turning around, he forcefully grabbed her with one hand.

'That hurts. It hurts!' she wheezed. 'You're tearing my head off!'

'Where do you live?' Ivlev asked, leading her around the bench and pulling her between his knees.

'On Old Mares' Avenue.'

'That, pardon me, is where?'

'That's what a friend of my father's calls it. It's actually Old Stables Lane.'

'In the Arbat? We can get there in an hour.'

'We can. But what about your wife? She'll be worried.'

'She's used to it.'

Ivlev took Nadya by the hand, and they went out on to the half-lit street. Most of the street lamps were out, to save on electricity. Snowdrifts, black with soot, lay along the footpath, surrounded by huge puddles. A truck rumbled by – construction materials were delivered in Moscow by night. A police patrol car drove past them and slowed down. The policemen looked suspiciously at Ivlev and Nadya but were too lazy to get out and check their documents.

'I love Moscow at night,' she said dreamily. 'There's no crowds, no queues, no rudeness. I especially like it after a snowfall. Everything's clean.'

'Snow does look like washing powder.'

'No! Like white sheets!' she turned towards him, walking backwards, and kissed him on the cheek. 'You know, I always thought that it would happen in a double bed, like in foreign films. A sheet with little flowers on it. And in the morning you open the curtains and outside the window there's sunshine, and the woods are covered with snow.'

'It was nicer on the editor's desk.'

'The office is a whorehouse, you said that yourself.'

'You remember that?'

'I remember everything you say. I'm so happy today! I managed to get you, anyhow. I got you!'

Ivlev grinned and started to say something, then thought better of it.

'You know, this is incredible, even . . .' she continued. 'Tell me – am I a woman now?'

'Not yet.'

'No? But I thought . . . Well, when, then?'

'What – when?'

'When do I become a woman?'

'How would I know? Most likely whenever you stop asking me about it.'

'The newspaper office is a whorehouse,' Nadya said dreamily. 'Two sociologists are collecting material for their dissertation in our department. Yesterday, when we were left alone in the room, one of them came up to me and put his hand on my waist. "Nadya," he says, "I've got a request for you." "If you please," I say. "Will you kindly throw out any letters with an anti-Soviet content so that we won't have to read all our mail?"'

'What used to happen to them?'

'Before, I used to hand those letters over to my superiors, like they ordered me to. I didn't know, after all. But today I understood.'

'Why today?'

'Well, I found a *samizdat* manuscript in the editor's desk. When *you* get the duty, you'll have to read what's in the grey folder. Just don't tell anyone. I've told you, because . . . I don't have anybody else. This is my Old Stables. That's Khrushchev's entryway.'

'Is he guarded?'

'All the entrances in our building are guarded. Come on in, don't be afraid.'

They stood for a while in the darkness until the caretaker had gone to his desk in the corner of the hall. The lift gates clapped shut, and her slender fingers stuck out through the grille. He began kissing them, one by one.

'Have pity on me!' she whispered. 'Otherwise I'll die – of unrequited desire.'

# 31

# Meeting at the Kremlin Hospital

The danger had passed to the extent that Makartsev was transferred to the new hospital building in the pine groves on Rublyov Chaussee. But he stayed flat on his back. At first he flinched at the penetrating alarm that rang periodically in all the wards.

'Now don't you worry yourself,' the pretty nurse tenderly soothed him.

'But what's the matter?'

'The alarm's just a warning for the hospital staff. As long as it's ringing we can't go out into the corridors, because a Politburo member has arrived for treatment. But when it stops we can go out again.'

And Makartsev grew used to it. It even got to be pleasant to hear when the alarm rang: in the hospital it meant he was still close to the leadership. Yesterday, after his regular visit, Professor Myasnikov had promised that he was going to allow him to turn over on his right side. 'Another month – well, month and a half at most – and you'll be as sound as a bell . . . well, one you can't ring, yet, for a while.'

'I need a telephone,' Makartsev demanded.

'Telephone? No! No way! You need to have positive emotions.'

He was permitted to read a little. He talked the nurse into bringing him the library copy of *Trudovaya Pravda*. He read his newspaper now the way everyone did, in the morning instead of the day before. He closely inspected every issue that had come out in his absence.

'No, just think about it, Zina!' he said agitatedly to his wife. 'What are the pages full of? Storms in a teacup, when I told them a hundred times: raise significant issues; don't be petty. Why did I agree to take on Yagubov?'

'Don't worry,' she said, trying to calm him down. She tenderly took the copy of *Trudovaya Pravda* out of his hands. 'After all, it wasn't you who picked Yagubov. Of *course* you would have found your own sort of man. But you'll be out of here soon, and this Yagubov will be back carrying out *your* orders again.'

Yagubov, so to speak, came along with the job. The newspaper had been given yet another deputy editor, but, of all people, Makartsev certainly should have understood what the whole thing smelt of. All his deputies had dual subordination – to him and to the Central Committee. Yagubov, without a doubt, had to be among those with yet another subordination – to the KGB as well. *What's all this overcontrol about? Mistrust, underhand tricks . . . I thought we'd finished with that sort of thing, and now here it is again. There's something here I don't understand. I always put out the newspaper myself – you could say I was inspiring my people. And now secondary functionaries decide things in my place and consider me old-fashioned – me, of all people – for coming in at night to check the proofs. They call it 'micromanaging affairs' – pure atavism. Lenin was right, after all, to say that if there was anything that would be the undoing of the Soviet regime it would be bureaucracy.*

'Did you call Rappoport?' he impatiently asked his wife. 'Where the hell is he?'

'Of course I called him. He said he was coming. I'm going to wash your back now. I hope I can do a better job than the nurse, although you'd probably prefer if she was doing it and batting her eyes at you the whole time.'

'Don't talk nonsense.'

He closed his eyes in half-sleep, while Zina washed his back down to his tailbone with an alcohol swab, to ward off bedsores. She sat down again, opened up his copy of *Trudovaya Pravda* and looked through it. She did this from time to time but only in front of Makartsev. She was thinking about how successfully she had managed to pass an expensive present to the ward head, a woman physician. For some dollars left over from her husband's last trip abroad, knowing that the doctor had an adolescent son, she had bought a denim suit and a Japanese watch at a *beryozka*, a store for foreigners and people with hard currency. The doctor had been very pleased and straight away informed Zina that she had already been promised new Swiss medication, obtained by some serious string-pulling, something that you wouldn't find even here in the Kremlin hospital if you looked for it in daylight with torches, and she was going to use it all up on Makartsev. Zina promised her a Japanese umbrella and asked what her shoe size was, after which they parted, pleased with one another. There wasn't any reason to tell her husband about it, of course.

The pretty nurse half opened the door and said softly: 'You have a visitor. Shall I let him in?'

'Go ahead,' he said.

Zina had made a present of a bottle of French perfume to this nurse not long before. Makartsev liked the way his nurse had asked the question, and his eyes grew brighter. Patients who were on the mend, and who had once more become people in charge, got to instruct the medical staff whether or not to let people in. Slowly and clumsily Rappoport walked into the ward, holding a white smock closed at his throat with a hand that was hairier than his head. He waved his hands and shifted his weight back and forth, spraying saliva.

'Makartsev, Makartsev! Did you get permission from someone to be sick? I'm the one who's suppose to be rattling around in hospital, according to all the known facts, after all.'

'Why you?' said Makartsev, smiling weakly.

'Just like a Young Pioneer, I'm always ready – for the hospital.'

'You don't look much like a Young Pioneer. Does he, Zina?'

She smiled politely.

'I've mustered for roll-call in a different kind of camp, which is why I don't look particularly fresh. I have a hundred ailments, but you've robbed me of my whole quota!'

'You'll get your own back! I'm glad to see you, old man. This is my wife. Zina, this is Rappoport – you've heard me mention him.'

'Rappoport,' Rappoport said, introducing himself.

'We're already acquainted.' Zina held out her hand. 'Over the phone.'

'I only accept Party resolutions over the phone. But beautiful women, you know, are so few and far between that you've got to look at them in person.'

'My husband doesn't appreciate me,' she said, stroking Makartsev's head.

'You've been sitting around here long enough!' Makartsev slapped her hand. 'Boris is going to come home for dinner and you won't be there. Don't worry about me. Rappoport and I are going to talk over newspaper affairs for while – it won't interest you.' He pulled his wife to him by the hand and kissed her on the cheek. Zina nodded to Rappoport.

'I beg you, not for long. You have to do as I ask. I'm telling you this as a doctor.'

'You're not a doctor. You're the wife of a senior executive.'

She pursed her lips in evident offence and quietly closed the door behind her.

'What's going on at the office? Tell me!' Makartsev greedily threw himself on Rappoport as soon as his wife had barely disappeared behind the door. 'By the way, in my spare time I got to read your article "Writers Are Ideological Warriors". It was a sensible and, most important, *correct* generalization. What are you laughing at?'

'Writers come in two categories,' grumbled Rappoport. 'Those who get written for and those who write for others.'

'But surely there are real writers?'

'I'm afraid they aren't warriors on any ideological front.'

'Well, God help them all!' Makartsev pretended that Rappoport had said something else – something not subversive. 'We have enough trouble with our own writers. So we'll think about them.'

'If that's the case . . .'

'Here's what, Rappoport. I'd rather you told me about the *subbotnik*. What's the latest plan of action?'

'What's there to tell you? The fraternal socialist countries have given their support. Our whole camp is coming out with shovels in hand. How much further can we go?'

'What scale! You've struck real gold there! That's journalism for you, as I understand it. I congratulate you from the bottom of my heart. Just you wait – I'll get out of hospital and propose a motion to award you the Journalists' Union Prize.'

'I don't need it. I don't need any prize.' Rappoport waved his hands. 'You'd do better to put a leash on that Yagubov.'

'Is he getting in your way? That son of a bitch! Hasn't got a clue about the importance of a project. My deputy – what a limited horizon he has!'

'It's not that. He does understand that much! Look . . . I know it's necessary to be an anti-Semite –'

'Nonsense!'

'– but you can't do it like that, right between the eyes.'

'That scum! Don't let him scare you, Rappoport! As long as I'm the editor-in-chief of that newspaper nobody's going to lay a finger on you. I know that for a fact. Here's what to do. Prepare a report for the next Party meeting – something on the demands of ideological work in these new conditions.'

'Me? My own report for the meeting?'

'You, yes, you! I'll give Yagubov his instructions. It'll be important for your prestige in the Party. There'll be representatives of the district committee, the municipal committee and the Central Committee at the meeting.'

'Please, suit yourself.'

There was a pause in their conversation, and Rappoport once again wondered what Makartsev needed him for so badly. Not so that he could finally congratulate him on the birth of his idea for the anniversary *subbotnik*. And even less so that he could commission a report for the Party meeting. Surely he was worrying about the grey folder again.

'By the way, before I forget . . .' Makartsev broke into the silence, grimacing with pain. 'Do you remember the folder?'

Makartsev's thoughts had been going back to it again and again while he had been in hospital. The Marquis de Custine was giving him no peace. Of course, Makartsev had done the right thing back then. But the circumstances had changed. Something in his desk might be needed, and they'd go searching. You couldn't rule out Kashin or some bystander doing it. And what if someone started thinking that Makartsev was informing on his employees? Makartsev's chest started hurting at the thought.

'So, about that folder,' he repeated, angry with himself, glancing at the door. 'For some reason it's really weighing on me. I'm obliged by my position, you know yourself! If it's in my possession, that means that I'm connected with it. Stupid, right?'

'I hope you're not going to make me take the thing voluntarily to the Lubyanka?'

'You think so badly of me! It's just that while I'm sick we'd better hide it, get it out of harm's way, so it's not lying around the office. Anything could happen.'

'That makes sense,' Rappoport said, shaking his head. 'I'll take it away – nobody will even know about it.'

'It's in the middle drawer of my desk.'

'Might as well be in the middle drawer. I'll hide it somewhere away from the office, right?'

'Exactly.' Makartsev's eyes lit up. 'As long as it just isn't there. No evidence, no trial!'

'I'm sure there's a court somewhere that could put you away, evidence or no evidence! But why leave any extraneous evidence around?'

'Exactly! So, you'll do it?'

'Sure.' Rappoport stretched his hand out to Makartsev. 'And don't you worry any more about that folder. Keep your pecker up, Makartsev! I'm gone, and I was never even here.'

After coming down to the marble vestibule Rappoport handed over his smock to the cloakroom lady and was pulling on his overcoat, grunting, when Zina walked up to him.

'You?' said Rappoport in surprise. 'Haven't you gone home yet?'

'I've been waiting for you. Tell me, what did Makartsev ask you to do?'

'Where'd you get the idea that he asked me to do something? What if it was me asking him?'

'No! He . . . Nobody would come here looking for something from him. I wouldn't allow it.'

'Well, fine. Let's say he did. Surely it's nothing that would interest you? This sort of problem is a long way from women's business. And it would take a long time to explain from the very beginning.'

'A long time? Who cares! You know, I've been feeling that he's been hiding something from me. Whenever I ask, he just shushes me.'

'Your husband takes the prestige of the newspaper close to heart. That's why he gets so upset. We've just started a campaign on the scale of the entire socialist world.'

'The *subbotnik*?'

'Exactly. And there is a real danger – something that alarms Makartsev most of all. Truth to tell, I think it's something that's not without foundation.'

'Danger?'

'The danger that the campaign – to put it as nicely as possible – will be appropriated by other newspapers or by the Party apparatus.'

'What's wrong with that?'

'That the work won't be considered our own.'

'Well, so what?'

'And it won't be Makartsev who gets any advancement out of it from among the candidate members of the Central Committee but somebody else. Did you want to ask me something?'

'You said that I'm a beautiful woman. Did you have in mind that I'm an idiot?'

'How can you say something like that?'

'Then what was it Makartsev asked you to do?'

'From tomorrow we're going to be stressing in all our articles that the campaign was started by *Trudovaya Pravda*. That's not too tactful, and the Central Committee might not like it. But before they figure it out we'll have already staked our claim, and it'll be that much more difficult to steal the campaign out from under Makartsev.'

She didn't swallow it, and he started respecting her a bit more.

'Are you going back to the office?' Zina asked drily. 'I'll give you a lift.'

He had imagined that he would be dragging himself to the bus now, to freeze at the bus stop for a long while, then have to go down into the damp Molodyozhnaya metro station and sit on the icy oilskin subway seats for half an hour until he got to the centre of town, where he'd have to change yet again . . . Makartsev's Volga sedan was warm and clean. But Rappoport had already given it a miss on his way to the hospital.

'You know, it's been ten years since I was out in the woods,' said Rappoport, indicating the window with his hand. 'I've forgotten what it smells like, and now, they say, it's spring. I think I'll go there for a stroll, if you don't object.'

'As you like.' Opening wide the glass door Zina walked proudly out.

# 32

# The Existence of
# Zina Makartseva

Although Zina never mentioned it to anyone, even Makartsev, she had been born into the family of Count Zhevnyakov, who had received a splendid education at the Sorbonne and Heidelberg and held an estate in the south of Russia, a gift to his ancestors from Empress Catherine II. After the Revolution the young Rostov lawyer and landlord lost everything that belonged to him, so he concealed his titles and went to work in the court system as soon as the Soviet regime had need of lawyers. Defending others, he managed to defend himself as well; he stayed in one piece by some miracle and married a teacher for love but then died soon after, leaving behind two daughters.

The sisters grew up to be beauties of not immoderately southern and swarthy tones, but there was something cold in their beauty. Their mother called them little countesses when nobody was around. Life in Rostov was hard and hungry for them. During the war they found themselves in Central Asia. Zina graduated from her ten years of secondary school and entered the medical institute that had been evacuated there. The teacher of the general therapy course was a Professor Fleytman, who at once turned his attention to his beautiful student, who was intelligent to boot. Fleytman's wife – a surgeon who had voluntarily gone off to the front – had been killed at the start of the war. Fleytman proposed to Zina; it would have been stupid to turn him down. She graduated from the institute, and the professor, through a colleague who was at the time working at the Ministry of Health's Fourth Directorate, got her a job at an out-patient clinic for government bigwigs.

Out of the blue, Professor Fleytman announced to Zina that he had a presentiment that it would be better for them to get divorced. She didn't understand and proudly walked away from him. After she became Makartsev's wife Zina found out that Fleytman had been dismissed from all of his posts and later on imprisoned during the Doctors' Plot. By getting a divorce Professor Fleytman had saved her. He loved her.

Makartsev guarded her from unpleasantness with the same care as her first husband. She had stopped working long before and had never returned to it. She never had to think about her well-being either: it was there, always, even when Makartsev was a hair's breadth from downfall. Zina grew accustomed to the difficult position of a high official's wife and steadfastly bore her burden. Even though she was already forty-four years old, time hadn't touched her, it seemed: her face, her figure, her walk – everything was good as could be. When she walked down the street holding her son by the hand an age difference could be seen, of course, but not the real one. Makartsev was getting older faster, but it could have been the other way around.

He was proud of the fact that his wife was so beautiful and was delighted whenever they got to go out together. But this seldom happened. She scarcely had to start saying that she missed the fresh air and he would pack her off to their government *dacha*; she scarcely had to hint that she was tired and within the hour he would be on the phone telling her that he had booked her a trip to a health resort. She loved to go on holiday at Likani in Georgia, at the restricted Central Committee sanatorium near Borzhomi. The old palace of the Romanov tsars was in a fabulously beautiful forest; there were few people there, and the waters were salubrious. It was as if her family past were opening out in front of her dark eyes.

Zina didn't accept sanatorium morals. She was indignant at the lack of restraint of the men and especially the women, lightly colluding for a single evening. There was something catty about it: she would make a wry face, squeamish, and try not to make the acquaintance of anyone, so that she wouldn't have to hear the inevitable 'We drank some brandy and then . . .' Sometimes she would try to feel sorry for the women, to understand them. But then she would think fastidiously: 'Makartsev and I have a lot of troubles of our own, after all, but neither he nor I would ever stoop to something like that.'

She would do everything in her power to make Makartsev get better – to cure him. Other people had two or three heart attacks and went back to work afterwards, no problem. The only one who evaded the logic of her life was her son. On the other hand, though, everyone was having problems now with their children. Boris would grow up and get wiser. If her husband would help, intervene a little more often, then she would worry less. But he relied on his wife in this matter. Zina had frequently begged him to get seriously involved with their son, to be a man to Boris. Makartsev would promise and intend to do it for a long time; he would think it over, try to do it and put it off. And now that he'd taken ill, she thought: 'Well, right: now Makartsev will have time to think about his son, and the boy's going to become more patient with his father. And everything's going to come out right.'

# — 33 —
## I'm Going to Kiss You Anyway!

Nadya was certain that she was going to calm down, now that Ivlev, whether he wanted to or not, was hers (however seldom she managed to exert total power over him). After all, she didn't need anything from him, and what had been needed was obtained. Love brought with it a condition of discomfort only so long as the love remained unsatisfied: Nadya had picked that up from a book somewhere. But now her interest in Special Correspondent Ivlev was supposed to subside, since everything had happened and nothing more could come of it. It was just something that didn't fit into her plans. Now she'd served out her Ivlev jail sentence. But there was to be no amnesty for Nadya.

*It'll pass,* she told herself sternly. *It'll be enough to see him, even if seldom, and nothing more. Well, and hear him talking* – even if not to her but to others. *The important thing is to latch on to something different: after all, everything is over and done with!* But now some kind of new power was ruling Nadya. If in her thoughts at work or at home, going to bed well past midnight, it had been enough previously for her to talk to him, listen to him, stroll down the streets together – now she was left with a sour taste in her mouth; she wanted another bite of the apple. She was ashamed. She assured herself that it was beyond her strength to play a modern, active woman for very long.

The only thing that stopped her was the fear of scaring him off completely. She didn't know what to do with herself. That evening she told herself that tomorrow she would go up to him and ask him to go to the pictures with her. So she bought some tickets, but when she saw him at the office there he was, pursuing whatever his goals were: notions whose content and depth were beyond her, or seemed secondary to her, after what had gone on between them. He was arguing with somebody in the corridor, swearing horribly, and she hurried to pass him by, even though she heard his appalling language without any hostility. He didn't have any time for her. She ran to the women's lavatory and tore up the tickets. After flushing the pieces down the toilet she wept. Then she stood for a long time looking out the window at the printing plant block, where the rotary presses were roaring, and waited until the redness had gone from her eyes.

'Listen,' she chirped cheerfully, running into Ivlev in the corridor as if by accident.

'Hi!' Ivlev looked at her distractedly and waited for her to continue.

But she choked and her words got all mixed up, enough lightness in her only for the one word.

'What's up with you?' he asked in surprise.

She clenched her fists. Her long nails dug into her palms. After a very long, drawn-out pause she finally remembered what it was that she'd thought up in advance. In a whisper, slowly squeezing out the words and making herself smile carelessly, Nadya said: 'By the way, I'm celebrating an anniversary today.'

'Congratulations. What kind?'

'It's exactly three years since my appendix was out.'

'You should tell Rappoport. Let him write a leader about it.'

'I think not! But if you'd like, we *could* celebrate it. Well, for instance, we could go to Journalists' House. I've got some money.'

'You know –' He stopped short. 'I'm flying out tonight.'

'Where to?'

'Novosibirsk. Rappoport asked me to whip up an article about the *subbotnik* for the provincial committee secretary. Rappoport doesn't like going to Siberia – I've got to give the old man a hand.'

'For long?'

'A week.'

'And what about this evening?'

'What – this evening?'

'Nothing!'

Nadya flared up, suddenly hating him. She felt like making a sharp retort or hitting him, to put a full stop to the whole thing. But she just smiled and walked away, trying to step lightly and independently. The day stretched out tediously, like a tape on a machine with dying batteries. But in the evening Nadya borrowed some pink frosted lipstick from Inna in the typing pool, applied it and went off to Journalists' House. Alone. With the firm intention of drinking, in defiance of propriety, to the glorious memory of her appendix.

Nadya couldn't bring herself to go into the restaurant, though. She bought herself a cup of coffee and a glass of brandy at the bar. She found herself an unoccupied table, littered with sweet wrappers, next to the wall. She sat with her back to the entrance, so as not to see anybody. Nadya warmed up after a swallow of her brandy. Ivlev was going to change his mind and come here for half an hour before his flight. She swallowed some more, and Ivlev grew more indistinct. She took out a cigarette, hoping that the bad-tasting residual memory of that scoundrel would vanish along with the smoke from her cigarette – the only drug (if you didn't count alcohol) allowed in her native land for some reason. She didn't have a match, so she looked around.

'Allow me.'

A tall, thin man in a checked pullover lifted up a beautiful foreign lighter to her face, adroitly turning it around in his fingers and flicking it, illuminating her smooth brow.

'And for that,' he asked, 'would you give me a cigarette?'

'I'm not going to give you anything for that. I'll simply give you one – you're welcome.'

Without any further ado he sat down next to her and lit up. The boy was younger than Nadya and presented nothing of practical interest. Right off she should have told him politely that her husband was on his way. But Ivlev hadn't vanished quite yet, and she wanted revenge. Nadya wasn't really up to the role of fatal seductress, but, so long as her voices were telling her to get revenge, she would go along with them.

'I've seen you here several times already.' He said what he should and nothing more.

'You have a good memory,' Nadya said.

'Even my parents admit it.'

'Why "even"?'

'Because everything about me irritates them. I can imagine how my mother would jump out of her skin if she found out that I want to get married.'

'Congratulations!' Nadya pronounced the word with Ivlev's intonation and got angry with herself for doing so.

'Thank you. It's just that I haven't got a bride yet.'

'Well, that's no problem.'

'It is. I have strict requirements: five foot three, seven stone and a bit, with a D-cup bust. Just like you, in fact.'

*I'm a size C,* Nadya's tongue was itching to say. But she decided that it would be improper to corrupt this youngster with any more vulgarity than he already had in sufficiency, without any help from her. 'Listen to the Sheikh of Araby!'

'Let's have a drink.'

'A cup of coffee each.'

'And a brandy, too!'

'Surely you've been drinking already?'

'And you,' he riposted. 'I've only had four tots – that's about half a bottle, no more.'

'So how much can you hold?'

'I've drunk up to a whole bottle,' he said modestly. 'Never attempted more than that. Shall we try?'

*Do your mummy and daddy get angry with you?* she might have asked. But she wasn't going to humiliate him.

'No, it would cost too much. But one each, a teeny one . . .'

They drank.

'Have you ever drunk Mexican spirits?' he asked. 'There's a little sack of pepper tied to the bottle and a pickled worm swimming around inside it. It gives a special bouquet, you know. They put another glass on the table and kiss the worm instead of eating any *hors d'oeuvres*.'

They drank another three tots apiece, and Nadya thought that the fact that she had got drunk on her own without Ivlev was in itself a nice revenge for his selfishness. Her new friend helped her put on her fur coat, not very skilfully. While doing it, as if by accident, he touched her neck and hair, and she, as if by accident, pulled away. On the street he took her by the arm and led her to a beige Moskvich. The cold engine didn't want to start for a long time, and it seemed like it was never going to go at all. Nadya sat in the cold car with her nose buried in her fluffy fur collar. The engine caught, and her new friend, not waiting for the engine to heat, abruptly drove off. The unwarmed engine missed, jerking and spluttering. There weren't many cars, pedestrians or police on Nikitsky Boulevard; a light, dry snow was falling, running away from the car in different directions along the blacktop. Hurtling out of the tunnel, the Moskvich braked at the intersection: there was a red light.

'Here's an idea. Shall we go for a drive in the woods?'

'At night?'

'What are we – children? Let's go for a stroll.'

'In the cold?'

'I'll turn on the heater.' He turned the handle.

The ventilator made a chirping noise as it came to life, blowing warm air on their legs.

'Some other time, all right?' Nadya said tenderly. 'My father's waiting. He'll get angry. This way to my place.'

'I'll see you upstairs.'

'You don't have to. I can manage.'

'I will!' he said stubbornly and walked with her into the entrance.

The caretaker looked him over carefully, but, understanding that he was with Nadya, said nothing, just followed them with his eyes as they went up the stairs.

'What about a kiss?' he asked, when she gave him her hand.

'Kiss who?' She raised her eyes in surprise.

'You.'

'Isn't it a little soon?'

He clumsily pulled her to him. Nadya turned away and tried to free herself.

'Let me go. I'm not a Mexican worm. You can't do that!'

'Why can't I?' he said stupidly. 'I can!'

'And I say you can't!'

She bent down and darted under his arm, then started searching in her bag for her key.

'When can I, then?' he asked, rocking back on his heels.

Nadya shrugged and stuck the key in the door.

'Let's stand here a bit longer. I don't want to go home.'

'Better another time. Can you memorize my phone number?'

He wrote the number down on his cigarette packet. 'Maybe we'll go for a spin now, anyway?'

But she'd already opened the door.

'You won't mix me up with some other Boris when I call? Do you know any other Borises? I'm Makartsev. Do you know my father, Makartsev? Everyone knows him.'

'Makartsev?' she asked. 'Who's that?'

'How did you get into Journalists' House? Where are you studying?'

'I work in a tailor shop,' she said. 'As a tailor. Some friends of mine brought me along to Journalists' House.'

'I really want to kiss you.'

'I've already told you: no!'

She hurriedly closed the door behind her. He pressed his mouth to the keyhole and said through it: 'I'm going to kiss you anyway, you'll see! On the mouth.'

Boris Makartsev skipped down the stairs five at a time and nearly fell at the turn. At the last moment he grabbed the banister with one hand.

# — 34 —
## The Circumstances Accompanying
## and Impeding Boris Makartsev

Makartsev had no doubt that his son, like all the children of Party members in his position, would enter the Institute for International Relations, and a 'satisfactory' grade on his school-leaving examinations wasn't a very big defect if you could pull strings when necessary. Makartsev wanted his son to become a journalist, too, but he appeared to have no vocation in this sphere. Or in any other sphere, to tell the truth. All he could do was hope the boy would wise up somehow. If he ever wanted to enter the Moscow State University journalism faculty all Makartsev had to do was telephone Zagulsky, the faculty dean, whose exposés of Western ills *Trudovaya Pravda* published after each of his trips abroad. Everything would work out its own way; you just had to be at the proper starting point. And Makartsev had the influence to put his son in the front ranks when the time came, for sure!

That's what his father thought while Boris was in his last year of school. But after he finished he announced to his parents that he was going to leave his diploma with them as a souvenir, since he was going off for a break. He wasn't about to enrol in any international whatever, since it was only mamas' boys and fashion slaves who studied there, and he certainly wasn't interested in flashy threads.

'So why did you take French, then?' Makartsev asked. It turned out that Boris and his friends had mastered French in order to blather over the telephone while remaining incomprehensible to their parents. 'So you consider my life uninteresting?'

'Sure. Any proletarian workhorse is a hundred times happier than you!

They knock out their eight hours, knock back their glass of vodka – no worries. While you shiver all night worrying whether you made any mistakes that evening and if they're going to fire you the next morning.'

'Wouldn't you like to live abroad?' his father said, trying to buy him off. 'Interesting diversions, films and whatnot, that we don't get here?'

'Do you think I don't know what you're allowed to go abroad for? Anton's father was made the director of an institute. And for what? For stealing a few ampoules from some company where he was getting work experience in England.'

'That's an extreme case!'

'That's industrial espionage. That's your external trade. And journalism! Have you ever published anything of what you saw abroad? You only publish something after you've blackened it a hundred ways.'

'You're taking everyday ideological games to heart.'

'Nothing of the kind. I take it to the place where it fits.'

'All right, Boris. You go to work in some factory.'

'No way! Let the stiffs do the work.'

'So you're going into the army?'

'No, I'm not. You'll make a phone call and they'll say I have a heart murmur and leave me in peace.'

'I certainly won't. I swear to you!'

'Mother will lean on you – you'll make the call.'

'I'm telling you this in front of your mother. Do you hear me, Zina? Your son – a sponger, a parasite? I won't let that happen! I'll call the Ministry of Defence myself in the autumn. They'll come and get you. You'll go into the navy – service there is even a year longer! But there is an alternative.' Makartsev hesitated but decided to try to strike a bargain. 'Enrol in an institute, and I'll buy you a car. Your mother and I will have to scrimp, but I'll buy one for you. And remember – my word is good as gold.'

'Your word is full of shit!'

A month later, though, Boris informed his mother that, sure enough, he was going to enrol in an institute.

'Which one?'

'The Maurice Thorez Institute of Foreign Languages. Did you hear me? I'm going to be a *tolmach*.'

'A what?'

'An interpreter, Mother.'

'Why that institute in particular? Your father had in mind something more prestigious.'

'My spies tell me that the girls there are good-lookers, right? But if Father's going to pull strings, then I'll piss off – you can tell him that!'

'Fine, fine! He won't lift a finger.'

Makartsev had wanted to telephone the vice-chancellor of the institute, but his wife talked him out of it. 'God forbid! If Boris finds out you'll ruin everything.' His parents' mood lightened. Boris had overstrained himself; he'd been having a nervous breakdown, but now everything was getting back to normal. A son of Makartsev's couldn't do otherwise – that much was clear! Let him graduate from some institute or other, at any rate. And once he'd sown his wild oats his father could always find him a launching platform to blast off into a real orbit. When they found out that Boris had become a student at the institute Makartsev brought home champagne and said that he'd already rung the manager of a factory, who had promised to set aside a car from his outside-the-queue quota. In short, he was going to get the promised Moskvich by his eighteenth birthday.

The student took his car for granted. Neither his life nor his attitude towards his parents changed. His textbooks lay on his desk. He came home late at night, just as before. If his mother weren't in bed yet she could tell from a distance that he had been drinking again. Showing up early sometimes, he would pop his head into the kitchen: 'The fascist around?'

'Don't you call your father a fascist!'

'*Pardonnez-moi, madame,* I forgot. I'll call him a Nazi.'

He would flop down on to the ottoman with his shoes on and phone all his friends. Mixed in with the French that flew into the telephone was enough foul language to give Zina a migraine.

Soon a company of five or six would gather. New fellows, who had never been in the apartment before. Boris would get some glasses from the kitchen and close his door. Zina could never understand anything but the dirty words in the snatches of conversation that drifted through to her. They wouldn't talk about girls or politics or what was going on at school or hockey. It seemed to her that they just smoked and drank. Sometimes she would bring them food. They would say they didn't want it, but then demolish the lot, leaving the dirty dishes on the floor. What motivated them? What actually mattered to them? They just listened to idiotic music for hours and had nothing to say to one another.

'It'll be a month soon since your father went to the hospital. Don't you have any time to visit him?'

'They don't let anybody in to see him, you said so yourself.'

'They've been letting people in for a long time. You should support your father.'

'So when are they letting him out?'

'The doctors say that we can't even think of that right now. Maybe in a month.'

'We'll see each other then. Give him a break from me. And me from him.'

'I'm tired of telling lies about all your seminars, lectures and colloquia.'

'Never mind, Mother. Keep on lying. He's used to lies.'

# 35

# Friday, 6 a.m.

Zina hadn't gone to sleep. She had come home late from Makartsev's bedside, seen that the dinner she had left out for Boris was untouched and realized that he hadn't been home. She watched television until it went off – sports and the latest news – and then donned a scarf and went out on to the balcony. Sometimes Boris would stand with his friends around the gazebo down in the courtyard.

Zina finally got undressed at half past one. She stood for a while in front of the large mirror in their bedroom, hoping for some distraction by concentrating on herself. She poked at the excess bits on her belly and hips sceptically; they weren't that noticeable anyway. She was still very pretty and thought not without pride that there was nothing more harmonious in the world than the female figure. Zina was eating very little now and trying out all the latest diets, but they had suddenly stopped working. She could still fast at the clinic of the very trendy Dr Nikolayev, with whom, they said, it was impossible to get an appointment. Of course Makartsev could get her into the place at the drop of a hat. But, to her, fasting seemed to be cruelty to oneself. Anyway, any excess weight was only visible when she was naked, and when she wore a girdle – not a thing!

She lifted up her breasts, which had been the object of Makartsev's special pride but which now kept their shape only inside French brassieres. Her breasts had lost their shape because of that good-for-nothing Boris, who wasn't going to show up at all for the night or even ring, apparently. Putting on her English silk nightshirt, covered in lace, Zina lay down on her half of their wide Finnish bed. She read a little more of some sort of nonsense in her fiction magazine, *Roman-gazeta*, turned out the lamp and, counting on hearing Boris's tread, drifted off.

She was awakened by the telephone on Makartsev's side of the bed. *He's ringing after all!* she thought, waking instantly. *At least he has a sense of filial duty. But what time is it?* It was ten minutes past six on her favourite gold watch, a wedding present from her mother. She picked up the receiver.

'I'd like to speak to the father of Boris Makartsev,' said a hoarse male voice.

'He's not here.'

'Where is he?'

'He's in the hospital, didn't you know? What's the matter?'

'And what are you to him?'

'His wife.'

'You'll be the mother of Boris Makartsev?'

'Yes. Has something happened to him?'

'This is Captain Uterin, senior inspector with the Moscow Criminal Investigations Department. Your son Boris Makartsev, while in an unsober state, ran down two pedestrians last night on Kutuzovsky Prospect. One of them died on the spot, the other in hospital.'

'And Boris?' she asked, not understanding very well what she was hearing. 'How's he?'

'He's alive and well, sleeping it off here in a holding cell.'

'Thank you for calling. I'll come right down and pick him up.' Zina had already completely woken up, as if she'd been prepared in advance for this.

'Pick him up? Well, no. There's going to be an investigation.'

'Investigation? Tell me –' She stopped short, realizing how important it was to maintain her dignity and not show that she was frightened. When push came to shove, they couldn't do anything to her boy against her will, whatever had happened. But she wanted to find out as quickly as she could what all this meant, what she was up against. And she finished her sentence: 'Tell me, what's going on – is it serious?'

'Up to ten years' incarceration under Article 211 of the Criminal Code, plus aggravating circumstances – another five years. But that'll be for a court to decide.'

'Court?'

'Well, what did you think? Can you come down here straight away? Bring your internal passport with you. Did you write down my name? U-te-rin . . .'

Not getting out of bed, Zina looked around her bedroom as if she were in it for the first time. *Up to fifteen years? Boris! What kind of nonsense is that? He'll eat his words, that Captain Uterin, he'll be sorry he threatened me. Makartsev, as if out of spite, is in hospital. Otherwise he'd phone who-ever was necessary and settle everything at once. Fine, I'll go down there myself.* Zina put her hand over her mouth, trying to concentrate, then turned and began leafing through the phonebook lying on Makartsev's bedside table. She telephoned the dispatcher and, when a sleepy voice answered, drily requested: 'Send a car for Makartsev's wife.'

'When?'

'Right now. It's urgent.'

'All right,' answered the voice.

Zina heard a sigh and some short ringing tones. She got up and began dressing quickly, throwing unsuitable garments out of their drawers on to the floor. She brushed her hair without looking in the mirror, went into the kitchen and, after some hesitation, took several jars of red and black caviar out of the fridge that she had been keeping to slip into the hospital attendants' pockets. The caviar might do some good right now. It occurred to her that she would need some money. But there wasn't much at home, and the savings banks were closed at seven in the morning. Putting on her boots, fur coat and the fur hat that made her look younger as well as looking good on her, she locked all three locks on the door of their apartment and went to summon the lift, but it was occupied. She nervously knocked on the door to hurry whoever was in it. The lift stopped at her floor, and Aleksey stepped out.

'Did you ring for me?'

'I did, Aleksey. Let's go, as quick as we can.'

When they got into the car Aleksey lit a cigarette and silently looked at Zina, waiting for orders. She hesitated to say where she was going, but then she decided she wouldn't hide it anyway.

'Do you know where the Moscow CID is?'

'Petrovka Street, 38. Who doesn't know that? You want to go there?'

'Yes. Here's something for you, before I forget.'

She dug around in her bag and handed Aleksey a jar of black caviar.

'Thanks,' he said. He started the engine, stepped on the accelerator and then with a deft motion tossed the tin into the glove compartment as they moved off. 'How's Mr Makartsev feeling? It's already long past time for them to turn him loose. Everybody misses him.'

'You're telling me, Aleksey! I can't wait, myself.'

Zina answered mechanically. She took the scrap of paper with the crookedly written name 'Uterin' out of her purse. Aleksey wondered if he should ask her to remind Makartsev about his promise to call Sovtransavto about a job for him. But it would be better to be patient a while longer, until the boss came out himself, and not ask via a third party. Aleksey wasn't going to bother Zina with his usual conversation about this and that; he just raced down the empty streets towards Petrovka.

# 36

# Captain Uterin's Career

After accompanying the cipher clerk Kashin back from Havana, Vinogradov, the deputy head of Moscow Centre's cipher group, entrusted Junior Lieutenant Uterin with the task of deciphering the word 'daehtihs', which was done by Uterin without the help of any decoding tables. Uterin smirked at it, and the lieutenant colonel came to the conclusion that he knew about the insult. Vladimir Uterin, reduced in rank, was transferred just like Kashin to the tenth section of the *Semyorka*, the internal surveillance service. Laconic and efficient, he received number 43-85 there and settled in. The work turned out to be livelier, demanding a knack, and that knack was something Vladimir had been born with.

The flatfeet were brought to their objectives in small groups. The senior man assigned everyone their spots, passed out the photos, explained who was to hand their objective over to whom in case of a pursuit. In the main their objectives were foreigners and the Soviet citizens who met with them. The agents memorized who it was they spoke to, photographed their meetings with mini-cameras through openings in the tops of their raincoats. Vladimir never allowed any errors in his work and soon was appointed to the post of operational group senior. His second screw-up wasn't his fault either.

On this occasion the internal surveillance agents had their various current assignments cancelled and were brought back to the Directorate. A colonel in civilian clothes dealt with them, someone the flatfeet, strangely enough, had never seen before.

'Our intelligence informs us, comrades, that a certain Mr Siegmaringen, a modest German businessman, a great lover of art and symphonic music, will be arriving at Sheremetyevo from Frankfurt-am-Main in the guise of a tourist. In reality this Siegmaringen – alias Meier, alias Luettgens – is an important West German agent. The trip is classified to such a degree by the intelligence service that the only thing left for us is to be on the alert. You all understand what sort of responsibility falls on your work, I hope? First-class work is demanded from you. Mr Siegmaringen mustn't have a clue that he's being followed.'

It was a difficult two weeks for Uterin. When the businessman and symphonic music connoisseur Mr Siegmaringen – a not-very-tall, greying man in a cheap grey overcoat – came down the gangway with a radiant and sincere smile and his female interpreter stepped up to meet him, the senior man in the surveillance group reported over his walkie-talkie: 'We have acquired our objective. We're off!'

Their visitor went uncaring to symphony concerts all over Moscow, strolled around Tbilisi, flew off to Tashkent and Samarkand and for two weeks never even once stopped to talk to passers-by in the street and never once showed any interest in chemistry, which was what he had made himself out to be a specialist in.

'What did he come for?' Soviet intelligence at every level tried to figure it out.

'I should like to extend my visa for two weeks,' he told his interpreter. 'If that's not a problem, of course.'

'Was there something you didn't get round to doing? Can I be of help?'

'Well, yes, I haven't managed to see the whole Hermitage and the Russian Museum.'

His visa was extended. Uterin was summoned to a new conference: that dastardly Mr Siegmaringen was going to torment them for another two weeks!

'Redouble your vigilance,' the colonel warned them. 'As old hands at this, we can't rule out that he's covering his tracks, lulling us into a false sense of security, and ultimately will try to bring something off.

Unfortunately a thorough study of the contents of his suitcases hasn't had any results. All our hopes are with you.'

After being handed over his objective from a colleague 43-85 kept his eyes rigidly on him. Fortunately their visitor wasn't in the habit of looking behind him, although he did walk around gawking on all sides. Sometimes he would run, holding his female interpreter by the hand, so that Uterin and his colleagues managed to catch their breath only in their cars.

Siegmaringen didn't leave on schedule but a day early, suddenly changing his ticket for a night flight and rousing his flatfeet out of their slumbers. At the gangway their visitor kissed 21-14, his lady interpreter, on the mouth and handed her a tip of a hundred dollars that she later handed in to the Intourist accounting section in exchange for a receipt.

'Everything is clear now,' the greying superior summed up. 'Siegmaringen has got old and decided to part ways with his criminal life. He was here in our country on holiday. We did good work, comrades – we did everything we could.'

Two weeks later, though, Soviet intelligence sent home from Israel a copy of a message about an illustrated account sent off by Siegmaringen to the intelligence services of all countries friendly with the Federal Republic of Germany. While studying Soviet art, their visitor had photographed the better part of all the internal surveillance service agents tailing him, so as to make them known to interested parties.

In the course of the following month Uterin's colleagues were sorted out and scattered to the winds. And he was called in for an interview.

'How's your diction?' asked one of the members of the committee. 'Did you learn any poems in school?'

'"*With GLOOM the STORM blots OUT the SKY, the AW-ful BLIZ-zards WHIRL-ing,*"' declaimed the former 43-85.

'Not bad for a start. We'll catch up on the rest!'

Uterin was transferred to the cheerleaders, where he liked it straight away. Those who were in the group dressed a lot better; they always went around in snow-white dress shirts and ties, some of them even with a handkerchief in their breast pocket. The head of the cheerleaders introduced them to Prov Tsarsky, People's Artiste of the USSR, the Maly Theatre Communist Party Secretary, to whom had been given the honour of training them for their job. All his life Tsarsky had played the contrary Chatsky on stage, but offstage he was agreeable to everyone. He started off with diction and made Uterin repeat tongue-twisters over and over.

'So – now we'll sing out *Glory be to the Communist Party* – beautifully, resoundingly!'

Uterin's squawked. Tsarsky made a wry face.

'Softer, dear heart! *Glory be* – intonation up – *to the Communist Party* – intonation down. And with more feeling, sincerity, passion! Here, listen . . .'

The song came purling out in his velvety professional voice. His intonation went up, hung there awhile and solemnly fell again. The former flatfoot was a long way from the People's Artiste.

'Got it?' asked Tsarsky, pleased with his own talent. 'Let's sing it all together, friends: *Long live* – intonation upwards, pause – *our dear* – small pause – *Soviet* – even smaller pause – *gov* . . . *ern* . . . *me-e-e-ent.*'

The piano confirmed the correctness of the thought with a majestic major chord.

'Don't make it so bassy! More tenderly, intimately! So that everyone sitting around you in the hall will feel like singing it along with you. Here we go,' – the artist glanced at his sheet music – '*Glory be to the mighty vanguard of our Party, its Lenin's* – and resoundingly now, like an echo – *Po* . . . *lit* . . . *bu-u-u-u* . . . *r-r-ro-o-o-o-o!*'

After the lessons Uterin's artistic mastery gained ground. But neither did he lose his previous expertise. At congresses and Party conferences the cheerleaders were evenly distributed around the hall on such a basis as to have every agent responsible for a particular group of deputies or delegates. Vladimir kept watch on the hand motions of his allotted audience members. He could imperceptibly distinguish with an elbow what the contents of a passer-by's pocket were, press a thigh against a briefcase to ascertain the hardness and weight of any object located inside it.

Texts for the cheerleaders were handed out in advance, marked with ticks indicating which cheer to give after which words in the speeches, when to lead the applause, when to applaud stormily, after which paragraphs not to fall silent for a long time and when to get up and lead a standing ovation. Their duties included getting the people around them to applaud and yell 'hurrah!' as well. This is the way they did it: whenever the speech got close to the words that were supposed to be followed by applause, Uterin would turn to his neighbours to the right and left and, smiling with delight, say: 'Well said, wasn't it? Brilliant! Let's give him a hand!'

Here the speaker would break off (he would have tick marks in his text, too), and Uterin would instantly break into applause, drawing in the people sitting round him by his example. And the difference between those who applauded out of the fullness of their hearts, those who did out of politeness and those whose job it was would have been impossible to establish.

The organization of the end of the Leader's speech was the most complex and responsible task. A special mastery was called for in order to set the whole hall, thousands strong, on their feet in one single rapturous burst. After all, the boss wasn't going to give a signal for when applause had to shift abruptly to a stormy ovation and when during the ovation the whole hall was to get to their feet. Therefore the group participants had to undergo special training, where, having begun their applause, they counted out twenty seconds in their heads (at two claps per second) before shifting to stormy applause (four claps per second), drawing in everyone in the hall. Then they would count out another twenty seconds exactly before beginning the ovation proper, during which, as if accidentally, unco-ordinated shouts of 'Hurrah!' and 'Hear, hear!' would ring out. Finally, at the end of another twenty seconds (eighty claps), all the cheerleaders would rise from their seats, continuing to applaud stormily, only now with their hands over their heads. Simultaneously, they would invite their neighbours by gestures to get up and themselves shout out cheers, memorized beforehand, in honour of the Leader. This was the apotheosis, after which the cheerleaders had only routine shadowing measures left to do on those sitting around them.

Uterin worked conscientiously, but now he had some free time in the evening. He decided to become a police detective, and after his second year at law school he was transferred to the Soviet Ethics Violations Group. There were various sorts of jobs in this group. Agents of the group would stand on duty around churches on holidays, where, after taking them aside, they would beat up any young people trying to go to church. They would similarly beat up Jews wanting to emigrate to Israel, out of sight, just inside building entryways. On the instructions of the adjoining department they would ambush students, pull the *samizdat* literature out of their briefcases and beat them with brass knuckles. But they beat people without doing any injury, inasmuch as these were measures of a purely educational character.

Then he did a stint with the filler-uppers. The filler-uppers would occupy all the seats at public political exercises before anyone else got there. Anyone who wanted to could get into court sessions, too, but there were never any seats. If it was necessary to seat somebody, one of the filler-uppers would get up and walk out, as if fortuitously, freeing up exactly one place. Uterin had had to help fill halls when an American senator and a Politburo member of the Italian Communist Party – people who might say something awkward – gave speeches in front of students; he filled the hall of the Library of Foreign Literature when a sociologist from West Germany gave a speech there; and he filled halls whenever exhibitions of foreign paintings were mounted, as well as filling the streets in front of foreign embassies, holding placards in joint operations with the cheerleaders' group – and if it was necessary to break some windows he would do that alongside the Soviet Ethics Violations Group, giving vent to the rage and indignation of the Soviet people.

There came a day when Uterin reported to his superiors that he had graduated from the university and that his higher education could be considered complete. He was promoted from KGB junior lieutenant to police captain and appointed to the post of senior inspector at the Moscow Criminal Investigations Department.

From his Petrovka office Vladimir would, even now, frequently walk home from work (as far as the metro, anyway), slowing his pace when he got near the Lubyanka. The flatfeet strolling along the building's front would be pretending to be passers-by. And the passers-by would be pretending not to have a clue who they were. Uterin would walk slowly along, winking at every one of his former colleagues.

'How's it going, Vladimir? How much are they paying you?'

'Things are great, on the up and up,' Uterin would answer softly, pretending to be looking at the bronze statue of Dzerzhinsky. 'And you're still pounding the beat?'

'Yeah, well, you know, they're never going to let me into the cheer-leaders.'

'Right! Well, see you!'

And Uterin would walk on. The flatfoot would rub his ears in despair and, in order to get warm, would throw himself all at once on some boy from the provinces who was taking a picture of the Dzerzhinsky monument.

'Photography here is forbidden,' he would say severely, snatch away the camera and expose all the film.

# 37

# Got to Find Some Channels

Zina waited in the pass bureau for about half an hour before she was called to the window and handed back her internal passport with a slip of paper attached. Her heart was pounding, and her thoughts were flying around in disorder. But she was trying not to allow herself to weaken and was thinking about how to break the news to her husband and even whether he should hear it in his present condition.

Makartsev had frequently reproached her for living as if she hadn't a care in the world. 'If I die, how are you going to manage?' She would laugh and answer him that if she had to she'd learn but that she was sure that with his energy he would outlive her and marry again. Of course she wouldn't want it to happen that way, but it wasn't in her power: all men were the same. And now an opportunity had presented itself for Zina to prove that she could take care of things on her own. It would have been better still if there weren't any such necessity. Why had God become angry with her? She was recalling God mechanically, in connection with the trouble that had overtaken them. The rest of the time he wasn't any use to her.

They told her how to get to Senior Detective Uterin's office. The door was locked, so Zina stood in the corridor leaning against the wall. People in police uniform and civilian clothes scurried past her in a businesslike manner. She tried to ask one of them something, but he shook his head, like a deaf mute, and she once again just stood and waited. There was no one to protect her from this inattention, to come to her aid. Nobody in this place was obliged to her, but she was dependent on each and every one of them, and that was humiliating to her. After around forty minutes (maybe even an hour) had passed, an athletic and somewhat simple-looking man with shoulderboards on his uniform came to the door. He pulled a bunch of keys out of his pocket, found the right one and opened the door.

'You're Makartseva?' he asked hoarsely, not raising his eyes. 'Come in.'

He led the way into the room, jingling his keys. Zina wasn't accustomed to being treated like this and was ready to start howling in anger. But she was supposed to be making do without Makartsev, to behave like a man herself, so she squeezed her lips tightly together.

'Have a seat.'

Uterin never even glanced at her. He unhurriedly lit a cigarette, adroitly chucked the match out the open window ventilation pane and silently buried himself in a folder. The smoke of the cheap cigarette floated towards her, and she coughed.

'Makartsev, Boris, born 1950, ethnic Russian, Young Communist – your son?' He finally looked up at Zina.

'Mine, mine, of course!' She tensed up as though they were about to tear her son out of her arms.

'So-o-o. Does he drink a lot?'

'No,' Zina answered, after a bit. 'He just drinks juice – he likes tomato juice a lot.'

'Likes tomato juice . . . That's nice.'

'Well, maybe he has a little one with his father during holidays.'

'With his father? Here's the notes from his first interrogation. "On the evening of 15 March I met up with Kotlov, my former school friend . . . We bought a bottle of vodka and went to his house for a heart-to-heart talk. Another friend came by, Demchenko. We poured him what was left of the vodka. Then I drove over to Journalists' House, where I met a girl, I forget her name . . ." Who's this Demchenko?'

'Kotlov is a classmate of Boris's. But Demchenko – that's the first time I've heard that name.'

'Don't you know the name of the girl either?'

'I don't,' Zina answered softly, her eyes closed.

'Right. "I treated her to some brandy and suggested a drive out of town. She refused, since she had to go home. So then I headed off for a drive in the country by myself. I noticed the two people who were crossing Kutuzov Prospect only when they were right in front of my radiator, because it was dark. I hit the brakes and turned sharply to the right, but they ran to the right, too, and I hit them. I wanted to brake, but while I was wondering if I should stop or not I'd travelled on a bit further, and then I stepped on the accelerator. After driving on to Minsk Chaussee I thought better of it and stopped. And I got out of the car myself, straight into the highway patrol . . ."'

'He's slandering himself,' Zina said. 'He's bragging about it!'

'Let's see . . .' said Uterin, leafing through his papers. 'Here's the medical examiner's conclusion. "One hour and forty minutes after the occurrence . . . strong degree of alcoholic intoxication."'

'He couldn't have drunk a lot!'

'Around two whole glasses of vodka or brandy, no less!'

'But nobody saw him hit those people! It was somebody else, and you're pinning it on him!'

Uterin smiled for the first time. 'Here's the testimony of an eyewitness: Mamedov, driver of taxi number 13-77 MMT. "I was following behind Makartsev's Moskvich at a distance of a hundred yards. I saw what happened and rang the police from the nearest pay phone." After this a patrol car set out in pursuit. The driver of a street-sweeper, licence number 91-54 MOR, Okun, was driving down the left side of the road towards them. The road-accident report said: "Driving over the speed limit at sixty miles an hour. On the right fender and hood of the Moskvich are marks from the impact and traces of blood."'

'And the two people?' she stumbled, not knowing what to call them or how to ask. 'They're . . . what?'

'I just brought the pathologist's findings with me. The autopsy showed that both of them had a quantity of alcohol in their blood – to a moderate degree.'

'So it was their own fault!'

'And, moreover, they were crossing the road in the wrong place.'

'There, you see what I'm saying! They've paid for it themselves with their lives.'

'They did themselves, indeed,' Uterin said, scratching the back of his head. 'That alleviates some of your son's guilt. But there's still a lot left. Driving under the influence, for one. Second, exceeding the speed limit. Third, both of the victims were fatalities. Fourth, not stopping to render assistance. It'll be for the court to decide.'

'Court? Wait a minute . . .' Zina's eyes filled with tears, and all her resolve disappeared. 'Tell me what I have to do so that it won't have to go to trial.'

Uterin looked closely at her. The remark could be interpreted in various ways, but the suggestion itself testified to the fact that the woman had definite opportunities to do just that, beyond the reach of normal people.

'I can't give you any advice like that. You'd be better off deciding that for yourself.'

'I have to talk to my husband. But he's in hospital right now. Do you know who he is?'

'I do. That's not hard to find out.'

'I think so, too. Tell me, can I see my son?'

'Are you asking for a visit?'

'Yes, yes! A visit!'

Uterin carefully stubbed out his cigarette against the heel of his shoe and threw it into the wastepaper basket, rose slowly, placed the file in his safe, locked it and walked out. Zina managed to stop weeping, wiped her eyes and carefully rearranged herself. Her eyes remained red and swollen, though. She'd never felt so old before.

'Because you're the wife of Makartsev they've permitted you a visit,' Uterin pronounced from the threshold, 'but your son refuses to see you.'

'That can't be!' exclaimed Zina, shocked more by this than by anything else that had gone before. 'It's not true!'

'If you want,' Uterin said drily, 'we can bring him to see you.'

'By force? Of course not! Am I free to go?' She rose proudly from her seat.

'I'll have to sign your pass.' Uterin looked at his watch, wrote down the time and signed it. He looked at Makartseva as she went out. A thought flitted through his head: *The prettiest women pick out the bosses for themselves.* But there was no envy in it.

Zina walked out through the gates, not feeling her legs under her, then stopped, not knowing where to go, what to do, whom to turn to. First, Makartsev's heart attack, and now a second blow had come falling on her. But she wouldn't say anything to her husband. She would struggle through on her own.

Makartsev was ill, but in his position he was still someone to be reckoned with. She had no right to weaken, to allow misfortune to overwhelm her nerve. She would figure out how Makartsev would ordinarily do things, starting with the basics and not the secondary things, and act as if this weren't her own son but somebody else's, as if this were merely her civic duty – saving some child who had got into trouble. Once having thought the words 'civic duty' she walked determinedly up to the car. Aleksey was dozing placidly behind the wheel. He had tucked his hands into his sleeves to keep them from getting cold and was finishing catching up on the sleep he had missed the night before.

'I won't be going anywhere. My place is right near by. You can take off.'

'Right. And what happened here on Petrovka?'

'Public affairs,' she smiled carelessly. 'Go on back to the office.'

It was morning, bright and cheerful. The working day had begun, and people hurried past her, conversing as they walked. Perambulators and pushchairs rolled out of apartment-building entrances. Everyone around her knew where they were going, what they were doing and why. Even though she'd already taken the decision to act, Zina was trying convulsively to keep her thoughts on the one track. But they spilled over in confusion, and a different, unwanted and desperate one came to the fore:

what was going to happen now? The thought knocked the others away, hampering them, creating a panic in her soul.

She needed someone qualified to talk to. Not some woman friend who would 'ooh' and 'ah' and then call all the rest of their friends and say, 'Have you heard what that son of the Makartsevs has got up to?' A lawyer, that's what she needed! She would have to look up Samuil Koren as quickly as she could.

Koren, one of the deputy chairmen of the Moscow Municipal College of Barristers, was a friend of her first husband's from the old days. They had been imprisoned at the same time. After their rehabilitation he had telephoned Zina several times, ready to restore old ties of friendship, but she hadn't wanted any recollections of her first husband, since Makartsev's position obliged her to think about the status of her acquaintances. Now, after searching out several two-kopek coins, she got through to Koren without any particular difficulty. He seemed sincerely glad to hear from her and started asking her how she was. But when he found out that she had a problem he told her he'd be waiting for her forthwith.

Zina stopped her taxi at an old, run-down building. Without taking her coat off she walked into a room full of desks and people and quickly searched out Koren, now corpulent and stooped. He got up to greet her, hugged her and kissed her on both cheeks, as he used to, then afterwards sat her on a chair to one side and asked her to wait for a bit. Koren had aged: his baldness had spread to all sides, his blue cheeks with their red veins and his flabby chin all drooped, and his black suit, covered with dandruff and ashes, hung off him. It occurred to Zina that his kidneys probably weren't working well and that his heart wasn't either. *Jews always mature early and grow old before their time.* That applied not just to women but, strangely enough, to the men, too. She was surprised to find herself not thinking about Boris now, but her thoughts were floating here and there, not obeying her.

'Well, now, I'm entirely yours, madame!' the barrister said gallantly, shaking the ashes off his jacket. 'I hope your husband isn't planning to divorce you, Zina!' Back then Koren had quickly seen their divorce through the courts, at Fleytman's request. She couldn't bear the thought of any joking and glanced around to see if anyone was listening.

'Don't worry.' He touched her on the shoulder with his gnarled fingers. 'Everyone minds their own business here.'

'Boris hit two people with his car,' she blurted out. 'They're dead.'

Zina squeezed her mouth to hold back her emotion, but the tears ran down as if a dam had burst. She took out her handkerchief; it was wet. Koren, without consoling her, waited for a while.

'He's an adult? Does he have his licence? Was he in his own car? Was he sober? How fast was he going?' The questions poured out one after the other, and she just nodded or shook her head, in agreement or negation.

'He didn't stop? Well, that's not the worst blunder. What? He took the wrong steps, one after the other, each one worse than the other. That's natural in his position. Where had he been before this? Who with? What did he do? What, you don't know any of this yet! All right, we can clear this up. But the fact remains: they don't have to throw the book at him – he's a boy! If he were older, he would have known: once it had happened, you have to abandon the car and run away. Yes. Phone the police and tell them that your car's been stolen. Who knows if they'd be able to prove it or not. By the way, what about your husband, Zina?'

She explained the situation. Koren put his head in his hands.

'Why did you come to me? Even if I found you the very best lawyer . . . you wouldn't stand a chance.'

'What'll I do, then?' she asked, barely audibly.

'Look for channels. But you won't be able to do anything without your husband. Go ahead and try, of course, but it's unlikely. Don't lose heart, though. Do everything in your power . . .'

'What can I do? What?'

'In any case, you have to get acquainted with the families of the victims. You're going to have to help them, do everything they want. How much money do you have in reserve?'

'Fifteen hundred roubles in the account, no more.'

'That little?'

'Well, we never put anything aside, and we have lots of expenses.'

'You're going to have to slip things to the families. The wives will testify, after all.'

'How will I set about finding them?'

'Is the case still with the Moscow CID? Which inspector is handling it? I'll try to find out. Phone me. I haven't even paid you a single compliment. That's what life's become – a madhouse. We see each other when something happens, but without anything happening nobody needs you. Would you believe, I don't even have any relatives left. That is, they're still alive, but we only see one another when somebody dies. Maybe we'll get together in the next life. Anyway, don't get too downhearted, Zina!'

On her way out she glanced at the watch on her wrist. Time to go to the hospital. If she didn't show up on time Makartsev would get worried. She flagged a taxi and rode down Rublyov Chaussee, promising herself that she would smile as if nothing had happened. Before even going to the ward she rang the garage from the lobby and ordered out the car.

Makartsev was feeling better; they had connected up his telephone and he'd taken heart. She one-sidedly inquired as to his well-being, grumbled a bit about the telephone and generally conversed eagerly on various themes, hoping he wouldn't get around to asking about Boris. But he noticed something anyway.

'What's up with you, Zina?'

'What are you badgering me for, Makartsev? That time of the month. You're always trying to figure out what makes me tick.'

She grumbled exaggeratedly, so as to discourage any cross-examination. And in fact she drove off successfully enough. Only when she got home did Zina realize that she hadn't eaten a morsel for hours; she persuaded herself to eat something just to keep up her strength. While she chewed away automatically, not tasting or smelling her food, she was wondering if it made any sense to phone Makartsev's friends – or would that make things worse? The thing could never be covered up anyway. But who else was there to help, if not those people? After all, he was always ready to come to their aid. She knew that Makartsev seldom turned to his fellow Central Committee workers for favours but, rather, used his friends in the ministries and departments. Zina decided to do the same.

She carried the telephone over to the couch and called the Deryugins. Pavel Deryugin was one of the deputy chairmen of Gosplan, the state planning agency. The Makartsevs and the Deryugins had spent their holidays together for many years; their *dachas* were next door to each other, their children had grown up together. Natalya, hearing Zina's voice, was delighted.

'How come we haven't heard from you?' she pronounced boomingly, in her simple, almost rustic, way. 'How's old Makartsev? The doctors going to let him out sometime soon?'

'Pretty soon. But we've had some misfortune, Natalya. With Boris . . .'

'What sort?'

Zina began relating what had happened, twisting it around to sound as if the police were waiting for some sort of direction from above and if the right call came they'd let Boris go.

'Well, how is this *murder*?' whispered Natalya. 'And, then, who do you think should be calling them?'

'I was thinking that Pavel could do it. After all, he could ring up Shchelokov on his hot line. Not to put any pressure on, no, just to hint that the thing doesn't get settled on their level but higher up.'

'I'll pass this on to Pavel, of course,' Natalya decided, after a pause. 'But it's unlikely he'll agree to it. After all, this is entirely outside his brief.'

'Maybe I should ring him.'

'What's the difference? I have to call him now anyway to remind him to drink his mineral water. He had heartburn all last night. If he agrees to do it I'll call you back. But, well, if he doesn't . . . you know yourself how fussy he is about personal issues. But I really feel for you!'

After sitting a moment, holding her finger on the hook, Zina dialled another number. She reached Rigo Badalyan himself, the chairman of the State Atomic Energy Committee, at home (what luck!). Rigo was sincerely upset. Makartsev's son – that was the same as a son of his own. He was ready to do everything in his power, and he did have some power. He would take up the issue forthwith, but, unfortunately, he had a flight to catch in an hour and a half. He was flying to India and would be back in Moscow a month later. Then it would be possible to get back to the issue and think about who best to ask.

'Thanks, Rigo! That'll be late, but thanks.'

She leafed through the telephone book a bit more and found the number of Ignat Shaptala, written in hand by Makartsev. Shaptala had worked together with Thick Eyebrows on the Dnepropetrovsk provincial committee and the Kazakhstan central committee and now was the deputy head of the Administrative Organs Department. A call from him could change a lot of things. The Shaptalas had been by to visit the Makartsevs. Makartsev and Shaptala had travelled abroad together on several occasions. Zina had twice stayed at health resorts with Shaptala's wife, Tamara, and had become good friends with the round-as-a-cupcake grandmother with the cheerful Ukrainian way of talking, who was always trying to appear younger.

Tamara happily started nattering away, talking about her (improbable, given her age) grandsons, who were keeping her very busy. 'Well, and how are things with you?'

Zina explained the situation. Tamara fell silent and then suddenly asked: 'How's this going to affect Makartsev?'

'He doesn't know. I don't want to worry him.'

'I'm not talking about that, dearie. I mean how is this going to reflect on his position? His son, in prison!'

'I'm not going to let that happen!' exclaimed Zina. 'If Ignat could help me and call Shchelokov –'

'And how could he do that? After all, that'll undermine his authority.'

'Tamara, my dear, ask him, I beg you!'

'I won't ask him! In his position do you think you can do things like that? After all, whoever he asks will be the first to reproach him for it later on down the line. Don't ask, Zina. That's breaking the law!'

'Let it be breaking the law!' Zina cried out in despair. 'Just one single time! Let it be untrue, unfair, whatever! This is my son, after all! I won't have another one.'

'I'm a mother myself, grandchildren already. But we'd better not mix Ignat up in this. Zina, sweetheart, you understand yourself, you'd better not even phone us again until this has all been worked out. Who knows what could happen? After all, for the sake of your husband, you'd do the same thing in my position.'

Throwing herself back on her pillow Zina stared dully at the ceiling for a while. Later on she roused herself. No, she wouldn't give up! She would carry on. She telephoned Koren.

'Zina, I've already found out something. The two who were killed were unskilled labourers, chronic alcoholics. Both were on the books; one of them had undergone compulsory treatment. The wife of the other one was even glad that her husband was dead. She says she's going to breathe easy at last. They have a six-year-old child, and there's two in the other family. One of them's mentally retarded. Maybe you could get the moron enrolled in a children's sanatorium? Win them over, promise them something, sweetheart. In any case, take down their addresses.'

# 38

# Yagubov's Hour

'Can I speak to Comrade Kashin? Kashin, is that you? Has your voice changed or what?'

'Who *is* this?'

'You don't recognize your own? Uterin.'

'Vladimir! Long time no see!'

'Kashin, I want to ask you something, as a friend.'

'For you – anything!'

'Then listen up. Makartsev – anybody by that name there?'

'You don't know?'

'How could I not? His wife said to me, "Do you know who my husband is?"'

'Well, what's the matter then?'

'Matter? Their son's a perpetrator, in my custody. What are you keeping quiet for? This is why I'm making this friendly call to you. On the one hand, to bring you up to scratch and, on the other, so that I don't get stuck as well. Why would I be butting in? You have your superiors, and I have mine. But we have some in common, too, right? And where are they going to turn – to my people or to yours?'

'It's hard to answer that, Uterin. I'll have to mull that one over. I think we'll have to defer to our own, before anything else. And then the people on top will correct your superiors, if it comes to that. After that you can do what your boss tells you to again. You keep me in on things and I'll do the same for you – all right?'

After putting down the receiver Kashin sat for a while, his gaze on his fish tank. He had seen Makartsev's son on two occasions when he'd had to take some urgent papers to their house that Makartsev had forgotten to sign before leaving on a trip out of the country. The fellow had seemed ordinary enough, nothing suspicious. How was the situation going to resolve itself now? In any case, Yagubov had to be placed in the know, urgently, by Kashin himself.

Yagubov was leafing through something, not listening very attentively, but at the words 'two fatalities' he got up and started rocking back and forth on his toes. His eyebrows knitted into a single line over his nose.

'What a calamity! You could even say a tragedy. What'll that get him? Did you find out?'

'Up to fifteen years.'

'Well. A tragedy for all of us here at the newspaper. Who've you spoken to about this?'

'Nobody! After my friend from the Moscow CID phoned, I came straight to you.'

'I approve! We don't want too many boots muddying the waters.'

'Right.'

Once alone again, Yagubov scratched his chin and walked over to the window. He pushed his face closer to the glass – the cold air from the ventilator pane helped to cool him down. What had happened would have been impossible to foresee. What bad luck Makartsev was having! First the heart attack and now his child! You just had to hope that they'd take it the same way Upstairs.

But, on the other hand, there would certainly be people of a less sentimental stripe who would decide that it might have been possible to foresee it. A candidate-member of the Central Committee ought to devote considerable attention to his son's upbringing. The boy had got out of hand a long time ago – Makartsev himself had complained about it more than once. Misfortune is misfortune, but guilt is guilt. And then they would look at the situation differently in the Big House.

*The heart attack? One doesn't want to think it, but let's be objective: Makartsev's lifestyle is less than ideal. He says he's been going to start doing exercise all his life. But later on he'll say that he'll start doing it when they haul him off to Novodevichye cemetery: he'll get up early, when there aren't any tourists there, and run around his own grave. In our circumstances, considering the tension inherent in Party work, the absence of rude good health is a vital shortcoming. A worker like that ought to be replaced for the general good.*

*They'll have a look to see whether the Makartsev style has spread around the whole workforce. And I'll have to say this in all honesty: there is a disorderliness, an absence of efficiency; discipline has been impaired. In circumstances like these even political vigilance gets undermined. And where there's damp, there'll be mould.* Today it was worrying him, Yagubov – tomorrow the municipal committee, and the day after tomorrow they would start talking about it in the Big House itself. *What's happened to Makartsev's son is an alarm signal, and we'll find that we have made a mistake if we don't come to some conclusion about it. It'll be in Makartsev's own interests . . .*

# 39

# You Have to Grumble,
# Even If You Don't Want To

At the very moment that Zina was coming out of the entry checkpoint of the Moscow CID, Rappoport was waking up. For him, this was two hours earlier than usual, and he groaned for a long time, snorting and wheezing until he got out of bed. And after getting up he wandered semi-dressed around his room and his kitchen for half an hour, muttering into his beard about how the authorities wouldn't even give him any peace in his sleep. Nevertheless, he dragged himself into the office a whole hour and a half earlier than usual.

The *Trudovaya Pravda* building had been built at the beginning of the 1930s, when Constructivism and the influence of Le Corbusier still existed in Moscow architecture. For that reason, the building still looked more contemporary than its post-war Stalinist-Baroque wing, a third of a century later. At first Rappoport had planned to get the key to the editor's outer office from the security woman downstairs, straight away. But he would have had to sign for the key, once taken, in her day book. Of course, he could have signed any old name, but she might recall who he was later on, and that didn't enter into Rappoport's plans at all. So he just glanced at the clock, went up to his own office and sat down to wait.

'You're already here? I was just looking in – it wasn't locked. Do you want me to clean up or not?'

Masha, a corpulent woman in a black smock, in men's shoes with drooping stockings held at half-mast by rubber bands, stood in the doorway with her bucket and rag, waiting for an answer.

'Clean up, clean up for sure, Auntie Masha,' Rappoport said. 'My office is chock full of rubbish!'

'You've been drinking again, I dare say. Got any empties? You just wait: I'll tell on you!' The regular receipt of collected bottles provided a serious makeweight to Masha's modest salary, and grumbling about people's drinking was just her way of wishing they drank more.

'Maybe there's one. Look around,' Rappoport strung her along. 'I'm going out, so you won't bother me.'

The lift took Rappoport up to the corridor leading to the editor's office. The door to his reception was open. The cleaning woman always went down every corridor first of all with her bunch of keys, unlocking all the doors of the newspaper office (except for the sealed ones, of course), emptying all the wastebaskets, pouring their contents into large paper bags meant for mail and only then swabbing the parquet floors with a wet rag wrapped around a broom head. Because of this the floor was a dirty grey colour and all cracked, but it was more convenient for Masha to wipe it down than to polish it. She cleaned the sealed rooms during the day in the presence of the people responsible for them.

After glancing around, Rappoport stepped into the outer office. It was uncustomarily quiet in there. The chairs and armchairs ranged along the walls for visitors were empty, the telephones silent. The yellow antechamber clashed hideously with the door, covered in dark-red leatherette: on the door was a black glass plaque with the legend 'Igor Makartsev'.

Not losing any time, Rappoport opened the door of the left-hand cabinet of Anna's desk, which wasn't kept locked. The top drawers inside the cabinet were full of bundles of papers, forms and envelopes. In the bottom drawer were the shoes that Anna would change into every morning, a soap-dish, scissors, a screwdriver, a bottle of nail varnish, hand cream and a packet of tea. In behind all these things, under an old issue of the fashion magazine *Siluet*, lay a paperclip box. Rappoport brought the box out with his fingers. Instead of containing paperclips (and everyone at the office who had ever done night duty knew it), it held the key. Masha would clean up the editor's office only after Anna had arrived.

The curtains in Makartsev's office were pulled, and it was in half-darkness. Rappoport slowly made his way around the editor's huge desk and sat down in his armchair. He pulled out the middle drawer, looked deep inside it and started carefully lifting the documents. The grey folder was not to be found. Rappoport pulled the drawer all the way out, set it on his lap and began digging through everything more thoroughly. The folder that he'd held in his own two hands in front of Makartsev in this very office was not anywhere to be seen, either within its envelope or without it.

Rappoport lifted all the papers out on to the desk and checked the contents of the side drawers, which were also unlocked. There was no folder in them either. *You have to grumble, even if you don't want to: circumstances compel you to.* The experienced camp inmate could feel that he shouldn't stay in the office any longer. He looked around to see if he'd left any traces, locked the office up, put the key back in its place, carefully looked out into the corridor and, enervated, walked over to the lift with a sluggish gait. The lift was occupied, and it rose, stopping at the floor he was on. So as not to run into whoever was getting off, Rappoport retreated several steps up the staircase. Anna came out of the lift and with mincing steps hurried into the reception room. Waiting until she was out of sight, Rappoport slouched into the lift and took it to his own floor. Masha had finished cleaning and was walking down the corridor, trailing her mop and locking one door after another.

'Don't lock mine, Auntie Masha!' he yelled.

She nodded silently and shuffled on, her huge shoes clumping along the floor.

# 40

# The Screws Tighten

At midday Anna ran through the office from door to door. She held out a pen and a list to everyone she met, sitting or walking: 'There's a meeting in Yagubov's office at sixteen hundred hours. Attendance is strictly mandatory! Sign here.'

Taking back the list, she ran on. Nobody had ever been summoned to a meeting this way before. And it wasn't just the careerists who were tearing along after the first phone call, sitting down and looking to see who was late and who was ahead of them, already sitting closer to the leadership, thereby demonstrating their energetic qualities. Everyone hurried to it: after all, people's situations at the newspaper depended on how well they were informed. The more you knew about what's going on, the greater your own power was. Who had been on the carpet. Who was for the chop. Who was going to get the praise? Just as Christian ritual was incomplete without a liturgy, so there could be no Party newspaper without a meeting.

'We have to sign up?' they asked Anna. 'What's going on, do you know?'

'Not a clue.'

'Maybe there's something wrong with Makartsev?'

'No – I'd know about that!'

'Maybe they want to make an announcement about his son.'

The news about Makartsev's son had flown around the office since morning and was sucked dry. The signers got lost in speculation, cancelled appointments, postponed international negotiations. Those who were getting ready to slip away changed their plans. Meanwhile Anna was already opening the next door: 'At sixteen hundred . . . Sign there . . .'

'For you,' said Rappoport, 'I'll sign anything your heart desires.'

'Oh, you're always joking!'

'Not a bit!'

Ivlev flew back into Moscow from his Novosibirsk assignment and called Rappoport half an hour before the meeting.

'The article's ready for you.'

'I figured as much. When are you showing up?'

'Rappoport, you offered me the keys to your place.'

'I get the hint. Anytime . . .'

'Then I'll take a cab.'

'Perfect. Only bear in mind that there's going to be a meeting here. Yagubov is tightening the screws. So you're going to have to either show up or be considered still away on assignment. I'll go out on the street – stop your taxi around twenty yards from the entrance.'

When he got back up to the office after handing over his keys, people were already converging on the reception area. Anna was running back and forth carrying chairs from Makartsev's office to Yagubov's. The staff crowded around the door. Yagubov loomed over his desk, seated on the new leatherette cushion that Kashin had brought in just before the meeting itself. He was smoking elegantly, and from time to time he would indicate – either with the two fingers holding his cigarette or his free hand – unoccupied spots where people could squeeze in.

'How come we're here and not in the auditorium?' someone asked, carefully. 'It's crowded in here, you know.'

'This is a working meeting, a business meeting,' Yagubov explained, adroitly rolling his cigarette along his lip from one corner of his mouth to the other. 'The more the merrier. Am I right, Rappoport?'

Rappoport was just then in the doorway, his glasses in his hands, looking for an empty spot with his poor eyes.

'Sit over here,' indicated Yagubov. 'Polishchuk asked me to reserve the seat for him, but inasmuch as our executive secretary is unexecutively late, we'll scrap his reservation.'

The seated people broke into smiles. Polishchuk had to take a modest seat on the edge of a chair by the door. Yagubov tapped his pencil on his desk.

'Well, shall we begin?' he asked and, taking the suddenly extinguished rumble for approval, proceeded. 'Anna, close the doors, please – and make sure there aren't any unauthorized people outside the door. So, comrades!' He stubbed out his cigarette. 'We're not going to be talking in elevated phrases about what's going on in our country. We all live for our lofty goals. Today, let's have a businesslike talk about what's bothering us, what's putting the brakes on our road to the very heights of endeavour, which are now nearer than ever before.'

*Nearer, again?* Rappoport suddenly thought in fright. While he did so he nodded to Yagubov to signify his approval and snorted.

'I think you all agree with me', Yagubov continued, 'that our newspaper must not only talk boldly about what's good but must also boldly criticize shortcomings. It goes without saying that neither one nor the other should be done without a sense of responsibility. We serve the Party, and we'll fight our war not only against ideas that are harmful to us but against harmful facts as well, if they keep us from moving ahead. After all, when an issue of our paper comes out, the printed word also becomes historical fact.'

*He thinks the same as I do,* thought Rappoport. *Why have I been less than fond of him? Is it because he says it too ponderously, perhaps?*

'You know yourselves,' said Yagubov, 'the more we become the creators of historical facts, the closer we are to scaling the radiant heights.'

*So he's a mountain climber!* thought Rappoport, once again. *And he's hauling us along, making us clamber along after him, and we won't be able to do anything about it. Or, more likely, do something only after we make it to the top of the hill.* Rappoport again nodded to the deputy editor as a sign of solidarity with his progressive thoughts.

'Recently,' Yagubov continued, 'the departments have been filing stories that the secretariat has had to send back. Surely it's time for the departments to understand the level of the new requirements? Let's approach the issue dialectically, the way the state does. Surely the Party organs know about any shortcomings. They do! Is it worth it to write about temporary difficulties when it's clear to everyone that these will be overcome? Is it worth it to write about shortcomings at all, if in a short while they're going to become the distant past?'

*Our shortcomings have become so abundant that our accomplishments aren't visible.* While he was thinking that, Rappoport shook his head negatively, agreeing with Yagubov that writing about shortcomings made no sense at all.

'Well, if it's necessary for a Communist to raise a question of principle, he has to have a developed sense of foresight: what are the people Upstairs going to say? Let's speak in concrete terms. You and I have two masters: the Big House and the reader. But the reader isn't ever going to give us the sack!'

Rappoport blinked, took off his glasses and, closing his eyes, started to wipe the lenses. *How sensibly and to the point the deputy editor is speaking. I underestimated him. Is he really cleverer than me? Craftier, that's closer. And around Makartsev he was quieter than water, lower than grass. And now he's blossomed. How quickly people grow up in this country!*

'Let's be frank,' smiled Yagubov. 'Sometimes we want to talk about shortcomings in one sphere or another, but, in order to make a more passable article we start with achievements. In the Big House I was shown an article by an English journalist. He wrote that articles in the Soviet press have to be read from the point where the word "however" is encountered. Let's not appease the taste of the bourgeois press. I ask you not to use the word "however" any more.'

'Can we use the word "but"?' came from the rear of the assembly very quietly.

Yagubov caught it. '"But" is all right,' he answered. 'Although, generally, I think that jokes like that are inappropriate. Someone called me today about our review of a play. We'd criticized it, while our comrades from the Big House saw the play and liked it. I called up the department editor. "Whose agreement did you get for this?" I asked. It turned out he hadn't agreed it with anybody. But, after all, there's always someone somewhere to get agreement from in advance.'

'Get *everything* agreed to?' asked Alekseyev.

'If you want to work without making mistakes – everything!'

'With who?'

'Just think, and you'll always find somebody. If it's too hard, talk to me about it. The press can be a genuine weapon only in strong hands. Let's say that a writer's stance doesn't suit you – you know better than I what to do. You're his editor. First of all, explain to him that the article is sensible but that he has to take out whatever conclusions the intelligent reader will make for himself without any prompting. The writer redoes the piece. Then you ask him to soften the title and the opening, so he doesn't smack everybody right between the eyes. And then change the middle a little bit, so the article reflects not just his personal opinion but editorial opinion as well. Then the writer's position has become more Party-minded. So now you have an experienced sub-editor bring it up to scratch. And we can all relax, and the author isn't going to run into any trouble. Straying from the ideological point, innuendo – these are dangerous things. What did the weakening of the Czechoslovak press lead to? We all like Makartsev, of course, but it seems to me that he's understated the dangers of apolitical criticism. The more so as the situation in the period of his absence has changed. In particular, let's put out less literature and art, less sport and more propaganda material. Every one of you is mobilized to do this.'

It was already quiet in the office, but now the silence thickened, becoming positively morose.

*There's going to be a war with China,* thought Rappoport.

'What are you doing, keeping quiet over there on the side?' Yagubov turned his head to Kashin. 'Now a word from you!'

Kashin rose, a little confusedly, stamping his wounded leg, jumpy ever since the accident, and leaned against the back of the chair in front.

'Well, it's like this,' he said, smiling guiltily. 'We have a problem with discipline here. Employees are coming to work later than they're supposed to, leaving earlier and sometimes not showing up at all, without offering any documented excuses. And where are we supposed to look for them when they're urgently needed? And there've been some instances of indulgence in alcoholic beverages. I'm not going to tell you who you are to your faces: whoever wants to can figure it out. By decision of the administration, there's going to be a log book for people coming in and going out, as of tomorrow. If an employee has to go on an errand the next morning, for example, he has to write down the night before where he's going and who's sending him and when he's going to arrive back. The rest have to go up and log in with Anna every morning.'

A low buzz ran around Yagubov's office and died down again.

'Furthermore . . .' Kashin smiled guiltily again. 'A pass system is being instituted, and all staff personnel will be obliged to present their credentials to security on their way in and out. Everyone else will have to request a pass by telephone. Upon exiting the building, department editors have to sign the pass, indicating the time. And they will be stamped personally by the secretary, Anna, as done in other organizations. And there's more: employees are also required to maintain order in their desks, the contents of which will be checked once a month by a commission of three people – '

'– under the leadership of managing editor Kashin,' Yagubov finished for him. 'This, comrades, is a necessary measure as well, since some people forget that they have possession of Party documents that are supposed to be kept in safes.'

'And you'll lock your offices behind you when you go out,' concluded Kashin.

'As our editor-in-chief likes to repeat,' said Yagubov with a smile, 'order broadens the mind.'

'A *new* order . . .' whispered Rappoport but quietly enough that no one would hear.

At the end of the meeting Rappoport began to grow restless, sneaking glances at his watch. Ivlev was waiting for him at home and couldn't leave.

He probably wasn't bored there, but, as a family man, he was surely in a hurry to get home.

Yagubov meanwhile looked around at everyone, paused as if in two minds about whether to bring up such a delicate trifle and then decided to. 'And there's one more request, comrades. We're not at a football stadium here; therefore I ask that the men show up for work in jackets and ties and the women in more modest clothing than at present. I have in mind, so to speak, skirt length. We'll stick to the example set in the Big House. Yes, by the way, Kashin: here's the list of people who came to this meeting. Check out why several employees are absent. We have democracy in this country, as you know, and that means that discipline is one and the same as much for editorial board members as for Auntie Masha. There's one conclusion alone: we'll strengthen our vigilance, towards ourselves and others.'

'Strengthen it . . .' muttered Rappoport, not to anyone in particular and this time sufficiently loud and boldly.

Finally they were all let go, and, shoving aside two elderly women employees, he pushed his way through to the door and went down to his office. Rappoport cursorily glanced at his desk, didn't clear anything away, took his hat from the cabinet and pulled it down over his head, wound his worn-to-threads scarf around his neck and reached for his overcoat. It wasn't on its hanger. Rappoport looked around in surprise at the hanger, looked down (maybe it had fallen off?) and looked behind the cabinet. He was too surprised even to curse.

The corridor was still full of people coming from the meeting. They were stopping to confer, then disappearing behind their doors.

'Colleagues!' Rappoport wailed to the people in the corridor. 'Did you see who went into my room? My overcoat – it's gone!'

'A good overcoat?'

'Not so much a good one as the only one I've got.'

'I wouldn't steal an overcoat like that one,' said Alekseyev. 'And if someone stole it from me I'd be glad.'

'But I don't have another one,' Rappoport said, blinking in dismay.

'What a day this is today – happy news from morning to night!' said Yezikov, the deputy secretary, turning his tiny head on its long neck. 'So how come you haven't got another one? Are you hinting that your royalties are getting cut down all the time?'

'Well, it's true, I still have the quilted jacket I returned from the camps in.'

'They're not going to let you into the Central Committee in a quilted jacket.'

'How am I going to go out into the cold without my coat?' said Rappoport, very downhearted. 'I have back trouble.'

'That's because it's on the threshold of the *subbotnik*,' Yezikov said, not easing off. 'You're going to get a prize for the *subbotnik*, Rappoport – you can buy yourself a new coat with that.'

'No, he can't,' Alekseyev objected. 'The prize isn't going to be more than fifty roubles. And Rappoport is going to have to split it with Lenin. The *subbotnik* idea occurred to both of them!'

'Joke all you want,' said Rappoport. 'But my coat's gone!'

'They didn't steal anything else?' pondered Yezikov. 'Well, then. Let's check it out!' The three of them went into his cubicle.

'My briefcase!' yelled Rappoport.

'There you are! And you were going on about your overcoat. Was there anything valuable in it?'

Usually Rappoport had something or other in his briefcase that he wouldn't want other people to read. He thought about it right away. But today, fortunately, there wasn't anything of the sort in it. Better still, he hadn't found the folder in Makartsev's office.

'Valuable? Well, just . . . Nothing.'

'You have to inform Kashin,' decided Alekseyev. 'Let him make a complaint to the police. What's going on around here? I don't remember anything like it, even though I've been on the paper since 1945. Here he is, himself. Speak of the devil!'

Kashin glanced into the room, dragged his trailing leg in, quietly closed the door behind him and smiled.

'What's happened here?'

'My overcoat and briefcase,' Rappoport said, spreading his hands and saying no more.

'Right!' Kashin nodded. 'Please come to my office.'

At his office he brought out Rappoport's briefcase and overcoat, tidily folded with the lining outwards.

'What are you playing at, Kashin?'

'Playing? You systematically leave your office unlocked. And I'm the official with the material responsibility. Why don't you safeguard your personal property?'

'Safeguard it from who? What idiotic regulations these are!'

'The regulations aren't mine. I'm just carrying out orders. And as for what kind they are – that's none of my business. Go and complain, if you want.'

'I will! If you don't, they come down on you like a ton of bricks!' Rappoport determinedly snatched his overcoat and briefcase out of Kashin's hands and headed for Yagubov's office in a rage.

Anna, noticing him, threw herself in his path. 'Yagubov hasn't called for you, has he?'

'Him? Call for me?' Rappoport failed to understand.

Anna lowered her voice. 'Yagubov has ordered me to let in only those who he's called in himself."

'What else is he going to come up with?'

Rappoport shoved Anna aside and resolutely threw open the door to Yagubov's office.

'Look here!' he yelled from the doorway, holding out his overcoat and briefcase.

'What's happened?' asked Yagubov eagerly. He was standing at his window holding a saucer in one hand and in the other a cup of tea. After taking a swallow, he placed the cup back on the saucer.

'This is a disgrace!' Rappoport declared. 'A proper disgrace!'

'Calm down,' said Yagubov, putting the cup and saucer on the windowsill. He took out a spotless handkerchief from his pocket and wiped his lips. 'The call to vigilance is a general directive for the whole office and touches everyone on the staff, including me and you. Be thankful it was Kashin who did it and not some stranger.'

'And he couldn't just have said something? He couldn't?' complained Rappoport. 'Today he takes our things, and tomorrow he goes through our pockets?'

'Well, I don't think so,' smirked Yagubov. 'He probably didn't go looking in your pockets. However . . .'

'However what?'

Yagubov hesitated. *However, if you don't like working at* Trudovaya Pravda, *on the editorial board and in the Party bureau, I think I can meet you halfway. No, Makartsev would get angry at a step like that, and besides there are people on the city committee and the Central Committee who still need Rappoport to write their speeches for them. If he wasn't certain of his strength, he wouldn't talk to me in that tone.*

Hearing that 'however' Rappoport perceived what Yagubov meant to say. *He hates me, that's clear. But now I'll tell him what I think of him. I haven't got anything to lose.*

'So – "however" what?' Rappoport repeated determinedly, expending all his reserves of rage on the question.

'However,' Yagubov pronounced, after a certain amount of thought, 'Kashin did overdo it a little. Everyone has their weakness. Here you are yourself, a bundle of nerves. Over nothing!'

'Nothing?' Rappoport switched his ire over to complaint. 'Just how am I supposed to work in conditions where I get no respect as an individual? Maybe somebody doesn't like me on ethnic grounds? Here, at the paper, that was something I never felt before.'

'And now you do?' Yagubov burst out laughing. 'Or do you have me in mind, specifically? Think about it: how could we – Party workers – be anti-Semites? For us the important thing is our convictions. Although we're from different ethnic groups you and I are still in the same camp, aren't we? It's only individuals from your tribe who commend themselves poorly.'

'And who was it who made the Revolution?'

Yagubov didn't answer. *Jews participated in the Revolution, but what for? Rappoport just doesn't know the latest currents of opinion Upstairs. They got into the Revolution so they could seize power and start the subsequent propagation of Zionism in Russia. It's a good thing the Party and Stalin managed to cut short that dangerous tendency in time. But we still haven't managed to carry that line all the way to its end. It isn't fascism that's a danger to mankind but the Jews. They strive towards power, and in the USA they've already succeeded. They want to rule the world. And in so far as Communists express the interests of all peoples, our historical mission is to save mankind. So, anti-Semitism as a whole, if you understand it from a progressive viewpoint, is a humane policy in the interests of the vanguard of mankind. Speaking among ourselves, Marx spoils the whole history of the Communist movement. Its history should start essentially with Lenin now and not go crawling around in that deep medieval shit.*

'It wasn't just Jews who made the Revolution,' Yagubov remarked, smiling politely. 'I have to say that I dislike only those Jews who are fighting on the other side of the barricades. But then I don't like that sort of Frenchman, Englishman, Spaniard or Russian even. I think you dislike that sort, too – don't you, Rappoport?'

'Of course I do,' choked Rappoport. He finally understood that he had to shut up, since Yagubov was going to be right whatever the case. And he was tired, and his stomach ached from hunger. 'I'm only offended because I've been a Party member since 1934!'

'I know.' Yagubov decided to draw suspicion off himself entirely. 'And, believe me, I love Jews, and I have friends who are Jews. There are Party members who consider Jews to be more industrious and persistent than other people. They break through quicker than others and occupy all the positions of responsibility. At least that's the way it was in the thirties! Surely that's not right, for Jews to govern Russians? Partisans of that point of view ask what if it were Russians governing in Israel? I'll repeat it yet again: it's only certain people who feel that way – I'm in determined disagreement with them! Let me help you with your coat.'

Yagubov took Rappoport's overcoat from his hands and, shaking it out, held it in expectation for him to stick his arms fussily into the sleeves. Rappoport was a head taller and considerably fatter. But then Yagubov was an athlete.

'By the way,' Yagubov recalled, 'I've been meaning to get some advice from you for a long time. It's just been proposed that I write my dissertation for the Higher Party School. The theme is "The Role of the Press in Communist Education of the Workers, According to Material from the Newspaper *Trudovaya Pravda*". That, after all, is a subject you know a lot about. You won't object if I dwell a bit on it?'

'Why should I object?' Rappoport understood that to avoid getting the sack he was going to have to write this dissertation for Yagubov.

'Will you help me select some material? I'll free you from work for the time you'll need.'

'Lenin said: "The Party is mutual aid,"' quoted Rappoport. He was making up these words of Lenin's himself on the spot.

'That's it precisely!' Yagubov confirmed. 'So, we have a deal.'

Standing there in the middle of his office it suddenly occurred to Yagubov: was Rappoport engaging in a little provocation, here, drawing pronouncements out of him with his conversation? It was conceivable that he had been an informant in the camps and someone was still pulling his strings. And now, when the leadership of the newspaper had passed to him, Yagubov, the KGB wouldn't be averse to getting interested. He called to mind the entire conversation and came to the conclusion that he hadn't said anything untoward.

Stomping off down the corridor Rappoport was wondering whether Ivlev was cursing him up and down – now there was nothing to do but blow his money on a taxi.

'I beg your pardon, are you Rappoport?' In front of him stood a moon-faced young Georgian in a checked overcoat, a large suede cap and a sporty flowered silk scarf.

'Well,' said Rappoport, 'I'm in an unbelievable hurry!'

'The thing is,' continued the young Georgian in a thick accent, 'my

name is Zurab Makashvili. I have to tell you something. May we go to
your office, my dear man?"

'You can't do it here?'

'No, there's no way I could tell you here! I won't keep you long.'

'What, are you giving me no choice?' asked Rappoport, walking on
to his department.

His room was open; he'd gone off, forgetting to lock it again.

'Are you really Rappoport?'

'I swear on my mother's grave. Go ahead!'

Zurab carefully closed the door, unbuttoned his overcoat and jacket
and pulled out a grey folder that had been clamped to his stomach by his
trouser belt. Rappoport recognized it straight away as the very same folder
that Makartsev had shown him and that he'd searched for unsuccessfully
that morning in Makartsev's office. Rappoport's brow furrowed deeper,
his lips squeezed together. He attempted to avoid appearing to recognize
the folder.

'What's that paperwork?'

'You don't recognize it?'

*I've done it now. I've done it totally stupidly, not by my own fault even.*
*For now I'll deny everything, down to the very last. But only if they don't beat*
*me on my spine. I won't be able to take that a second time; I'll grass, I'll let*
*everybody down* . . . 'Haven't got a clue,' he said indistinctly.

'Don't get excited. I'll explain,' said Makashvili. 'Kakabadze is an old
friend of mine. He and I shared a school desk until the sixth grade. I called
him yesterday and told him that I'd flown in from Tbilisi for one day on
a business trip to get a project authorized, and he came by my room at
the Rossiya Hotel last night. I always stay at the Rossiya Hotel: I stick
twenty roubles into my internal passport when I check in and no worries! Kakabadze arrived, we drank a little Georgian home brew, and he
showed me this folder. He told me that everybody at the newspaper was
reading it with great interest. I asked him to leave it with me overnight,
but he didn't call me the next morning. I have to fly back to Tbilisi. I've
looked for him all day – he didn't spend the night at home.'

'What has this got to do with me?' asked Rappoport, calming down a little but still cautious.

'You? He told me everything about the *subbotnik* last night – I laughed and laughed. He showed me a photograph: the professors from some institute or other chipping ice off the pavement in front of a kebab house. It would be fit for a Chinese newspaper. You're a genius, Rappoport! Kakabadze praised you to the skies.'

'What other slander did he get round to?'

'You don't have to be afraid of me. Zurab Makashvili – quiet as a grave, understand? I hate them! Here, tell me what you think of Stalin.'

'Look, Zurab, I have to respect your feelings as a Georgian . . .'

'Forget it! Stalin was a bastard, a Nazi! He slaughtered three-quarters of our family just because my grandfather knew something about him. They studied together at the seminary. My grandfather was a Communist, while they called Dzhugashvili "*Kinto*".'

'What's that, *kinto*?'

'*Kinto*? That's a vagrant, a tramp. My grandfather buried his mother; she died before the war. Kinto didn't even come to see her off. A Georgian can't do things like that! So you don't have to be afraid of Zurab Makashvili. So where is Kakabadze then? Just between the two of us, he got that folder from the editor's office. I hope they don't find out.'

'You're a naive hayseed,' muttered Rappoport. 'All right, damn you, give it to me!'

— 41 —
# At Rappoport's

When everyone had sat down and Yagubov was knocking his pencil on his desk to begin the meeting, Ivlev and Nadya were sitting in a taxi. Ivlev had telephoned Nadya straight after Rappoport's call.

'I have the key,' he'd told her. 'Can you sneak off?'

'Now?'

'Of course.'

'What about the meeting with Yagubov?'

'They won't notice. And if they do – you had a toothache. Anyway, I'll be sitting in a taxi twenty yards from the office.'

Now they were driving off, and Nadya didn't ask where to. He had called, and here she was with him. The driver went fast, jerking and braking sharply. On the turns Nadya would grab Ivlev's knee, so as not to lose her balance, and then remove her hand in embarrassment. Scarcely after drawing away from him, though, she would calm down, because he didn't give the least significance to any of these trifles that seemed so important to her.

'Izmailovo?' she said in surprise, peering out the window as if she'd been under the impression that he was taking her to the Fiji Islands. 'So have you had dinner yet?'

'A hungry male,' he said, smiling at her logic.

'Then we have to get something to eat.'

'And drink . . . Hey, fellow!' he said to the driver. 'Stop at a food shop!'

At the shop Nadya got in line in the delicatessen section and Ivlev in the liquor department. They met up at the exit. Nadya had ready-made mince rissoles in her hand, and he had four bottles of beer.

'Now for some bread,' said Nadya, and went on in a German accent, 'Rghrashans ligue a lodd uff brghrett.'

They went into a bakery.

'And oil? Is there any oil for the rissoles where we're going?'

They drove another two blocks.

'Don't fuss. I'll pay for it,' she said and pulled a three-rouble note out of her bag.

Ivlev put the bottles down next to the door and fiddled with the key for a long time, not knowing in which direction to turn the thing, looking around to see whether anyone was coming up or down the stairs. Finally, they stepped into Rappoport's hallway. Two pairs of green eyes shone in the darkness.

'Oh Lord! You sweet things!'

Two cats, one grey, one black, rubbed themselves against Nadya's legs, willingly letting her pick them up, and she walked into the room with them. She moved cautiously, as if afraid of finding someone else there. After confirming that no one was there, Nadya moved along the wall as if in a museum, looking at all the photographs, the books on the shelves, the dishes on the sideboard. There was dust on the books and on the dishes, too.

'Can I do what I want here?'

'Sure.' Ivlev stepped up to the cupboard with a businesslike air.

'Yikes!' Nadya shook her head. 'Digging around in other people's things . . .'

'I'm just following orders,' Ivlev explained and pulled out a clean sheet.

Nadya, trying not to be offended by this masculine efficiency, bent over the gas hob. Neatly covering the ottoman with the sheet, Ivlev moved the coffee table over and spread a copy of *Trudovaya Pravda* on top of it. Nadya brought in the pan containing the steaming rissoles, sliced the bread on a plate, whipped up a kind of sauce, put out two glasses and then, after wiping them with a napkin, knives and forks. After cutting off a piece of meat each for the cats she put a single plate on the floor for them. Then she invited Ivlev to the table with her eyes.

'Get undressed first,' he said.

'Completely?'

'Completely.'

'For shame! What'll the cats think of us? And you first, anyway!'

She waited while he took off his jacket, then turned on her heel and went into the kitchen. Ivlev breathed in the smell of the rissoles; it was starting to make his head swim.

Nadya appeared from the kitchen naked in her boots and stopped in the doorway, admiring the effect she was having. A small silver cross hung down between her breasts on a fine chain. Ivlev looked her over bit by bit, without the strength to take his eyes off her. Finally, sensing her power, she magnanimously came down to his level. He took her fingers and sat her down beside him on the ottoman. She was barely perceptibly shivering, either because of him or from the cold.

'The beer!' he remembered. 'Where's the beer?' They'd left it outside on the stair landing.

'The floor's cold. You'll catch your death!'

Ivlev leaped out into the hallway and, cocking his head, listened for a moment. It was quiet on the other side of the door. He undid the lock and looked out. Nobody. And the beer was still there. Ivlev happily grabbed two bottles in each hand and closed the door behind him with his naked foot.

'What if the door had slammed shut on you?' she asked, narrowing her eyes.

'You would have let me back in.'

'It wouldn't have crossed my mind! I would have lain back on the ottoman with the cats and waited for the owner to come home.'

Opening a bottle, he kept silent, grinning, then turned abruptly to Nadya and sprayed her back and forth with the beer.

'You madman!' she laughed, covering herself with her arms instinctively. 'Idiot! You're going to ruin the wallpaper.'

'And you?'

'You've already ruined me.'

He poured out a bit, then sprayed Nadya with beer again, put the bottle down on the floor and fell on top of her, licking the drops of the bitter, foaming liquid off her skin.

'Do what you want with me!' she said. 'Anything you want, only quick!'

She tried with all her might to help him, then, suddenly forgetting him, she started to tremble, her head rocking from side to side, her body writhing all over the ottoman; her back arching and her head thrown back, she let out a guttural shriek like a jungle bird's.

She quickly subsided and, after lying still for a moment, pulled away the hair that was in her eyes with a weak hand and guiltily pressed her nose against Ivlev's cheek.

'What kind of person am I?'

'You're great!' he praised her, indulgently.

She laughed weakly, like someone sick. 'Am I a woman now?' she asked, not opening her eyes, and answered the question herself: 'Yes, a woman!'

'A real woman,' he affirmed. 'I could issue you a diploma.'

'You don't have to tie yourself down.'

They sat up and started annihilating the tough-as-rubber rissoles, drinking down their beer. Nadya cut off pieces of her portion and imperceptibly slipped them on to his plate.

'How nice it was on the sheet, just the two of us,' she said. 'It was nice on the glass as well. But on the sheet was better. I'm ashamed of the fact that I'm not a bit shy in front of you. You know, I've understood what love is about. To my mind, love is about souls being naked.'

'And bodies, too . . .'

'I know whose apartment this is,' she said, pointing at an envelope lying next to the ottoman.

'He calls it his pencil-box: long and narrow.'

'It seems to me you're falling asleep.'

'I flew all night from Novosibirsk to get to you.'

'Hey, you get some sleep, and I'll go to the bathroom.'

Momentarily weakened by the fact that he had no need to be polite or attentive, Ivlev fell fast asleep, as if he'd collapsed. The cats were napping on the carpet on the floor. Entering the little combination bathroom (toilet and shower), Nadya sighed, glanced in the mirror and was left unsatisfied with herself. Turning on the taps and getting the water just right, she stepped under the shower. Turning her back to the mirror she caught sight of an old pair of Rappoport's long underpants hanging on a hook and ashamedly turned her eyes away. But she noticed some faded grey letters on them and carefully spread the seat out with two fingers so she could read it. The seat was stencilled with 'GULAG MVD SSSR'. Spelled out, it stood for 'Chief Directorate for Corrective Labour Camps, Ministry of Internal Affairs, Union of Soviet Socialist Republics'.

Because the towel seemed of dubious freshness Nadya didn't bother drying herself. Ivlev was asleep, lying diagonally across the ottoman. She stealthily arranged herself alongside him.

'He's so sweet,' she said into his ear. 'He's got his lucky lottery numbers pasted up on his bathroom door: 13, 19, 25, 31, 41 and 49.'

'Silly,' Ivlev murmured through his slumber, 'those are the BBC frequencies.'

'But where's his wife? I've never heard anything about her.'

'We carried her out of here three years ago. They wouldn't take her in the hospital, because they didn't want to increase their cancer mortality statistics.'

'He's got a lot of books. What kind are they?'

'You've got to know everything! He collects Party literature, mostly old stuff that gets chucked out of libraries. He digs around in junk shops, swaps recent publications for them.'

'What for?'

'He probably likes to.'

'Maybe I could open his bookcase?'

'You can't. He doesn't like anyone touching his books.'

'But why does he write such pretentious articles? They're unreadable.'

'He doesn't read them either. He pastes them together.'

'But does he think about other people when he's pasting them together? He doesn't believe it, at all.'

'And you – do you believe it?' Ivlev looked closely at her.

'Me? I'm from a different generation. I'm ashamed of it. But he's not!'

'How do you know that?'

'Him? He's not ashamed! He's full of irony. Irony is a kind of indifference, I read somewhere.'

'And I feel guilty next to Rappoport. Imagine: I was studying in school, blathering on about the meaning of life, studying at Moscow State University – and he was in prison the whole time. I had my girlfriends – he was in prison. These people served time for themselves, for me, for you, for us – for everybody. Rappoport hasn't got any strength left. He's tired.'

'And he's become a toady. Rappoport is a slave. A slave by conviction!'

'You dummy! A slave in chains isn't a toady. Try swimming against the tide yourself!'

Nadya kissed him on the throat.

Ivlev reached out for his trousers, pulled off the belt and, slipping it around Nadya, tightened the buckle up around her belly. She watched what he was doing in silence.

'Does that really look better?'

'That's not it! It's something to hang on to.' He pulled her to him by the belt.

'What's this?' he asked a little later, moving back, noticing a tiny, neatly stitched scar on her abdomen for the first time.

'My appendix. Is it ugly?'

'Beautiful!' He kissed the seam.

'Strange,' she said pensively. 'Strange, that you love me afterwards. Or are you just doing it for show? If you are, you don't have to. I'll go.'

'Are you afraid of seeing Rappoport?'

'I don't want him to see you with me.'

'Nonsense!'

Ivlev lay on the couch and read. Nadya, so as not to bore him, put her clothes on, sat on a stool in the kitchen and smoked cigarette after cigarette.

'Smells like someone's been frying something,' said Rappoport cheerfully, entering the room in the company of both cats, who had met him in the hallway and wound themselves around him. Rappoport sucked in the air through his large-nostrilled nose. 'How could I ever have doubted Ivlev's good taste?'

'Thanks,' she said politely. 'I'll cook something right now.' Nadya was overjoyed to have something to do and ran into the kitchen. 'Men are such gluttons!'

'Gluttons?' Rappoport replied. 'Ivlev, she's insulting you!'

'Well, of course,' Nadya chirped. 'All you want to do is guzzle and screw.'

'But even better', Rappoport intoned dreamily, walking into the kitchen, 'is to guzzle and chat. Hope nourishes the young, but it's the bane of the elderly. You did right, kittens, to leave me something to guzzle!'

Seating himself on the ottoman, he added quietly to Ivlev so that Nadya wouldn't overhear: 'We accept payment in beer for the amortization of equipment! Even though I can't drink beer! So why haven't you asked me what the meeting was about?'

'Jan Zizka, the Czech hero, demanded that his skin be made into a drum-head after his death,' Ivlev said, screwing up his eyes. 'Probably precisely the way Yagubov has decided to stretch not only Czech skins but ours as well!'

'Yes, a new broom does sweep clean,' said Rappoport. 'He wouldn't let a story of Zakamorny's run. The money'll have to be subscribed to some other name. The screws are tightening, kids.'

'Makartsev or Yagubov, what's the difference? They're both trained Stalinist falcons!'

'I'm afraid there is a difference, Ivlev: one of them really is a Stalinist hawk, but the other one now – he's a Stalinist raven, a bird of ill omen.'

'They're both as bad.'

'Well, the first eminent Nazi was, as everyone knows, Ivan the Terrible,' Rappoport pronounced. 'When the Russians captured Polotsk they found some Jews. They asked the Tsar what to do with them. He commanded: "They shall turn to our faith or be drowned in the river." To make things simpler, they just drowned them.'

'The poor damned Jews!' said Ivlev. 'They founded Christianity, created Communism. For what? Protest is in their blood. Then afterwards they suffer themselves.'

'How different Muscovites are!' Rappoport continued, in the same vein. 'My neighbour on the other side of that wall died five years ago. But his name is still hanging on his door. It makes no difference at all to the new tenant. Apathy . . .'

'Nadya, time to go!' said Ivlev, when she set down the steaming rissoles and beer in front of Rappoport. 'We can talk at work, too.'

Sticking a chunk of bread into his mouth, Rappoport jumped up and, chewing, helped Nadya on with her overcoat.

'Well, how'd you like it in my crypt?'

'I was happy here.'

'Little girl . . .' sighed Rappoport and didn't go on. 'By the way, kids, Kakabadze has disappeared.'

'What!' whispered Nadya in alarm. 'He's on a shoot. Or he's away on assignment.'

'Er, no. A friend of his came by. Kakabadze left him last night and never got home.'

'Go on!' said Ivlev. 'He drank too much and he's sleeping it off.'

'He doesn't drink like that.'

'We'll find out from Inna in the morning,' Ivlev said to calm her down. 'Let's go!'

'Why should she know?' said Nadya in surprise.

'Don't ask stupid questions!'

Rappoport crammed a large piece of meat into his mouth and threw a morsel to each of the cats. They crawled up beside him, warming themselves, purring. He took the heavy grey folder out of his briefcase. He opened it up and, continuing to chew, began unhurriedly reading through *Russia in 1839* by the Marquis de Custine, taking in the Marquis with his rissoles and his liver-busting beer. But, the book being even more dangerous, the danger from the beer diminished. Rappoport chewed slowly, lazily, taking pleasure in the forbidden beer and the forbidden reading material, as well as the silence, something still permitted to him for a while anyway.

# 42

# The Stages of
# Inna Svetlozerskaya

She came in response to an advertisement for a typist, and Managing Editor Kashin signed her up without any recommendations at all, forgetting even to enter her month's trial period in his hiring order. One could only guess at the reason for such decisiveness and boldness in Kashin.

This is how it came to pass. She opened the door to his tiny cubicle and froze on the doorstep, holding her handbag behind her. Kashin looked at her inquiringly, but she silently afforded him the opportunity to look her over better, with the light from the window full on her. Not overly beautiful, her face was too crudely stuck together, a bit too simple, with her nose overflat and her eyes so small that eyeliner didn't help, all only just compensated for by her radiant and placid smile. But her figure! To call her a Venus would be to offend her, inasmuch as Inna Svetlozerskaya had all the basics for her own standard of beauty. Her figure, from neck to toe, radiated good health, a harmonious definition of line and the unique combination of incorruptible chastity with immediate readiness. Kashin swallowed air and nearly choked. His gaze simply stuck to her; he had to force himself to look out the window, but his eyes would every now and again run up and down his visitor and down and up and then once again, as if indifferent, turn away. Now, after the pause, understanding that she was victorious, Svetlozerskaya modestly uttered: 'I'm a typist. I came about the ad.'

'Where have you worked?' Kashin used the question as an excuse for a more thorough eyeballing of his visitor.

'At the newspaper *Krasnaya Zvezda*.'

'And why do you want to move here?'

'I like your newspaper better.'

'And wages?'

'The girls said that they're the same.'

'Well, what the heck?' the managing editor leaped up out of his seat considerably more expeditiously than usual. 'Here's what we'll do: sit here at my desk and fill out this application form.'

Sitting on the edge of the chair, Inna stretched her long legs out to one side. Kashin walked over behind his aquarium so that her legs and what was above them were visible to him and started pouring out fish food. The inmates strained towards his hand.

'Oh, how charming!' she batted her eyelashes with joy.

'Indeed,' agreed the flattered Kashin.

He wasn't very good at shifting from official tones to personal ones when talking to women; and as for going from personal to intimate he was even worse. He went into a panic around beautiful women, got completely confused and blushed. Because of that he had come to the conclusion that plain women were easier to get. The face on this new girl was homely, and the managing editor decided in a flash that this was very good indeed: on the one hand, he liked her and, on the other, she wasn't pretty. That meant that she wouldn't think too highly of herself and would appreciate the depth of his, Kashin's, future feelings.

Inna brought with her from the Volga her light-brown hair, tied up in an old-fashioned bun that suited her, and the handicap of a round, provincial pronunciation of her vowels, something that Jews, even with all their imitativeness, had never been granted mastery of.

There were more than enough problems with her qualifications, but Kashin was already so set on employing her that certain flaws (such as an unhappy family life) he evaluated as pluses for him personally and others (such as the absence of a residence permit for Moscow) he took as an advantageous step towards what he was after. He, Kashin, would be able to get her a residence permit if she commended herself well.

The temporary residence permit that she did have was for Vladimir province, nowhere near Moscow, and Inna had her own reason for that. After deciding to get a divorce from her second husband, Gryaznov, she had started life anew by coming to the capital. Here, on Gorky Street, Inna took up her favourite pose as a statue of a contemporary Aphrodite, with her handbag behind her back. Right off the bat, an Italian coming out of the Central Telegraph Office latched on to her. He turned out to be a technical representative for Olivetti, which had just concluded a contract to supply special furniture for the Party's Central Committee. Inna saw Aldo in his room at the Hotel Berlin twice a week over the course of three months, and, although he spoke Russian very poorly and Inna's Italian was limited to the word 'Ciao!', she felt that he'd opened up for her a whole world of passions that no one had ever explained to her before. Inna was noted down in the books of the internal surveillance service. She had no record, the Italian was supplying equipment to the Central Committee, and nobody had received any orders to offend him. It was assumed that Inna would meet other foreigners after his departure. And then the KGB organs would decide what to do with her. But Aldo had scarcely gone when Inna disappeared from Moscow.

She showed up in Kirzhach, just outside of Vladimir, at the house of Gryaznov's mother. Here she bore the Italian a son, honestly informing Gryaznov's mother about everything. The granny, however, became attached to the little boy and, after the departure of her former daughter-in-law, hurried down to the local registry office and contrived to adopt the skinny black-haired boy in return for a present of a chicken and two dozen choice eggs. And the only thing she demanded from Inna now was money for the maintenance of Inna's temporary residence permit, for which she had to pay a three-rouble bill every month to the local policeman.

Freed of the Italian and his son, Inna couldn't settle and out of boredom agreed to marry a professional soldier, Alfred Svetlozersky: his name reminded her of Aldo. There weren't any other points of comparison. She hadn't managed to hang around him for very long. He was physically repulsive to her, and his stupid jokes made her screw up her face as if from a toothache.

After deciding to make a fresh start she went back to Moscow and got a job as a typist, registering as the holder of a street-sweeper's job, since that was the only position she could get without a residence permit. She worked in a place surrounded by the same sort of obtuse people as her last husband, only these were half-military, half-journalist. She continued to wear the clothes that Aldo had given her, and there was no fending off the officers who swarmed around. She liked working at a newspaper, but she wanted a more intellectual milieu. In the prime of her physiological powers she found herself at *Trudovaya Pravda*.

In the typists' pool the talk was only of clothes and men, and in the breaks between conversations they did some typing. Sharp-tongued and clever, Inna settled in straight away. To the query 'How many men have you had, Inna?' she would come right back with the question 'When? Today?' For up till the day before there had been 481 men in her life. The first hundred names were beginning to fade from her memory, but she never lost count.

'From whatever angle you look, Inna has the best figure in the office,' said the typists with pride. 'It's a pity she can't walk around naked. Any clothes, even imported things, just spoil a figure like that.'

'They don't spoil it!' Inna put them at rest. 'If you get undressed straight away then you've got nothing to promise. And if a fellow's drunk, whatever he's offered is going to be beautiful. So, girls, don't get upset about it!'

With such worldly wisdom, if she'd had any kind of higher education Inna could have gone really far. That's what her friends thought. But she was trying to persuade not so much them as herself: 'What are you on about, girls? I'm not messed up by the lack of a diploma but by the fact that I'm a woman: the hormones will get you every time.'

'But don't they get the lads, too?'

'They do, but then they give them a break,' said Inna, defending her point of view. 'But we get it non-stop! If it wasn't for hormones I could have reached such heights!'

She was entrusted with the most responsible work at *Trudovaya Pravda*.

Literacy was in her nature – where else could she have got it from, with her six and a half years of education? She had a typing speed that was beyond all praise, and her fingers never grew tired, and she was never off sick, even after one of her abortions.

'The unhappiest people on the newspaper are us, the typists,' she philosophized. 'We have to thoughtfully transcribe with both hands the same rubbish that they scribble in their departments with their right hands alone and with never a thought about it.'

From her village childhood she had brought with her the ability to read fortunes in the cards, which began to draw the women to her, secretly curious. She told everybody's fortune – everyone had misfortunes or indeterminate situations. All the men at the newspaper from Makartsev down to the alcoholic pressmen in the print shop had their fortunes told and retold hundreds of times, were dealt kings and jacks crossed by various queens. Knowing as much as she did, Inna could have played on anyone's beliefs, but she never did. The males in the office thought of her as one of the lads, even though there were fewer and fewer of them who remained personally unconvinced that she was a woman.

# 43

# The Only Way Out

The next morning Ivlev ran straight to Inna first thing. Spying him at the door, she waved a hand at him not to come in, quickly got up from her seat and made her way between desks to the exit, bent over like a cat. She had a particular way of talking to everyone in a corner in the corridor: she would lean against the wall on one arm, the other hand holding a cigarette, and get her half-opened lips so close to the person she was talking to that it seemed as though they were getting it on there and then. The door to the typing pool was always opening and closing, as employees collected material left from the night before, but in the corner it was quiet and dark.

'What have you done with Kakabadze? Don't cover up!'

'Where do you get this from?'

'It's not important. His mother phoned. She's going crazy.'

'No kidding!' Inna drawled. 'I swear to God, I have no idea!'

'Was he with you the night before last?'

'No! He promised to come by, that's a fact. A friend of his from Tbilisi showed up. I waited for him till one o'clock, listened for footsteps outside the window the whole time. He likes to come by when I'm already in bed, so I go to bed before he gets there. I waited and waited, but next morning I woke up all alone. I'm speaking absolutely frankly to you, which I wouldn't do with anyone else . . .'

'What have you got going with him – something serious?'

'Oh, sure! He said himself: "You suit me perfectly as far as sex goes. But Mummy isn't going to let me marry you." As if I needed that! The most important thing is, he can do the business – I yell my head off. The bruises don't fade for two weeks. What a guy!'

With both hands she adjusted her bra, which had slipped with her two-handed, over-emotional explanation to Ivlev.

'All right, Inna,' Ivlev patted her on the shoulder. 'We'll find your Georgian. Go on back and get clattering.'

'I don't clatter. I type. Well, then, block the corridor for me; I'm going to pull up my stocking.'

'By yourself, or do you need help?'

'You're all the same!' she pouted. 'First you want to button me up and then later unbutton me.'

His desk was strewn with unread letters and old notebooks. Ivlev pulled the telephone over to him, piled the telephone book on top of it and wondered where to open it. After hesitating, he started off with the morgues.

In those five where Kakabadze might accidentally have ended up he didn't feature among the identified corpses. He could get to the unidentified ones later, if other approaches failed to yield results. If Kakabadze was alive the task would be a lot easier.

It occurred to Ivlev that Kakabadze could have dashed off to his native Tbilisi and be sitting with his friends sipping Izabella wine. But he said no to that version straight away. Either his friend from Tbilisi or his mother would know about it. He could telephone the duty city police desk right now, but his conversation would be taped, and Ivlev didn't want to kick up a fuss before it was necessary, to avoid causing Kakabadze any trouble. With the telephone in his hand he let his fingers do the walking around the various ambulance-bay emergency rooms. Nope, they hadn't picked up anybody like that. According to the police there hadn't been any road accidents involving anyone answering Kakabadze's description either. A dead end was looming when his phone rang.

'Ivlev,' he heard Rappoport say in official tones. 'Come straight to my office, now.'

Rappoport was pacing around his room waving his hands, a sign of extreme agitation. A miniature old lady of about eighty years of age was perched on the edge of his chair. Her face was a wrinkled fist with eyes like beads. She was blinking like mad, hypnotizedly turning her head to follow Rappoport's pacing back and forth.

'Sit down, Ivlev.' Rappoport made a broad gesture with one arm and said to his elderly visitor: 'Could you please repeat the story?'

'From the beginning?'

'Why not? This colleague of ours has to hear the whole thing as well.' Turning to Ivlev, Rappoport added: 'She's a long-time subscriber to our newspaper, a former teacher, loves art, in particular music and painting. She's been retired for a long time now, and she does volunteer work down at her local housing office. Besides that, she's a person with principles.'

'No, that's not the point! It's that I live on the second floor.'

'Remember that, Ivlev, on the second floor!'

'And there's a police station on the first floor, right below me. I live alone. It's always quiet at my place. I just *despise* television! And because of my insomnia at night I can hear every rustle. I hear doors being locked and unlocked downstairs, what people are yelling. And whenever they're beating somebody up I can hear every blow perfectly. By the way, they beat people up every night, but usually drunks, juvenile delinquents and people like that. That's the sort of pedagogical methods they use. But the night before last I took two sleeping pills and went to sleep, because I had travelled to see my sister and was very tired. However, I woke up in the middle of the night. They were beating somebody so hard that the building was shaking.'

'Pay attention, Ivlev!' ordered Rappoport.

'The person they were beating up was trying to explain that his name was Kakabadze and that he was from *Trudovaya Pravda*. Naturally I didn't believe that someone entrusted with a high public position like that could ever engage in hooliganism. Something wasn't quite right. I got up, went to the phone and rang the police, and I said to the municipal duty officer that my patience had run out. How was it that people were being tortured in Soviet police stations? What do we have law-enforcement agencies over us for? I told them that if they didn't take steps I was going to get an appointment the next day with the minister.'

'And did that have an effect?' asked Ivlev, silent until then.

'It certainly did!' she said with pride. 'Around fifteen minutes later a bus full of men with machine-guns drove up, and they burst into the station downstairs. I saw the whole thing, standing at my window. What they did down there I don't know, only everything grew quiet. And a little later they led out several policemen in handcuffs and drove off with them.'

'Now,' Rappoport interrupted her, 'tell the most important thing.'

'The important thing was that I got to sleep afterwards. Then in the morning I woke up because somebody was ringing my doorbell. A young man came in, very elegant, in a beautiful uniform – I even thought at first that he was a general. But he introduced himself as a police major. A very well-bred young man, fifty years old or so, no more. When he came into my room, he wiped his feet beforehand, and he even took off his cap. Imagine!'

'She has a well-developed sense of humour,' interjected Rappoport.

'And what did you expect? I could tell you even better things! So, this general, that is, major – he was pretty as a general – says: "Pardon us for disturbing your sleep. As a result of your call we've taken steps, so there's no need to alarm anybody further. Whoever deserves it will be punished. Don't worry about a thing." "What do you mean," I said, "don't worry? What about that young man they beat half to death?" "How could they have beaten him half to death", he says, "when he's alive and well? This is a congenital hooligan, and he's going to be punished in accordance with the law." So then I tell him: "You know, I can hear them beating people up every night. And I have my suspicions, because I know who this person is!" "You'd better not interfere in this, Grandma," he says, "or else you'll be charged with unauthorized disclosure of official secrets."'

'He said that?' Ivlev said, smiling.

'It didn't bother me that he was trying to intimidate me so much as calling me grandma. I think the department of Communist Education is obliged to intervene!'

The old lady got up, held her thin, dry hand out to each of them in turn and darted out the door.

'Well, what do you say, Ivlev?' Rappoport stopped in front of him, his feet set wide apart and his hands thrust into his pockets.

'Any normal newspaper in the world would remake their front page and put an account of this on it!'

'Don't get all steamed up, Ivlev. You're not a tea-kettle. Better give some thought to it: if the police have busted Kakabadze for doing something genuinely illegal, how come he's not on the List?'

Any Party worker, actor, journalist or other member of the elite fraternity who committed an anti-social act in the course of the previous twenty-four hours was included on a list prepared by the Internal Affairs Directorate of the Moscow Municipal Executive Committee and placed every morning on the desk of the first secretary of that body. If Kakabadze was on the list Kashin would have already been informed so that he could take the appropriate measures.

'What are you suggesting?'

'They must have had some reason for not including him on the List.'

'Snouts in the trough?'

'And then, if they're clearly guilty and hide it from the city committee, to save Kakabadze we can remind them that we're the Central Committee paper. And, so to speak, fighting for the honour of the uniform. True, Yagubov is a pathetic slug. But maybe it would work if we involved Makartsev.'

'The newspaper against the Ministry of Internal Affairs?'

'For starters, the Ministry of Internal Affairs isn't the KGB, and we would be observing the appearance of legality. In the second place, this is just the city administration, and we're not subordinate to the municipal hierarchy. If something sensitive comes to light it'll be more convenient for the ministry to dissociate themselves. What do you say, Ivlev: are you going to risk it? Then I'd better go and talk to Kashin.'

'Why?'

'My dear departed wife's first cousin works as a bookkeeper in the shop at the Zoo.'

He walked solemnly into Kashin's office, the way people do who are coming to congratulate somebody. 'I'm sure I have good news for you. Do you need any hard-to-get baby fish?'

'Do you have channels?'

'Do I ever! You can get rare specimens through the back door. And, most importantly, without any profiteering, absolutely legally.'

'That's unbelievable!' Kashin got up out of his chair. 'I'm obliged to you.'

'Don't think about it! Well, I'm off.' Rappoport turned to the door. 'Hey, by the way, did you hear about Kakabadze? He's in trouble, a good man, a Young Communist . . . He wasn't on the List, was he?'

'I'd know if he was,' said Kashin offendedly. 'What about him?'

'That's just what I thought. So he didn't do anything.'

'What's this about?'

'Well, they're saying that he was beaten up for no reason at all at a police station. We've got to get to the bottom of it. Do you have anybody in the Ministry of Internal Affairs? We should find out. After all, we're the Party newspaper, you and I – we're stronger than them!'

Kashin gave it some thought. Finding out what had happened to an employee of the newspaper was his direct responsibility. He dialled Uterin's number and asked him to make an inquiry regarding Kakabadze. Kashin and Rappoport were talking about fish when Uterin called back.

'Aleksandr Kakabadze – one of yours? We've got him! In the prison hospital in a serious condition. Fighting while in a drunken state.'

'Then why's he in the prison hospital?'

'It means he's guilty of something. They're going to sort it out.'

'While they're sorting it out I have to answer to my superiors. What am I supposed to do – bat my eyes?'

'We have to get to the bottom of this ourselves,' interrupted Rappoport.

'Get us a visitor's pass,' Kashin continued into the telephone. 'We're going to send down one of our employees. That suit you?'

Rappoport burst into the special correspondents' office. 'Kashin's helped get you into the CID, Ivlev. Just be careful. They'll stitch you up in the affair, too, at the drop of a hat.'

'I won't let them do that!'

'Then get on it.'

Buttoning up his overcoat as he went, Ivlev ran down the stairs and stopped the first passing vehicle. It was a tipper lorry loaded down with snow. For three roubles the driver agreed to take him where he wanted; he really didn't give a damn about anything, even running red lights. The rapid delivery, however, didn't help: an hour and a half went by on the pass-obtaining process.

'I'll permit you to talk only for a short while,' said the surgeon in officers' shoulderboards, with ostentatious severity. He was long and thin. It seemed as though he didn't have any shoulders at all.

'What's wrong with him anyway?'

'Are you going to write about this?' the surgeon inquired. 'You'll write it up beautifully; you know how to do it. Drunken fighting and that sort of thing. You take trouble over people like that and wonder if it's even worth while. A fracture at the base of the skull, two ribs broken, compaction of his right kidney, face messed up.'

The surgeon turned and walked out. His footsteps echoed down the corridor. Ivlev took a four-rouble note out of his pocket and, after glancing around, held it out to the young and pleasant-looking guard.

'I want to talk to him alone. Don't worry. Nothing will happen.'

The guard looked around, tucked the money into the top of his boot and stepped out into the corridor. There were twelve cots in the ward and a stinking smell; everyone was gravely injured. There were two barred windows up by the ceiling, which was covered with yellow stains – it was oozing out somewhere through the lagging on the sewage pipes. Ivlev went from bed to bed, looking for Kakabadze.

'You?' Kakabadze wanted to smile but couldn't. His eyes filled with tears that spilled out instantly. Ivlev went down on his knees on the filthy floor, so as to get closer to the bandaged head, a perfect sphere.

'How did you manage to get in . . . here?' Kakabadze whispered, barely audibly. 'I was thinking I'd die and nobody would know . . .'

'Nonsense! You know that we don't take no for an answer. We haven't got a moment to spare. You're not allowed to talk. Keep it short, can you?'

'They'll beat me up again if I say anything. It hurts . . .'

'For what?'

'Just because . . . the sadists . . .'

'Who? Who is, old friend?'

'I was looking for a taxi.'

'Hurrying to get to Inna's?'

'She told you?'

'She did. That Inna's a brick. She'd give you the shirt off her back.'

'I know. Don't tell Nadya.'

'Nadya? I won't tell her. You were looking for a taxi, and . . .'

'Uh-huh! There was a policeman on the sidewalk. I was trying to flag a car down, but they wouldn't stop. He comes up to me and says: "Stopping's forbidden here – nobody's going to stop for you. Shift yourself out of here." I got angry: I was frozen, and there he was in felt boots and with nothing to do. I said: "I'll make you a bet. If someone stops, you pay me a tenner – if nobody does, I'll pay you! Somebody'll stop right away, you'll see!" And he says: "That's right! Somebody will!" And I look, and straight in front of me is a police car with two men in it. "Get in!" they tell me. I say to them: "This doesn't really suit me. I need a taxi." "Get in," they say. They grabbed me and pulled me in and drove straight off.'

'Where to?'

'To the district police station. But I only understood that the next day, because they started beating me straight away while I was still in the patrol car, when they were searching me. They tied my hands with my belt and beat me up. They were thinking: a Georgian – lots of money. And when we got to the station the duty officer joined in with them. I said to them: "I'm not a typical Georgian, I'm poor." "We'll teach you to chat up our Russian girls, you Georgian monkey!" he says. They kicked me and worked me over with brass knuckles and threw a stool from corner to corner that hit me in the head. And they asked me again where my money was hidden. And when I couldn't move any more they stood around me in a circle and pissed on me, everyone trying to piss straight into my mouth. I choked . . .' Kakabadze squeezed his eyes shut, screwing up his face either from the pain or from the recollection. 'They say they're going to bring me up on charges. But for what? Watch out for them!'

'Calm down. We're involved now. If we have to, we can ask Makartsev for help.'

The ward door opened. The skinny surgeon beckoned to Ivlev who stroked Kakabadze's face with his fingers, wiping away his tears, and walked out.

'So, you're from *Trudovaya Pravda*?' A captain in police uniform pulled Ivlev's sleeve. 'Senior Inspector Uterin, pleased to meet you. I've been assigned to have a chat with you. The press writes about us a lot. We're not complaining; it's just that not everybody understands what we're supposed to do. Let's go up to my office.'

They walked down the narrow cellar corridor, under lamps covered by metal grilles. Their papers were inspected twice. In his room Uterin showed Ivlev a chair.

'You have a difficult task,' said Uterin, getting straight to the point. 'I'm not handling this case myself. My colonel instructed me to explain it to you. The evidence against Kakabadze is serious. You have doubts: to wit, you think he was beaten up at a police station. Between ourselves, it does sometimes happen that people get beaten up – we have all sorts on the force. But this was a fight. He doesn't have any witnesses –'

'He does,' Ivlev said drily.

'You found one?' Uterin was surprised. 'I called Kashin about you, checked you out. He commended you as an intelligent and experienced journalist.'

'Thanks.'

'You and I, we're both subordinates. I have my superiors; you have yours. It's better not to argue with your superiors, right?'

'Exactly.'

'Incidentally, how is your Makartsev – is he still in hospital? What bad luck: a heart attack, and now this thing with his son. I would have been happy to find some extenuating circumstances – but there weren't any to be had! The boy's going to have to serve fifteen years. He's a goner. My superiors think that we can meet each other halfway. Talk it over. No one's going to say anything like that officially, of course – understand?'

'I understand you.' Ivlev got up.

Uterin stood as well and smiled guiltily. They shook hands firmly, like old friends.

On the pavement a cold wind was blowing debris off the street, spinning it around in the air. On Tver Boulevard children were playing on little islands of dry asphalt between the puddles. 'Agree to it!' Rappoport was going to say to him. 'No articles of any kind!' was what Yagubov was going to declare. 'Criticizing the police means criticizing the authorities. Exposing the perpetrators is a matter for the punitive agencies. We're just propagandists.' 'There is a whiff of something in this transaction, but it's an accidental affair,' Makartsev would say. 'We're talking about life here, after all. Imagine your own son getting into trouble, Ivlev.' *I wonder what Polishchuk is going to say?*

# 44

# The Twists and Turns of
# Lev Polishchuk

In his last year of secondary school Polishchuk, an ambitious young man, became a candidate Master of Sport in the game of hundred-square draughts. When he applied to the Bauman Academy, the most patriotic department of the institute – sports – pressured the selection committee, and Polishchuk was accepted, even though he was one point short. He became a Master of Sport in his second year and did less studying than travelling around to competitions. For being a sociable person he was elected a member of the Young Communist League committee and then nominated for the position of secretary. Before him loomed the sparkling prospect of scoring big. After getting his engineering degree, the rosy-cheeked Young Communist leader Lev Polishchuk, having an irreproachable résumé (no one knew that his grandmother was Jewish), was recommended for the job of executive organizer in the science department of the All-Union Lenin Young Communist League's central committee. He began supervising young people at the new Siberian academic towns.

Polishchuk had a serious shortcoming: he trusted people. It was something that never really messed him up at student level but afterwards caused problems. Because people would let him down. Twice he approved something along the lines of a public discussion of issues in the academic city of Novosibirsk. However, the discussions quickly grew from being purely scientific into something social, and a directive was issued to close down the Young Communist café. The Young Communist League central committee first secretary, Pavlov, called in Polishchuk and explained it briefly to him: 'There isn't going to be any more of this striptease.'

Following in the tracks of Semichastny and Shelepin, Pavlov was dying to get into the Central Committee of the Party or, failing that, into the KGB. Polishchuk, like everyone in the leadership of the Young Communist League, understood that the leadership of the country itself needed rejuvenating, and the foremost candidates for this were in the Young Communist League, the foremost assistant to the Party itself. If for Polishchuk this rejuvenation presented a way out of stagnation, however, then for Pavlov and people who thought like him the goal was personal advancement. One way or another, the elders understood that they had only to let a single Young Communist leader into the Big House – and behind him would come the rest, like mountain climbers tied together on a rope. And although both grey buildings stood facing one another between the Party and the League there was a transparent and insurmountable wall. Polishchuk finally understood this when the embezzling Pavlov was named chairman of the Sports Committee, leaving to him the sporting Olympus but for ever closing off the Party one. Around this time Polishchuk himself began losing enthusiasm for his organizational work.

His friends were cobbling together their dissertations, having a good time. During the shake-up in connection with the change in the country's leadership Polishchuk managed to move to an institute where, after a break of many years, the science of sociology was being taken up again. Whatever side of life they took for their sociological studies, though, there was never any question of publishing their results, since they 'just wouldn't do'. The leadership would run the secret reports past the people Upstairs, but there they didn't like what was said either. Polishchuk already had his dissertation on 'The Strivings of Soviet Youth and Their Realization' ready when the directive came to cut short all specifically sociological projects. From now on the institute had to pursue tasks in which the conclusions that were to be reached were indicated in advance.

Fortunately Polishchuk had already passed through an excellent school for getting the feel of these things and was prescient enough to make the jump – before the organizational closures – to the new futurology section at the International Workers' Movement Institute. There they were preparing a complex computer program to show how far Communism had come in comparison with rotten old capitalism. The work was going ahead successfully; there were already several post-doctoral and a host of doctoral dissertations written up. The computer was operating in a festive atmosphere, and the Institute administration promised Upstairs that they would have results in time for the forthcoming Party congress. Unexpectedly, however, the machine revealed that the 'international workers' movement' had no material significance, Communism was not moving ahead and capitalism wasn't rotting. Moreover, ideology, from the point of view of futurology, played no role in economic development. Capitalism and Communism were even converging at a certain point. The altogether temporary role of ideology sufficed merely to slow the convergence down, impeding it, declared the computer.

It was impossible to punish the computer for its anti-Leninist approach, but the futurology department was shut down in its turn. Polishchuk was going crazy searching for another job and didn't get out in time. This is when he got overtaken by a reprimand for ideological negligence (with an entry on his record card), even though Polishchuk hadn't been directly connected with the computation.

At this point Makartsev, concerned about rejuvenating his own *Trudovaya Pravda* staff, was looking for an executive secretary to replace old man Ovseyev, an old-timer on the paper who was being retired with honours. Makartsev understood that if he didn't find some sort of neutral person on his own the Central Committee would send round someone who would carry out not his, Makartsev's, will but that of whoever had got him the job. Polishchuk, who had been recommended to him through friends, was an instant hit with Makartsev, who generally liked or disliked people straight off.

In his new position the Master of Sport in hundred-square draughts soon felt himself as at home as a fish in water. All of his earlier organizer's experience came in handy. The mechanism of the newspaper fascinated him. The dangerous trait of trust in people – that Polishchuk had never overcome – afforded him good relations with all of his co-workers. The only thing that drove him around the bend was the need for frequent trips Upstairs. Fortunately Makartsev loved doing that himself, and whenever he couldn't he mitigated Polishchuk's fate by sending one of his other deputies. About this time Polishchuk's career prospects faded again. It was as if he could feel himself butting against the ceiling.

Yagubov was very surprised when he heard that Polishchuk rode to work on the metro, with a transfer to a tram, when he was entitled to a personal car. And he ate his lunch at the Young Communist League central committee private dining-room, to which he was admitted by habit, and not at the Big House one. Polishchuk heard out the observation without any objections, accepting Yagubov's point, but nothing changed. When Makartsev gave the order to publish irate reviews of Solzhenitsyn by working-class people, Polishchuk, declaring himself to be ill, asked for someone to replace him as duty editor and went home. The issue was passed for press by Makartsev himself.

Two or three people would sometimes gather in Polishchuk's office for a chat. And, smiling sadly, he would venture the opinion that, since Moscow's streets were being renamed after Soviet and foreign Party leaders and they were putting up monuments to them everywhere, the city was starting to look like a cemetery for the Communists of the whole wide world.

'Once when we were in Sweden,' he recounted to some close friends, 'the mayor of Stockholm rushed up to hug us. "I deeply respect you Soviet journalists. You're so intelligent! Our journalists are a bunch of primitives in comparison with you. After all, how do you contrive to write anything at all under the kind of censorship that you have in your country?"'

Polishchuk stayed just within bounds, trying not to do anything too awful. In order to stem the tide you would have to be a hero, and he was just an ordinary sort of fellow. He would take care of business, trying not to participate in any baseness, and not voluntarily pour oil on any fires.

He could get into deep trouble with the odd trifling honesty, too, though.

One day when Nadya, in Yagubov's absence, brought the latest bundle of post to Polishchuk he looked it over and took out several too-nasty letters from the pile, tore them up along with some open letters in defence of political prisoners and threw them into the wastebasket.

'You didn't see anything!'

Nadya nodded, and they had no further conversation on the subject. Among Polishchuk's friends at the newspaper was Raisa Kachkareva, the editor of the arts and literature desk. People talked about them. She had energy in abundance. Raisa would drop by for a cigarette and stay awhile to natter about life, giving advice (wise, as a rule) on how to behave and who with, when to be more leftish and when to hold back so as not to get burned. She understood Polishchuk better than anyone else did. Polishchuk's wife knew about this friendship and was jealous, even though she tried to conceal it.

His former Young Communist colleagues had jobs in various organizations. One day Polishchuk's League central committee boss, who now worked for the KGB, found out that he had become a journalist, and, after chatting about life in general, he proposed: 'Listen, why don't you come and work for us? Two years in a special school: languages and a speciality. And then you'll go abroad for your *Trudovaya Pravda* or some other paper. We'll send you with your family, no worries. You'll be an accredited journalist, collecting information that we need. Under present conditions it isn't hard to do.'

'Tempting!' responded Polishchuk, but the next day he turned the offer down. Raisa had talked him out of it.

'What a stupid thing to do!' said Makartsev, when the executive secretary related the story to him, even though he himself wasn't at all fond of the KGB.

On one occasion Polishchuk seriously offended his editor-in-chief, and if the latter had been a bit more stupid he would never have forgiven him. The information department had selected a likely lad and wanted to employ him. The newspaper was suffering from a lack of good reporters, every issue had to have fresh material in it and this fellow ran around with a will and wrote quickly, but Makartsev dug his heels in, citing the fact that the young man was non-Party.

'We'll co-opt him into the Party,' Polishchuk said, trying to argue him round.

'It'd be easier to hire somebody already in the Party,' Makartsev objected. 'Anyway, we're not a kindergarten here. We need experienced people, from other newspapers.'

'But he suits us, to judge by his professional qualities.'

'Let's get this clear: I'm answerable for the staff's politics as a whole, and you're concentrating on professional qualities alone.'

'I never knew you had it in for Jews!' Polishchuk squeezed out as he left.

'Hang on!' yelled Makartsev. 'If that's the case, no way, hang on! Look at what goes on at this paper! And compare it with the others. There are poison-pen letters against me for having too many Jews here and not against you! You know what? You go to the Central Committee and tell them that I'm an anti-Semite. Say it loud. Then they'll knock me a lot less for it!'

'I'm not going to say anything there,' the secretary objected. 'On that level, it probably wouldn't be enough. And here . . .'

'Look at the liberal!' Makartsev suddenly laughed. 'I'll never understand what it was they taught you in the Young Communists. All right! Where's the application? Let's process it!'

They never once returned to the subject, but a coldness remained between them. Makartsev hadn't got angry. It was just unpleasant to get accused of being what you really weren't.

# 45

# Behind Yagubov's Back

Without taking off his coat Ivlev went straight to the executive secretary's office. He had a working friendship with Polishchuk. They didn't get together outside work, but here, feeling what they had in common in their estimate of a range of issues, trusting each other more and more, they drew closer and got deeper into the kind of debates that had been impossible not long before.

'Well, what's happening with Kakabadze?' Polishchuk covered the pile of galley proofs on his desk with one hand, so that they wouldn't blow away in the draught.

Ivlev fell into the armchair still in his coat and gave a brief summary of the situation, including Uterin's proposal.

'I'm sorry for Makartsev,' said Polishchuk. 'But we weren't hired to spit in our own faces. The issue isn't even Kakabadze; it's the newspaper. I'm for publishing the story. Otherwise we become the same sort of criminals as these Interior Ministry types. Why don't you say something?'

'Suppose we hold back on the article and they let both of them go. Is Kakabadze going to have to go around in disgrace the rest of his life because of Makartsev's brat?'

'So who's going to put it on the page? Surely not Yagubov?'

'You know, Yagubov might just go for the article.'

'For what reason?'

'Because it gives him a chance to stick it to Makartsev,' said Ivlev. 'If the paper publishes something against the police, they're going to come down like a ton of bricks on his son.'

'That's it!' grinned Polishchuk and touched the brush of his moustache with his tongue, as if checking to see whether it had grown at all; but the enthusiasm then faded in his eyes. 'But what if he chickens out?'

'Well, what about you?'

'Me? I'd risk it, probably,' Polishchuk said, running his fingers around on his desk, prolonging his coming to a decision, then glanced at his clock. 'Yagubov leaves around eight o'clock. The material should all be ready about then. And no noise. Will two hundred lines do?'

'I'll fit it in.'

'My son!' pronounced Rappoport, tiredly massaging his eyes with his fingers after hearing a brief summary from Ivlev. 'If you want to see the affair to its conclusion don't have any generalizations in the piece. The most important thing is to stress that our police are the best in the world and that these three policemen are just some sort of aberration.'

Following him out with his eyes, Rappoport suddenly thought: *Was it Polishchuk who put the grey folder on Makartsev's desk? No, not very likely. Polishchuk is all words, and he's a lot more moderate when it comes to deeds. It is pleasant, though, when someone turns out to be better than you thought he was.*

Locking himself in, Ivlev got down to writing the article. He was distracted from his work by a rustling under the door. A piece of paper appeared on the wooden floor. Ivlev picked it up and read: '*Let me in for a minute.*' He turned the key. Nadya, glancing round to see if anybody was there, slipped inside and locked the door behind her.

'Are you busy? I want to show you my new trousers. Do you like them? They're not too tight here? Touch them.'

Politely he touched her, and she leaped on him like a cat, wrapping her arms and legs around him. Ivlev staggered but remained standing, grabbed hold of her and lifted her up on to the desk, messing up the carefully laid-out notebook sheets. Nadya slipped down, continuing to squeeze him with her arms and legs.

'Let go, you little snake!'

'Work away. I won't bother you,' she said, releasing her arms and legs.

Flopping into his chair Ivlev put his head down on the manuscript, trying to calm his aroused heartbeat and gather his remaining still-unwritten phrases. He heard the squeak of a parquetry block and then felt her stroking his knees like a cat, and he kicked at her lightly. But no way would she leave him alone.

'Now you're mine!' her voice carried to him joyfully from under his desk. 'If you resist, I'll rip it completely off!'

He bit his lip, stretched out a hand under the desk and stroked Nadya's hair. The room rocked, swam and suddenly stopped. Nadya sat on the floor for a few moments longer, then stood up and made her way to the door, trying to tread noiselessly.

'Lock it behind me, you toiler.'

Ivlev flung the window open, and the damp evening cold reached into the room. The sheets of paper on the desk blew around. The damp made him shiver, but it brought him to his senses. He locked the window again and made himself concentrate on the article.

Pieces that didn't have the *Direct to Issue!* stamp were typed up by the duty typist late in the evening for the next day's issue. Ivlev had barely walked into the typing pool when Inna took the sheets out of his hand without asking, as if she sensed what they were about. Before she reached the end of the first page she stopped typing and picked up the manuscript, fixing her eyes on the slanting lines of Ivlev's minute handwriting. Twice in this way the machine-gun clatter of her Kontinental typewriter broke off: not believing her eyes, she had to read how Kakabadze had been beaten up. Both times Inna stood up and drank down half a glass of cold water. After banging out the article she ran over to Ivlev.

'I'm going to him,' she said, putting the article down on the desk. 'Right now!'

'You're not going anywhere, dummy,' he reasoned softly, putting his hand against her ear. 'It's a prison hospital.'

She sat down on a chair and wept. He raised her head with both his hands, saw how the tears were flowing past the corners of her nose and into her mouth and slowly kissed first one of her eyes and then the other.

'I'll go anyway,' she said stubbornly.

'You won't,' he repeated wearily to her, as if to a child. 'The most I can offer is to replace him for a while.'

'Cretin! You're all cretins!'

Rappoport cut one paragraph from the beginning of Ivlev's article and two phrases from the end of it, silently nodded and returned the pages to Ivlev. Polishchuk, without reading the article, switched on the intercom while he took a deep breath.

'Is Yagubov gone?'

'Just left.'

Polishchuk slowly read the article, 'Muddy Water', now and again taking out his handkerchief and mopping his brow. He didn't notice Rappoport come in and sit down, snuffling, next to Ivlev. Waiting until Polishchuk finished reading, Rappoport hissed: 'You know the difference between you and Zoya Kosmodemyanskaya? They'll never put up a monument to you. The only thing that excuses you is good intentions and dilettantism. But it doesn't matter: they're going to kick you out of the Party and your job and mess you around. We'd be better off doing it this way, boys. We'll get the article set, print out a page and call in a representative from the Ministry of Internal Affairs to read it. You get my drift, I hope? One way or the other. A half-hour for vacillation and then agreement. Most likely they won't want the publicity and will close the case against Kakabadze. It'll never enter their minds that we aren't really going to print the piece. And then we kill the article at the last minute!'

'Blackmail?' whispered Polishchuk.

'But for a noble purpose.'

Closing his eyes, Polishchuk sat in concentration, weighing Rappoport's proposal. Boldness and cowardice had taken on such a symbiosis in him that the boundary between them had generally ceased to exist.

'Fucking hell,' Polishchuk squeezed out, angry as anything. 'My whole life has been total compromise. We all help one another to be dishonest.'

Rappoport remained silent. Polishchuk jerked at a knob on the intercom, got through to his deputy in the compositors' shop and was asking him to set type as quickly as possible and think about what to take out so as to free up a hundred and eighty lines on page two, when Yagubov rang from home on the city line. He was curious about what was going on with regard to passing the issue for press.

'We're on schedule,' Polishchuk reported in a cheerful tone, winking at Ivlev. 'Pages four and three are passed, and I'm waiting for the rest from minute to minute.' Hanging up the phone, Polishchuk transferred his gaze to Rappoport.

'I don't like this mess. Oh, how I don't like it!' muttered Rappoport. 'Believe me, I'm a fight-scarred old jackal.'

While they awaited the page pull the two of them discussed how to carry on the conversation with the Ministry of Internal Affairs representative. Polishchuk had dragged his official-use-only phonebook out of his safe and was getting ready to make the call to them when the intercom buzzed.

'This is Volobuyev. There's something I can't find anywhere in the registration book. You do have permission for the piece called "Muddy Water", don't you?'

'It's a one-off case. Why does it need a stamp?'

'Stamp? So that everything's in order. Does Yagubov know about it?'

'Of course he does! I'll send Ivlev down to you right now. He'll set your mind at rest.' Polishchuk switched off the intercom in a frenzy.

# 46

# The Victories and Defeats of
## Delez Volobuyev

Not a single feature on Volobuyev's genealogical tree could have foretold
that he was going to work as a censor. His father, although barely literate, had been passionately devoted to the Bolshevik-Leninist cause. That
was where he got his son's beautiful name. On the one hand, it sounded
like something splendid and oriental; on the other, it signified an
abbreviation of *Delo Lenina zavershim* or 'We will conclude Lenin's work'.

Volobuyev senior had been sent with a Red detachment to fight the
*bai* and the *basmach*, the Central Asian landowner class and others resist-
ing the establishment of Soviet authority there. At the time, the Emir of
Bukhara, an ardent foe of the Soviets, was suffering greatly from
syphilis. And in medical science the discovery had already been made that
all illness sprang from nerves, except for syphilis, which sprang from pleasure. In order to cut short the illness the court physician, who had almost
finished his studies either at the Sorbonne or in Makhachkala, recommended that the Emir entirely replace the contingent of girls in his harem
with new, clean ones so that the Emir's health would be restored. The
Emir's henchmen, armed with rifles, seized suitable girls and brought
them to Bukhara.

After arriving on the spot, the Bolshevik Volobuyev decided that the
best way to bring around the Uzbeks that were unconscious of their social
obligations towards the Soviet regime was to oppose the Emir's curing
himself at the expense of working-class women, since these women were
bound to belong to the Uzbek workers' and peasants' classes. But when
the four Red Army soldiers with their bold commissar liberated three

young girls from the Emir's clutches and got a look at them without their veils, three of them promptly married them. It soon became clear to the two left unmarried that they were fighting for nothing. Among the married ones was Commissar Volobuyev.

After victory over the Emir, Volobuyev occupied the post of Deputy People's Commissar for Enlightenment and worked at that job until 1937, when he was shot as an enemy of the Uzbek people 'for attempting to turn the republic back into the Bukhara Emirate'. Delez was eighteen and his early-widowed mother thirty-four. She had five children left on her hands and was carrying a sixth.

When the war began Delez Volobuyev decided to wash his father's disgrace from their family with his own blood; they and their mother had entirely disavowed him. In the tank forces he was first a mechanic, then a driver, then a tank commander. He got surrounded and broke out, his tank was burned up, he rammed various things. He sought death with desperate doggedness, but the scythe never mows down people like that, as everyone knows. Medals showered down on him. He would have received a second Hero's Star, but he'd only got his first one with an effort because of the opposition of the political commissar, who had been bothered by the defects in Volobuyev's background. The front-line newspapers glorified his exploits, though, and even ascribed a magical significance to his name.

Throughout the war Volobuyev tore articles about his heroism out of newspapers, in the hope that the number of praiseful lines would outweigh the single 'Son of an enemy of the people'. And they evidently did outweigh the one, inasmuch as he was detached for study at the Armoured Tank Academy. After attending the academy Lieutenant Colonel Volobuyev, Hero of the Soviet Union, commanded various formations and served on the General Staff, where he was involved in Stalin's secret plans for the complete liberation of Europe for the final victory of Communism.

In the evening he liked to get out his old newspaper clippings and read about his exploits. It was sad only that for fifteen post-war years not once had anything more ever been written about him. Volobuyev decided that he would write a book about himself – it wouldn't be any worse than the stuff that was coming out. Moreover, it came suddenly to him – someone who had honourably earned the title of Hero – that he would write about how it really was, in contrast to all those frothy, sonorous words in the books familiar to him.

His wife uncomplainingly troubled herself over their children while he wrote. He wrote a great deal and began making the rounds of publishers. Everywhere they took it to read eagerly enough, but everywhere they turned him down. The problem was that his emphasis was not quite what it should have been: either the Russian units robbed the local populace after capturing a German town, or the soldiers settled in to spend the night in a mansion after chasing off the owner but keeping his daughters. Or the Poles and Czechs appeared in his recollections shooting at the Russians. And the heroes of Volobuyev's literature went into battle with the cry 'For the motherland! For Stalin!' on their lips, while since 1956 they hadn't been fighting for Stalin any more but for the Party. Finally the unsuccessful author broke his manuscript down into two parts: 'can' and 'can't'. There was so little 'can' left in comparison with the 'can't' that virtually nothing was left of Volobuyev's production.

By this time he had already retired from the army, since a year in the army counted for two, and he decided to fly back to his homeland, to Tashkent. Next to him on the aeroplane sat a small man with a familiar face, but Volobuyev at first didn't recognize him. When he nimbly rolled a cigarette from one corner of his mouth to the other with his tongue Volobuyev recalled who he was. This was the man who had been in charge of his tankers and drivers when they had cleared the corpses off the streets of Budapest in 1956. They had even had a conversation standing on the bridge between Buda and Pest, estimating how much work was left for them to do. Their names had appeared on the same list of medals awarded for the affair.

Volobuyev had heard that Yagubov was in charge of publishing at the *Novosti* press agency. He decided that this was fate and that what he'd writ-

ten would finally see the light of day. In Tashkent Volobuyev took Yagubov
over to the bust of his father that had been placed there *in memoriam*. This
was where Yagubov offered to get Volobuyev a job as a censor.

So now Volobuyev was taking a vigilant look at the work of other
authors to make sure nothing of the sort written by him ever crept in. He
didn't keep up any outward association with Yagubov, inasmuch as they
were on different levels, but when Yagubov got transferred to *Trudovaya
Pravda* he shifted Volobuyev along with him. Now his censorial talents
began knocking things to pieces in earnest. Not publishing other people
turned out to be more interesting than getting himself published.

He didn't start off with just prohibitions either but with painstaking
explanations to his co-workers about what they shouldn't be writing and
why. The exact distance between two cities turned out to be a state secret,
as well as any absolute industrial-production figures (percentages alone
were allowed). Any mention of opium-poppy-growing collective farms
was forbidden. You couldn't criticize the insufficiency of any goods if they
were exported from the country, since that undermined external trade.
Volobuyev progressed from explanations to the education of his newspaper
colleagues.

'The duty of the entire newspaper collective', he said, speaking at a
daily meeting, 'is to aid in censorship. Undertake this initiative: whenever you get a rejection as a writer don't blame the censor but your own
decisions.'

In individual conversations Volobuyev asked that he not be called a censor. There was a waft of something cold in the word. 'I'm just a simple
political editor.'

This irritated Makartsev. Out of the delicacy characteristic of him,
though, he didn't interfere in the decisions of people who were not subordinate to him. However, at heart he felt that he wouldn't let the censor
interfere with any issues that he himself answered for to the Central
Committee. But Volobuyev himself never pushed things to boiling point.

'My business is to bring something to your notice and keep my superiors informed. But the decision as to whether or not something concerns

specific state secrets or specific listed restrictions – that decision is your own, of course!'

The phrase 'of course' would always calm Makartsev down, and he would forget about their latest conflict. Volobuyev's professional energies were looking for an outlet, but a sense of danger existed, too. Heroism away from the front lines was merely an irritation and its absence preferable in journalism. Acquiring a taste for his new profession, Volobuyev came to the conclusion that his function didn't afford complete results, since he was setting to work on already-prepared material. So, if the censor could link up with the author at the thought stage, then the necessity of squeezing out extraneous things would never arise.

Volobuyev was fifty years old in January 1969. Yagubov commissioned Kashin to prepare a congratulatory address to Volobuyev on his jubilee, and of course Rappoport wrote the speech under his pseudonym of Tavrov. Kashin went around to all the departments with the letter. Everyone in the office, including Makartsev, put their signature under the words: 'We wish you, dear friend of our newspaper, good health and further fruitful work in the field of the glorious Leninist press.' Matrikulov, the staff artist, fleshed out a notion of Rappoport's by drawing a picture on the envelope: Volobuyev holding a sickle in one hand and a hammer in the other. Rappoport had explained to his friends that the censor hit authors on the head with the hammer and used the sickle to cut off their . . .

# 47

# Unmonitored Associations

On the door to his room hung a sign: *No Admittance*.

'Well, what?' Ivlev asked from the doorway, then without any particular warmth shook Volobuyev's hand and sat down.

His host smiled politely at him. 'Listen here, Ivlev! I'm new here, but I ask – I *demand* – that you people bring me your material in advance, even a week, if possible. After all, I've got to get the agreement of my superiors. But no! You're always pushing till the last minute.'

'We're a newspaper! Who the hell needs week-old news?'

'That's an incorrect understanding. Am I the one who makes up these restrictions? Those people Upstairs aren't fools. They've set up a group there to keep an eye on the subtext of 'unmonitored associations'. I have my instructions: first, read the text, second, the subtext. Formerly the most important thing was monitoring and prevention of textual violations; now it's subtextual violations. For example, if an author is discoursing on the Middle Ages the reader might imagine that things are worse now. The text might add to Soviet authority, but the subtext impairs it.'

'And what does this have to do with "Muddy Water"?'

'I'll clarify that now. You're criticizing the police, as if there were nothing dangerous in that. But the reader will understand that the muddy water is the system as a whole – understand?'

'What kind of logic is that?' Ivlev stood up and, turning the chair around by its back, banged it against the floor.

'And don't you go looking for logic. What we could print yesterday we can't today. Today we can have caricatures of the leaders of certain foreign countries, tomorrow other ones. I just obey the latest directive, that's all.'

'All right,' Ivlev pretended to retreat. 'You're right, as always. We'll take out the piece, don't worry!'

'It's not me who's worried – it's Yagubov.'

'He's gone.'

'I had to call him at home. Turned out he didn't have a clue about the article. He'll sort it out, if he hasn't already.'

'At home?'

'Why at home? He's on his way here.'

Ivlev stared straight at Volobuyev, wondering if he should tell him what he was thinking or just spit in his face – so round, so healthy, so placid. He did neither the one nor the other but just walked out, neatly closing the door.

The warm, just-cast silvery stereotypes for pages three and four, already passed for press by Polishchuk, the duty editor, had long since gone down to the print shop. The printers, tearing themselves away from time to time to drain free milk out of paper cartons, had taken up the heavy blocks and set them into the rotary presses. The pre-production prep was under way. Slowly turning the drums, the workers adjusted the castings, filing them down, pressing them in, so that the offprints would be even.

Page two – the lower section of which was occupied by Ivlev's 'Muddy Water' article – was held up in the compositors' shop. Workers were coming up and reading the mirror-image article. Things like that happened rarely: the printers despised their own paper and got their information at home, through the radio jamming.

The compositors were holding up the print shop, and that was holding up the whole process. There were vehicles waiting to take sacks full of matrices to various airports, from where they were taken away by plane to the cities where *Trudovaya Pravda* was printed, coming out in the morning along with the local newspapers. A delay of several minutes to the schedule held up the delivery of the newspaper to kiosks throughout the country. Millions of people going to work wouldn't be able to buy the paper, and the edition would have to be pulped.

A hush set in around the newspaper office in expectation of the order to get on with it. Bursts of laughter carried from Rappoport's office, where, in addition to Rappoport, sat Zakamorny. The door to the letters department was half open. Nadya, listening for footsteps in the corridor, was quietly registering the day's post, although she could easily have done it the next day. Ivlev might notice that she was here, and then they could walk to the metro station together. Kashin was in his office feeding his fish, and he had already decided to show up on Inna's way home when the typist went off duty. The duty typist had to wait until the all-clear came, just in case the duty editor needed something for the issue. Meanwhile Yagubov had already walked into the compositors' shop, his gait urgent. The bosses of the print and stereotype shops barely managed to get there in his train. The compositors' shop boss hurried to meet them.

'Where's the nearest telephone?'

They showed him. Yagubov was pale and a little dishevelled. His jacket, hastily donned over a powder-blue silk undershirt, had all its buttons fastened, not just the middle one as usual. Walking over to the phone Yagubov dialled Polishchuk's internal number.

'I'd like you to come down to the shop at once.'

Not waiting for an answer Yagubov replace the handset and, stretching out a hand, demanded: 'The page!'

They held out an ink-smelling sheet to him. Yagubov immediately fell to reading as if the people standing around him waiting for instructions didn't exist. After reading it to the end he neatly folded the sheet and began tearing it into small pieces. After it was in tiny pieces he crumpled them together, then unclasped his hands over a wastepaper basket, pouring the fragments into it. 'How many copies did you pull?' he asked.

The compositors' boss bent down his fingers one by one: 'The duty editor, the censor, the "fresh head", the corrections bureau, the special correspondents' and the proofreaders' – six in all, as usual.'

'Gather up all six immediately. For any missing one every one of you will lose your Party cards. Warn the workers, the foremen, security . . .'

'Yes, sir!'

Polishchuk walked in. The people moved away, giving him a chance to talk to Yagubov. Polishchuk was clearly embarrassed.

'That didn't work,' he said in an attempt to soften the conflict. 'I didn't warn you, and took all the responsibility on myself. But we weren't actually going to print it, after all. It was just for bargaining with. After all, it's not fair to Kakabadze –'

'And it is fair to me?' Yagubov said slowly, without hearing him out. 'Or maybe I'm not your colleague? But more on that later.' He turned to the compositors' shop boss: 'What are you standing there for? Get the page into the frame. Or are you going to hang around here all night?' He bent his head, as if he was going to butt the people around him, and moved towards the door, not looking at anyone. He went up to his office and opened it with his key.

'Sit down, Polishchuk,' he said. Now that measures had been taken and the executive secretary was in his hands, Yagubov calmed down and became more pleasant. He merely sat and smoked pensively, cigarette after cigarette. 'Now, that's over with! How do you expect me to take all this? After all, it's not me you've tricked – I'm a rank-and-file Party man. You were trying to deceive the Party!'

'Makartsev would support me on this issue.'

'That's a dangerous game! I think that Makartsev would place the honour of the newspaper above personal likes and dislikes.'

'What's personal about this? On the contrary. This is a defence of the paper's honour!'

'That's pulling a switch of the meaning! Can you vouch for Kakabadze the way you could for yourself? You see? Why the hell put a blot on the newspaper's record for the sake of one employee? Besides, frankly speaking, I'm sure of this: in this country of ours someone can't be arrested unless they're guilty of something!'

Polishchuk narrowed his eyes and tensed his lips so as not to answer back right away. And he swallowed his retort.

'Don't you agree?' Yagubov continued. 'Let's suppose that Photo-correspondent Kakabadze really *is* innocent. He wasn't drunk; he didn't get into any fight. Let's suppose! Who gets to do that sort of thing then? That has to be decided at the highest level. Then I would be for it. You're a clever man. I'm sorry for you: the Central Committee doesn't forgive things like this, you know yourself. You, with your great CV – you're finished. You know, I could try to talk to my own people Upstairs about putting a stop to this affair, take a part of the guilt on myself, fire somebody from among the people who did it. But I'll tell you straight – something would be necessary from your end as well. Not right now and not for me – I'm someone without anything to gain from this. But the people who are going to pull you out of this will risk disgracing themselves.'

'What do I have to do?' Polishchuk said dully.

'We're not hagglers by trade, after all,' laughed Yagubov. 'I don't know yet myself. Let's say that when the Party bureau makes the decision on how to improve the paper's health you have to be for . . .'

'For you and against Makartsev?' Polishchuk elaborated, clenching his fingers into fists. 'And what if you lose?'

His gesture didn't go unnoticed. A smile played over Yagubov's mouth.

'The Americans think that a good boss is the one in whose absence everything goes smoothly. But, between the two of us, Makartsev's style is yesterday's – arrhythmia. Give some thought to whose side you're on.'

The intercom phone rang.

'How many?' Yagubov queried. 'All right. I'll deal with it myself.'

Putting down the phone, he got up and walked over to Polishchuk. 'By the way, let's have a little chat. Even though we consider that "Muddy Water" never was, I've just been informed that they've got back only five pulls. One of our colleagues has hidden away one of them, despite everything.'

'Who?'

'What are we going to do with that fellow?' Yagubov continued, not answering.

'Depends on what his reasons were.'

'That's just what I was thinking. What are they? The reason could even be something that's not for us to work out.'

'Somebody just took it to read it,' Polishchuk said straight away, think-ing that it would be better to suggest the lesser of two evils. 'Let's raise the issue at the Party bureau meeting. Our comrades can decide what to do.'

'Then include the issue of Party Member Rappoport in the agenda.' Yagubov watched Polishchuk closely, trying to read the effect of the name on him, but he just turned away and walked to the door.

Polishchuk telephoned Rappoport from his office. 'Is anybody in the room besides you?'

'Uh-huh.'

'Then just listen. Yagubov knows who took the pull. To avoid more trouble take it straight to Kashin. Tell him that it has to be passed on to Makartsev. Got that?'

'So it hasn't worked?'

But short beeps were already coming from the receiver. Rappoport looked around gloomily at Ivlev, Zakamorny and Nadya, all sitting around him. Nadya hadn't waited for Ivlev to look in on her and had gone to Rappoport's.

'It's logical!' Ivlev got up. 'We should have figured that one out. We've underestimated Volobuyev. He's Yagubov's watchdog.'

'There is an amazing creature called a praying mantis,' Zakamorny said prettily, gazing at Nadya for his inspiration. 'It catches insects. Its vision is constructed so that it won't see an insect if it doesn't budge or if it crawls really slowly. Its retinal nerve is activated when a subject moves quickly past. That's when the mantis strikes! The censor notices abrupt motion, too. But if you do it in a lot of trifling little interspersions, then you can write the baldest anti-Sovietisms for the intelligent reader.'

'You're our Aesop!' Ivlev clapped him on the shoulder. 'Just imagine: several lines go by containing nothing but the repeated phrase "hurrah!" If you take out the exclamation point just once the mantis flinches. And zap!'

'Everything's a lot simpler than that,' Rappoport said, rubbing his back.

'Yagubov wants to bury Makartsev alive. Makartsev made the paper into something grey; Yagubov is making it brown. In the camps, kids, I cooked up a newspaper for convicts who dreamed of becoming free. And now I publish a newspaper for readers who are entirely satisfied with the fact that they're sitting behind barbed wire.'

'Don't get upset,' Nadya said, stroking his shoulder with the tips of her fingers. 'You'll get a stomach ache.'

'As always, the woman is right,' Rappoport agreed, after snorting. 'Let's go home, Chekists!'

In the lift Nadya stuck her hand into Ivlev's pocket, and he squeezed her hand in his own inside it. They ran into Yagubov at the stairway gate. The deputy editor pretended not to be surprised at all by this night-time company; it was just the way things were. He didn't even have any doubt that it was these people who were waiting for the article to come out. Whatever else, he knew about people. Yagubov walked past, giving a small nod, and went into Volobuyev's office. The latter got up to greet him.

'Thank you,' Yagubov said, firmly, shaking his hand. 'I'm much obliged to you.'

'Hey, never mind. It's nothing.'

Having accomplished this brief friendly gesture Yagubov walked out as fast as he had appeared.

# 48

# Rain

The next day passed in endless suspense. Rappoport remained working at the office until well into the night and was dozing at his manuscript-heaped desk when he was woken by the telephone.

'I need to talk to you, Rappoport.'

'Makartsev! Where are you calling from?'

'The same old place. Unfortunately.'

'How are you feeling?'

'It's all taking its time. They're allowing me out – two hundred yards a day. You know, therapeutic gymnastics, lying on my back. I'm tired of it.'

'Tired of being sick? That's something I understand!'

'No, not of being sick. What's Yagubov up to? And they're all sticking up for him! I should stop what he's doing, but I haven't got the strength yet.'

'You'll have enough fighting to do later on!'

There was a pause. It was hard for Makartsev, and Rappoport didn't hurry him.

Having achieved nothing, Zina had finally shared her secret with her husband.

'My son's a murderer?' Makartsev had yelled at her. 'I haven't got a son! My life's gone completely haywire!'

'Yes, you do,' she'd objected coldly. 'We can do without your posturing, especially me. You at least have to get well enough to save Boris!'

Makartsev had never seen his wife so pale and stern. After she had gone he was in torment, grinding his teeth, grunting, incapable of mastering himself. Finally he decided to phone Rappoport.

'Maybe I should think about retiring. What do you think?'

'You called me for that?'

'No. Why beat about the bush? My son's in trouble.'

'I understand.'

'Do you have any channels . ... to bring pressure to bear? If I was well I could push buttons in a flash. But I'm temporarily out of the game . . .'

'I can try.'

'Do. After all, you've got a son yourself.'

'Emotion isn't called for here.'

'Well, sorry to lumber you with this, Rappoport.'

'Don't worry. Get better. Everything will work out.'

'You think so?'

'I'm sure.'

It seldom rains in Moscow in April, and the thin, slick mist clinging to his hands and face made Rappoport mutter unfair generalizations. On top of that, hardly any of the streetlights were on. They were conserving electricity. Rappoport stumbled over the cracks in the pavement, stepped into a pothole full of water, and his generalizations degenerated into ordinary swearing.

He was walking the streets in search of a public phone. The hands on his watch showed nearly one o'clock in the morning. In the first phone booth he located the receiver had been ripped off, the cable hanging loose. Rappoport tramped another half a block. His hat was wet through, and as soon as his shoes got sodden his back was going to start aching. At the second payphone the receiver was in place, but when his coin dropped he just got an engaged signal. The machine didn't return his coin. The third phone, right next to the second one, gave no signs of life. His generalizations exhausted, foul language alone was all that was left. Rappoport moved on, but now there wasn't any public phone in view, not even a broken one.

He saw poorly even in good light, and now he was simply putting one foot in front of the other at random. The one thing orientating him was an immense neon sign on the roof of a building: 'We Are Approaching the Victory of Communist Labour!' The first two letters in the Russian word for 'victory', *pobeda*, were missing, making the word into *beda* or 'misfortune'. There wasn't anyone to share this discovery with, but there wasn't any point in storing it up in his memory either, since life in its own sweet time would always come up with something funnier when he needed it. And when he didn't need it, too. And anyway it was uncomfortable craning his neck up at the roof. Rappoport recalled Zakamorny's characterization of journalists as moles. They couldn't look at the light; they might go blind. They sat in their cubby-holes until nightfall, scribbling their mean, deceitful drivel, then crawled out at night satisfied with themselves, sleeping the sleep of the just through till morning, their dreams never troubled by the things they had done the day before.

He finally found another payphone. He didn't have any more two-kopek coins, so he had to drop in a ten-kopek piece. The third time he put it in it was accepted, and the number rang.

'Sagaydak? Are you asleep?'

'Who is this?' a voice answered. 'I can't hear you very well. Call back.'

Instantly turning the receiver around, Rappoport yelled into the earpiece: '*Allo!* Don't hang up! This fucking payphone doesn't work!' He again quickly switched the handpiece around and put it to his ear.

'Rappoport? Is that you, dear boy? Where are you calling from?'

'I'm telling you, from a public phone!' He'd already got used to moving the earpiece back and forth from his mouth to his ear. 'I have to see you! Got a little business.'

'See me? It would be better if you didn't have any business. But on business is all right, too. Come on over!'

'Right now?' Rappoport glanced at his watch. 'When am I going to get some sleep?'

'At our age we can do without sleep.'

'That depends on who . . .'

'What? Come on over, I tell you! We'll have a cup of tea.'

'I'm on my way!' barked Rappoport and threw the receiver into a corner of the phone booth so hard that he would have broken the side of the booth if it hadn't been made of scrapped tank armour.

Once more he plodded along down the very edge of the pavement, now and again looking around to see if a taxi might be flashing past. He didn't like going on foot. 'I've already had enough walking, riding, flying and sailing, boys,' he would say. 'Well, travelling with my kind of history, you understand, don't you? The only thing left for me is to keep on going, somehow.' Keeping on going between two enormous puddles, he flagged down a taxi.

# 49

# Sisyphus Sagaydak,
# Impotentologist-General

Sisyphus Sagaydak expressed his life history thus: 'I was born on the barricades of 1905 to a family of fiery Bolshevik-Leninists. My father, a Russian revolutionary, a friend and comrade-in-arms of Lenin, died defending the Soviet regime. As a representative of the working class I was sent to study at the Medical Institute, from which I graduated as a sexopathologist. Since that time my whole life has been devoted to combating sexual illness among the workers. I joined the Communist Party in order to facilitate the speedier construction of socialism by my efforts. Being a Doctor of Medical Science, a professor, I pay a lot of attention to social work and the propagation of a Marxist sexual education among the populace. I am the founder of a new branch of Soviet medicine – impotentology – and am the author of a range of research papers. A true and loyal son of the Communist Party, I consider all my advances to be inspired and organized by it.'

This, though, is the footnote that Sagaydak wrote exclusively for himself on the copy of his autobiography that he kept at home: 'I wasn't born around any barricades. My father, a Jew baptized as a Christian, a commercial traveller, was killed in an attempt to cross the border into Poland. It isn't known if I ever had a mother. Homeless, a waif, I lived by stealing, and then I traded two loaves of bread for a diploma saying that I had graduated from the Saratov Medical Institute. I never wrote any dissertations myself, but I did defend them personally. I'm a jailbird by profession. They made me join the Communist Party. Without that, they never would have conferred a doctoral degree on me. I propagate knowledge only for money, although it doesn't always have to be for cash, exactly. I became the founder of a new science only thanks to the low level of science in this country. It is the sacred truth, however, that it's the Party that inspires me to do research in the sphere of impotence.'

When Sagaydak turned sixty he intended to observe the occasion modestly with his narrow circle of friends at the Aragvi restaurant. But Rappoport told him: 'There's no way they can forget about you!'

And, in truth, on his birthday the telephone rang in the Sagaydak home.

'I wish you a happy birthday, Comrade Sagaydak, from me personally.'

'Thank you,' he said, pleased as punch. 'Thank you very much!'

'You're probably already aware, aren't you,' continued Thick Eyebrows, 'that the Presidium of the Supreme Soviet has awarded you the Order of the Red Banner of Labour? I'm very pleased for you!'

Sagaydak didn't have a clue about the decoration, but that very day they sent a car for him; Thick Eyebrows himself, with a smile, pinned the medal on his chest and gave him a long, manly handshake. The Ministry of Health started making a fuss over him after that, not knowing what else to do. The fact was that Sagaydak wasn't employed in any scientific establishment anywhere, didn't hold a post anywhere. But he wrote out his prescriptions on beautiful forms with purple letterhead that said:

*Sisyphus Sagaydak*
*Professor, Doctor of Medicine*
*Impotentologist-General*

How to celebrate the jubilee of a specialist like this wasn't exactly clear either to the people at the Ministry of Health or the people in the Academy of Medical Sciences. And they hadn't received any directive on the subject. Just in case, a delegation from the Ministry of Health led by a deputy minister showed up at Sagaydak's home. He met them in his dressing-gown, listened to their congratulatory address, treated them to some brandy and then, in his answering speech, said staidly: 'I thank you on behalf of the Secretary General and on behalf of myself, personally.'

'You screwball!' Rappoport gently reproached him. 'Did you ask him to get you the Bolshoi Theatre for your birthday celebration? He wouldn't have turned you down. Do you actually imagine that there's any-body else on earth that he would have called to wish a happy birthday? Never in his life! But he defers to you. He's afraid of nothing but his inter-nal organs!'

You couldn't actually say that Sagaydak was without education. He really had gone carefully into the contents of the dissertations that he had defended, read all the books, familiarized himself with folk medicine. Intelligent by nature, he winkled the rational kernels out of everything and achieved a high mastery in his sphere. As a result, treatments for wide-spread pathological conditions were actually advanced at his hands, since the treatments had never been approved by any government agencies. Better still, it was possible to approach him in confidence. So Sagaydak wound up being unofficially more important than Academician Lopatkin, the chief urologist of the Ministry of Health of the USSR. The mean age of Party and government leaders was such that there were few people who didn't consult Sagaydak.

'Do you know So-and-so?' Sagaydak would ask, smirking.

'Of course!' they would answer.

'I took his prostate gland out,' he would say off-handedly. 'Do you know Such-and-such? I took out his prostate. For a lot of other people, too. But have you heard of Such-and-so? I didn't take his out. Doctor Rabinovich in Riga took his out. Do you understand what a government without any prostate glands is like? They would ban not only sexual lit-erature but sex itself. It's just that they don't know any other way of making young Leninists.'

If Rappoport wasn't able to get through to Sagaydak on the phone, he knew that someone Upstairs was having trouble passing water. If he did get through, but Sagaydak asked him to call back in an hour, that meant that he was glued to a microscope while alongside him, red as a beetroot, sat a highly placed KGB officer who had caught gonorrhoea or some minister telling him in a whisper about how he wasn't able to get it up. All his patients were less fearful of disclosing state secrets than venereal ones. That was understandable: state secrets were state ones, while venereal secrets were one's own. Everyone carefully hid from one another that they were coming to see him. Some of his patients hinted that the KGB organs were aware of his anti-Soviet jokes. They couldn't frighten Sagaydak though.

'I've got them all right here!' he explained to his friends, raising an index finger. 'Just like them, I work in the organs. And the organs, under my management, always work better.' This notion reached the very top, where it was appreciated. It got a laugh, Upstairs.

'I don't see anything funny!' Professor Sagaydak quickly reacted. 'Stalin was following in the steps of Academician Pavlov. He believed that it would be possible to instil conditioned reactions in the populace, to train people like dogs. I go further. I consider a real scientist to be someone who, like me, has the absolute ability to inculcate conditioned reactions in our leaders.'

Sagaydak loved to sit at home in the den of his Moscow condominium. He would lie on the sofa in his dressing-gown and watch hockey on television. He had an excellent library. He studied unacknowledged philosophers, read good poets and forbidden literature and looked at the pictures in foreign journals as well. All these things were brought to Sagaydak by KGB types receiving treatment. To those of them who brought with them truly special forbidden books Sagaydak would give a short course in sexual fitness and show them certain yoga exercises that increased their potency. Generals, ministers, colonels, mastering the exercises, would scamper around the room on all fours, holding their breath and getting covered in sweat, while Sagaydak would stand on his sofa with a whip in his hand yelling: 'Livelier! And faster, now, you salty dog!' While this was going on he would confide in them that this sort of autogenic training would be of no help to stupid people.

Certain of his more curious patients wondered how things stood on this question with the doctor himself.

'For you it's a question,' the professor would answer, 'but for me it's an exclamation mark!'

Sagaydak dreamed of getting the position of Impotentologist-General included in Communist Party regulations. Sagaydak's *magnum opus*, 'The Theoretical Bases of Impotentology', was written by Rappoport, of course, and published at the express order of the Chief Censor of the USSR, whose prostate was getting massaged by Sagaydak. In this same way the Znaniye publishing house had a popular-science brochure put together for it entitled 'Nobody in This Country Is Impotent!' Rappoport knocked that one out with particular satisfaction. He himself flatly refused any treatment, declaring that, for him personally, life on this earth was a lot more peaceful that way.

Sagaydak was thinking about how much he would like to go abroad and see something of the world. But he understood that he would never be allowed to under any circumstances. On one occasion Sagaydak read in Winston Churchill's memoirs that people in positions of power should be physically healthy, otherwise their condition might be reflected in the decisions they made. The Impotentologist-General was the possessor of terrifically secret government information in this sphere.

# 50

# The Tenth Circle

On Festival Street, two streets away from Rechnoy Station, Rappoport got out of his taxi. Although he had been here often he stood for a long time wondering which of the two dozen identical buildings he had to enter. There was no one to ask at this hour of the night. Finally he worked out which entrance he needed and went up to the apartment on the highest floor; the tenant there couldn't stand people walking around over his head. A dog barked as soon as he rang the bell, and then he could hear measured steps. Sagaydak, a gigantic man in every respect, with a leonine mane of curly white hair, in a dressing-gown that looked like something made from an entire blue-and-white-striped roll of terrycloth – the sort of thing an old prisoner would wear – enveloped Rappoport in an embrace. Kisa, his snow-white lap dog, squeaking with delight, jumped up and down all around Rappoport, contriving at every bound to lick his hand.

'Hey there, you jailbird! Damned glad to see you, *tyr-pyr-tyr*!' Sagaydak added a long tirade that a passer-by would understand only after translating it from thieves' cant into prison slang, from prison slang into obscene speech and only then into Russian. 'Fucking hell, get your coat off. Right now I'm . . .' Shuffling his carpet-slippers, Sagaydak tramped back into his living-room and picked up the telephone receiver that he had thrown on to the sofa.

After flopping down into a low armchair Rappoport half closed his tired eyelids, vacantly running his eyes over the familiar objects. The dog lay down beside him, thwacking its tail against his muddy trouser-leg. Sagaydak's apartment was the complete antithesis of his own. Carpets

covered the walls, sofa and floor. Antique vases, candelabras, lamps, lacquered boxes, statuettes – half and wholly undressed figures in frivolous
poses – chaotically filled the flat expanses of the sideboard, the writing
desk and the bookshelves, standing out vividly on shelves in front of books
and in between porcelain and silver dishes dully glimmering in the half-
darkness. To the right and left of the door stretched two tapestries, one
Japanese, the other Chinese. The crystal chandelier hanging from the ceiling could have found a rival only in its identical twin in the Bolshoi
Theatre.

'Excuse me.' Sagaydak took the telephone into the corner and covered it with a tea cosy in the shape of a woman in a Russian peasant dress.
'That's life. It couldn't be worse. Perhaps we'll get some rest in the world
to come.'

'You could probably get some rest there,' said Rappoport, 'but it'll be
even worse for me in the afterlife.'

Sagaydak strolled around the room, halting to pose artistically now
in front of the Japanese tapestry, now against the background of a Persian
carpet. 'Could it be any worse?'

'It could, old friend. I'll prove it to you right here. Hand me that thick
volume in the sumptuous binding.'

'Dante? I thought you read only our leaders' speeches.'

'Shut up!' Rappoport opened the heavy binding. '"*This earthly life but
half passed through, I found myself in gloomy woods, strayed into a darkling
valley from the righteous way* . . ." Here it is, *The Inferno*. Let's find a
circle worthy of me.'

'Well, so which one suits you?' grinned Sagaydak, coming up behind
him and looking at the engravings alongside the text.

'It's complicated by the fact that the whole place suits me. There's a
spot for me in any circle of Hell. Look: I go through the Gates of Hell –
there sit the nonentities. Could I sit alongside them? What do you think?'

'Well, let's say you could.'

'We go further. We go down into the First Circle, plausibly described
after Dante by Solzhenitsyn, with his knowledge of secret slave-scientist

prisons. Here, by the way, are the unbaptized and the virtuous heathens. Would that do me? With the greatest of pleasure! After all, just look at the company here in the First Circle: the greatest philosophers – Socrates, Plato, Seneca, Cicero. True, it doesn't say that Karl Marx is here. Dante hasn't yet been forced to adjust to our socialist realism. Maybe I could be alongside the greatest philosophers? No way! They would shove me down further, into the depths of the Devil's funnel!'

'And what's there, down lower?'

'In the Second Circle? Voluptuaries. Fantastic women, too. Great company! Oh, how I love to talk about sex!'

'You love to exaggerate your weaknesses.'

'I don't exaggerate, Sagaydak. I extrapolate. To put it simply, I look ahead. The Third Circle is for gluttons. The less I eat, the more this one appeals to me. The Fourth Circle is for misers and wastrels. Well, I'm not stingy; that's for sure. But it's a fact that I'm a spendthrift. I squander my whole self. I let my life blow away in the wind. The Fifth Circle's for the irate. Boy, am I ever irate, you urologist, you! I'm ready to blow my top right here in the Fifth Circle.'

'Very amusing,' Sagaydak muttered through his teeth.

'Let's press on, Brother Virgil! The Sixth Circle is for – guess who? Heretics! My soul would delight in how warm the gang is there. Epicurus wound up here, by the way. That's the guy to have a cup of tea with! Green tea would be best – I've switched to green tea now; my heart doesn't palpitate so much. Down, down ever lower! The Seventh Circle: those guilty of violence upon their neighbour and his property – that's the first ring. The very place for journalists with Communist Party cards! The second ring is for people guilty of violence upon themselves and their own property. I can sit with my arse on both those benches at once. Yes, and the third ring, that is, bench, is the one for me: I'm guilty of violence against the Deity, Nature and Being!'

'Stunning!' chuckled Sagaydak. 'What a cross-section of reality in its glory!'

'Save the emotion. Let me finish. The Eighth Circle: deceivers of the mistrustful. We go down into the first pit of the Eighth Circle: pimps and seducers . . .'

'You're not a pimp!'

'Then you just try to borrow the key to my flat! The second pit: flatterers. The third pit: simonists.'

'Who are they?'

'Those who have summoned others to the bright future that they themselves have no intention of going to. In the fourth pit of the Eighth Circle are the soothsayers; in the fifth, bribe-takers. And what about me – you think I write that shit for free? The sixth pit holds the hypocrites. Well, that suits me fine, you can't deny it! The seventh pit is for thieves. Am I a thief? I am! When I write I rob people of their last hopes.'

'Don't blame yourself. People aren't that stupid!'

'People don't realize it, but Dante's grey cells were working! That's why he puts cunning counsellors even lower – in the eighth pit. And in the ninth pit are the sowers of scandal and schism. I could find myself a place there, too. The tenth pit holds falsifiers of metal. Dante was a great Aesopian! God knows what he had in mind! In any case, the tenth pit of the Eighth Circle is where the counterfeiters of people, money and words suffer. Hey, that's where you'll meet the entire Journalists' Union!'

'So who's in the Ninth Circle? I don't recall.'

'The Ninth Circle, professor, sounds fantastic: that's where the deceivers of the *trustful* are.'

'The trustful – that's the readers of *Trudovaya Pravda*?'

'Them in particular. Well, what do you think?' Rappoport looked proudly at Sagaydak, as if he'd written *The Inferno* himself. 'This is what. The first ring of the Ninth Circle holds traitors to their kin, the second, traitors to their homeland and like-minded people, the third, traitors to their friends and guests, the fourth ring – traitors to their benefactors.'

'You've never been a sell-out like that!'

'How would you know who was and who wasn't? Well, anyway . . . Lowest of all, at the centre of the Earth, are traitors to human and divine majesty. Of course, I'll go to any circle the Party tells me to, but best of all, of course, would be here to the Ninth. But I have to tell you: these nine circles aren't enough for me. Dante didn't live in the twentieth century; he was naive. I need a Tenth Circle, something Dante didn't have. Dante didn't foresee it, but I deserve it.'

'That's laying it on a bit thick!'

'I'm not! In the Tenth Circle there'd be corruptors not just of particular people but of whole nations, whole peoples, maybe even the whole of mankind. Do you know who would be in the Tenth Circle? I see Lenin, Hitler, Stalin and Mao there, yeah, and even littler dogs, unconstrained politicians and their journalists. Somebody will probably make room for me in that frying-pan. I've been barking for them all my life. And I know in advance what my punishment will be: an eternity of reading aloud my own articles from morning till night, with feeling. And maybe they'd even let me write speeches for Satan himself. I'll make up slogans: "Devils of the world, unite!" "All roads lead to the frying-pan!" And what if they've never heard of *subbotniks* in hell? I'll help them out! If I can only get into the Tenth Circle! I want so badly to take my rightful place finally. What do you think? Will they trust me?'

'They will, Rappoport, they will.'

'If they do, I won't go. That'll mean they want to cheat me again and squeeze out more than they put in!'

'With the sort of integrity that you have, you can think about repentance. And then you've got a chance to get to Heaven!'

'I've already been in Heaven. I've had enough of it! It's too late for me to think about integrity, and as for repentance – what do I care about that?'

'That may be!' agreed Sagaydak. 'To repent would mean writing a book called *In the Second Circle*. And then *In the Third Circle* and so on. No one person would have the strength to do that. That would call for an entire collective of healthy authors. And where would you find authors like that – healthy ones?' Sagaydak flopped down on his sofa and lifted his hands up to the ceiling in supplication.

'Only in Hell!' reiterated Rappoport. 'Maybe I should send in a request! "I request that you send me to the Tenth Circle of Hell." I've already written one actually.'

'When?' asked Sagaydak, in fright.

'When I was a kid I wrote asking to be sent to Spain. I was afire with world revolution. My mother was already in prison by then. For the sake of the world revolution I disavowed my own mother. I believed that she'd betrayed Stalin.'

Sagaydak got off the sofa. 'I beg of you, that's enough. Pascal said that there are two kinds of people: the sinners who consider themselves just and the just who consider themselves sinners. With all of your self-flagellation you've proved only that you belong to the second bunch. And forget about Dante! Anyway, why have you come here in the middle of the night?'

'On business.'

Suddenly a soft arm twined around Rappoport's neck. His nostrils filled with the bewitching scent of fine perfume. A golden shower of hair played across his face, obscuring Sagaydak's carpets and valuables. A cheek pressed against Rappoport's lips – tender skin, a transparent silhouette. Rappoport gave two smacking kisses to the cheek, felt her soft, full lips slide past his mouth, just barely touching it, and then he kissed her other cheek.

'Hello, titch!' said Rappoport tenderly, clumsily hugging her slim waist. 'You haven't gone to sleep yet?'

'She just got up,' Sagaydak explained.

Alla stroked Rappoport's unshaven cheeks and soundlessly sat down beside him on the Egyptian pouffe, not drawing closed her bright dressing-gown, covered all over with golden firebirds' tails. The gown hung down loosely on both sides of her hips, covering Rappoport's shoes, unshined since the previous autumn.

# 51

# From the Life of St Alla

And when she was born on the foam in a year unknown, a Voice from above commanded: 'She shall be of such beauty that your eyes shall not be taken off her, of excellent health, and her function on this earth will be to bring joy to men.'

She grew up like a flower in the field, knowing neither rickets nor bronchitis. And, once grown, she never used any cosmetic chemicals, even imported ones. Alla soon achieved enough adulthood for her vocation, and time itself stopped for her from that time. She began living in the foreknowledge of peace and bliss, hearing around her the voices of heavenly angels.

And she met her earthly angel in Moscow, near the Uran Cinema – Sagaydak, the servant of God, just then released from prison under an amnesty. They went in to see the comedy film *Springtime* at her expense and began living together as man and wife.

True, a rumour had been floating around Moscow at one time that Alla had previously been making a living picking up officers at Kazan Station and then later had progressed to the Tsentralny Restaurant and become known in actors' circles by the name of Mirror Alla after her interest in observing certain processes in the mirror. But this could be considered not to have happened at all.

Patients came to Sagaydak in an endless herd, but the pantocrine injections he prescribed – to say nothing of the imbibing of ginseng tea or extract of five-prong deer antler – far from always had a beneficial effect. And the observant Sagaydak noticed that the effectiveness of an injection considerably increased when the shot was given by a nurse and not by him.

The analyst's exceptional mind felt that here opened the door to the Discovery of the Century.

And one day when Alla, smiling tenderly, was swabbing the skin of a patient with alcohol in preparation for an injection, the Impotentologist-General walked out of the room saying that he'd be back within half an hour.

Neither Alla nor Sagaydak had cottoned on that this was an unearthly being appearing to them in the form of a patient so that Alla could finally begin to fulfil her destiny. A miracle came to pass. The patient found his desired potency. As far as Alla was concerned, she sensed her Big Opportunity. Soon Doctor Sagaydak had worked out a special quasi-secret Method.

According to Sagaydak's plan, Part A of the Method – a series of injections – was administered by the Impotentologist-General himself. Part B began with an overture, the purpose of which was the creation of a sudden 'lovemakey' situation. When the patient's desires had caught fire, the impotentologist would disappear. The patient sat on the sofa and looked at a bunch of photographs. He would begin to peruse them, observing astounding natural scenes featuring a young Butterfly, something that would bring the patient to a quivering mental state.

Now the Butterfly would flutter into the clinic, almost as if it had flown in here by accident, looking for a flower on which to alight and suck up its sweet nectar. Under no circumstances would the Butterfly appear in a white assistant's smock but – on the contrary – in a miniskirt and airy blouse with maximum décolletage.

The patient would gaze now at the photo, now at the Butterfly and perceive the identity and the difference. The difference lay in the quantity of clothes on the Butterfly in front of him and on the girl in the photograph. According to the Method, this created in the patient a special craving for what could be called carnal knowledge. Alla, smiling smile No. 2, gradually progressed to No. 3, creating an atmosphere of psychic sympathy, which was strengthened by the administration of a scientifically measured dose of alcohol. Professor Sagaydak, positioned by this time at the remote-control panel, would turn on soft music and lower the illumination in the sitting-room by 74.3 per cent. Part C of the plan would ensue in the remaining light.

It would be dark but not so dark that you couldn't see how gorgeous Alla was. She would gaze lovingly at the patient, carefully touching her ethereal fingertips to various erogenous zones indicated by arrows on the Method charts. When a sufficient 'lovemakey' level was achieved, the patient, at a prearranged signal from the Impotentologist-General, would be taken into the bathroom by Alla or left on the sofa. In difficult circumstances the Specialist, in accordance with paragraph D, would undertake telepathic massage of various organs and the hypno-arousal of animal instincts or certain other means known only to her in her capacity as both a woman and an expert in the field.

If Alla didn't successfully achieve, for any reason, the desired result (diagnosis: pathology of abstinence, fear, etc.) from the telemassage, she would progress to physical massage. An apparatus was always used first. In circumstances where it didn't help the Specialist would get down to the personal approach, and it would have been difficult to rival her in this. It was no accident that, in response to numerous petitions from his patients, the Impotentologist-General had awarded Alla the honorary title of Best Blowjob in the Soviet Union.

After the strictly scientific execution of Method instructions A, B, C and D the session would be successfully concluded with Part E. Alla loved everyone like a first love, and she appeared the very embodiment of innocence and purity for every successive client.

In accordance with the Method, Alla held in reserve (and carried with her on visits to patients outside her workplace) yet another scientific aid, designated in the Instructions as the ASS – the Ancillary for Supplementary Sensation. The little dog Kisa sat in a suitcase with air-holes. The Specialist herself had taught Kisa, on a conditioned-reflex basis, by personal example. Before entrusting Kisa's work to their patients Professor Sagaydak had checked it out on himself. 'Oh, what a little licker you are!' he had been moved to say.

In a speech as yet ungiven anywhere, the professor declared: 'My fundamental research has given the Specialist the opportunity to realize the process of de-impotization in such a way that, in principle, she could arouse the dead . . .'

Usually breaches in the observance of the Method came at moments when the course of treatment had reached its end and the Impotentologist-General had transferred his Specialist to another subject. Alla would hand her patient a card that read: *'You are now completely cured: make love to any woman you like! I wish you success in your job and in your personal life for the good of the workers of the world!'*

The now ex-patient, however, would not want to love other women, since, as Professor Sagaydak divined, those other women had not yet achieved the 'lovemakey' level of his Specialist. The patient would insist on an extension of Part E in order to consolidate the results of the treatment. And the Impotentologist-General would be forced to interfere personally once again.

'For now, you cannot,' the Impotentologist-General would explain to his VIP patients. 'Such a time will have come for everyone when the Communist Party of the Soviet Union implements its programme for the harmonious development of the personality. But this won't happen until a developed Communist society is completely constructed, and you know better than I do when that will be. For my part, I myself am doing everything possible to make a lofty Communist level of treatment obtainable right now. For the time being, it's not for everyone, unfortunately, but only for those who are particularly worthy. Consider this an establishment for sexual enjoyment that is restricted to a clientele that no longer includes you. It's not my fault: I've received a directive to transfer my Specialist to Comrade So-and-so . . .' Here the Impotentologist-General would pause in a significant way, after which he would firmly shake the patient's hand.

Alla had several minutes in her packed production schedule during which to relax and engage in some political self-education, for her duty under the Method included a spiritual concord with her clients. Most of all she loved reading in the newspapers about the long and stormy standing ovations that the attendees met with at solemn convocations of the leadership. Then there would follow a list of all her best patients. She was irreplaceable to all of them. One name in particular did Alla – the Young Communist – preserve with special attention and care, in connection with the fact that they had not succeeded in carrying the course of treatment of this most important patient to its conclusion.

These Very Important Comrades were attracted to Alla still more by the fact that she was mute or, more properly speaking, a deaf-mute. The Lord had probably arranged that specially, having in mind to present the Politburo with the ideal woman, one who wouldn't tell others what she had heard. Her deafness and muteness promoted the development of other means of communication – by using her hands, her lips without any sound, her legs and certain other parts of her wondrous body. Besides that, she could lip-read the words of her scientific director and their clients, and in emergencies she could rely on the hand-alphabet.

There had been a time when Sagaydak had maintained a whole company of pretty Young Communists to provide collective service to whatever great and wise patient came next. Alla on her own surpassed the capabilities of the collective, though, and consequently turned out to be much more useful from an economic point of view.

Alla was constantly engaged in the perfection of her knowledge and experience, never resting on her laurels. Her motto was 'Do it better today than yesterday and tomorrow better than today.'

'She'll never stoop to hack work, no doubt about that,' Sagaydak one day praised her to Rappoport. 'If you could only see how she gets into her work! She spares herself nothing in the interests of the Communist Party.'

And, really, over the long years of their life together, on only one occasion after a hard day's work did she object – and only to Sagaydak. In translation from the sign language Alla declared: 'I have endured the kind of men on top of me that not a single woman in the world would have been able to stand. I'm a saint. And, besides, workers have the right to a vacation!'

Sagaydak, the servant of God, was so surprised by this objection that on the very next day, using his connections, he got her a reservation at the most exclusive health resort.

# 52

# A Shot of Tea

Sagaydak touched Alla's shoulder. 'Well, here's what, titch. Enough lovey-dovey. Make some tea, and we'll have a chat.'

Alla nodded with a smile, got up and with a carefree and beautiful gesture tossed her amazing hair back on her shoulders. The skirts of her gown closed, concealing her splendid legs. But at the same time her wide, delicate sleeve fell back, exposing her swan-beautiful arm all the way to the shoulder. *Look at what I am, delight in me! Remember me, carry me away with you, recall me at night, in your dreams, in whole and in part, in detail. Be aware that I am an empress and you are all my slaves. All you people of the opposite sex are ready to kneel before me and do anything that I wish. I need nothing from you at all. I come to work for you, but I live in a completely different world, one inaccessible to you. I hear the clouds rubbing against one another; I dream in colour. I sense through you. And whom can you sense, apart from yourself?* She tenderly drew her arm past Rappoport's lips. For an instant he smelled her elusive scent, and something – far away and entirely forgotten – just barely stirred, aching in the pit of his stomach, then died down and extinguished. Alla had gone.

'What is it you want, you jailbird?' Sagaydak asked to his face, stopping in front of Rappoport.

'I'll tell you. I have to get help for Makartsev.'

'Yikes! Has he caught the clap? They're all even more afraid of getting registered in the special out-patient clinic than they are of the diseases. That's a pleasure beyond all compare – studying the diseases of your subordinates.'

'This is a special matter.'

'Special? If you're counting on my giving him the special Method treatment you've dragged yourself up here in vain! After all, Makartsev is just a *candidate* member of the Central Committee. Alla isn't for people of his rank. Tell him to hurry up and get on the Central Committee.'

'Give him time and he'll be a candidate member of the Politburo!'

'Makartsev? With his mistrustfulness? As President Kennedy put it, I'll allow myself to note – not, however, condescending to argument – that if he has yet to become a somebody it'll only be a candidate for the removal of his prostate gland.'

'Listen!' begged Rappoport. 'Shift your mind around in another direction! Makartsev is in hospital with a heart attack.'

'Really? Been overdoing it?'

'And his son ran over two people when he was drunk. If it goes to trial they'll give him fifteen years.'

'Murder? The son of a Party executive? Let him go to jail! Don't even ask!'

'But in principle? In principle, is it possible? Bearing in mind that there aren't any laws.'

'There aren't? On the contrary, we've got far too many! Some for the masses, others for those on top, a third bunch for the lackeys, a fourth for foreigners, a fifth . . .'

'So, is it possible? Do it then! Not for Makartsev but for me.'

'God, he's sucking the juices out of you! You're breaking your back while he's acquiring more capital. They didn't treat even plantation slaves that badly!'

'Let it be that way. We're of an age when it's time to think about God. Help me!'

'And your god is Makartsev? All right, fucking hell! Purely for the sake of our friendship, jailbird!' Sagaydak spat out in anger, and the dog looked at her master in alarm.

'Right, for friendship's sake. But bear in mind that Makartsev will be able to do you a good turn as well.'

Angels on the Head of a Pin

'How's that?'

'Wouldn't you like to get the Lenin Prize?'

'And where would I stick your damned Lenin Prize? And why would I need Makartsev? So he could print an article entitled "Professor Sagaydak's Heroic Deed"? If I want to get the Lenin Prize I'll find out whose prostate needs massaging. Well, maybe if he ran an article for me, about my new discovery! But nothing's going to come of that anyway.'

'What discovery?'

'I've discovered Sagaydak's Basic Law: in Party VIPs sexual impotence and political impotence are communicating vessels. One flows into the other.'

'No kidding?' Rappoport raised his unclipped eyebrows. 'You discovered that?'

'I did! And who better? I could get the Nobel Prize for that law. I've already worked out a course of treatment, in theory, only there's no way I can check it experimentally. I propose to treat impotence by means of withdrawal from one's political career. But nobody wants to quit out of those that I've hinted to about it. So how can I test it?'

'And you can't try it out on rabbits?'

'Not on rabbits, no. I'm afraid they'll never give me the Nobel.'

'Well, how can I make it up to you?' Rappoport uttered sadly. 'You yourself understand: this is a gateway, an opening for everyone . . .'

Alla came noiselessly in with a tray. She set down three tiny little cups of Chinese porcelain, a teapot and a sugar bowl. An aroma exuded from the teapot. Alla again sat down on the pouffe near them.

'Good girl,' Rappoport praised her. 'What a good girl!'

'I'll pour you some now,' said Sagaydak. 'Camomile tea at night is very good as a soporific, and it hasn't got any chemicals in it.'

Silently they each drank two little cupfuls apiece. Rappoport drank his with double pleasure, feasting his eyes on Alla, who was sitting opposite him.

'That's it, my children! I have to get to work tomorrow. And you're tired, titch. Farewell, you divinity.'

He kissed Alla first on one cheek, then on the other, slobbering all over her. She wound her arms around his neck, clinging to him. Rappoport, stooping, moved into the corridor. The lap dog wearily got up and followed him as far as the door. Sagaydak handed him his overcoat.

'Thanks, jailbird.' Rappoport prodded him in the stomach with a fist. 'You're a real . . .'

'All right! It says in the Scriptures: you don't have to click your heels! Today's that sort of day. Or, rather, it's already tomorrow now. How could I turn you down?'

'What is today?'

'The seventeenth of April! The two of us were born today: Khrushchev and me.'

'Happy birthday.'

Rappoport opened the door. Sagaydak, still in his dressing-gown, thrust himself out on the landing and felt around in the opening of his mailbox. All the other tenants in the building had to go downstairs for their post but not the Impotentologist-General.

'You're waiting for something,' noted Rappoport. 'But I have a jailbird's feeling that I live in a box just like that. Sometimes the slot opens, and I can see the world through it. And then once again I'm in darkness. And I read the newspapers that they stick in on top of me.'

'Go to you-know-where. Get some sleep!'

'I get the hint,' said Rappoport. He nodded and started slowly walking down the stairs.

Alla had turned down the bedclothes and lain down. The dog was asleep at her feet, yelping softly in a dream. Sagaydak took a shower and, not putting his dressing-gown back on, shuffled across the room and flopped down on the bed. Alla took a jar of fragrant oil out of the bedside table and, pouring some into her hand, began rubbing it in all over Sagaydak's body, starting with his feet and working up to his neck. Now and then she tickled or kissed him, and he would make a wry face, pretending that it was unpleasant. Getting as far as his neck, Alla turned her subject on his stomach with an effort and, pouring out a little more oil, once more went from toe to head. When the procedure was complete Sagaydak opened his eyes. Alla lay quietly on her back and waited, her eyelids dropped. Sagaydak poured some oil into his palm and started rubbing his wife's body in the same sequence. After the massage they fell asleep, content with each other, and slept peacefully, evenly and long.

# 53

## *Subbotnik* at Nadya's

Nadya was struggling with herself with all her might. Every time, though, it turned out to be pointless, and she would give in.

In the morning she would rise, make coffee, get herself ready for work and rush to the hairdresser's for a hairdo or to get colourless nail-varnish applied and then hastily make her way to the office. She would look at her watch and tell herself proudly that a whole hour had gone by without her once thinking about Ivlev. *So it'll pass. Soon I'll forget about him completely, and when I meet him in the corridor I'll just smirk and think: What's so special about him? Why did I go for him and he for me? He's just a guy like any other; scruffy and not even tall, and I like them tall. And with an ego the likes of which has never been seen on earth.*

Encountering him in the corridor Nadya barely perceptibly nodded to his brief 'Hi!' and hurried on past, as if she had somewhere to get to. She always had things to do in the evening: shopping, films to see, girl-friends, and – incidentally! – lectures at the university, at which she had to show up sometimes, as well: next summer Nadya would have to defend her bachelor's thesis, finally.

Tired, she would look in on her father in his room. He usually came home late and sat for a long while behind his desk, reading; he would go to bed and then get up again and walk around his room. She would drop in on him before he went to sleep, kiss him on the balding spot at the back of his head and ask if he had been late to the swimming-pool that morning because she had overslept and hadn't made him his coffee. No, he hadn't been late to the pool. He loved his daughter, and after the death of her mother he probably loved her twice as much. He would tenderly smack her on the bottom, like a child, and say: 'Well, you go ahead! I've got something more to do.'

Nadya would take a shower, apply nightcream to her face, admire herself for a minute in the mirror with a smile (*What a waste!*), put on the pyjamas that an old friend of her father's had recently brought back from Brussels and, throwing the half-read issue of *Novy Mir* on her pillow, would crawl under her bedcovers. Picking up the magazine, she wouldn't read it, but with it opened out on top of her face would recall the day that had passed – its pluses and minuses. And she would be proud of herself – she hadn't once thought about Ivlev for any length of time. Meaning it was all going to pass. A day was like a year and a year eternity.

She would lift the magazine, making a decision to read, but after several lines she would feel that she was losing concentration, that she was falling asleep and didn't have the strength to resist. She would put out the light, and then Ivlev would appear. 'No, we shan't have any of that!' she would declare confidently. But pushing him away was beyond her weak powers.

Now she would be afraid even to move lest Ivlev disappear again. Well, maybe she *was* letting herself fantasize a bit: he was more tender and active than in reality (which is what she wanted), while she was restrained and cold (as she had never been). And he would say things to her, too, lots of disconnected words. He would continually say the things about her that she desperately wanted to hear but about which he always maintained silence.

Then he would fall quiet, and she could almost hear him breathe in her ear, now faster and faster. And she would start to moan, very softly, so that her father wouldn't hear on the other side of the wall. Now she would roll over on to her back, ready to become as resistless as a throw rug. After a few moments she would come back to her dream reality. Full of inertia, she would kiss Ivlev on the neck in gratitude. He would raise himself up on his arms, turn a proprietary gaze on her and say: 'Time for me to go.'

In the mornings at the office Nadya would sit like someone just brought back from the dead. Of course Ivlev wanted to be with her, even more than she did. That feeling is always stronger in men. He held his silence merely because there was nothing he could do about it. They weren't sending him on any assignments, and Rappoport's son came by too often. But if they could see one other the whole thing would pass more quickly.

That day Nadya was walking around the canteen with her tray, looking for an unoccupied seat. Noticing Ivlev eating his lunch, she wanted to walk past as usual and sit by herself, but he pulled out a chair and invited her to sit down with ironic gallantry.

'Slop!' He pushed away his plate. 'They steal everything – if only they'd cook what's left properly!'

'Do you want me to feed you some real mince rissoles? I made them myself last night. As well as a delicious spicy chilli sauce!'

'Where?'

'At my place.'

His eyes flared up and died down again. 'At home? All I need is to run into your parents!'

'Would I have asked you if there was any danger of that? Shall we rush over there? The rissoles just need heating up.'

Thinking it over, he looked at his pork chop with hatred, stuck his fork into it and held it up to the light. 'See, it's as transparent as a soap bubble.'

'And my rissoles are so thick', she enticed him, 'that X-rays wouldn't even go through.'

He threw the chop back on his plate. 'Let's go!'

'We won't drink anything, just have the rissoles and the sauce,' she said into his ear in the taxi on their way.

Drinking was giving him less and less pleasure. Any arousal quickly turned to apathy, and that was irritating. Nadya didn't want anything that would add something artificial to her feeling; she wanted it to be the pure thing and nothing else that made her heart beat faster.

While Ivlev took off his overcoat and looked around the enormous apartment Nadya dived into the kitchen, turned on the gas and put the rissoles from the night before on the hob.

'Come on in. That's my room,' she said, indicating her door to Ivlev after coming back into the corridor and taking off her fur coat and boots. 'I'm afraid I wasn't able to make the bed. Although today, by the way, is the nineteenth of April, *subbotnik* day . . .'

'And here we are, getting down to work!'

They got straight into bed, and everything went the way she had dreamed it at night.

'Oh, Lord, the rissoles!' she started, barely managing to return to reality.

The kitchen was full of smoke. Smiling guiltily, Nadya carried the frying-pan into her room, and with their forks they scraped the middle bits from the burnt-black rissoles, spread the red chilli sauce on bread and stuffed it all down with gusto. Then they got under the covers again. Ivlev started feeling sorry for Nadya and a little bit for himself. Her confusion made her so tender and obedient. As if she could feel that there was no longer any place for her in his heart. He understood her but couldn't help her. She had figured it out.

'I have the feeling that this is our last time together. Every time – the last time . . .'

'That's a good thing,' he nodded. 'That means that every time afterwards is like a gift.'

'Yes. But that's scary.'

'On the contrary, it's good! Anything otherwise is just a bore. Kakabadze wants to get married as soon as he gets out of hospital.'

'And I want to choke you!' She grabbed him by the neck and lay on top of him. She raised herself up on her arms so that her breasts hung pointed and then flattened them against his chest. She kissed him on the eyes.

'I want you to go blind and never look at anyone but me!'

'That's what all women want. All they need to do is give birth to men as blind as kittens.'

'I'm going out of my mind with desire!'

'Put a wet towel on your stomach, the way Italian women do.'

'I'm a Russian, my dear! I'll put a sheet of paper on my stomach.'

'And then what?'

'And then I'll write a complaint to the Party bureau. "He loved me in un-Party ways." They say that by using yoga a woman can keep from getting pregnant, by sheer willpower.'

'Then steel your will.'

'I was! As long as I didn't see you.'

She ran into the bathroom, her robe flung over one shoulder. Ivlev got up from the bed and roamed around the room, looking over the knick-knacks from various countries and little bottles of a kind he had never seen before. He tried on Nadya's brassiere. She didn't come back, so he set off in search of her.

Ivlev found his way without difficulty around Nadya's huge apartment (the kind they don't build any more) with its moulding on the ceilings and frosted-glass windows. He padded barefoot through the living-room and stuck his head through yet another door – it was a gentleman's study, the kind you see only in museums these days. One wall was completely filled with books from floor to ceiling. Ivlev walked down past the shelves, which contained a multitude of luxurious albums full of reproductions, old encyclopaedias, gold-tooled volumes of monographs from the previous century. A stepladder stood opened out and on it lay two books, taken from their places or awaiting replacement on the shelves. Both of them were poetry in the pre-Revolutionary orthography by poets that Ivlev had never heard of. Across the room, with its back to the bookshelves, stood a narrow little couch; on a shelf alongside it was an ashtray with cigarette ends in it, a small transistor radio and a telephone. Facing the window was a huge, sprawling writing desk with carvings on its claw-legs, covered from one side to the other with books and magazines in English, as Ivlev rapidly ascertained, and in German. He leafed through them. The magazines had translations appended to them – a complete service. Psychology, philosophy, psychiatry . . . an absorbing selection. And this?

This was the occult sciences, if Ivlev understood correctly – telekinesis, telepathy . . .

He punctiliously refrained from reading the manuscript sheets strewn over the desk. His eyes, sliding from item to item, plucked out three thick volumes from all this abundance; they were bound in a non-mass-produced way in bright red cloth covers. Ivlev opened the cover of one and read in a corner of the page: 'Top Secret.'

He could no longer hold back. He read the title: 'State Security Major-General V. Sirotkin. *On the Question of Possibilities for the Control of Thought Processes in the Ideological Struggle.* Dissertation for the scientific degree of Doctor of Philosophy.' Ivlev made a quiet sound of surprise and immediately wanted to start reading it, but he heard steps in the corridor. He quickly closed the book cover and was heading for the door when it opened.

# 54

# 'Excuse Me,
# I Seem to Be Bothering You . . .'

At the door stood a broad-shouldered man of about sixty in a top-quality grey suit. He had intended to come in but now was confused at the sight of the naked Ivlev. For a while they were both silent, not knowing how to act or what way out to offer the other. They simply looked one another up and down. Finally the man said: 'Could you explain to me what this means?'

Ivlev spoke his line with dignity: 'Allow me to get dressed first.'

'As you please! And where, damn it, is Nadya?'

'In the bathroom . . . with a girlfriend,' muttered Ivlev without batting an eye, passing sideways down the corridor to Nadya's room.

'With what girlfriend?'

'With hers. That is, with mine. Excuse me!' As if he needed Nadya's father, too! Finding himself in Nadya's room, Ivlev bundled some clothes into his arms and hurtled into the bathroom.

'Your father!'

'Where?' Nadya's eyes grew wide. 'He's never come home during the day before!'

'Don't waste any time. Get dressed.'

'You know what,' whispered Nadya, 'it was our neighbour who called him! She's a schizophrenic, retired, a former major. A light goes on in her place when anyone rings the doorbell just to borrow some salt. You stand there like you're being interrogated. She started visiting my father a lot after my mother died, and now she keeps her eye on me.'

'Right. I'll disappear, if I can. Remember: I came here with a girlfriend of yours. And how come you never told me who he was?'

'Everybody knows who he is except you. And would you have trusted me any less?'

He shrugged his shoulders. 'It's awful!'

'For me, too. But he *is* my father!'

'And what if you'd had a slip of the tongue at home?'

'It's the other way round, you nit! If they come to him, it's as a last resort.'

'Of course, your father isn't going to let them hurt you.'

She pressed against him. 'He's nice,' she said. 'He loves me and gives me money. Do you despise me? Fasten my bra!'

Ivlev patted her on the head and looked out into the corridor. There was no one there, and he gradually eased himself out to the stairway gate. Nadya went off to the kitchen.

'You!' she yelped, feigning surprise at the sight of her father.

General Sirotkin was slamming down saucepan lids. 'I came home to eat the rissoles you cooked for me last night. By the way, where's your girlfriend and her nudist?'

'They've gone.'

'That's what I thought. Without even introducing themselves!'

'Don't start!' Nadya said drily. 'They haven't got anywhere else to get together.'

Her father looked at her closely, wavering over whether to explode or hold back. He suddenly felt afraid of his daughter.

'They should get married,' he said. 'Then they'd have somewhere.'

'I'll tell them that.'

'So where are the rissoles?'

'We finished them. Sorry.'

'I understand. It was for the sake of my health. Listen, my girl! It's long past time that we had a chat. I've kept on putting it off, but now is obviously the time. It's true, my time is limited . . .'

'What about, Daddy?'

'You're living a secret life, a life I don't understand.'

'Me? Everything about me is out in the open. It's just that you never ask me about it. That's *your* style – everything top secret.'

'You know very well what my work is like, and we're not going to go into that!'

'So we won't. Suit yourself. You started this!'

'I started it because you're my daughter. I want to know what's going on in your life.'

'You can't stop being a KGB man even when you're playing the father, Daddy! You think you've got to know everything about other people. But about yourself – nobody knows, not even your daughter!'

'I'm a Chekist, my girl.'

'I know that, Dad! I've heard you go on about it for twenty years. But now we're both grown-ups, and Mum isn't around any more to keep the peace between us. And she, by the way, asked *me* to look after *you*. Let's play it this way: if you want to know about me tell me about yourself, you Chekist! If not, then not.'

'Someone's inciting you to take a leftist point of view.'

'Nobody's inciting me to do anything. Calm down.'

'And what do they say about us at your newspaper?'

'What, you want me to tell on my friends?'

'You've been picking up some stupid ideas! Even if those are your own convictions you have to be more restrained.'

'I don't know what other people are saying about your institution, but *I* tell everyone that there's a portrait of Pushkin hanging in your boss's office.'

'Pushkin?' he smiled with the corners of his mouth. 'Why?'

'Dad, he was the one who said: "Beautiful are the urges of the heart!"'

'I've heard that,' laughed her father. 'Not too witty, I must say. We don't deal with beautiful urges. We've got no time for that sort of thing.'

'You deal with forcing people to stop thinking altogether!'

'Oh, Nadya.' He made a wry, squeamish face. 'You're not a child any more! Agencies with real power exist in every country. Menzhinsky, my girl, put it very clearly: "We are the armed wing of the Party!" And that's what we are! None of your intellectuals bothers me personally. But there are definite principles held by the government, and if the majority of the people follow them our task is to defend that majority from the upstarts. A society can't live without discipline. Our enemies are just waiting for us to come unstuck. We have to be monolithic. Water seeping through a crack can wash away a gigantic dam if the hole isn't filled in time. I hope I live till the time our organization is completely abolished. But in order to do that the whole of society needs to have an elevated consciousness.'

'So that everyone turns into robots.'

'And it's a normal thing in your opinion when upstarts and drop-outs want us to let them write and say whatever comes into their heads? As a matter of fact, it's not Chekists like me who dislike people like that but the People themselves who demand their punishment. Imagine, we have to guard Solzhenitsyn around the clock. He's not stupid, but he'd never understand that. It's only a few hundred sensitive intellectuals, and nobody else, who need all those critical notions of his! If his programmes were realistic and useful they would have long since broken through into our lives. I know of a hundred times more cruelties and injustices than he does. I reinforce the country, though, while he pulls it down. I serve the People, and who does he serve? What is he – a single man who's cleverer than the whole Party with its fourteen million people? Who could seriously believe that?'

'The people you persecute!'

'Well, if you don't want to subscribe to the norms that exist for everyone else, then you have only yourself to blame! Of course, we try to educate that sort as well, but it doesn't always work out.'

'And your Stalin did a particularly good job of educating people!'

'Stalin's not mine, Nadya. Stalin was just an upstart and a very dangerous one in so far as he concentrated too much power in his own hands. If Solzhenitsyn, say, was to be given unlimited power, nobody knows what sort of laws he would establish. All of today's fighters for human rights – if you let them start acting in the open, they'll be dying to get into the driver's seat. We have humane laws, but we can't let that happen.'

'But isn't today's man at the top just the same?'

'Today's is just someone carrying out the will of the Party. He signs whatever he's supposed to, after we decide it, my girl. Get this straight. It's not because we're the KGB – those times are long gone. We're a force because we're the middle link of the Party. We decide what the Politburo should know and what they shouldn't. We had to kick Khrushchev out the minute he went too far. And we'll get rid of anybody who gets in our way, because we collectively express the will of the People, and there *is* no force that can get in our way. Got it?'

'And how!'

'Well, if you do understand, then let me know about *you* now, since according to your formula I've explained myself. What's his name, our guest?'

'What's that to you?'

'Surely your father has a right to know who his daughter is seeing?'

'His name is Kulikov. Andrey Kulikov.'

'Does he work with you?'

'No, he's an engineer. Works in a secret establishment, tucked away just like you, and I never asked him about it.'

'His face is somewhat familiar.'

'He's got that kind of face. Looks like a lot of people. I get him mixed up myself. You know what, Daddy? Don't even think of checking up on him or putting him under surveillance or anything like that. If I find out that you have – I'll leave.'

'What do you mean, leave? What are you on about, Nadya?'

'What you heard me just say.'

'But where'll you go?'

'I'll leave, and you won't find me!'

# 55

# The Rise of
# Vasilly Sirotkin

Everything that Major-General Sirotkin had achieved in life was the result of his own efficient qualities and abilities. If he failed to master something it was because people or circumstances prevented him.

Sirotkin did not like to recall his childhood and even less his youth. Back then, in childhood and youth, he had been insignificant, in no way distinguished from others. But he had long since become accustomed to people relating to him with particular respect even when he wasn't in his general's uniform. He was used to speaking slowly and weightily. And his every word was immediately taken as a command.

In moments of frankness with his subordinates at work Major-General Sirotkin would say that everything he had achieved he had attained thanks to his ideological convictions, his faith in the rightness of the cause that he served. His views, however, had developed over the course of his life, even though he considered them to be as unshakeable as granite. In his youth people had been divided for him into the proletariat – that is, good people – and the bourgeoisie – the enemy. He himself was one of the good people. The idealism of his youth was replaced by ideological pragmatism, that is, the use of ideology for promotion in the service.

After obtaining high rank Sirotkin involuntarily began dividing people up differently: ours (KGB operatives) and theirs. Convictions (Communist, non-Communist) didn't play a role like that any more. Today you might be a Communist, but tomorrow you're a traitor to the motherland. But if you work for the KGB, that's for ever. Traitors to the motherland got branded with infamy and, if they came home, were given ten years. Traitors to the KGB were exterminated by the organization itself, without trial or investigation, hunted down in whatever country they hid. Sirotkin considered devotion to the motherland the most important buttress of his life, but in practical terms he understood this to mean devotion to the KGB.

Occupying a stage at a middle link of the managing apparatus at a time when the power of the organization was a bit limited, Sirotkin was satisfied with that. It was his business to fulfil his function in the general expanse of the leadership of the state. He even used to say that the KGB was needed now for the defence of Soviet attainments from unbridled Stalinists, volunteer informers who demanded the imprisonment of everyone they didn't like. But even in later times the Party made mistake after mistake in their management of the country, and those mistakes were correctible only by people like Sirotkin, provided they were in power. This was impossible, though, for a whole range of reasons. At that time Sirotkin's colleagues had been going on about unifying the Party and the KGB, having in mind that after such unification they would find themselves in even stronger positions. As far as their views went, the task of convictions – in so far as theory aids practice – was to aid someone in the realization of his own plans. Sirotkin continued to bide his own time, although chances were getting fewer and fewer, as he saw it.

Sirotkin had never once been out of the country. This situation grieved him when he was still just a department head and thinking about getting transferred to a different directorate, Intelligence. Foreign languages turned out to be his stumbling block. Twice he undertook a study of them in special courses, where things were done straight up, Chekist-style, and each time he fell uselessly behind everyone else in the course. His pronunciation was so terrible that his strict former-deep-cover teachers would make sarcastic remarks, and he had to quit so as not to undermine his authority.

Certain people might have thought that Sirotkin had wound up in Internal Affairs because of his lack of ability with external ones. But that wasn't true. The majority of the intelligence-apparatus managers didn't speak any languages. It was just that here, in the struggle against the penetration of bourgeois ideology, Sirotkin had solid experience. After the war it had been his initiative to set up jamming apparatus – brought in from Nazi Germany – in all the major cities, so as to block foreign radio broadcasts. Consequently the production of similar apparatus was adopted in the Soviet Union. Sirotkin hadn't been able to foresee the dark cloud that was hanging over him, though. He suffered under strange circumstances, unclear to himself.

'Where's Petrov? I've come to arrest him.'

'But he just left to arrest you!'

There were jokes like that going around at the time. Sirotkin's location didn't change. He just didn't go home. They took him down in the lift to the jail six floors below. He wasn't beaten, tortured or interrogated. He remained one of theirs. 'They just put me on ice for a while,' he would joke afterwards. He was held in privileged conditions, and he read a lot.

Neither could you say that he got out of the Lubyanka after his rehabilitation. When first they rehabilitated KGB operatives Sirotkin simply got into the lift and went up six floors. From there he rang home. Sirotkin hadn't known that his wife had disavowed him in writing, because she worked in the KGB, too, with the rank of captain. Her deed he took to be reasonable and even necessary: she had been left with Nadya on her hands. After disavowing him, as was expected, his wife was dismissed from the organization, but she found a job and awaited her husband's return. When Sirotkin rang home and Nadya answered the phone, he immediately realized that this was his daughter. Once he was home his wife disavowed her disavowal, and they got on with their life together. Nadya called her father 'uncle' for a month and then got used to him.

His daughter had been born fairly late in Sirotkin's life when he was approaching forty. And when she grew up, he was left without a wife. He became a solicitous father, even though he didn't have a lot of time. He had invested too much in her, and now she had her own life, one that was unknown to him and therefore utterly wrong. Without noticing it, he was becoming captious in his efforts to put his daughter on her guard. He would assure himself that this was just the desire to do right by her, and he couldn't stop it. Evidently the death of his wife had had a big impact on him. To his subordinates, on the other hand, he had begun to get soft with age, less frequently punishing them for not carrying out his orders. Of course this sentimentality didn't extend to people of other convictions. But, in a certain sense, they weren't even people, after all.

Sirotkin had served in the Secret Political Security Service for many years and had risen to be deputy to its chief when, in 1965, in connection with the danger from intellectual ferment, the specialized (Fifth) Chief Directorate was created, and General Sirotkin was appointed to command it.

Cases that came under the new directorate passed through all the levels of the organization, from district to provincial and republic agencies. His central apparatus picked out the most interesting, the ones that had important significance, and sent back the others for further inquiry. The most difficult subjects, the ones with connections abroad who represented a significant danger to the state, Major-General Sirotkin passed on to his section chief, Shironin, a man who was tidy and methodical if not too deep. Comrades from Shironin's section provided shadowing, bugging and the discovery of the addresses of people visited by the subjects, of their interests, their ties, the circle of their relatives and friends – in brief, they kept the subject covered.

Shironin never had enough personnel or equipment. Subjects such as Solzhenitsyn demanded more strength than did the anti-Soviet organizations that arose from time to time, the quick arrest of whose members allowed the transfer of freed-up agents to the next operation. Shironin had frequently suggested isolating Solzhenitsyn from society. Sirotkin reported this upwards to Kegelbanov. But the proposal languished in the Politburo, which was playing a double game with the West. But the difficulties and special conditions of the Fifth Directorate's work were noted Upstairs anyway, and additional means were thrown into the fray.

Affairs in the new directorate weren't going as well as was being written in the accounts presented to the Chairman of the State Committee.

And worst of all was the *samizdat*-combating section, headed by Yudanichev. The complication was that *samizdat*, despite confiscations and special orders for nicking the persons guilty of spreading it, was being created anew all the time. It was necessary to nip that in the bud. At Sirotkin's suggestion the Supreme Soviet passed a law that gave the process of writing it a considerably harsher punishment than, say, the unlawful possession of firearms.

*Samizdat* resisted, floating out of reach, while Sirotkin expected trouble even without that. There was a massive commissioning of officers going on at the Ministry of Defence, and Sirotkin was afraid that this rejuvenation would affect the KGB organs as well. That would be unfair, to replace experienced Chekist personnel with green youngsters. He was absolutely positive that there was still much he could do. They wouldn't be able to do without his expertise. He got down to writing his dissertation, separate bits of which had been assembled at the directorate that he'd been entrusted with. In the near future this realization of Sirotkin's thoughts was going to have a significant effect on the safeguarding of the socialist camp from penetration by pernicious Western influences, as well as on the flow of undesirable information abroad.

Sirotkin had had a reverence for books since his childhood, considering them the source of knowledge. He loved to read not only service manuals but the slanderous *samizdat* productions procured by his staff as well. He would often go to the bookstall at Kuznetsky Most and buy old Russian poets under the counter and leaf through them at night. He took an interest as well in certain literary and philosophical works on stylistics.

Sirotkin was struck by the abstract, Partyless quality of these researches. From his point of view, contemporary stylistics could become a more refined science for determining the authorship of anonymous works, that is, a science to aid the Party in carrying on the struggle for the Leninist Party spirit in literature. In the meantime, though, works on stylistics were limited to discussions of the style of classic authors. The thought occurred to Sirotkin of creating a special group of stylistic philologists within the directorate that could work out clear-cut criteria for the evaluation of an individual style. Then, however much a writer tried to hide under another name or write on an unregistered typewriter, he could be detected in the same way as by fingerprint identification. A special group of students, selected from the military, was already studying at the philological faculty of Moscow State University, and they were to be sent to work for the KGB organs.

Sirotkin had other ideas as well, ones that in their significance went far beyond the bounds of the directorate entrusted to him. The Party had charged the KGB with looking after ideological purity among the ranks of the workers, but the Party press acted sometimes at odds with that. When intimidation was called for they wrote about the development of democracy. Whenever it was time to do the expedient thing and praise unanimity, they would discuss the various currents in Party literature. And, most importantly, the press wrote a lot about the 'wisdom of the Party' without ever bolstering the authority of the KGB (without which the Party was nothing) among the People. Instead of respect, they were inculcating fear. They praised intelligence agents operating in other countries; they praised the Border Guards – but the most difficult concern for operatives of the KGB organs was working among their own people, a task that demanded tact, fortitude and a particular artistry. This honourable mission remained unsung. The very programme of the Communist Party of the Soviet Union for the construction of a new society would be more speedily realized if all the information media – press, radio, television, film – were given over to the KGB. After all, Lenin himself wrote that newspapers represented 'the most primary and most vital branch of our military activity'. Major-General Sirotkin was saving up this quote for a rainy day.

An organized and temperate man, he even took his vacations in an organized fashion, as someone of his rank in the organization should. The holiday destination would be settled on in advance. On Friday evening four or sometimes even six cars, not counting bodyguards, would set off for the hunting reserve, where the huntsmen would already be in preparation, the servants heating up the Finnish bath. Groceries would have already been delivered that morning from Moscow. The members of the shooting party would vary – that was the way it went. But most frequently they were the directorates' chiefs and their deputies.

Sirotkin knew all about hunting. And as far as hunting weapons went he was the unsurpassed master. There were over two dozen shotguns and hunting rifles in his collection, kept in a special cabinet. He never hung on to any mediocre ones – he'd give those to his colleagues. In general he loved to give presents: books, souvenirs, expensive porcelain. His late wife used to get very angry about this trait. He kept the best guns for himself, with their silver-and-gold-chasing. On the hunt he would bring his double-barrelled gun with the telescopic sight, the one that Beria had personally given to him for his excellent work. That gun never let him down.

Sirotkin had learned to shoot without ever missing – even on rough terrain or in the semi-darkness of a foggy morning – in his youth, when he had been called up to serve in the forces of the People's Committee for Internal Affairs, the NKVD. He had served first as a prisoner escort in the north and had then been appointed to a roving search party up there. That group tracked fugitive prisoners: they had to shoot under difficult conditions and kill escapees on the spot. And sometimes, following orders, they were supposed to wound them in the legs or, as an exemplary punishment, in the lower part of the stomach or back so that their inevitable death was long and tormented. The ones like that they registered as dead and left in the woods, still alive, for the wolves to eat. Sirotkin worked in that sort of group for five years and became the leader of one of the roving parties, then the head of a camp, working for the provincial KGB apparatus. In short, he was never an upstart of the sort that appeared from time to time as a result of patronage.

He had only faced disgrace now, in the recent past, in March 1969. Towards evening at the hunting reserve, dinner had been prepared and the fireplace lit. Everyone drank a little, listening to organ music – Bach – on the record player. Sirotkin's deputy, Colonel Shironin, was a big fan of Bach. The moist spring weather was persisting. They ordered the huntsmen to let the dogs into the room. The animals, poorly looked after, lived in a barn, and they stank with their doggy smell. After some discussion the leaders decided to issue a directive for the establishment of a position of Master of Hounds at their hunting reserve. And so off they went to their rooms, remembering that tomorrow they had to get up before break of day. The bull moose that had been set aside for them had already been captured and was fruitlessly gnawing and butting at his fence.

That morning they put on their Japanese sporting jackets, pulled on their rubber boots, covered their upper parts with hooded green cloaks, took up their guns – barrels downwards so as not to get wet – and moved out through the woods. Huntsmen without any guns (since huntsmen on reserves like that were forbidden to carry them) had already let the moose out, placing salt licks for it in particular places, and had spread themselves out through the woods so as to prevent the beast by their shouts from heading in any undesirable direction. They had asked first if their illustrious guests wanted the moose tied up so they could shoot it more conveniently, but those worthies had declined. They had also turned down an opportunity to shoot from special platforms, just so that everything would be as real as possible.

That night a light snow had fallen on the slush, and the early morning wind was whipping the powdery snow off the bushes, impeding vision at any distance. They caught sight of the moose as it grew light. They started shooting at him, and they wounded him; but he was frisky, and he bled and crept on ahead through the cutting. Then their ammunition, as if in spite, ran out, Sirotkin having the last remaining round.

'Well, then,' they told him, 'it's time for you to prove your mastery of the hunt.'

Without any fuss Major-General Sirotkin fired, and when the beast fell everyone let him know how delighted they were. But when they approached the fallen moose they saw he was still alive and not about to let the huntsmen approach and cut his throat, even though he couldn't move. Sirotkin had broken the moose's back near its rump; the beast was crawling along the ground, and there was nothing to finish him off with

– too bad for the beast. They urgently sent a huntsman for more ammunition. Sirotkin was upset by his poor shot; he decided that he was getting old. His comrades tried to comfort him: snow was whirling around on the ground and making everyone's eyes water, so the moisture had obviously distorted the precision of his aim. The moose grew motionless from loss of blood and turned a vacant gaze on the guests. And only when they once again drew near, after reloading their guns, did he begin to toss again, even though it would have been better for him to have them end his suffering. They shot the moose point-blank with all four guns, while he strove forward on his forelegs.

Knowing that the tastiest part of the moose was his liver, they ordered the huntsmen to cut it out hot so that they could taste the fruits of their labours. They left the rest of the carcass behind. The huntsmen later dragged it away with horses. Sirotkin was sorry that Nadya hadn't come with him on that hunt. He would have been glad to have his daughter with him, and she would have provided feminine company for the others. But Nadya had flatly refused.

# 56

# Reception at the Chairman's

Holding the slim folder under his arm, Sirotkin quietly crossed the reception hall diagonally in front of Kegelbanov's office and silently shook hands with his executive secretary, Shamayev. The latter half rose, tearing himself away from his papers briefly.

'He should be soon . . . ?'

'I'll wait.'

Sirotkin never made his subordinates wait. He didn't bother sitting down but walked over to a window, distractedly looking down at the ring road around Dzerzhinsky Square, intricately outlined in its springtime punctuation of fresh white paint. The flow of cars from Marx Prospect twisted around the monument and streamed apart down the various roads. Sirotkin stood looking for half an hour, not outwardly showing any feelings and afraid to absent himself, as then he might lose his chance to go in first. Two more heads of directorates came into the reception hall, wondering when Himself would be in. They shook hands with Sirotkin, exchanged a few phrases about the weather and went out.

But now the traffic policemen around the monument started energetically waving cars over to the kerb with their batons, freeing up the middle of the square, and Sirotkin understood that he didn't have much longer to wait. A black Volga sedan with a flashing yellow light flew past with two more behind it. 'Stop! Pull over to the kerb!' *They're trying!* Sirotkin smiled to himself. They were proving to the Boss that the wages they earned were not in vain. And his five-ton black ZIL-114, made of tank armour with bullet-proof glass, was now hurtling towards the

Lubyanka. And behind it a Volga full of boys in bullet-proof jackets. Sirotkin didn't curl his lip, didn't sigh. *It has to be that way. Chairmen come and go, but we abide. Today it's Kegelbanov, tomorrow he'll vanish, like all his predecessors, without exception: Yagoda, Yezhov, Beria, Serov, Semichastny – all of them, just like the last one, Iron Shurik Shelepin, that hard-assed Young Communist switching over here with all his hangers-on, done in by the ire of the old men. Today's man has been hanging on for a long time, but he'll burn out, just the same. They change, and we go on doing our work. Anyone can give orders, but the KGB needs thinking leaders, men with an understanding of what the prospects are. The trouble with every one of our chairmen has been that they didn't have enough genuine intellect. What causes me the most pain is the fact that it's impossible for me to implement the achievements of science in real life, of perfecting the work of the department as a whole.*

*Take, let's say, the conservatism of that directorate that works on the 'outside'. What ridiculous aloofness! What goals do they have? The non-conformity that we've been struggling with for several years already comes from the West. Only from the West! The basis of all our bases – ideology – is suffering. But that directorate keeps on talking about industrial espionage, about our people in the West purchasing this firm or that bank. It would be better if the KGB trained philosophers, writers, journalists and publishers here especially to go out there, to fill not just the Communist world but the whole world's press, radio and television with our people, so that the whole of the more liberated literature of the West would be what we need it to be. That would be when real peaceful coexistence would come along. People like Kegelbanov don't understand that. They say that it's all very expensive and its effectiveness isn't obvious. In reality, it's just adventurism to waste money on the arms race, on the means of physical annihilation, when the enemy needs to be annihilated spiritually. And here I am, wasting my strength on petty intrigues in order to oblige the leadership.*

Shamayev dived into the study and quickly came out again. That meant the Chairman had already come up in his lift and appeared in his study through his secret door.

'Kegelbanov requests that you wait a little while.'

Nodding in understanding, Sirotkin drummed his fingers on the folder lying on the windowsill. Soon, however, the buzzer sounded.

'You can go in now.'

'Sir!' Sirotkin said in military fashion, standing at attention in the doorway.

'Come in, Comrade Sirotkin,' said Kegelbanov cordially, touching the bridge of his gold-rimmed glasses with his ring finger. He was standing in the corner of his study next to the television set, in the bright sunlight from the window, arranging red carnations in a vase. Kegelbanov wiped his hands with a handkerchief and sat down behind his desk.

'Excuse me for keeping you waiting. Make your report, Comrade Sirotkin; I'm listening.'

Sirotkin took the typed report out of the folder and, bending down, set it in front of Kegelbanov. He himself sat down in the armchair to one side, which turned out to be lower than the chairman's, so that he had to look up at him from below.

'Spring?' Kegelbanov nodded in the direction of the windows, and the eyes behind the glasses crinkled merrily.

'That's right, spring,' Sirotkin bantered.

Kegelbanov sighed and began to look the text over. At one point, without taking his eyes from the line he was reading, he patted his hand around on the desk, feeling for a pencil; he took it and placed a fat red tick in the margin. Craning his neck, Sirotkin understood which part of the report had attracted Kegelbanov's attention and, pulling another sheet out, was already holding it in readiness so that at the end of his reading Sirotkin could place it on his desk. But, without reading the first one to the end Kegelbanov said: 'And that one?'

'A list was drawn up as well,' Sirotkin reported. 'A lot of work was done on it, as ordered.'

After reading through the list Kegelbanov looked over at the bunch of red carnations in the far corner of his study. 'That's all very well . . .'

he drawled, thinking of the conversation that he had just had half an hour ago with the Man Who Preferred To Stay In The Shadows. 'So, you think that we have complete unity on this?'

'In what sense do you mean?' asked Sirotkin carefully, divining that there was a logical dirty trick here but not yet understanding what kind.

'I have in mind a dialectical unity,' said Kegelbanov, and his eyes looked at Sirotkin with what seemed to be mockery. 'On the one hand, there *are* no political crimes in this country. And on the other? On the other, they all get successfully solved – is that what you mean?'

'Something like that,' agreed Sirotkin, for appearance's sake, appreciating the humour. 'But you *could* consider it slightly differently, after all: crimes are successfully solved, thanks to which they might not ever have existed.'

'They might not exist. But they do.'

Sirotkin was an experienced hand and kept silent so as to give his boss a chance to develop his train of thought.

'Of course, from an operational point of view, the faster it goes, the fewer the worries,' said Kegelbanov, standing up and again walking over to his flowers, where he once more began rearranging them. Glimmers of light from the crystal vase ran along the ceiling. Sirotkin got up as well and, standing, turned to keep facing the pacing chairman. 'Well, it's not a big deal. We could allow you to do it. But prospectively we should demonstrate the unity of the Party and the People at the threshold of Lenin's hundredth anniversary; and not a dialectical unity but a total one! What do you think – won't these preventive measures of yours conflict with the directive on complete unity?'

'We're still sorting out Czechoslovakia,' Sirotkin carefully reminded him. 'After all, that's something, too . . .' He fell silent because he felt that his reasoning wasn't quite in unison with the leadership's. His report on the completion of the work wasn't having the right effect. Something had changed, and the preceding task wasn't of any interest to the leadership any more. What was going on? Which aspect of what had been accomplished should he emphasize, so that it would be approved? 'If I understand you correctly, hearings in open court are now uncalled for?'

'Open ones? Let's think about it . . . You undertake these court hearings, but the West is attacking the Politburo. Who, then, I ask, are we guarding and from whom?'

'But there was formerly a political expediency, after all, and it produced its own results –'

'Here's what you do, Comrade Sirotkin,' Kegelbanov interrupted quietly. 'You act within your professional guidelines, show some initiative. We appreciate you for that. But don't go getting into politics. Leave that to us, the Party workers. Do you have any objections?'

'I'm a military man. I carry out my orders.'

'That's good. So, you understand that the situation has changed. Although not enough yet that we can relax. Educating the intelligentsia is necessary, especially in connection with ideology. But the less they see of you the better.'

'Can I try out any new methods?' asked Sirotkin carefully and as if in passing.

'If the doctors have approved it I can't forbid you to. But not on all of them at once. Just try one, not more. On somebody who's unknown in Europe.'

'We'll find one!'

'Of course you will. But, I repeat, keep out of politics. Vary your methods. Why should I be teaching you this? And the rest of them you can leave to the Moscow Directorate for the time being – let them keep an eye on them, and we'll see what's there, after the centenary.'

'That's clear enough,' said Sirotkin and nodded. 'I brought the file along with me. Would you like to take a look?'

But Kegelbanov was already thinking about other, more governmental things. 'Let's not mark time here,' he said, his face screwing up. 'In a couple of days the issue of the funding necessary for a broadening of our organization is going to be debated. We'll have to get them interested in significant measures we've undertaken in order to warrant attention. Do you have any suggestions, Comrade Sirotkin?'

'I'm not strictly ready, but, taking a general view, we need funding for some experimental research . . .'

'On people?'

Sirotkin nodded in silence. Kegelbanov pondered for about half a minute. The earpieces of his gold glasses scintillated in the sunlight.

'That's interesting, but it's still early days. Work the thing out in theory first. Anything else? The requirements of your directorate should be submitted in written form, then we'll think about them. Is that all?'

'One tiny question.' Sirotkin understood that his audience was at an end. 'I got a call from the Ministry of Internal Affairs. There's a murderer breaking into people's apartments with a file. He kills women; several of the corpses had been raped as well. Around forty victims. They can't find him by themselves, and they're asking us for help.'

'Help? What do they think – that we've got lots of free time? Or extra personnel? What do *you* think?'

'That's just what I told them,' said Sirotkin and nodded his head one more time.

# 57

# Such Is Life in the Party

Only after eight o'clock at night did Thick Eyebrows finish signing papers and send his three assistants out of his office. It fell silent right away, so much so that it was hard on the ears. He didn't like that kind of silence; it oppressed him. He walked over to a window draped in thick white curtains and looked through the crack. Out there it was quiet as well. The cobblestoned square with its little park was empty, from in front of his window all the way to the Tsar Cannon. The populace wasn't allowed into the Kremlin any more. There were only two cars parked down below, at the entranceway. His new ZIL wasn't there, so that nobody would be able to determine where the master was at the moment. His bodyguard thought up their own ruses.

He was tired. His eyes, overstrained by long exertion, watered periodically. His lower abdomen was giving him discomfort, an unpleasant sensation from which he had been able to get no relief for some time. But he smiled and gazed around the square with a curiosity undiminished by age, and his mood lifted somewhat. The day had gone well, he'd had a great deal of success, but he now felt the value of passing time more sharply, even though he hadn't lost any irony with regard to himself. This helped to preserve his reserves of optimism and firmness of mind, something the majority of his associates had lost.

Right now, recalling something, he harrumphed, stepped over to his desk and, after rooting around in a bottom drawer, took out a small coloured reproduction of a painting by the artist Nalbandyan. Stalin, in military uniform, standing in this very same office. True, the furniture had been changed. The edges of the reproduction were crumpled; it had been lying there for a long time, of course. When he was familiarizing himself with these premises he, the new master, had found it in the desk of one of his executive secretaries and taken it for himself. Stalin was barely perceptibly smiling.

Thick Eyebrows took a pair of scissors out of the middle drawer of his desk and neatly cut out the Generalissimo's head, endeavouring not to touch his collar and marshal's star. Picking up the head with two fingers he tidily dropped it into a wastepaper basket. Then, after rooting around a little more, he took his own photograph, of a similar size, out of the drawer and put it underneath the reproduction. His head turned out to be a bit bigger, and he had to cut some more around the edges of the opening.

He gazed at himself in the uniform of the Generalissimo and came to the conclusion that the uniform looked good on him. If he had obtained this power when he was younger he could have done a lot more than he had now. He started counting up the number of orders and medals that he and Stalin had between them. He laid them out in columns, neatly writing out the numbers reduced to carry from one unit to another in subtraction. Stalin's awards turned out to be eleven more than his. *But, after all, Stalin isn't getting any more medals, and the motherland will be able to award me more if I work honestly, with full expenditure of my strength.*

This thought delighted him. Stalin had never taken these baubles seriously, even though he had been assured they were important. *It's impossible to resist certain traditions. And the more power you have, the less you can do.* He had been his own master from an early age, in minor positions. But here things had their own momentum; they all whirled around apart from one's will. Any subordinate could order him around, and *en masse* they did what they wanted. Sometimes matters were taken care of before he even had a chance to figure them out. The telephone rang. He picked up the receiver and coughed.

'Do you want Comrade Sagaydak? May I connect you? Connecting . . .'

'Sir!' he said in military-style greeting. 'How are you feeling?'

'And you?' asked Sagaydak. 'If my memory doesn't betray me it's time for us to meet. When can you find half an hour?'

'Let's do it tomorrow . . . although, no, tomorrow's Wednesday – a meeting of the Council of Ministers . . . so Thursday . . . Thursday I have the Politburo. Friday won't work either: that's the Central Committee secretariat . . .'

'Then when?'

'How about right now?'

'Hmm,' said Sagaydak. 'I'm ready.'

'Good! I'll send around my car.'

He scooped up the Nalbandyan reproduction with the hole cut out where the head should have been and, tearing it into tiny pieces, consigned it to the wastebasket, when his other phone, the direct line, rang.

'This is Kegelbanov. Sorry to bother you. Could you let me in for a short report?'

Comrade Thick Eyebrows breathed heavily into the phone, hard pressed as how to answer. He couldn't refuse to receive Kegelbanov – it was evidently something important that he didn't want to talk about over the phone. But he would have to respond, make a decision, and he was tired; he needed a rest.

'This is what we'll do,' he said, recovering. 'As soon as I'm free I'll call you. Where will you be? At your *dacha*? Good!'

He glanced at the electric clock: it was past eight thirty. They would be bringing Sagaydak very soon. He listened for steps outside his door. That was probably him right now.

In the company of a grey-uniformed deputy of the Kremlin guard commandant the rudely healthy Sagaydak really was approaching, walking at a staid pace down the corridor. He was dressed in a suede jacket the colour of a tanned woman's back and a pair of well-ironed grey-flannel trousers, swinging his doctor's bag. Alongside him minced the miniature Alla, with her restrained gait, from time to time touching her shoulder against their companion.

Sagaydak had been more than a bit surprised at being invited to the Kremlin and not Thick Eyebrows' *dacha*. He had walked into the loggia, where Alla was lying naked taking an air bath.

'Get ready, my girl, quick now!' said Sagaydak. 'I'm going out on a call, and you'll be needed, too. Only dress a bit more modestly, and don't forget your Young Communist badge.'

Now Alla was walking down the corridor in a severe suit, something similar to what the stewardesses on Aeroflot's international flights wore but with a skirt all of eight inches above her knees. On one of her pointed little breasts shone her Young Communist badge, on the other a tag that read 'Exemplary Socialist Competitor'. The soft-green colour of the walls, on which lay the barely noticeable shadows of the pleats in the white silk curtains that completely covered the windows, created a pleasant half-light. Bright parquetry, of an ideal cleanliness, gleamed at their feet. A soft strip of carpet over it muffled the sound of their footsteps. At every turn stood an unarmed soldier in a brown tunic and brown beret, looking simultaneously down both branches of the corridor.

The deputy commandant stopped and asked them to wait. Sagaydak nodded and, leaning his case against a sofa, sank into a soft armchair. Alla, clasping her hands over her clenched knees, sat modestly next to him. They didn't have to wait long. The major had barely managed to throw the door panels wide when Thick Eyebrows emerged, hurrying towards them, spreading his arms in readiness to embrace the rising Sagaydak.

'Hello, my dear!' he exclaimed. 'So glad to see you. Thanks for not forgetting about me!' The guest had to bend down a bit while their host had to stand on tiptoes in order for their heights to coincide, and then they hugged. 'Madame!' the host then pronounced in dashing tones, turning to Alla and kissing her willowy hand. Alla touchingly blinked her long lashes.

*He's started dyeing his eyebrows*, noted Sagaydak, continuing to smile.

'You haven't been here with me before?' their host asked. 'Then come on in. I'll show you around.'

He opened the door and invited them in with a wave of his hand, solicitously allowing them to go ahead. In a long room with walls of red wood panelling there were chairs upholstered in green leather arranged neatly around an endless table covered in green baize. On the table in front of every place lay four neatly sharpened pencils and a clean writing pad.

'The Politburo holds its meetings here,' said their host. 'As they say in the papers, it's one of Lenin's traditions, so we're not about to break it.'

Sagaydak looked closely at the speaker. Solicitude and loathing mingled somehow incomprehensibly in Sagaydak's mind, his human dislike of certain people with his physician's duty to cure them. Like a toothache that can reduce the splendid health of a body down to nothing, this suffering was the only flaw in his otherwise happy, absolutely cynical existence. *Surely it's not the fault of this patient of yours*, he once again asked himself, *that on God's earth no lesser position had been found for him? Surely he'd like to hide himself away somewhere in the country, raise his grandchildren? Surely he's in a tragic situation?*

'Excuse me, my dear!' Sagaydak forced himself to relinquish these inappropriate thoughts because his host was saying something to him. 'I didn't quite catch what you said.'

'I'm saying that over there, at the head of the table, sits Comrade Thick Eyebrows,' he laughed, inviting laughter at himself. 'Here he makes his speeches. And here he checks over and signs important papers in the presence of members of the Politburo. Here is where it comes clear who gets to say nothing at all and who doesn't.'

'Right!' Sagaydak smiled sympathetically. His host started laughing as well, and his eyes shone. He rocked right and left with his laughter, and the diamond pin on his red tie twinkled. Alla attended politely. She could read their lips, but she had the ability to let things pass that were of no interest to her.

'And where does this door lead?' asked Sagaydak.

'That's the walnut room. Go on in, don't be afraid. This is where they sit around discussing issues before our meetings. Democracy! Well, come on into my study. This is where I manage things from,' he said wearily, opening his arms wide.

'Can I try?' smiled Sagaydak, politely making his way to the armchair.

Part of the writing desk was occupied by a glass hemisphere with stuck-on golden coins. Next to it lay copies of *Izvestia*, *Pravda* and *Trudovaya Pravda* and on the other side of them Wulf ballpoint pens from Germany.

'What's this?' Sagaydak pointed at a group of telephones on a small table.

'Connections with every point in the country.'

'But the buttons? There have to be around fifty of them.'

'The top ones are every Politburo member, the lower ones the Central Committee secretariat, the rest – the Council of Ministers, the State Planning Committee, various ministers . . .'

'Right! And what's that red thing over there?' Sagaydak swivelled around in the chair.

'The red phone is a direct line to the leaders of the Warsaw Pact countries.'

'And this?'

Under glass sat two telephone sets, a grey one and a red one. And beneath it one, two, three . . . fifteen buttons. Their host squirmed.

'Ooooooh!' Sagaydak said, unoffended. 'Looks like you've got a line straight to the Lord and all his apostles . . .'

'Precisely!'

'Well, what about me? Do I suit the place?'

'Sitting in the chair there, you look good,' his host eagerly agreed. 'But what next? How are you going to direct things? What are you actually going to do? It's easy enough to sit at home in your easy chair and tell jokes about your leaders. But how would you manage the helm? If something went wrong, you know yourself . . . We'd better have a cup of coffee, my dear doctor!'

He pulled aside a curtain and revealed a secret door made to look like a bookshelf. In the adjoining room stood a bed, lacquered armchairs and a mirror, all very homey. A couch was spread with a flowered rug. On a brown table next to a television set lay a lighter and cigarettes. Alla picked up a coloured photograph from the table. On it was a picture of Thick

Eyebrows in glasses behind his desk. He was writing something.

'They make me look younger in my photos,' said their host. 'But that's a falsehood!'

'It happens!' Sagaydak offered, indeterminately.

'Happens? But who's forcing them to write nonsense? We demand, we remonstrate, and it's in vain! After all, there's nothing to read in the newspapers at times.'

After cautiously knocking at the door a waiter came in and started setting the table.

'Shall I put out some brandy?'

'Not under any circumstances! You're free to go.' His master followed him out with his eyes, placed a finger to his lips and only then walked over to the door of the safe hidden in the wall.

'We won't be doing any drinking,' he said sternly. 'But a swallow apiece, for the sake of our getting together . . . After all, it was only a short while ago I was drinking a lot and eating a lot and was as strong as an ox. But you're giving me a reproachful look: I mustn't gain weight; I mustn't sit around all day! But how else am I going to manage the country?'

'Maybe you can manage it standing up?' Sagaydak proposed to him in the same tone.

The Secretary General chuckled and rubbed his leg where a bullet was lodged. Sagaydak knew how it had got there. In the heroic battle of Malaya Zemlya the colonel, who didn't at the time have such majestic eyebrows, was caught by another officer on the couch with his wife. The colonel tried to jump out a window, but a bullet caught up with him.

'Does it hurt?' Sagaydak asked solicitously.

'Just aches a little . . .'

'Then let's move on from international affairs to internal ones.' Sagaydak got up, opened his case and took out a crumpled white smock. 'Where's your sink? Urinate for me! I'll check your stream pressure.'

'Is that really necessary?' his host said warily, looking askance at Alla.

'Very! She'll turn away. There . . . Nothing wrong with the pressure yet. Not bad.'

'Well, hey! I tell you, I can do some more! Listen. Tell me as a friend: what kind of pressure does you-know-who have, the Man Who's Always In The Shadows?'

'Well, now –' Sagaydak started to answer.

'I know, I know! Medical ethics . . . But can't you tell me confidentially? Worse or better? I won't say a word, after all!'

'What can I do? Of course . . .' The doctor tried to wriggle out of it and finally figured out how. 'I have to tell you straight up: both of you are fine in this regard. The both of you are ready right now for the *subbotnik*. We'll have a look, however . . . Take off your trousers and get down on all fours, as usual. Alla, my girl, hand me my glove and the vaseline.'

Obediently dropping his trousers, the patient climbed on to the couch. His upper part in shirt and tie remained the Secretary General, while his lower, with its pale skin, seemed an ordinary part of a rank-and-file member of the Party. With practised movements Sagaydak pulled the rubber glove on to his right hand while Alla opened the jar. Scooping a portion of the vaseline on his index finger and slapping the patient with his other hand, the doctor made him move aside and sat down on the edge of the couch. He drew his finger down the patient's body, dividing it into two halves, as if distinguishing a site for resection, then groped for the necessary spot and inserted his finger with an abrupt motion.

'Oho!'

'Hard to cure, easy to bury,' joked Sagaydak. 'Well, sir, let's look and see how things are in there . . . Have you heard this joke? The urologist says to the patient: "Please bend over, sir." And the patient says to him: "Listen, my dear man! In such intimate moments you can dispense with the formality!" Does that hurt?'

'Not much . . .'

'How about this?'

'Ouch! That hurts!'

'By the way, I have a small request. There's this fellow Makartsev, the editor of *Trudovaya Pravda*.'

'I know who he is.'

The doctor tenderly drew his finger over the man's prostate gland.

'Well, the police have got ahold of his son.'

'Shchelokov does?'

'Well, maybe not personally him . . . Couldn't you close the case and let the boy go?' Sagaydak pressed harder.

'Oy-yoy! That hurts!'

The doctor glanced at the telephone connected to the Warsaw Pact countries out of the corner of his eye. It was a good thing the patient couldn't reach it or heaven alone knew how this massage would end!

'I understand that it hurts,' he said, suddenly and cruelly, 'but massage is imperative, my dear boy! Your capacity for work as well as your general tonus will improve. So what about Makartsev's lad?' And he pressed still harder.

'I'll try . . .'

'That's nice then.' Sagaydak's finger became more sociable and tenderly resumed its back-and-forth massage. 'Well, that's enough for today . . . My girl, give him a novocaine injection.'

Nodding, Alla quickly pulled out a syringe and broke the head off an ampoule. Wiping the skin just below his spine with a cotton swab soaked in alcohol, she skilfully gave him his injection and kissed the swabbed spot.

'You can put your clothes on,' Sagaydak said, pulling off his rubber glove. 'I'm satisfied.'

'Thanks, you ministerial mind, you. Listen, since we've been talking about Makartsev. After all, he was the one who came up with the idea, and now every department is looking for funding from the *subbotnik*. What would you use the money for?'

'If you're not joking, let's have some for impotentology, eh? After all, the future of mankind depends on it!'

'I know, I know what the future of mankind depends on!' his host patted the doctor on the shoulder. 'You think it depends on people's willies. And the Minister of Defence thinks it's missiles. Who am I supposed to believe? Oh, if only I could just decide that by myself! Everything has to have a way cleared for it, has to be sneaked in, agreed to. Sometimes you lose heart. Power these days lies with everyone. Every cook and bottle-washer has power. If she doesn't want to, she won't feed anyone, and there's nothing you can do to her. Everyone has power, because this is a democracy. I'm the only one who's powerless. I depend on everyone. Here I just went, promising to do something about Makartsev's little son. Makartsev is one of ours. So how to do that I still don't know. You wind up running around like a hamster on a wheel . . .'

The lights changed to green at the Spasskaya Tower gates in good time, and the policemen on the beat straightened their backs. The car sped through Red Square past Lobnoye Mesto and the monument to Minin and Pozharsky towards Kuybyshev Street.

Sagaydak stared silently at the road. The more use he made of Thick Eyebrows, the more liking he felt for him. *Of course, he does treat me bet-ter than he treats other people. The whole Fourth Chief Directorate of the Ministry of Health is on duty around him day and night. But I'm the one who looks after him. He doesn't trust those people! Why should I care about those others? He has fun, he jokes around, but not out of happiness. It's just danc-ing on his grave. Everyone in the country is unhappy, and he's even less happy than the rest. He hasn't been lucky in life. Everyone else is one of the lads, and he's the Leader. By comparison with him, I'm a free man! By comparison with me, he's a slave. The Man Who Preferred To Stay In The Shadows stands behind his back and pesters him, but he's no more in charge either. My God, what frightful power! Everyone chained together and constantly pulling on one another, not knowing where to go. Rappoport is right: this cage was made for everyone. Isn't that so, my girl?*

Alla dropped her eyelashes in token of agreement. She could always read his thoughts and most often accepted them without objection.

# 58

# 777

Sitting at his desk, Comrade Thick Eyebrows wrinkled his nose and massaged his eyebrows with his fingers to help him get rid of the dandruff there. He opened the middle drawer of his desk and took out a packet of cigarettes. He was struggling with himself, trying to protect his vocal cords, which were now in a state of chronic inflammation. He had been ordered to limit himself to a single cigarette per hour, and they had brought him an imported automatic cigarette case with a clockwork mechanism that opened the lid only once every hour. But twenty minutes after a smoke he could never wait any longer for the thing to open up again. So he had to resort to guile. In another pocket of his jacket and in his desk he kept packs of cigarettes in reserve and smoked them in the intervals. But he told his doctors that he was smoking less, thanks to the automatic cigarette case. The ringing of the telephone distracted him from his cigarette. Hearing the voice he felt happy, and his eyes lit up.

'Dad, when are you coming home?'

'Hello, my girl. I've got a lot of work . . . I'm just finishing up now.' He was happy that she had called. He didn't want to go home. Moments of complete peace like this seldom came along.

'Come home quick! My brother has just flown in. And I can't wait for you to get home.'

'Yes, you can. Since the whole family's together now, tell your mother I'm coming straight home.'

His wife hadn't gone to bed; she was dozing, sitting in the kitchen. She heard the lift door slam and went to open their door herself, not waiting for the bell. Two dogs – a Great Dane and a Siberian Layka – threw themselves with a yelp into the entrance hall in front of their mistress. Both of them leaped up and down, trying to lick their master's face. He calmed them down, patting them tenderly and scratching behind their ears.

'I beg you, don't get mad at our daughter,' his wife said quickly, forestalling any possible trouble. 'She wants to borrow three and a half thousand roubles. We have to give it to her . . .'

'I know what she means by "borrow",' he laughed.

His wife hung up his fine fur-lined raincoat. 'You don't look very well. Have you been smoking again? Do you want some dinner?'

'No time. I brought home some papers, I have to work for a while . . .' He looked at her round, kindly face with its unsightly uneven teeth. 'Give her the money. Of course, give it to her. What can one do with her once the bit's between her teeth?'

'I already did.'

It bothered him that his daughter treated him like a commodity and gave him no little distress. *She had her baby girl, then left her here with us and went off sleeping around. She makes scenes in public; she gets up to mischief; she drinks. It's nice that at least she gets to travel abroad incognito. Now they inform me that she's met a police lieutenant colonel and is seeing him. He'll have to marry her: I've had enough of her disgracing me. After all, she's not a girl any more – she's forty!*

After kissing his daughter he didn't stop to talk to her but headed off to his room, where he had a desk and a couch, intending to lie down and read through several papers. His son was lying on the couch with his feet up on the back of it. He hadn't removed his shoes. A bottle and a shot glass sat on the floor next to the couch. The dogs ambled in behind him and lay down on the carpet, thumping their tails against the floor.

'Drinking like you used to, eh, Son?'

'I'm fine, Pop! You've been out partying yourself.'

'Let me lie down on the couch, and you sit somewhere else.' The father bent down and kissed his son and, while leaning over, saw that the bottle on the floor was mineral water. 'Have you come back to Moscow for long?'

'A day or two, if you don't help me stay a little longer.'

'Sweden getting you down? What is it that you'd like?' *How come my children never ask me how I feel, how things are? How come they remember their father only when they need help? It's my own fault. Whatever way they've turned out, it's my fault. At his age I was making something of myself, while he gets everything done for him. But, essentially, he's a good boy.* 'How are my grandchildren doing over there?'

'Fine. They told me to give you a kiss. I'm going to bring them to the *dacha* this summer.'

'And what kind of help do you want from me, Son?' The father had stretched out on the couch, while the son had perched himself in the arm-chair.

'Well, nothing special. I was thinking it's something good for you, as well . . .'

'What, exactly?'

'Install me as KGB chairman, Pop.'

'You?'

'Why not? I'm not any dumber than Kegelbanov. He'll sell you out at the first hint of trouble. You'll rest a lot easier this way.'

'Well, what the hell . . . It's not a bad idea, Son. But can you handle it? Let's give it a try. So that nothing gets put off, this Monday you go and start work at the Lubyanka.'

'Seriously? Or are you joking?'

'Joking? And . . . what? Kegelbanov's people are really tiresome, watching over you and not letting you fall into the hands of the bourgeois press? And here they hide your girlfriends from your wife, pay your bills for you, drive you around, watch over you . . .'

'Why not live it up when you've got the chance? You didn't waste any of your time either, after all. And it's not me they watch over but you, Pop!'

'So be it. And who would you have been if it wasn't for me? And don't yell like that. They can hear upstairs.'

'The Kegelbanovs are at their *dacha*, Father, I went by their apartment. You should have moved to a mansion a long time ago. A five-room apartment on the fifth floor . . . In Sweden anybody with a job lives better than that! I'm ashamed to tell people in the West.'

'Well, Son, I don't live for the West. I'm a Russian. I serve the people. Kegelbanov obeys my every word, but let me make you the chairman of the KGB and you'd jail your own dear father! I'm joking, of course. But that job is *not* for you!'

'Forget it, Pop. I was joking, too . . . I don't need a position like that. I can make my own career. Let's drink to that.'

'To that, sure . . .'

A bottle of brandy and thimble-glasses filled to the brim were brought from the sideboard. They clinked the glasses.

'Are you going home or are you staying with us tonight?'

'I'll go home, Pop. I'll get a good night's sleep, and then in the morning I'll get to work on my career.'

'Then go and give me some rest. It's almost one o'clock.'

The father watched through the space between his floor-length curtains. He waited for his son to get into his car and drive off. A second black Volga rolled up after him and concealed itself under an arch. The father stretched out on the couch, pulling a Japanese transistor radio over to him. With a wan hand he turned the dial, located some music and then heard himself being mentioned in Russian. 'The Kremlin overlord soberly debated the –' From that point an unbroken howl of radio jamming kicked in, and he didn't find out what he had soberly debated.

He tried to snooze a bit, but he could feel a slight pain in his groin. *It'll ache and then it'll go away by itself.* Now he remembered Sagaydak's request. Tomorrow, affairs would be in a whirl and catching him up – he wouldn't be up to it. What would be the best way to do it on a principled basis? He quietly got up from the couch, and the two dogs instantly stood up and moved towards the door, following their master.

'Ssshhh!' he said, wagging his finger at them.

Everyone in the apartment was asleep. His daughter hadn't gone out; she'd stayed for the night: her raincoat was hanging from the coat rack. *She's decided to sleep alone*, her father thought, querulously. He took down

his overcoat and, without putting it on, shifted the heavy bar and pulled
back the two locks.

'What are you up to?' came a cranky whisper from behind him.

'What did you get up for, Mother? Don't stick your nose into other
people's business!'

His mother in her eighty-second year was strong, and she had never
known any illness. She treated her son strictly, being of the opinion that
children were always children and give them one indulgence and they'd
be running after another one straight away.

'How's this none of my business?' she whispered. 'Come time to take
the dogs out for a walk in the rain, that's my business, but all of a sudden it ain't. You just turn yourself around and come inside! What are you
up to in the middle of the night?'

He stood there and laughed. He liked his mother shouting at him like
at a little boy. It made him feel younger, more energetic. He hugged her
and kissed her white hair.

'Go to bed, Mummy. Get to sleep. Don't you worry. I've got some government affairs . . .'

She stepped away and continued sternly: 'What sort of government
affairs are in the middle of the night? I know what kind! Turn around,
I say!'

The dogs began snarling, feeling a conflict brewing, but with their
simple minds they couldn't decide whether it was serious or whose side
to take, and therefore they were snarling in an indeterminate sort of way.
Their master had, in the meantime, opened the door; the dogs, always
ready for a walk, slipped out on the landing and thus were on his side now,
growling at his mother. He managed to pull the door closed behind him
so that she couldn't come out on the landing as well.

'You just wait. You'll be up to no good' could be heard from behind
the door. 'I'll take down your bloody pants and take your own belt to you.
I won't care if you're ashamed. Then you can go out and have more fun!'

He and the dogs were already descending in the lift. From the lobby
behind them leaped out two sinewy young men in light-blue Japanese

sports jackets, wiping their eyes and yawning.

'Ssshh! Stay there, boys, I'll go on my own.'

He hurried to the Mercedes that had been given to him as a present not long before and got behind the wheel. His bodyguards ran to their Volgas.

'Hey!' he yelled to them, wagging a finger. 'I said stay here!' The dogs in the back of the car growled their displeasure.

'We can't. You're not supposed to go out without a bodyguard. We'll get into trouble . . .'

'I'm coming straight back, boys. Don't tell on me, and nobody will know. Go back to sleep!'

They pretended to obey him and turned back to the entranceway. He started the engine and made off without letting it warm up. His bodyguard waited a bit and then surreptitiously plumped into their cars, so as to give him a lead but not lose him from sight.

On Kutuzov Prospect, wet after being washed down, he glanced into a police booth: there was no traffic policeman there. He turned right towards the Arch and its Borodino panorama, then thought for a moment, picked up his telephone and dialled a number.

'Kegelbanov?'

'Yes, sir!' a sleepy voice answered shortly. 'Has something happened?'

'What are you doing? Are you in bed?'

'No . . .' the man answered in confusion.

'I need you.'

Kegelbanov had already been informed about it, and he was ready with a response, although he had reproved the service: Politburo members had long ago agreed not to eavesdrop on one another. 'I'll be there in twenty minutes,' he said.

Thick Eyebrows' heart warmed at such expeditiousness from his KGB chief, but he said: 'Here's what. I'll drive over to your place. Only don't make a big deal out of it.'

The watch on his wrist showed twenty minutes to two. The night was transparent, still, the sky full of stars. The Mercedes turned off the Minsk

Chaussee on to the Rublyov, from the Rublyov on to the Uspenskoye and sped along the empty road, down the white central strip, making the turns with tyres screeching. Thick Eyebrows loved driving fast.

The guard around Kegelbanov's *dacha*, forewarned, recognized the visitor and greeted him. Kegelbanov, dressed in a dark suit and a snow-white shirt and tie, his overcoat slung over his shoulder, hurried to meet him along the asphalt driveway, lit by daylight-coloured lamps. The only thing he hadn't managed to do was shave. The door of the Mercedes opened wide, but the driver sat and waited for Kegelbanov to come closer. The dogs, not waiting for a command, squeezed out from behind the front seat and, baying, broke free. Kegelbanov raised a hand in welcome and smiled, even though he was taken aback at the sight of the dogs.

'Come on into the house,' Kegelbanov said, stretching out a hand to help his visitor out of the car.

'Nice *dacha*,' his guest said dreamily, looking around at the structure, overgrown with wild grape vines. 'I remember everyone who's lived in it . . . We won't go into the house. Let's talk here.'

Shivering in the damp night, Kegelbanov stood in front of him, muffling himself up in his overcoat. The sky in the east was starting just perceptibly to brighten.

'Where do you think we should channel the money from the *sub-botnik*?'

Kegelbanov was expecting a different topic of conversation, the one that he had been informed about, and didn't have an answer to this question ready. 'Well, if they want to have it go on strengthening the organs, we wouldn't say no . . .'

'That's it exactly: strengthen the organs,' his guest laughed. 'Some people are of the opinion that we need to develop the field of urology.'

'Urology? What's that? The one that –'

'Exactly! We're falling considerably behind the West in it. We have to think about future generations, and they depend, first and foremost, on urology. You don't believe it? Let's talk to the Minister of Health.'

The visitor went back to his car, lit up a cigarette, picked up the phone and dialled a number.

'Petrovsky? His wife? And is he asleep? Wake him up. I'll wait . . . Listen, Comrade Petrovsky. I'm holding a little conference here. Tell me, is urology of any significance? It is? Very much so? That's what I thought. But Kegelbanov here has his doubts. Some people are of the opinion that the funds from the all-Union *subbotnik* should be set aside for the development of urology. What? And oncology, yes . . . The Ministry of Health won't object? Goodnight, then.'

The visitor put down the phone and walked over to a rose bush, already with its winter wrapping off, and touched the thorns on the stems.

'By the way, the *subbotnik* idea was proposed by the editor of *Trudovaya Pravda*, Makartsev, our man . . .'

'I know,' nodded Kegelbanov, satisfied that his service hadn't made a mistake and that the conversation was heading in the anticipated direction. 'He's got some trouble with his son?'

He said this half-inquiringly to make sure that the other unpleasantness awaiting Editor-in-Chief Makartsev was something his guest was still unaware of. Makartsev himself didn't interest Kegelbanov, but he knew that the man carried out functions for Comrade Skinny, the Man Who Preferred To Stay In The Shadows. Comrade Skinny had told Kegelbanov not long before to let certain people go ahead and think that they were the ones who ran the country. The hint was taken unambiguously. *But it can have a flip side. It's always nice to have a trump card. Have to keep it in my hand, though, and when and how to use it, time will tell. His son, now – he's just a minor issue.*

His guest walked a little way down the drive, then turned around and said: 'Maybe Makartsev doesn't need this trouble – he's got enough on his plate with that heart attack.'

'I've got you,' nodded Kegelbanov. 'In the morning I'll go in to the Committee, and together with the Ministry of Internal Affairs we'll resolve this issue positively . . .'

Right there Kegelbanov steered the conversation on to a different subject, and his visitor liked that. *Stalin was a good organizer*, he thought, *but*

*he was afraid of his comrades-in-arms and was always getting rid of them.
I trust my comrades, though, and they're all true to me. Right now the
apparatus is working well; it's reliable precisely because everyone has known
each other for many years, grown up together, made their way up the ladder
together.*

'Shall we have some supper?'

'What kind of supper at this hour? It's time for breakfast!'

They laughed and shook hands. The visitor whistled for the dogs, got
them into the car and, turning sharply, drove back down the drive between
the trees. The inside guards had locked the gate. Now that it was almost
dawn the sky had grown brighter still. He stopped and got out at the
guardhouse, out of curiosity. Under the roof gutter stood an old white bathtub to collect rainwater. There wasn't any water in it now, and something
was moving.

Fat spiders crawled along the slope of the roof, hung on cobwebs over
the bathtub, lowered themselves down and climbed up again. He
passed a hand through the air, and several spiders fell into the bathtub.
They were unable to make their way back up its smooth enamelled walls.
Some of those in the tub, already chewed up by their brethren, lay unmoving, legs upwards; others still struggled, trying to climb back to the roof.
But up there, on the webs they had spun, other spiders were already in
residence, awaiting their prey, and it was unlikely that they would feel like
sharing their food with the former owners. Those in the tub scuttled
around, spasmodically moving their legs, crawling over the bodies of their
kin and sliding with a rustle down the slippery walls. He picked up a twig,
tracked a spider that had made it up the side further than the others and
knocked it down. His brethren below fiercely threw themselves on him.
After gazing a little longer at the spiders' struggles he tossed the twig away
into the bushes and summoned the guards.

Once through the gates he yawned and stepped on the accelerator, rac-
ing back into the city. Tiredness was taking its toll, and he screwed up his
eyes so they wouldn't stick together. Then he saw them in the mirror: two
black Volgas with red lights on their roofs were on his tail. They weren't

going to let him off; they were working, their wages wouldn't be in vain. He slowed down and waved to them. They waved back at him in greeting. But he again pressed down hard on the accelerator and sped up.

'No way! You won't catch me!'

They fell behind again. He had a Mercedes, and they had Volgas, cars that still hadn't achieved a world-class standard. On Kutuzov Prospect the needle on his speedometer reached a hundred miles an hour. He flew down the middle lane, in between the two solid white lines, moving to one side only at the Triumphal Arch. At Building 24, his own, stood another two Volgas full of young men. Evidently they were all seriously worried. He tore past them as well, flew over the bridge next to the Hotel Ukraina and suddenly caught sight of another two black Volgas ranged across the middle of the bridge, the lads trying to flag him down.

He braked sharply, and the back end of the Mercedes went into a slight skid on the just-watered asphalt. His right side slammed into a Volga, crumpling his fender and door, and his engine died. The boot flew open from the blow. They were soon surrounded by more cars, the ones that were finally catching up. The boys in their black uniforms with ties, calling to each other, poured out of their cars and rushed over to help him out.

'Caught up with me at last, have you?' he said, crawling out of the car. 'The Old Guard never surrenders! Who's got a smoke?'

The dogs crawled out after him and stood beside him, wagging their tails. He laughed. And they all laughed, satisfied that their duty had been done, that he wouldn't be upbraiding them and that all had ended well. He tossed away his cigarette end.

'Here's what, boys. Here's an idea!'

He walked over to the open boot, glancing at the crumpled fender on the way, and pulled a bottle out of the cooler. The bodyguard smiled, buzzing approvingly; everyone began rubbing their hands.

'Well, hey, get that cork out! This is that classy port Three Sevens. We'll have a shot each.'

'What are we drinking out of?'

'Get you, lads – aristocrats! From the bottle of course.'

The boys produced a corkscrew – 'the agitator's companion' in Party jargon. Taking the bottle from the hand of the detachment chief, he threw his head back and a fine red stream flowed into his mouth. He drank calmly, in small swallows, and then took the bottle from his mouth and looked to see how much he had drunk.

'Hey! Come on, drink up . . .'

The bottle went from hand to hand; everyone drank from it, everyone was having fun, when the phone in the car rang.

'That'll be my wife, boys!' he said. 'It's a good thing you can't hear smells over the phone, right?'

He was handed the receiver.

'Yes, it's me. Coming right now. That's it!'

'Time for you to get some rest,' said one of his bodyguards solicitously. 'You're tired, I'll bet.'

'I'm strong as an ox! Nothing can shake me up!'

He suddenly had an irresistible urge to do what he hadn't done for a long time, and he looked around in search of a spot. Undoing his fly, he walked over to the parapet of the bridge, accompanied by the dogs. His bodyguards were right behind them.

'Hey, screen me off!'

They surrounded him in a thick wall, leaving him facing the parapet. Down below, past the black wrought-iron grille of crossed hammers and sickles, ice floes floated silently by in the dark waters of the Moscow River. Cold and damp wafted off it.

'I'll tell you this for nothing, boys. The most important thing is your health!'

He felt a slight pain at the very start, but then his stream flowed normally. The pressure was good, you could even say perfect – too bad for the enemies of Peace, Democracy and Progress.

# 59

# Hockey Fans

Kashin tore himself away from his papers and, putting his head in his hands, followed the lazy movements of the fish in the aquarium. He was thinking about mermaids – they would have to have an enormous aquarium, a whole swimming-pool. Mermaids were better than ordinary women in that they lured and seduced you; with women you had to take them out, propose to them, talk them into it, and you still didn't know if it was going to work out or not. Kashin tried to analyse his mistakes, shuffling and reshuffling all the possible and impossible variants yet again. But meanwhile he couldn't forget the objective deficiencies of the girls and women he was coming on to.

He'd had an eye on Anna for a long time. But she refused to understand what he was after, although he had shown her signs of attention for a good long while. First of all, he had talked to her more cordially than to the other women; second, he had given her chocolates; and, third, he had shared his personal agonies with her. But Anna? She had scarcely even hung around in his office for an extra minute. She would pick up an order and run straight back to her Makartsev. And she'd been single back then! When on one occasion he had got up the courage and put his hand on her waist she had immediately jumped back.

'What are you doing, getting up to mischief like that?'

'Mischief?' he took offence. 'I'm serious!'

'If you're serious, it's even more not on!'

Figure that one out! Well, after that he hadn't even tried any more. And if you took a peek at her records you would see that she was seven

years older than Kashin, so she could have toned down her expectations
a bit. In case of love ever raising its head, the prospects of marriage and
the possible begetting of a child (also something to consider!) were nil.
And Kashin had no respect for any other sort of relationship, not only out
of the obligations of his service but also by virtue of his own morality,
although he might have allowed for the possibility of such casual
liaisons existing. He wouldn't have turned one down, though, if invited,
but no one had ever made him such an offer.

In this respect Inna would have suited him best: some kind of
unknown radiation emanated from her. And if you chatted her up you
got the feeling that not only might desire arise but prospects for the future
as well. True, she never said anything about long-term prospects, but she
*had* declared that all men were just lechers, which was something you
couldn't say in Kashin's case. After all, he did show her sincere marks of
esteem: he spoke to her more cordially, not the way he talked to others;
and of course he'd given her chocolates and shared his agonies with her.
He had never touched her. But when he'd tried to ask her out for a meal
she had said: 'Some other time.' Meanwhile four other men from the office
had had entirely frivolous affairs with her, something that had raised sudden urges of an irresponsible sort in him. And she was the one who lured
people on, after all! She would smile tenderly and walk past him in that
special way that made him forget what he was talking about, if he was
in conversation with somebody else at the time.

Now, take that editorial staffer Nadya Sirotkina. Kashin liked her, too,
although she was far too young. Someone like that you would have to
marry. And even though there was the problem of the difference in their
ages, in principle this very much suited him, especially taking into account
his high regard for Nadya's father. Of course, if he got married to her he
himself wouldn't say a word about it, but if his father-in-law troubled himself to reinstate his son-in-law in the KGB organs – from which he'd been
thrown out for nothing at all really – Kashin wouldn't object. As far as
Nadya went, he had thus been especially sincere when he showed her signs
of interest. Whenever he got the chance, he talked to her more cordially

than to the others, he gave her boxes of chocolates on three occasions and shared his personal recollections on two. He had asked her once to the pictures and once to the circus. Both times she had answered with a refusal: she hadn't felt like going to see a film, and she didn't like the circus.

As a reserve, there was always Raisa Kachkareva. But her manner was crude, and he liked a woman to be unassertive, at least in certain regards.

All in all, you couldn't say that Kashin didn't have any choices. A man could never be satisfied with just fantasies about mermaids. He had choices, and pleasant future prospects opened up to him whenever he imagined in detail what it would be like to be now with the one, now the other. But the actual realization of his designs was for now just at the development stage, and he was going to have to work on this problem a bit more. If it weren't for his workload at the office it wouldn't be that difficult. But from morning till night he was up to his neck in work – logistical, administrative and organizational.

Kashin glanced at his watch. He'd been called in for 4 p.m. So, as usual, Kashin set off on the metro for his meeting with his handler. There were lots of people at Revolution Square; the Hotel Metropole was crowded with foreigners and foreign cars surrounded by gawkers staring inside them. The day was altogether hot and so sunny that you couldn't even look at the windows of the upper storeys, they shone so blindingly. So he didn't look up. Moving slowly towards Neglinnaya, he looked only at women, as if he'd never seen them before.

Winter over, they had taken off their warm clothing, and it was as if they had all become better built and had stripped off especially for him. Skirts had risen to show their knees, and some of them were entirely barelegged, without any stockings on. Thin blouses. Those parts of the body that stick out in front and back were now thrown into relief, and their utter and complete nudity was blocked from Kashin's sight only by insignificant light fabric. His heart was pounding. Women had become more accessible to him; he felt that with his entire body. There they were, right next to him. Pick any one – they're all yours! His mainspring was wound to breaking point, but consciousness of his duty would not permit him to stop or to walk after any one of them.

At the entrance to the Hotel Armenia, across from the rear of the Maly Theatre, Kashin looked around out of habit to see whether anyone he knew might be walking by. The clock in the lobby showed three minutes to four. Kashin went up to the second floor, walked past the woman on duty, who didn't challenge him, and knocked on the door of Room 27.

Behind the desk in the room sat a man somewhat younger than Kashin. Kashin had never met him here before. The man got up in greeting, introduced himself as Pokhlebayev and with a happy smile firmly shook Kashin's soft hand, from which Kashin had just transferred his keys. Offering him a seat, the host sat down next to him in another armchair and not behind his desk.

'You were highly recommended to me. They said we can rely on you. Especially as you're one of ours.'

'Strictly speaking, I'm not formally working for the organs now.'

'I know. But now a lot of people are being attached to the operation.'

'Against *samizdat*?'

'That's it! An order from the directorate. We're to clean it up and get rid of it as quick as we can.'

'I was thinking about that,' nodded Kashin. 'I haven't been at the paper very long. I see workplace discipline going down the drain, but they tell me: "This is creative work – you put the screws on and people will stop writing." And conversations like that go on among the newspaper's managers, which is really strange!'

'I don't entirely understand: what's the connection?' Pokhlebayev said.

'A direct one. Let's say that in every classified institution the engineers are obliged to pack up their notes and drawings in their numbered briefcases and hand them over to the Special Department. It's forbidden to throw any notes into the wastebasket. But what goes on at this newspaper? Of course I'm the one who's supposed to selectively check up on desks and the contents of wastepaper baskets, but how can I keep track of everything? Who goes off where, what they see, what they write about? It's a complete mess. This is a national newspaper, after all!'

'That *is* a serious issue, but it's not up to us to resolve it. We've got a concrete task at hand. A fellow called Ivlev has cropped up in our card index.'

'We've got one by that name. Born 1935, ethnic Russian, Communist Party member, higher education, salary 180 roubles. But surely he's not . . . ?'

'We're checking up on him. If he *is* . . . naturally, he would *want* to get into contact with people from abroad. Why wait? We'll help. Basically, you invite Ivlev to a hockey game.'

'Hockey?'

'Why not?' Pokhlebayev rose, walked over to his desk and took some tickets out of a folder. 'Hockey's a long way from our sort of business, so there won't be any suspicions.'

'How would I know if he's a hockey fan or not?'

'Personnel director and you don't know . . . The match is already sold out, so there shouldn't be any questions. You go along with him, drink some beer together or something stronger, so as to put him at ease. Got it?'

'Got it.'

'Sit in the stands so that he's in seat 22 and you're in 23. There'll be a foreigner sitting in 21 from West Germany, who's also one of our people.'

'I understand.'

'If you understand, then go to it. I won't keep you any longer.'

Kashin hobbled back down Marx Prospect as quickly as he could. So there was, after all, a range of issues that the organs couldn't resolve without turning to him, Kashin. Now he was going to prove that his dismissal back then had been a mistake. Kashin wasn't looking at women any more, even though some of them – it was rush-hour, after all – brushed against him in the crowd and leaned against him on the metro. Right now he was hurrying back to the office and in his haste was limping even worse than usual. Hobbling down the corridor and smiling affably at everyone, first he walked past the door with the 'Special Correspondents' sign on it, and then came back, as if he'd just then remembered something – it would look better that way. Ivlev was sitting at his desk reading a book.

'The joint is really jumping,' said Kashin jovially. 'Hey, what if you and I went to a hockey game? It'll be a first-class match, they say . . .'

Ivlev picked up a clean sheet of paper from the desk, neatly stuck it between the pages and set the book aside. 'And what if you and I went to the Bolshoi Theatre?'

'Why the Bolshoi?'

'Why a hockey match?'

'Because I've got an extra ticket to the match. It's sold out.'

'If tickets are impossible to get, why should I take up a seat? Find a hockey fan. He'd at least value it. But I don't care any more for hockey than I do for ballet.'

'Hey, I offered it to everyone – they're all busy!' Kashin persisted. 'You and I haven't ever gone anywhere together. We'll have a beer or two . . .'

Ivlev goggled at him. 'I've never been to a hockey match, and I never intend to! That's a moron's pastime.'

'Maybe you'll change your mind by tomorrow?'

'Leave me alone.'

Kashin withdrew, thinking about how hard it was to work at the newspaper. He had his orders, but he had to pussyfoot around. They messed him about, they didn't want to do this, didn't want to do that. Even in Cuba, when the heat got unbearable, things had been easier.

Ivlev regaled Rappoport with his conversation with Kashin, playing both parts. Rappoport didn't say anything. Wheezing, he got up and walked to the door. Opening it, he muttered: 'Can you wait for me, old man? Something's griping my stomach.'

Nodding, Ivlev looked out of the steamy window at the long clouds, like crumpled white terry towels, that were slowly crawling past the upper left corner of the window.

'As I thought, my boy.'

'About what?'

'About the hockey. Kashin didn't ask a single one of the hockey fans. Just you.'

'How did you find that out?'

'I asked four of them – the ones that live and breathe the game. Do you know how surprised they were that Kashin was going to that hockey match? They would all go with pleasure, but they can't get hold of any tickets anywhere. I fear Greeks bearing gifts.'

# 60

# Permafrost

Nadya came to a stop at the door to the typing pool, waving a letter in the air. 'Girls! Who wants to get married?'

Everyone instantly raised their hand, except for the elderly Nonna Abeleva, the department head. 'One was enough – I've had my fill!' she said, drawing a finger across her throat.

The typewriters had stopped clattering, but their voices were muffled by the soft upholstery on the walls.

'What about *you*, Nadya?' said Inna, out of curiosity. 'Or is it addressed to you?'

'Not enough guts to throw on the saddle yourself?' someone called out.

'He doesn't like them as skinny as that.'

'Eat more bread – you'll soon plump up.'

'You're all too excited,' Abeleva muttered. 'You should have asked who's on offer first.'

'Well, you just listen to what kind of bridegroom you're missing!' said Nadya. '"*I appeal to your newspaper for help. I want to get married, since I have need of an eternal friend and comrade with whom I can go through life. I am an Old Bolshevik with service since 1918, a veteran of the Revolution and the Civil War. I am eighty-one years old, I have gone blind, and I need a guide.*" Signed . . .'

'Mother of mine!' Abeleva blubbed.

'Girls!' exclaimed Inna. 'He's seen Lenin, I'll bet!'

'He might have seen Lenin, but he won't be able to make out *your* charms.'

'I've got somebody else besides him to look at me,' Inna said, offended. 'Nobody wants to get married!'

'So you're up for it?' Nadya said, to clear things up. 'I'll answer him: "Towards meeting the wishes of the workers, the editorial staff of *Trudovaya Pravda* is assigning you a guide-wife, quantity, one."'

'He's a worker? He's a special-pension parasite!'

'And what was it you wanted?' said Abeleva indignantly. 'To have a husband and him to feed you? There aren't any like that around any more!'

'Does he have a sword?' asked Inna, narrowing her eyes.

'Of course he has!' Nadya asserted confidently.

'So, he's a real man!'

'To my way of thinking,' Abeleva pronounced, 'it isn't a sword that makes a real man.'

'What does, then?'

'A hobby.'

'A hobby!'

'You misunderstand me! I mean, him being a sports fan or an alcoholic or a stamp collector . . . Well, that's it, girls!' Abeleva sternly put them in their place. 'You've had your laugh. Now get back to work.'

Nadya walked out of the typing pool to the laughter of the typists. Inna jumped up and followed her.

'Hang on,' she said in a hoarse whisper and glanced around, looking for a more secluded corner. 'Listen, here's a laugh for you. Kashin insulted me last night . . .'

'Wow,' Nadya said, coming to a halt. 'How did that happen?'

'This is how. He's been staring at me for a long time. But I always had other plans. But last night he bumps into me on the street, as if by accident. And he started asking me again to come to this *shashlyk* restaurant with him. Well, I felt sorry for him. He's a fellow, after all . . . "Shashlyk," I says, "I can cook that at home in the frying-pan if you buy me some meat at the delicatessen . . ." He was so happy! He splashed out not only on the meat but for some vodka as well. We drink it up, scoff the *shashlyk* –

and there we sit. I say: "It's hot! Take off your coat . . . And *I'm* going to put on my housecoat, if you don't object. It's springtime, after all." I took off my clothes, didn't bother buttoning up my housecoat and came out. Well, he gets a little lively now and takes off my housecoat. I tell him: "I'll freeze. It's cold!" And he says: "You just said it was hot!" And he hands me my housecoat to put back on. "All right," I say, "I'll put up with the cold . . ." Only now he starts taking off his belt. A military one, with the big star. And then he didn't do a thing. Not . . . a . . . thing! The arsehole!'

Nadya smiled politely.

'What are you laughing at? He's dishonoured me! Nobody has ever done that to me! I've been freaked out about it the whole day. I'm thinking – maybe I'm getting old? I can't take that sort of insult. After all, I'd already thrown him out of my plan, the idiot.'

'Out of what plan?'

'Out of the three guys I haven't slept with yet. As soon as I've slept with everybody I'll quit. I'll either move to another newspaper, like *Izvestia* or *Pravda*, or I'll die of boredom! They say there's a lot of young guys over at *Komsomolskaya Pravda*, haven't you heard?'

'Listen, and how does Kakabadze look at this?'

'Kakabadze? Georgians are better than Russians, that's a fact, of course. But, in the first place, he doesn't know anything and, in the second, he hasn't been promised anything. What am I? A dog on a leash? And men? They do worse things than that! To hell with them all! It's just pleasant when they humiliate themselves and tell lies and aren't even sorry for blowing their money on you when they want to. Tomcats is all they are! You could castrate them all, except then life would be even more boring. Even half a drop of sperm is better than none at all. I came here and thought I'd start from the top down . . .'

'How do you mean?'

'Well, with Makartsev, love. Twice I was typing something urgent for him in his office. His eyes were starting to glint. But Anna figured out what was going on: "Don't you get up to anything like that," she says. What a goddamned bloody saint! I'd already figured out how to get the saddle on the horse when Makartsev goes and ruins it all with his heart attack. Now, probably, I'm not going to be able to wait for him. So I'll go after Yagubov in the meantime.'

'But isn't he disgusting?'

'Disgusting? Everyone else slags him off, but I like him. For me, he's got lips I'd give anything to touch.'

'Go ahead!'

'But he won't go near me. Maybe it bothers him that I'm not a Party member?'

'He's a dwarf!'

'They say dwarves have big . . .'

'Nonsense!'

'I believe only my own eyes, Nadya.'

'Inna!' Nadya said, then hesitated. She had wanted to know for a long time and kept talking herself out of it, but now she made up her mind. 'Can I ask you something, if you promise to tell me the truth?'

'Why would I lie? It's just between you and me.'

'Is Ivlev part of your plan?'

'Nope . . .'

Nadya blushed, although she hadn't been expecting any other answer.

'What's with you, you idiot?' Inna hugged her. 'If you really want to know, it was just the one time, on a nature hike, and only for the plan.'

It was stupid, of course, but the tears came out anyway. Nadya blinked in dismay.

'Don't cry, you ninnie! A wise woman should be happy that her man is sleeping with other women. It means there's nothing wrong with him. As long as he doesn't go kissing women in entryways. If he sees them home, that's offensive. Hang on a minute! You mean you two aren't seeing each other? If you haven't got anywhere to do it, come over to my place. You can even have a wash there, as long as you don't make a mess of the floor. Remember to mop up afterwards, otherwise the landlady will start yelling, and you won't calm her down for anything! And bring a sheet with you. Or, if you prefer, we can do it without any men at all!'

'What are you saying?'

'So what? I tried it with Raisa Kachkareva. True, she's even worse than a man – rougher than a truck driver.'

'Well, that's not the important thing for me,' said Nadya, blushing. 'You know, I want to go to the theatre with him . . . I've never had anybody to go to the theatre with in my life. I've made up my mind: I'm breaking up with him.'

'You're talking nonsense!'

'You don't know me. If I decide to, I'll break up with him!'

Turning away abruptly, Nadya returned to her own department.

'Where have you been?' the letter-registry girls demanded. 'You've been called three times. Run down to the Special Correspondents' room!'

And off she went, at long last deciding to say no. In the Special Correspondents' room she pulled the door closed behind her and leaned against the doorframe without looking at Ivlev, who was sitting behind his desk and copying something out of a book. She drew a bit more air into her lungs, preparing herself to speak to him calmly and with dignity. Calm and dignified, without fail. And without any pauses.

'Nadya,' he said, not taking his eyes off the book, 'come here, I'll give you a kiss.'

'No,' she answered quietly.

The greater part of the decisiveness that she had amassed with such difficulty into a single point of consciousness was exhausted on that 'no'.

'Shall we take a ride out of town?'

'What for?'

'To a friend's *dacha*.'

'What for?' she repeated. 'I'd rather go to the theatre.'

'What about hockey? Wouldn't you like to go to a hockey game?'

'Why to a hockey game?' Nadya came to life. 'With pleasure, for sure. Wherever you feel like, only we'll just go there. We won't lie down.'

'Are you feeling all right?'

'Never better.'

'Then let's go for a little trip.'

After a brief hesitation she submitted, telling herself that she would break up with him there, so as not to cause a stir in the office. Nadya asked for around three hours off. Ivlev waited for her at the metro, screwing up his eyes against the sun. Riding as far as the Komsomolskaya stop, they got out and walked to Kazan Station, and the machine spat out tickets for them as far as the station at Udelnaya. Peasant women with sacks crowded around on the platform. The heavy stench of unventilated village huts filled the suburban *elektrichka* train. On the way they gazed silently out of the window. Ivlev became gloomy, and she felt sorry for him.

'Lord, how fantastic! Just look!' Nadya grabbed Ivlev by the hand and pulled him away from the platform down the little road that lost itself in a forest of pines. 'Sunshine, birds and air good enough to blow your mind!'

Her raincoat swung open, touching Ivlev's hand. Nadya ran ahead, and he plodded after her, heavily and slowly, saying infrequently: 'Right. Straight. Look out for the puddle . . .' The *dachas* stood blindly, their windows boarded up for the winter against thieves. On the hillocks around, where the snow had already melted, the warming grass of the year before showed yellow, and a light steam was rising from the reviving earth. Alongside a clayey precipice little coltsfoot flowers were sticking up and getting ready to turn gold. And above the cliff grey alders were swelling with buds, about to put out their catkins.

'Don't run off! The second house around the corner is ours,' said Ivlev. 'The owner said there's firewood there. We'll light the stove – the house will be damp, for sure. Hang on – what's that?'

Barely around the corner, Ivlev came to a halt, squeezed Nadya's hand and pulled her back. In front of the *dacha*, the keys to which were in his pocket, two black Volgas were parked. The boot of one of them was open. Stepping back out of sight, Ivlev bit his lip and screwed up his face as if a tooth had started aching. His brain, enfeebled by the wide-open spaces of the countryside, his brain, occupied with thoughts of Nadya, lightly and happily skipping ahead, that brain now switched back on and returned Ivlev to reality.

'What's going on?' asked Nadya, looking at him with alarm. 'Is it occupied?'

Her thoughts were still tripping down the rutted road, and Ivlev didn't answer. They still hadn't been noticed: both cars were empty. But they could be spotted at any moment, and they had to get away.

Firmly squeezing Nadya's hand as before, Ivlev moved a little bit back around the neighbouring corner house. The garden was visible through two separate fences of wide-spaced stakes, and the naked bushes, not yet in leaf, didn't hinder their view. Five men were walking around the garden, now and again bending over as if looking for something. A sixth person walked up to them. They all gathered together; the five took off their raincoats and handed them over to him, and he carried the raincoats out to one of the cars.

'Who are they?' Nadya mouthed silently.

'Them,' he mouthed back.

Nadya blinked in understanding. 'What are they looking for?'

'A hiding-place with some manuscripts, if they haven't already found it.'

'But who buried them?'

'It seems I did.'

The men on the other side of the two fences split up and once again began bending down and straightening up, moving in various directions. Now long, thin steel bayonets were visible in their hands, glinting in the sunshine. Ivlev winced, as if they were sticking them into him and not into the soil of the garden.

'Lord!' said Nadya softly.

'I've been meaning to move them for a long time. I didn't get round to it, because it was winter.'

'You should have given them to me.'

'To you?'

'Of course! It's safer at my place. Let's get out of here. I'm afraid for you. I beg you, let's go!'

Nadya rubbed her forehead against his cheek, then led him away by the elbow. He submitted. Without turning or looking around, they went on through the row of *dachas* and then walked around the pond. There were no more houses. The little road, wet and slippery, continued towards the forest. The shadows of the tree trunks and the branches fell on their faces; the dense birch grove accepted them into its realm, concealed them, cut them off from the rest of the world. Nadya now and again looked at Ivlev with concern and to calm him down stuck her hand inside his flapping raincoat and hugged him round the waist, walking sideways, with her head stuck under his arm.

'That must be awkward for you,' he said, grabbing her by the neck.

'So just stop right here.'

They stood for a long while hugging in front of three birch trees on the dry hillock, reminiscent of a grave. Nadya started to tremble.

'Are you cold?' he asked.

'What are you on about? It's just that I don't want to go to the theatre with you . . .'

'Where to then?'

'Over to the grass.'

It went quickly and poorly. But she was trying to make him forget, even if for just a moment, what had turned him into someone possessed. And she succeeded, getting carried away by him and slightly overplaying her passion. She had learned how to do this and got so thoroughly into the role that she forgot she was playing a game.

'When you stand up the grass seems warm,' said Nadya. 'But the ground still hasn't thawed out. Excuse me, but it's colder for me than you.' Nadya looked him steadily in the eyes. Now they had died down again. Cares, troubles, losses – what was in them? Old age! He'd got older. Some grey hairs had been added to his temples today. 'Do you want me to have a daughter for you?'

'For my complete and utter happiness?'

'Sorry, I'm an idiot today. It would be great if I could live just for love.'

'You'd get bored.'

'So what can I do?' Nadya asked quietly. 'Remember, you said once, "Life is a river." I remembered that. When I was little I couldn't swim, I didn't know where the deep spots were, where the whirlpools were. But now I can swim. Only where to?'

'To where everyone does, Nadya. Life offers you a hundred different streams: human relations, everyday life, service. Most people swim with the current all their lives.'

'I would be, too, if it wasn't for you.'

'I'm no better than anybody else. When I try to swim against the current it carries me away. And nobody appreciates it.'

'Let's leave. Let's run away! The river's freezing over and the shore's permafrost!'

'Jump across into another river? But I'll just want to swim against the current there, too.'

'It's Rappoport who's influencing you!'

'I have that cast of mind. Journalism is dissatisfaction and not a pot of honey.'

'What's going to happen now?' she said, nodding in the direction of the *dachas* on the other side of the trees.

He shrugged. 'Just before we skipped out of the office my wife called. From a payphone, she said.'

'Tonya loves you,' Nadya said politely. 'Hang on just a minute longer. And then you'll belong to her for ever.'

'I love you,' he said.

'And her?'

'Her, too.'

'Surely you can't love two people at once.'

'If I can't, then let's split up, Nadya. Split up nice and pretty, like they say in Odessa. Things will get easier right away.'

'You put that well: split up nice and pretty. And will we walk to the *elektrichka* together or separately?'

'Together, of course. But just as friends.'

'Fine. Just as friends!'

# 61

# The Joys and Sorrows of
# Tonya Ivleva

In 1938 the publishing arm of the People's Commissariat for International Affairs proposed urgently to the London newspaper the *Daily Telegraph* that it recall its Moscow correspondent as quickly as possible for attempting to interview people coming out of prison. His place was soon taken by a younger reporter, Donald Oakesby, a Cambridge graduate and a not particularly fluent speaker of Russian.

At his very first discussion with the People's Commissariat for International Affairs they had explained to Donald which aspects of Soviet life a foreigner needed to interest himself in, and he understood perfectly. Oakesby punctiliously took whatever material he was sending to his newspaper to the People's Commissariat for International Affairs for inspection and obediently expunged whatever they asked him to.

Oakesby held views utterly sympathetic to the Communists' notion of universal brotherhood. One day, needing some photographs for an article on the lives of Soviet workers, he went to the photo archives of TASS. He picked out several shots featuring grubby, smiling tractor-drivers and ditch-diggers. They explained to Oakesby that, as the photos were destined to be published abroad, it would be necessary to touch them up yet again. The retoucher said to Oakesby that she would stay behind after work and do them all, since he needed them urgently. He would have to come back in three hours. The girl's name was Ksyusha. For three hours Donald Oakesby, *Daily Telegraph* reporter, strolled around Moscow and, so as not to forget, kept on repeating the retoucher's strange name: 'Kiss-*you*-sure,' he pronounced. 'Kiss-*you*-sure – that's simple enough!'

This repetition of her name over the course of three hours led to absolutely no good at all. When Donald got back to the photo archives Ksyusha still hadn't managed to get the grime off all the cheeks in the pictures and draw in suits and ties in place of their overalls. Mister Oakesby leaned over Ksyusha to see how skilfully she was doing the job, but he couldn't tear his eyes away from her translucent little ear and the locks of red hair around it. The locks swayed with Mister Oakesby's breath, and he completely ceased breathing, afraid of hampering the exacting work of the retoucher.

When the photographs were ready Oakesby volunteered to take 'Miss Kiss-*you*-sure' home. She appeared very frightened, and he didn't understand why. They went on foot. In the whole period of his being in Moscow Mr Oakesby never walked as much as he did that day. The *Daily Telegraph* reporter and the photo-archive retoucher began to meet every evening. And after two months, before leaving for London for several days, Donald proposed to Ksyusha. Once again she got very frightened, but she accepted his offer.

After filing their declaration of intent to marry Oakesby flew to London, intending to drive to his parents' house for their blessing. Ksyusha counted the days. Donald was long since supposed to have returned, and there was no sign of him. After a month Ksyusha was sacked from the TASS photo archive for having relations with foreigners. She was at her wits' end from uncertainty. Her girlfriends advised her not to live at home – after all, she was bound to be arrested. Another month passed and the new *Daily Telegraph* correspondent managed to find Ksyusha, through one of her girlfriends who also worked at the archive. Mr Oakesby, he said, had been denied a re-entry visa on grounds of his amoral behaviour in the USSR. He earnestly requested that 'Miss Kiss-*you*-sure' travel to join him in London. His parents were amenable to the marriage and as a wedding gift had decided to give them their farm in Scotland. Ksyusha broke into a happy smile but for some reason didn't get to go anywhere and after another six and a half months walked alone into the tranquil reception room of Grauerman Maternity Hospital No. 7.

She named her daughter Tonya. On her birth certificate there was a dash in the place of her father's name. Ksyusha was afraid to try to get a job, because then she might be arrested straight away. She cleaned people's apartments, washed windows, and during the war she evacuated to the far side of Lake Baikal in Siberia, where she worked in the fields of a collective farm. After the war ended Ksyusha went back home so as to get a better education for her daughter. Everyone said the little girl had a real gift for music – 'Just look how flexible her fingers are!' When Tonya got her internal passport, like every sixteen-year-old, it was 1955.

The letter from her father came entirely unexpectedly. But it reached them. It had been posted in Moscow by some unknown foreigner. Mr Oakesby wrote that he had waited for his beloved for six years, but then, out of an absence of any sort of information or even hope, he had married, and now he had two daughters: Carol, named after her mother, and Susie, named after Ksyusha. Similar enough, right? He was sending this letter just in case, without any particular hope that it would find the addressee. Ksyusha hid the letter from her daughter and never answered Mr Oakesby, even though she didn't feel any malice towards him but rather gratitude for his attention.

Tonya grew up an obedient girl. Whenever something was going the way it shouldn't, her mother (whose nerves were ragged) would start to cry, and her daughter wouldn't be able to bear it and would obediently agree to do whatever it was that she didn't want to do. She wore her Pioneer scarf even at home; she became troop leader, then a Young Communist. She was good at everything: her schoolwork, her socialist obligations, her music. The rented piano had to be paid for – it wasn't going to sit around their apartment for nothing.

Tonya wasn't any Plain Jane either. She was shapely, with long legs (revealed when she had a nice dress to wear), a lovely neck (when it was bared), wavy hair (if she combed it the way it suited her), and noble features (if she took care not to get a rash on her chin from rubbing against the coarse fabric of her school uniform). Everything at school was explained to her, spelled out to her, indicated to her – how to understand this or that phenomenon or subject or system. The only thing that was never explained to her was how to understand her being born a woman on this earth.

That was how she was when she graduated from the music school and went off by herself to Siberia. After working out the three years' assignment required of her, Tonya returned and met up with her schoolfriends. Life had got somewhat easier in Moscow. Foreign clothes were making an appearance. Her girlfriends were dressing up, putting on makeup, living incomprehensible lives. They practically had to drag Tonya to a party. She sat in a corner, not knowing how to dance. Nobody even looked at her. She howled the whole night long after she got home, stuffing her pillow in her mouth, trying not to wake her mother – all they had was just one room in a communal apartment, and her mother had to get to work early. Ksyusha was working as a retoucher in a print shop.

The following day Tonya found an advertisement and went off to a fee-paying contemporary-dance school. At the time establishments like this were beginning to open up here and there. Before that people had been allowed only to dance the waltz, the two-step and, in exceptional circumstances, the tango. At the cultural centre an elderly, bow-legged manageress with a hussar moustache ordered everyone – who had paid the cashier their money a month in advance – to form themselves into two rows: the young men on the right against the wall, the girls on the left. The first person in each row went down each rank, collecting the receipts.

The manageress counted up first the receipts and then the number of participants. The numbers tallied, and she solemnly announced: 'Attention! Gentlemen, step up to your ladies. Forward – march! Now take the right hand of your lady in your left hand and place your right hand on your lady's waist. Very good!'

Although Tonya the music teacher was twenty-three years old, nobody had yet put either his right or his left hand on her waist. In her agitation she didn't even look at her partner. She just tensed up at his touch and moved a bit further away from him.

'Hold your posture the way I've told you to!' shouted the dance mistress. 'I'm going to walk by and check every one of you.'

It was uncomfortable, even shameful, for Tonya to stand there. Everything was stupid, so terribly stupid that she wouldn't have believed it herself if someone had told her.

'And you, girl, don't stick out backwards like that! I'm talking to you – yes, you. What's your name?'

'Mine?' Tonya said, waking up. 'Kosykh.'

'Remember this: sticking out backwards is just as unattractive as plastering yourself right up against him. Have you got that?'

'I'm not sticking out,' Tonya timidly objected, feeling the colour flood into her face.

'Don't argue with me. I can see it better than you!'

Tears flowed from her eyes. Tonya freed herself from her partner's hands and ran off. On the other side of the door she leaned against a pillar and gave vent to tears. Something was happening to her. She had always been able to manage herself with ease – her desires, her disinclinations, her feelings, her actions. She had always been surprised at how other people gave in to sudden weaknesses, things that were completely unfounded. But now . . . Now it felt like the hand was once again on her waist. Tonya moved away, but the hand stayed.

'Don't be upset! She's just an ass . . .'

Tonya opened her wet eyes and recognized her dance partner with difficulty. He had come out of the hall after her. It turned out that he was at the dance classes for the first time as well. And from his elaborate justification as what he was doing there Tonya understood that it was for the very same reason as her. Ivlev was twenty-seven.

He turned out to be the same kind of person she was, both in terms of his past and present. You didn't have to explain anything to him, nor did you have to justify yourself. Nor to her. With a smile she recalled the things that had interested her when she was a Pioneer and a Young Communist – they seemed so paltry and pitiful in comparison with the altogether important thing that had sprung up between her and Ivlev.

His parents went off to the Crimea on holidays. Tonya took to staying at Ivlev's. Her mother went bonkers, afraid that her daughter was going to repeat her fate. But he soon showed up at their place and inquired as to whether Ksyusha would object if he and Tonya got married. This was sensational news: Tonya was marrying a journalist! And he was a nice fellow, too, and not some kind of lout. The news flew around Tonya's girlfriends.

A rather strenuous happiness ensued for Tonya. After a while Ksyusha admitted to her daughter that she had been seeing a man for a long time and would like to go off with him. He was an artist, a portrait painter. Ksyusha had been too shy to do it before.

Tonya was packing her things to leave her mother's when she found the hidden letter from Donald Oakesby. She took it away with her. She started daydreaming about seeing (just seeing!) her father, but she understood that it wasn't going to happen. Starting a correspondence was out of the question: her husband worked for a newspaper. And just suppose she did find her father. He would be anxious that she was trying to foist herself on him as his daughter – after all, he had never even heard of her. If she could only go to England on a holiday! True, she would never be allowed to absent herself from the group of Russian tourists she travelled with. But at least she would get to see her father's homeland.

Tonya put this notion of hers on the back burner when her son Vadik was born. There were three of them now, and the boy took all her attention and all her care. She was happy, and she never noticed anything, although she did feel that her husband had changed. She couldn't have explained herself what the difference was. Everyone changed with time. Not long after the incident of Ivlev's telegram to Solzhenitsyn the lady director of the music school called Tonya out of her class. A young man sitting behind the director's desk started asking her questions about her work, her family and her husband.

'Excuse me, but who exactly are you?'

'I'm from the KGB. We would like you to exert some influence over your husband.'

Tonya compressed her lips tighter, so as not to betray her agitation. 'I don't understand what you're on about . . .'

'He has some dubious connections. Our task is to educate him, to warn him. Help us – it'll be in your interests, too.'

'He's an independent person.'

'Even more important then! Why does he have to get involved in these disreputable things, things he can get severely punished for? By the way, does he do any writing at home?'

'No.'

'Does he read any manuscripts?'

'No.'

'I can see you're not very communicative. A pity! After all, we just want to help you preserve your family.'

'I don't need any help.'

'Then I want to warn you: you can't say anything about our discussion here.'

'You want me to hide something from my husband?'

'Are you a Soviet?'

'Yes. And I don't have any secrets from my husband.'

'Well, then, you'll be sorry.'

'Are you threatening me?'

'I'm warning you.'

Tonya never said anything to her husband about this conversation, not because she was afraid but so as not to worry him.

Before this, when she had been offered a trip to Bulgaria she had agreed to sign up for it. Her trade-union committee had allocated the music school an out-of-season trip, and they couldn't find any takers straight away, much less ones with any money to spend. Tonya was thinking that it would be good for Ivlev to miss her for a while. He was too accustomed to her always being at home waiting for him, meals cooked and ready for him and everything generally spic and span. She was an independent person, too, after all! Moreover, she would have to travel to a socialist-bloc country at some time, otherwise she would never be allowed out to a capitalist one. Her dream of going to England to see her father had never left her. And now her trip to Bulgaria fell through.

For some unknown reason the word 'happiness' in Russian exists only in the singular, while the word 'unhappiness' has both a singular and a plural.

# 62

# Don't Write Down Any Phone Numbers!

Tonya got up at seven in the morning to take Vadik to her mother's before work. Ivlev was still asleep, and she quietly slipped out from under the covers without waking him. Vadik was sleepy, too, and he whimpered. They drank down one cup of warm, sweet tea between them, and Tonya dressed him in his cap and jacket. Calmed down now a little, he put on his own shoes.

In front of their entryway Vadik stumbled, fell down and burst into tears. His shoelaces were undone. Tonya sat him down on a bench and squatted in front of him. The yard-woman was sweeping the footpath, and she stopped and waited for them to leave.

'That's a Volga,' said Vadik.

He knew the make of every car. A man in a greenish raincoat and hat got out of the Volga. He stopped for a moment and pulled a polythene bag out of his pocket, removed a pair of rubber surgical gloves from it and walked towards the entryway, donning the gloves as he went. Tonya was surprised.

'Who's that?' she asked the yard-woman.

'That feller?' the woman waved her broom in the direction of the entryway. 'How would I know? He comes here every morning and digs around in the dustbins. I ast him how come he's a-littering up all around the bins, and he said he's from the *housing authority,* he says, checking out the peelings, what kind of rubbish is being thrown away. Or maybe he's looking for summat else. How would I know?'

The man didn't go into their entryway but disappeared through the basement door. Tonya tied Vadik's shoelaces and lifted him off the bench.

After taking her son to her mother's, Tonya made her way to school. She had four classes and a teachers' council meeting. She excused herself from the meeting on the pretext of feeling ill and ran first to one shop and then another: there wasn't anything at home either for supper or for breakfast; nor was there anything in the stores. But she bought a few things to eat anyway. Then she stood in a queue at the laundry to collect Ivlev's shirts: there wasn't a single clean one at home. Her bag had grown heavy with music sheets and groceries, and now she had the package with the shirts in it under her arm as well. She hurried home so that she could use her son's absence to do a bit more round the house: vacuum the room and clean the kitchen floor, wash her clothes and Ivlev's socks, shampoo her hair and dry it, get ready for the next morning's classes. It was a good thing that they weren't letting her go abroad. After all, cobwebs would grow over her two men if they were left alone for two weeks! And who knew how Vadik would take her absence. At the entrance to their courtyard her way was blocked by two men. She decided they were drunks, and she stepped back to run past them, to duck under their outstretched hands, just as she used to do when she was a little girl.

'Hang on a minute!' said one of them. 'Where are you going in such a hurry?'

'It doesn't concern *you*!'

'It might concern us,' said the other, firmly grabbing her by the elbow.

'Let me go!' yelled Tonya.

'Don't you get upset, my girl! We're police. So don't be afraid. Can I see what's in that package?' Not waiting for an answer, the first one pulled the bundle from under Tonya's arm.

'You don't have the right!'

'We do. Give it here.' They quickly unwrapped it, but catching sight of the shirts they neatly stuck the edge of the paper back under a fold and wrapped it up again. 'That's all. You're all nervous about trifles like this? Goodbye.'

Politely stepping aside, they let Tonya past. Several seconds later, when she looked around after opening her entryway door to see if they were coming after her, they were already gone. Tonya was so nervous that she couldn't find her apartment key and had to rummage through her bag. When she finally entered it seemed to her that there was an unfamiliar smell in the apartment. She got alarmed, thinking it meant she was pregnant, but then she straight away reassured herself that this couldn't be the case. Tonya opened the door of the kitchen and only then realized that it was the smell of cigarettes, only not the ones that Ivlev smoked but sweeter ones. Yes, that was it: he had sat at home that morning, sorting out his papers. Scraps of manuscripts and whole pages were lying on the floor next to the rubbish chute. He hadn't been able to get hold of his usual cigarettes, so he had smoked whatever was at hand.

In the bedroom Tonya took off her skirt and blouse. She drew a finger across his desk – she should dust it. On it lay folders taken down from the shelves. Ivlev had been looking for something in a hurry and hadn't even tidied up after himself. She didn't touch anything but put on her housecoat and went into the bathroom to wash.

At around eight in the evening Ivlev walked into their building, tired and sullen. Nadya hadn't wanted to go home, and she had ridden on the metro with him. Ivlev had let her, even though he was straining to be left alone. He had tried to say goodbye at the turnstile, but she had begged permission to come up to the top with him. And at the top of the stairs she said that she would walk him as far as his home.

'Are you trying to make sure my wife sees us?' he asked. 'Is that what you're after?'

'I'm not after anything,' Nadya replied quietly. 'I've already got what I want. I got you. I don't need anything else. Goodbye!'

She impassively kissed him on the lips and ran to the metro doors without looking back. He stood there, following her with his eyes, then shrugged and headed home. He had barely walked into his entryway when he was jerked to one side by his sleeve.

'That him?' asked a lazy voice in the darkness.

'It's him! Who else? Take this, you fucker!'

They hit him in the stomach. Ivlev writhed from the pain. They knocked off his hat and yanked his hair from behind, pulling his head back. They were kicking him. How many were there? Three, four – he couldn't tell. They beat him silently, from different sides, until the entry-way door opened and three of his neighbours appeared – husband, wife and child. The men who were beating him let them past into the entry hall and one after another leaped out into the street. His neighbours walked past Ivlev without noticing a thing.

He lay there for a while and then got up. He looked at himself in the lift mirror. There wasn't a single bruise on his face. His back and stom-ach ached. He felt himself over: at least they hadn't broken his arms or legs, and his skull was in one piece.

At home he made his way in quietly, slowly took off his raincoat, washed himself for a long time with cold water and then walked into the kitchen and silently sat down at the table. Tonya quickly got up to feed him something, not saying a word. He ate, stood up, kissed her on the cheek as he walked past, went into their room and came straight back out again.

'Tonya! Who's turned everything upside down?'

'You did!' she said, putting down the knife that she was using to slice onions, and looked at him in alarm. 'Who else?'

'Me?' he asked, in bewilderment.

'Surely it was you throwing things out?' Tonya pointed a finger at the floor in front of the rubbish chute, where she still hadn't had a chance to clean up.

Ivlev got down on one knee. Every movement caused him pain. He picked up a scrap off the floor. It appeared to be part of a page of one of his unpublished articles.

'What scum touched my things?'

'When I came in it seemed to me . . .'

'So whatever they didn't need they simply tore up and threw down the rubbish chute? I'm going to the police!'

The lieutenant on duty at the police station listened wanly to the complaint and didn't write anything down. He asked for Ivlev's name and place of work.

'All right, we'll look for the people who did it.'

'Nobody's going to have a look around the scene?'

'To look at what? It's clear as a bell – you were robbed. I've already told you: we'll look for the people who did it. What was stolen?'

'Stolen? A French language textbook . . . They beat me up, lieutenant!'

'I'll tell you this much anyway,' said the lieutenant, looking at Ivlev ironically but not without sympathy. 'Keep your nose out of this! There's no way to catch *those* people, you know?'

Tonya was still pottering around in the kitchen. He sat down on a stool in the middle of the kitchen, sorting senselessly through the scraps of notes and rough drafts that were on the floor. Tonya got down on her knees next to him.

'Did you take my notebook with the phone numbers in it?' he asked.

'I didn't touch it.'

'Then it's clear what else they stole. Zakamorny even has a poem about it:

> *'Don't write down your friends' phone numbers!*
> *Better just remember them.*
> *Such are the conditions of these times*
> *And of simple human decency . . .'*

# 63

# The Typewriter

Inna got home from the office around ten. She stood at her half-open window, pulled down the zip of her dress, removed both it and her brassiere and sighed. She knew that she was visible from the street below, but this didn't alarm her. The spring air tickled her nostrils. Inna stretched blissfully, glanced under her arms and decided to shave right away before she forgot. She had picked up her razor when her buzzer sounded.

Covering her breasts with her arms, she opened the door. Ivlev was standing on the threshold.

'Come on in! Sorry, I'm not dressed.'

'I can tell,' Ivlev said, setting down his briefcase at the door. 'You're even better-looking that way. You'll excuse me for being so late. Give me the manuscript!'

'But I haven't even finished yet.'

'It doesn't matter how much you've managed to do. And . . . give me your typewriter.'

'What for?'

'Here, I've brought you a new one, better than yours.'

'Huh?'

'Don't be silly, Inna. They're coming after me. Do you want them to catch you in all this?'

'Me? What would they come after me for?'

'Because you've been typing things for me, stupid!'

She whistled. 'Come on in. Take off your raincoat.'

The landlady was bustling around the kitchen; she didn't come into the room, as she could hear that someone had come to see Inna.

'What's that?' asked Ivlev. A tiny stream of blood was running down her arm.

'Nothing! I cut myself with my razor. Want to lick it off?'

Ivlev took her by the shoulders and kissed her, licking off the blood with his tongue.

'Thanks,' she said. 'Do you know how to use a safety razor? Then shave my armpits.' She raised both arms and turned towards him until he had done it.

'Men – they're something else. They know how to do everything. Do you like my knickers?'

'Very much!'

'They're Italian. They're getting a bit old, but they're still better than ours! Look how these little laces untie from the front.'

'Cover up!'

'Whatever,' she said, without offence. 'I wanted to make it better for you. Anyway I've already told Nadya that we've slept together.'

'What did you do that for, stupid?'

'There's this thing that happens to me: if ever I lie about someone having slept with me, afterwards I've got to do it. Then the lie comes true! Understand?'

'Oh, I see!' He put down the razor. 'But what about your landlady?'

'Whenever a man comes to see me, she goes and sits in the kitchen. After all, I pay her for it.'

'For what?'

'For every single man. That way she's even happier if more men come by. She's an absolute miser: she even listens to hear how many sheets of paper you tear off in the toilet.'

Placing a mirror on the table across from him, Inna started winding locks of her hair round curlers. Then she covered her head with a flowered scarf.

'What a heatwave! Don't you look at me – I'm ugly in curlers. Besides, I'm getting old, and it's time for me to start a career, just like everyone else.'

'What for?'

'Because people like you are already starting to just sit here with me.'

'I'm the one who's old. Just a simple Soviet impotent. Don't judge everyone by me.'

'Do you think I've still got my charms?'

'Everything's in place. I'm not worried for you.'

'Yagubov told me today that everything was in order with me, too. True, he did have my personal records in mind. He said he'd recommend me for Party membership.'

'Well?'

'I just told you – I'm going to have a career. He promised to make me head of the typing pool.'

'Oh-ho!'

'Of course, he's giving me a recommendation so that as a Party member I'll keep quiet about the fact that he wants to sleep with me. But why should I care about that?'

'Too bad.'

'Too bad? And what about all of *you*?'

'I joined up when I still believed. But now it's only idiots and careerists who join.'

'Right! And that's just what I am, both the one and the other. If I join, maybe they'll let me go on a tourist trip. To Italy. I'd really like to go to Italy.'

'What'll you do there?'

'The same thing I do here, only openly. After all, the men there aren't any worse than ours; that's a fact. None of you nice people are going to help me, but Yagubov will. It'd be stupid not to use him while he wants me.'

Ivlev stood up. 'You're a nice person, Inna. You're sincere. Give me my manuscript so they won't involve you in this. Otherwise your career will go up in flames because of me.'

Pulling a folder out of her bedside table, Inna held it in her hands, slow to give it up.

'Ivlev,' she asked quietly, 'is it true that you came here for my sake?
You know, so I wouldn't get in trouble?' She came close up against him.
'Humiliate me. A lot. Be as foul-mouthed as you want. Come on! Insult
me. Tell me I'm a slut or cut me with a knife or knock out my teeth. Don't
be afraid. I won't yell. I'll take it. Come on!'

He looked into her eyes. They were dry, crazed. 'What's up with you?'
he said in perplexity.

'I'm a bitch, Ivlev.'

'Why?'

'Because! Everything you asked me to type four copies of I typed five.'

'What for?'

'One of my clients asked me if he could read an extra copy. He paid
me the same for the fifth copy as you paid me for the other four. And I'm
always in need of money, you know yourself. I thought he was just going
to read it. The swine! When he comes, I'm going to bite off his . . . ! Don't
be afraid of them. They won't do anything. Don't be upset. Right now
I'm going to cheer you up!'

Taking her guitar down off its nail Inna drew her thumb across the
strings, tuned it and coughed. 'You want a drink?'

He shook his head. Inna picked up a bottle of vodka from the windowsill, poured out what was left into a cup, drank it and licked her lips,
waiting until the vodka penetrated her system.

'Listen to this:

> *'What's the Party going to give us?*
> *That's what people want to know.*
> *Ask not what your Party gives, just*
> *Keep in mind it's not a whore. Hey!'*

— 64 —

# The Once-Over

On the old ladies' bench opposite the entryway sat a young man in a dark-blue sports jacket, gazing at the door. Coming out of his building very early in the morning Ivlev wouldn't have paid him the slightest attention if the fellow hadn't stood up far too hastily. His footsteps echoed in the archway, and Ivlev understood that he had picked up a tail. That meant that they hadn't backed off, and yesterday's events were just a link in the chain.

Ivlev forced his way into the thick of the crowd closest to the edge of the footpath, waiting for the trolley bus. When it came, Ivlev moved straight through the mass of them towards the rear door, but then squeezed past it and ran behind the tram to the other side of the street. He flagged down the first vehicle that came by, going in the opposite direction. It was a van with a sign that said 'Cakes & Pastries'.

'Not far from here, just three streets away. I'll give you this three roubles. Just take me there!'

Glancing back, Ivlev saw that he had two men on his tail, and they were boldly running across the street after him. Once around the corner he asked the driver to stop, threw the money on the seat and dived into a schoolyard. He skirted round the building. He knew where there was a hole in the fence behind the school. He went through the hole on to the neighbouring street, and here he got lucky: he stopped a taxi right away. He had shaken his tail. He got out in the city centre, where there were always lots of people, and rang Rappoport.

'When are you coming into the office?'

'Do you need my keys, Ivlev?'

'No, I'd like to meet you somewhere.'

'Has something happened then?'

'Sort of.'

'I'm ready, old man! Just let me shave and have a cup of tea.'

'Of course. I'll be waiting for you at the entrance to Izmaylovsky Park metro station.'

'Surely that's not very near your place?'

'I haven't got anything else to do. I'll be there.'

Ivlev didn't have to wait long. Rappoport, in his hat and with his far-too-long raincoat dragging on the pavement, slowly crossed the road.

'Are there really cataclysms on this earth that can make somebody willingly do without enough sleep?' Rappoport stretched out a gnarled, hairy hand. Trying to avoid emotion Ivlev recounted the facts to him.

Rappoport didn't interrupt; he just snuffled, glancing to one side. Only at one point did he raise an eyebrow and ask: 'Inna? If I hadn't heard that from you, Ivlev, I wouldn't have believed it. Evidently I haven't spent long enough in jail.'

'What can be done?'

'You see? And now you're asking me what can be done! Who am I? Chernyshevsky? Did you ask me that when all this started? And none the less I warned you! You've done something even worse than Inna!'

'Me?'

'Of course! As far as people like Inna go, Zakamorny would say in the words of the Gospel of St Mark: "Father, forgive them, for they know not what they do!" But you know what's what! Or were you studying French just to translate approved French Communists?'

'De Custine was really afraid of falling into the clutches of the Third Department. But who would have thought that he'd fall into their clutches a hundred and thirty years later!'

'Not him, but you, my boy. And what are you going to prove with your heroics? That nothing has changed since the time of Nicholas the First? "Oh," you'll say, "it's got even worse." Sure, Russia hasn't been lucky –

she was prostrated under the Mongols, when it should have been under the French, or even better under the English. Then when *they* left we could have been impregnated with their democracy and not this swinishness. And do you think we didn't know that, even without your de Custine? So what do you want now?'

'I only wanted to warn you that they're after me.'

'Thanks! But I always live as if there's a tail on me. And particularly right now.'

'Why?'

'It's that kind of year! The ninth wave is rolling over us. Pretty soon it's going to crash down. I've been caught by the wave more than once, but I always managed to get back up before. This time I won't get back up. Upstairs they were wavering, up till August 1968. They were afraid. But now they've strangled the Czechs, and they got away with it! They realized that if even in Czechoslovakia, a foreign country, people put up with everything they do to them, then in their own country that's what Lenin himself ordered them to do. Now here come the first ritual sacrifices. You're a talented man, Ivlev. There's no place for talented people in our system. And maybe not even in our solar system – how would I know? Let's get to work. Kashin's at the entrance now, mornings, taking down the names of people who arrive late.'

They went down into the metro and there in the crowd, while they rode, they talked about other things.

'How are things between you and Nadya?'

Ivlev shrugged.

'Of course, it's none of my business, and you can say that I'm old-fashioned, but it'd be better if you didn't mess her head about like that.'

'In principle I understand that. But when I hear her voice my hands itch to unbutton my trousers all by themselves.'

'Stop pretending to be a sex maniac, Ivlev. I'm talking to you like a father.'

'As a father you're too late, Rappoport. It's all over.'

'And a good thing, too! Cheat on your wife with girls less pure.'

Riding up the escalator, they separated so that they wouldn't be seen together. Ivlev stopped at a kiosk to buy some cigarettes and got to the office a minute later.

Rappoport flopped into his chair without taking off his hat or raincoat, then unlocked the middle drawer of his desk and pulled it open. On top of all the other papers in the drawer lay a thin folder with *Personal* written on it. This was just a ruse. In the folder were several meaningless clippings from *Trudovaya Pravda*. But in among the clippings lay little hairs that had been plucked by Rappoport out of his own hairy chest. He opened the folder and carefully lifted the first clipping – the hair beneath it was nowhere to be seen. He slowly lifted the second – the hair had been knocked to one side.

'*Pe-pe-pe*,' he sang.

He didn't have to look any further. He wasn't afraid of getting the once-over. Everything in his office was clean. And it had never entered into his head to struggle with this phenomenon. He simply wanted his finger on the pulse. The search gave him more information than it did the person who had performed it. There was a knock at the door.

'May I?'

He wanted to tell the visitor off for knocking, but he was suddenly too lazy.

Two round-faced young men came into the room, one in a black suit, the other in grey. Their faces seemed familiar to Rappoport. He didn't like faces like that, and for that reason didn't recognize them straight away.

'We're from the Young Communist League central committee,' the guest in the pin-striped grey suit reminded him. 'You remember, about climbing the mountain . . .'

'Of course!' Rappoport said, coming to life. 'You were going to carry a bust of Lenin . . . er . . . up Elbrus?'

'Up Mount Communism. So, anyway . . .'

'Did you make it? There were three of you, weren't there?'

'Stepanov, who was carrying the bust, slipped.'

'Did he drop the bust?'

'And fell to his death. We managed to get him posthumously awarded his Master of Sport qualification, of course.'

'Too bad about the bust,' said Rappoport, looking searchingly at the younger generation.

'Too bad about Stepanov, too. But this fellow here, he's decided to try the ascent a second time.'

'What's your name?' asked Rappoport.

'Rodyukin.'

'Are you going to carry the bust?'

'Of course!'

'But, after all, we've already agreed, boys: as soon as you get the bust in place up there, tell us. But beforehand . . . you understand yourself, now . . .'

'You see, Yagubov got a call from Upstairs. We just came from his office. He said, "The most important thing is to grab the public's attention, since nobody's going to be able to see the bust behind the clouds."'

'So why are you beating about the bush, my lads?' Rappoport burst out. 'You should have told me right away that you'd agreed everything with my superiors. So, now . . . Just tell people about it? Too shallow! That's not enough scope. But, Rodyukin, what if you come forward as the initiator of a new campaign? Let's say . . . something like this: "A bust of Lenin on every mountain!" Well, we'll think about what to call it. After all, his centenary is coming, and what a lot of nature sites there are that we still haven't enveloped in propaganda! Come on back after the holiday – we'll get down to it.'

His telephone rang. Rappoport firmly shook his guests' hands and showed them to the door.

'Hey, there, jailbird!' rumbled the voice of Sagaydak in the receiver. 'What's the news?'

'I did what you asked, Rappoport,' said Sagaydak modestly. 'Makartsev's pup has already undergone a psychiatric examination at the Serbsky Institute. It's established that he's in good health now but at that moment he had a temporary loss of consciousness owing to nervous overstrain. There won't be any court case, and his parents can come and take him away.'

'Good man! I never doubted that you're a mighty lecher.' *Saving Makartsev's puppy turned out to be easy. Makartsev is going to say, 'Those are the rules of the game. Change the rules, and we'll play it differently.'*

# 65

# The Return of the
# Prodigal Son

Zina had called for the car to take her home at twelve thirty. Aleksey drove out of the garage a bit early, as usual, after telling the dispatcher that he was heading for the office. But he phoned Anna from a payphone and told her that he was busy with Makartsev's wife. *You understand yourself what kind of a day this is!* Now Aleksey was free until twelve thirty, but he wasn't even thinking of doing any moonlighting. He quickly turned on to the Volokolamsk Chaussee and, breaking the law, sped down the middle lane past lines of trucks to his own Anosino.

There they had buried his grandma Agafya the preceding Sunday. Aleksey and Lyuba were there, too, of course, at the funeral; they'd come down on Friday, after Klavdiya had discovered the old woman dead in a bent-over position, face down on the floor in front of an icon. Agafya hadn't died of anything but her eighty-two years. To her very last day she had worked on her garden and kept seventeen chickens there, if you counted the cockerel.

First, they were thinking of taking her to Zvenigorod for her burial service, but Aleksey went to the church on his neighbour's motorbike and arranged with the priest to conduct the service at her place for thirty roubles. When he found out that Agafya had been the Chief Beggar at Anosino Convent the priest knocked five roubles off the fee.

The cemetery at Anosino sits on a hill that is visible from every side, even though it's in the woods. His grandmother's grave was dug out on the edge of the cemetery, in between two iron fences (every Russian tries to fence off the grave of his dear ones ever higher, so that nobody will trample on it or mess it up, and even puts spikes on the fence so that people won't climb over it). The pit they dug wasn't very deep – the earth had yet to thaw out, and it didn't want to accept Agafya. The wake was a big affair, noisy, with the empty vodka bottles alone that they now had to take back to the store numbering nineteen, along with seven empty smaller vodka flasks and two bags full of fortified-wine bottles. They scraped the bottom of every dish at the wake, so that Grandmother Agafya would rest in peace and the earth over her would be lighter than a feather.

On the way Aleksey decided to drive first to Pokrovskoye, to the governing board of the Lenin Collective Farm, to try his luck talking to the chairman. *You know, my own dear grandmother's dead, and now we've got to convey her property – that is, her house – to her grandson. The house, all the same, is worthless, rotten, straw-thatched, and I'm the legal heir; if there's any problem I'll get it re-registered at the notary's with a wink, since I work you-know-where.*

Over the three days that had passed since his grandmother's funeral Aleksey had realized that he wasn't going to be building an extension to his parents' house but putting the money and effort into Agafya's house – and consequently having his own *dacha*. That was something not just anybody could dream of.

So Aleksey rolled up to the office of the collective farm in style and parked the car so that it would be visible from the chairman's window. The chairman turned out to be there. He had known Nikanor Dvoyeninov since after the war, but he still wouldn't support the initiative.

'Rights are rights, but, Aleksey, you haven't been a registered member of the collective for a long time. And the plot's in a great spot. We'll hand it over to a member of the cooperative. They'll build a new house so that the collective farm's prosperity won't be put to shame if any high officials drive by on the highway.' So nothing was going to come of it. 'Well, heard anything interesting there at your Central Committee?' the chairman said, changing the subject.

'Everything's all right there,' said Aleksey.

'All right? That's good,' said the chairman. 'In fact, if you think about it, there's only the one way . . .'

It occurred to him that chauffeurs such as Aleksey weren't just lying around in the streets. And if he had a chauffeur to drive him around who had formerly worked for the Central Committee it wouldn't look bad at all.

After getting the invitation to move back to the collective farm, Aleksey, of course, was laughing inside, but he didn't show it. 'If I build myself a house, and get my family used to the village,' he answered evasively, 'then I might think about it. But, on the other hand, the house was Agafya's, after all. You can't simply . . .'

'No,' the chairman agreed. 'But the owner of the property has died, and the land is neither yours nor mine. It's the collective's, whether under the house or around it. So we can.'

Then it suddenly occurred to Aleksey. 'But if my mother and father get divorced, can the house be registered in my mother's name? *She's* a member of the collective, after all!'

'Is that any reason to get divorced?'

'They aren't getting a divorce because of that. They've been going to for a long time.'

'Well, that's up to the court to decide.'

On the way to Anosino Aleksey slammed on the brakes in front of a shop and bought a bottle of vodka without having to queue. As soon as his mother, bustling around, had put food on the table he plumped the bottle down. He wasn't drinking himself.

The bottle emptied quickly. Nikanor offered to run out and get a second one, since it was such a sudden holiday, but his son then said that he'd met the chairman who was worried about what was to become of Agafya's house. However, there was a way out.

His mother, who twigged right away, agreed instantly to divorce Nikanor in her son's interests. His father burst into tears.

'I fought in the war. Surely I wasn't fighting for that?'

'Shut up!' Klavdiya shouted at him. 'It's for the good of the family! Shut up, if you don't know what's going on!'

Nikanor nodded his head, as if in agreement, but the tears streamed down. 'I'm scared, anyway; scared.'

'Afterwards we get back together again, dummy,' Klavdiya explained calmly. 'And until then we can live in sin . . . You haven't got it up in a long time anyway. The important thing is to get Mother's house registered in my name so they don't take it away.'

She started telling Aleksey how they had sorted things out at Agafya's house after the funeral. 'I carted out a heap of rubbish, and there was still some left. Take a look. It might be some good to somebody.'

'On foot or shall we drive over?'

'We could go on foot. Our feet won't fail, but it is a bit far . . .'

She wanted Aleksey to drive her through the village. They drove off. Aleksey himself unlocked the padlock and walked into the house, looking around with fresh eyes and sizing it up for his and Lyuba's arrival in the summer. None of the junk there was useful.

'Burn the lot of it, and that's it,' Aleksey decided.

An entire wall and corner, as far as the window, was occupied by the iconostasis that his grandmother had saved from the convent in the nick of time. Aleksey straight away started taking down the icons and stacking them in the middle of the room. Klavdiya silently watched, understood and didn't interfere.

'Whoa!' said Aleksey edifyingly, finishing the job. 'There'll be more room and less dust! And we have to consider my position. Let's go, Pa. It's all going out to the garden!'

'Long past time!' declared Nikanor, making up for his defeat on the issue of the divorce and looking triumphantly at his wife. 'It's what I've been saying all along!' They began dragging the heavy copper-bound icons out and stacking them on the vegetable bed, still damp from the just-melted snow.

'Those icons are good for keeping troubles away, you know,' muttered Klavdiya, trailing behind them.

'If you don't understand something just shut up!' Nikanor admonished. 'Otherwise I might just get married to somebody else after our divorce.'

'Who needs you, you piece of trash? You're barely able to stand up!'

'That's not important. I'll find someone younger, don't you worry! I know my own worth.' He fell suddenly into a mischievous mood and dragged the icons from the house out to the garden at a trot, egging on his son. Aleksey heaped up old clothes and two broken stools on top of the pile of icons, shoved a bundle of old newspapers under the lot, took his beautiful Ronson lighter – a gift from Makartsev – out of his pocket and set fire to it. The heat of the dry newsprint started the rags smouldering and smoking. The stools began to char. The icons themselves snapped and cracked, but, covered in paint and metal, didn't seem to want to catch fire.

If the escapade had been Nikanor's idea Klavdiya would have clobbered him with whatever was at hand and pulled the icons out of the fire. If they couldn't stay in the house, then let them lie in the barn, at least, preserved. Just in case. This was God stuff! But her little son knew everything; he'd been an officer, after all, and now he was working for an organization more important than any other on this earth. He knew what he was doing, for sure. Maybe the order had come down again to destroy religious things, or maybe the icons would spoil something for him if someone denounced him for it. A summer vacationer, an artist, had come to Grandma's the year before. He had said that these icons were old, from the seventeenth century or something. He had offered eighty roubles apiece for them. And Agafya had over a dozen of them. He might even have come up with more, but Grandma told him that the icons belonged to the convent and that selling them would be the worst of sins. So Klavdiya wasn't going to say anything about it now, because of the sinfulness attendant on it. It would be better to let them burn. After all, fire was a natural calamity, while money was nothing more than cupidity.

Aleksey and his father went back into the cabin to talk about the renovation, to estimate how much timber would be called for and where the wood had fallen in from rot and needed replacing. They decided to do the whole thing themselves and not hire anyone else.

'We'll get started over the May Day holidays. Only you have to get divorced as fast as you can.'

'All right, all right!' grumbled Klavdiya. 'Tomorrow we'll go. Only what reason are we going to give for the divorce?'

'Tell them he drinks. Say he's an alcoholic and that's that.'

'Me, an alcoholic?' his father said indignantly. 'Well, what a thing to say! I can drink, of course, but an alcoholic – that's someone who . . . and . . . me?'

'What, Pa, are you a little kid? "Me, me!" Isn't it all the same thing to you?'

'Don't listen to him, Son. He's talking nonsense, really and truly! For shame!'

'It's only for the piece of paper,' Aleksey clarified.

'Well, then, if it's just for the paper, then of course!'

When the Dvoyeninovs went back out to the garden the icons had already caught fire. They blazed away with a pure orange flame after their long ordeal, without fumes or smoke. Everything else had already deposited a lot of ashes around the yard.

'It'll be good fertilizer,' observed Aleksey, looking at his watch.

'How's that boss of yours doing?' his father asked. 'Has he got himself out of hospital yet?'

'Actually, today's the day I pick him up.'

'Meaning he's got over it. But he could get stuck in the hospital if they find something else. My wounded leg has started getting unsteady, too.'

'Drink less,' suggested Klavdiya.

'The doctor says, the word I forget . . .'

'Thrombophlebitis,' his wife pronounced, without stumbling.

'That's it, the very one! With that, you can get into hospital. But why would I go there when I can still walk? When I'm not able to walk, that's when I'll go – have I thought it out right, Son? Go to hospital or not, you're still going to die in the end.'

'Who knows!' said Aleksey. 'For sure, you have to go to the hospital, get yourself examined . . .'

'That's all I need, to get examined! Just let them do it and they'll find things that'll send you straight to your grave. And we've got to renovate the house.'

'Well, I'm off.' Aleksey got himself ready. 'Lyuba and I will be show-ing up here for the three days of the holidays if they don't make me duty driver. And we'll grab some food on the way.'

Aleksey went out through the gate, and the black Volga sped off right away, disappearing into the woods before Klavdiya managed to run down to the fence. Aleksey was late, but he supposed that on such a happy day they wouldn't swear at him. Zina had already come down to the street and was waiting for him. She was upset and told Aleksey to hurry up. The hospital had promised to hand Makartsev over to them at 2 p.m. after his consultation. Zina rang her husband from the lobby.

'Why so late?' he asked. 'I'm sick of waiting.'

'Have they discharged you?'

'Long ago. I'm already dressed,' said Makartsev, even though the doc-tors had only just left him and he'd only just got his pyjamas off and put his trousers on.

He was being helped by a nurse so that he would move less. In the lobby he appeared with the woman who headed the cardiology depart-ment, supporting him by one arm. Makartsev stepped forward to his wife by himself and kissed her on her lightly painted lips. She blinked rapidly to restrain her tears.

'Lord, surely it's all over now,' she said joyously.

'Nothing is over yet,' said the department head. 'Makartsev has to get back to normal. A strict regime in everything: food, rest, walks, sleep, no kind of overindulgence in anything.' She looked at Zina.

'All right!' Makartsev said, spreading his hands in resignation. 'What kind of overindulgence could I get up to anyway?'

'Don't try to laugh it off, Makartsev! You may *not* go to work. You have to rest in a sanatorium for six weeks or so.'

'Leave it out!' he replied. 'You've already tortured me enough here with all your rest! For me the best sanatorium is my work.'

'If you don't obey, I'll phone the Central Committee and complain about you.'

'All right. For a week at least at home and then off to the sanatorium.'

'And it has to be a hospital regime at home, too. I'm coming to check on it.'

'What a despot you are!'

Zina handed her husband his overcoat, buttoning him up herself and checking to see whether his scarf covered his neck, even though outside it was warm and sunny. Leaping out of the car, Aleksey opened the door for his boss and waited, smiling.

'Good man!' Makartsev said cheerfully and shook Aleksey's hand as firmly as he could. 'You were probably thinking I wasn't going to make it, that it was curtains for me!' Makartsev guffawed. He was happy.

'What are you talking about, boss? You got a little sick, and that was it. It happens! My father's sick, too . . . And that's all there is to it!'

'Did you know, Zina, how scared he got when I collapsed?' said Makartsev, getting into the front seat with a groan and turning his head back towards his wife. He opened the glove compartment with his right hand. 'Well, Aleksey, where are some cigarettes for me?'

'Igor!' Zina entreatingly put a hand on his shoulder. 'What for?'

'There, you see, brother, the domestic dictatorship of the proletariat. You can't do this, you can't do that! Now it starts. Can't smoke even one damned cigarette. You and me, Aleksey, we'll have to smoke only when we're driving, on the sly, so that nobody catches us.'

He liked this sort of democratic conversation with his chauffeur. Aleksey sped down the ring road so as to turn off Leningrad Prospect to Makartsev's building and then drive back to the office to tell everyone all the news.

'I wrote out a menu for you from a book, Makartsev,' Zina recalled. 'How an American millionaire eats. At nine, oatmeal porridge without milk and a quarter-pound of boiled veal. And a cup of green tea. At twelve thirty, ten ounces of boiled deep-sea fish without any salt, five raw quail eggs, a cup of coffee and a piece of cheese. At five, half a glass of strong bouillon, wildfowl lightly fried all over, two ounces of caviar with lemon, and two apricots. At eight thirty evening tea . . .'

'Where am I going to get that – deep-sea fish? And where's the brandy?

Or maybe I missed that, eh, Aleksey?'

'Brandy separately, on the sly, like the cigarettes . . .'

'Why haven't you said anything about Boris, Zina?' Makartsev asked drily, suddenly serious.

'I didn't want to remind you. They telephoned last night with permission for us to come and get him today.'

'Today? Why the hell didn't you tell me?'

'I thought that I'd take you home and then go and get him.' She closed her eyes and her mouth broke into a smile. 'That's what my day's been like today, nothing but running around for other people.'

'No, it won't do, that way. We'll go together!'

'You can't!'

'Positive emotions are allowed! Here's what, Aleksey. Let's go, brother. Turn that wheel around. You know where to.'

'Petrovka 38?'

Aleksey glanced momentarily into his side mirror and then moved abruptly to change from the left to the right lane, skirting around the shoal of cars heading for the left turn. Everyone was silent, not saying a word to one another, until the chauffeur braked at the gates of the Criminal Investigations Department.

'I beg you, stay in the car. I'll go in.'

'And you can manage without me? After all, I'm . . .'

'Don't get up, don't get up.'

When his wife had disappeared through the gates Makartsev pulled a glass phial out of his pocket and shook two tablets out of it into his palm, then threw them into his mouth, putting a finger to his lips as a sign to Aleksey that his taking the medicine had to be kept a secret. Aleksey nodded: that much was clear.

They sat there for nearly forty minutes, and Aleksey started thinking about Anna. She would be certain that he had taken Makartsev home a long time ago and was now moonlighting, chasing all over Moscow. And here he was, sitting here without making anything on the side, while Makartsev, always so busy, was also just sitting with him inside the car, waiting in silence. Aleksey hesitated over whether or not to ask Makartsev about his transfer to Sovtransavto. But he decided that now wasn't the time. He would just say anyway that Aleksey should remind him about it some other time.

At first Makartsev didn't recognize his son with his head shaved. Boris appeared from behind the gate in his jacket but without his fur hat, with a distracted expression on his face. Zina trotted along after him, her outstretched hand holding his hat that he had evidently refused to put on. Aleksey discreetly turned his head away so as not to show inordinate curiosity. Boris opened the door and got into the rear seat without saying hello to his father or even seeming to notice him. He addressed the chauffeur. 'Give me a cigarette!'

Aleksey cast a sidelong glance at Makartsev. The latter had become all tense and sat without stirring, staring straight ahead. Aleksey slowly pulled out a packet of cigarettes, shook it so that a cigarette protruded and clicked his handsome lighter.

'Let's go,' Makartsev squeezed out, after Zina had sat down next to Boris. 'Home, and quickly.'

'What did you get me out for?' asked Boris.

'Don't go on like that, Boris,' Zina said quietly.

'Who asked you to do it?'

'Look, we'll talk about it at home,' Makartsev cut in.

'Hey, Dad has just got out of hospital, and he came straight here to get you.'

'And where have I come from? They brought me here from the loony bin.'

'Are you hungry?'

Boris didn't answer. He spat on the carpet and smeared it with his foot. He didn't utter a single word all the way home. When they turned on to Petrovsko-Razumovskaya and stopped in front of their entryway Makartsev said, holding the car door open: 'Here's what, Aleksey. Tell them at the office that everything's fine with Makartsev. He's feeling fine, and he'll soon be up and about. But as far as everything else – don't . . .'

'Of course I won't,' said Aleksey, offended. 'I'm not a kid.'

'Don't do this. *Don't* tell them that I'm coming in soon, got that?'

'What you tell me to say is what gets said.'

Makartsev slammed the door shut, and Aleksey drove off.

'Why did you get me out?' yelled Boris from the doorway.

'We're your parents,' his father said. 'Makartsev's son should be at home, not in prison.'

'And what if he's better off in prison?'

'Think about your father, Boris! He's had a heart attack. Think about his position: after all, he's a candidate member of the Central Committee!'

'And why do I have to think all my life about his damned career? What am I supposed to do? Quake along with him?'

'Don't you understand', said Zina, 'that the road to full membership of the Central Committee may be barred to him now, and that you're the cause?'

'Then there'll just be one less Nazi. And if you want to know, I ran over them on purpose, those two, just to get you into trouble!'

'Me?' Makartsev, still in his overcoat, stood in the corridor in dismay, and sweat covered his forehead. 'You're making it up, you little bastard! I'm your father, after all!'

'Any old wino would be a better father than you!'

'Hey, look here . . .'

'You're not worried for my sake – you're trembling for the sake of your own skin. At home you come on all principled, but at your Central Committee you kiss the arses of those creeps. And if you want to know, people like you are going to get strung up soon. You've ruined my entire life, you filthy Stalinist!'

'You little fool!' Makartsev tried to smile in order to assert his superiority, but his hands were trembling from weakness. 'I almost suffered myself in the years of the cult of Stalin. We never mentioned it to you.'

'"Almost suffered . . ." It would have been better for you to have rotted honestly in the camps and not be a disgrace to me!'

'Son, did it ever cross your mind that it was for your sake that I kept your mother and me safe? And improved my position, so that you were well off? And if they'd raked me in they would have sent you off to a KGB orphanage. If I hadn't preserved my position, my prestige, my background, you'd never have got a look in at any institute. They would have thrown you out of school like a dog to run a machine in some factory. But you're nearly living under ideal communism, and you blame your father just for the sake of it. First off, at least find out what you want out of life!'

'And how am I going to find out if they jam every broadcast? How?'

'All right, I'll bring you French newspapers and magazines.' His father switched over to his tried-and-true method of education through bribery. 'Or even American ones.'

'You could have been bringing them home for a long time.'

A quiet settled on them, and Zina felt that the conversation about politics had exhausted itself as usual, ending in nothing, with tones softening all around. She decided to divert the men's discussion into practical channels and thus unite them.

'You've missed a lot. We're going to have to settle your conflict with the institute.'

'With what institute?'

'Yours.'

'You idiots! There isn't any institute! You're not saying that for a whole year you thought there *was*!'

'Then what is there?' Makartsev decided that Boris was pulling their leg.

'Nothing! I never even enrolled anywhere.'

'Then what was it you were doing?'

'Drinking. Listening to music. Bringing girls home during the day. Surely my mother told you?'

'Zina?' yelled Makartsev. 'Do you hear this?'

She didn't look around but went out.

'Could it be that you're not even a Young Communist?' his father said quietly.

'Of course not! I burned my card after I got out of school, so as not to pay my dues!'

Makartsev gritted his teeth and leaned his forehead against the door-jamb. 'What is all this?' he said once again with difficulty. 'It's like I'm not in my own home at all. Well, all right, Boris. We won't delve into the past. We'll just put a cross through it. Let's try to start life anew. Let's think about what you're going to do. Work? Take a course that'll get you ready for college?'

'If I go anywhere, it'll be to a religious seminary.'

'You believe in God?'

'What does God have to do with it? I'll go just to spoil your career!'

'There you go again! You have to engage in some kind of self-improve-ment, build yourself some kind of fundament . . .'

'You've already built me one! Anyway, is there anything to eat in this house? Or am I going to die of hunger? In the nick they at least give you slop . . .' Boris went into the kitchen.

Zina came back into the corridor. 'I've made up your bed. Go and lie down.'

'Well, there's a nice little coming-home present to make things all right. I might as well go back to hospital.'

'Calm down, I beg you.'

'I *am* calm. I'm absolutely calm, Zina. It's not that easy to get me down. I didn't clamber up my own egotistical stepladder, after all; I climbed the Party stairway. And it was hard, to be sure! The Georgian mafia came – I escaped destruction; the Ukrainian one came – I held on. And the snivellers, the ones who now are running around stealing without any principles, without faith, without convictions, they're not going to bring me down. I'll keep on fighting! Boris's cynicism is because of his age. It'll pass. I myself don't want him to go into Party affairs. As long as he doesn't steal or kill anybody . . .'

Makartsev realized that he was talking stupidly. He waved a hand and went into the bedroom. There, still agitated, he walked from the door to the window and back again, feeling his heart pounding. It would be bet-ter to lie down.

Somewhere to one side of Makartsev there was a rustling noise, and the Marquis de Custine stepped towards him, smiling guiltily, and tenderly placed a hand on his shoulder. Makartsev instinctively leaned away. Amazement sprang up, but no question escaped from his mouth; Makartsev just breathed in the refreshing scent of his strong eau de Cologne and silently looked at his uninvited guest, who was dressed to the nines: a waistcoat with pale blue stripes harmonized with his dark-blue frock coat. A carefully – even coquettishly – tied cravat complemented the outfit. Glints from the diamonds on the Marquis's fingers ran along the walls of the bedroom when he moved his hands.

'How unpleasant this all is,' said de Custine thoughtfully, pressing his sword to his hip. 'In our time, just imagine, things went just about the same with our young people: drunken ones chased around on horseback, knocking people down, avoiding punishment through connections. Send the boy out of the country, if you can. There he'll have a chance at some alternative . . .'

'Are you joking?' said Makartsev, smiling sourly. 'Who would let him go? Because of him, the road there is closed even for me right now! And how all the rest of it is going to come out is shrouded in gloom.' They fell silent.

De Custine looked around him. 'Excuse me for this indiscreet question: do you sleep on that bed with your wife?'

'At times,' nodded Makartsev.

'In what sense?'

'Most often she's asleep while I stay up. I'm a senior executive, after all. A so-called *apparatchik*.'

'Yes, of course, and let's hope that you'll be able to move higher still, even though that's difficult for you right now . . .'

Makartsev felt a weakness in his knees and sat down on the bed. 'I'm in bad shape, Marquis,' he admitted, suddenly enervated. 'Internally I'm in bad shape, and externally there's trouble! Life is making me sick . . .'

'I understand,' de Custine said, stroking Makartsev's elbow. 'I had these sorts of grave moments in my own life. That's why I have appeared, so as to express my sympathy. I feel sorry that I can do nothing to help you, although – believe me – I would consider it an honour to do so. Right now you have to take a sedative. And lie down on your bed. If you'll permit me, I'll stay here a while beside you . . .'

De Custine looked on in silence as Makartsev slowly undressed, poured out two tablets on to his palm and swallowed them, got into bed, covering himself with his blanket, and closed his eyes.

He could hear footsteps, and the door opened a crack.

'How are you doing?' his wife asked.

He ran his eyes around the room. De Custine had disappeared. In his place stood Zina handing him some sort of potion. Placing a hand on his palpitating heart he assured her and himself that his heart was healthy and should not be ailing him any more.

# 66

# Personal Indiscretion

Anna could unerringly guess when to put calls through to her boss without asking him. They rang Yagubov while he was getting together his documents to go to the Central Committee. Yagubov didn't know who was talking, but he was from 'that place'. The caller was interested in Ivlev. Yagubov reined in his normal haste and answered calmly, with dignity, but he also refrained from giving a direct evaluation, so as not to influence his comrades with his own point of view. He said that this employee had been hired by Makartsev, and the editor-in-chief was ill.

'We won't be waiting, most likely, Yagubov. We have enough material on him, and everything is already agreed.'

'I understand you,' Yagubov answered. 'We, on this end, will take your signal under advisement.'

Even though Yagubov was running late, he decided to delay a little bit longer and solve the problem expeditiously, guided by the principle learned by him from American businessmen's instruction guides: don't consult the same piece of paper twice. He had consciously refrained from clearing up anything over the telephone that would let him be freer in his actions. On his return, Makartsev was going to go all sentimental about how they had to take care of their gifted employees, to correct their errors tactfully. *He tries to be nice, but he not only acts to the detriment of Party principle, he gets out of step with everyone else, unfortunately. He doesn't understand that there's a process going on of full amalgamation of the Party leadership and the KGB organs. And pursuing a common policy – that means helping one another and not fighting. Makartsev not only doesn't have any connections to the organs, he deals with them condescendingly as well. Not to beat about the bush, leaders like that under these new conditions will put the brakes on our perfecting the Party-governmental apparatus.*

He called Anna. 'Get me Kashin, right away.'

Yagubov walked around his desk, waiting for him. Kashin came in, smiling affably.

'What fantastic sunshine there is today! It must be on account of Lenin's birthday . . . Maybe we can change the curtains in your office to something more summery – brighter, happier on the eye?'

'You can,' Yagubov agreed, not getting drawn into his chatter. 'Listen: what's the best statute for sacking Ivlev?'

Kashin, thinking furiously, fixed a more serious gaze on the deputy editor. 'I've found out something about Makartsev,' he pronounced, as if by the way. 'He'll be showing up after the holidays . . .'

'I know.'

'And the Party bureau wants to expel Ivlev on what grounds?' Kashin said, in an attempt to clarify the situation. He was continuing to weigh things up.

'We'll include it in the Party bureau records afterwards.' Yagubov made a wry face at the managing editor's slow-wittedness. 'What, don't you get it?'

'*They* called *you*?' Kashin elucidated, pointing a thumb over his shoulder. 'And *they* didn't suggest which statute?'

'If they're going to suggest everything, what are you and I here for?'

'Fair enough! Then how about this one . . . under Article 47 of the Labour Code, the paragraph entitled "Untrustworthiness"?'

'That would be very point-blank,' objected Yagubov, slowing down his pacing. 'There'll be talk . . . By the way, what are his morals like?'

'As far as his morals go, anything bad, of course, remains to be seen . . . But what if we do fire him on that account? There was a circular not long ago with a new formulation, "Personal Indiscretion". It specifically concerns workers on the ideological front. And under this statute the courts are forbidden from investigating cases of unfair dismissal.'

'That'll do it!' agreed Yagubov. 'Make out the order as quick as you can. And another thing: date everything – let's see – a week earlier. Otherwise it'll look as if we missed it ourselves, waiting for a directive from them.'

Kashin nodded and dragged his trailing leg to the door. Following him with a condescending look, Yagubov sat down behind his desk and removed a folded piece of paper from his wallet. Two columns of names were written on it. Over the left-hand column was a minus sign, over the right-hand one a plus. Yagubov passed his eyes down the left-hand column. He started with Polishchuk. Next to that name were two question marks, and Yagubov now confidently crossed them out. Next came Rappoport, Matrikulov (with a question mark), Ivlev, Kachkareva (with a question mark), Zakamorny (already crossed out) and a few more names. Last in the column was Makartsev. Yagubov took a pen out of his pocket, clicked it to expose the ballpoint and neatly crossed off Ivlev.

After that he let his gaze wander over the right-hand column with the plus sign. These were those reliable comrades that he had known in his previous jobs, who had proven by their loyalty to Yagubov that they were of like mind, people that he could depend on. On this list Volobuyev's name was crossed out, since he had already successfully transferred to *Trudovaya Pravda*. The rest of them were working in various places – on district committees, at institutes, in the KGB – and everything had already been agreed with them in principle. True, the majority of them had never had anything to do with journalism, but their organizational capabilities were not in doubt.

After looking down the column Yagubov placed a fat mark alongside the name Avdyukhin. Avdyukhin worked as an instructor in the Agitation and Propaganda Department of a city committee and in his time had been together with Yagubov in Hungary. *A reliable fellow, a man of few words. He knows how to gather information, and that's the most important thing for a special correspondent. To begin with, we'll entrust Rappoport with the writing of his pieces; let him share his experience with a comrade . . .*

His reflections were interrupted by Kashin. 'It's all sorted,' he said, putting the order on the desk.

'But what do I need this for?' Yagubov said in surprise, replacing the list of names in his wallet.

'For your signature. Good riddance to bad rubbish.'

'Kashin, my dear man! I'm starting to worry about you. Call in Ivlev and have him submit his resignation, at his own request. Afterwards, explain to him about his personal indiscretion. Get all the paperwork done correctly, then come back for my signature.'

Kashin silently took the order and went out in embarrassment. Yagubov shrugged and began walking around his office, thinking things through on the hoof. He congratulated himself on his boldness. After all, the editor-in-chief was gone – Yagubov had taken over his responsibilities, even though Kashin had tried to remind him that Makartsev had ordered that no personnel issues were to be decided in his absence. But Makartsev could hardly get indignant about it. Now he'd got caught with his own snout in the jam-jar, and he'd have to swallow this particular pill. Somebody was covering for Makartsev in the Central Committee. But if the Politburo got all the facts the axe would fall right away. *The issue isn't my own candidacy*, Yagubov thought at this point, *not mine at all! The issue is Party principle. Makartsev even once spoke positively about Dubcek after he'd already been kicked out.*

Thinking over what he needed to do, Yagubov walked past Anna into Makartsev's office and phoned Shamayev, Kegelbanov's secretary, on the secure line. Yagubov guessed that Kegelbanov, as soon as he was informed about Yagubov' situation, would understand that his countryman wasn't going to bother him with trifles on the phone. Shamayev sounded friendly enough to Yagubov, but at his request for a personal interview with Kegelbanov he asked to be told briefly what it was about. Yagubov explained concisely and forensically, leaving himself out of it. H[e] alluded to the opinion of the Party bureau and the editorial staff whos[e] will he, Yagubov, was expected to carry out. He had hesitated over remind[ing] them that Makartsev had hidden himself out of reach of the K[GB] organs at a time that had been difficult for the Party, but then decided [that] this fact would come in handy later. He mentioned only Makartsev's

'Did you get that down?' asked Yagubov, after waiting.

'Everything gets recorded,' Shamayev reassured him. 'I'll pass it on.'

Yagubov went out into the reception room in an elated mood. 'To the Central Committee!' He whistled softly.

Aleksey jumped up and ran ahead of Yagubov, untangling the keys on his ring. The engine was already running by the time the deputy editor-in-chief got into the car. Two employees bowed politely to Yagubov, and he gave them a brief nod, thinking that it wouldn't be long before the chauffeur started opening the door for him. That wasn't done for anyone who ranked lower than head of a Central Committee department. The issue was inconsequential anyway, since it wasn't exactly arduous for him to open the door for himself. There was a special sort of democracy about the whole thing.

Kashin observed Yagubov's departure from his window. He was standing, and Ivlev was sitting behind his desk.

'Who's the resignation addressed to?'

'Address it to Makartsev. The way it should be.' He looked at Ivlev in sympathy. 'I don't have anything to do with this, after all. You understand that I'm just the one who carries it out. They order me, and I do it. If it up to me, you could carry on working here until you retire – no prob- Maybe you can get a job somewhere . . .'

able to restrain himself, Kashin added off his own bat what he upposed to: the statute under which Ivlev was resigning excluded ssibility. Ivlev didn't know this, but he wasn't even paying any his managing editor's last words.

with this newspaper!' Ivlev said light-heartedly. 'That's not out.' He flattened out the resignation sheet with a sweep- ed it and held it out.

little later for your work book, all right?'

Ivlev stopped, wavering. He decided that he would leave , so that he wouldn't run into anyone, wouldn't have have to listen to words of sympathy. Then it least Nadya. But straight away he convinced himself that it would be better not to drop in on her either. She would hear it from the others when he was no longer there. It would be better not to show up at Rappoport's either. As a result, he looked in on nobody but Polishchuk.

'I'm clearing out.'

'On assignment? Then why don't I know about it?'

'Evidently Yagubov didn't allow himself to discuss it with anyone. I'm out of here altogether.'

'What! Explain clearly! After all, Makartsev has forbidden . . .'

'I heard that, too, Polishchuk. And you should be a little more cautious yourself: I've got a tail on me.'

'Nonsense! They're not going to get away with this!' Polishchuk switched on the intercom.

'Anna, is Yagubov in?'

'At the Central Committee. He'll be back in a couple of hours.'

'Right.' He pressed another button. 'Rappoport, could you come up here urgently? Thanks.'

'I'm getting out of here,' said Ivlev cheerfully.

'Hang on!'

'You know, I'm not in the mood . . .'

'We can turn the tables on them, I'm certain!' He was talking to Ivlev's back. The latter shrugged and walked swiftly to the lift, so as not to run into Rappoport.

Polishchuk's desk was covered with material prepared for the ninety-ninth anniversary of Lenin's birth. Today's issue, entirely devoted to that wondrous date, accommodated just a few of them. Right now Polishchuk was deciding which pieces wouldn't get too out of date before Lenin's next, one-hundredth, anniversary, which ones to release gradually in the run-up to the jubilee year, which ones to send back to their various departments for reworking with new facts and which to throw out completely. The executive secretary moved the still unconsidered pieces to one side, took out his official-use-only telephone book and quickly leafed through it.

Polishchuk's gaze fixed on the name Khardankin, who was somebody he had worked with on the Young Communist central committee. Khardankin had been keen to get on the fast track; he was the sort who delighted in the benefits but never trampled on his comrades as he rose. When he was offered a transfer to the KGB he first carefully found out what conditions he was being offered and only then agreed.

On getting through to him on the phone, Polishchuk asked for advice. So much and so on, an intelligent fellow, a pity . . .

'We don't occupy ourselves with fools,' Khardankin answered seriously. 'There's the police for that.'

After asking for Ivlev's name, he promised to make inquiries. He told Polishchuk to call back in three days or so. Polishchuk, making a gesture of helplessness with his hands, explained to Rappoport, who had just come in, that he was trying to clear up at least some of what was going on.

'These are Yagubov's little jokes. He's even trying to run me over with his car. Makartsev will come back and reverse this command.'

'Jokes come in various forms,' Rappoport noted philosophically after snuffling for a while. 'Yagubov called me in and asked, "What are you thinking up campaigns for? That's not right. Campaigns come from the People! You can't make them up. You have to take them from life." "There's a thought!" I told him. "Whenever you see one, grab it!" Since that time he hasn't said a word about campaigns.'

'Fucking idiot!' Polishchuk squeezed out.

'Not at all,' objected Rappoport. 'Have a look at today's front page. There's a campaign by the workers at the Flame of the Revolution factory to save enough steel for an eighty-foot-high statue of Lenin. In reality, the steel is going to be used for new tanks, but that's just a detail. Last night Yagubov crossed out the byline of the author of the article, the not-unknown Y. Tavrov, and wrote Y. Sidorov. "Why?" I asked. "The readers get tired of seeing the same name over and over," Yagubov told me. "Anyway, the name Tavrov will remind people of times long since condemned by the Party and now forgotten. Get yourself a new pen-name, Rappoport." "Fine! I'll use 'Rappoport' as my byline . . ." "Your humour is inappropriate," he says. "Use Ivanov or Petrov – aren't there enough names out there for you to choose?" I think this is a sign . . .'

'A sign?'

'Why, yes. It used to be that a Jew could get published if he went under a Russian last name. Now they ask: "And what's his real name?" And then they don't publish him! So Yagubov, as I interpret it, is like the indicator on a barometer. But the mainspring . . .'

'But what about Ivlev? To do that without involving the Party bureau or the editorial staff . . .'

'Yes, they do seem in a bit of a hurry. Where is he, by the way?'

Emerging from the newspaper office Ivlev walked slowly, feeling the sun baking down. He unbuttoned his raincoat, then took it off and hung it over his arm. He tried to concentrate, to decide where to go and how to get by. His thoughts ran in circles, tumbling one over another, overstepping one another, and melting, possibly, in the heat. Ivlev decided to walk home, then sit behind his desk and try to concentrate there. And begin a new life. A new one, for sure. It wasn't clear yet what kind, but it was clear that it couldn't be the one it had been. It was a good thing that the newspaper had torn him away from his old life. The quagmire had sucked at him, and he had never had enough willpower to pull himself free. 'Writing for a newspaper', he recalled Rappoport's words, 'is the same as shitting in the ocean.'

There were Intourist buses packed everywhere on the squares and at the hotels of the city centre. The foreigners were all sporting movie cameras. They smiled at passers-by, and Ivlev slowed his pace, trying to catch snatches of unfamiliar language. He walked down Marx Prospect past his old university. There were fewer people here. A group of silent youngsters overtook him. When they drew level with him they suddenly pushed Ivlev against the boundary wall.

'Just keep quiet,' a voice said right above his ear. 'Get into the car!'

They twisted his right arm behind him, and he groaned with pain. He strained in resistance to this absurdity, this low behaviour, this coercion.

'Let go!' He jerked and managed to break free for a moment, but then they grabbed him again from both sides. One of them spat at him, 'You filth!'

'Hey, people!' Ivlev yelled with all his might, and the foreigners who at first weren't aware of the fight looked round at them. 'Hey, look, everyone! I'm being arrested, just like under Stalin! I'm innocent! For what? Look, this is the KGB!'

Instantly he felt as though he was being stupid, but those last words saved him. The youths ran off in all directions, pretending not to be involved. The car drove off. Ivlev stood for a moment, brushing the yellow chalk off his sleeve where they had pinned him against the wall, and then made his way on. His thoughts now had stopped being wan and were beginning to spin around in a dance together. He had to disappear as quickly as possible, get away, hide . . . Where? He couldn't go home; even less go to any of his friends'.

Ivlev walked another half a block in tense perplexity. He decided to cross the road and hail a taxi. To get out of there, even though he still hadn't come up with a plan; split, so that he would be lost to sight. He went down into an underground pedestrian crossing and ran through it.

The Marquis de Custine appeared in front of Ivlev from nowhere and spread his arms wide, ready to take him into his embrace. So as not to get knocked off his feet, the Marquis had to lean back against the dirty tiled wall between two booksellers' stands. Ivlev came to a halt for a moment. His dismayed eyes got the impression of a strange man who looked like an ageing musketeer or an actor emerging from the prop room of some sort of old play. They looked each other in the eye. The moment lodged in his memory, and Ivlev would wrack his brains long after trying to remember where he had seen the man before, but he never would recall.

He ran further down the crossing, and de Custine, holding on to his sword, strove to keep up with him. Some of the passers-by in the tunnel stepped aside and looked around at them; others paid them no attention at all. The young men were waiting for Ivlev around the corner at the base of the stairs. There were six of them. He had scarcely appeared when they surrounded him in a thick circle and jammed a tennis ball into his mouth. His jaw muscles cramped and he wheezed with pain, but now he couldn't yell out.

They speedily dragged him up the stairs to the footpath and threw him into the rear seat of a black Volga that had been driven up close to the footpath. So as to eliminate the possibility of presenting an unattractive spectacle, they put a cardboard box over him, one that had contained a television set. The doors were slamming shut and the car moving away by the time the Marquis de Custine, panting, reached the top the stairs from the subway crossing and ran up to it. His blue cravat had been knocked askew, and his pomaded hair was dishevelled. He drew his sword, ready to enter the fray, but there was no longer anyone to fight.

'Curses!' the Marquis panted. 'I didn't interfere a century ago, and I've obligingly put up with everything that I see now, but this is too much!'

On the run, raging, he thrust his sword into the rear tyre of the Volga, pulled it out and plunged it in again.

Withdrawing it the second time, de Custine examined it. It was shorter: the broken-off tip remained in the tyre. The car drove off, but there came the sound of air hissing out of the ruptured tyre and then the dull sound of the wheel rim scraping along the pavement. The Marquis should have looked around, because brakes squealed behind him and other agents were now running towards him. Within a few seconds they were twisting his arms behind him.

The Volga with Ivlev in it came to a halt. The people in it slipped out and called for help from a nearby payphone. Without removing the television box, they dragged Ivlev into the rear seat of a second Volga, and it sped off with its siren going. The grey cardboard wall grew dull in front of Ivlev's eyes, and the smell of varnish and plastic was enough to make him choke. He was not aware that they were taking him in the direction opposite to his home – to the KGB's Lefortovo Prison.

A number of gawkers had collected on the footpath, and a policeman appeared, suggesting in no uncertain terms that they disperse. The passersby saw a man in a strange get-up, like someone from the last century, being led by two men in civilian clothes to a third car that drove up. It looked as though they were making a film.

Without putting up any resistance the Marquis de Custine silently climbed into the car, and when the door slammed behind him he disappeared. Not believing their eyes, the agents rummaged frantically through the interior of the car. There was nobody there.

# 67

# This Too Shall Pass

'Comrade Rappoport! Armoured Forces Marshal Katukov is on the line.'

'All right,' Rappoport wanly responded. 'I'm listening.'

'Comrade Rappoportov!' declared the Marshal. 'I want to remind you about my article. It has to be published for Victory Day.'

'Yes, of course,' mumbled Rappoport. 'Don't worry . . .'

'I'm not worried,' the Marshal snarled. 'If it's not, bear this in mind: I'm going to drive my tanks into your newspaper!'

Rappoport closed his eyes. He had chucked out Katukov's article ages ago. He didn't have the strength to throw himself under a tank with bottles of flammable liquids yet again. The telephone rang once more. Rappoport decided that he wasn't going to answer it; he was too tired. But the ringing wouldn't stop, and he exasperatedly picked up the receiver. 'Well?'

'This is Tonya,' he heard a woman's voice say.

'Which Tonya?'

'Tonya Ivleva.'

'Oh, of course. I had no idea! Forgive me!' Rappoport thought that Tonya had heard something about Nadya and was going to ask him to use his influence on her husband. That was easy enough. Of course, he would assure her that Ivlev didn't have anyone else on the side, that it was all gossip. If she was bright she would have to go along with the reassurance.

'I don't know what to do. I don't know who to turn to . . .'

'What's the matter, Tonya?' Rappoport asked innocently and kindly.

'The most important thing is not to worry.'

'They've arrested Ivlev . . .' Her voice rang out and then died.

'What?' Rappoport gulped air and held it in, afraid of letting it out, as if he was afraid that they wouldn't give him any more if he did. For the first time in his life he had failed to guess in advance what somebody wanted of him. After a pause he said: 'How did you find this out?'

'They rang me themselves. They said that I wasn't to worry and I wasn't to search for him. That he was in . . .'

'Where?'

'Their place.'

What service! Now they were telephoning people themselves. They phoned her to find out who she was going to call, where she was going to go. They needed his connections. Rappoport snorted. Tonya understood.

'I'm calling you from a payphone, a long way from my house, so . . .' That was a weak consolation, given that Rappoport wasn't talking on a public phone.

'Have you gone to anyone for advice?' he asked, for no real reason.

'I rang his mother. She shouted that her son was a traitor to the motherland and that he should pay for his crimes. That she was ashamed that she'd given birth to him. What can I do?'

'You shouldn't cry, Tonya! I beg you.' Rappoport avoided the danger and asked: 'And what is he accused of doing?'

'They say it was for hooliganism. That he started a fight; with witnesses and everything . . . There'll be an investigation. It'll be settled, they said. A trial, of course. Everything according to the law.'

'According to the law? Well, yes, of course, according to the law . . .' *That's an old song; we've learned it before. O Lord, everything's starting up again. The Inquisition bonfires are smoking.*

'Please do something! It's not true, after all. He can't . . .'

'Do you think I doubt that, Tonya? But what can I do? When things like this happen, who can help? Perhaps King Solomon . . . Maybe it'll all blow over. They'll interrogate him, hold him a while and then release him. We'll just have to hope. Ring me and keep me posted on how things are with you. And I'll ring you.'

Rappoport went up to Polishchuk's office. Beckoning him into the corridor and putting his gnarled fingers on his shoulder, he blurted out the news. Polishchuk pulled a long face. His plan for Ivlev's reinstatement had now evaporated like dry ice, without a trace. There weren't going to be any questions raised about it, neither with the Party bureau nor with the editorial board. Makartsev's arrival wouldn't change anything; he wouldn't even be able to raise the issue. Calling Khardankin would be tactless, too: that would mean questioning the KGB's actions. All that was left was to hope. And it was imperative to keep quiet, so as not to spoil anything. You wouldn't help Ivlev, and you would hurt other people. And yourself as well.

'That's that!' was all Rappoport could say.

*There it is, the payback for the Czech carnival*, he muttered to himself, storming down the corridor. *The fireworks are over, the lamps are out, time to go home. Nothing like that can happen here; we're the monolith. The bonfires are smoking and flaring again. Anyone who's close to them is going to burn up like a moth. It stinks of burning human flesh. If I were younger and didn't have a slipped disk maybe I would try to do something. But now . . . there's only one thing I want – my pension; and they're not even going to count time spent sitting in the camps as time in Party service. Such a piddling thing, but they won't include it. If only I was retired now; I wouldn't read a newspaper from morning till night! But if I stick my nose into this now, once again . . . It won't help Ivlev, and they'll just give me salt herring, and then they won't give me any water, and I'll be telling them myself where his papers are hidden at my flat. I don't have any strength left. If they put me away again I'll hang myself in the first lavatory I come to. I always carry a tie around with me, in my pocket, just in case.*

Rappoport was somewhat uncomfortable with these thoughts. Wheezing, he set off for the letters department.

'Nadya,' he said, stopping in the doorway. 'Could you give me a hand sorting out some letters? Otherwise I'll sink so deep in them I won't even gurgle.'

'When?' asked Nadya with a smile.

'Right now.'

She readily got up from behind her little desk. Rappoport looked her over with satisfaction and let her go ahead. On the way he told her what had happened. He took her into his office and sat her down in his arm-chair. She shrank into the chair, her mouth and nose covered with her hands, looking at him with numbed eyes, waiting for him to tell her something even more terrible.

'I do understand that this is hard for you, Nadya,' said Rappoport, and two deep furrows running from his nose to his chin divided up his face.

'For me? What about him?'

'That's his fate. He knew what he was getting into.'

'Do something!' Nadya's imploring eyes looked at him fixedly. 'Surely *you* can!'

'Me! Why does everybody ask me? Who am I? A pitiful old ruin. Sure, I can whip up campaigns to make nobodies famous throughout the whole country and maybe even get them into the Central Committee. But when I get them in they aren't beholden to me any longer, Nadya. It would be better to talk to your father. It's hardly worth it, but if he can't help nobody can!'

'Nadya, are you here? I've been looking all over the office for you. I've seen everybody but you . . .' Flinging the door open Kakabadze stood on the threshold, his legs wide apart. He had just been released from hospital, and he looked drunk with the sensation of freedom.

'Kakabadze, are you all right?' Nadya said, pleased to see him.

'The policemen were convicted. I testified against them. God exists, truth exists, you see?'

'And you have no criminal record!' said Rappoport cheerfully. 'Good boy!'

'You'll excuse me, of course. I guess you've got business with Nadya. But I missed her so much I simply can't stand it! Nadya, come on out, talk to me a bit . . .'

'We'll consider those letters sorted out by you and me, girl,' said Rappoport. 'Off you go, children!'

He bent his heavy head over his papers, pretending to take no further interest in Nadya and Kakabadze. Out in the corridor Kakabadze bent down, pulled a camera out of his case that was propped against the wall and started taking pictures. Nadya thumbed her nose at him and gave him the finger, but nothing deterred him. So she covered her face with her hands and turned to the wall.

'Oh, Nadya! Stand right there like that – you're even more beautiful from behind! You know I came home from hospital and realized that I haven't got a single picture of you. How can this be? I've taken pictures of the entire country, but there weren't any of you! Listen, when I was in the hospital I did a lot of thinking. I've come to a conclusion: we have to get married right away.'

'You've lost your mind!'

'Nope, I'm absolutely certain. I told my mother, and she was very happy about it. I've decided to get married, and it's serious.' Replacing his camera in its bag and paying no attention to the few individuals coming along the corridor, he took Nadya by the elbow.

'Let go, you hear! Let me go!'

'No, no. I officially offer you my hand plus my heart. Don't have any doubts, Nadya. We'll get married and go off to Georgia on our honeymoon. We'll be welcomed there with open arms, just see!'

'To Georgia? But what about Inna?'

'What does Inna have to do with this? Did she tell you something? That's another thing entirely. I can't do without women altogether. Don't be jealous.'

'I'm not jealous.'

'Good girl! Let's get married, and there'll be no more women. I'll be a one-woman kind of man! Why are you crying? Who's hurt you?'

Two tears hung in Nadya's lashes. Pressing her back to the wall she fixed her gaze on Kakabadze. Suddenly she threw her arms around his neck and sobbed, burying her wet nose in his neck.

'Hey, what's the matter? Why cry? Your face will get all unphotogenic. And I want to take some more pictures of you. I'm going to photograph you for the rest of my life, from every angle.'

'You can't, not from every angle!' said Nadya through her blubbing. 'They'll put you away again for that.'

'If it's your wife you can! No one will know. So, you agree, then?'

'No, no! Where did you get that from? We're friends. But getting married, no, I can't.' She unclenched her hands and moved a bit further away from him. He was dismayed.

'Winter is past, summer is coming, thanks be to the Party for that! Knock me down with a feather. Fine. I'll wait. I'm going to marry you anyhow! Anyway I wanted to talk to you about something. Tomorrow's the Party meeting –'

'You're not a Party member!'

'But maybe I should join? After all, sooner or later everybody joins, you know. Surely nothing's going to change because of it? Yagubov called me in and asked me to speak on behalf of the Young Communists about Ivlev's expulsion.'

'And what did *you* say?'

'Am I any different? Everyone else is going to spit on him – one gob more isn't going to change anything. He'll understand that I'm not doing it willingly. I'll ask for his forgiveness afterwards. And if I refuse to do it, that'll mean that I'm on his side, right? This is all crap; you think I don't understand that? At the slightest provocation they'll accuse me of being for Stalin's personality cult because I'm a Georgian. I'll have to speak. I can't get out of it.'

Walking past them, Rappoport clapped Kakabadze on the shoulder. 'Hey, you conspirators, break it up!' Rappoport wrapped his raincoat around him, glanced at the lift, decided not to wait and went down on foot.

Zakamorny was waiting for him on a bench in the little park. After the introduction of the pass system he had been coming into the office for a while on one-off passes that Rappoport ordered for him by telephone.

But Yagubov got wind of it, and Kashin made a call to the pass bureau.

Zakamorny was relaxed, half lying on a bench not far from the children's sandpit. Rappoport realized that he already knew about Ivlev. He sat down alongside him on the bench, looked around to make certain that no one was interested in them and snuffled.

'How many times have I told him', Zakamorny hissed, 'not to throw his drafts down the rubbish chute! Only into the lavatory and then only in tiny pieces. Great people are undone by trifles.'

'Calm down. It's not just a matter of rough drafts. Inna typed up *five* copies.'

'Christ!' Zakamorny said, spitting. 'If I'd known that I wouldn't have slept with her. But then if it hadn't been her it would have been somebody else. Somebody has to carry out that function on this earth! Just think: a government that's capable of annihilating the whole world is afraid of one little person squeaking a pen on a piece of paper. When they get bored of fleeting glimpses of wings in front of them they impale the butterfly on a pin and hide it in a box. It was only in the seventeenth century that they needed Don Quixotes. And that was in Europe. But in Russia the crowd pointed their fingers at them and wanted to hang them by their heels and impale them on stakes. Any normal system would cherish its critics, because without them it decays, like a woman without any male hormones. But here?'

'Here? I've said it before and I'll say it again: keep your noses out of it, kids.'

'That smells of lack of principle!'

'Lack of principle – that's when you betray your ideals for the sake of your friends. Principle is when you betray your friends for the sake of ideals. Which is better?

> *'Whenever I see Rappoport,*
> *The question's clear and undistorted:*
> *How come Mummy Rappoport*
> *Didn't get herself aborted?'*

'You're repeating yourself, boy!'

'As far as keeping our noses out of it goes, I have an idea. Our borders are under lock and key. Customs agents rip out the lining of our coats, gynaecologists in shoulderboards poke around in the rest of the places. But birds just fly across borders for some reason! They fly wherever they want to, and even though they might be ringed nobody knows whether they come back or not.'

'So what are you proposing?'

'Erect nets all along our borders, up to the sky, so that not one single Soviet sparrow can fly off. To say nothing of cranes and swans, the scum! They aren't even worth the excrement of my friend Ivlev. Surely we're not going to let them get away with it this time, Rappoport. Rappoport! Why are you so silent, you old jailbird? Speak out as the initiator of a *decent* campaign for once in your life. Tell them: "Burn your newspapers without reading them!" Explain that to all your subscribers: each one of them has to burn their copy of the paper. Rip out the wires in their radios and televisions. The regime will go deaf and dumb. It'll choke on its own bile.'

'Let's go for a drink,' Rappoport proposed. 'Maybe we'll feel better then.'

'Not in the mood. Sorry.'

Without saying goodbye Zakamorny marched off. Rappoport followed him with his eyes, then got up and headed off in the opposite direction, hunched over. At the corner, in front of a shop, he stopped.

'Hey, pal, you want to go three for a bottle?' The fellow, his eagle eye picking Rappoport out of the crowd, was haggard and unshaven.

'Is there a third?'

'There he is – standing over there with two empty bottles. We'll join up with him! The crockery is ours – you want to add some change?'

'Sure,' said Rappoport.

The one with the bottles was already standing in a queue, impatient. They handed him two roubles in notes and change. Then the three of them trooped over to some bushes in the park, no one falling behind by so much as a step.

'Maybe we should get a bite to eat as well?' Rappoport proposed cautiously.

'What are you? A snob?' the second fellow asked. 'Get a bite at home.'

'So come on, come on, let's get stuck in. I haven't had a drink since this morning!' The unshaven one ripped off the foil stopper with his nail. 'Let's drink from the neck so there won't be any cheating!' He tipped up the bottle and started swigging.

The second fellow moved his lips, counting each swallow. 'Halt!' He pulled the bottle down like a knife-switch, stopping the flow of the drink with the sharp downward thrust. 'Go chew on a twig while I take a turn.'

The second one stopped on his own. If he took more than his share it wasn't by much. Rappoport closed his eyes, getting ready to do the same. He could already feel his creeping ulcer beginning to stir in his stomach; the pain travelled throughout his entire belly, settling in his liver. But there was no place to retreat to. He drew in some more air and took his time.

'What are you? A yid?' the second one said, trying to figure him out.

'A little,' Rappoport admitted.

'Yeah, I can see you hesitating. It don't matter. Drink up. Make you a human being!'

They didn't laugh; they just waited. Rappaport took a deep breath again and started to drink. The bottle swung between two clouds that had stopped above him in the sky. The sky was bottomless, the vodka poured down from above, and it seemed there wouldn't be an end to it. But, after all, his share was only something like five ounces or so, all told. When he had finished he wiped his mouth with his sleeve in a manly fashion and returned the bottle to the second fellow. They both looked at Rappoport.

'We should get some more,' said the unshaven one. 'That went down real good. Should get some more. Let's get some more – it'll get even better. But I haven't got any . . .'

'Got none either,' said the second, staring fixedly at the third member of the party.

'I'll pay for it, boys,' Rappoport immediately offered. 'Since we need some, I'll pay.'

'Are you in business?' asked the unshaven one.

'Something like that.'

'Then you pay. Blow it on a new bottle!'

The second one, not lingering, rushed off.

'Don't be scared. He's not going to run off with it! You know, as soon as I saw you I knew you was a shop manager. You got the look of a shop manager.'

'I'm not a shop manager,' Rappoport explained. 'I'm Rappoport.'

'What do I want to know your name for? What am I, a personnel clerk? You drink, so – drink up!'

After that they were quiet for about twenty minutes, turned away from each other and separately experiencing the same warming of their organism. Then the second man ran up, an untouched bottle under his arm.

'Me first!' Rappoport declared.

'Oh, he's a smart one,' the unshaven one said to the second one. 'Yeah, a smart one.'

'I'm not smart! I'm a piece of shit! Give it to me. I'll go first. Otherwise you fuckers won't leave me enough!'

Squeezing his thumb to the one-third mark he drank his share and then waited while they drained the bottle.

'I'm shit!' Rappoport stubbornly repeated. 'Manure that flowers grow on!'

'Did you walk out on your family?' the unshaven one asked sympathetically. ''Cause if you did, they're better off without you.'

'What's this got to do with my family? The most important thing is to burn your newspapers! Burn them without reading them!'

After shaking their hands he walked off, trying to place his steps so that the footpath under his feet wouldn't slide to one side. They wouldn't let Rappoport into the metro. Feeling as if he was about to fall down, Rappoport talked a taxi driver into taking his sagging body to Izmaylovo, after paying him five roubles in advance. But the journalist Rappoport, the one they called Tavrov, wasn't the kind of person who would simply pass out.

Barely managing to get his key in the lock, the first thing he did was to go into the living-room without taking off his raincoat and move the bookcase. Tilting it on its side, Rappoport pulled out from underneath it a fat grey folder and some sheets of paper. The sheets he threw on the floor. In the bathroom he untied the ribbon, lit a match and set fire to page one of the Marquis de Custine's composition. On top of the burning sheet he placed another, then another, and soon a fire was blazing in the bath-tub, the ceiling blackening with soot. Rappoport began coughing furiously from the smoke. Choking, he burned the manuscript to the last page, turned on the tap so that the remains would stop smoking and stumbled out of the bathroom. He remembered sitting on the floor in the front room, without the strength to make it to the ottoman, and after that his memory failed him.

He opened his eyes to find someone shaking him by the shoulder. For a long time Rappoport couldn't make out what it was that they wanted. He had been dreaming that they arrested him twice, and he was con-sidering himself lucky for that: when you're half awake nothing bothers you at all. He was afraid only of physical pain, and the fingers were dig-ging into his shoulder so hard that he groaned.

'Don't . . .' he begged plaintively, 'don't beat me.'

'What's wrong, Dad? Wake up! Are you sick?' Kostya was on his knees in front of him.

'Son,' Rappoport said, not opening his eyes, 'I'm fine. It's just that my head hurts.'

'I can tell, Father. I'm just glad you haven't choked to death.'

Kostya had come in through the unlocked door and seen his father stretched out on the rug in front of the ottoman. Both cats were sleep-ing curled up on his stomach. Frightened, Kostya had instantly imagined the worst and everything else that would follow after the worst. But straight away he had realized that the cats wouldn't be warming themselves on Rappoport if he were dead. His father smacked his lips and from time to time repeated, 'Burn your newspapers without reading them!' The smell of vodka seemed even to emanate from the cats. Placing a pillow under his father's head Kostya sat down at the table to read the sheets of paper that Rappoport had thrown on to the floor.

The pages appeared to be a piece written by Rappoport the journalist in a genre that he had invented, to be able to call himself a newspaper 'calumnist'. This piece was a 'calumn' on himself. Rappoport wrote for everybody and about everybody, but nobody ever wrote about him (if you didn't take denunciations into account). Therefore Rappoport had decided in advance – in case it was ever needed – to prepare an article about himself that could be published at any given moment. After all, if you don't worry about yourself it will be done for you – and, worse still, with insufficient professionalism. So his 'calumn', entitled 'Newspaper Traitor', was composed in the best traditions of patriotic Party publishing. The 'calumn' used the full range of labels from the Rappoport manual: double-dealer, decadent, traitor to the motherland, internal émigré, sell-out to the Zionist secret service, malicious renegade, dirty provocateur.

'What's this, Dad?'

'This?' Rappoport sat up, leaning his back against the ottoman. 'Who knows, Son? Maybe it's something that'll be needed soon.'

'You wouldn't want to go away, would you, Father?'

'Me? Are you trying to compete with me? I've been put away twice already. No, Son. You're young – you at least have some feeble hope. But me . . .'

'And you're not fed up with this place?'

'Oh, how fed up I am indeed! But I'm going to watch this film to the end! I'm going to throw up, Kostya.'

'Why did you get drunk? To become a nationalist?'

'What's going on is making me throw up.'

'You were the one who told me, Father, that King Solomon had engraved on his signet ring the words "This too shall pass . . ."'

'Yes, I did. But it doesn't matter what I said. And if I had a signet ring, even, I'd have engraved on it the words "They're not going to get away with it!"'

# 68

# Fille Fatale

There was a queue stretching along the wall outside the savings bank on the Old Arbat: elderly men and women waiting for their pensions. Nadya asked them to say she was next in line at the end, walked over to the counter and, opening a savings book of her father's (in the name of Gordey Severov, with the right for his daughter to use the deposits for the course of three years), filled out a withdrawal slip. There was over two and a half thousand roubles in the account. Her father hadn't touched it since her mother's death.

The odd few roubles Nadya wasn't concerned about, but she withdrew two and a half thousand roubles after waiting in the long line. Nadya was told to sign for it three times – she was agitated, and her signature came out differently every time. Finally she was made to produce her internal passport, and the woman inspector wrote down its number and where, by whom and when it was registered in Moscow. Only then did Nadya receive a counterfoil with a number on it that she handed over to a cashier, who counted out the money. How much it was Nadya couldn't actually see, because of the height of the cashier's window, but she wasn't going to count it out herself. She stepped over to the counter, took out an office envelope with a *Trudovaya Pravda* logo on it from her bag, put the money into it and sealed it.

Nadya travelled on the metro as far as the Universitet station with a determination that diminished somewhat as she went up the escalator. Usually when she was with Ivlev he didn't want her to accompany him to his building; so she would stay in the tunnel and the escalator would carry him up alone. But sometimes he would be talking and not notice that she was already on the escalator, and she got to walk with him as far as the metro entrance. On those days Nadya would be happy.

Now she walked into his entryway. She went directly up the stairs, as if she'd been to Ivlev's place a hundred times. She wanted to meet Tonya, and she was afraid of her. It was a sort of game that Nadya had played with herself when she and Ivlev first got together. Tonya had been her teacher at Music School No. 38. As a girl, Nadya had loved her and quickly forgotten her, like all her other teachers, but then had remembered her again when she found out that Special Correspondent Ivlev was her husband. In her time, her teacher had spoken about him (what an intelligent and exceptional person he was – something like that anyway), and Nadya, when she first got a look at him at the office, was curious about him.

Exactly when it was that the game and her half-childish calculations had become serious Nadya hadn't noticed. All she noticed was that she loved Ivlev, and she not only felt good about that but bad as well. She had never even told him that she knew his wife.

'Nadya!' Tonya said in surprise, recognizing her as soon as she opened the door.

Tonya stood there in a multicoloured housecoat with a dish-cloth that had seen better days in her hand. She scrutinized Nadya, dressed to the nines.

'I just came by for a minute.'

'Well, come on in. I'm afraid it's a mess here. Take off your coat. I'll be right back . . .'

While Nadya was removing her raincoat Tonya powdered her face in the bathroom to try to conceal the bluish swellings from her tears and her sleepless night. She cast off the housecoat, quickly pulled on trousers and a blouse, passed a brush over her head twice and walked out of the bathroom.

'I know everything,' Nadya said straight away, so as not to beat around the bush.

'What do you mean – everything?'

'I work with Ivlev. That is, I'm a minor technical employee at the office.

He's not guilty of anything, I'm sure of that. They have to let him go! They just have to!'

Tonya didn't say anything. She just shook her head and tears flowed, leaving two tracks on her hastily powdered cheeks.

'I really do know it! The newspaper is going to speak out for him, and people listen to the opinion of the paper. Our boss, Makartsev, is getting out of the hospital soon. He's got a high regard for Ivlev. He understands that he's a talented man. He'll make a call and all that stuff – you'll see!'

'Call where? You're the same naive little girl you used to be!'

'No!' protested Nadya. 'Well, maybe I am naive but not in the way you think. Just believe me, that's the most important thing!'

'I'll try.'

'Oh, and I almost forgot. I've brought you your husband's royalty payment – the accountant's office asked me to give it to you.' Nadya took out the envelope and put it on the table. Tonya didn't even glance at it.

'Well, how are you getting on yourself, Nadya?'

'Me? Marvellously. Great! It's all such a whirl – no time to even look around. I'm studying at the university in the evenings, and I'm about to graduate. Generally things are fine.'

'I could envy you . . .'

'A lot of people envy me. It's even a bit embarrassing when everything is going well for you. So how's your son?'

'Right now he's at his grandmother's. He's growing . . .'

'Well, I'm off,' Nadya said, standing up. 'Excuse me for bursting in on you uninvited.'

'On the contrary, I'm very glad. Sit back down and we'll have a cup of tea'

'Another time. I'll look in as soon as I find out something.'

Closing the door behind Nadya, Tonya smelled a familiar perfume. The scent had been bothering her for a while, although she hadn't accorded it any significance. Only now did a weak conjecture come into her head, but she didn't allow the thought to develop and startle her consciousness with an unexpected discovery.

Back on the street Nadya skipped along, satisfied with what she had done. Slender and purposeful, she hurried smiling to the metro and passers-by followed her with their eyes. She had a feeling that her father would be home. But when she found him in the kitchen she remembered. That morning he had said that he was coming home early after a conference and then was going off to spend the night elsewhere. She was certain that he had a woman; it couldn't be otherwise. It was just that he considered her a child and was hiding it from her. In the past he sometimes used to declare that he wouldn't be coming home that night: he was off on an assignment. But now he hadn't specified the reason – he hadn't wanted to lie. That was progress of a sort.

'Hello, Daddy!'

Sirotkin was sitting in his white shirtsleeves, with his jacket off and his tie loosened, munching away. She hugged her father around the neck, pressing herself against his back. Soft and tender music emanated from Nadya's room.

'Did you turn on my record player?'

'Yes.'

'What are you – in love?'

He smirked silently.

'You're shaved more carefully than usual; and there's the music . . .'

'I got a shave at the Central Committee barbershop, and the record was given to me by my deputy. Is that all?'

'No. Where are you off to?'

'Well, to be frank, I'm off to the *dacha* to play cards.'

'I hope there'll be women there. It's long past time . . .'

'Time?' Sirotkin smirked again. 'No, there won't be any women there. And what does that mean: "it's time"? I'm not telling *you* that it's time for you to get married.'

'Well, you don't tell me that because you're a tactful person. And what if I did do that? I've got a new boyfriend. He takes me so seriously it's scary.'

'A new one? Who?'

'A military cadet. He's doing his last two years at Zhukov Academy. What do you think about that?'

'Me? In my opinion, if you have to ask you're not sure yourself.'

'Oh, I'm sure,' she whispered into his ear. 'But I don't know how you're going to take to him. After all, the last time, you –'

'The last time? With that anti-Soviet? The one you lied to me about back then? His name is Ivlev, and he works with you.'

'There you go! Yelling at me from the very beginning of our conversation. It's been over with him for a long time. But, if you want the truth, he's no anti-Soviet. He just translated a book from French, one that any mortal can get from the Lenin Library. And it's not in any special collection; it's on the ordinary shelves.'

'That book isn't the issue! The fact is that this man could write something he shouldn't.'

'That's scary?'

'That depends on who it's for. For people who are ideologically unsound it's dangerous. The majority of the People, unfortunately, can't tell the difference between good and bad and might get caught by the snares of people like your Ivlev. I meant to say your *former* . . .'

'You're right, Daddy! I understand. It's lucky that this all has just a theoretical significance for me.'

'Well, there, you see . . .'

'Tell me, how did you manage it? Surely you aren't so important that you can just jail him?'

'Nonsense! This isn't a personal matter. I hope you understand.'

'And can you let him go? Tell me – can you?'

'How do you mean?' he asked, standing up and straightening his tie.

'Don't you see – we break up and then you jail him. If you let him go I would quietly go and get married to my cadet, but otherwise . . . Please! I rarely ask you for anything.'

'No! You don't understand the nature of our work. The issue isn't Ivlev. Right now we don't want to isolate everyone who for one or another reason is dissatisfied with our ideology. The work we're carrying out is *preventive*. But to let him go would mean showing that we're weak, that anti-Soviets can carry on with their activities. And it's not me who decides this.'

'Then who?'

'The Party, the People. When are you finally going to understand that? You'd be better off forgetting about Ivlev!'

'All right, Daddy, I'll try. By the way, how's your dissertation coming along?'

'I hope it's all going to come out all right.'

'I'm so happy! Hey, let's drink to everything being all right with you.'

'Well, let's, if you insist.'

Sirotkin took out a bottle of export vodka from the bar and filled up the two thimble-glasses that Nadya held out. They drank them down. He pulled on his jacket and kissed her.

'How elegant you look! And very young for your age . . .'

Picking up a comb, she combed back her father's greying hair, curly over his ears and on the back of his head. 'Somebody's missing out on a man like you!'

'Don't be naughty!' he said, slapping her lightly on the hip.

After closing the door behind her father Nadya grabbed the bottle from the kitchen and went to her room. She put a record on and poured out some vodka.

'To your health, Daddy!' she said aloud and drank it down without pulling a face.

Nadya poured herself another and again drank it down. Then she got up and twirled around the room in a pose suggestive of someone being held by the waist, until she reached the piano. She sat down and played along with the melody, rattling the keys with unpractised fingers, and continued to think out loud.

'Thank you, Daddy, for making me a free woman again. I never even suspected that it was you. I'm not just Nadya Sirotkina. No, I'm a real *femme fatale*! Anybody who comes into contact with me is going to be sorry. Thanks to me Boris Makartsev killed two people. Because of me

Kakabadze was beaten half to death. I had only to give myself to Ivlev and he's already in prison. Who's next? Who's going to risk kissing me? And, after all, I'm still a young thing, I haven't had a single abortion. I still haven't learned how to love properly. And when I learn it'll be even worse! Wherever I pass by there'll be prison and death. I'm a witch – only still an apprentice. I'm no more and no less than the daughter of a KGB general. And when I grow up . . . Ivlev, forgive me!'

The music finished, but the record kept spinning on the turntable. Nadya didn't pay it any attention. She gently let herself down on to the ottoman and stretched out a hand to her bedside table. By feel she pulled out a box of sleeping pills, lay back and lazily chewed the powdery, foul-tasting tablets. Her agitation passed. She lost all desire to speak any more. She was just tired. She raised her head only because the door squeaked. There stood Ivlev.

'Hello,' she said, and a blissful smile came to her face. She wasn't in the least surprised: she hadn't had any doubt that he would come. 'Don't just stand there like you're in the wrong place.'

Ivlev shook his finger at her and stood there without moving. Nadya grew cheerful. She laughed loudly and unconcernedly, rolled over on to her back and held out her hands to him, beckoning him with her fingers. He walked slowly over to her bed and fell on top of her as he was, fully dressed, and straight away her arms and legs locked around him. Bare birches, leafless, shook their slender branches with last year's yellow tassels over Nadya's head. And all around shone puddles and patches of snow and old, soft grass.

'Never!' Nadya exclaimed, smiling a happy, distracted smile, stroking Ivlev's badly shaven cheeks. 'It'll never be as great for me as in the woods, on the damp ground, under the birches! People want so many things to make them happy. But you don't really need much to be happy.'

# 69

# The Pale-Blue Envelope

Taking off his raincoat, Yagubov held it out to Anna. 'Nobody gets in to see me!'

'Shamayev rang.'

'On the regular phone? Why didn't you say so right away?'

Anna didn't react and walked to the door.

'A glass of tea, hot and strong.'

Since Shamayev had phoned him on the regular line Yagubov rang him back over the regular system as well, but he just got an engaged signal. Trying to collect his thoughts, he pressed his hands to his temples. It was half dark in his room, even though the morning was bright with sunlight. The window of his office had been covered over by a portrait of Karl Marx put up on the building wall the night before for the May Day parade. His shoulder, cheek and a part of his beard shone through the window; the entire picture obscured four windows on two floors and made a scraping noise as the breeze made it sway on its ropes.

Anna brought in the tea, together with a folder of papers awaiting his signature and the proofs of the leader page, and quietly walked out. Yagubov took several swigs of tea, and his drowsiness left him. He stretched, feeling a pleasant tiredness in the muscles of his arms and chest. Unusually, he hadn't been to the swimming-pool this morning. Yagubov made a wry face, recalling the previous night, and now was sorry that he had let it happen. Yesterday he had compiled a small list of tasks with a view to strengthening ideological discipline at the office. These tasks demanded immediate resolution: the errors hadn't disappeared from the pages of *Trudovaya Pravda*. Every one of his paragraphs held concrete proposals and punishment measures. He hadn't wanted to bring this project to the attention of the newspaper's employees before it was time, however, since among them there were a number of people on Makartsev's side. They would hurry to advise him of the document. Vacillating, Yagubov had asked Anna to send the typist Inna to him.

Inna had entered his office and halted not too close to Yagubov's desk, so that he could see all of her, but not so far away that her parts and her odour would be lost to sight and smell.

'Would you please fulfil a personal request of mine?' said Yagubov, cursorily paying attention to what he was supposed to.

'At last!' she pronounced with delight, beaming.

'At last, what?'

'You've finally noticed me, Yagubov. If you don't pay attention to a woman she withers away. Of course, I'll do anything you want that's within my power.'

He was slightly perturbed by this turn of the conversation. 'Well, to tell the truth, it's not such a big thing. I need to have several pages typed up – something that nobody in the office should know about.'

'I understand. Will you dictate it to me yourself? And where shall I type it? Maybe we should do it at my place?'

Dictating it, and at her place, had never crossed his mind. He had wanted to explain this politely and entrust her with typing it up and bringing it back to him. But something occurred that was beyond his control and – looking into eyes that gazed back at him so devotedly – he unexpectedly found himself saying the opposite of what he had intended. 'Would that be convenient?'

'For sure!' she exclaimed joyously. 'When are you free?'

'In about an hour . . .'

'In an hour I'll be waiting in the metro station, by the front carriage of the trains going towards the centre of town.'

'But wouldn't it be better to take a taxi?'

'Then at the bakery entrance – it's easier to get one there.'

He closed his eyes in agreement, and Inna disappeared. His heart was pounding, and his brain immediately settled on several tasks. Yagubov had never before allowed himself this sort of thing, and every part of his body, without asking permission, was up for the game. He hadn't yet decided anything, but everything had been decided already. He calmed himself down with the fact that nothing was going to happen, since it couldn't, for a host of reasons. *And if something does happen, it'll only be an exception, and nobody will ever find out. After all, she's apparently in love with me!*

All his other affairs moved to the background. He phoned home and told his wife not to wait up. He had been summoned to a government bigwig's *dacha* to put together a very important document – what exactly he still didn't know himself – and he would call her tomorrow; it was nothing to worry about. He told her to kiss the children. And then he got through to Polishchuk on the intercom to ask him to take over the reins since he was being called away on urgent business.

In the taxi he sat in the front with the driver, while Inna was in the back. Half turned round, he asked her about things in the typing pool and the typists' needs, promised to give his attention to improving their working conditions, and he made her happy by telling her that the typing pool was being given a hundred-rouble bonus for the holiday.

Her landlady, hearing from behind the door that Inna wasn't alone, went off to the kitchen and didn't show herself.

'You must be hungry!' exclaimed Inna. 'I'll just rustle up something.'

When he walked into her cubby-hole of an apartment he involuntarily made a face and carefully sat down behind the table with the typewriter that Ivlev had brought. Inna bustled about. Shifting the typewriter, she covered the table with a clean newspaper and put out two glasses, some bread and some sausage and then sliced an onion.

'Your living accommodation is a bit inadequate, Inna.'

'It's what I've got.'

'I can probably help you.'

'But I haven't got a Moscow residence permit.'

'We'll get you registered, too.'

'Come on, Yagubov!' She froze, with an open bottle of vodka in her hand that she had just taken out from under her bed.

'What, Inna – you don't believe the word of a Communist!'

'Of course I believe it!' she beamed, setting the vodka down on the table. 'Let's drink to you! For being such a down-to-earth kind of man. And I was so afraid of you.' She poured out the vodka for him and herself until their tumblers were three-quarters full.

'Thanks, Inna,' he said, clinking glasses with her and drinking it down. Growing slightly flushed, he didn't notice that he had slipped into more informal speech. 'And you're an interesting person. How come I never . . .'

'Well, when did you ever have the time? The whole newspaper is on your shoulders. Would you like me to tell your fortune?'

'Well, sure, let's risk it!' he laughed.

'All right, so . . .' She laid out the cards. 'A public building . . . A trip . . . Luck . . . And here, look, the King of Hearts is hindering you, but it won't be for long.'

'That's all nonsense, Inna,' he said, putting his hand on the deck of cards, stopping her chatter.

Throwing down the cards, Inna went to the mirror as if to assure herself that she looked all right. He got up as well and observed her reflection in the mirror.

'You looking at me like that makes me embarrassed.'

'Me, too,' he answered simply, not taking his eyes off her.

She stepped up close against him, so that he could feel her nipples through his jacket. Inna was over half a head taller than he was, but now she bent her knees. They looked each other in the eyes.

'What's first?' she asked. 'The typewriter or . . .'

'Or?'

'Or me?'

'Whatever you say. A woman's word is law.'

'Then let's have another drink.'

They each drank down another half a glass.

'Now, since you're the man, kiss me. Because I'm too shy in front of you.'

What happened next Yagubov could recall only fragmentarily. Sometime around midnight Inna got out of bed, fetched her guitar and, sitting on his stomach, sang him ditties to which he sometimes sang along. Then they got up and drank the rest of the vodka. He took the guitar out of her hands and put it on the floor and sat Inna on his lap.

'You're an amazing woman. I didn't even think women like you existed.'

The landlady woke them in the morning, and only then did Yagubov realize that Inna's living conditions were even worse than he had supposed the night before. There wasn't any bathtub at all. The old lady had slept in the kitchen on chairs pushed together and demanded a double fee for the discomfort – six roubles.

'What happened between us never happened,' he said before he left. 'I hope you understand?'

'I'm as quiet as a grave,' she answered simply.

On the way he stopped off at a barber's for a shave. He was afraid that Inna would take it into her head to come to see him that morning, and that's why he had ordered Anna not to let anyone in. Yagubov recalled individual details of the night before. She lived in conditions like that and was happy anyway. What they said was true: you should make love to happy women – and not to talkative ones, of course.

Finishing his tea, Yagubov put the glass to one side and opened the document folder. His secretary came in, and he made a face.

'Excuse me. Kashin is asking to see you. He says it can't be put off. Shall I let him in?'

'We'll have to let him in. What else can we do?'

In the middle of the previous night Inna had said suddenly, while she was kissing Yagubov: 'Not all men at the office are like you. Kashin, for instance . . .'

'What about Kashin?'

'He locked the door to his office. I says, "The fish are looking at us. I'm too ashamed!" "Let the fish look," he says. "Let them look!" He undressed me then, but he couldn't do anything. I thought I'd bite him, to bring him to life. But he just goes, "Ouch! That hurts!" And he shuts his mouth with his own hand so as not to yell. I bit him all over, but there wasn't any sort of result.'

'None?' guffawed Yagubov. 'That was because he was on duty.'

'Happy upcoming May Day!' Kashin, interrupting Yagubov's musings, presented himself cheerfully. He sat down on one of the closer chairs, preparing himself to relate his urgent news and anxious to see his boss's reaction to it.

'So? Haven't got a lot of time right now.'

'Excuse me, Yagubov. I'll be brief. Just the most urgent stuff. Nadya, from the letters department, poisoned herself.'

'How's that?'

'She took an overdose of sleeping pills. She was taken unconscious to the hospital last night. I rang and found out what was happening: they'd pumped out her stomach and given her a blood transfusion. They put her on a dialysis machine. Her father – you know who he is – well, he prodded the doctors into doing something. They say that she'll live.'

'Did she show up on the municipal committee list?'

'I checked that out, too. No. They registered her at the hospital as a student. *Trudovaya Pravda* doesn't figure in this.'

'So – the reason? Did you find out the reason?'

'Not exactly, of course, not yet. But the typing pool says that she's pregnant, by Ivlev.'

'By Ivlev?'

'Inna, the typist, said so. "The silly girl," she says. "What on earth would she do that for, over such nonsense? Men", she says, "are all scum, without exception!"'

'Without exception? Did she say that?'

Kashin nodded and went on: 'What can we do? If it was anybody else we could fire them. But she's . . .'

'We won't discuss that,' frowned Yagubov. 'Is that all?'

He was thinking that when he met up with General Sirotkin at the swimming-pool after the holidays he was going to have to express his condolences. Or maybe it was best to pretend that he didn't know anything about it.

'About the parade,' Kashin continued. 'The lists of people who are to be right-flankers and banner-carriers have been drawn up. The people have been given their instructions to march in step, eight to a row and no more. Here, sign this, and I'll take it for stock-taking. And a second copy for the bookkeepers for the sum indicated: five roubles each for carrying the portraits and banners – it all adds up.'

'That's not right! The banners should be carried for free.'

'Of course, that's the way it should be . . . but everybody can be counted on if there's money involved. We've done it this way for a long time.'

Not objecting any further Yagubov signed.

'And one last thing,' said Kashin. 'Makartsev is coming to the office.'

'How come you didn't tell me that right away? Where's this information from?'

'Anna telephoned him. He, like, asked her not to tell anybody at the office.'

'He wants to show up here out of the blue? Here's what you'll do. Get together a surprise party for him, the way it should be. Flowers, maybe . . .'

'Flowers on which account? Should we take it from the editor's fund?'

'What a bureaucrat you are!' Yagubov said in reproof. 'Here, take this. Send a courier to the Central Market.'

Kashin took the five-rouble note held out to him and folded it in half, putting it in his pocket. 'Yes, sir!'

Yagubov got up to show that the audience was at an end. He dialled Shamayev's number once more, but again there was no answer. With the prospect of his editor-in-chief putting in an appearance Yagubov decided to do the rounds of all the departments to check on how work was progressing on the May Day issue.

The edition was being put together without any fuss or rush, most of the material having been prepared in advance. Some of the people had a whiff of the barley about them, but everything was going smoothly and Yagubov came back satisfied. He picked up the leader-page proofs but then decided to let Makartsev read it; it would be nice for him.

Underneath the proofs lay a large pale-blue unsealed envelope, a thick one without any address on it. Yagubov picked it up, not understanding how it had got there. Inside the unsealed envelope was crammed a thick manuscript, written on paper about the size of cigarette paper. The pages were densely typewritten – single-spaced and without any margins. '*Impotentocracy*,' Yagubov read on the first page. '*The Physiological Reasons for Ideological Decrepitude. Samizdat, 1969.*' Yagubov mumbled something, leafed through the tiny pages, catching several sentences of a very critical nature.

'A provocation,' he decided at once, as if ready for it. 'On the eve of May Day!'

He had no fear. He just had to analyse the situation efficiently and find the correct solution.

'Anna.' He called in his secretary. 'Did you put this here?'

'I haven't been in. I've never laid eyes on it.'

'All right, I'll sort it out myself. By the way, what about Makartsev? They say he's dropping by.'

Anna blushed but said nothing.

'Fine. Since he told you not to say anything I won't be angry. Bring me some cigarettes from the speciality shop.'

He picked up the leader proofs and the blue envelope from his desk, opened his door and – first making certain that the reception room was empty – walked quickly into the editor-in-chief's office. The room was half-dark, just like Yagubov's: two-thirds of the window, located symmetrically with Yagubov's, was occupied by a portrait of Lenin – a shoulder and a gigantic ear were visible. Yagubov put the envelope with its manuscript on Makartsev's desk and the proofs on top of it. He walked over to the secure line and dialled Shamayev's Central Committee number.

The incident with the envelope was something opportune, confirming Yagubov's alarm, and his comrades at the KGB Central apparatus would advise him on what to do.

Shamayev was there; he just hadn't been answering his regular phone. He listened attentively and said that he would pass the information on.

The past of Editor-in-Chief Makartsev couldn't interest Kegelbanov, since everything about it was known. The Central Committee knew about the ideological and personnel policies pursued by Makartsev. There was somebody there that these policies suited. There was just this matter with his son left to consider. Shamayev briefly informed Kegelbanov about this, among other issues, citing Yagubov as the source of this information.

Kegelbanov set his cup of tea with lemon to one side and pushed aside the piece of paper in front of him and, to Shamayev's surprise, showed some alarm. He didn't like it at all when his people took it upon themselves to remind him of their existence. But here the issue was something else. It hadn't been long ago that Comrade Thick Eyebrows had said to him that Makartsev was one of their lads. And all of a sudden one of Kegelbanov's own people was hinting that Makartsev was *not* one of theirs! It seemed like Yagubov was in too much of a hurry to get ahead, since he was trying to prompt him as to what to do. And perhaps he had a real opportunity to do this and Makartsev's standing was already changed? If so, by whom?

'We're not going to react to that message,' Kegelbanov said, once more moving the glass closer to him and taking a swig of the now cold tea. 'And, by the way, Shamayev, find out who else Yagubov is working for.'

'Well, I think . . .'

'Don't think. Find out!'

They put taps on Yagubov's telephones. Returning to the reception room Yagubov heard the intercom buzzing in his own office.

'You already know, of course,' said Polishchuk, 'that in every TASS piece on the Secretary General they've started writing out the word "Comrade" before his name in full?'

'It's about time,' said Yagubov. 'Alert the secretariat, the departments, the typing pool, the proofreaders and the issue duty editors. Recheck all material in the columns and quotations and the captions under photographs as well. This directive is terrifically important!'

'I thought so myself,' replied Polishchuk.

# 70

# Tomorrow Is the Holiday

Makartsev was pining away as he slouched around his apartment from first thing in the morning on 30 April. Doctors liked to play it safe, everybody knew that. But the newspaper wouldn't be able to get along without him on a day like this. *It's important to remind them not to make the issue too dry: it's a holiday, and the reader's supposed to have a laugh as well as a break. Yagubov doesn't understand the value of humour. But the most important thing is for me to wish all the staff a happy holiday. After all, they respect me and, I think, love me. Which means they're waiting for me to pick up the reins. I'll drop by for just an hour. Whatever else, I was prescribed positive emotions! I'll explain to Zina that I was called in urgently, and then I'll come home and take it easy the rest of the holiday.*

From the far end of the apartment, when Zina was in the kitchen, he had called Anna and asked her to send his car, warning her not to tell anyone. He could tell that she was genuinely happy. He was arriving unannounced, and he would be able to tell instantly by minor details how things were at the newspaper.

Makartsev swallowed tablets from three bottles on his bedside table, slipped his nitroglycerine and some other imported medicine into his pocket and put on the rest of his clothes. After telling his wife that he was going for a stroll around the Dinamo Stadium fence he went out through the building gates so the woman porter wouldn't notice him getting into his car.

A dismayed Aleksey was hurrying to pick Makartsev up. That morning he had managed to drive to Anosino and found out that his parents had got their divorce without any red tape. Klavdiya had barely had to say any more than that her husband drank without restraint and beat her severely. Nikanor had screwed up his face and grunted but admitted to it, and he'd had to pay thirty-five roubles for the divorce. That hurt him as well, of course, on his pension of twelve roubles a month. As far as registering the house went, though, things had got tricky. Klavdiya had gone to the collective farm administration the day before. There the bookkeeper had explained to her that she was now, in effect, a stranger to the collective, as she hadn't been considered a member for half a year, since she had got a job in the workshop gluing together cardboard boxes for clocks. The wages there were up to a hundred and thirty roubles a month – double what they got on the collective farm. But now the shop had been put under the clock factory's authority, and she had been struck off the roster of collective farm members. Consequently, Grandma's house wasn't within their reach. They shouldn't have got the divorce, of course, but the couple were afraid to go against their son's instructions and took the affair to its conclusion.

Today Aleksey's father had been snivelling, pestering him. 'Tell me, when can we get back together again? Will they let us?' Aleksey roared at him but didn't know what to do. 'Go get married again, as often as you want,' he yelled, waving him away. 'Or maybe you'll step out yourself, Pa? Why don't you do that?' That amused his father. He started speculating about that course of action out loud, and Aleksey drove off.

He was surprised to see his boss waiting for him on the street. Makartsev smiled and slowly climbed into the car, afraid of making abrupt movements.

'Do you have a cigarette for me?' Makartsev looked questioningly at Aleksey and opened the glove compartment.

'You can't do that, now . . .'

'I know I can't!' Makartsev slammed the compartment shut. 'So is it all right just to talk about smoking?'

'Why not?' Aleksey said, bursting out laughing. 'Where can I take you?'

'To the office, as fast as you can.'

'Sure.' Aleksey had already turned on to the road skirting Dinamo Stadium, and in the empty left lane they hurried towards Leningrad Prospect. 'I thought you weren't going there before the holidays. How's your heart?'

'Fuck it!' Makartsev said unexpectedly, stooping to democratic language that he had never allowed himself before. 'I'd rather you told me about yourself.'

'What's up with me? Actually something not right at all. I jump out of a fighter plane, the medal's hanging on the wall of my garage. But when I need a piece of paper they tell me: nobody knows for sure if you're a hero or not.'

'What are you on about?'

'All about that one thing, about Sovtransavto. I went there and told them my background. They say it would be a good thing to have some sort of document from the Ministry of Defence to prove my heroic deed. Well, I went to the Ministry for an interview. And this colonel there said straight to my face: "I don't see any heroism. If you'd burned up with your aircraft, then there wouldn't be any doubt at all. For that, you get the posthumous Order of the Red Banner, something better than any supporting document. In your case, however, military equipment was destroyed but you're still alive. It's good that you were left in one piece, but how did that happen? Whose fault was it? If it was yours, then you should be court-martialled." I tell him: "Check and see whether I'm to blame or not. I preserved my life for my country – not for me." And he goes: "If everybody throws themselves out of their aeroplanes we're not going to win any kind of war. So go back to your civilian job, and don't come claiming any certificates from the Ministry of Defence!"'

'All right, Aleksey. So you had a run-in with some idiot colonel. An untypical occurrence! I promise – I'll make the call.'

'Thanks. You look after yourself now. Your wife is devastated without you. And they can't wait to see you back at the office.'

'Right now, Aleksey, I have to learn to walk on my own two feet.'

'How's that?'

'Well . . . I've decided to walk to the Central Committee. Not at once, of course. First a block or two, then halfway.'

'I can drive alongside you in first gear.'

'Passers-by might not understand. You'll wait for me at a designated spot. We'll start after the holidays.'

'Or maybe you can go swimming with all the generals at the Army Central Sports Club pool, like Yagubov?'

'Yagubov's a youngster. Let him swim. I'll just walk on foot, on foot . . .'

Flags and panels with slogans on both sides of the streets flowed together into one red stripe. *It's in bad taste; they don't have any sense of proportion,* thought Makartsev. *The resources put into all of this are enormous, after all. We'll have to cultivate their taste* . . . Portraits of the first leader of the country and the present one flashed past here and there, those of the entire Politburo less frequently. Makartsev imagined himself up there on the edges, as someone newly admitted to the Politburo, and made a wry face. No, he was not only unthreatened by that fate, he also didn't want it. He was a toiler for the Party, an ox pulling a cart. *And let those who can't do without it cream off the glory.*

'They all look too young,' Aleksey said, looking askance at the portraits.

'All right! Never mind that – tell me: have you ever cheated on your wife?'

'Have you?' Aleksey instantly retorted.

Makartsev hadn't expected that question. 'Well, I . . . that's something different. I don't have any time for that, you know yourself.'

'Right. "The Party is our helmsman!"' Aleksey read aloud when they stopped for a traffic light, right behind a garbage truck.

'What, you have any doubt about it?'

'Me? Nope. If you say so, that's what the Party is. Us drivers, we just sit behind the wheel.'

The truck abruptly moved off, and several crumpled newspapers flew out of it. One of them smacked into the windscreen of Makartsev's Volga, flipped over, spread itself out and then flew off to the side in the stream of air. Makartsev glimpsed that it was a copy of *Izvestia*.

'That arsehole's going to leave the whole street in a mess! Overtake him, Aleksey, and tell them to arrest him.'

A feeling of proletarian solidarity lurked at the bottom of Aleksey's consciousness but didn't take shape. He braked in front of a traffic policeman, opened his door, indicated behind them with his thumb and drove on. In the mirror he saw the policeman waving his stick and ordering the truck to stop.

Driving up to the office, Makartsev felt younger. He wasn't in pain; he was healthy and back in action. Aleksey ran ahead to the lift, twirling his keys like a propeller. He whispered to the security man that the chief was coming, so that no misunderstandings would arise. The new security man had never seen the editor-in-chief before and stood to attention. Everyone greeted him with joy, wishing him a happy upcoming holiday. At the lift a spotty young female proofreader stood to one side to let the editor go ahead, but he gallantly let her in first, shaking her hand in the lift, and she blushed to her very roots. On his own floor he was already moving in the middle of a retinue. Bureau editors came running up, asking how he felt, shaking his hand. *So they really do love me. I'm not wrong. And they're all dear to me, too, my workmates. What am I without them?* Makartsev took Rappoport, who had also appeared in the corridor, to one side by his sleeve.

'What about that problem, Rappoport? Taken care of?'

The feeling of danger had flown away into the remoteness of time, and he was asking more for form's sake than anything else.

'How could it be otherwise?' rasped Rappoport. 'Don't worry. I burned everything, just in case. If we don't have something then we'll have to do without it.'

'Thanks!' Makartsev said, shaking his hand. 'Have a good holiday.'

'Right.' Rappoport screwed up his eyes. 'Actually, for the sake of the children, it should have been the other way round.'

'For what children? Other way round how?'

'Burned the newspaper and kept the grey folder.'

'That's a bad joke!' Makartsev said and walked into his reception room, taking off his raincoat as he went.

Aleksey had barely appeared at the doors when Anna jumped up and, straightening her skirt, ran to open the door of the editor-in-chief's office wide for him – clean, aired out, with a cup of tea, not too hot and not too strong, on his desk.

'Greetings to the boss!' Makartsev said on entering the reception room, his grey hair flopping as he bowed to her.

'Well, how *are* you?' she asked with alarm and joy.

'As strong as an ox. We Bolsheviks are tough . . .'

Grabbing Anna by the elbow, Makartsev kissed her on the lips. She pressed against him for an instant but didn't feel anything. Probably because it was right in front of everyone. Absolutely nothing, even though she'd been waiting for this moment for nearly nine years. And his lips were cold and tasteless, while it had always seemed to her that they should be hot, with the flavour of American cigarettes, the smell of which Anna liked a great deal. She went into his office behind him, closing both doors tight against all the curious people.

'You look sad, Anna. It's a holiday, after all . . .' Her tears had appeared in an instant but just hung in her lashes rather than running down her face.

'My husband has left me . . . Don't pay any attention to me.' She hadn't wanted to say that to him; it just popped out by itself.

'What do you mean, left? Why?'

'A car ran over our dog, and he left.'

'What's the dog got to do with it?'

'He said it was the dog that kept us together. Well, what's there to understand? He left me for somebody younger, and the dog was just an excuse.'

'Oh, Anna!' He patted her head like he would a child. 'I've always said: you've got to love nice elderly men. Like me, for instance!'

'Like you?' She stopped weeping and stared at him in surprise.

'Somehow I don't remember you ever saying that to me.'

'So, I was thinking it.'

'You're joking . . .'

'Well, all right, we'll talk about it later. How long is it till the planning session?'

Anna glanced at the tiny worn-out wristwatch on her arm, which had told all her nine years at the *Trudovaya Pravda* office. 'Thirty-five minutes.'

'That's fine. I'll make a few phone calls before they come in.'

'I bought you some painkillers just in case. In the right drawer of your desk, at the front.' She was already in the antechamber between the doors.

'Thank you, o irreplaceable one!'

Putting on his glasses, he wiped his hands and sat down in his armchair, which he hadn't occupied for sixty-two days now. He'd been keeping count. The moment had come to take the paper back into his own hands. But he still existed separately from it, and the newspaper continued to exist without him. He decided to find out – before he forgot – what he could do for Aleksey. Makartsev understood that drivers who got to go abroad were selected by an entirely different department, but since he'd already promised Aleksey he decided to give it a try. On the secure telephone he called Stratyev, the Deputy Minister of Foreign Trade, with whom he'd worked together on various assignments for Khrushchev. After two or three general inquiries about each other's health (*He doesn't know I had a heart attack – that's good!*) Makartsev said: 'By the way, Sovtransavto is over at your place. Its international authority profile, they tell me, still isn't very high. Maybe we can bring it up in the newspaper?'

'It never hurts to get brought up,' said Stratyev, after thinking a bit. 'But on whose instructions? Maybe we should finish our reorganization first.'

'Which one is that?'

'Well, we're introducing a more progressive system, so as not to have to send our drivers abroad. At all border-crossing points we're going to transfer all the trailers over, so our drivers will come back with the incoming load. It's more convenient that way and – most important – considerably cheaper.'

'When are you going to put that into effect?' Makartsev realized that Aleksey's request was a dead duck, but he went on talking.

'Probably a month or two, at most three.'

'That's a deal,' agreed Makartsev, so as to forget about the Sovtransavto thing. 'Are you heading off anywhere yourself?'

'Well, I just got back from Finland yesterday, signed an agreement. Got to catch my breath.'

'Well, catch your breath. Happy holidays!'

Makartsev thought with sadness about how he hadn't been anywhere for a long time. And now he wasn't up to it. He was going to bring the newspaper up to scratch, put Yagubov in his place, mobilize the people. And then there might be a little trip abroad. He hadn't had a pen in his hand for a long while. It was time to show the youngsters how to take the bull by the horns! Makartsev had the feeling that his brain had got enervated over the course of his illness and was shirking, didn't want to work. He had to discipline himself. He pulled out all his desk drawers to check if everything was in its place. He dragged over the proofs of the leader page, looking at them with a smile. Dry as dust. They could have quoted some poetry at least! He drank his now-cold tea and tossed the proofs aside.

A blue envelope had been lying under the proofs. The editor opened it, read its title and winced. His heart still hadn't reacted, but it seemed to him momentarily (out of fear maybe?) that it was already pounding, beating arrhythmically, lapsing into silence just as it had back then in front of the Central Committee. Forgetting all about the poetry that the leader needed, he started reading the manuscript, hatred suddenly aroused. It was entitled *Impotentocracy*. Realizing what the manuscript was about, he flung it down in a rage. His fingers were trembling, either from weakness or from indignation. *Again? What is going on here?* He wanted to get up quietly from behind his desk, slip out of his office, sneak past his secretary and the porter and make his way home without his car; crawl headfirst under his blanket and just lie there as if he'd never got up at all.

What stupidity! He pulled the folder full of pages over to him, raking them together with his frenziedly disobedient, trembling fingers, and stuffed them back into the envelope.

His door opened, and a KGB lieutenant with a briefcase walked in. Makartsev squeezed his lips tight.

'Hello. Courier mail.'

The lieutenant opened his briefcase, took out a book sewn up with twine, with a pendant wax seal, and indicated the column with his finger. Without relaxing his lips, and feeling his heart resonantly rising up and floundering under his gullet, the editor-in-chief signed the sheet. Tucking the book back into his briefcase the courier left a small white envelope on the desk and went out. It turned out to be a confidential directive about the increasing use of narcotics, particularly among young people, and, in connection with this, it specifically prohibited the publication of any material on the subject.

Blowing out his cheeks, Makartsev stuffed the decree into his safe. As a result of his abrupt movement the pain that he had feared appeared under his left shoulder-blade. He hurriedly took out a tablet and started to suck the nitroglycerine.

Anna opened the door and said smiling: 'The whole office knows that you've shown up. Everybody has something for you, and everyone swears it's urgent. I'm not letting anyone in.'

Anna's voice was distant, like an echo, and didn't reach him right away.

'Tell everyone that we'll get together in the auditorium for ten minutes after the planning session. I'll wish the staff happy holidays. Is the bonus order ready?'

'I think so. I'll ask Kashin. And another thing . . .' Anna hesitated. 'Yagubov is asking to come in.'

'Why so official? Yagubov can come in without permission.'

Yagubov appeared immediately, as soon as she went out. Makartsev had meanwhile put another tablet into his mouth. It got easier to breathe with the nitroglycerine, although the pain hadn't gone yet. But at least he understood better what Yagubov was saying.

'I'm very glad that you're well again. To be honest, it got a bit hairy without you. I'm pleased, too, that everything worked out all right with your son. There was some talk in the office, but I soon put a stop to it! I have to inform you, though, so that you'll be aware of it: we've had a staff problem. Even though you left a directive not to resolve staff issues in your absence – something we've rigorously adhered to – I violated it on one occasion against my will. Special Correspondent Ivlev has been arrested by the KGB. We've fired him by order, although the order is still unsigned . . .'

Makartsev suddenly realized that he loathed his deputy and had to put him in his place. He drew air into his lungs and, forgetting the pain under his shoulder-blade, said sharply: 'You fired him straight away? Instead of trying to defend the man. As if you, Yagubov, aren't welcome there and don't know who to turn to! There can be no return to the times when people were arrested in broad daylight. I tell you that with all my authority as a candidate member of the Central Committee!'

Harsh words indeed, but he spoke them only to himself. In fact, he just drew in air and looked silently at Yagubov, suppressing his hatred. Makartsev suddenly felt that he was taking off from the earth, hovering around the ceiling, and that the space around him was filling up with shreds of something white: either fog or cotton. There in this space next to Makartsev hovered someone else, wearing a frock coat and knee breeches. Makartsev recognized him immediately, and the Marquis de Custine winked at him and beckoned him to follow, with both hands.

'Where is it you're going – heaven or hell?' asked de Custine, and his eyes shone with an unearthly glint.

'I . . . I . . .' Makartsev stalled, at a loss, and looked down towards Yagubov. But he couldn't see him through the fog.

'Ah, be so magnanimous as to forgive me,' the marquis hastened to correct himself. 'I forgot that you don't believe in God. Your heaven and hell are both on earth, right?' They were sailing along together, and the shreds of cotton were touching Makartsev's face, sticking to his eyes, fes-

tooning his lips. The marquis, it seemed, paid no heed to this, and floating along for him was easy and comfortable.

'I feel bad,' rasped Makartsev, not taking offence at the irony. 'So bad
that God alone can help me. But can I . . . can I go to heaven?'

'That's something, monsieur, for them up there to decide,' de
Custine said, waving a hand vaguely upwards.

'What!' Makartsev said indignantly and stopped slurring his words.
'You want to tell me that even there my fate is to be decided Upstairs, while
I can't defend myself? I can't stand up for myself . . . stand . . .'

Makartsev felt an unimaginable pain under his shoulder-blade; the
pain passed to his neck, his arm started aching, and his body suddenly
became heavy and started to fall. De Custine grabbed him by the elbow
to support him.

'It is true, there are things that are stronger than we,' he said. 'But when
you feel human affection it becomes easier to bear. Loneliness in eternity
is much worse than in earthly life, believe me. I dare to hope that you and
I will meet again.'

De Custine disappeared into the fog, and Makartsev sank into his armchair. Yagubov appeared through the fog and stood in front of him, small
and dim.

'You don't have any objection?' asked Yagubov.

'Wha' are you talkin' abou'?' slurred Makartsev. The cotton stuffed
into his ears and mouth made it hard to make out his words.

'About our firing Ivlev . . .'

'No,' Makartsev spat out the cotton that was preventing him from moving his tongue. 'You acted properly. I'll sign the order.'

Straight away it got easier, because now he didn't have to act, to take
the responsibility on himself. He, Makartsev, was too honest, and he was
settling the score with his own pain, damn it!

'The bosses all together!' Polishchuk said, looking in at the door.
'Happy holiday, comrades! There are issues that need settling by you,
chief!'

Issues again. Once again, needing to be settled. There was still more cotton all around. *Maybe I should tell them I feel ill? But, no, my subordinates shouldn't know that. For their sake, I'm well.*

'We'll settle them,' he muttered, glancing at his empty glass and licking his dry, swollen lips.

Polishchuk stood next to Yagubov. For two days after Ivlev's disappearance he had gone around shattered, forgetting that there was a threatening cloud hanging over him as well. The statistic attesting to the fact that the mortality rate among journalists was higher than among any other category of white-collar worker never left his head. Transferring to the newspaper had been a mistake; it would be stupid to deny it. It would be better to go back to the institute, write some sort of dissertation and quietly give lectures on some trivial subject or other. After thinking that, Polishchuk took heart. One on one with Makartsev, he could speak frankly. The boss could help get him permission from the Central Committee for a transfer. But Yagubov was hanging around the office, as if out of spite. Kashin thrust himself through the door, rattling his keys.

'Happy holiday, boss,' he said, smiling. 'A double holiday for you. Your latest medical certificate is already in Accounting. Anna will bring your money later. Congratulations on your commencing execution of your duties.'

*Execution? What's he talking about, some crime?* Makartsev couldn't hear him. *Maybe I should ask him about it?* But it was too hard to move his tongue. It had swollen up; his mouth was getting full. The pain hadn't receded for a long time; it was time for it to go away . . .

'I wanted to ask you when I should lock down the typing pool for the holidays.' Kashin shook the brass seal on its cord. 'This year there was an additional directive: to secure each typewriter separately, running a cord through it so that the case can't be opened from the rear. I've already sealed all the typewriters except for the one that's left, and there's a queue formed up at it, everyone with something urgent. But the directive was to lock down the typing pool by four p.m.'

'That's a technical matter,' said Yagubov. 'We'll solve that one without the editor-in-chief. Don't you see how much is on his plate?'

*So Yagubov has noticed that I'm feeling unwell,* thought Makartsev wryly. *My head's buzzing, I can't hear very well. From the cotton in my ears.*

'There's a call on the secure line,' Yagubov politely pointed out. 'Let's have a little quiet, comrades!'

The secure telephone, like an emperor's sceptre, served as both the real and the ceremonial attribute of the power that Yagubov wasn't entitled to. The editor-in-chief could hear it buzzing now himself. *How inconvenient it is that the telephones are on my left, since it's so hard for me to reach out with my left hand. I'll have to ask for them to be shifted round after the holidays.*

'Makartsev,' he said into the mouthpiece, trying to keep his disobedient tongue from drawling or slurring his words. In the receiver he could hear the voice of Khomutilov, the assistant of the Man Who Preferred To Stay In The Shadows.

'I'm calling you in advance, Comrade Makartsev, since the holidays are . . . Write this down: eleven thirty on the fifth of May.'

'To see Himself?' asked Makartsev. 'On the fifth? That's press day.'

'That's the way it is.'

'What's it about?' He had instantly divined the alarm in Khomutilov's tone.

No answer was forthcoming, and Makartsev realized that things were even worse than they had seemed.

'Has something happened?' he repeated, although he knew perfectly well that asking at all, never mind for the second time, was forbidden.

'I don't know,' sighed Khomutilov. 'After all, as you know, I'm just somebody who carries out instructions.' Low, short tones buzzed in the receiver.

'It's time to start the planning session.' Yagubov's voice carried to him. 'Will you conduct it, or would you like me to?'

'I will,' Makartsev whispered sharply. 'I'll conduct it myself . . .'

But his words sank into the cloud of cotton, and he couldn't tell if he had uttered them or only wanted to utter them. If he wanted to conduct the session or had already conducted it. If he wanted to wish the staff a happy First of May or if he'd already done it. If he was alone in his office or if people were standing around him and looking at him, not understanding what was happening to him. He suddenly shrank in size, became a Lilliputian, and everyone around him was enormous. Fearing that they would stamp on him, he began pouring with sweat and opened his mouth in an attempt to breathe in more air, to stock up so that he had enough air for his next breath, but they were using up all the air in his office; there wasn't anything left for him except cotton.

He tried to stand up so that he could open the ventilation pane wide, and he propped his hands on the arms of his chair but forgot that he was still holding the telephone in one hand. It fell, dangling by its cord, continuing to give off disquieting beeps. Then they stopped and a voice asked: 'What's the matter? Why hasn't the receiver been hung up?' Yagubov flung himself on the phone, bending across the desk to reach it, and placed it back on its hook. Unable to rise, Makartsev groped around on the telephone stand with one hand until he found the buzzer switch.

Anna ran in and saw that Makartsev was sinking in his chair and that his face was grey.

'It's uncomfortable to sit!' he said to her. 'Cotton's getting into my mouth . . . Stifling!'

'Lord!' Anna exclaimed. 'What are you all doing just standing there?'

She hurtled to the window, but she couldn't open it: the frame of the portrait hanging outside was obstructing it. Kashin went out to the reception desk and dialled the Kremlin hospital and an ambulance, cupping his hand over his mouth so that nobody could overhear. Makartsev the whole time followed Anna's unsuccessful attempts at opening the window with his eyes.

'When there's air it's easier to breathe,' he said distinctly.

Or maybe he didn't say it but again just thought it. He suddenly realized that he was dying. He didn't know how it was supposed to happen; he'd never had to die before. He could feel the back of his armchair with the back of his head, and his consciousness suddenly became clearer than it ever had been before. Because of his uncomfortable pose the back of his head began to grow numb. The numbness spread to both sides, upwards, downwards; he was dazzled by reflections of sunlight, and darkness fell. Makartsev had his last insight: death begins at the back of the head.

'Well, here we are together, after all,' said a pleasant voice right above Makartsev's ear. The voice didn't resemble anyone's from the office.

The Marquis de Custine had once more appeared out of the fog, jangling his sword, and made a welcoming gesture, either towards the ceiling or in the direction of the window.

'I feel sorry for you, but your mortal vanity has ended,' he said to calm Makartsev down. 'Time to clear out, as I think they put it here. It's nothing so terrible. Believe someone who made the crossing a good while ago and feels an ineffable affection towards you. Maybe even love . . . Another instant and you will be at ease and, perhaps most important, free at last. Soon we will have more than enough time to get closer and to discuss everything . . . ing . . . ing . . .'

De Custine dissolved into a white mist, but the fog around Makartsev turned grey, then violet, then red and suddenly blackened. Makartsev suddenly started blowing bubbles like an infant. A large bubble, shot with violet highlights, hung on his lower lip, ran down his chin and burst. The last thing that Editor-in-Chief Makartsev saw in this world was Lenin's enormous ear.

The office was filled to bursting with people who had come to the planning session and were now crowding back against the wall in dismay. Makartsev sat in his armchair, his hands on the arms of it, and looked into the distance directly in front of him. He was still officially the editor-in-chief of *Trudovaya Pravda*, its director; he still represented the link in the chain between the newspaper and the Central Committee. But he wasn't any more really: although the rest of his body still functioned, sort of, his eyes had grown cold and his brain had extinguished.

'Where to?' asked the strapping country-boy ambulanceman in a dirty white smock. Holding out his medical case in front of him, he unceremoniously used it to push his way through.

'You got here quick. Good lads!' Yagubov praised him, indicating the way with his hand.

The ambulanceman unhurriedly put his case down on the editor's desk, opened it and took Makartsev's arm. His hand wouldn't release its grip on the chair arm, and the man pulled it away by force. For several seconds he felt for a pulse, then grabbed the editor by both sides of his head and shook him.

'No reaction. Did you see?' said the ambulanceman, turning to Anna. She stood next to them, her hands to her throat.

'Give him a shot of something!' she ordered him. 'So he can make it to the Kremlin hospital.'

'So who is he?'

'A candidate member of the Central Committee!'

The man pulled down Makartsev's lower eyelid.

'What are you doing? That must hurt him!'

'It doesn't,' the ambulanceman said in a businesslike manner. 'It's not hurting him any more. Has he had heart attacks before?'

'He did,' Anna said, 'on the twenty-sixth of February.'

'We'll take him to the morgue. It's forbidden to bury people during holidays. He'll lie in the morgue until the parades are over. Help me put his body on the stretcher.'

Yagubov ordered Kashin to help. The ambulanceman wetted a piece of cotton with alcohol and wiped his hands and then the edge of the desk where his medical case had been. A trace of coagulated blood that the alcohol loosened from the desktop showed up on the cotton. It was Nadya's blood, left there from her long-ago encounter with Ivlev. The ambulanceman tossed the cotton into the wastebasket.

The internal telephone rang, and Yagubov surreptitiously lifted the receiver.

'This is Volobuyev, Makartsev. Happy holiday! Well, and congratulations on your improv –'

'Volobuyev,' interrupted Yagubov. 'Makartsev's not here any more.'

'Not here? But I heard that he'd showed up. You see, we have to delete the words about the demonstrators marching eight to a rank out of all the articles. In the West they've been writing that we've organized the nation-wide rejoicing in advance. Just write "in columns" and that's all!'

'Don't fuss, Volobuyev. We'll take them out. Makartsev's just died.'

'Died? What about the newspaper?'

'The newspaper? It'll come out, even if we all die!'

The news about the death of their editor-in-chief flew through the bureaux and the printing plant. The workers, seeing their shop bosses run upstairs, pulled out the bottles that they had laid by for the end of the day and started drinking to the repose of Makartsev's soul, dunking fresh galley offprints into their glasses. The lead-laden ink shortened their lives, but it killed the smell of the vodka.

They carried Makartsev's body out slowly from the corridor to the stairway. A herd of people moved along behind the stretcher. The security man, pushing against them with his shoulders, opened both sides of the main lobby door. Two people in white smocks were hurrying towards them.

'Stop!'

'Too late,' said the ambulanceman, 'too late for resuscitation . . .'

In train behind the stretcher, on which rocked Makartsev's corpse covered by a sheet, the procession poured out on to the street. A thin drizzle was falling. The Kremlin doctors and the city ambulancemen argued over who was going to take the body away and could come to no agreement. Suddenly from somewhere above them a song began to howl deafeningly:

> *We're born to make our fairytales come real,*
> *To bridge together what was far apart.*
> *Now Reason's given us new wings of steel*
> *And flaming motors in the place of hearts.*

It was being played to check the loudspeakers on the roofs along the route of the next day's parade.

MOSCOW, 1969–1979